FIRE *of* *the* SPIRIT

The Journey of Sam Mahoy Begins

JOHN PONTIUS

Latter-day
Legends
Salt Lake City

ISBN 13: 978-1-944200-66-4

Published by Latter-day Legends, a division of Digital Legend Press & Publishing Inc. Salt Lake City, UT 84121
www.digitalegend.com

Inquiries or permissions: info@digitalegend.com

Cover design by David Christenson
Interior design by Jacob F. Frandsen

Printed in the United States of America
First Edition; Second Printing, 2020 V1.

BOOKS BY JOHN M. PONTIUS

Visions of Glory
Journey to the Veil
Following the Light of Christ into His Presence
The Triumph of Zion: Our Personal Quest for the New Jerusalem
We Three Kings

Journey to Zion

Fire of the Spirit—Book One
Angels of Fire—Book Two

SPECIAL OFFER

Go to www.JohnPontius.org to download
previously unpublished works by John
including fireside, papers and essays.
Also receive advanced notification and news on
Book Two of *The Journey to Zion* series, as well as
watch video interviews with John's family and best friend.

ACKNOWLEDGMENTS

For those who have read John Pontius's *UnBlog My Soul* postings from 2010–2012, many of which I included in the book *Journey to the Veil* after John's passing, you will notice that a few of his early-life stories have been retold in this novel. That is because back in the summer of 1997, John penned the entire *Journey to Zion* series, loosely using a few stories from his own life in this first book. John often told me that he took significant "poetic license" with this series, since these novels were clearly fictional. However, the reader should note that the posts John wrote for *UnBlog My Soul* (and those included in *Journey to the Veil*) are accurate accounts of actual events, which John originally intended for his beloved posterity.

I hope you'll enjoy these novels of passion and spirit and perhaps even find them life-changing as you progress through your own mortal experience.

Terri Pontius

CONTENTS

INTRODUCTION

All the stories in this book are fictional. Their primary value is to illustrate the process of spiritual greatness. Even though many of these stories are based on real events, none of them are intended to represent real people. I have carefully changed names, places, and surrounding events where necessary. These stories are not intended to establish doctrine or propose that all people must, or even might, walk a similar path.

It is my profound belief that this life has a single, grand purpose. That purpose often has little to do with what we spend the majority of our time actually doing. To learn what that grand purpose is, we must pierce the confusion of this world and find the path of righteousness. However, just understanding the purpose of life may not necessarily give us a concrete means of achieving true joy.

One of the rather recent additions to my testimony of Jesus Christ and His glorious gospel is the witness that, in addition to being true, it works. In other words, the promises are profoundly true! We can—you and I can—achieve every promised blessing by ordering our lives to follow the voice of the Spirit. There is nothing withheld, nothing missing, and nothing omitted that we must have in order to walk the path to great righteousness and its promised rewards. Having found this to be true, it has fallen sweetly on my understanding that the principal outcome of living the gospel is the happiness and meaning of life that we all seek.

If you feel nothing else from reading Fire of the Spirit, I hope you will feel, at the very core of your being, the witness that is possible for you, regardless of your limitations or self-doubt, to luxuriate in that joy which surpasses the understanding of man. All things really are possible to those who believe.

John M. Pontius

JIMMY

Jim Mahoy stuffed the tractor keys into his pants and bent to ruffle Jimmy's hair. His son's temper was still aflame.

"Thtop it, Daddy!" he said, pouting.

"You hurt the kitty, Jimmy. That's why she scratched you."

"No. Kitty hurt me!" Jimmy countered with perfect two-year-old logic.

"She was afraid. You need to hold Kitty easy, like a baby. Be nice to Kitty."

"You be nice!"

"Don't talk to Daddy that way . . ."

"Kitty hates me. You hate me. I don't like you!" he shouted, his arms rigid at his sides.

"Jimmy, that's not true. I love . . ." Just then Mom called everyone to breakfast. Jimmy spun around and was gone before Jim could say another word. It was a typical exchange with Jimmy. Not typical in its anger, but typical in its abruptness and in Jimmy's surprising certainty that he was right.

Just as Jimmy disappeared around the corner, the Spirit whispered to Jim, "This is the one." Jim was stunned. His heart cried, "Oh, no! Not Jimmy!" The feeling did not subside as he joined his family for breakfast. Jimmy was a vividly happy child. He was always busy, always challenging, and always experimenting with his new world. He was unusually willful, seldom willing to take second seat, even to his parents, and yet, he was unselfish and loving. He started talking at a young age, apparently out of the sheer necessity of having a way to take control of his little world. He spoke with a vocabulary worthy of a child several years his senior. His hair was bright red, almost orange, and he possessed a sudden Irish temper. He was the youngest of seven and the joy of every member of his large family, which consisted of his two brothers and four sisters.

Jimmy's dad, Jim Mahoy, was a man of medium height, almost as broad across the shoulders as he was tall. He came from a long line of burly Mahoys who, for four generations, had coaxed crops from the fertile Utah Valley. He was a quiet man, wise in his own way, and deeply spiritual. While his education stopped one year short of a high school diploma, he could add a column of numbers of almost any length simply by glancing at it. He could multiply, divide, figure square root, and convert from metric to English measures, all in his head.

As breakfast ended and each family member piled their dishes into the sink, Jimmy's mom turned on impulse just as Jimmy ran from the kitchen after his big brother Sam. A strange feeling of concern touched her, but she had things to do. She smiled and busied herself with assigning cleanup and chores to the older children.

Jimmy's mom, Laura Mahoy, was forty-two, a blond beauty from California. She was soft spoken and through the years had grown infinitely patient. Still, Jimmy had inherited his quick temper from her. It made her chuckle to watch him stomp his feet and put his fists on his hips. Sometimes his face would turn red, simply because his two-year-old vocabulary did not have enough words in it. She saw herself in her youngest child's fiery ways.

Sam almost fell over as Jimmy eagerly wrapped himself around his brother's leg. Sam set down the milking equipment and knelt in front of his little brother. As he did so, Jimmy flung his arms around Sam's neck, so that their noses were almost touching. "Pleath, Tham. Pleath let me go to the cowth with you," he begged, his lisp somewhat exaggerated due to his excitement. Jimmy's lisp was completely absent at times and only surfaced when he was upset or especially excited. Sam smiled. He loved it when Jimmy called him "Tham." Sam and Jimmy had a special relationship, one which neither understood, yet one in which they both rejoiced.

Because their family was so large, the last three children had been tended and raised as much by the older children as they were by Laura. Consequently, each of the babies had bonded with one of the older children, creating an almost paternal relationship between them.

Jimmy was Sam's baby. They were bonded by the purest love siblings can have. It wasn't uncommon for Jimmy to run past his parents to Sam to seek sympathy or to show a hurt. It was certainly to Sam he came to seek justice from, or more commonly, revenge on, an older child.

He was almost never disappointed.

"You have your pajamas on. Big boys don't milk cows in pajamas, and I have to go now," Sam told him. Besides, Sam knew what a bother Jimmy was in the milking parlor. It took as much work to keep Jimmy out from under the cows as it did to milk them.

"I will dreth me," he said, pulling at his pajama tops with chubby little hands. "I can milk cowth and feed the baby cowth. You will take me to the cowth? Pleath?"

Sam was the second oldest after sixteen-year-old Emily. He was fourteen and stocky like his dad, but not at all eager to farm for a living. He hated milking cows. At fourteen, he was nearly the strongest boy in his school, and the slowest afoot. He could lift the back end of a VW beetle but finished last in every race he entered. He was quiet, made friends slowly, and was often the brunt of teasing; but when he found a friend, that person remained his friend for life.

Sam had inherited his father's hands but his mother's fingers. His hands were broad and powerful, his fingers long and agile. Even at fourteen, few adult men could outgrip him. He had a heart so big and tender that it ofttimes felt on the verge of breaking.

These were his blessings. His curse was that without glasses he was virtually blind. Behind the heavy lenses, he could see just well enough to get along. The thick glasses made his eyes look smaller, giving him an almost-unintelligent appearance. He had never caught a ball in his life, except perhaps on accident. He could not see well enough to catch anything, so if someone actually did throw to him, the ball usually hit Sam, which would make the other kids laugh.

In a desperate gamble to give her young boy a chance to succeed, when he was six years old, Sam's mother started him playing the flute. Why the flute? Because, for some odd reason, they had one. He took to it with delight, and by age fourteen, he was a surprisingly accomplished artist. He read music well, but his most beautiful songs came from deep within him: music that was at times bright and prancing, sometimes soft and wistful, occasionally thundering, and often brilliant. But even this talent made him seem odd. The small silver flute looked misplaced in his big hands, and his peers misunderstood his gift. From a body that big, one expected a grunt or belch, not a haunting melody. Consequently, he never played for anyone not directly related to him, and no amount of coaxing could convince him otherwise. Even Miles, his best friend, didn't know he played like an angel's dream.

Sam lifted Jimmy and swung him around until he laughed. "I don't think I can take you, Jimmy. Tham is in a hurry today," he said, using Jimmy's pronunciation of his name. "Maybe tomorrow, okay Sport?"

"Okay, Tham. I love you, Tham. You are my biggeth, betheth brother. You milk cowth today, and me milk cowth tomorrow and feed baby cowth," he said, shaking a small finger in Sam's face. As far as Jimmy was concerned, they had a contract. Sam put on his most serious face and nodded solemnly. It was all he could do to not laugh at his baby brother.

Jimmy loosened his grip on his big brother's neck. Just as they broke contact, Sam suddenly felt like taking him along. He was about to say something, but Jimmy was already off onto something else and out of sight. Sam heard the kitten complain as Jimmy picked it up in the other room. The love Jimmy felt for his kitten was not mutual. Sam walked through the garage and loaded the milking equipment into the old GMC truck. He stopped for a moment to examine his bicycle. He and Jimmy loved to ride together. They rode long distances, with Jimmy astraddle the center bar; but when Jimmy had graduated from diapers, the bar hurt him. They taped a bath towel around the bar for a while, but that had a tendency to roll sideways. Dad had helped Sam weld another bicycle seat to the bar just behind the handlebars. Sam smiled to himself as he remembered how much Jimmy loved it! This way he had his own seat and could hold onto the handlebars. They even welded on some footrests to keep Jimmy's feet safely away from the front wheel. Sam promised himself that after chores, he and Jimmy would go on a long ride together.

Sam wasn't old enough to legally drive, but in a farming community, boys were expected to be able to operate all the equipment. Because of his size, he had driven early. Driving the farm truck was old hat for him now.

As Sam turned onto the lane to the barn, he had that uneasy feeling again and almost went back to bundle up Jimmy and take him along. But Sam had work to do, and he pressed the accelerator hard. He would hurry back.

Chores usually took several hours, but this morning, one of the cows, Rosie, had been reluctant to enter the stanchion, and it had taken longer. Sam fed the calves, mixed chopped grain and water for the pigs, fed fifty rabbits, broke open twelve bales of hay for the cows, loaded nearly forty gallons of milk in ten-gallon cans onto the truck, washed the milking equipment in large sinks of scalding hot water, pressure cleaned the parlor floor, and started back toward the house.

All along the half-mile lane back to the house, that uneasy feeling persisted, making the ride seem longer. He wanted to speed up, but if he did, the milk cans would slide off the truck. He came to the bridge over the big irrigation ditch behind their house. He glanced at his watch to see if there would be time to take Jimmy on that bike ride before his nap. It was two minutes to eleven.

As he came off the other side of the bridge, he saw Jimmy's kitten standing on the bank. It was soaking wet. Sam had a sudden urge to look up and down the ditch, but the feeling was indistinct, and his need to concentrate on steering the truck across the narrow bridge quickly swallowed it up.

Once beyond the bridge, Sam felt he should go back to the ditch, but the milk needed to go into the cooler. He sped up, and as he approached the house, his mother was standing on the back porch. Her hand shielded her eyes from the sun as she scanned the backyard.

"Mom, where's Jimmy?" Sam asked from the truck, struggling to keep his voice calm.

"I was just looking for him. I heard him asking to go with you to milk the cows. I thought you had taken him."

A lump rose in his throat. "No, I didn't."

Laura swallowed but calmly said, "Well, he's around here somewhere. You check the chicken coop. You know how he sneaks out there sometimes."

"Mom, I'm going to look in the ditch."

His mother flashed him a frightened look. "Why? He never goes near it."

"I saw his kitten by the bridge. It was soaking wet. I'm afraid he threw it into the ditch. Maybe he fell in too. I don't know. I just have a bad feeling."

Without another word, Laura headed toward the bridge. The kitten was still there, licking himself off. The ditch was full and moving slowly.

They walked to the first bend and then to the next, but found nothing.

"Go get your dad," she commanded, and strode off downstream. Sam complied and trotted toward the house.

Sixteen-year-old Emily bolted from the back door, alarm showing on her face. "What's wrong? Why is Mom walking the ditch?"

"We can't find Jimmy. Go get Dad, will you?"

Emily nodded, dropped the dishtowel she was holding, and ran toward the south fields. Then she stopped, ran back, hopped on her bike, and raced away.

Sam loudly called Jimmy's name. Seconds later, their only close neighbors came out onto their porch. The Carters lived directly across the street and had heard Sam calling. Without asking what was going on, they ran across the street to the ditch behind Mahoy's house. There was no hesitation; they just did what had to be done.

The Carters were inactive in the Church but had been good neighbors for many years. Mr. Carter jumped into the water above his waist and started pulling boards from the dam. The water changed course and dumped into the drain ditch. He hung onto the metal frame of the dam to keep from being washed away.

"I'll stand in the water here. If he's in the ditch, he won't go past me. Besides, it will stop the water from going further downstream."

Sam nodded. The ditch went underground shortly after it left their farm. Sam turned to rejoin his mother.

Laura had walked almost a quarter mile and was in the middle of the hayfield. Sam was halfway to her when she suddenly jumped into the ditch and frantically called for help. Sam shouted to the Carters and broke into a run. Mrs. Carter shouted something about an ambulance. Sam got to his mother just as she was climbing out of the ditch with Jimmy in her arms. The little boy was blue and not moving. Sam tried to take Jimmy, but Laura ignored him. She quickly laid Jimmy on the grass and felt for a pulse.

Sam rubbed Jimmy's arms. They were ice cold. Jimmy's eyes were closed, his lids almost black, his lips a dark blue.

Laura bent Jimmy's head back and leaned over, blowing air into his mouth. A gush of water came from his mouth. With an icy calm, she cleared his mouth and blew repeatedly. She then pushed on Jimmy's chest. Sam didn't know what she was doing or why, but he trusted his mother. She knew things he didn't, and was dead calm in emergencies.

For Sam, time seemed to stand still. His father arrived, and following Laura's directions, he started pushing on Jimmy's chest.

After a long time, Laura straightened. Her face, a mask of exhaustion and grief, was streaked with tears. Her eyes were puffy and her lips were purple and swollen. Oddly, except for being discolored, Jimmy's mouth looked perfectly normal.

Jim gently pushed Laura aside, and they changed places. Laura rhythmically massaged Jimmy's chest, while Jim blew air into his son's mouth.

After what seemed like a long time, which in reality was over an hour, Jim straightened up and felt for a pulse at Jimmy's neck. Tears coursed down his face.

"Honey. Laura. I don't think we should continue." Laura didn't seem to hear. "Honey, it's no use. He's gone," Jim said softly.

"No!" she screamed. "He's not dead. We have to try longer. Do it!"

The intensity and volume of her response shocked everyone. Jim nodded and resumed his work.

By this time, a sizable crowd had gathered. Some had walked, a few had driven tractors, and several cars had driven out onto the hayfield. The wail of a long-awaited siren punctuated the distance. Laura looked across the crowd of dismayed, sympathetic faces, and they stared helplessly back. A few glanced away.

She looked at Jim and knew he could not stop working on her son to give Jimmy a blessing. Her eyes were frantic as she scanned the group of onlookers.

"Don't we have any priesthood holders here? Someone give my baby a blessing!" she shouted. The entire crowd took a step back, a dozen active priesthood holders among them. She flared at them.

"You! Rulen Carter. You're an elder. I know you hold the priesthood. You give my baby a blessing!"

Brother Carter was the only inactive priesthood holder in the crowd, and the only one who had not taken a step back. He hung his head.

"Sister Mahoy, I can't. I ain't worthy. I've been inactive more'n twenty years. I don't even remember how." It was the first time he had ever called her "Sister Mahoy." For years, he had just called her "Laura."

"My baby is dying! God will bless my baby. You only need to say the words. Please!" she pleaded.

He looked helplessly to the left and right. Every face he saw glanced away from him. A look of grim determination mixed with tremendous anxiety settled on his face, and he slowly came around and knelt by Jimmy's head. Tears were coursing down his leathery face. He placed his large, callused hands on Jimmy's tiny head, and after a long pause, in a voice almost too soft to be heard, he said, "Heavenly Father, I know I'm a sinful man. Please forgive me, and please don't hold my sins against this little baby. Jimmy, in the name of Jesus Christ I command you to live, amen."

The blessing was so simple, so direct and honest that Jim Mahoy stopped working on his son and looked up at Brother Carter.

Unexpectedly, Jimmy coughed, and a spatter of muddy water sprayed from his mouth onto Laura's dress. She gasped. Jim pressed his fingers to Jimmy's neck.

"I feel a pulse!" he cried. People applauded. A hundred "thank God's" were mumbled simultaneously. "Roll him onto his side. Here, raise his hips. Come on Jimmy, cough it all out." People were laughing, crying, and hugging each other. Sam found himself hugging Emily. Other brothers and sisters joined them. Brother Carter knelt in stunned silence as if he had been turned to stone.

By that time an ambulance had arrived, and Jimmy and his parents were loaded into the back, still working with him, urging him to cough, and speaking words of love and encouragement.

The ambulance was one of the old models that looked like a pregnant station wagon. A piece was missing from the oxygen bottle, and the drivers fumbled with it, trying to make it work. Jim grabbed it from them and got it going. By cupping his hands around Jimmy's face, Jim improvised a way to replace the missing piece. He ordered them to drive. They slammed the back doors and were shortly gone in a cloud of dust, sirens, and flashing lights. In those days, ambulance drivers were trained to do little more than transport sick people. The idea of trained paramedics treating someone at the scene was an idea still years away.

*   *   *

Sam couldn't remember walking back to the house or putting the milk into the cooler. He couldn't remember finishing the rest of the chores, which could not be postponed, even for something as terrible as this. The worst part was the grief-stricken quiet. For a house full of seven kids ranging from sixteen to two years, silence was an ominous thing. It was probably the first time the house had ever been silent in the middle of the day. Emily urged the kids to complete their chores to take their minds off Jimmy. They plodded ahead slowly, each struggling with fear, hope, and disbelief.

What little talk there was centered on the idea that Jimmy was breathing. Their hopes were that their parents and he would come home from the hospital together and their lives would be whole again. Emily spoke words of hope and assurance, drawing deeply from the fragile resources of her own hope, pushing aside logic and reason in favor of comforting the little ones.

Sam walked back to the bridge. The kitten was still there, looking at the water as if waiting for Jimmy to return from it. Mr. Carter had replaced the dam, and the ditch was once again full. Sam found a piece of wood and tossed it into the ditch. It floated away slowly. He timed it until it arrived at the place where they had found Jimmy. It took thirty-six minutes to arrive at the spot. He had heard that three minutes was the most a person could go without oxygen.

He knelt on the bank and cried.

*   *   *

When the phone finally rang, it was like a cannon going off in dead silence. For the briefest moment, no one moved. Finally, Sam answered it. It was their dad. The news was not good but not without hope.

Jimmy was breathing on his own, and his pulse was strong and steady. His body temperature had returned to normal. The only problem was that he had not regained consciousness. The doctors were amazed that he was alive. To further confuse the issue, his lungs were completely free of water. It was a miracle by any measure. The doctors speculated that he had been without oxygen for over an hour.

They all agreed that if Jimmy did regain consciousness, at best, he would surely suffer some sort of brain damage. At worse, he would never awaken.

Neither parent came home that evening. Someone brought food, and Mrs. Carter stayed long enough to see that the children were tucked into bed. Her demeanor was kind and grandmotherly, and everyone appreciated her care. Sam cried himself to sleep, as did many of his siblings.

Jimmy did not improve or deteriorate, but simply remained asleep, breathing easily. Each of the kids was allowed to go to the hospital to visit him. Each came away with the feeling that everything would be okay. The mood in the home brightened after several days. Laura refused to leave the hospital, so Dad came home each evening, ate, held family prayers, slept a few hours, and returned to the hospital. Sam tended the farm. Emily watched the family. They would make do. After fourteen days, Jim finally prevailed upon Laura to go home and sleep. She had eaten little and had not bathed for over a week. She had changed from her muddy dress only after insisting that the nurse let her change by Jimmy's bedside.

That night Jim and Laura stood by Jimmy's bed, their arms wrapped around each other. Laura gently stroked Jimmy's forehead, and Jim held his small hand. The boy's flesh was warm and alive. In a few minutes, Laura would leave. Unexpectedly, Jimmy's eyes fluttered open and focused on his mother.

"Hi, baby," she whispered lovingly.

"Mommy, I love you," he said. Jimmy smiled softly and closed his eyes again. His breathing continued undisturbed.

Jim and Laura hugged for a long time, confident for the first time that everything would be okay. They knew Jimmy could not speak or remember who they were if he had any brain damage. Laura hummed to herself as she made the long drive home.

After family prayers, Laura tucked her loved ones into bed. Even Sam, and those too old for such things, were tucked in and kissed goodnight.

After a long, hot bath, Laura fell to her knees beside her bed. She shed many tears of gratitude for a blessed spark of hope. For the first time in many days, she climbed into bed with a peaceful heart.

She slept for what seemed to be the entire night until she had a dream. She dreamed she was sitting down to do genealogy. Their family group sheet grew large in her vision, until she focused on the last entry on the page. She read Jimmy's full name, birth date, and place of birth. Then her eyes drifted to his death date—24 July 1965—that very day. Laura awoke suddenly and sat up in bed. Oddly, there was no panic, no grief, and no wrenching anguish—just peace. It was meant to be. It was a little after midnight. Seconds later the phone rang. It was Jim. Jimmy had passed away peacefully just moments before.

* * *

The death of a child is a tragedy felt by everyone in a small community, and Jimmy's funeral was overflowing with people. A small, baby blue casket, covered with countless flowers, stood in front of the pulpit.

All of Jimmy's family sat in the first row, with dozens of aunts, uncles, and cousins in the rows behind. Behind them, a sea of mourners flowed into the cultural hall and out onto the grass. Sam thought the funeral seemed to go on a long time, but in reality, it was only as long as necessary.

Finally, the bishop stood and said, "I was just passed a note that one of the family wants a few minutes." He returned to his seat.

Almost a full minute elapsed in silence before anyone stirred. When Sam finally did stand, every eye in the large assembly turned toward him, but he did not feel them. He walked to the small, blue casket, and without turning to face the people, he brought his flute to his lips.

He heard his mother weeping, and his father drew a ragged breath. Finally, he blew a quivering note, and softly, ever so softly, he played "I Am a Child of God." It was Jimmy's favorite song, which he had played for Jimmy many times. The music was sweet, pure, and haunting, like an angel's hymn at evening. Then, quite unexpectedly, the music danced away, laughing, playing, bubbling with little songs Jimmy had loved and sung: Primary songs his mother had taught him, nursery tunes, the theme from Sesame Street, Mister Rogers, and others. Next came a thundering passage from Bach, and then a magical, aching tune from deep within Sam. At last came a lullaby. The music was so pure, the tone so clarion and sweet, that the words seemed to float in the air. "Lullaby, and good night, may angels attend you. Lullaby, and good night, my little one, good night." It was as if there were no one else in the chapel but Sam and Jimmy, and their love touched hearts until every eye was flowing.

The music ceased. Sam stood there for a long time, reluctant to finally say goodbye. At last, he gently laid the precious flute beside his baby brother and slowly returned to his seat without looking up. This was the last time he would play the flute until Jimmy, in his joyful, innocent way, once again asked him to play "I Am a Child of God."

* * *

It seemed like an invasion, all the people who came to their home. For hours they came, bringing food, leaving food, eating food, and clearing away food. And all the while, they remembered, laughed, and cried. Some brought a photo or two they had taken of Jimmy, and others offered help.

Rulen Carter didn't come to the house along with everyone else. Instead, he got on his tractor and baled the hay that Sam hadn't been able to get to. It was his way of being there for them in their hour of need. Of all the flowers, food, and warm wishes they received in those days, Brother Carter's gift was the one that most touched their hearts. Finally, the company all left, and miraculously, so did all the clutter they brought. Jim and Laura collapsed onto the big sofa, and after a few minutes, the entire family gathered around them. It would have been a typical evening at the Mahoys, except that every heart was burdened beyond tears, and each had sought their parents in the hope of receiving comfort. Mother spoke first.

"Kids, you have all been brave these last few days. I'm proud of you. But now that this is behind us, it's time to cry." The kids exchanged confused glances.

"What I mean is, it's important to let your feelings of hurt come out. One of the worst things we can do is let Jimmy's death ruin something inside us or make us angry with God. The time will come when you feel like crying for days and days. When that happens, I want you to know that it's okay, and that you should go ahead and cry until there are no more tears. We will all understand."

"Mama, I already feel like crying for days and days," Beth exclaimed, her bright blue eyes wide and shining with tears. Beth and Angela were twins—blonde, blue eyed, mischievous, and dressed in ruffles and ribbons. They were twelve years old, going on twenty-one. "Me too, Mama," Angela replied in her twinnish way. They arose simultaneously and snuggled on either side of Laura, who tucked them against her.

"Mama, me too," little Rachel sobbed, not sure what it all meant. At five, and suddenly the youngest again, she had yet to fully understand why Jimmy was getting all this attention and why he was "spending the night" somewhere else. She took a place on Laura's lap. The twins both reached up to take Rachel's hands.

"I don't need to cry," Benjamin interjected gruffly, lowering his voice for emphasis. At seven years, he was going through the tough stage.

Jim responded, "I used to think that big boys don't cry, and I suppose when it comes to a cut finger or a black eye, maybe they don't. But when the hurt is coming from your heart, then it's okay to cry. Actually, I think that if you don't cry, it will eventually build up inside until you explode with sorrow. If that happens, you will hurt yourself, and maybe hurt others that you love, too."

For a moment, there was silence, and a few sniffles from the twins. Finally, Dad knelt down. It was their silent cue for family prayers. They all shifted to the floor, but before he called on someone to pray, he said, "In a few days, after we have cried all our tears, we'll talk again. It's been my experience that people sometimes feel angry after they feel sad. After that, they might blame themselves for what happened. I want to talk about those feelings, because no one is to blame. Jimmy's death was . . ."

"My fault!" Sam bellowed, as if the burden of his guilt would burst his soul. Everyone was stunned by Sam's fury. He jumped to his feet. "I should have listened! He didn't have to die! It's my fault! It's the same as if I had killed him!" His fists were clenched, his body rigid, veins standing out on his neck and face. He turned as if to leave the room but stopped abruptly when his mother calmly asked, "Was this when Jimmy asked if he could do chores with you?"

"How did you know? How . . ." he stammered, his face contorted with grief and confusion.

"Because, just after breakfast, I had a feeling like I should keep him near me. That's why I thought maybe you had a similar impression."

"The point is," Sam interjected, his voice icy with self-indictment, "I didn't listen. If I had listened, he . . ."

"If I had listened," his mother interrupted, "he would still be here too. If anyone is guilty, I am! I'm his mother, for crying out loud!" She choked back an angry sob. "It was my job to keep him safe. I . . ."

"While I was washing dishes," Emily interrupted, her voice choked with emotion, "I had a feeling several times to go find Jimmy. I could see the bridge from the kitchen window. If I had even been responsive enough to just look up, I would have seen . . ."

"While I was feeding the chickens," Benjamin interrupted in a whisper, "I felt worried about Jimmy, and I thought about the ditch. I just ignored it, because I thought it was stupid. The ditch goes right behind the chicken coop."

There was a painful silence. After a moment, Sam sat down on the floor, and everyone returned to their seats.

"I also have a confession to make," Jim admitted. Every one turned their eyes toward him, including Laura. She had no idea what he was going to say. "Three days ago, as I was fueling up the tractor, I looked into the backyard where you were all going about your chores. For some odd reason, you were all there. You were so happy and beautiful. I thought to myself how lucky I was, and how I loved each one of you. I distinctly heard a voice say, "One of these will shortly be called home. Their work is done." There was a feeling of peace that came with it, and I knew that one of you would be leaving our home." He stopped for a long while as his body was racked by a silent sob.

"I knew it was from God, because of the peace I felt. I have long known that one of the things Satan can't imitate is peace. I knew better than to try to beg the Lord to not let it happen. What I was hearing wasn't a prophecy as much as it was a loving word to prepare me for these last few days.

"That morning, as I was helping Jimmy because his kitten had scratched him, I heard the Spirit whisper that it was Jimmy who would be called home. I don't know why, but I knew then, and I know now, that it was Jimmy's time to leave us."

"Then, if it was inevitable," Emily asked aloud, giving voice to the question they all wanted to ask, "why prompt so many of us to feel something that would have saved him? And why did we all ignore it? Why? It seems so futile, and so . . . so unfair!"

Jim hesitated before replying. "Well, I don't know the answer to that. I still have questions myself, but I think it has to do with agency."

"In what way, Jim?" This time it was Laura's heart begging for understanding. She had a master's degree in marriage and family counseling, yet nothing in her extensive training had prepared her for the devastation she had experienced in the last few days.

It was obvious to all, especially to Jim, that he was struggling for understanding, even as he was trying to explain it to his loved ones.

"Perhaps it works like this. Heavenly Father knew that Jimmy had to come home, that his work was done. He wouldn't just strike Jimmy down. We have great faith that He wouldn't do such a thing, and we pray constantly for His protection.

"Perhaps Jimmy decided to throw the kitten into the ditch to punish her for scratching him that morning. Jimmy was a little like that, you know. Somehow, Jimmy also fell into the water. Perhaps Kitty scratched him, or hung onto him, and he got too close. I don't know, but he fell into the water because of poor choices on his part, not because God pushed him in, or sent angels to do it, or anything else like that. He fell in because of his poor use of agency. However, it was God's plan to call him home, so he allowed this error on Jimmy's part to accomplish that.

Jim looked at his family lovingly. "He forewarned us, because we love Jimmy, and the Holy Spirit always warns and protects. He forewarned us because it's our right to receive such promptings. We didn't listen because we were busy. Just like Jimmy, we used our agency unwisely, and Heavenly Father used this also to complete His plan. I think any one of us could have stopped Jimmy from drowning, but since we didn't, Heavenly Father used our actions to bring Jimmy home. Heavenly Father allowed our weaknesses, including Jimmy's, to accomplish His divine will."

"Then, what is the point in warning us?" Laura asked, as much for her benefit as for her children.

"Because, I suppose, we have the right to the promptings of the Holy Spirit, and because He wanted to teach us a lesson we would never forget. I don't think He took Jimmy home to teach us. I think He just used his passing as an opportunity to teach. I believe Heavenly Father loves us enough to use even a tragic event like this to teach us a lesson we must learn before we can reach the celestial kingdom."

"What lesson were we supposed to learn from this?" Angela asked dubiously. Beth nodded in twin-like agreement.

"What do you think we were supposed to learn?" Jim asked in response.

Angela thought awhile, but Beth replied, "I think we are to learn that Heavenly Father loves us. I think it was loving and kind of Him to warn us and give us the opportunity to save Jimmy, even though He knew we wouldn't do it. Imagine how we would all feel if He hadn't told Daddy that Jimmy's work was done and that He would be going home. We would all feel like we had killed Jimmy ourselves by not listening or watching him closer."

"I think," Sam added quietly, "that we are to learn to listen and to obey the promptings we receive. At least, that's what I'm going to do. I'll never ignore another one if I know it's from God." A chorus of "me either" followed.

"I think," Emily said slowly, her voice nearly a whisper, "that He warned us because He loves us, not to make us feel guilty. I don't think He'd do that. I know He wouldn't."

Laura nodded at her daughter. "It breaks my heart that Jimmy is no longer with us." Her voice was soft but certain. "Yet, he is sealed to us in the temple, and I know he will always be a part of our family. His life had meaning. He brought us love, happiness, joy, wonder, and laughter. He brought us all these things and more. His being a part of our family had a great purpose, and when that purpose was completed, he went home to Heavenly Father. I promise each of you, and I promise Heavenly Father, that I will never forget Jimmy, and I will never forget the lessons he taught me in his short life, nor the lessons Heavenly Father taught us in his passing. This I promise."

"This, I promise," Sam said to himself, and he meant it more than any promise he had ever made.

CHERYL

By the time December rolled around, every tear that needed to be shed had rolled from reddened eyes to the floor. With the final drop, a semblance of normality came upon them, and the joy of the upcoming Christmas season slowly warmed them.

The Mahoys loved Christmas more than any other time of year. With so many kids in the house, a sense of breathless wonder hung in the air, like crystalline snow on a winter's eve, sparkling like diamonds in the moonlight. Christmas was Laura's season of joy, and her happiness blanketed the entire family like a warm comforter. For her, Christmas meant secret plans and special gifts, surprises, decorations, and fun. It meant remembering old friends, Christmas cards from far away, and new friends unexpectedly made. It meant walking through crunching snow with frozen toes to sing carols at friends' doors. It meant shopping for hours for that special gift, wrapping it just so, and thrilling inwardly for days at the joy the receiver might feel when it was finally opened.

Jim Mahoy's favorite part of the season was watching Laura. He never loved her more than when she was alight with the Christmas spirit. At times he felt his heart would burst from sheer love. It seemed as if she were superhuman, inexhaustible, and angelic—all packaged in a soft, womanly bundle. For Jim, Christmas was the Christ Child born in a manger, and it was Laura. He cared but little for gifts, bright paper and ribbons, Christmas trees and ornaments. The thousand feet of outdoor lights he hung each year were hung for Laura. He didn't care about caroling and the like, but he would have wrapped the entire world in strings of Christmas lights just to see his precious wife laugh and clap with joy like a four-year-old when he plugged them in each year. It was as if she had never seen them before, and her happiness was so pure it was spiritual.

Emily's favorite part of Christmas was cooking. She loved to bake, and Christmas was a blank check to cook anything she could conceive. And cook she did: cookies, cakes, pies, candies, pastries, gingerbread houses, and much more. Some of her creations were too beautiful to eat. For weeks the air was filled with a carefully orchestrated symphony of sweet spices. The aromas wove a tapestry of Christmas more beautiful than any masterpiece on canvas, and she loved every moment she spent weaving it.

Emily also cherished another part of Christmas. She had never told a soul, and probably never would, but she loved watching her papa watch her mama. Deep inside, she understood his passion, and everything feminine within her thrilled that a man could love a woman so. Every Christmas she renewed her vow that she would also have such a love.

For Sam, the best part of Christmas was the tree. Each year he would hunt for the perfect evergreen, and when he found it, he would bring it home. It would first spend a few days in the barn, then in the garage, and then in the back room to gradually warm up. It took Sam more than a week to get the tree into the house. But with Sam in charge, it had to be done just so. Finally, the tree would stand unadorned before the big living room window, carefully watered, until its branches relaxed enough to suit him. In the meantime, he planned how to decorate it. One year he flocked it white with small red lights, big red bows, and candy canes. Another year it was blue lights, white origami birds, and silver garland. This year, it was going to be multicolored lights, large calico bows, strings of red popcorn garland, and a large angel in calico coveralls on top. He didn't even try to explain the angel, and no one asked. One does not question the master, and when it came to the tree, he was in charge.

For Angela and Beth, the twins, Christmas meant snow—snow to play in, build forts in, and sled on. Soft snow, hard snow, powdery or wet—it didn't matter. The only way to ruin Christmas for them was for it to be snowless. If there was snow outside, they were outside. It seemed as if the only time they came in was to get warm enough to go back out.

For the first time ever, five-year-old Rachel was melancholy during the holiday season. No one understood why, least of all Rachel, but it seemed as if all she could do was to gaze out a window or at the tree hour after hour. It was so unlike her that Laura worried about her and tried to draw her into the festivities. But Rachel resisted gently, and wisdom seemed to dictate to Laura to let her find her own solace.

It was a perfect Christmas Eve. Fresh snow was falling, so Angela and Beth were breathless with anticipation. All the presents were carefully wrapped and hidden, cookies and cakes covered every flat surface, and a quiet calm had fallen over the house. In the background, the Mormon Tabernacle Choir quietly sang "Away in a Manger." The entire family had gathered near the tree, now perfectly resplendent in its calico bows and red popcorn stringers, to hear their father read the account of Christ's birth from the Gospel of St. Luke. They had scarcely begun when the phone rang. It was nearly 10:00 p.m. and unexpected. Laura hurried to answer it, expecting a late holiday greeting from family far away. After a moment, she handed the phone to Emily, a look of concern on her face.

Emily took it in Jim's small office, and after a while, she came back to where the family sat waiting to resume their Christmas Eve devotional.

"Mama, Papa, that was Cheryl. You know, Cheryl Cantello, the inactive girl? Well, she needs a place to stay, just for tonight. I guess her Dad threw her out of the house. She says she'll call her married sister in the morning and work out something with her."

Jim and Laura exchanged glances, nodded, and in a way that completely mystified the younger kids and thrilled Emily, they made a decision without a single word being spoken.

"Of course she can spend the night, Honey," Laura told her. "You and I will go get her. It's too stormy for you to drive alone tonight. Call her back and tell her we'll be there in about half an hour."

Emily shook her head. "Mama, Cheryl is at the gas station pay phone. The station is closed. She walked there without a coat, and she was crying. She's really cold and afraid. Can't we go get her right away?"

Laura quickly dialed elderly Sister France's number, who lived next to the gas station. Sister France was on her way out the door to get Cheryl almost before hanging up the phone.

"Come on, Emily," Laura said. "We'll pick her up at Sister France's home. It will still take us about twenty minutes to get there. We'll have to drive slowly in the snow, but she will be safe until then."

After they departed, Jim gathered the family around him.

"You all heard what is happening. This means Cheryl doesn't have any Christmas. The stores are closed by now. Let's come up with some ideas for a Christmas for Cheryl."

"How old is she, Dad?" Sam asked. He couldn't remember her too well.

"She's Emily's age, and about the same size, I'd say. Any ideas?"

"Daddy, you got each of us a couple of things, right?" Beth asked contemplatively. Jim nodded. "Well—you and Santa know what they are," she added with a quick glance at Rachel. "Would any of them be good for Cheryl? I mean, she can have one of mine."

"Yeah, mine too," Angela agreed. Beth nodded enthusiastically and added, "And we can hang another stocking and share our candy."

"I wanted a teddy bear. If you—I mean Santa—was going to give me one, I want Cheryl to have it," five-year-old Rachel volunteered happily with an "I already know about Santa" glance at Beth. It was the first time in days that she had risen above her melancholy.

"I don't know what to give her," seven-year-old Benjamin said. "I doubt if any of my gifts would work for her. I'm just a kid, and she's a grown up," he added, which brought a chuckle from the older family members. He was so busy thinking that he didn't notice. Finally, his face brightened. He ran from the room and returned holding Jimmy's kitten in his arms. It lay there listlessly. "You know how Kitty hasn't been playful since . . . well, you know, since Jimmy left? We thought she was sick, but she isn't. I think she needs to be loved again by someone special. Well, I think Cheryl needs to be loved again too. Maybe they need each other. Maybe this is their Christmas to find a new family for both of them."

Jim was touched by his son's compassion. "I think that's a wonderful idea. Why don't you make her a gift box with holes in it and a soft bed inside? You all have come up with wonderful ideas."

Only Sam had not come up with a gift. It was hard for him to imagine what Cheryl needed or wanted, especially among the things he possessed. Finally, his face brightened, and he knew what to do. "I have an idea," he said, and he walked away to work on it.

Cheryl was the last one to walk through the front door. She was taller than Emily by almost an inch and was as pretty a girl as Sam had ever seen. He wondered why he hadn't seen her at school. Her hair was almost the color Jimmy's had been—dark red, almost chestnut.

She was clutching a paper shopping bag to her chest. It contained everything she possessed. Her eyes were red and frightened, and she looked at the floor as if wishing she could sink into it and disappear.

Emily and Mom hustled her upstairs and drew her a hot bath. They found her a nightgown, and without another word, tucked her into the spare bed in Emily's room.

Christmas morning was the most magical morning of the year. Jim and Sam left the house at 4:00 a.m. to milk the cows. When they arrived home, the festivities would begin. They returned around 6:00, and the entire family gathered around the tree. Jim and Laura studied their family with wondering eyes, wanting to hold onto this moment in their memories. Jim snapped a few pictures and handed the camera to Laura since she was a better photographer, and family tradition demanded that Papa hand out the presents.

"Where's Cheryl?" Jim asked. Emily gave him a sideways look. "Still in bed."

"Well, go get her. It's Christmas morning."

"I already told her, but she said she doesn't want to interfere with our Christmas."

"Our Christmas? It's hers too! You go tell her we aren't starting without her."

"Yeah, and tell her to hurry, too!" Rachel added enthusiastically. Finally, Cheryl came down the stairs, wrapped in Emily's thick, blue bathrobe. She smiled weakly and took a seat on the couch, as far from the tree as she could get and still be in the same room. She folded her arms across her chest and lowered her head until her long, red hair hid her face.

"Let's see," Jim said, "the first one here is for Rachel." Rachel laughed happily and hopped up to grab her gift. Without returning to her seat, she ripped off the wrapping paper. It was a doll, with long, blonde hair, just like hers. Everyone was appropriately impressed as she hugged the doll to her chest and rocked back and forth. Mama flashed a picture of her.

The next one was for Benjamin, who received a baseball glove.

They continued from youngest to eldest until each had a gift. Angela received slippers with bunny rabbit faces on the toes, and Beth got a pair of fluffy mittens. Sam got a harmonica, which he immediately began to play as if he'd had it for years. Emily received the new blouse she had been hoping for.

"Well, look. This one says, 'To Cheryl, from Santa.'" Cheryl looked up for the first time, a look of disbelief on her face, tears beginning to form in her eyes. She honestly believed they were mocking her and wanted to run away. But no one was laughing, and Jim really was holding out a Christmas gift to her. Slowly, with wonder in her eyes, she stood and walked to where she could take it.

"There must be some mistake. I didn't . . ."

"Open it, honey," Laura urged. She slowly undid the ribbon and removed the paper with great care. A small, blue teddy bear was inside. She took it and pressed it to her cheek. From where Sam sat, he could see a tear trickling down her cheek.

Suddenly, all the rest of the presents were forgotten. Someone pressed another box into Cheryl's hands. It contained a pair of bunny slippers exactly like Angela's. Another box held mittens, exactly like Beth's. Another, bigger box contained a winter coat with a faux fur collar, exactly her (and Emily's) size. Sam shoved his gift into her hands. She looked at him with a shocked expression and then at the box. She carefully unwrapped it and removed the Christmas tree angel wearing calico coveralls.

She cried and then laughed. "It's true," she said. "Angels do sometimes wear coveralls. I just never realized it before." She gave Sam a meaningful smile, and he blushed.

Benjamin handed her the box he had wrapped. "This one is moving!" she exclaimed gleefully. She carefully opened it and lifted out the yellow and white kitten. As soon as she touched the small animal, it began to purr in a loud, contented way.

"See, Daddy? See? It loves her!" Benjamin exclaimed happily.

Cheryl didn't know, but everyone else knew that the kitten hadn't purred since Jimmy died five months earlier. Cheryl just stood there, holding her gifts, pressing the kitten to her cheek, her eyes aglow with wonder and happiness. "You guys. How did you . . . ?"

"Santa did it!" Rachel declared.

"Baby Jesus did it," Benjamin corrected, and everyone laughed. "Hey, here's a gift for Mommy," Jim said, handing his wife a shiny box.

Cheryl knelt down among her gifts and new friends and laughed happily as they finished their Christmas giving. Every so often, her voice would grow quiet, and she would have to wipe away tears before she could laugh again.

When it was all over, the room looked like the aftermath of a cheerful tornado. Everyone carried their treasures to their rooms, but Cheryl continued to sit amidst the bright Christmas clutter, stroking her kitten, rocking gently from side to side, and humming softly to herself. It was a time of sweetness for her, and everyone sensed it was also a time of healing.

* * *

Later that evening, they knelt for family prayer. Cheryl knelt next to Emily. Her eyes were bright and happy, and she held her kitten in her arms, its kitty motor purring loudly. "Before we pray, can I say something?" Cheryl asked timidly. Jim nodded and smiled.

"This has been the happiest day of my life. Since my mother died when I was seven, we haven't had Christmas. I have hated Christmas all these years. I think I hated it so I wouldn't have to be sad at not having it. I didn't realize that until this morning.

"My dad kicked me out last night because I didn't have dinner fixed when he came home. He was drunk, and he didn't realize it was almost ten o'clock. We had eaten without him hours earlier. He grabbed me by the hair and threw me out into the snow. He said I was a worthless bitch, even more worthless than my mother had been. I lay down in the snow and cried. I wanted to die! I wanted him to find my frozen body when he left the house the next day. I wanted him to know how he has made my life miserable all these years, and how much I hated him. He opened the door and threw a paper bag of my clothes at me. He didn't even care that I was lying in the snow without a coat.

"As I lay there shivering, a feeling of warmth came over me. I thought about my mother, and I knew she wouldn't want me to die this way. I got up and stumbled a couple of blocks to the gas station. It was closed. I had forgotten it was Christmas Eve. I just stood there shivering, thinking about dying, until this warm feeling came over me again, and I thought about Emily. I knew she was warm, safe, and loved. I thought if I could just spend one night being loved like Emily . . ." She stopped. Her voice wouldn't go on. She wiped tears away with the back of her hand and smiled sadly. "I thought if I could spend just one day being like Emily, then I would be happy to die. I wasn't going to let my father cheat me out of that one day, so I called Emily. I called because I hoped that somehow I could experience love, even for one day." There was a long pause.

"I know you don't love me like one of your own, like you do Emily, but I have seen the love you have for each other, and you have shared more love with me than I thought existed in the entire world. I got my wish. I got my day of love. I'll go to my sister's house tomorrow or the next day, but I wanted you all to know how special you have made me feel. I've never felt so loved. I just wanted to thank you. That's all, I guess." When Jim finally spoke, his voice was husky with emotion. "You were only wrong about one thing, Cheryl. We do love you like one of our own." A chorus of agreement filled the room. The twins rushed over to hug her, and everyone joined in. For a few minutes she was surrounded by love more powerful than she thought possible. It was more than her fragile soul could stand, and she wept openly for joy. These were not just words; this was love, pure and unfeigned. It warmed her through and through, and the icy pain deep within her began to melt away.

* * *

Several days later, they all gathered for family home evening. It was Angela's turn to give the lesson, and, naturally, Beth did exactly half of it. Cheryl was still there. She had not been able to reach her sister by phone and had written a letter instead. It would be a few more days before she left. No one was in a hurry for her to leave, especially Cheryl.

"Tonight's lesson is on what is good," Angela said in her best Sunday School teacher voice. "Who can tell me what is good?"

"Love is good," Cheryl said and blushed. It was one of those comments that opens a window into another's heart.

"I think Christmas is good," Rachel said in her enthusiastic way. "I especially liked the part about giving Cheryl presents she didn't expect." Everyone agreed. Again, Cheryl blushed.

Angela cleared her throat importantly. The room fell silent again. "How can you tell if something is good?"

"It makes you feel good inside," Laura answered, a thing she had discovered for herself.

"It makes me want to thank Heavenly Father," Jim added. He always felt like praying when something good came his way, even something as ordinary as a beautiful sunrise or a bird's song after a summer rain.

"Daddy, would you please read Moroni 7, verses 12 and 13?" Jim waited until everyone found the scripture. Then he closed his eyes and quoted it from memory.

> Wherefore, all things which are good cometh of God; and that which is evil cometh of the devil; for the devil is an enemy unto God, and fighteth against him continually, and inviteth and enticeth to sin, and to do that which is evil continually. But behold, that which is of God inviteth and enticeth to do good continually; wherefore, every thing which inviteth and enticeth to do good, and to love God, and to serve him, is inspired of God. (Moroni 7:12–13)

"So," Angela continued, "if something makes us feel like doing good, then that thing came from God. Does that also mean that if something ends up being good, then the things that made it happen were good too? Is that right Daddy?"

"I think that is generally true, especially if it felt good inside."

"But what if you didn't feel good inside, like you were sad at the time, but later it turned out good?" Beth wanted to know.

"Then, I suppose you could say that Heavenly Father made good come of it," Jim replied.

After a silent, twin-like signal, Beth took over the lesson.

"Okay," she said, drawing a deep breath as if preparing herself. "Here is what the lesson is about. We think this is the best Christmas we ever had. And we think it's because Cheryl was with us. Daddy, do you think this was good, I mean, like Heavenly Father wanted Cheryl to spend Christmas with us?"

"Very much so," Jim said, smiling.

"Okay, then, do you remember when she said she got this warm feeling at the gas station that made her want to call Emily? Do you think that was Heavenly Father too?"

Instead of answering, Jim asked, "What do you think, Cheryl?" Cheryl nervously looked around the room and cleared her throat.

A calm feeling came over her, and she smiled. "I was thinking about that this morning. It's funny that Beth brought it up. I do think that the warm feeling and my thoughts about Emily came from the Spirit. The other thoughts I was having were that I wanted to die."

"See? That's what we mean," Angela took over as if it was all in the script. Beth looked at her sister with an expression of perfect harmony. "On the one hand, she had this bad feeling that told her to lie down in the snow and die. But then she also had a warm feeling that told her where to find love. I think that's what Moroni was trying to tell us in the scripture. Things that tell us to do bad come from the devil, and everything that tells us to do good comes from God."

"That is really neat," Cheryl volunteered with wonder in her voice. "I hadn't realized that. I was actually in a battle for my life and was receiving real revelation from Heavenly Father on how to win. I didn't realize . . ." She fell silent for a moment. "I didn't realize how much Heavenly Father loves me. I had no idea. I thought I was nobody, a total write-off. I thought God only loved the prophets—and Emily." This brought a collective smile from the Mahoys, but Cheryl was serious. "Boy," she continued, her voice almost too quiet to hear, "this really is turning out to be an amazing Christmas. It seems as if I am suddenly surrounded by love."

"There's one more part to our lesson," Beth added without missing a beat. "We think that since Heavenly Father sent Cheryl to us, she should not be in such a hurry to leave. If Heavenly Father wanted her here, maybe she should find out if Heavenly Father wants her to stay here, like, for a long time. I mean, if it's all right with Mommy and Daddy."

"Oh, yes, Cheryl," Laura interjected enthusiastically. "I was thinking just this morning how sad it will be when you leave. I think Beth and Angela . . ."

"Angela and Beth," Angela corrected.

"She was born first, Mama. You know the ABCs. Angela and then Beth," Beth added teasingly.

"Angela and Beth have given us an inspired family home evening lesson," Laura said with a smile, and turned to her husband. "I hope you'll consider their words, Jim."

All eyes except Cheryl's turned on Jim as he searched for the right words. This was unexpected, yet it had the feeling of truth to him.

"Cheryl," he said as her big, brown eyes finally turned to look at him. "You are family now, whether you leave tomorrow or stay here for the rest of your life. Always remember that you have a home here and that you'll always be loved." A tear rolled down Cheryl's cheek.

After a moment, Jim slid to his knees and everyone followed. As he looked around the room, waiting for the Spirit to whisper who should pray, his eyes fell upon Cheryl. Her face was bright with the light of Christ. "Cheryl, would you pray tonight?"

Her head snapped up. She was startled, and for a moment, she looked as if she might say no. Instead, she bowed her head, and they waited for her to begin.

"Dear Heavenly Father, I think you are the most wonderful Heavenly Father in the whole, wide world. You treated me so nice to let me have Christmas with . . . with my new family. I didn't know you loved me . . . it surprised me to learn that you did . . . that you do. God forgive me for not knowing sooner . . . God bless Mama Laura. God bless Papa Jim. God bless Emily and Sam, Angela and Beth, and Benjamin and Rachel, . . . and please tell Jimmy we love him. God bless Kitty and the angel in coveralls. God bless Jesus, amen."

No one moved for a full minute. "I don't think I did so good," Cheryl said timidly. "I've never prayed out loud before, actually, or to myself either."

"It was the most beautiful prayer I've ever heard," Sam said quietly, mostly to himself. A chorus of happy hugs assured her that everyone present agreed.

MY ANGEL IN COVERALLS

Cheryl never did move to her sister's house but stayed with her new family. The next year she turned seventeen the same month Sam turned sixteen. He was a junior in high school, and she a senior. It was the fall of 1967.

Fall had gripped the air, and Halloween decorations hung all throughout the school. When you're a senior girl, the most important consideration is who will take you to the senior prom, which was only three days away. Cheryl held no hopes that she would be asked. She was not popular at school, because she did not participate in the things that would have made her so. She was too shy to join in without being almost forced to participate. Still, her heart ached to go to the dance. Sam was sweet on Jenny, a dark-haired junior from the seventh ward. Jenny was pretty and a cheerleader. She was popular, bubbly, and enthusiastic. Sam was hopelessly smitten with her. He thought

Jenny was perfection wearing lipstick.

Sam was now on the football team and had acquired considerable talent in that sport. By his junior year he was the varsity center, and, consequently, more popular with the other kids. The best thing about that position was that he didn't ever have to catch the ball—a skill he was still not good at.

He had grown nearly two inches the past year, had gotten contact lenses, and suddenly his broad features and dark hair were attractive. It was as if the old Sam had moved away and his handsome cousin had taken his place. He was still rather shy, but too caught up in the momentum of his new life to be overly affected by it.

He and Jenny had planned for weeks to go to the prom, and he had arranged for a tuxedo, corsage, and dinner—the works. Cheryl watched all this from a distance. She was sincerely happy for Sam's good fortune, yet she was saddened that she had not found the same. The night before the prom, Sam called Jenny. After a long conversation, a thousand promises, and tears from Jenny, Sam successfully arranged for her to go with her cousin and Sam's good friend, Tim. Sam told her he had a family obligation he could not shirk, and he would see her at the dance. Jenny understood and admired him for his decision, but still, she was not pleased.

The evening was waning to darkness when Sam approached Cheryl, who was sitting at the kitchen table, studying for an algebra final.

"Cheryl? Uh, I have a problem. I have spent all this money, see, and made reservations and all, and Jenny says she has to go with her cousin to the prom because her parents insisted. I was wondering if you would like to go with me. I know we're family and all, but if you weren't, I mean, given other circumstances, I would have liked to go with you. You're real pretty and fun to be with. I mean, what do you think? Go with me?"

Cheryl laid down her pencil and eyed him dubiously. "As a favor to you? To save you money?" she asked.

"Well, yes."

She shook her head. "I don't believe a word of it. I talked to Jenny yesterday, and she was so excited about the prom she couldn't think straight. It was all she could talk about. Her parents were happy about it too. Tell me the truth or forget it."

Sam gulped. "Well, it's sort of the truth, except that . . . I kind of asked Jenny to go with her cousin. I didn't want you to miss the only senior prom you'll ever get to go to. You are more important to me than a date with Jenny, and we will have our own senior prom next year. You can bet that if you say no, Jenny will still go with her cousin just to spite me. So you are doing me a favor."

Cheryl thought about it. "Yeah, she would do that, and I probably would too. You will have to do some awful fancy footwork to get back into Jenny's good graces." Sam shrugged. He knew what she said was true. "Well, as long as it's only as a favor to you, not because you feel obligated to take me."

"As a very big favor to me," he echoed, and Cheryl smiled a big smile.

"I don't have a dress! I don't know how to do my hair! I don't have high heels or anything! This is awful! Actually, it's very sweet." She kissed him on the cheek, and hurried off to find Emily and Mama Laura. Actually, Sam had already discussed it with them, and they had been working on Cheryl's dress all afternoon. They had lengthened one of Emily's dresses and borrowed a pair of shoes. Preparations were much further along than Cheryl could have ever guessed.

That next evening, when Cheryl came down the stairs, Sam had to struggle to keep his mouth from falling open. Since Christmas Eve a year ago, he had looked at Cheryl as his sister, not as a dateable female. What he saw coming down the stairs could have walked across any beauty pageant stage and won hands down. Her dark red hair was done up with large ringlets falling softly by her cheeks. Her dress was black and was stunning on her figure.

"Wow, you look fantastic!" he gushed. "Who are you? Where's Cheryl?"

She hit him playfully with her handbag. Sam pinned a corsage on her, and she pinned a boutonnière on him. She took his arm and they left in the family car. Jim and Laura stood on the porch, huddling against the chill, and inwardly glowing with contentment.

The dance was the highlight of the school year. There were kids in tuxedos and tails, and others in leather jackets and faded jeans.

Cheryl was graceful on the dance floor. Sam had secretly taken lessons from his mother for several weeks, and he knew the basics. Before long, they were oblivious to anyone else and danced in a cloud of discovery and happiness. It surprised him when he felt a tap on his shoulder. He did not recognize the boy, but the boy was dressed in a suit and looked harmless. Cheryl shrugged and smiled, so Sam stepped aside. That he was a much better dancer than Sam was obvious from the second step, and Cheryl glided away like magic.

Suddenly alone, he thought of Jenny, and after a few minutes found her dancing with her cousin. Following the stranger's example, he tapped in and was soon gliding around the floor with Jenny. She was pleased to finally dance with him and didn't show any sign of being angry.

"I understand why you wanted to come with Cheryl," she said finally. "It would be a shame for her to miss this." He was grateful she understood. "Look how much fun she's having." Just then, the crowd shifted and he caught sight of her dancing away. Her partner had drawn her close to him, and they were spinning around the floor. All he needed to see was the smile on her face to know he needn't hurry back.

He and Jenny talked and danced for most of an hour before he again caught sight of Cheryl. The music had slowed, and they were dancing very close, except that Cheryl was arching her back, trying to keep his head off her shoulder. He was leaning into her with his hands low on her back. Too low.

"I think I better go rescue Cheryl," he said, nodding toward Cheryl and her partner. Jenny gasped and released him. He immediately walked away.

"Excuse me. May I cut in?" he said, tapping the boy on the shoulder. The look of relief on Cheryl's face was enough to tell him that he had come just in time.

"No!" the boy said at the same moment Cheryl said, "Sure." He danced away with Cheryl, and Sam followed. "I'm cutting in," Sam said.

Cheryl turned to join Sam, but her partner jerked her back. "Please. It's been nice, but I'm tired now. Thanks," Cheryl told him. But the boy wouldn't stop. Finally, Cheryl stopped dancing, and the stranger had to stop also. Sam held out his hand and she reached for it, but the stranger gave him a menacing look. Sam returned the glare without lowering his hand. The stranger gave Sam a dangerous look. "She's dancing with me, and if you know what's good for you, you'll leave. You can have her back when I'm finished with her. Now beat it!"

Sam took Cheryl's hand without blinking an eye and pulled her away.

The stranger shrugged. "Well, I guess I lose." He started to turn away, but added, "On second thought, you lose." Without warning, he spun on one foot and swung at Sam. Sam wasn't expecting an attack, and the blow caught him on the side of the head. Sam stumbled one step, his head ringing, and his ear turning puffy. The fellow swung another time, but Sam stepped into the blow, and the boy's fist hit Sam's shoulder.

The same defect that made him poor at catching a ball also made him a poor fighter. Sam knew he had one chance to end this fight successfully. He waited until the fellow swung again. He ducked beneath the blow and with all his strength hammered the stranger under the chin. The fellow's head snapped back. He fell backward with a loud thud onto the polished floor. Sam took four quick steps and grabbed him by the suit lapels. In a single motion, he lifted him until only his toes were touching the floor. The stranger was still gasping for breath as Sam shook him, the boy's head snapping back and forth. Two boys in leather jackets and jeans pulled their friend from Sam's grasp and were about to finish the fight for him when several teachers appeared. They separated them and kicked the stranger and his friends out of the dance. Sam didn't realize the music had stopped until it began again, and people started to turn away in disinterest.

Cheryl was instantly by his side, inspecting his ear. It was sore, but not bleeding. "A cow can kick harder than that fool can hit," he said quite honestly. He should know. He had taken blows from many cows. Cheryl chuckled, put her arms around his neck, and kissed him on the forehead.

"You really are my angel in coveralls, aren't you?" He blushed as he took her hand and they danced until the band put away their instruments.

There weren't very many cars left in the parking lot when Sam and Cheryl came out. Sam helped Cheryl into the car, but as he was doing so, he spotted four cars parked on the far side of the lot. Only the glow of cigarettes in the dark told him that someone was there. He had a sinking feeling and knew that he and Cheryl were in trouble. He slammed her door, dashed around to the driver's side, quickly slid behind the wheel, and locked all the doors.

"What's wrong?" Cheryl asked in a worried voice.

"I think those punks waited for us. It's a long drive home, and they may be planning something."

"Let's go back inside and call Mom and Dad," she insisted. Sam thought that was a good idea, but they could see the janitor locking the doors to the school.

"Cheryl, you pray, and I'll drive. We'll be all right. What can they do to us as long as we drive straight home? They surely won't run us off the road."

"I suppose you're right," she said nervously.

Sam started the car and pulled away. After watching for a while, it didn't appear they were being followed. They began to relax and talk about the dance. They approached an intersection where they had to turn left to go home. If they turned right, it took them down a long, winding road in the hills, which eventually dead-ended at a lake. When they came to the intersection, they were shocked to see three cars completely blocking the left road. Sam panicked and started to back up, but several cars came up directly behind him, honking their horns. Sam had no choice but to turn right. He knew the road was a dead end, and hoped they could find a way to turn around before the other cars caught up. He gunned the car and sped off. After a mile, the road turned to dirt.

Sam didn't dare go too fast, mostly because he didn't want to reach the dead end anytime soon. But he did want to find a place to turn around before they caught up. All of a sudden, a car loaded with teenagers roared past them like they were standing still. Before he could react, another car zoomed past, its exhaust squealing loudly.

Cheryl screamed in fright, and turned terrified eyes on Sam. "Whatever happens," Sam told her, his fists clenched white on the wheel, "I won't let them hurt you. They want me, not you. When they start on me, run away into the woods. Take off your heels, and run barefoot. I've seen you run on the farm, and you can really move. You have on a black dress, and they won't be able to find you."

"I couldn't leave you. I couldn't!" she protested. "You have to!"

"But I won't!"

"Promise me you will if it comes to that!" he nearly shouted. "Okay, I promise. If I have to, I'll run. But I won't like it."

"Listen, they can't hurt me too much. I'm tough from football and working on the farm. I'll fight them a little, and then I'll roll up and pretend to be whipped. They'll get tired and leave. I'm afraid of what they might do to a beautiful girl in the middle of the night. You must remember your promise. I'm going to get it either way. It will only make it worse on both of us if you stick around."

"Okay, okay!" she said, her voice angry. "Let's figure out a better solution before it comes to that."

At that moment, the two cars in front of them pulled next to each other and braked. Sam had no choice but to slow down. Four cars pulled up behind them, swaying back and forth, honking, and flashing their lights. They were obviously spoiling for whatever they had planned. It only took them a few minutes to force Sam to a complete stop.

Sam knew better than to get out of the car as the boys from the front car started walking back toward him. One of them was the stranger in the suit. He had a baseball bat in his hands which he was swinging back and forth. He walked straight up to Sam's car, and without saying a word, shattered the windshield. A million pieces of glass sprayed into their faces and laps. Cheryl screamed in terror.

He leaned through the broken windshield on Sam's side, his face plastered with an evil smirk. Cheryl cowered back into her seat. Suddenly the rear window exploded as someone else smashed it.

"First," the boy glowered, "I'm going to beat the living crap out of your boyfriend here and make it so he never thinks about another girl as long as he lives. Then you and me are going to finish what we had going at the dance. And you're going to like it, whether you want to or not!"

As he was saying this, Sam was praying silently. He knew only a miracle could save them. At the exact moment the threats ended, he had a wild idea. It was impossible, dangerous, foolish, and a hundred other things, but with the idea came a feeling of peace. His father's words rang in his ears: "Satan can't imitate peace."

Sam lunged forward and grabbed the kid's tie and a part of his jacket. Luckily, it was not a snap-on tie. Sam wound a beefy hand into the fabric so that nothing short of a crow bar could have opened it. With his other hand, he shifted into reverse, grabbed the steering wheel, and simultaneously jammed his foot onto the gas.

The family car was a new Rambler Ambassador station wagon. It outweighed the punks' cars by almost a thousand pounds.

His action was so sudden, so unexpected, that the kid in his grasp dropped the bat and screamed in wide-eyed terror. The big V8 engine roared as the car slammed into the car behind them. A side window exploded from an invisible blow. Shouts, screams, and curses were rending the night air.

"Get down!" Sam shouted at Cheryl, who complied the best she could. He jammed the car into first gear and gunned the motor. He didn't dare hit the front cars as hard. He had watched a few demolition derbies and knew that to puncture the radiator was to lose. He picked the smaller of the two cars in front of him and hit it as hard as he dared. It jolted forward six feet. He was hardly aware of the screaming face still suspended in his front window as he jammed the car into reverse and plowed into the cars behind. The car he hit jumped ten feet.

Sam jammed into forward and hit the other car. People were running everywhere, trying to get out of his way. There were four cars behind him, and they were having a hard time getting away. Sam hit them repeatedly. Finally, there was an opening between the two cars in front of them, and he sped through the opening, letting go of the punk on the hood just as they cleared the two cars. He saw him flip end over end onto the side of the road. He hoped he hadn't hurt him too much and simultaneously hoped he was stone dead. Sam steered the car down the winding road in total darkness. He had smashed out the headlights in his escape. Cheryl was sitting up, blinking in the rush of wind through the open windshield.

"That was the most amazing thing I have ever seen!" she exclaimed without taking her eyes off the winding road. "I think your Dad is going to kill us when he sees what we have done to his new car!"

Sam thought about this for only a second before replying. "Maybe, but I'll bet he'll consider it a small price for bringing you home safe." She looked at him with a strange expression on her face.

"You really would have let them beat you up if it would help me escape, wouldn't you?"

He just shrugged. "It isn't over yet. This is a dead-end road. I doubt they will give up after I messed up their cars like that. We have to figure out something else." After what seemed like too short a time, they arrived at the small campground on the lake. It was deserted.

When they pulled into the parking lot, six other cars immediately surrounded them. Sam couldn't tell that they had been followed because the punks' headlights were also smashed. This time they pulled in bumper to bumper. Sam gunned the big engine, but the wheels just flipped gravel and billowed smoke. It was no use.

"Okay, this is back to plan A," he said. He reached up and ripped the dome light off the ceiling with one effortless movement.

"When I jump out, you wait five seconds and head off the other way. If you do it right, they won't see you. Remember, you promised. No matter what you hear, keep running." Cheryl nodded, wide-eyed, tears streaking her face.

He pushed his door open the few inches he could and climbed out onto the hood of the car that was blocking him. A head appeared and he kicked it. Whoever it was fell backward and didn't return. He jumped up onto the roof of the car blocking him, jumped over a baseball bat that someone swung at his legs, and ran down the trunk. He didn't even look back to see if Cheryl had followed his instructions. He had his work cut out for him at that moment. He knew where he was headed. He had spotted an old fire pit not far away, and it had branches hanging out of it that he could use as a club. He almost made it but was not fast enough. Someone tackled him from behind. He fell, skidding forward, someone clinging to his legs. He easily pulled a leg loose and kicked the offender in the face.

Just then, a terrible blow landed on the side of his head, and he was momentarily dazed. He could feel other blows coming down on him. He could feel himself contorting, trying to roll into the fetal position. He had never felt such pain, and his mind seemed to grind to a stop.

Sam forced himself to think. His vision cleared just as a fist came at his nose. Reflexively his hand shot out and caught the fist. He closed with all his strength and twisted. He felt the other's bones breaking, accompanied by a scream of pain. It was a sickening feeling, but he was fighting for survival. He rolled onto his knees and was immediately bowled back over by a kick in the ribs. The only thing that was saving him was that there were too many attackers on him to swing a weapon without hitting one of their own. It was small consolation.

Blackness was just about to overcome him when he saw a body fly over his head. He dimly heard someone curse, and the beating seemed to slow and suddenly stopped. Dimly, he identified the sound of another fight going on nearby. He had a sinking thought that Cheryl had returned, but the blows were too solid. His vision cleared a bit, and he saw a black-coated punk spin away and drop to his knees. Sam sat up and saw his attackers converge on a single person standing in the headlights of an old truck, his legs spread.

Whoever it was moved like a ballet dancer, swinging what appeared to be a shovel. The improvised weapon moved too fast to follow in the dim light. It blurred this way and that. All Sam knew was that his attackers were screaming and running away as fast as they could. Within less than a minute, it was all over. Engines gunned, and cars sped away into the darkness.

It wasn't until his unidentified benefactor leaned over Sam that he realized it was his dad. Jim Mahoy still had the shovel in one hand, his eyes wary and scanning the campground. He examined his son, and satisfied that his injuries were not life-threatening, helped him stand. Sam felt like passing out and throwing up at the same time. He hurt in every part of his body. He took a step and realized he had been kicked in the crotch.

Just then they was alarmed to hear a shuffling noise in the darkness, just to their right. A moment later, Cheryl trotted into the circle of light, crying with relief and joy. She threw herself into Papa Jim's strong and welcoming arms. She was completely exhausted and emotionally spent, but she was miraculously unhurt.

Sam fell asleep on Cheryl's shoulder as they bounced to the hospital in the old truck. His dad said nothing, his face a grim mask of anger and pride. Cheryl told Jim the entire story as he drove, while Jim concentrated on not hitting any bumps that could make Sam groan in his sleep.

The hospital treated Sam immediately, administering tests and x-rays, and setting his broken bones. When they all returned home early the next morning, Sam went straight to bed and slept for three days. When he finally looked in the mirror, he was surprised to see a black and blue stranger looking back at him. In the final tally, he had four broken ribs, three broken fingers, two black eyes, a concussion, and a zillion cuts and bruises—but he was alive and Cheryl was unharmed. He tried to smile at the thought, but it hurt too much. The station wagon was a total loss. The insurance company took one glance at it and wrote it off. Most of the punks were caught and punished. Several received prison sentences. They weren't hard to identify. They drove battered cars and most had broken bones and bruises the shape of a shovel.

Sam later found out that the story had been in the newspapers and on television. He was a kind of hero, which made him feel uncomfortable.

* * *

Cheryl was in charge of family home evening the following Monday. Sam hobbled downstairs and was greeted by a room full of balloons and crepe paper. A large cake Emily had baked was on the coffee table. On its surface, Emily had very carefully crafted a frosting angel wearing coveralls.

Cheryl's lesson was a retelling of their experience. None of them had actually heard it from start to finish, and they all listened with rapt attention. She was gushing in her praise of Sam, and of Papa Jim. When the telling was all done, and they were about to kneel down to family prayers, Sam asked the question that had been tickling the back of his mind for days.

"Dad, where did you learn to fight like that? You weren't in any of the armed forces. How did you do it? And how did you find us? We were miles off the road to home, and it seems like a miracle you ever found us."

Jim straightened in his chair and considered his answer. "Well son, we called family prayers about eleven o'clock that night, and while your mother was praying, I had a feeling come over me that something was very wrong. It was just a feeling, but very clear. I knew you two were in danger. I didn't wait for the prayer to end, but jumped into the old truck and drove toward the school. As I went, I prayed. You know how the Lord and me are. I do everything He says, and He makes it rain on my crops. Well, I needed some rain, and I told Him so."

Laura smiled at this, then nodded for her husband to continue. "I about drove past the turn-off to the lake when I had the strong feeling that I should turn up there. It was a long shot, and I knew it, but I had asked for help and it seemed absurd to ignore it when it came. When I turned onto the road, I knew I was on the right track when I saw hubcaps, fenders, and glass all over the road about halfway there. I drove as fast as I could until I came upon the station wagon surrounded by cars. From its condition, I knew you had tried to get away by bashing into them."

Jim grimaced at the memory, then continued. "It was also obvious you hadn't been entirely successful. I saw a pile of guys off to the side, and knew you were under them. As I was getting out of the truck, I had the thought to grab the irrigation shovel. I did, and when they came at me, I just did everything I felt impressed to do. I swung, ducked, kicked, punched, and fought by the Spirit. It was the most incredible experience I've ever had. It was as if I were another person. During it all, I had a perfect sense of calm come over me. When it was all over, I found myself just standing there, holding the shovel." Jim looked intently at Sam. "Son, the answer to your question is that I did it by the grace of God. I think this is what Moroni meant when he said God strengthened their arms so they could defend their families from the armies of the Lamanites, even though they were vastly outnumbered.

Jim gazed around the room at his family. "I'm certain that had we not discussed what we did following Jimmy's accident, about listening to the Spirit and following directions even when it's hard to understand, and had I not taken it to heart, that both you and Cheryl would have died out there."

Everyone in the family soberly nodded. Then Sam said, "You know what I don't understand, though, Dad, is the difference in the promptings. You described the feelings you had as being quite clear. I can see how that could be the Holy Ghost directing you to come save us. But for me, the promptings are so quiet, so difficult to hear, so . . ."

"Still and small?" Jim interjected.

"Exactly. Sometimes I can't tell the difference between the whisperings of the Spirit and my own thoughts. Yeah, I usually get the big promptings, but the little ones I miss a lot."

Laura cleared her throat and everyone turned toward her. "The same thing has bothered me since Jimmy's passing. There were both kinds of promptings for me that day. I had many little promptings, and I ignored them because I didn't recognize them as promptings. By the time the big one came, I had waited too long . . ." Her voice trailed off. "I have often wondered why Heavenly Father didn't warn me more loudly so I couldn't miss it. Why even use the still, small voice if we are so prone to not hear it?"

Benjamin interrupted them. "We keep talking about two voices, the still, small voice and the louder one. Are there actually two voices? Or is it just that we have our ears turned low some times, and it sounds still and quiet?" he asked, a note of confusion in his voice.

Jim turned to Cheryl. "Is it all right with you, Cheryl, if I take a minute and explain what I think is going on? I know it's your family home evening." Cheryl nodded willingly. "Please do. I'm as confused as I can possibly be. I have heard both of these voices, too. I always assumed it was because I just don't listen well enough, or that if I were more righteous, the voice would be louder. Please explain it to us!"

"Thanks, Cheryl," Jim replied. "There is only one Holy Ghost, but it seems that He speaks in two different ways."

"Why Daddy?" Beth asked in unison with Angela.

"Well, you know how Bishop Connell serves as our bishop but he is also our home teacher? When he comes home teaching, does he act and speak differently than when he's being the bishop at church?"

"Oh yes—he smiles and laughs more when he's our home teacher," Rachel observed enthusiastically. "When he's the bishop, he acts all serious and stuff."

"Well, it's kind of the same thing with the Holy Ghost. One of the great blessings that Jesus Christ has given us is that the Holy Ghost can also act as the 'Light of Truth.' Has anyone heard that term before?"

"Is that the same thing as our conscience?" Sam asked.

"It is. It's something that every person has, and it has the job of teaching every person right from wrong. This is the still, small voice we keep talking about. We have it because of the Atonement. It's one of the many precious gifts from Jesus Christ. The scriptures indicate that one of the reasons Jesus had to suffer so much was so that He would know how to guide us when we have problems."

"Wow. I didn't know that," Cheryl said, putting her hands on her cheeks and resting her elbows on her knees. "So does the still, small voice only tell us not to steal candy bars and that kind of thing? Or does it have another purpose?"

"It has several purposes, in addition to helping us discern right from wrong," Jim explained. "The greatest of these, and the hardest to learn to hear, are the promptings to do good things. It sometimes seems a lot easier to hear the promptings to avoid evil than it is to hear the promptings to do good."

"You mean, like, say your prayers, be kind to someone—that kind of thing?" Benjamin asked. "I've heard those a lot. Sometimes I ignore them because they always seem to want me to do something I don't want to do. I thought they were just my own thoughts and not important."

"I think we all have done that, Ben. I'd like to share a scripture," Jim said, and drawing on his unique memory and love of the scriptures, he closed his eyes and recited,

> *And the Spirit giveth light to every man that cometh into the world; and the Spirit enlighteneth every man through the world, that hearkeneth to the voice of the Spirit. And every one that hearkeneth to the voice of the Spirit cometh unto God, even the Father. (D&C 84:46–47)*

"I think the important part here is the last sentence. 'And every one that hearkeneth to the voice of the Spirit cometh unto God, even the Father.' That's the whole purpose of life, to return to Heavenly Father. It says that we must learn to hearken, or obey, the still, small voice in order to return to Him. Unless you realize that these promptings are actually revelation from God, then you may feel free to just ignore the ones that are inconvenient."

"Boy, I do that a lot," Emily commented. "But you know what? I always feel kind of empty inside when I do."

"Me too," several family members said at once.

"But I'm still confused," Cheryl said as she leaned forward in her chair. "How do I tell the promptings apart from my own thoughts? I always thought they were just my own thinking."

"Well," Jim began, "here's how I do it. I still miss some, but this helps me. It's like the scripture in Moroni we read in family home evening a while ago. Everything that is good and teaches us to love and serve God, to pray and be kind, comes from God, and we should always obey those promptings. Everything that teaches us to do bad, to be mean, or to not pray, those things come from the devil."

"I can see that," Laura interjected. "But I also hear confusing things. I hear a lot of discussions, questions, and even arguments in my head. I hear the good and the bad, and then I hear myself debating about what it all means!"

Jim nodded. "We all do that! It's my opinion that this is our own mind working. I think what happens is the Holy Spirit prompts us to do good. After that, the devil tries to get us to not do that good thing, and then our minds try to decide what to do. What we are hearing is that argument going on in our minds."

"Hey!" Emily said enthusiastically. "I think I understand. It's called the still, small voice because it sounds like our own thoughts. But it's not—at least, not all of it. The Holy Spirit says to do some good thing. It just says 'Say your prayers,' or something like that. After that, you hear reasons from Satan why you shouldn't, like you're too tired or too mad to say prayers. After that, you hear your own voice trying to decide what to do. I get it. This is how revelation works. We get prompted by both sides, and we must decide what we will do."

"Yes, Emily! Let me read another scripture," Jim said. He turned to the Book of Mormon lying on the table, and read.

> *And they are free to choose liberty and eternal life, through the great Mediator of all men, or to choose captivity and death, according to the captivity and power of the devil; for he seeketh that all men might be miserable like unto himself. And now, my sons, I would that ye should . . . choose eternal life, according to the will of his Holy Spirit; And not choose eternal death, according to the will of the flesh and the evil which is therein, which giveth the spirit of the devil power to captivate, to bring you down to hell, that he may reign over you in his own kingdom. (2 Nephi 2:27–29)*

"I think this is a great key," Jim observed. "I believe almost all revelation works this way, that it comes quietly, and we receive our greatest blessings by being obedient to what is sort of a divine hint or suggestion. Promptings aren't the same as commandments, but they are personal revelation to us, and anyone who learns to obey them will eventually enter the celestial kingdom."

"So," Laura added, "we choose eternal life by choosing to obey the Holy Spirit, and we choose captivity and eternal death by choosing to obey the will of the flesh, which is what Satan uses to tempt us. It all seems so clear and precise when you look at it that way. This will sure make it easier for me to decipher the crazy conversations I hear in my head!" She laughed and reached for her husband's hand. "Jim, this is so exciting to understand! It makes me wonder why we have never understood it before."

"I think it has crystallized in my own mind only in the last little while. It's been a principle I've apparently been having trouble learning myself."

Benjamin had a question. "But then, what is the louder voice, Dad?"

"I believe that the louder voice is the Holy Ghost speaking in His other role as a revelator," his dad explained. "It seems to me that these louder messages are reserved until after we have become fully obedient to the still, small voice."

Sam was confused. "Dad, why do you suppose you heard the louder voice to warn you to come help Cheryl and me? Why didn't you get the still, small voice like when Jimmy was in trouble?"

There was a conspicuous silence before Laura said, "I think I can answer that. Since Jimmy's death, I have seen a tremendous change in your father. I can honestly say that I have never seen anyone try harder to hear and obey every prompting than your dad. I think because of his obedience and faithful heart, it wouldn't have mattered how loud the voice was. I think Jim would have heard and come to save you even if he had only heard the tiniest whisper from the still, small voice. I personally feel that because of his perfectly obedient heart, when a time of danger for you and Cheryl arrived, the Holy Ghost spoke in an unmistakable voice. Perhaps if we use our agency wisely and are obedient in all things, then Heavenly Father will speak to us in a louder voice when it really matters."

"All I know," Jim said, "is that I am grateful beyond words to Heavenly Father for allowing me to come to your aid. It has given me greater faith in Jesus Christ and in the promptings of the Holy Spirit. It has caused me to be even more diligent in obedience. I can honestly say that my cup of joy is full and runneth over. I'm sure that this experience was partly to teach us this lesson."

"And," Cheryl added with great soberness, "I'm just as sure that all this was meant to teach me a lesson. Sam was motivated by kindness to take me to the prom, and then he was inspired in the way he handled that awful situation. He was my angel in coveralls. Then Papa Jim was inspired to find and save us, and he was my angel in coveralls, too."

Cheryl stopped to think, then continued. "Before, when I wanted to die, Heavenly Father wouldn't let me. Now that I want to live, I seem to keep getting into life-threatening situations, and God keeps bailing me out. This has never happened to me before. It's more than my poor brain can grasp. Someone please help me understand all this!" Benjamin observed, "I don't think the war you won at the gas station is over. I think Satan is mad because you got away from him the first time."

Six-year-old Rachel raised her hand, and Papa motioned to her. "Cheryl, I think it's just Heavenly Father's way of saying He loves you and that you matter a whole lot."

"You matter enough that he is willing to send angels to save you," Laura added quietly.

"Angels in coveralls," Cheryl whispered reverently.

* * *

The following Sunday was fast Sunday. In those days, Sunday meetings were held in two blocks. In the morning, priesthood began at 9:00 a.m., and at 10:00 a.m., the sisters and children came for Sunday School, which lasted until 11:30 a.m. After that, people went home, fixed and ate their Sunday meal, did necessary chores, and rested. At 7:00 p.m., everyone returned for sacrament meeting, which lasted until 8:30 p.m. Fast Sunday usually meant fasting until testimony meeting was over in the evening.

It was the first time in Cheryl's life that she had fasted, and her tummy rumbled fiercely. Yet even with the discomfort of hunger, she felt the warm glow she had only recently learned to recognize as the presence of the Holy Spirit. She fidgeted with her hands, fighting the urge to stand and bear her testimony. She desperately wanted to but could not overcome her fear. There was a long silence, during which no one stood. Cheryl was just about to stand when a brother walked past their row. Startled, and simultaneously relieved and disappointed, she quickly relaxed. She didn't recognize the man who slowly walked to the stand.

He stood before the pulpit for a long time before taking a step closer. Then, with trembling hands, he pulled the microphone toward him. It groaned loudly in protest.

"I hope ya all'll forgive me for coming to the pulpit today," he said, his voice subdued. "I knew I didn't have the courage to stand and bear my testimony, but I reckoned I could make my feet walk up here. I just figured once I got up here, I'd think of something to say." A soft chuckle flowed across the congregation.

"For those of you who don't know who I am, the name's Rulen Carter. I live 'cross the street from the Mahoys. I bin a member of this church all my life and ain't seen fit to darken the doorway for longer than most of ya all've bin alive." This he said with some emphasis, as if he felt some justification for staying away.

"I ain't proud of it. I knew ever Sundee that I should go to church. I done raised my whole family without the gospel, and . . . until a short while ago, I didn't care one whit.

"Before I lose my starch, I gotta tell you why I'm here today. I hope Brother and Sister Mahoy will forgive me, cause I sure don't mean to play upon their loss, but I gotta do this if they'll forgive me." Brother Carter looked meaningfully at Jim Mahoy, who nodded. Brother Carter smiled as if relieved.

"Not long ago, little Jimmy Mahoy fell inta the irrigation ditch and drowned. Ya'll know about that. What ya probably don't know is that I was there. I helped hunt for Jimmy and was standing there while Brother and Sister Mahoy was tryin' to get him to breathe.

"I knew Jimmy was dead, and it made my heart ache as if it had been my own baby layin' there. I was about to turn and go back to my own house when Sister Mahoy looks directly at me and says, 'Somebody give my baby a blessing.' Well, her words drove through me like a sword. I was stunned, cause I knew she was talking to me. I looked around. I knew a dozen other priesthood holders were there, and when I looked, they all turned away.

"Laura looked directly at me, and said, 'Brother Carter, you're an elder. You give my baby a blessing.' I ain't proud of what I said. I says, 'I ain't worthy and don't know how on account a bein' inactive all these years.'

"I don't know why she said what she said next, but it was words that echoed in my mind ever since. She says to me, 'God will bless my baby. All you have to do is say the words.'

"Well, I kneeled down and asked God to forgive me and not count my sins contrary to little Jimmy, cause God knows, and ya all know I'm a sinful man—was then, and still am now. But I fixed my mind on those words, and I knew they was true. I did my best to say the right words, and to let God give that baby a blessing. Well, I wanted to say beautiful, powerful things, but instead I was sayin' all the wrong words. The feelin' was right though, and inside me, I knew God would bless Jimmy."

He paused to swallow back emotion. When he continued talking, his voice was soft. "Then Jimmy takes a breath. It was the most fantastic thing I ever heard. Jimmy coughed and started making noises, and he was alive. I knew it was the power of God what brought him back.

"Well, they took Jimmy away, and he stayed alive for a couple weeks until God made it right with Laura and Jim, and then he took Jimmy home. But that don't make no never mind to the fact that he came back to life.

"Now, here's the thing what has got me inside this here church after all these years of sinnin'. It's that God sucker-punched me. I know that sounds bad, but it's kind of what He did. You see, I was living my sinful life feeling content, and by bein' in the wrong place at the right time, I was called upon to use my priesthood, what I plumb forgot I even had. So here I was, kneeling there with a stone-dead baby, surrounded by Jimmy's angels, and I put my hands on that baby's head, and by God, he looked past me, and plumb poured out the power of heaven into that baby through my soiled hands. Brothers and Sisters, I felt it. I was there. I was an instrument in God's hands. When He coulda picked a hundred better men, he picked me. I'll live the rest of my life without knowin' why. But, by God, by all that's holy and all that's true, I'll live it with my heart and hands clean before God. Maybe it was plumb orneriness, or stupidity, or just bein' too busy, but whatever my reasons was for not serving God before have been flat washed away, so's I can't even remember what they all was.

"Well, I'm here before ya all to ask God's pardon, and ya all's pardon, and the bishop's and who all else I gotta beg forgiveness to. That's what I'll do. I'm here to serve God and to try to make myself worthy of the miracle what God wrought through my soiled hands."

Brother Carter stood there in the stunned silence that followed. His eyes misted over, and he gripped both sides of the pulpit. His head fell, and his voice quivered as he said, "I most humbly bear my witness that God lives and that he loves us. I also bear witness that Jimmy's death has bought me salvation. Brother and Sister Mahoy, if Jimmy's death means nothing else, to me, it is the key that unlocked my stony heart. God forgive me for being so wretched that a baby's death was the only thing that could touch me. It's a terrible price to pay. God forgive me."

He hung his head and stumbled back to his seat, never lifting his eyes from the floor to see the tears on every face in the congregation.

4

CHRIS

It isn't often that identical twins have different birth dates, but Angela and Beth did. Angela was born May 1, 1956, at 11:49 p.m. Beth was born May 2, 1956, at 12:02 a.m. It made perfect sense, therefore, at least to Angela and Beth, to celebrate their fourteenth birthdays at midnight. Mama and Emily made a cake with two identical halves—each with fourteen candles. As the grandfather clock was striking twelve, they blew out the candles on their cakes. Such a clatter of clapping, clocks, and cheering followed that they didn't hear the doorbell the first time it rang. Jim hurried to the door the second ring.

It was Grandma Pearl, Papa's mother. She excused herself for calling so late and stepped into the entryway. Behind her came a small boy holding a little battered suitcase without a handle. His hair was almost black and was cut very short. He was barely four feet tall, with bony arms and wrists. His black eyes were sunken, giving his face a feral quality. His face was emotionless, even while he exuded fear.

"Jim, this is Chris. He's my niece Lois's boy. He's six years old, and he needs a place to stay for a few days. His real name is Buddy Brown, but he was born on Christmas day and goes by Chris. Lois and her husband are having marriage difficulties, and, well, he needs a home for a few days."

"Hi, Chris." Laura bent over and smiled at him. "It just so happens that we have an extra bed in Benjamin's room." It was Jimmy's bed. She hadn't been able to bring herself to let anyone sleep in it since he had died. Yet, Chris's plight now was more important than a sentimental silliness. "We were just having carrot cake and ice cream. You want some?" Chris nodded enthusiastically.

"Wait!" Grandma Pearl commanded, and Chris halted mid-stride. "Let's look at the list." She produced a three-page document from her purse and studied it a minute. "Nope. No wheat. No nuts. Sorry, Chris honey. No cake, but it lists ice cream as being okay. You will have to have a shot before you go to bed, okay?" Chris smiled and nodded. By this time, the rest of the family had gathered around. Angela and Beth each took him by a hand and led him into the kitchen.

Emily, Sam, and Cheryl stayed with the adults who moved into the family room.

Grandma Pearl unbuttoned her sweater and took a seat in the recliner. She was so short that her feet dangled six inches from the floor.

"I went to visit my sister, Maryanne, Lois's mother, yesterday. They live side by side in a development outside Salt Lake City. As I was driving up to Maryanne's house, I saw Chris sitting on the front doorstep of Lois's apartment. It was late in the afternoon, and he was sitting there in his pajamas. I walked up to him and he smelled like urine. His pajamas were horrible. I could see he had been crying. He looked at me with those big brown eyes and said, 'Will you be my mommy?'

"I tell you, it melted my heart. I scooped him up and banged on the door. It took a long time for her to answer. When she came, she was still in bedclothes. I told that young woman that I wanted Chris's clothes. She bundled them up and handed them to me without asking where I was taking him. I'm not even sure she remembered who I was. The only thing she said was that Chris was being punished for wetting his bed last night. The poor thing hadn't had breakfast or lunch. I didn't know what to do with him, so I brought him here. I'll work things out with my sister tomorrow. I appreciate you taking the boy in. He's a handful. He's a full-blown diabetic. He's hyperactive and can't eat a blessed thing. He's allergic to everything under the sun. Every one of his teeth are rotten. I'm so mad I could skin someone alive!"

Grandma Pearl scooted forward and slid off the big chair. She buttoned up her sweater, said her goodbyes, and vanished.

Chris was finishing his second bowl of ice cream when they entered the kitchen. He ate like a wolf, food flying off his spoon, running down his chin, and splattering all around his bowl. He was reaching for another helping when Laura intervened and sent all the kids to bed.

Chris still smelled like urine, even in his street clothes, so Laura hustled him off to the bathroom. She started a tub of water running and pulled his shirt off over his head. Her heart sank and tears came to her eyes. She opened the door and called to Jim, who was beside her in an instant. After closing the door, she turned Chris's back toward Jim. His back was a mass of scars and bruises. Old cigarette burns were everywhere, and long red welts ran across his bottom. They questioned him about how they got there, but he would only say, "I fell down playing." It was the only answer he dared give them.

All her other kids could bathe themselves by the time they were six, but Chris didn't have a clue what to do. Laura scrubbed him from stem to stern and rubbed him dry. He stared expressionlessly at her the whole time. She found a pair of Benjamin's pajamas that would fit him and showed him his bed.

"Need shot," he said emotionlessly. Laura had forgotten about it. He retrieved his insulin kit from his small suitcase. She had seen these before and quickly filled the syringe. He pulled down his pajamas, and she administered the shot in his hip. He didn't flinch.

"Are you a big boy and won't wet the bed, or do you need to wear diapers to bed?"

"Big boy!" he said with a wounded voice.

"That's a good boy. I'm glad you can spend the night. My room is right down the hall. The door is open all night. If you need something, you come knock on the door, okay?" He nodded. She kissed him on the forehead, kissed Benjamin who was already asleep, and turned out the light. Chris rolled onto his side and yawned. It had been a long day for him.

Laura had earned a master's degree in marriage and family counseling, which she had set aside to raise her family. She often felt grateful for her education, especially when their family accommodated foster children, some of whom, like Chris, needed special attention. Her gentle ways and love of counseling made it possible for her to draw the foster children out of their frightening worlds and into her circle of love. She loved being a mom, and in spite of occasionally feeling as if she wanted to scream, she wouldn't have traded it for anything.

Neither Laura nor Jim could sleep. The memory of Chris's back was haunting them. It troubled them both deeply that anyone could harm a child, and they needed to talk. They finally turned out the lights at 2:00 a.m.

"I didn't put away the cake," Laura mumbled as she rolled over. "It will have to take care of itself until morning." Sleep had already taken her away when she suddenly sat up. She glanced at the clock, which said 3:00 a.m. She had little difficulty arousing Jim, who was a light sleeper.

"Jim, I just realized I ignored a whispering of the Spirit. I said I didn't put away the cake, but what I was really thinking about was the candles and matches."

"I'll get them, Honey. You've had more than your share of troubles today." Jim swung his legs out of bed and pulled his pants on, looping one suspender over his shoulder. When he pulled open their bedroom door, a strong odor of smoke swirled into the room. Laura was at his side instantly.

"You get the kids up. I'm going to stop the fire. Get everyone out, and then come back and help." Jim ran down the stairs. Bright flames danced on the floor at the bottom of the stairs. He turned left toward the family room and skidded to a stop, momentarily immobilized by what he saw. Chris was standing in front of him, a single flickering match in his hand. The wrappings from the birthday presents were burning hotly, and suddenly the couch was on fire. As he watched, the fire jumped to the curtains behind the couch. Chris was transfixed, as if hypnotized. He grabbed Chris by the pajamas and yanked him away from the flames.

"Fire," Chris said almost reverently.

Jim flung open the front door and tossed Chris onto the grass. The garden hose lay sprawled across the lawn. He spun the faucet and ran to the sprinkler. He twirled it off as he ran back. By the time he got the hose to the fire, it was too hot to approach. Behind him, terrified kids were streaming through the front door. He aimed the hose at the fire, and knew almost immediately it was hopeless. The glass in the window behind the couch burst at the first sprinkle of water, and the fire roared bigger with the fresh oxygen. The paneling on the walls was beginning to buckle and burn. The carpet was burning, making a choking, blue smoke.

At the moment he decided it was hopeless, he heard the glass break on the opposite side of the room, and a thick column of water roared past him. The fire retreated against the blast of muddy water and in minutes was defeated. Jim used his garden hose to put out the remaining hot spots.

Sam had run into the house from the back door. He had started the sprinkler pump and turned one of the big flexible hoses from the garden into the house. His quick thinking had saved their home, but the aftermath was unbelievable. What was not burned was soaked with muddy water. The smell was a nauseating combination of acrid smoke and pond water.

Cheryl tapped Sam on the shoulder. He turned his stare from the devastation in their family room to her. "You better put on your coveralls, or I'll have to start calling you my angel in underwear," she said in mock seriousness. He looked down, and as if for the first time, realized he had on nothing but his underwear. He disappeared into the back hall and returned wearing a pair of muddy coveralls.

"Mama, look!" It was Angela's voice. She was pointing out onto the front lawn. Chris was standing in the blackness of the morning, his face visible only by the flickering light of the single match he held in his hands. His eyes were glazed and hypnotic, his pajama bottoms dripping with urine.

It took months to repair the damage, both physical and psychological. Insurance paid for all the repairs, but the worse damage could not be repaired with money. No one trusted Chris. Everything he ate made him hyperactive. Sugar put him into a zombie state, and he started lighting matches again. Already he had burned down the chicken coop and a neighbor's pasture before they figured out the sugar connection. Everyone except Laura wanted to strangle him.

The most frustrating thing about Chris was that punishment had no effect on him. After he burned down the chicken coop, Jim had spanked him, a rare occurrence in their home, but not unheard of. Chris had taken the spanking without emotion or crying and had walked away apparently unfazed. Moments later he purposely broke one of Benjamin's toys by smashing it against the wall of the house. Jim spanked him again, this time more soundly. Again, no tears from Chris. Moments later, Chris went out to the chicken run, caught a chicken, and kicked it until it stopped moving. When Jim and Laura found him, he was standing there with the dead chicken dangling from his hand. They were both furious and wanted to punish him in anger; but some greater force prevailed. Laura knelt down before the boy so that they were almost eye-to-eye.

"Chris, I know you are angry and that you are breaking things because you think we are punishing you out of meanness. Maybe some big people did that to you in the past, but not in our home. In our home, we only punish when you do something wrong. What you have done here is wrong. Do you understand that it's wrong to kill things out of anger?" Chris nodded, and let the chicken drop to the ground. "Do you understand that when we do wrong things, that painful things happen back to us? Sometimes it's a punishment, sometimes another thing?" Again, Chris nodded sullenly.

"Do you remember when I spanked Benjamin the other day? What did he do?"

"He cried." Chris shoved his hands into his pockets and wet his pants. Laura ignored the latter.

"That's right Chris. Little boys cry when they are hurt or when they are spanked. Why don't you cry, Chris? You don't even cry when you hurt yourself."

"My papa says if I cry, I get more. Only babies cry, and babies get more whippings. If I'm bad and cry, then Mister Cigarette will punish me. I'm too big for Mister Cigarette any more," he said with an air of fear and defiance.

"Your papa was wrong, Chris. Mister Cigarette is always bad, and Mister Cigarette should never punish little boys. Mister Cigarette can't come here to our house, and we will never let him punish you, sweetheart, ever again. Do you believe that?" Chris nodded uncertainly. "Chris, I want to ask you a question. Will you try to tell me what you are feeling no matter what, even if it scares you a little?" Again,

Chris nodded, his face a mask of uncertainty.

"First, will you smile for me?" It was such an unexpected request that Chris's eyes grew wide. Laura smiled broadly, and after a moment of silence, Chris smiled back.

"That's much better. I want you to smile because what I'm going to ask you is a happy question, and not something to be afraid of. So, you can answer without feeling afraid, okay?"

"Okay," he mumbled.

"What makes you feel the worst inside? Was it Mister Cigarette hurting you or was it that your papa helped Mister Cigarette hurt you?"

"My papa," Chris said quietly. When he glanced up into Laura's eyes they flashed with anger and betrayal.

"Chris, will you smile again for me?" Laura asked. "Why?" Chris asked.

Because it is against the law of our house for Mister Cigarette to come here. You never have to be afraid again. Does that make you feel like smiling?"

"Yes," he replied, and a little smile appeared on his face. "Good. There's one more law at our house that is also happy, but might seem a little hard to understand. Will you help me with this other happy law, Chris?" she asked tenderly, gazing into his eyes, both hands on his shoulders.

"Yes," he responded carefully. Still, he answered without asking what the law was. Trust was slow to form in his heart.

"Thank you Chris. I really need your help with this one. This law is that when little boys feel sad inside, they cry until they don't feel like crying any more."

"Really?"

"Look into my eyes Chris," Laura instructed gently. "See these tears in my eyes?" she asked. Chris nodded slowly. "I feel sad inside my heart because of what Mister Cigarette did to you. So, I'm going to cry for a few minutes because of your sad experience. Will you cry with me?"

Jim felt his own eyes flood with tears as he saw tears streak his wife's face. But he resisted the urge to swallow back his tears or to hurriedly wipe them away as he had done all his life. Chris looked up at Jim just as the tears fell from his chin.

Suddenly, as if a great dam broke somewhere inside Chris, he began to sob. At first it sounded like a bleating goat, "Blaaaa! Blaaaa!" It was as if he had never cried before and didn't really know what sound to make. Then it changed. "Bluuuur, Bluuuur, Bluuuuur," he cried. Laura held him close to her and whispered love to him.

"That's right, baby. Cry now. Cry hard. Cry those nasty feelings out. Cry until it doesn't hurt anymore. Mama will hold you until you no longer hurt inside. Cry away all those bad feelings." And he did.

For a long time, and during it all, Laura held him, rocking him back and forth, kneeling there in the chicken coop. When Chris finally exhausted his pent-up emotions, he was a little boy again, and they were both covered with chicken manure, urine, snot, and smiles. Afterward, the sweet spirit that was the "real Chris" was finally liberated from the terrible prison Mister Cigarette had put him in. Before, he was a tough little boy who wouldn't have cried if he broke his arm. Now he cried over everything, and Mommy Laura, as he called her, would hold him until he no longer needed to cry.

In time, with good fresh farm food and an abundance of love, Chris outgrew his insulin dependence and was able to eat anything. He discovered a world filled with love, family, and strawberries. He would do anything for a fresh strawberry, a bribe that worked until he discovered that the precious little gems grew on plants in the garden. They considered putting an electric fence around the patch, but in the end, it became Chris's strawberry patch. At least they always knew where to find him.

Months later, Jim and Laura were lying in one another's arms, as was their happy custom just before going to sleep. Jim tenderly swept a stray lock of hair from her face as he spoke.

"Do you remember when you cried with Chris until he cried?" He felt Laura's head nod against his chest. "At the time it was very uncomfortable for me. I was standing there with anger in my heart while you were administering love. I'm ashamed to say that I thought you were wasting your time. I just want to say that I'm sorry for doubting you."

Laura looked up at him and gave him a kiss on the cheek. "You know, it was a unique and wonderful experience for me," she said. "All my training, everything I knew about mothering, seemed to be useless at that moment. But inside, I heard the Spirit telling me what had to be done. It took a lot of faith to do what I knew to be right. But as I was doing it, I felt the Lord not only inspiring me, but empowering me to do it. It was one of the most humbling moments of my life."

"Just watching Chris since that day has vindicated your inspired therapy. He is a happy little boy, and if we can just get him to quit wetting the bed, he will be quite well adjusted," Jim commented.

"He's almost there, Praise the Lord!" Laura said happily.

"I can't quit thinking about that day. I was ready to hog tie him and send him to a mental institution. But you, in a single act of inspired love, changed him." Laura shook her head slowly. "It is rare for a life to be changed so suddenly. Most problem children like Chris take years and years to reach. What occurred that day in the chicken coop was an act of God—a miracle—and had little to do with me."

"You are far too modest, Laura. As I watched you that day, I was awed—overwhelmed. I am convinced that through your obedience, you saved his life, and possibly his soul. If you had failed to act as Heavenly Father wanted you to, who knows what would have become of him. Perhaps he would have ended up in prison, having killed some innocent person out of anger." Jim fell silent.

"I just did what the Spirit directed. I'm no heroine. I'm just a mom. Besides, remember that I almost burned the house down by ignoring a prompting."

"You are a heroine to me. You heard the prompting, and your spirit was sensitive enough to truth that it later woke you back up. You saved our home, my love, not almost burned it down. And, with Chris, you had the courage to do what was right in a very difficult situation. In my book, that makes you a heroine. More specifically, it makes you my heroine."

"In my book," she said happily as she snuggled closer, "that makes you the person I love most in the world. Want another kiss?"

5

THE FARM

No one except Mom and Dad was sure why they all loaded into the station wagon early one morning and drove for a long time. Excitement and secrets were in the air.

After the car warmed up and the scenery began to roll by in monotonous reiterations of sameness, they quieted down and played "I spy" games.

Finally, the car followed a series of dirt roads and pulled into an abandoned farm. It was an impressive place—a large brick home with two new barns, six grain silos, and row after row of big tractors and equipment. The newest barn had two huge combines and a variety of new farming implements. To the children's amazement, their dad took a key from his pocket and ushered them into the house. It was large, with five bedrooms, a living room, a family room, two bathrooms, and a roomy kitchen. Someone had spent a lot of time and money decorating it with long beautiful draperies and deep carpets. Everything about the farm spoke of prosperity and security. They explored for hours before they finally returned to the car. It was a warm spring day with patches of snow still on the north side of the buildings. Laura spread out their picnic lunch on the tailgate of the station wagon.

"Well, what do you think?" Dad asked, a strangely neutral expression on his face. Various expressions of "Big, new, pretty, and amazing" sounded from the children.

"How big is it, Dad?" Sam asked.

"It's 840 acres, all sprinkler irrigated. It produces an average of eighty bushels to the acre of wheat and barley. It has eighty acres in alfalfa, and . . ."

"Dad," Sam interrupted, anxious to get to the point, "why are you showing us this place?"

Jim glanced at Laura, who gave him a sly grin. "Well, we're thinking of buying it. What do you think?" The excitement in his voice was too much to suppress, and he sounded like a kid who was on the verge of fulfilling every dream he'd ever had. The family all started talking at once, and rushed up to give their Papa a big group hug. They had often heard him talk about his dream farm. To Sam, this farm seemed to fit that description in every way. It was a wonderful place, and a thrill of excitement built up inside him.

They all loaded into the car again and drove around huge fields thick with grain stubble. The farm was long, narrow, and "L" shaped. It stretched two miles in one direction, and one mile in the other.

The fields were a quarter mile wide in most cases. There were three other homes on the farm, one of which was still inhabitable, and had its own small collection of barns and a milking parlor. The others had long been abandoned and had at one time or another housed cattle. One of the small homes had twelve small triple bunk beds built along the walls of two small bedrooms. They learned later that a family named Christiansen had raised a wonderful family of twelve kids in that small home.

This Idaho community was small, but large enough for two thriving wards. Their church was an old converted grade school, complete with flagpole. Comically, the bishop's door still had "Principal" lettered on the glass. The other farms in the area were well kept and prosperous looking. Everyone they stopped and talked to was enthusiastic about the farm they were proposing to buy and welcomed them as potential neighbors. It was a wonderful, positive day, and they all returned home exhausted but happy.

The papers were signed two weeks later, and Sam moved onto the new farm immediately to begin spring plowing. The family began packing for the unbelievable task of moving twenty years of accumulated possessions into their new home.

It was with a sense of adventure and exhilaration that Sam went out that first morning to hook up the plow. He selected the largest of four tractors. It started like a dream. No grinding noises, no spraying starting fluid, or hunting for booster cables that he was used to. He selected a six-bottom plow and hooked it up. He chose the field closest to the house and lowered the plows. They slid into the rich, brown soil and started rolling deeply into the earth.

Sam had spent hundreds of hours plowing—albeit, never on a rig this big—yet his senses told him something was wrong. The tractor was jerking, and that concerned him. He stopped and walked back to the plow. To his amazement, he was picking up large stones. He was plowing too deep.

Back in the big cab, he turned the dials to adjust the plow depth. Again, he picked up stones and had to raise the plows to where they were almost not able to roll over the dirt. After a whole day of fighting the shallow soil, he moved to another field and found it the same.

With a heavy heart, he called his dad and told him about the shallow soil. They consulted for a while and decided it was not a tragedy. It would take a different tool to till the ground. Still, they wondered why the plow was on the property if it was not usable.

The new disk was sixteen feet wide with twenty-four-inch diameter disks. It could be adjusted from inside the cab to cut exactly six inches deep. It rolled the soil as neatly as any plow with half the effort, and it didn't pick up rocks. The big tractor pulled it like it wasn't even there.

Sam hooked the big set of harrows behind the disk and began preparing the soil with a single pass. The big equipment worked like a dream. In the air-conditioned cab, you could turn on stereo music and drive for hours without so much as a moment's discomfort. With their old, open-air tractors, plowing was a freezing, runny-nosed, dusty, bouncy, exhausting job. With their new tractors, it hardly seemed like work. The hardest part was the amount of time it took. A quick calculation told them they would have to plow almost twenty-four hours a day to be done in time. It became obvious why the big equipment was there. Not for comfort but for speed. They settled into six-hour shifts. Sam plowed for six hours, and then Jim took over. It took almost two weeks to prepare the fields. Spreading fertilizer took another week.

They hooked two smaller tractors to the seeders, and Emily and Cheryl each took one. At seventeen, they were adept drivers, careful to not miss a patch and mindful to keep the hoppers full. The girls worked at it about ten hours each day, and then Sam and Jim took over. Finally, after six weeks of around the clock labor, it was done, and the entire family slept for two straight days.

The spring was glorious, with flowers blossoming and green appearing everywhere. When the grain finally peeked through the soil, it was a wonder to look across eight hundred acres of rolling fields carpeted with a haze of green. It was the miracle of spring as far as the eye could see, and it was the hope of a future filled with promise slowly peeking through the soil.

Shortly thereafter, it was time to start irrigating. The big pumps were carefully oiled and adjusted. There was no way to test the sprinkler equipment other than to pressurize it with water, so after as many tests as could be done dry, the big pump was switched on. The water exploded into the big mainline with a roar like a jet engine. The first mile of mainline was buried until it reached the two irrigation circles. An irrigation circle is a large irrigation machine. One end is anchored in the center of a large 160-acre field and pivots around it. The machine itself looks like a quarter-mile-long suspension bridge on wheels. The wheels slowly turn as it slowly moves around the field like the large hand of a clock. As it goes, it sprinkles water on the thirsty ground. The farther from the center, the larger the sprinklers become.

In mere seconds, water streamed from the first sprinklers.

As the water moved down the quarter mile length of the big circle, the Rainbirds clicked their life-giving rhythm, each one slightly larger than the one before it, until the mighty nozzle on the end burst to life spraying its one-inch-thick jet of water over fifty feet as it came to the corners of the field.

Their new ward was wonderful and welcomed them with enthusiasm. They were loved and accepted from the first day at church. It was like finding family, like coming home, and the entire family basked in the warmth of their fellowship. Their chapel had been a small gymnasium in the old school, and the organ was pedal powered and sounded asthmatic. To make matters more frustrating, not a soul in the ward could play more than one hand. Sam could play one hand and a finger, so he was instantly called as the new ward organist. He took the calling seriously and spent hours practicing until he could squeeze as much music from the old gasping organ as was physically possible.

Not long after they moved in, the ward announced plans to modify the old church house and add on. In those days, the ward members were either expected to raise half the money or do half the labor. Since money is not a surplus item in a farming community and work is second nature to them, they opted to do the labor. Each priesthood holder was asked to invest two hours a day or ten hours a week to build the church. Sam and Jim accepted the challenge. So, in addition to the physical demands of activating and maintaining a new farm, they happily worked on the new addition to the church.

Six months after moving into the ward, Jim was called as bishop. It was a surprise to Jim, who considered himself a plow horse suitable for the fields not a racehorse to prance in front of people. He accepted with as much humility as a human soul can possess and still be able to breathe. His sweet spirit touched the hearts of the ward members, and things began to happen. He plainly confessed to everyone his lack of knowledge and understanding on how to run a ward, especially to Heavenly Father. As a result, he relied entirely on the Lord and inspired decisions were made.

Bishop Jim, as the ward members affectionately called him, found there were many inactive members in his ward. He visited them wherever he could find them. New faces showed up at church, and their marvelous little ward loved them so openly that they came back every week. It was a time of great spiritual growth for Jim as the mantle of his office settled upon his shoulders, and it was a time of rejuvenation for his ward.

For Sam, the change that came over his father was startling. Jim's quiet humility seemed to deepen, but the power behind the quietness was the most amazing of all. The power was accompanied by a quiet dignity that made Jim seem majestic in an unassuming away. Sam watched with wonder. His dad was still human, prone to err, and occasionally moved to anger. This might have seemed hypocritical, except that Sam knew his father well enough to know that his heart was rock solid in his faith. Sam understood that his dad wanted to be perfect, both personally and as the bishop; yet he also knew him well enough to know that he did not pretend perfection. With Jim Mahoy, his exterior was a perfect reflection of his soul. He spoke and acted the same on the fields as at the pulpit.

On one occasion toward the middle of the summer, Sam and his dad were loading sacks of chicken feed at the feed store when another truck backed up beside them. A man with a full, black beard climbed out. He was unfamiliar to them, and in the way of country folk, they immediately shook hands and introduced themselves.

The man's name was Jake Please. Sam had heard the name many times, and had remembered it well. Whenever the subject of enemies to the Church came up, this man's name always seemed to top everyone's list.

Jim smiled at the man, and before he could withdraw his hand, he said, "Jake, I'm your new bishop."

Jake's eyes narrowed, and he forcibly withdrew his hand. "Ya ain't my bishop. I don't belong to your Church. And if you know what's good for you, you'll drop the subject." He glared for a second and then walked away.

Sam breathed a sigh of relief. Jake Please was a large and powerful man, and his face had an edge of steely sharpness that made Sam want to follow his advice and let the man leave. Jim, however, walked right up to him. "I need you to be my ward clerk," he said, loud enough that everyone on the loading platform stopped and looked up. Nearly all of them were members and knew of Jake Please's reputation for antagonism toward the Church. But it was noisy, so they couldn't hear much of the conversation that followed.

"I told you. Let it drop. I don't want to have to rough up a good man just because his mouth got to runnin' away with him." Again, Jake turned away.

"It isn't going to be easy," Jim said, just as loudly as before.

"What isn't going to be easy?" Jake demanded, thinking Jim was saying it wouldn't be easy to rough him up; but a slight edge of curiosity softened his hostility.

"Getting you ready to serve the Lord as my ward clerk," Jim replied matter-of-factly.

There was almost an explosion of anger, but Jake's curiosity won. "What are you talking about?" he demanded vehemently.

"I'm probably going to have to excommunicate you first," Jim replied with a thumb and finger on his chin, as if considering the situation carefully.

"You can't excommunicate me! I ain't done nothin' that bad!"

"Then why don't you come to church?"

"Because I don't like it, that's all! I ain't been to church since I was ten years old. Didn't like it then, and don't like it now."

"I always found that when someone doesn't like church, it's because they've done something that they need to be excommunicated for. So that's what I'm gonna do."

"But I ain't done nothin' that bad!" Jake protested.

"What have you done then? You better fess up so you can be my ward clerk like the Lord wants and I don't have to ex you. It's up to you."

Jake had to stop and think. "Well, me and the wife, we 'bout broke every commandment there is, I suppose, except for the really bad stuff. But nothing to get exed for! My wife would kill me if you exed us!"

"Hmm. Well, maybe we can get this cleared up after all. But you and the wife had better come see me tonight at the church. Come prepared to get your lives in order, and we can maybe avoid the excommunication. Seven o'clock okay?"

"You're damn right, it is. We'll be there! And don't you go exin' us before we get there, you hear?"

"I'll wait for you. Don't be late. Nice to finally meet you, Jake."

"Yeah, maybe." They shook hands, and Jake stomped off.

Jim stepped over to his son and smiled at Sam's dropped jaw. Sam didn't realize he was standing there agape. They loaded the feed in silence and started home.

"Dad?"

"What is it, Sam?"

"How did you know Jake wouldn't punch you for saying what you did to him?"

"I didn't."

"What you said, though. You can't excommunicate someone like that, can you? I mean, just because they don't like coming to church?"

"No. Of course not."

"Then why did you say you would?"

"To be honest with you, I don't know. I felt the Spirit come over me as soon as we shook hands. I have learned over the years that when the Holy Spirit touches me, I say or do whatever I'm told to say or do. I have had some amazing experiences, and this one was one of the strangest. It was probably the only thing I could have said to get them into the bishop's office. Whatever the eternal truth of this matter is, it was what the Lord wanted me to say. I said it, and Jake responded. That's what really matters. When they come tonight, I'm going to explain the entire process of Church discipline so they understand. I'll set it all straight so they aren't acting under a misunderstanding. However, they are coming, and that's a wonderful start!"

"Is he really going to be the ward clerk?"

"As soon as I touched his hand, I knew I was supposed to call him to that position. If he carries through with his part of it, I will call him to that position, just as the Lord wants." Brother and Sister Please kept the meeting with the bishop that night and were both disfellowshipped. Part of the conditions of their repentance was that they could not miss a single sacrament meeting for six months. Accordingly, the next Sunday, they came to sacrament meeting. Brother Please wore his work clothes but had buttoned up his collar and tied a dark string tie around his neck. He looked extremely uncomfortable, but plowed his way bravely through the small crowd of faithfuls. He shook everyone's hand with a painful grip, laughed with a loud voice, and acted like he had never missed a Sunday in his life.

With his full, black beard, Brother Please looked like a charging bear. Even so, not a single member backed away or acted surprised to see him, and the elders fought as to who would sit by him in Priesthood. Sister Please wore a red miniskirt, red high heels, red beads, bright red lipstick, and a hairstyle full of red hair. She looked like a lady of the night and was the exact opposite of Jake. She spoke to almost no one and clung to her husband's hand like a frightened child. It took three sisters to lovingly pry her loose from him to attend Relief Society. They had three children—all girls—who were dressed in worn jeans. They ranged from nine to fourteen, and desperately wanted to be somewhere else.

Before church had even begun, they had accepted a dinner invitation to a neighbor's home that evening, and the magic of the Holy Spirit and love began to work.

As the weeks progressed, the Please family continued to come. Each week, Brother Please's beard grew shorter and Sister Please's dresses grew longer. The third week, all three girls showed up in cute dresses, and each carried a new copy of the Book of Mormon. The transformation that gradually occurred was a miracle as surely as the dividing of the Red Sea. In exactly six months, Brother Please accepted the position of ward clerk, and Sister Please, a position in the Primary presidency. Their girls looked as if they had never missed a day of church in their lives.

The most amazing transformation of all occurred in Brother Please's soul. Where once there was bitterness and a hardened heart, now there was a gentleness that only the influence of the Holy Ghost can bring. On the day he was called to his new position, the bishop asked him to bear his testimony. He walked slowly up to the pulpit and steadied himself with both hands.

"I want you to know that Bishop Jim tricked me into repenting!" This brought a ripple of laughter, but Brother Please was serious.

"The first time we met, he threatened to excommunicate me if I didn't become the ward clerk. At that time, I was an angry, violent, unforgiving person. Everything inside of me told me to beat him senseless.

"I once spent a week in jail for hitting someone who shoved religion in my face. But something was different about Bishop Jim. I could feel his love for me. Or, probably what I was feeling was Heavenly Father's love for me. But it felt good, and I desperately wanted to know why it was coming from Bishop Jim when he should have been afraid of me. I wanted it bad enough to go to the bishop's office to find out.

"Over the years I had convinced myself that God didn't love me, so I didn't love Him. I believed I was too nasty for anyone to love, including God. I thought my wife stayed only because I fed and housed her. I didn't think anyone, including her, could love me. But it was that morning when I met Bishop Jim that I felt God's love for the first time.

"Since that time, I have come to the amazing realization that not only does God love me, but my wife and girls do too. Oh yeah, I admit that I don't deserve their love. But now realizing they do has literally melted my soul. I feel inclined to forgive Bishop Jim for tricking me, because I know he was acting as the Lord's servant. Besides, he told us straight out that first meeting that he owed me a better explanation, so he didn't really trick me. As I think about it, he probably said the only thing in the world that could have gotten me to set foot inside this church."

He chuckled at the truthfulness of what he had just said, then became sober again. "You have all witnessed the change that has come over me and my family. Look how beautiful my daughters are in their new dresses. They had never worn a dress before in their lives. I can hardly believe how beautiful they are. Look how my wife glows with the Holy Spirit. I've seen her in every kind of clothing imaginable, but I have never seen her look as beautiful as she does this very minute, radiating love and goodness." He smiled at his family on the third row, and they squirmed uncomfortably.

"Thanks to you all," he said. "I have come to the startling conclusion that not only is the Church true, but the gospel is too. By that I mean that not only is this His true Church, but it also works. It blesses lives. It changes people. It purifies and uplifts. It takes mean, nasty, sinful people like me and helps them repent, which leaves them feeling clean inside. For that, I will be eternally grateful. In the name of Jesus Christ, amen."

Brother Please remained at the pulpit a few more seconds before adding in dead seriousness, "I offer as a witness the fact that I just said that whole bit without cursing a single time. That, in itself, my brothers and sisters, is a miracle." Those who knew him, nodded vigorously in agreement.

* * *

During this time, the farm continued to look more dismal. It was exhausting, unrelenting, and hopeless work. There was not enough water. As the summer progressed, even the big well lost pressure and started sucking air. They had to throttle it back, and the water going onto the fields was insufficient. The grain suffered and matured slowly. Over two hundred acres were lost to faulty or missing equipment.

Harvest was frightening and exciting that year. They prepared the big combines, swept out the grain silos, put the grain bed on the truck, and made everything ready. Jim lowered the cutter bar and started into the grain on the field beside the house. Sam was riding on the combine, making adjustments and helping. After a few minutes, a trickle of grain flowed into the hopper. It gradually increased to a stream, and then a steady pour. After many stops to adjust the settings on the big machine, they were ready, and the grain poured into the hopper. The fields were forty acres each, and before they had gone all the way around the first field, the combine was full. They pulled the big truck beside the combine and transferred the burden of golden wheat. It made a surprisingly small pile in the bottom of the truck. They would repeat the process over a thousand times for nearly two weeks.

Once harvest began, it would continue nearly twenty-four hours a day until it was done. If it was during the day, they drove the truck to the local mill where the truck was weighed and the grain dumped. If it was night, the grain was pumped into their own big grain silos where it would wait until after the harvest. When the fields were bare, they would take a truckload at a time to the mill.

The precious wheat was most vulnerable during harvest. As the days progressed, the stalks and heads grew more fragile, and even a brisk wind could knock grain onto the ground. Once on the ground, it could not be recovered. No effort was spared to get the grain in as soon as possible. If a frost came, the heads would swell and the combine could not efficiently harvest it. If it snowed or rained, the brittle straw stalks would become soft and lay down where the combines could not pick it up.

Nearly every hour the combine had to be readjusted to accommodate the changing conditions. As the days warmed, the grain heads grew dryer, the grain lighter, and the combine fans and screens had to be adjusted. As the evening came, the chaff became damp, and the fans had to be set higher to blow it away without blowing the grain out the back end of the combine.

Jim and Sam ran the big combines. Cheryl and Emily, who had both graduated from high school now, drove the big truck. Angela and Beth baled straw, and Benjamin, now age eleven, drove the gas truck out to the combines to refuel them.

Running a combine is the nastiest job man has invented for himself to do. The combine engine runs at full throttle. The belts, chains, fans, and machinery scream and shake as if they are going to fly apart, and the roar is deafening. The big cutter head hovers just above the ground, requiring constant adjustment. To pick up a rock or dirt is to damage the machine and cause hours or days of repair. The back end of the combine dumps out the straw and chaff. By far the worst, the chaff hovers in the air in a choking cloud, not unlike some ancient pestilence decreed by the voice of an angry God. It fills the cab until the windows are coated, the driver's skin itches, his nose runs, and his eyes are red and puffy. Jim and Sam coughed and sneezed constantly. Before long, they wrapped scarves around their faces, but the scarves were not sufficient. They tried gauze masks, but they were plugged in minutes. Finally, they bought big dust masks designed especially for mines. The masks kept the chaff out of their lungs, but not their eyes. Every so often, they had to run the windshield wipers to knock the dust off the window, and every few minutes, they had to wipe the inside of the glass with a rag. During the day, it was hot and dusty. During the night, it was cold and dusty.

They were amazed at how much grain they harvested. From the fields with adequate water, they harvested thirty-five bushels to the acre. Even on the fields that had suffered most, they harvested enough grain to break even. Before long, it became apparent that they would have a good harvest after all. They rejoiced as truck after truck of grain went to the mill.

By the end of the harvest, they had delivered over 21,000 bushels of grain to the mill. The current price of grain was $4.35 per bushel. Simple math told them they could make all their payments and still have plenty to live on until the next year. It wasn't as good as they had hoped, but it was enough.

Every aspect of farming is a gamble, but deciding when to sell your wheat is the biggest gamble of all. The price of wheat is always lowest during harvest since there is an abundance of grain and many farmers must sell immediately. Because of this, the supply is more than the demand. Most grain mills offer to store the wheat for a few pennies a bushel until the farmer is ready to sell. If you could hold off, the price usually rose by the first of the next year. It was considered prudent to wait as long as possible to sell your harvest. Accordingly, Jim decided to wait. Even a few pennies per bushel raise yielded thousands of dollars in additional income.

It was September 21, 1972, when the news came. The United States announced a total grain embargo against the Russians. Frantically, farmers rushed to sell before the prices plummeted. The mill immediately suspended all grain sales. All across the nation, farmers watched helplessly as the price of wheat slid and finally stuck at $2.85 per bushel. Without hope that the price would rise any time soon, Jim sold the wheat for a huge loss. Their actual cost of growing the grain was $3.95 per bushel.

Expecting the worst, Jim and Sam went to the local bank they had borrowed money from to grow their crop. To their surprise, the bank was willing to wait to be paid back, and they loaned them money for the next year's crop. They saw the good job that the Mahoys had done with their farm, and they knew the price of wheat was beyond their control. It was the best they could expect, and they mentally prepared themselves to do much better the next year.

They worked steadily during the winter, rebuilding several engines, repairing equipment, and welding sprinkler pipe. They worked every daylight hour and many dark ones. It was a peaceful, happy time, and one of almost total poverty.

Christmastime found them without funds except for the barest necessities. They gathered the family around and explained the situation. Rather than feeling dejected, the kids welcomed the challenge and enthusiastically set themselves to making gifts. They plotted, planned, schemed, and worked their magic in secret little huddles. Instead of Christmas lasting a week, it lasted a month, because their preparations were so lengthy.

The girls sewed, painted, knitted, wrote poetry, made photo albums, cooked special treats, and invented a hundred small but loving gifts. The boys built, sawed, welded, and otherwise crafted thoughtful and fun gifts for everyone. Jim built Laura an apple cider press from old machinery parts and wood, something she had often spoken about. Sam made her a butter mold from a small but perfect piece of maple he found. It was a time of joyful anticipation, and very little money was spent.

Christmas morning was magical. Cheryl put her angel, still wearing coveralls, atop the tree, and everything was perfect. There were fewer gifts to give, but each was highly special, both in thought and in the amount of effort and time it had taken to create it. The gifts were unwrapped slowly with everyone else watching. Many tears were shed, both by the receiver and the giver.

They spent the day appreciating their gifts, laughing about their efforts and joys, and making fresh apple cider. The press worked perfectly, and they sipped the sweet cider as if it were the nectar of life. Far sweeter than the juice was the love that flowed in glorious abundance. For many years thereafter, everyone would say it was the best Christmas ever.

After days of fasting and prayer, they decided to hang on and farm again the next year. They were, after all, farmers, and the decision was as much genetic as it was logical.

Even more important was their attachment to the ward. Their father, Bishop Jim, was making dramatic headway in reactivating lost members. The ward had grown in size by almost half again, all of who were previously inactive members. At one point, nearly ten percent of the adult members in the ward had been disfellowshipped. One family simply showed up to church and never wavered thereafter. Their reason? "To keep from having Bishop Jim come to their home and disfellowship us too," they laughingly insisted. It wasn't really their reason, but it played a part in their thinking.

Early the next spring, the Mahoys dug new wells, deepened and improved old ones, and bought enough sprinkler equipment to cover the entire farm. When the freeze left the ground, they worked around the clock.

No effort was spared. They labored like dragons, and after four weeks had all eight hundred acres seeded. The new sprinkler equipment functioned perfectly, and the farm turned a lush green. They waited with breathless suspense for something to go wrong, but nothing did.

The crops came up, the water burst from the ground as if by a miracle, and hope returned.

During this time, they labored on in the Church as before, fasted weekly, studied the scriptures, held numerous callings, sang in the choir, and taught classes. It was a time of sweet joy and a joyful season in the sun. They did develop one unique farming practice, which their neighbors thought would cost them their farm. After much discussion, it was decided that moving the sprinklers on Sunday was breaking the Sabbath, and they decided not to do so. Jim said, "The Lord called me to be bishop to labor in his kingdom, and He expects me to keep the Sabbath day holy. The Lord needs a bishop, and I need a miracle so the crops won't die without water on Sundays. We'll both do our jobs." And they both did. Jim's fields were a wonder to behold. People drove a hundred miles to see the crops that didn't need water on

Sundays, shook their heads, and drove away thinking it was a trick.

Chris turned ten that year and started first grade. He was a little old, but he was just now ready. His little body was stunted by years of malnutrition and was about the size of a six-year-old. He hadn't touched a match in three years and was a happy, loving—and loved— child. His thick black hair still had two wild tufts where the hair grew around large scars left by "Mister Cigarette." Laura's heart ached every time she combed his hair before school, but Chris seemed to have forgotten those days.

Laura had taught him the alphabet, and he could read fifty words from flash cards. He could recognize all the numbers and knew all the "dos and don'ts" about school: Do say please and thank you. Don't pick your nose or forget to zip your pants after going to the bathroom. He knew that schoolboys don't wet their pants, hit other kids—especially girls—or throw things. They mind the teacher and pay attention whenever she is talking. The fact that Chris understood such things was a miracle. He came to them with almost no social skills and lacked even the most basic reasoning. Mommy Laura, as Chris lovingly called her, had drilled him endlessly until he knew all the rules, and probably a few extra just in case.

For unsophisticated farming folk, getting a certified letter was a rare, frightening experience. Before Angela was back in the house from the mailbox, the entire family knew about it from her excited shouting. It was addressed to Jim Mahoy, and Laura dispatched Rachel to get him from the equipment shed. The return address was from the State of Utah, Department of Family and Youth Services.

Jim sat down and carefully opened the letter with his pocketknife. He read it before handing it to Laura. She read for a few minutes before having to sit down, and her eyes filled with tears.

"What's wrong?" Beth demanded.

Cheryl reached for the letter, which Laura let her take. She read it and looked around the room as if searching for someone. All of the boys were outside.

"Chris's father wants him back," she said quietly, still looking at the letter. She looked up to see if she had spoken out of turn, but both Jim and Laura were looking at her as if grateful she had spoken the dreaded words. She read on. "There is to be a hearing before a judge to determine custody. Papa Jim is supposed to appear with Chris a week from Monday."

The next Monday morning, Laura packed Chris's small suitcase, as well as a larger one. He had little comprehension of what was going on, and laughed excitedly as he lugged his luggage to the car. Each of the kids gave him a hug, told him they loved him, and walked him to the car. Jim and Laura got into the front seat of the station wagon with Chris between them. They drove away and were gone, but not before Cheryl was in tears. This was too close to her own experience, and she had a bad feeling about it.

The drive seemed to go by too fast. Before they were ready, the Mahoys were sitting in a small room, oppressively dark with wood paneling and worn red carpeting. Chris squirmed between them and seemed both excited and afraid. They had told him this was a meeting to see if he wanted to live with his real father again. When Chris saw his father, he hesitated and then ran to him and gave him a hug. They both seemed happy to see each other. The man was with another woman who was obviously not Chris's mother. She also gave Chris a hug and seemed pleased to meet him. Jim and Laura waited patiently. Tony, Chris's father, walked up to Jim and shook his hand.

"I want to thank you for taking care of Chris these last few years. I'm sorry I haven't contacted you sooner. This has been a terribly difficult divorce. I knew Chris was safe and that he was being spared much of the pain in our lives. As you can see, I have remarried and made many personal improvements. I'm sorry for any pain taking Chris back might cause you. I can see you love him. What you can't see is that I do too. I'm ready and anxious to be his daddy again."

Tony had a lawyer who presented their case and read from state statutes. The judge listened attentively and nodded frequently. When it was their turn, Jim stood and began telling about how Chris had come to live with them and his deplorable physical condition, but the Judge interrupted him and said it was irrelevant. Jim tried to explain that Chris had been burned with cigarettes and beaten. The judge asked curtly if they had evidence that Chris's father had done it, or if Chris had just said that his father had done it. They had to say no. The judge wouldn't listen to more. He simply said that the law stated that natural parents had a right to their children unless there was obvious evidence of their being unfit, unable to provide, or abusive. He banged the gavel, and Chris no longer lived with Papa Jim and Mommy Laura. His new family swept him away, and before they could even say goodbye, he was gone.

Laura cried all the way back home, and Jim drove with grim determination. She could hear his teeth grinding. When they returned home without Chris, Cheryl ran to her room and stayed there the rest of the day.

That evening, just before family prayers, everyone was quiet and an air of sadness hung over them like a rain cloud. Laura, obviously fighting back strong emotions, said, "Kids, I know it's hard to see Chris leave after living with us for four years. We all loved him. Sometimes patients in a hospital fall in love with their doctors and the doctors love them back. But the time always comes when they have to leave, because they can't live at the hospital. It's better that they get well and return to their real lives. We were Chris's hospital, and because we loved him when he most needed it, he got well. While he was getting well with us, his father was getting well at his own hospital. Now they are together, and we mustn't mourn the fact that he has his family back. Let's be happy for him and remember him with happy hearts."

Jim felt like giving her a standing ovation. His heart swelled with pride for her courage and pure heart. He slid to his knees, and in his soul and prayer that evening, he wished everyone could be blessed with a mother like Laura to love them so perfectly and to heal their young lives. When he finished, he looked up to see Laura staring at him, a radiant look of wonder and tender love on her face. Her words had healed the family's hearts. His prayer had healed hers.

* * *

The spring of 1973 was slow in coming, and by the time the ground was thawed enough to begin planting, it was almost summer. In order to have a reasonable expectation of a good harvest, the planting had to be done by the first week in May. They started working the soil the first day of May, leaving them less than a week to complete a four-week project. Their only choice was to purchase another tractor. It arrived in a few days, and they worked around the clock until the crops were in. They did it in exactly ten days. This feat left them semi-conscious from exhaustion, but it was done and done well.

Emily and Cheryl left to attend Ricks College that spring. It was an exciting time for them, and they departed with many tears and much laughter. They arranged to share a dorm room at college and took comfort in the fact that they were together.

Emily was a whiz at school and could give Cheryl much needed help in her classes. Cheryl had shed her defensive shell and had become a natural with boys and in social settings. She helped shy Emily find a comfortable niche in college society. Together they eased their mutual transition into college life.

Jim and Sam had learned much over the winter. They read many books, consulted with neighbors, hired an agricultural specialist to calculate optimum fertilizer rates, and set schedules for spraying. They carried out their plan like clockwork, and the crops grew. Again, they refused to water the crops on Sunday, and, oddly enough, the crops didn't seem to mind. They grew thick and lush. The fields were solid green as far as one could look in any direction. In their community, no crop of grain had ever been as lush as this one was. Neighbors stopped their cars beside the fields and walked out into them, just to experience the rich feeling of such a lush stand of grain. They returned to their own fields with renewed determination and faith in the valley and its thin but fertile soil.

Sam turned nineteen that fall and received his mission call to South Africa. The family had to get out the big atlas to see where he was to go. They rejoiced, his mother cried, and plans were made to take Sam to the mission home right after harvest.

The chill of fall was already in the air, and the sprinklers had been turned off weeks earlier. The fields were a golden sea, heavy with grain. Old timers could not remember a time when such a crop of grain had been grown in the valley. Jim cut a ten-foot square piece of ground, thrashed it by hand, and measured the results. It represented over one hundred bushels to the acre. That Sunday the family held a special day of fasting to thank Heavenly Father and to rejoice in His blessings and kind favor.

The new church house had been dedicated the week before, and their long labors in building it suddenly ended. It truly was a time of joy.

Sam pushed open the big, double doors of the red barn and backed a huge combine out into the yard. Even though combines are as big as a small house, they are complex, finicky machines, prone to breakdowns and failures. They require constant maintenance and careful operation to keep them from breaking down. Both he and his dad had worked until noon on the big machines before they were comfortable that they were ready to go.

Sam was working on the John Deere combine when he felt a chill blow through the cabin. He glanced up to see a black cloud rolling across the valley. It looked like a thundercloud, but much lower to the ground. Within several minutes, the ferocious cloud had reached the far edge of the Mahoy farm, and immediately unleashed a devastating barrage of hail. The cloud swept across the farm from end to end, changing course to make the L-shaped turn of the last field. Then as suddenly as it came, the cloud lifted and blew off into nonexistence.

Sam ran into the fields with his father. Within minutes, the entire family had joined them, and they all stared at the ground in wordless shock. The fields were a perfect sheet of golden grain and glistening hailstones. Little, if any, grain remained on the stocks. The entire field of wheat was destroyed. There was no point in driving the combines out into the fields since there was no way to adequately recover grain on the ground. The loss was tragic and complete.

Weeks later, the banks foreclosed on the Mahoy farm. Dealers came and repossessed sprinkler equipment and tractors. Everything was mortgaged to pay for the massive loans they had incurred, and within weeks, an auction was held, wherein everything they possessed of any value was sold to pay the debt: furniture, clothing, tools, jewelry, and vehicles. Even a stack of fence posts was sold. In the final analysis, the Mahoys had lost everything. They were penniless, homeless, and destitute. The farm was repossessed, and the proceeds from the auction barely canceled the mortgage debt. They still owed over a hundred thousand dollars to the small bank that had loaned them money to operate the farm.

The night before they were to leave their once-beautiful farm, Sam did not eat. Even though they had spent the day loading their old GMC truck with their last few possessions, he had fasted. His heart was heavy and his faith shaken to the core. They had spent three years joyfully serving the Lord, obeying His commandments, fasting, and worshiping. They had risked all to keep the Sabbath Day holy. Their father had worked to exhaustion to serve as the Lord's bishop, and his powerful service was a great blessing to the ward.

Their farming had been a success; and yet, in an act that was apparently divinely engineered, they had lost everything. Theirs was the only farm affected by the hail, and the destruction on their lives had been thorough and complete.

That night Sam spent a long time on his knees, asking, wondering, begging, and even complaining. It did not seem fair. It seemed so unkind, so undeserved, and so unjust. He was young, and he knew he would recover in time; but his parents had lost a lifetime of work and savings. They had nowhere to go and no hope for the future. He climbed into bed with a heavy heart and slept fitfully. In the night, he was given a dream, one he would never forget. So impressed was he by the experience that he hunted up a few pieces of paper the next morning, and recorded it as follows:

Last night I had a dream. It was so vivid that I was unsure if it was a dream or reality until I woke up the next morning.

I dreamed I was standing in a field of ripe grain. As I looked out over this field of grain, I instantly knew many things about it, as if I had lived there all my life. The field was lush and deep, as rich a crop as ever was grown on earth. Along the borders of the fields were flowering shrub bushes that grew spontaneously. The roads leading to the fields were lined with flowering trees and bushes more beautiful than any formal garden I could conceive, yet they had not been planted but had grown there spontaneously or by decree. I knew that the rains had come to water the fields every night, and there were no weeds or noxious plants anywhere.

In one corner of the field, a huge machine was harvesting the grain. The machine made little noise or dust and never broke down. It moved across the fields, cutting the grain, which poured into the hopper in a heavy stream of gold. The man driving the machine barely gave thought to what he was doing but sang as he ran his hands through the flowing grain and danced on the machine as much as drove it.

Immediately in front of this huge machine were women and men dressed in beautiful robes of bright colors, with flowers in long streamers running through their hair and across their shoulders. They were singing and dancing, walking ahead of the machine as its big cutter bars bit into the thick grain. I instantly knew that they were not afraid of the machine because it was against the laws of nature for them to be harmed by it in any way. Neither they, nor the person operating it, had any fear that they could be injured. They simply were in the joy of harvest, and it seemed to consume their entire souls.

I somehow knew that the laws of nature had been altered and the law of opposition in all things had been done away with. Anything they tried to do yielded to their efforts. If they tried to move a rock a hundred times larger than themselves, it was obligated by divine decree to move. If they wanted to farm, they would be successful by divine decree. If they wanted to run a business, they would succeed by divine decree. I also understood that it was impossible for them to injure one another physically or in any other way. The laws of God would not allow it. Nothing could be lost, damaged, stolen, misplaced, ruined, or abused, and nothing was unusable, unattractive, or undesirable.

Their society was perfect, with no crime, taxes, corruption, or sin. Their government was by divine decree and perfectly just. There were no courts, criminals, or jails. There was no such thing as hospitals, doctors, illness, disease, or death.

I watched all this with a thrill in my heart, experiencing their joy, yearning to join them, and yet aware that I was still bound to this world where things were much less than perfect. I thought this must be the celestial kingdom and yearned with all my heart to be there.

As I watched, a kindly voice from behind me asked, "Sam, is this what you want?"

"Oh yes," I replied with all my heart. "This is the life I long for." There was a moment of silence before the voice replied, "What you see is the telestial kingdom, the least of all the rewards I give unto men. If you seek a life without opposition and refuse to learn the lessons of this life, this will be your reward. If you desire a greater reward, then endure with patience, and great shall be your blessings, even greater than the mind of man can comprehend."

It was then that I understood that these people had lost their agency. They could choose any righteous act, but it was physically impossible for them to choose to disobey or sin. We have always been free to choose righteousness. What I did not understand until then was that agency is largely the right to choose to do evil. They had lost this right.

I knew they were not organized into families. Their relationships were according to their chosen vocation and common interests. They loved one another but did not marry or have children. They were without authority except over their own possessions, and they could never progress beyond what they were at that time. They had no priesthood, and without it, they could never return to the presence of God.

No sooner had I perceived these thoughts than the vision closed, and I found myself sitting up in bed, marveling at all I had seen. I knew many *things about their world as if I had lived there all my life. I have recorded only a few of them that are of greatest interest to me at this time in my life.*

* * *

The next morning, Sam called the family together and related the dream he'd had and the impressions he'd received while in the vision. He told them that his greatest impression was that everything would be all right. Everyone took comfort in the dream, even in the idea that Heavenly Father had seen fit to bless them with this word of comfort at the very time they felt abandoned by Him.

As they loaded their last things onto the old truck, Jim took Sam aside. "Son, I'm so proud of you. I didn't have a vision last night, but I did have a peaceful feeling. I too know that everything is going to work out. The family really took comfort from your dream."

"Dad, I'll write a letter to the Church and ask them to postpone my mission for a year. I know we can no longer afford to pay my way. The ward can't afford it either. Besides, we're leaving town. I hate to do it, but I don't see an alternative."

Jim put his arm around his son. "This spring, as we were planting the fields, the Spirit whispered to me to take the money for your mission and put it in a savings account under your name," he answered. "I took five thousand dollars and put it in your name in a bank in Utah. You have your mission money. The Lord has seen fit to preserve that part of our dreams."

"But you and the family are penniless. How can I take all that money and leave you? You need me to help you start over. I'm sure the Lord will understand. This is just a delay, not an abandonment of my plans. Don't you see . . ."

"Now you listen to me, my young son. The Lord instructed me to set that money aside for your mission. I obeyed, and He sanctified that money to your use. Those funds are sacred, don't you see? We would have lost them along with everything else, but we didn't. It would be sacrilege to misuse them even to buy gas to leave the farm. We have enough money to see us safely to Salt Lake. From there you will go on your mission, and from there we will find a place to start a new life. As you said, it will all work out."

Sam could not keep the tears from his eyes, and merely nodded. He climbed into the station wagon with the family, and his dad got into the old truck. His moist eyes were only two of many as they pulled out onto the dirt road. A heavy snow began to fall, as if the heavens were mourning with them. They had one stop to make before leaving town. They still owed the bank a lot of money, and Jim wanted to stop and thank them for investing in his dream and to assure them that he would repay the debt as soon as he was able. In a small town, even the failure of one farm can burden a small bank. He felt bad that he had placed them under any hardship.

The bank was small, even by small standards. It consisted of one teller window and an attached room wherein sat the bank president, Paul Richards. Brother Richards was a member of the other ward in town and was fully aware of their plight. Brother Richards was the one who had loaned them money to run the farm. Even though he had not held the mortgage on their farm, his investment in the Mahoys exceeded $100,000 dollars. Had he been able, he would have loaned them enough money to farm another year, but it was beyond the resources of their small bank to do so. It was with much regret and many apologies that he had denied their request, and consequently, they lost the farm.

Jim and Brother Richards shook hands solemnly. Jim was the first to speak. "Brother Richards, we have said all we need to, except that I want to thank you for your kindness and to assure you that I will repay every cent of what I owe you."

Paul got a strange look on his face and responded, "But you don't owe me anything."

"You know better. I owe you many thousands of dollars."

"But you don't. I received payment just two days ago. Payment was made by bank draft transfer, and I assumed it came from assets you still held in Utah."

"I no longer own anything in Utah. There must be an error. Someone accidentally deposited those funds into my account. You'd best look it up and correct the mistake."

"Brother Mahoy, I checked and double checked. The money came from Utah and had your name on the draft. That's all I know. That's all I need to know. Your account is paid in full."

"Do you mean to tell me that I owe you nothing?"

"Actually, I owe you money. The bank draft was $10,000 more than the amount you owe. I have a cashier's check for you here." He pulled an envelope from his drawer and handed it to a stunned Jim.

"Are you sure? There's got to be a mistake. I—"

"Jim, I have lived in this area all my life. In forty years, I have never seen a family move into our area and do greater good, set a greater example, or live a richer, more Christlike life. You and your family practically built our new church. You have had a greater influence for good upon this area than you could possibly know. If you insist that this money didn't come from you, then it came directly from God, or from someone acting as His agent. Don't argue with God or with me. Take the check, and God bless you on your journey. I can assure you, for years to come, whenever people refer to 'the bishop,' they will be talking about 'Bishop Jim.' "

Jim swallowed hard, and wiped his eyes with the back of his hand before he spoke.

"I'll always remember this place as my first spiritual home. I'll miss you all powerfully. But I have to ask. Paul, is this money from you?"

"No. In all candor, I know only what I told you. It came from Utah with your name on it. Accept the fact that you have a miracle and rejoice over it."

They embraced, and Jim walked slowly out of the building, the check held out before him as if it were the most amazing possession of his life.

"Who could have done such a thing? Who could have paid all that money?" Laura exclaimed after she had heard the story.

Cheryl spoke with great conviction, "An angel in coveralls."

In reality, they would never know, and the origin of that vast sum of money would always remain a mystery.

In the final analysis, Cheryl had been right. As long as Cheryl lived with them, whenever she was asked to pray, she always said, "And God bless the angel in coveralls." They all knew she meant their unnamed benefactor.

6

NORTH AND SOUTH

The family arrived in Salt Lake City late in the afternoon on December 4, 1973. For reasons they did not understand, they drove directly to Temple Square. They parked and slowly walked across the temple grounds, brightly lit with a million colorful lights. It was like walking through a frozen celestial kingdom—so bright, peaceful, and beautiful. A sweet spirit was there, and it warmed their souls after their long, mournful journey from the farm. Because of slick roads and car trouble, it had taken them several days, during which time they had slept two nights in the car and eaten all their meals in their laps. They knew no one in the city and had no concrete idea of where to go. They just assumed they would find an inexpensive motel or some other meager accommodation. Even though they had the big check, they had not been able to cash it. It was drawn on an Idaho bank, and since they had no accounts in Utah, banks had refused to cash it for them. Consequently, they had been reduced to living on the few dollars they had scraped together before leaving the farm.

The visitor's center was still open, so they walked reverently into its vast foyer, savoring the warmth, peace, and richness of spirit there. They clustered together, almost as if afraid to be any distance apart. They moved as a group to the large paintings on the far wall. The life sized paintings of scenes from the life of Christ and were breathtaking. "Good evening." They turned to see a white-haired man behind them. Jim shook the man's hand. "My name's Elder Carlson. I'm the director of the visitor's center. Welcome to Temple Square."

Jim thanked him and was about to turn back to the paintings, but the man persisted.

"Have you had a long trip?" he asked, an edge of hidden meaning in his voice. Laura joined Jim and shook Elder Carlson's hand as Jim introduced her. The kids continued to look at the beautiful paintings. They were soon out of sight.

"We just drove several days from Idaho," she told him. "We don't have a hotel room yet, but several of the younger kids have never seen Temple Square at Christmastime, and we wanted to visit it before it closed." She wanted to apologize for their crumpled appearance, but she instinctively knew that the older gentleman hadn't noticed, or at least he didn't care.

"How did you know we've been on a long trip?" Jim asked.

Brother Carlson smiled. "Well, I didn't really. When you all came through the door, you just stood there as if you'd just stepped foot on foreign soil and weren't quite sure what to do. That usually means you are more than just visiting Temple Square. It usually means you are pilgrims, so to speak."

"What do you mean, pilgrims?" Laura shoved her hands into her coat pockets as if subconsciously seeking protection from the answer she knew was coming and didn't want to hear.

Brother Carlson smiled and shrugged. It was so gentle and disarming that they all smiled. "A pilgrim is usually someone coming from one place and going to another place that they have yet to determine. They are just traveling to an unspecified destination."

"Is it that obvious?" Jim asked, looking around to see if someone else might have noticed. There was almost no one else in the building. "Only to those who choose to notice," the man answered. "What brings you to Salt Lake?"

Brother Carlson motioned to a grouping of chairs and they all sat down. He pulled his chair around to face them and waited. Before long, they had told him the entire story. He listened carefully, nodding, frowning, and occasionally laughing. They really didn't know how long they talked, but by the time they finished, the custodians had locked the doors to the visitor's center. Jim looked at his watch and realized with a start that it was 9:00 p.m. They had stayed over an hour past closing. Elder Carlson stood as a white-haired woman approached. He put his arm around her and introduced her as "Sister Carlson, my bride." She shook Jim's hand and gave Laura a hug.

"Elder Carlson," she scolded, "you have kept these good folks talking so long that they have about missed supper." She put her arm around Laura's shoulder and walked her toward the elevator. Brother Carlson chuckled, and ignoring Jim's protests about needing to get along and finding a hotel room, he herded him into the elevator that descended one floor. They walked along a carpeted passageway until they arrived at a cafeteria. Only one table was occupied, and that was with the Mahoy's children. Before them was a mountain of food that was rapidly getting smaller.

"Come. You've almost missed it. We already said the blessing," Sister Carlson insisted as she pulled out a chair for Laura. Brother and Sister Carlson started eating, and Jim and Laura joined them. It was hot and delicious. They had forgotten how hungry they were. Sister Carlson disappeared into the kitchen and returned shortly with plates of pie and ice cream. Before long, it was all gone as well.

When they were finished, Jim reached for his wallet, but Elder Carlson caught his arm. "We have this wonderful arrangement. We are on a mission, you see, and run the visitor's center for the Church. One of our little blessings is that every evening we come down here and eat our dinner. This is the staff cafeteria and is under the temple annex. The cafeteria cooks always leave out something nice. We have specific instructions to share it with anyone we like, so you needn't feel obligated to pay anything. You are our guests."

Jim was about to express thanks and insist they needed to leave, but Elder Carlson again placed a hand on his arm. "Brother Mahoy, it's Christmastime, and every hotel and motel in this city is booked to capacity. I know you are capable people and don't need any assistance caring for yourselves, but we are elderly and have no family nearby to share the Christmas season with. We have a large apartment just a short distance from here, also provided by the visitor's center. We have two extra bedrooms and no one to help decorate our Christmas tree. We were even considering not putting one up this year. Look at these children. They need a Christmas tree."

Sister Carlson took Laura's hand. "Laura, I have been trying to finish a quilt for my daughter who is having a baby, and my slow old fingers aren't getting it done very fast. Besides, I miss having children in the house. Won't you please spend the holidays with us? At least until you are settled? It would be such a nice thing to do for two lonely people."

Laura sputtered, and Jim was wide-eyed. This sweet couple had turned the situation around so that it was a favor to the Carlsons for the Mahoys to stay with them. Jim had known it would be impossible to find a room and had secretly planned on spending another night in the car; yet this kindly couple was giving them exactly what they needed and then making it appear as if the Mahoys were doing them a favor!

Jim and Laura exchanged one of their meaningful glances, and Laura nodded. The relief and happiness in Sister Carlson's face was genuine and almost enough to convince them that the Carlsons did consider it an honor to host them.

They walked less than a city block on freshly-fallen snow to the Carlson's apartment. It was on the fourth floor of a large building. Their apartment was indeed large, and the Mahoys had two bedrooms, ample beds, and a bath all to themselves.

Upon waking up the next morning, they happily discovered that the Carlsons had already fixed a huge breakfast. They spent the morning putting up the tree, quilting, and baking Christmas goodies. The Carlsons were genuinely pleased to have company, and the Mahoys soon felt as comfortable as if staying with family.

The Carlsons left at noon to do their job at the visitor's center. They gave Jim a key to the apartment and told the Mahoys to join them in the cafeteria below the visitor's center at 7:00 p.m. that evening.

That evening as they were eating dinner, Sam mentioned that he was entering the mission home January 2 to go on a mission to South Africa. Brother and Sister Carlson stopped eating and looked at each other with widened eyes. Finally Elder Carlson explained, "Sister Carlson and I have been called to preside over the Johannesburg, South Africa mission. We will be entering the mission home on the very same day!"

The news was a very unexpected surprise, and suddenly everyone was laughing, shaking hands, and talking all at once. A sense of divine providence settled over them, and they let the joy wash over them and salve their wounds.

For the Mahoys that Christmas, time seemed to pass in slow motion, as if that glorious season would last forever. Every day was filled with wonders: Christmas shopping in the big new malls, visiting Church historical sites, and, best of all, listening to the Tabernacle Choir sing "Handel's Messiah." It was powerful, magnificent, and deeply spiritual. Christmas morning was also delightful, with laughter, hugs, and gifts for everyone.

After what seemed like months, January 2 finally came. The Carlsons arranged for the Mahoys to stay on at the apartment for another week after their departure. Jim drove the Carlsons to their destination in Provo, and the whole family fondly bid them goodbye. Later in the afternoon they took Sam to the mission home in Provo, and after many hugs and well-wishes, kissed him a tearful goodbye.

"Dad?" Sam asked as he picked up his bag. "Where will you and the family go?" Do you have plans?"

Jim and Laura exchanged one of those magical glances before Jim replied, "We have decided to go to Alaska. The economy is booming there. Uncle Ben lives there, as you know, and he tells me that I can find a job almost without trying. Your mother and I figure that the Lord wants to have an adventure!" A feeling of peace swept over Sam. He knew now he wouldn't have to worry about his family. He could concentrate on his mission and trust God for everything else. He had learned the lesson of obedience to the voice of the Spirit, and he suddenly felt unafraid. "Then north to your future, and south to mine," he said triumphantly.

Sam embraced his father and mother one more time, turned and strode through the big double doors of the mission home.

7

SOUTH AFRICA

A new world was on the other side of those double doors, a vast sea of white shirts, suitcases, and organized pandemonium. A white-haired lady with a gentle smile directed Sam to a table, and there he handed in his papers. He was shown where to deposit his bags, and before long, he was sitting in a large hall with nearly a thousand other prospective missionaries. The mood was apprehensive and yet calmly determined. He sensed the Holy Spirit warming his soul, and he felt at peace. Music began to play, and within minutes, they were singing "Ye Elders of Israel." The voices of missionaries drowned out the organ in a rendition so enthusiastic that it sent chills of joy up Sam's spine. A whitehaired man took the pulpit and introduced himself as Elder Whitehall, mission president of the mission home.

He heartily welcomed the new missionaries and instructed them. He then turned the time over to Elder Bruce R. McConkie, who delivered a stern yet inspiring message about personal worthiness, dedication, service, and personal integrity. He bore his strong testimony, and the words reverberated in Sam's soul.

The new missionaries were bused to the BYU campus and assigned a room in the ancient Knight Hall dorm. After meeting their new companions, they ate dinner and studied the scriptures for two hours. Finally, they fell exhausted into bed. The next day began at 6:00 a.m. with a shower, scripture study, companion prayers, and breakfast. Each newer missionary's companion had been there for at least three weeks and knew the routine.

These "seniors" enthusiastically instructed their "greenie" companions in their duties. By 9:00 a.m., they all gathered in a room no larger than twelve feet square that smelled of furniture polish. All four walls of the room—floor and ceiling—were wood. The room would have been oppressive if not for the bright overhead lighting. Twelve Elders were there—six senior companions and their respective greenies.

A skinny, serious-faced young man stood before the missionaries and introduced himself as their zone leader. Elder Toleman was a returned missionary from South Africa and would spend the next eight weeks teaching them Afrikaans, the language of their mission. He also informed them that they would be learning the discussions in both English and

Afrikaans since the mission field was bilingual, and both languages would be used for teaching. This brought a groan from the new missionaries and a sympathetic chuckle from the "seniors."

Elder Toleman asked everyone to stand. He said "Good morning" in Afrikaans and had everyone repeat it loudly. He then told them what it meant. They repeated the phrase several times. He then taught them "How are you," which they repeated endlessly in loud voices. This went on for three hours. By the time they broke for lunch, they were able to conduct a rudimentary door approach in Afrikaans. It was amazing, and the new Elders enthusiastically practiced their new language skills at lunch.

After lunch, they repeated the process and learned lines from the first discussion. By break time at 4:00 p.m., they could say the first two exchanges in the discussion, including "Brother Brown's" unrealistically golden responses.

From 4:00 to 5:30 p.m., they exercised vigorously and took a shower. Dinner was at 6:00 p.m., with more language training from 7:00 to 9:00 p.m.

Scripture study and journal writing were from 9:00 to 10:00 p.m., with lights out at 10:00 p.m. Every other day they had a devotional with a General Authority. Sundays were a spiritual feast, with more language training. Monday was preparation day, and they had four hours in the morning to roam BYU campus, write letters home, and otherwise unwind. The rest of the day was language training.

By the end of the eight weeks, Sam was supercharged spiritually. His prayers had found a dimension of communication he had never thought possible, and his bosom burned with the presence of the Holy Spirit. His whole desire was to do the Lord's work, and nothing else mattered.

Emily and Cheryl, who had both enrolled at BYU, came to see him off at the airport. They hugged Sam or held his hands the entire two hours they had together. His family had departed weeks earlier for the long drive to Alaska. His parents had each written him a long letter, with instructions that he was to open them on the plane and not before. When it came time to leave, Emily gave him a big hug and kiss. Cheryl held him tightly and kissed him hard. That surprised him and took his breath away. She pressed a letter into his hand and spun away as tears streamed down her face. Emily stayed to cheerfully wave as Sam walked down the ramp.

Sam's flight was scheduled to take him from Salt Lake City through Chicago, New York, and London. After almost a full day in London, he boarded another plane, which made several mysterious refueling stops in the Middle East at places the pilot claimed he was not at liberty to name. From there, it was a long flight to Jan Smuts Airport in Johannesburg, South Africa.

When Sam wearily stepped off the plane three days later, he could not believe he had finally arrived. For three days he had not slept anywhere but sitting up on planes. The saying popped into his head, "No matter where you go, there you are." He knew it was silly, but South Africa seemed much more real than he had expected. In his mind, his mission started the moment he set foot in Africa; but now that he had arrived, there seemed to be a conspicuous absence of heralding angels or a pillar of fire over the airport. It was just another hot, muggy place, and he was the same farm boy as he ever was—though much more tired, hungry, and dirty. His suit smelled, and his shirt seemed permanently glued to his back.

Four missionaries met Sam and his companions at the airport, shook their hands unceremoniously, and herded them into several vans. They crowded inside and drove a considerable distance through the bustling city of Johannesburg. Finally, they entered a quiet neighborhood filled with huge homes.

The elder driving their van explained, "When Israel became a nation again after the Yom Kippur War, many Jewish people in South Africa sold their homes dirt cheap and moved to Jerusalem. Homes were sold for a tenth of their value at that time. The Church bought a Jewish mansion for almost nothing, and it has served as the mission home ever since."

Sam later learned that there were few economies in the world like South Africa. Because of the rich natural resources and almost an un-limited supply of cheap labor, by 1972 there were more millionaires per capita in South Africa by almost double than in the United States. South Africa had almost no middle class; one was either mind-bogglingly rich or grovelingly poor. What middle class there was fell to those who chose a profession, such as lawyers, doctors, and the like. Thus, the middle class, such as it was, would be classified as wealthy in America.

Anyone of any race who made their living by the sweat of their brow eked out an existence on their minimal income by living in a tiny house and doing without many of the necessities of life. With labor so incredi-bly available and cheap, there was no pressing need to pay anyone more than survival wages.

About this time, Sam's van turned off a well-manicured lane onto the long drive of the mission home. The drive took them to a sprawling, red brick mansion with expansive glass windows, flowing architecture, and a five-car garage. They rounded a fountain and stopped before massive, double wooden doors. Sam was delighted to see Elder (now President) and Sister Carlson standing on the front steps. They had not gone to the language-training mission, but had come directly to South Africa.

President Carlson shook Sam's hand exactly like every other Elder, and Sister Carlson gave him a wink as she shook his hand. Sam didn't expect special treatment, but could tell they were pleased to see him.

The double doors opened into a broad foyer. A massive circular staircase dominated the room, and a six-foot-wide crystal chandelier hung from the high, domed ceiling. The stair treads were nearly three feet deep and rose a mere four inches with each step, which gave an almost fluid appearance to anyone climbing them.

They were ushered into a huge living room with a massive, white velvet couch and a ten-foot Steinway grand piano sitting in the bay window. A painting of exquisite beauty hung over the couch. It was nearly ten feet in length and pictured a peaceful, pastoral scene. It depicted small stucco homes with thick thatched roofs on a picturesque dirt lane bordered by a stream on one side and a meadow on the other. Sam later learned that the home was furnished when the Church bought it, and the art and furnishings were virtually priceless. The painting that hung over the couch was worth more than they had paid for the entire mansion.

Sister Carlson brought them sandwiches and milk while President Carlson interviewed each of them in turn. In what seemed like a brief time, Elder Mahoy was loaded into a VW beetle and driven several hours to his new area of Pretoria.

Elder Tilley met him in front of the boarding house where they would be staying. He was tall and blond with a perpetual smile. Sam decided almost immediately that he liked his new companion. Elder Tilley helped him unload his two bags and carry them through the house. It was oppressively dark inside, with small windows and high ceilings.

On their way to their room, Sam was introduced to a huge woman in a dirty apron. The introduction was done in Afrikaans, and he didn't understand any of it. He shook her plump hand and assumed she was the landlady. He could see into the big kitchen and was amazed that they were cooking on a big wood-burning stove. Several black servant girls were scurrying around the kitchen, and paid no attention to them. The missionary apartment was an attachment to the back of the house with an outside entrance. The room was about ten feet square, with a painted concrete floor and a high, sculpted tin ceiling. The room was unheated and had no plumbing. They had to go into the house to take showers. Sam remembered having been told this, but it finally sank home that they would not be cooking for themselves. They lived in a boarding house, which meant the landlady cooked for them. He flopped on his bed and let his eyes roll up into his head. He was exhausted to the point of death, having had no true sleep in three days.

Sam was no sooner horizontal than his companion prodded him in the side. He opened his bloodshot eyes to look at Elder Tilley, who had a broad grin on his face. He wasn't sure, but he suspected Elder Tilley enjoyed what he said next.

"Don't even think about going to sleep, Elder. We don't go to bed until 10:00 p.m. Dinner is in ten minutes. Then we have several appointments and some tracting to do. "

Sam rolled to a sitting position, a little chafed but glad to hear that missionary work was waiting to be done. Dinner consisted of two small fried beef sausages that his companion called "boer worst" or farmer sausage, two fried tomato slices with a couple of fried onion loops, a small pile of white rice, and a cup of tea. He couldn't believe his eyes or his stomach. The sausages were floating in oil, and he'd never eaten a fried tomato slice in his life. He detested rice, and he was relatively certain that tea was still against the Word of Wisdom. He looked at his companion who was slicing his sausage. Elder Tilley stabbed a piece of sausage while still holding his fork upside down in his left hand. He scraped a pile of rice onto the sausage with his knife, wiped the knife on the side of the fork, and stuffed the whole lot into his mouth, all with the fork still in his left hand.

Elder Tilley said something pleasant in Afrikaans, which Sam correctly interpreted as a compliment on the food. Sam blinked in surprise and sliced a piece of sausage. He nearly gagged. The sausage had no spices other than salt and a lot of pepper, and it tasted like lard. He forced himself to swallow. He then tried the rice, which was dry and tasteless. Surprisingly, the tomatoes and onions were wonderful. The problem was that they had almost no bulk. Sam forced himself to eat everything on his plate, which wasn't much.

When he finished eating, he felt no less hungry than before. Elder Tilley picked up his tea and stirred in milk and sugar. He leaned toward him and whispered, "It's herb tea, called rooibos, and we have permission from the First Presidency to drink it. It's almost a national drink. It is completely healthy and tastes good. Try it."

With considerable doubt, Sam watched his companion sip the tea. He felt as if he were watching him commit some grievous sin, yet a feeling of peace soon came over him, and he prepared his tea similar to Elder

Tilley's. He carefully sipped it and was surprised to find a sweet, full-bodied, earthy taste on his tongue. It was pleasant, and he enjoyed the entire cup. Had he been at home or been more confident, he would have had about three more cups of the tea and several more plates of something besides lard sausage and tasteless rice. As it was, they simply thanked the landlady and departed.

Pretoria was the capital city of South Africa and an important point of commerce. The wide streets were jam-packed with buses, trucks, cars, bicycles, and pedestrians. To make it more confusing, they were all driving on the wrong side of the street. Sam was amazed to observe that there were ten black faces to every white one, and everyone seemed to be shouting in a foreign language. He felt dizzy, tired, hungry, nauseated, and terrified—all at the same time.

He and Elder Tilley walked what seemed like a long distance before coming to a high-rise apartment building. One elevator serviced the odd-numbered floors and another the even-numbered floors. The thirteenth floor was "missing" since it was presumably unlucky, but there was a floor numbered twelve-and-a-half, which was apparently an odd number since the odd elevator stopped there. Sam found out later that some buildings skipped the thirteenth floor completely, since some of the more astute tenants figured out that twelve-and-a-half was just a ruse to cover up the fact that it was, in reality, the thirteenth floor no matter how you numbered it, which meant it was still unlucky.

In order to preserve the even/odd rhythm, there was also no fourteenth floor. In some buildings, the thirteenth floor was actually there but was used for storage or something other than apartments. The culture's extreme preoccupation with thirteen struck Sam as comical every time he saw a different attempt to avoid it.

Their appointment was on the eleventh floor, but the odd elevator was broken, so they rode the even elevator to the twelfth floor and walked down one flight.

Elder Tilley introduced Sam to Mister Van der Merva. Sam was able to say, "Pleasure to meet you" in Afrikaans and was pleased to have followed the conversation thus far. From that point on, he didn't comprehend a single word, not even one. They talked a hundred times faster than the teachers in the Language Training Mission, and they pronounced the words differently. Moment by moment, Sam felt his heart sinking farther into his empty stomach. After about fifteen minutes, Elder Tilley turned to him and asked him in Afrikaans to continue the discussion.

Sam barely understood what Elder Tilley said, but realized with a start that he was supposed to give the next concept. His brain flashed and a vague memory surfaced. He remembered some of the words, but without confidence, he felt he couldn't do it. He turned to Elder Tilley, thanked him, and asked him to continue. There was perspiration on his companion's forehead. Elder Tilley frowned, nodded, and continued. After a while, the discussion became heated. In spite of not being able to understand the words, it was clear that an argument had erupted. Mister Van der Merva fetched his Bible and began quoting scripture. A few minutes later, Elder Tilley stood without warning, politely excused himself, shook hands with Mister Van der Merva, and walked to the door. Sam followed, not sure what had just happened.

Once back in the elevator, Elder Tilley switched back to English.

"I guess he just wanted to argue. When the spirit of contention comes, I just leave. Some Elders like to argue. We call it bashing. But I refuse to do it. I'm here to teach the gospel, not to argue about it."

"Sorry about not doing my concept in there. I was lost, and I didn't understand a thing you two were saying," Sam admitted.

"Don't worry. It took me weeks to begin to understand what was going on. The LTM gives you a false sense of the language. It will click for you. Our other appointment is a few blocks away, and we need to hurry. She is an English-speaking sister. She's had the first three discussions. Do you know the fourth in English?"

"I thought I knew them all—in both languages," Sam said despondently.

Elder Tilley chuckled. "Ah, to be green again."

To call a missionary green was about the same as calling a teenager a baby. It was not a compliment, but Sam sensed that Elder Tilley didn't mean to insult him. He was just commenting on his own memories of being a "greenie."

The walk was short, and the apartment complex was newer. They took the odd elevator to the seventh floor and walked to apartment 722. A note was stuck to the door in a fashion Sam had never seen. The envelope had been licked and the flap stuck to the door. When Elder Tilley pulled it off, it left a white inverted "V" on the door.

Dear Mormon Elders,

I am no longer interested in continuing our discussions. Thank you for calling.

Eva

"Someone got to her," Elder Tilley lamented as he stuffed the note into his pocket. "It happens a lot. Well, our tracting area is not far from here. We still have several hours of daylight."

"Why didn't she call? It seems rude to just stick a note to the door," Sam complained as they walked briskly to their tracting area.

"We don't have a phone, as you may have noticed. Things are different here. Most people don't have telephones, and you have to pay by the call, so they are expensive to use. Most people only call for important things or emergencies. Because of this, we never use the phone since it scares people. They think only bad news comes when the phone rings. Besides, we can't afford it; you wouldn't believe the cost of getting a phone installed. And, I'm told there's a five-year waiting list!" Elder Tilley winked at him. "Don't worry, Elder, you'll get used to a phoneless world."

They turned several corners and entered a residential area of small homes. Sam guessed the homes were no bigger than one or two bedrooms at most. Each home had a tiny front yard surrounded by a short, ornate, concrete fence. The yards were immaculately kept, with breathtaking displays of flowers and shrubs. Africa was, after all, an arid, tropical climate, and flowers seemed to spring from the cracks in the sidewalks.

Elder Tilley walked up to the first gate. A pit bull ran from the porch to the gate and began barking. Elder Tilley pushed open the gate and strode toward the house. Sam hesitated and then followed. The dog nipped at his heels as he hurried to keep up.

The doorbell was a buzzer that reminded Sam of the timer built into his mother's stove. A woman in her forties slowly opened the door a few inches. When she saw who they were, or who she thought they were, she slammed it back shut.

"Foot sack!" she called from the other side of the door. Sam knew it was a curse, usually reserved for dogs and rapists. It literally meant "Go away, I say!" but carried an array of colorful threats and insults, several of which were threats of physical violence and suggestions of non-human ancestry. When someone said, "Foot sack," they really meant it. In reality, the word she said was Afrikaans but sounded exactly like "foot sack" in English.

Elder Tilley slid a blue pamphlet under the door. As they walked away, they could hear it being ripped to shreds.

"Happens a lot," was all he said. Somehow, it seemed to make it less disappointing, almost normal. But it still bothered Sam. He found himself wondering why the lady was so angry and if they should go back and reason with her. Elder Tilley seemed to have no such misgivings as he marched away.

The next house had a bullmastiff. It was so big that it could almost look them in the eye over the concrete fence. Elder Tilley marched right up, spoke something soothing to the dog, and opened the gate. Then he proceeded up the short lane. Sam followed, trembling with fear of the dog. Instead of biting him, it followed him, sniffing at his behind. Just as the owner opened the door, the big dog put its nose on Sam's heel and slid his big slobbery nose all the way up into his crotch. Sam couldn't keep himself from uttering a startled cry. The owner saw what had happened, laughed at them, and slammed the door.

Elder Tilley glanced at Sam as he wiped the slobber off his pants. "Happens a lot," he said.

After three more doors, Elder Tilley turned to Sam. "Elder, this one is yours. I do five, you do five."

"But!"

"If you get stuck, I'll help you, but don't expect me to bail you out until you are really stuck. I'm here, just relax and you'll do fine." He pushed open the gate and motioned for Sam to lead the way.

"But I don't know what to say."

"Say whatever the Spirit directs or whatever you have memorized, whichever comes to mind first." He chuckled.

"I'm not sure I can handle it if it's not in English."

"Okay, tell you what. If it's in Afrikaans, I'll take it. If it's in English, you take it. Now do it."

Sam took a breath and strode in. He didn't even notice the barking dog as he walked past it. He knocked and waited. Someone stirred inside and pulled open the door. A young woman stood before him. She was holding a little girl. The baby was about two years old and was one of the most beautiful little girls he'd ever seen.

His eyes were pulled toward the child, and for a moment, he entirely forgot why he was there. The woman turned the child toward Sam. He reached out to her. The little girl cocked her head and reached out a small hand with a big smile. Her hand was tiny compared to his, and it was sticky. Sam smiled, and still holding her hand, suddenly remembered why he was there. With a start, he turned back to the baby's mother. To his surprise, she was studying his face with interest. He forced the smile from his face and introduced himself in Afrikaans. He could do that much.

"I prefer English," she said in Afrikaans, then added in English, "and I think you might too."

"Yes, ma'am," Sam said with a little too much relief. "Today's my first day in South Africa, and I can't understand a word anyone says. Even the English people are hard for me to understand."

This made her laugh, which sounded musical to his ears. "You have an American accent," she observed.

"Yes, I suppose I do. I'm from Idaho, in the western United States. We're missionaries for The Church of Jesus Christ of Latter-day Saints."

"Mormons?" she asked.

"We're sometimes called Mormons. We . . ."

"I don't mean to be rude, but I'm not interested in your church. My husband and I are happy in our church. I hope you'll forgive me."

Elder Tilley turned to leave, and the woman started to close the door.

"Believe me, you are not being rude," Sam muttered as he turned. The door stopped closing. She had a quizzical look on her face.

Sam hurried to explain. "What I mean is, the previous five doors got slammed in our faces. I've almost been bitten by two dogs and was molested by a third. Not being interested I understand, but slamming the door or siccing your dog on someone is rude. You certainly haven't been rude. I thank you for allowing me to speak to someone who understands what being a Christian means."

She frowned at this and said, "If I truly understood what being a Christian means, I probably wouldn't turn you away, would I? But really, I'm not interested."

Sam had to think about this before answering. "I can't imagine you doing anything unchristian. Forgive me for intruding on your evening. It was worth it just to see your daughter. She's so cute. Is she about two?"

"She'll be two in three weeks."

"Reminds me of my baby sister when she was that age." Sam turned to leave, and the woman slowly closed the door.

When they were back on the sidewalk, Sam suddenly had an idea. "Just a minute," he said, and hurried back up the walk. He rang the bell. When she opened the door, he handed her a Joseph Smith tract. She seemed reluctant to accept it, so he handed it to the child who snatched it from him.

"Ma'am, I came over six thousand miles to be a missionary. So far, you're the nicest person I've met in this country, and the most wonderful thing I possess is in that pamphlet. I know you aren't interested and won't read it. Just the same, I wouldn't feel right about not giving you something in return for your kindness." He smiled and trotted back down the steps. When he closed the gate, she was still standing in the door. She had a confused expression on her face. Sam waved and in response, she took her daughter's arm, and waved it back at him.

As they were walking away, Elder Tilley put an X next to 355, their house number.

"Why'd you do that?"

"They sacked us. The X warns the next Elders not to knock on that door again," he explained matter-of-factly.

"I know what the X means. What I mean is, why did you X her? She didn't sack us," Sam objected.

"Did too."

"Did not."

"Are we in her house teaching her the first discussion?" Elder Tilley countered.

"Well, no."

"Do we have an appointment to come back?"

"No."

"She sacked us."

Sam stood his ground. "But I have this feeling. I think maybe we planted a seed."

"I have this feeling that maybe you wasted a Joseph Smith tract. Do you realize we have to buy those things ourselves? Give away ten of them, and it's worth one soft drink. Don't waste them, Elder. We can give out the little blue ones for free. If they sack us, give 'em a blue one, okay?"

"She didn't sack us," Sam insisted.

His companion moaned and muttered something in Afrikaans about greenies as he turned into the next gate. Ten slammed doors later, they headed for home. It took them almost an hour to walk back, and each step brought on more exhaustion until Sam was not sure he could make it home. The town was hilly, like San Francisco, and seemed an endless series of climbs and equally wearying descents. By the time they stopped at their boarding house, Sam was exhausted and completely lost. He didn't recognize the building and thought they were going to tract one more house before going home. He was startled when Tilley opened the door and just walked in.

When Sam got to his bed, he fell onto it and almost immediately began to snore. Elder Tilley rousted him and said something about scripture study and companion prayers. Sam felt he was talking to someone in a dream.

"Elder Tilley, did you ever notice how much bigger I am than you?"

"Yes, but . . ."

"This body is going to sleep, whether you or I tell it not to. If you want to knock yourself out trying to get it up, help yourself, but I'm not going to fight it or you. Good night."

"I'll pray for your soul, you sinful Elder," Tilley said in mock seriousness.

"Light a candle for me," Sam muttered and promptly fell asleep.

Elder Tilley let Sam sleep until about 8:00 a.m. the following morning, two hours past normal. Sam was still tired when he awoke. Elder Tilley was sitting on his bed, reading the scriptures. They made it to breakfast just in time. It consisted of a shallow bowl of white corn mush. With a pat of butter, salt, sugar, and milk, it was tasty, but only a quarter of what Sam's stomach was hoping for.

After breakfast, Elder Tilley announced they were going thumb tracting. Sam had no idea of what this meant but followed gamely.

They walked out onto a busy street, and Tilley stuck out his thumb. Sam did the same. In less than two minutes, a big, old Buick screeched to a stop in front of them. The brakes were metal to metal. In America, this car would have been a classic. In Africa, it was a taxi stuffed with about ten black people. Sam couldn't believe that many people could fit into a car. The springs were collapsed from the weight, and the bumper almost touched the ground. As soon as it stopped, the driver leaned toward them and spoke loudly with a big smile on his face. "Good morning, my bossies. Do you need a ride into town, my bossies? I have much plenty room, if you like, I drive you to town."

Sam had several African-American friends back home, but this man's face was truly black. His accent was lilting, with a singsong beat. Sam could not imagine what "room" he was talking about, but as the driver was speaking, four people got out to make space for the missionaries. Tilley thanked them and told them they would never make someone else walk so they could ride. After much persuasion, they went on.

"The blacks offer us rides about ten to one over whites. They know we are missionaries, and they have taboos and strong beliefs about missionaries. It's considered good luck to give a missionary a ride, and to give foreign missionaries a ride is a big honor. They were probably really disappointed we didn't take them up on it."

"Why did they call us 'bossie?' I once had a cow called Bossie," Sam observed dryly.

"Well, they call anyone they respect their boss. If they are speaking to someone younger, they often call them bossie. In our language, it's a compliment, like a small boss—bossie. See? But in Zulu, bossie means something like 'little smart ass,' or something like that. It's not a compliment."

"I thought you said they would be honored to have us ride in their car. Why insult us then?"

"Oh, they would have been honored. In that situation, they have the power, and offering us a ride puts them in a position of power over us. They weren't offering us a ride to honor us; they were offering a ride to honor themselves, to be able to have power over us."

"That sounds pretty cynical. Are you sure about that? It sounds petty and cheap," Sam said with a note of disgust in his voice.

"I have heard many people comment on that aspect of black culture."

"Have you ever heard a black person say that?"

"I don't speak Zulu."

"I won't believe all that until I hear a black person say it. Why don't we just take one of them up on their offer? Why not ride with the black people?"

"Well, there's two reasons," Elder Tilley explained. "The first is that I don't like the idea of putting four people afoot so we can ride."

Sam agreed with that.

"The second is that it's actually illegal."

"What?" Sam exclaimed. He could not believe his ears.

"It is," Elder Tilley insisted. "The Church has a binding agreement with the South African government that no LDS missionaries will meet with a group of blacks larger than four persons. It also absolutely prohibits us teaching them the gospel."

"You're joking," Sam said.

Elder Tilley turned to face Sam, his face stern. Sam could tell he was not joking. "Elder Mahoy, this is not America. The laws are different here. When we return to boarding, I will show it to you in writing in our missionary handbook. To avoid the appearance of holding meetings with black citizens, we do not accept rides from carloads of blacks."

"I think that's terrible," Sam said adamantly.

"Actually, I do too, Elder. I do too. But I can't change the way things are."

Elder Tilley was muttering something again about greenies when another carload of blacks pulled up. The missionaries turned it down, as well as another, before a white man pulled up in a car all by himself. They got in, and while driving to town, almost taught him the first discussion. He was nice but not interested, and the subject changed to the weather. He let them out near the center of town.

Pretoria was a bustling city of high-rise apartments. The street level held shops, stores, and businesses. The apartments above the shopping district were new-looking and appeared to be recently built.

The signs along the street were about half Afrikaans and half English. Sam could see Coca Cola, Kodak, General Electric, Sony, and a hundred other names familiar to him. They walked a short distance and went into the camera shop where Elder Tilley's camera was being repaired. He picked it up, and after paying, they looked around the store.

Everything seemed expensive. Everything they could have bought in a camera store in America was on the shelves, but was much more expensive. It turned out that Elder Tilley loved photography and came here occasionally to look at the latest equipment. His camera was new and expensive.

They decided to walk to the park and meet people there before lunch, but their attempt at proselytizing was a disaster. Every conversation they tried to start ended up in a curt refusal. It seemed that everyone was in too big a hurry to listen to their message. By lunchtime, they were both discouraged. They couldn't get home in time for lunch at the boarding, and Sam didn't have enough money to buy anything. Elder Tilley bought them fish and chips at a small shop. The little café was no bigger than a walk-in closet and had a line of people waiting. It was worth the wait. Sam finally tasted something he liked, but he could have eaten twice as much.

They decided to take the bus home and found the correct bus stop, which was not a simple task. They had to study the bus schedule for twenty minutes, tracing routes and studying maps to see which bus or combination of buses would take them nearest home. In the end, the fastest way home was a direct ride that left them within a half mile of their boarding. The combination of buses that would have let them off within a block of home would have gotten them back several hours later. Sam was surprised to learn it only cost five cents to ride the bus.

As they were waiting, Sam noticed that they were just a few doors from a music store. He missed music, and had left his harmonica with his parents. As they had a few hours to wait, Sam finally persuaded Elder Tilley to go in and browse around. They stepped inside, and Sam was entranced. Most of the instruments were used, showing obvious signs of wear, yet the shop looked prosperous.

Sam gazed at the instruments, wondering what stories each instrument could tell, who had owned them, and why they had sold them.

He was so deep in thought that he was startled when the store owner spoke to them in English. "Looking for something particular, gentlemen?"

"Huh? Oh, no. Mostly waiting for the bus. But I love music. Hope you don't mind," Sam said.

"Certainly not. Do you play?" The store owner was a young man in his thirties, dressed like an American hippie. He had long hair held back by a scarf tied around his head and was wearing a flowered shirt, faded bell-bottom Levis, and sandals over white socks. It was almost comical, but he seemed very comfortable in his attire.

"I used to play the flute and the harmonica. I tinker on the organ and piano. Nothing spectacular. I gave up the flute years ago."

"You're American!" The shop owner nearly shouted.

"Yes. We . . ." He wanted to tell them they were missionaries, but the man grabbed his hand and started pumping it up and down.

"I am too! Except that I've never been there, I mean. I love everything American. In my office, I have an American flag. I collect American stamps and anything American I can get my hands on. I love American clothes, American music, John Wayne, Walt Disney—American everything." He was so enthusiastic that Sam was embarrassed. Even Sam didn't love American everything.

"My name's Thomas Snodgrass. Pleased to meet you."

"Elder Sam Mahoy and Elder John Tilley," Sam introduced them. Tom finally stopped shaking Sam's hand and worked over Elder Tilley's. Elder Tilley was smiling like he was watching a comedy act. "Do you play Dixieland jazz? That's my favorite."

"I don't know that I've ever tried," Sam admitted.

"What! You said you are American. You really a Russian spy? Just kidding! I thought all Americans loved Dixieland jazz."

"Well, some do I'm sure. But . . ."

"No buts. Which instrument do you prefer? Pick one, and I'll get my trumpet."

Sam looked at Elder Tilley, who shrugged his indifference. Sam wandered over to a piano and sat down. Oddly enough—or perhaps not oddly at all—it was an American-made Baldwin baby grand. It was obviously a used piano, but it was in perfect tune. Sam played a Primary song, and peace came over him. The piano was in great condition, and he felt its music calling.

Tom returned with a long silver trumpet and blew an exuberant note. Without warning, he launched into "When the Saints Go Marching In." When Sam didn't play along, he stopped.

"What's the matter? You're a Mormon missionary, and you're from America! This is your American song. Don't you know it?" he asked in mock amazement.

"I've heard it, but . . ."

"Okay, I'll play the opening line, and whatever I do, you do the same thing. Okay? Good. Key of C."

"What is the key of C?"

"Oh, one of those. No black notes," he answered with surprising patience.

"Got it," Sam said, understanding perfectly.

Tom puffed out his cheeks and belted out the notes for the lyrics "Oh when the Saints . . ."

Sam hammered out the same thing. Tom played ". . . go marching in."

Sam copied him, but added a few chords.

They played back and forth until they had worn the song to a frazzle.

Tom would stop and periodically give him some instruction.

"Okay. Now go up a key: play a fourth, then the fifth, and then add the seventh. See how that leads to a natural key change? Now, you'll just play everything with two sharps, F and C." When explained that way, it made perfect sense to Sam. He played by feeling and hearing, and every previous attempt to explain music theory to him had gone over his head. But Tom had a way of teaching it that made sense. Sam played until his fingers ached and they had missed their intended bus.

By the time they stopped playing, the store was jammed with people who had come in to listen. Tom stood his horn on the piano and turned to the people. In a few minutes, he had sold one lady trumpet lessons for her son, and another man said he would bring his wife back to see the piano Sam had been playing.

"Hey, you Mormons are good for business," Tom proclaimed loudly. Many people in the store laughed. Tom disappeared and returned with a flute. He handed it to Sam, who took it reluctantly. "Elder, play us some flute." The people clapped and urged him on. Elder Tilley nodded at him to do it. But Sam laid the flute onto the piano and shook his head.

"I'm sorry. I don't play the flute anymore," Sam explained quietly. "That was a long time ago."

As they left, so did the crowd. One man wanted to know who they were, and several others asked if this was part of their mission. A woman wanted Sam to teach her daughter piano lessons. He explained that he was here to teach the gospel, not the piano. The woman considered this, and then invited them to come to her home to teach the gospel if he would play, too. They made an appointment with her.

While the Elders stood at the bus stop, they talked with several people about the gospel and made another appointment. By the time they finally arrived home, they had made three appointments, taught two discussions, and were filled with the Spirit. It had been a wonderful day.

After companion prayers that evening, Elder Tilley complimented Sam on his playing and the effect it had on people. He suggested they return every Tuesday and do the same thing. Sam was delighted, but admitted humbly, "Elder, all I can say is that what happened in that music store was a miracle. God knew I needed to play the piano, and He was the one who did it, not me!"

As the weeks progressed, their Tuesday "music tracting," as they came to call it, turned into Tuesday and Thursday, then Tuesday, Thursday, and Saturday. Tom loved it. People actually planned to be at his store, and a few made reservations. He had to have his wife, Linda, come to the store to man it so he could make music with Sam. Tom started handing Sam different instruments just to see what he could do. With a few dismal exceptions, Sam quickly learned to play most of them. The third week, Tom handed him a violin.

"Gosh. I've never touched one of these. Don't have a clue what to do," Sam said with some hesitation. Tom handed him the bow and showed him how to hold the violin. He showed him where to press down the strings to play the different notes of the scale. Sam was surprised at how simple it seemed to him. It made perfect sense, like he was learning to speak an long-forgotten native language. The violin suddenly felt like an old friend, and Sam rejoiced in the flow of the Spirit as he drew the bow across the strings. Under Tom's direction, he ground out a simple tune, adjusting the bow's pressure to create a sweeter sound. Tom picked up a violin from the counter for himself, and played a catchy line. Sam struggled but played the same thing, albeit with several squeals.

Tom played it again, and Sam did better. The fourth time, it was fairly decent. Tom played something harder and Sam copied. Tom's eyes widened in utter amazement; what he was witnessing was quite impossible, and he knew it. Tom then fired off a complicated melody, and Sam botched it halfway through. Tom repeated it, and Sam did it right the second time. People clapped. Tom's wife sold someone violin lessons.

By the end of the day, Sam was playing the violin fairly well, even achieving the beginnings of vibrato. He had felt the flow of the Spirit empowering his musical ability throughout the entire experience, and he offered up many silent prayers of gratitude and thanksgiving.

As they were playing the final passage, Sam heard a familiar melody in his mind. It was the song he had played at Jimmy's funeral—a haunting, passionate piece by Bach. He couldn't get the tune from his head. It called to him so loudly that it started coming from the violin. Sam closed his eyes and heard the music. It welled up in him like an irresistible force and spilled out onto the strings. He was there, back at the funeral, Jimmy's still little form before him. Sam threw his head back and played, his heart overflowed, and the strings cried out the precious feelings. Tears streamed down his cheeks, and he played as if nothing else in the world mattered.

When the music ceased, he was startled to hear someone sniffle.

He opened his eyes and realized that nearly fifty people were looking at him with faces filled with emotion, some with tears on their cheeks.

He lowered the violin and they applauded. He suddenly felt foolish, exposed, and embarrassed. It was too private a moment to have shared with so many people. He suppressed the urge to run away.

Sam's old feelings of never wanting to play in front of people dominated him for a minute, but quickly washed away. Suddenly he knew something about himself that he had never been able to understand. His soul was filled with music. He was so full of music that he heard it night and day. It was so real and so deep that it nearly flooded out conscious thought at times.

Like a new revelation, Sam realized that music was one of his gifts from God. He realized that music was not something that he had struggled and practiced a million hours to perfect. It wasn't even something he had asked for. It was simply and entirely a free gift from God.

Sam had known this on some level before, but it had never occurred to him how magnificent this gift really was. At that moment, he realized how wrong it was to hide it, and to not use it. The spontaneous and sustained applause of his listeners drilled this knowledge home to his soul, and in silent prayer, he thanked Heavenly Father and gave Him all credit. He knew where the music came from, and it wasn't from himself. Like all things of pure beauty, it was from God.

Tom and Linda drove them home that evening as they often did. Tom usually didn't want them to leave, and they would usually miss the last bus. As they pulled onto the highway, Linda sighed. She didn't often say much to the Elders. They were Tom's friends, and everyone in the car was surprised when she spoke directly to Sam.

"Elder Mahoy, I feel as if a miracle happened before my eyes today. I'm not sure what it was. I mean, watching you touch a violin for the first time and play it so beautifully just a few hours later, that was a miracle. But that's not what I mean. As I listened to you play and saw the tears coming down your cheeks, I felt as if God were in the store with you. When you stopped, your face was glowing, and my chest was burning like it was on fire. I've never felt that before. I felt as if I wanted to laugh, shout for joy, and cry all at the same time. I've never felt such a complex mixture of joy and yearning. I want to know why your face was glowing tonight, and why my chest was burning."

Linda turned to face Tom. "I know we kind of have an understanding with these young Mormon men. They just come and play and don't talk about their religion, but I simply must know. Tom, I want them to come to our house and answer these questions. If you aren't interested, you can go to another room or something. I'm sorry, Tom, but I have to know."

Then, turning back to the Elders she asked, "Will you come teach me about what happened tonight?"

Elder Tilley broke the silence that followed. "Elder Mahoy, what were you doing at the end of the music, when you were just standing there?"

Embarrassed, Sam cleared his throat. "I was praying," he said softly. "Why?" Linda asked impetuously.

Tom interjected. "Honey, maybe it's too personal," he said, although it was obvious that he wanted to know too.

"Sorry, I . . . you don't have to answer that," Linda apologized. "No. It's all right, Linda. Really," Sam said softly and smiled at her.

She relaxed. "I guess the easiest way to explain it is that I have always been musical and embarrassed about it. I'm a big guy, and playing music isn't a thing big guys are supposed to do. So I would only play for my baby brother, who loved my music. I used to spend hours playing my flute for him. He would sit on my knee, and I would play. He would sing mostly nonsense words, or ones he just made up. It was our connection. After he died, I never played the flute again. Except for my harmonica and some church music, I hadn't played any instrument much until I walked into your store a few weeks ago."

Tom nodded understandingly, and Linda turned around and knelt in her seat so she could face the Elders. Sam continued.

"Tonight, for a few minutes, I was back there at the funeral, playing that same music as I looked down into the casket. Back then, I laid my flute next to him in the casket and vowed I'd never play again. Tonight, I vowed I would play all I could to express my love to Heavenly Father. I think that's the miracle. I think a part of me came back to life tonight. In a small way, the musical part of my soul has been reborn. I was praying to thank Heavenly Father for that miracle."

Nobody spoke for the remainder of the drive. They pulled up to the boarding house. Sam was halfway out of the car when he paused and sat down. His heart burned within him. He didn't want to offend them, yet he knew what the Lord wanted him to say. He waited until peace swept over him.

"Tom. Linda. Tonight was a special spiritual experience for me, and you were an important part of it. Would it be okay if I said a prayer and thanked Heavenly Father for this blessing and your part in it?" They nodded their heads silently.

Sam bowed his head, and after a moment, he said, "Heavenly Father, I'm so sorry I hid behind my sorrow all these years. I know now that it was wrong. And I know that thou hast brought Tom and Linda into my life to teach me this. I just want thee to know how grateful I am. Please bless Tom and Linda and let them feel thy Holy Spirit as they drive home so they will know how pleased Thou art with them for helping me understand thy blessings to me and thy will for me. In the name of Jesus Christ, amen."

March 6, 1974

We have continued to go to Tom and Linda's store three times a week. It has turned out to be a wonderful experience. We keep busy teaching all the rest of the week from appointments we make in the store. Since we started this, we haven't needed to do much tracting. Can't say I miss it. It wasn't very productive.

Tonight Tom handed me a violin. I've never played one, but I was able to play it somehow. It was as if I had played one all my life. I wasn't thinking about how to put my fingers on the strings. I was hearing the music in my soul and causing it to come out of the violin. I have had similar experiences, like when I got my harmonica a few Christmases ago.

Something happened while I was playing. The Holy Spirit came over Linda and Tom and touched something in their souls. I hadn't really thought of them as investigators, just friends. We will begin teaching them next Tuesday after playing in their store. I know they are ready for the gospel. It will be a joy to teach them.

The hardest part of this evening was asking them to pray as we sat in the car. I felt my soul burning, and I knew what to do, but for some reason, I was afraid to offend them. But that feeling of peace flowed over me, and I did it. It was a wonderful experience. The Spirit was strong, and they felt it. I am learning to trust the promptings of the Holy Spirit, even more than I did before. I honestly believe that in order to be a good missionary, I have to be completely obedient to the Holy Spirit. Then I will be able to do His work, His way.

I think I learned something about missionary work tonight. We have been trying to influence people to listen to our message, and the ones we simply loved and weren't even trying to influence ended up being the ones the Lord has prepared.

I love missionary work. I love the Lord. I feel the power of His love as I speak to the people.

* * *

Tom and Linda's home was large and hidden deep in a lovely subdivision. Sam and Elder Tilley were impressed. Tom was obviously proud of his success, but brushed off their compliments. Linda beamed as she showed them around their place. The building was horseshoe shaped, with towers at both ends. A swimming pool was nestled in a lush courtyard formed by the house. It truly was impressive.

They suggested sitting around the dining room table for the meeting. Elder Tilley set up the flannel board and began the first discussion. Before Elder Tilley had finished the first concept, Tom seemed to grow restless and Linda was frowning. Elder Tilley made his voice more sincere, and tried hard to teach with the Spirit. By the time it was Sam's turn, there was a strained feeling in the room.

Sam didn't pick up immediately with the next part of the lesson but sat quietly, looking at his new friends. Elder Tilley assumed he had forgotten his part, and began with the second concept, but Sam interrupted him politely. Elder Tilley smiled and leaned back in his chair. "Linda. Tom. I want to tell you something I was taught by my family. Something very important to me that I hope will be important to you too." They both nodded and turned toward him.

"Ever since I was a little boy, I've had an active conscience. You know, the voice that stops you from doing everything you thought was going to be fun?" They laughed and made comments about how well they understood.

"I didn't realize until my parents taught me that the voice I was hearing is the Light of Christ coming from the Holy Spirit. Every person born into this world has a conscience and knows the difference between right and wrong."

"Everyone?" Tom asked doubtfully.

"The scriptures say that every person born into the world has the Light of Christ. The important point here is that the Light of Christ comes from Christ and is actually His voice in our soul. It is revelation to us."

"Wow," Linda said. "Are you sure? I mean, wouldn't that make us prophets or something? If we are receiving revelations?"

Sam nodded. "In some ways, it does, or at least it can lead to that point. What do you think the reason is for Christ giving us this revelation?"

Elder Tilley cleared his throat. "Elder, would you like me take it from here?" He gave Sam a pointed look to remind him that they were not supposed to deviate from the memorized discussions.

"Thanks. In a minute," Sam replied, his mind hardly registering his companion's words. "You both indicated that you'd heard your conscience guide you in the past. Did you follow that guidance?"

"Sometimes I don't," Tom admitted. "I have always looked at my conscience as a nuisance, not as a guide."

Linda leaned on the table with her elbows, and put her chin in her hands. "I try to but miss a lot, I think. I try not to do anything contrary to my conscience though."

"Why is that?" Sam asked.

"Well, because I always feel miserable when I disobey," Linda answered slowly.

"Could you say that in a positive way?"

"What? Oh, yes. Because I always feel good when I obey. Actually, that's true, but I had never thought of it before."

Sam nodded and asked, "Would it be a fair conclusion then to say that the purpose of the Light of Christ, or our conscience, is to make us feel good, to make us happy?"

Tom straightened a bit and thought about the question. "I think that would be a fair statement, but it strikes me as being too simplistic. I get the feeling there has to be a larger purpose to anything God does than just making us happy."

Elder Tilley coughed loudly, slapped a flannel cutout of Joseph Smith on the board, and began to speak. "Brother and Sister Snodgrass, as we were saying earlier, since all the apostles and prophets of Christ's time were killed by evil men, it became necessary for God to restore the things that were lost at their death. For this reason, in the spring of 1820, God again called a living prophet. He was fourteen years old, and his name was Joseph Smith. Why do you think God called Joseph Smith to be a prophet?" Linda looked a bit impatient, and Tom smiled woodenly at Elder Tilley.

"Elder Tilley, would you mind if Elder Mahoy finishes his thought before we get to Joseph Smith? I know about Mr. Smith and the gold bible, and frankly, I'm doubtful of the entire story. I want to know what Elder Mahoy is getting at. When he was talking to me, my soul seemed to be on fire. When you started with Joseph Smith, the fire went out. I don't mean to be rude, but could you kindly postpone your comments until Elder Mahoy is done?"

Elder Tilley's mouth was hanging open. "Oh, sure. Excuse me," he said.

Sam felt the awkward feeling in the room, and wasn't sure what to say, so he relaxed for a few seconds. Then he felt the peace of the Spirit, and spoke again with confidence.

"The scriptures indicate that man was created for the purpose of having joy, but the type of joy the scriptures are speaking of isn't necessarily the type we might get from winning the lottery or finding a buried treasure. It's the type of happiness that comes to a person when he or she finally enters the kingdom of God."

"So, what has that to do with the conscience?" Tom asked as if Sam still hadn't returned to the prior subject.

"If the ultimate object and outcome of God's plan for us is to make us happy, how would you expect to feel if you were on the correct course and successfully traveling toward that goal?"

"Happy," they both said simultaneously. Linda added, "But happy in the sense that I felt happy as my chest was burning after you played the violin. Happy in a deep, wonderful way."

"Exactly."

Sam paused, and they all sensed a sweet feeling present. "No wonder I feel miserable, frustrated, and unhappy most of the time," Tom said loudly, half joking. Linda jabbed him with an elbow, which he pretended really hurt.

"Every time we hear and obey our conscience, it brings us greater genuine happiness. Every time we disobey, we become more miserable."

"That's me," Tom said. "It often takes courage to accept what our conscience tells us, because it's often contrary to our own will, even contrary to common sense at times. But if we know it is the voice of Christ, and it is telling us to do something good, then we can be confident that obeying it will ultimately bring us great blessings, even if at the time we can't see how that could possibly be."

Tom leaned forward. "When we first met, I told you two that you could come to my store anytime, but you were not to talk to me about your religion. You honored that request right up until the other night, when you actually asked us to pray with you in the car. How did you know that your request wouldn't offend us so we'd just drive away?" Then he stopped. "Never mind. I know the answer."

Sam turned to Linda. "What do you think is the answer to Tom's question?"

"You felt guided by the Holy Spirit, and because of your faith, you knew it wouldn't offend us."

"Not exactly. I felt guided, but I didn't know what your response would be. I only knew what the Lord wanted me to do. We seldom know the outcome of our obedience, only that it is what is right."

"I see," Linda pushed her long hair out of her face. "I can see why obedience might be scary, except for the faith that one would develop through obedience."

Sam nodded at her and turned to Tom. "Tom, a minute ago you asked a question and said you knew the answer. What did it feel like when you suddenly knew that answer?"

"It felt complete, and comfortable, as if I had known it all my life. I just knew it, that's all," he responded.

"And has it brought you happiness? Has it been a blessing in your life? In other words, did that knowledge come from God?"

Tom smiled broadly, his voice certain. "I believe that it did. What you have already told me tonight is going to change the course of my life. I know what you are saying is true, and I have decided to live my life by obeying my conscience. I don't know where it will take me, but I'm going to do it!"

Linda slipped her hand into Tom's. "Me too. And I think I know where Elder Mahoy would say it's going to take us. Back to God. Right?" Sam did not speak, but beamed at her. She already knew the answer. Then he said, "I want you both to listen with your hearts for a moment, not with your rational minds. I want you to feel, to listen to that still, small voice, and after a moment, I am going to ask you to tell me what you feel. Elder Tilley, would you repeat what you started to say earlier about Joseph Smith?"

Elder Tilley was following every word and smoothly flowed into the account of the first vision. He told the events as if he himself had been there, with wonder in his voice and with a sense of great joy. He told it as he never had done before, and his heart soared as he recounted that holy visitation. When he was finished, he knew even more powerfully than he had ever known in his life that it was perfectly, profoundly true. He concluded and bore a joyous witness of its truthfulness, barely able to restrain his emotions.

Sam turned back to Tom. "Tom, what did you feel just now? You are a prophet, able to receive revelation for yourself. What did the Holy Spirit whisper to your soul as you listened to Elder Tilley?"

Tom cleared his voice and fidgeted in his seat. Linda placed a hand on his arm as tears pooled in his eyes. He looked at her, Elder Tilley, and back to Sam. His voice was barely audible as he said, "I know it's true."

Linda clapped a hand to her mouth in wonder and tears formed in her eyes. She gave Tom a hug and rested her head on his shoulder.

"Linda, would you like to add your feelings to Tom's?"

"I felt it too. It was like after the violin music. My heart felt like it was on fire. When Tom said it was true, I just knew with all my heart he was right."

Sam took a deep breath before he spoke the next words. "We are going to have a baptismal service exactly one month from today. Would you be willing to make the necessary preparations to participate in that service? Are you willing to commit your lives totally to obedience to the Lord and be baptized into His Church?"

They nodded without hesitation and kissed each other. For the briefest time, eternity paused, and a moment of joy was indelibly recorded in heaven.

March 23, 1974

Brother and Sister Snodgrass committed to baptism tonight. It was a wonderful discussion, but it got me in trouble with Elder Tilley. I didn't feel they needed to hear the first discussion, and when it was my turn, I taught them about the Holy Spirit and how to discern truth. When we did give them the first vision, they accepted it. They wouldn't have otherwise.

Anyway, Elder Tilley gave me a lecture about not deviating from the lessons and following his lead as long as he was senior companion. I felt like asking him who I should obey—him or the Lord? But I didn't. The important part is that Tom and Linda are committed to baptism. I hope we can teach them every time with the Spirit. I have a feeling that they will not respond to the missionary lessons exactly as they are written. They seemed offended when we start rattling off memorized words. In this, and in all other things, I will do as the Lord commands. It is my only hope and my only joy.

* * *

After scripture study the next morning, Sam finished a pencil sketch he had begun three weeks earlier. The image was clear in his mind as he worked. Sketching was another thing that came fairly easily to him, although he had never developed the talent past rudimentary art. He found a piece of stiff, white paper that worked perfectly. When he was finished, he showed Elder Tilley the sketch.

"I've seen this little girl before!" Tilley said in surprise.

"It's the little girl at the first house I did the door approach to three weeks ago. Remember?"

"Now I do. This is good. It looks just like her. Why'd you draw a picture of her?"

"On our way to the tracting area, I'll show you."

This was the only explanation Sam felt inclined to give. Elder Tilley accepted his answer, and they hiked off. They arrived at house number 355 about thirty minutes later. It was nearly 10:00 in the morning.

"I think this is going to turn out badly," Elder Tilley said as Sam led the way up the walk. He rang the doorbell and waited. After a long time, the young mother opened the door. Her eyes looked as if she had just been sleeping. She gave a small sign of recognition and a big sign of annoyance. She was not pleased to see them again, but didn't say anything.

Sam held out the picture without explanation, which she took after a slight hesitation. She studied his drawing with a dull expression, and then a smile tugged at her lips. Sam noticed what a beautiful woman she was. He also noticed that she was not a whole lot older than himself. She had short, dark hair and high cheekbones, portraying an almost noble appearance. Her lips were full and gave the impression of being willing to smile. Her eyes were a most startling brown, almost black.

"It's her birthday, isn't it?" Sam said, disclosing what the Spirit had whispered to him that morning. "I drew her a picture." She said nothing, but continued to stare at him with no expression. Sam was beginning to agree with Elder Tilley that this was going to go badly. He started to back up to leave, but felt a hand in the middle of his back.

He stopped, thinking he was about to trip over Elder Tilley, but realized with a start that his companion was standing beside him and had both arms folded across his chest. Yet, the hand on his back had been very distinct. A sweet peace settled over him, and he knew he should not leave until the Lord had finished whatever it was they were there to do.

Then a tear trickled from the mother's eye, and she held the picture to her heart. Her lips said, "Thank you" but no sound came out.

Sam didn't know what to do, and was grateful when Elder Tilley said, "Is there something we can do? Is everything all right?"

She shook her head, and Sam wasn't sure which question she was answering. Perhaps both of them?

Sam said, "Ma'am, is something wrong with your daughter? I'd like to help if I can." Instead of answering, she stepped back and motioned them to enter.

The living room was small and dark. It had a brightly polished hardwood floor and worn but functional furniture. They found a seat on the sofa. After closing the door, she took a seat in a big chair that groaned as she sat in it. A few more tears coursed down her face before she said, "Juanita is ill. She has a blood disease. The doctors didn't expect it to advance as quickly as it has. There's nothing they can do for her . . . I'm afraid . . ."

Just at that moment, a young man walked into the room from the back of the house. He was tall and blond. Sam thought he looked like someone had peeled him off a California surfer poster. He walked into the room to stand beside his wife, a look of displeasure on his face. Sam could almost hear him thinking, "What are these Mormons doing in my house?"

"Sean, these are Mormon missionaries. I'm sorry, I don't know your names."

Elder Tilley introduced himself and Sam. Their names were Connie and Sean Van Dangen.

"Look, Elder Mahoy drew a picture of Juanita," Connie said as she held the picture up for Sean to see. The hard expression on Sean's face softened.

"It's a birthday present for her . . ." she added, but her voice trailed off. A look of concern crossed her face.

"She's sleeping. I gave her another pill," Sean said in answer to her unspoken concern. He turned to Sam. "It's a beautiful picture. Her birthday's actually two more days away, but I'll give it to her . . ." Sam heard the rest in his soul. " . . . if she lives that long."

Sam's heart ached, and he remembered the pain of his little brother's death. He remembered the two long weeks when Jimmy was unconscious and everyone had hoped he would live, even though they knew he wouldn't.

Without realizing it, Sam bowed his head. He understood their pain perfectly, and it was more than he could bear to see them going through what he and his family had suffered. Tears fell onto his hands. After a moment, he realized he was weeping and wiped his eyes. He noticed with a start that everyone was watching him.

"Excuse me," he mumbled. "It's just that—my little brother died when he was two, and I remember the waiting and the wishing and the unbearable hopelessness. I guess I know a little of what you're feeling . . . it breaks my heart, I guess. Forgive me."

There was a moment of silence, and then Sean and Connie exchanged glances. He had seen his mom and dad do the same thing and knew they had silently arrived at a decision.

Connie stood and asked. "Elders, would you like some rooibos tea? I know you don't drink regular tea, but I heard you can drink rooibos tea." They accepted, and she disappeared into the kitchen.

Sean cleared his throat. "Please forgive me for being rude earlier. I didn't mean to be inhospitable. It's just that this is a hard time, and we don't want to get tangled up in religious arguments right now. You see, I'm studying at the seminary to become an Anglican minister. My father is an Anglican minister. So, you would be wasting your breath. I probably know more about Mormonism than you do," he added in a subdued but haughty tone.

"Connie already said you weren't interested, and we respect that. I just wanted to give Juanita a birthday gift. I have a little sister, and she reminds me of her. When I saw Juanita the first time, I guess it made me homesick. We'll be going soon and won't bother you again."

At that moment, Connie returned with a tray. "Please don't misinterpret our words. We do missionary work ourselves and know how hard it can be. I appreciate the beautiful picture you drew and you remembering her birthday. It's just that we are very comfortable with our lives and are happy with our involvement in our church. We are just not in the mood to have a religious debate at this time. Perhaps sometime later, after . . ." her voice caught, and she busied herself with the tea.

Sam sipped the tea. She had brewed it lightly, and the delicate scent seemed to echo her fragile feelings.

Unexpectedly, Sean broke the silence. His voice was searching, almost reverent. "You said your brother died when he was two years old. Did he have a disease too?"

"No. He drowned in an irrigation ditch. We didn't find him until he had been dead for over an hour."

"I'll bet your parents were devastated," Connie sympathized. "But you said you waited and felt hopeless at times. Why was that?"

Sam's mind tumbled about, groping for the right way to explain what had happened. He couldn't think of a way to explain it without interjecting his faith into the explanation.

"My mother pulled Jimmy from the irrigation ditch. She and my dad gave him artificial respiration for over an hour. After all that, he still was not breathing, and my mother asked a neighbor friend, a man who was an Elder in our church, to give Jimmy a blessing. Immediately after that, he took a breath."

"Oh!" Connie said. "Then he lived?"

"He lived for exactly two weeks. He was in a coma during that time, but his body seemed normal. One evening my mom and dad were holding his hands, and he opened his eyes and told my mom he loved her. When he told her that, my mom thought he would be fine. But shortly thereafter, he passed away."

Sean frowned. "Why do you suppose the blessing didn't work to keep him alive? It seems odd that it only worked for two weeks," he commented a little harshly.

"My family feels that Heavenly Father wanted Jimmy to come home to Him, because he could have let him stay. There was nothing wrong with his body. He didn't die because of the drowning. He just went home to be with Heavenly Father. I think he let Jimmy live the extra two weeks to soften the blow to my family."

Sean remained unconvinced. "Suppose it wasn't the blessing at all? Suppose it was that the artificial respiration finally worked and the blessing had nothing to do with it? I find it hard to believe that such miracles happen now, and even harder to swallow that a Mormon Elder has any power to order the dead back to life. I don't mean to be heartless, but the whole thing is preposterous." Sean folded his arms across his chest and awaited Sam's reply.

Sam was amazed that Sean could doubt such a blessing from Heavenly Father. It had never occurred to him that Jimmy's coming back to life might be anything other than a miracle wrought by the hand of God. His mind reeled at the suggestion that it was anything else.

When Sean saw that Sam did not have an answer he continued with a little more fervor. "Furthermore, I think it's cruel of any religion to teach their members that miracles can happen if their faith is strong enough.

When the miracles don't occur, it makes them think God doesn't love them or that their faith is too weak. It cheats them out of true faith, which is to believe in Christ Jesus."

Elder Tilley bridled a bit and leaned forward. "But Christ and his apostles worked miracles. If miracles occurred in the primitive church, is there any reason they shouldn't happen in today's church? If they had God's power, shouldn't Christ's church today have that same power?"

"Miracles were given in olden times to proclaim Christ and to establish the truth of Christianity. It was not given to divert their minds from their faith in Christ to faith in their own miracles. Today we are only required to have faith in Christ. The miracles have already testified of Christ and have ceased. They would serve no purpose in our lives today."

"But . . ." Elder Tilley began; however, Sam cut him off with a slight wave of his hand.

"Sean, we didn't come here to interfere with your faith or even to tell you about my little brother. I came because I felt impressed to draw a picture of your beautiful little daughter. My faith, my beliefs, and my perspective on these things are different from yours. I wish you well, and with your permission, we will leave. And I will pray for Juanita."

Sam set his teacup aside and stood. Elder Tilley followed. They were standing on the front porch when the Spirit moved within him. His face flushed and his heart pounded, but the peace came. He knew what he must say. He turned to Sean. "I know there is a power that can heal your daughter. I hold that power, and my faith is strong enough to use it to that end. However, it isn't my faith that is the determining factor. It's yours." He shook both their hands, and left before another word was uttered. He heard their door slam as he and Elder Tilley walked down the sidewalk.

March 29, 1974

Today we met with Juanita's parents, Connie and Sean Van Dangen. They are fine people, but Sean is very rigid. I drew them a picture of their daughter who is dying. I felt strongly that Heavenly Father would allow us to heal her with the priesthood, but not until her parents have more faith. I believe that Sean was right to some extent about miracles. Miracles are seldom given as a witness. They more often come as a confirmation of faith in Christ than a source of it.

This evening I prayed with great strivings for Heavenly Father to allow us to use the holy priesthood to heal little Juanita. I was startled when the Spirit plainly said that I could not. It further said that such a blessing would work as a condemnation to their souls, because they would reject it. I was stunned but immediately felt impressed to ask Heavenly Father to allow us to heal their daughter in such a way that it would not be a witness to the parents. I heard nothing but silence from the heavens after that.

Something else is happening. Elder Tilley is beginning to keep quiet around me. We don't laugh and chat about simple things anymore. I can't tell if he resents me, is angry, or what. I try so hard to do what is right and be obedient to the voice of the Lord. I don't think he understands that. I sometimes feel as if he misinterprets my yearnings for obedience as a form of arrogance or phoniness.

Tonight I was reading in Mosiah 5 about how King Benjamin's people were born again following his great discourse. I have decided to seek the rebirth. It came to me very strongly that the key to the rebirth is obedience.

They made a covenant to be obedient in all things in verse 5, and because of that covenant, they were changed. I want to have this mighty change in order to serve the Lord with greater power.

* * *

Three days before the Snodgrasses' baptism, the zone leaders unexpectedly showed up at Sam and Elder Tilley's boarding house.

The zone leaders went with them to their appointments. Sam and Elder Coleman, the senior zone leader, went together. That evening they taught Tom and Linda the sixth discussion. The lesson began well, and the Spirit was there, but it was rigid and given word-for-word from the memorized discussions. Sam was disappointed, and Tom and Linda wondered what had changed. They were used to a free-flowing, spiritual experience with Sam and Elder Tilley. About halfway through the lesson, Sam could stand it no longer, and following a question by Tom, began explaining the plan of salvation. The zone leader interrupted him and returned to the sixth discussion.

Sam waited patiently and then went back to their discussion of the degrees of glory. Tom had a particular question about his parents and where they would be going after this life. They were not members of the Church, and he was troubled.

For a few moments, Sam wondered if Elder Coleman would chastise him in front of his investigators or insist on returning to the memorized text, but he did not. When it became apparent that the discussion was permanently derailed, Elder Coleman relaxed and in time made several moving comments about the plan of salvation. He told of an experience he'd had when his grandmother died. She wasn't a member either, but he felt strongly that she would accept the gospel in the spirit world. The Spirit was strong and testified to all present. In the end, they reconfirmed their determination to be baptized on the upcoming Friday, just three days away.

Once they had regrouped at their boarding house, the four of them knelt in prayer and thanked Heavenly Father for the blessings of the day. Without warning, Elder Colemen announced that Sam was being transferred to Germiston, a suburb of Johannesburg. He was to leave that evening, at that very moment.

A thousand thoughts assailed Sam simultaneously, especially the thought that he would not be able attend Tom and Linda's baptism. Second was that he would not be able to speak to them before he left, to wish them goodbye, or to bear his testimony one more time, and he would not be able to play music again with Tom. It was heartbreaking to him, and tears welled up in his eyes. They were at Tom and Linda's just a short time ago, and yet he had not been allowed to say goodbye. It didn't seem fair. He started to ask the questions beleaguering his soul, but was cut short.

As Elder Coleman answered, he seemed twelve feet tall, and Sam felt like a child again. Elder Coleman simply said, "It's not my decision, nor within my power to change."

Sam and Elder Coleman loaded his things into the VW bug and drove the short distance to the main road. As they came to a complete stop, Sam suddenly straightened in his seat. He gazed around as if lost, and then a look of determination came over his face.

"Elder Coleman, we need to turn around."

"Did you forget something at the boarding?"

"No. We have to go visit an investigator."

"Elder Tilley can handle that. It's in his hands now. Relax. He's a good Elder," the zone leader replied. He steered the car out onto the street.

Sam grabbed the emergency brake handle between the seats and yanked it on. The car skidded to a stop. The zone leader turned to him with anger on his face.

"Look, Elder Mahoy. I'm the zone leader, and I have instructions. What you did was dangerous and rebellious. Now let go of the emergency brake. We have a good hour's drive ahead of us."

"Elder Coleman, as we were sitting at the stop sign, I felt the Spirit come over me and whisper that we needed to go give a little girl a blessing. It's someone we met while tracting. We haven't even given them a lesson yet, and I don't understand why we have to do it now. But I'm afraid if we don't, the little girl will die. This is not something I just thought up. It's what the Lord wants us to do. Please!"

The zone leader pondered Sam's words. He closed his eyes and said, "Okay. We're here to serve the people. The transfer can wait. Now release the brake!"

Sam whispered, "Thank you," and released the brake. They made a U-turn, and Sam directed Elder Coleman to their tracting area. As they turned the corner toward 355, Sam was startled to see flashing lights. An ambulance was parked in the street outside the house. A half-dozen other cars lined the street. Several of them were big Mercedes and other expensive cars. They quickly parked and hurried to the gate. A team of white-coated men were carrying a stretcher into the house. They didn't seem to be in any hurry. Sam and Elder Coleman followed. A large, black woman sat on the front steps, rocking back and forth, moaning loudly. Every once in a while, she broke into mournful singing in her native tongue. Once inside, the Elders saw that the small house was packed with weeping people. Sam noticed that two of them wore ministerial collars and were obviously consoling everyone. One of those with a collar was Sean.

Sam quickly made his way toward Connie and Sean. As soon as Connie saw him coming, she broke away from her husband and made her way toward them through the press of people. Her face held a mixture of grief and frustration. It was almost as if she were angry with Sam.

"Where have you been? You gave me hope! I prayed and knew your words were true, but you didn't leave your name, phone number, or address. For weeks I've hunted, watched every day for you to walk past, waited . . ."

She buried her face in her hands and sobbed. Sam was grief-stricken. He had not considered the possibility that they actually might try to contact him. He had been waiting for the Holy Spirit to direct him back to them, but it had not. Sam wanted to scream, explain, and beg forgiveness, but Connie calmed herself.

"It isn't your fault, of course. I'm sorry. I'm not thinking clearly right now." She waved her hand weakly, as if brushing away the entire affair.

At that moment, Sean came to her and put his arm around her trembling shoulders. He nodded toward the Elders, but said nothing.

Sam introduced Elder Coleman, who shook their hands. Sean introduced his father, a senior minister in the Anglican Church. They also shook hands.

"Please, tell me what has happened," Sam asked. By this time, the crowd had fallen silent, and everyone in the room had turned toward them.

Connie shrugged. "There's not much to tell. My baby just kept getting worse and worse. Tonight, about six o'clock, she . . . she . . . stopped breathing." She sobbed once, then recovered enough to continue. "The doctor came and pronounced her . . ." She couldn't bring herself to say it. Tears flowed down her cheeks, and she looked directly into Sam's eyes. She looked at him searchingly, but no sound escaped her lips.

It was Sean who spoke next. "Elders, thanks for coming. But this isn't a good time, as you can see. I'll have to ask you to excuse us."

Sam felt Elder Coleman put a hand on his shoulder, and he started to leave; but once again, he felt another hand in the middle of his back. This time, he did not try to figure out who it was. He stopped in his tracks.

"Can I see her, just for a moment? Then we'll go." Sean opened his mouth to object, but before he could, Connie was nodding and taking him by the arm. She led him a short distance to a small bedroom and opened the door. The room was painted pink, with ruffled curtains and bedspread. In the corner stood a pink crib, its side lowered. In the crib was a perfectly still, small form.

Sam stopped in the doorway and turned to Connie. "Would it be all right if just you and I went in?" She nodded and let him in, pushing the door closed afterward in the faces of her husband and Elder Coleman, both of whom were voicing protests.

Once inside, Sam turned to Connie. She looked into his face, tears streaking down her own. "I believed," she said. "For a while, I believed what you said, about your little brother, about the power to heal. I believed it with all my heart. But my faith was weak, and I'm afraid it's gone. My baby's dead now."

A feeling of calm flowed over Sam. Even still, he struggled to find consoling words to tell her. He opened his mouth to speak comfort to her, to tell her about how little children are saved by the Atonement of Christ, to tell her of the better place her daughter had gone, but that was not what came out. "She isn't dead, Connie. Just sleeping. I have come to awaken her."

They both started at his words—Sam as much as Connie. Connie took a step back and looked from him to the crib. She put a hand to her mouth, as if she would cry out, and then lowered it. She slowly nodded and smiled.

A feeling of peace came over Sam, and he walked to the crib. He looked down at the innocent little girl, and felt tears of gratitude forming in his eyes. Slowly, he reached out and brushed golden hair from her face, and then placed his hands on her head.

"Juanita. In the name of Jesus Christ, and by virtue of the Holy Melchizedek Priesthood, and according to His divine mercy, I call you back. Juanita, come back to your mother, amen."

He lifted his hands from the small head, and when the tiny eyes remained closed, he felt the calm flow even stronger. He took a step back and placed his hand on Connie's arm. Connie looked at him, a struggle of faith manifesting itself on her face. She looked down at her baby, and smiled.

Still as death, Juanita lay there not moving.

Sam turned her toward him and spoke the words that formed in his heart. "Go tell them. Go tell the others she was only sleeping."

Connie's face remained blank. Finally, she smiled weakly and nodded. She looked one more time at her baby and left the room, pulling the door closed behind her. As soon as it closed, Sam fell to his knees, praying earnestly. His prayer was not for the still form before him, but for her mother. Tears cascaded down his face, and he waited, praying in mighty strivings such as his soul had never before known. It seemed as if a silence passed over the room beyond the door.

Then Sam's prayer was answered. He heard Connie's voice explaining, "She was . . ." and then a long pause. "She was . . . only sleeping." A murmur of disbelief arose, and he sensed footsteps coming toward the door.

Sam quickly stood, and on impulse, reached into the crib and lifted the limp form into his arms. He was just turning as Sean burst into the room, a look of shock, anger, and disbelief on his face. His fists were balled, and he came toward Sam with violence written on his features. "Get your vile hands off my daughter!" he spewed. Connie quickly made her way around him and approached Sam.

Sam leaned forward and gave her his precious bundle. As he did so, a small arm looped around Connie's neck, and a sleepy little voice said, "Mama, why did you wake me up? I was sleeping."

A cry of astonishment came from everyone except Sam and Connie.

The word was quickly passed that little Juanita had only been sleeping. As warmth follows sunshine, sweet relief and joy swept through the house. Connie and Sean were swept into the living room.

Someone began singing, and a baby laughed.

Sam, alone in the small bedroom, fell to his knees, gratitude filling his soul to overflowing. After a moment, he felt a hand on his shoulder and looked up to see Connie, a look of solemnity on her face. "Thank you," she said, her voice trembling, tears of joy streaming down her cheeks.

Sam stood and said, "To Heavenly Father, she was only sleeping."

Connie nodded, a look of partial understanding in her red eyes. Sam joined Elder Coleman, who was waiting patiently in the hall. He smiled at Sam. He knew the child had only been sleeping, and Sam felt no need to tell him otherwise. They departed without further comment. No one noticed them go.

April 1, 1974

April Fools Day! I've been transferred. On the way out of town, we stopped and gave a little girl a blessing. The veil between life and death is thin. Heavenly Father saw fit to honor her mother's faith and awaken her from death. It was a precious experience and one I would not have had if I had not been obedient to the still, small voice.

Everyone, except her mother and I, believes that the child was only sleeping. Miracles are not given to force belief, only to bless those who believe.

It is interesting that Heavenly Father honored her faith; yet I doubt that she associates this miracle with His true Church. Perhaps in time, she will come to understand what truly happened tonight. What an interesting April Fools experience. Everyone in that house witnessed a miracle, yet no one recognized it.

I realize now that this is what I requested. I asked Heavenly Father to heal this child through her mother's faith, without it being a condemning witness to the child's parents. What a sweet, sweet blessing it is. I marvel at His mercy, love, and gentle kindness. With all my soul, I thank Him for allowing me this precious blessing.

It is three days before Tom and Linda's baptism. I hate missing it. I didn't even get to say goodbye. I hope Elder Tilley can make them understand. I love them and will miss them terribly. I don't even have their mailing address; I never thought to ask them. Elder Tilley promised he would write and tell me about their baptism and give me their address. I will miss playing music with Tom, and poor Elder Tilley will have to go back to tracting.

Tom and Linda have had a marvelous effect on my life, and I hope I have blessed theirs.

I am going to Germiston, about an hour outside of Johannesburg. I will be junior companion to a South African missionary named Elder Beesler. I don't know too much about him, but I hear he is a goof-off. The one thing I could not bear would be to waste this precious time. There is too much to do. Too many miracles need to be performed, and too many wonderful people need the gospel! My soul is on fire, and my every thought is to bring glory, honor, and souls unto the Lord. Blessed be His name!

8

BAR AND STRIPES

Sam and Elder Coleman arrived at the mission home late that evening and spent the night there. The next morning, Sam was called into the office to speak with President Carlson.

"Elder Mahoy, my boy, how are you? How did you like Pretoria?"

"President, I was transferred three days before a baptism. I loved Pretoria, but I'm devastated about missing their baptism. I could have spent the rest of my mission there and done a wonderful work."

President Carlson frowned and said, "I'm sorry, but this transfer was urgent. I have had to send a missionary home and needed a strong Elder to replace him. The Lord needed you in Germiston more than your investigators needed you at their baptism."

Sam considered this and nodded. He was willing to go anywhere, but it sure helped to understand why. "What should I know about where I'm going?"

"Your new companion, Elder Beesler, is a good missionary, but he's had bad examples. He and his last companion, the Elder I just sent home, got into some trouble. Bad trouble. Elder Beesler was only partly involved, but he is on a short leash. I need someone I can trust to not be sucked into his ways. I have to send you as a junior companion because he's already a senior. So, you can see why I needed you. I trust you to do what is right, no matter what." Sam hesitated. "It doesn't sound easy. I just want to do missionary work! I don't want to have to fight my companion to get it done. It shouldn't be that way."

"No, it shouldn't, but sometimes the reality of things isn't as perfect as our image of them. I know this will be difficult, but after much prayer and fasting, I am confident you are the right one for this assignment. If you can't influence Elder Beesler, I'm afraid he will be sent home too. It's a tragedy I hope to avoid. Will you accept the call?" Sam sighed resignedly. "Accept? Do I have a choice? Don't answer that! I don't want to know. I'll do as you say, President. I hope I don't let you down."

President Carlson smiled. He stood up behind the big, ornate desk. "I appreciate your faithfulness," he said and added, "There's something else I wish to discuss with you. I have had many reports regarding you. It seems you have a hard time sticking with the memorized discussions in spite of our instructions to do so."

Sam had no idea this was coming and was dumbfounded. He started to reply but decided there was no point in defending his position. Instead, he simply said, "Its true. I do deviate sometimes when I feel that an investigator needs to hear something different. I don't know what else to do but follow the Spirit."

"And how do your investigators feel about this? How do they respond?"

"Well, when I say the things the Holy Spirit wants me to say, it always works out well. Sometimes He wants them to hear the discussions, and sometimes He doesn't."

"And how can you tell the difference?" President Carlson asked as he sat down on the edge of the desk.

"I listen. When I'm in tune, I just listen, and then the peace comes.

Once I know what to do, I am given the courage to do it."

"I see." President Carlson stood and walked to the bookshelves that covered three walls of the office. He opened a leaded glass door and motioned to the books inside. "I love books. You may not know that I have a law degree and have read extensively on almost every subject you can name, and some you couldn't name, I imagine."

Sam stared at him, not seeing the connection. President Carlson continued. "When I first came to this office and saw all these books, I spent days reading titles and marveling at the value of what is sitting on these shelves. Almost every book in this room is priceless. I couldn't afford more than two or three of them if I sold everything I own. It's almost unbelievable to see such a marvelous collection in one room. Yet I imagine that few people who enter this room recognize their worth."

He pulled a book from the shelf. It was bound in rich leather and had gold lettering on the side. "This is a first edition copy of Charles Dickens's *Oliver Twist*." He opened the book and tipped it so Sam could see the signature inside. "It's signed by Dickens. It's exceedingly rare and fantastically valuable." He slid the book back into place and closed the door. "Yet, in an eternal sense, it's worthless. It has almost no redeeming value."

He picked up a paperback copy of the Book of Mormon from his desk. "This book sells for two dollars and is worthless by worldly standards. Yet, it has been the instrument of bringing millions of souls to Christ. Its value is impossible to overstate. It's the most perfect book ever written, yet it is not a part of this collection of valuable books. I have purchased a leather-bound edition of the Book of Mormon, and when I leave, it will be a part of this collection. If I could, I would get Mormon or Moroni to sign it. The difference between these priceless books and this perfect one is that the Book of Mormon was written under the influence of the Holy Ghost."

Again, he sat on the corner of his desk. "Missionaries are like these books. They are all of great worth and precious to the Lord. Even that Elder I sent home today is precious. Yet, some missionaries are not inspired, and to the extent that they are not, their value is not as great in missionary work. By my earlier comments, you may have thought I was upset by your deviating from the memorized discussions." Sam nodded. "I just wanted to ascertain that your deviations were being inspired by the Holy Spirit. I am comfortable that they are."

He leaned closer to Sam, and lowered his voice. "What I'm going to tell you now, you must keep to yourself, because others would not understand what I'm going to say. The memorized lesson plans are inspired, but they're not a substitute for inspiration. We have them to guide us until the Holy Spirit chooses to take over. When that happens, we teach by the Spirit. Until it happens, we teach by the book. Unfortunately, some Elders never reach beyond the book."

"This is my instruction to you, just to you. It's not instruction to the entire mission, and I urge you to accept it as such. You have my full and complete approval to teach whatever the Spirit directs, as long as it really is the Spirit. Just be certain that you are responding to the Spirit. If you do, all will be well, and you will serve a great mission for the Lord."

"President," Sam said as soon as it became obvious that President Carlson had finished. "I am relieved! I promise I'll make every effort to ensure that everything I say is under the direction of the Holy Spirit. You have no idea how relieved I am to know that what I knew was right is truly acceptable to you and the Lord. It causes my heart to rejoice!"

President Carlson placed a loving hand on Sam's shoulder. "And it causes my soul to rejoice to have such a faithful young man serving with me in this great work. God bless you Elder," he said as he stood. They shook hands and then embraced.

Not many minutes later, Sam met Elder Beesler, and they began the long drive to Germiston. While Sam was a large individual, Elder Beesler was even larger. He was the first missionary Sam had seen that could twist him into a pretzel. What caused Sam even greater wonder was that he was sure Elder Beesler would enjoy doing it.

"Elder Mahoy," his new companion began shortly after he had begun to drive, "I have to admit that today has been a shock. When President Carlson called me into the mission home, I thought he was going to make me a district leader out in Germiston. Now I find out that I'm in trouble because my companion was sent home. Well, all I did was follow my senior companion, just like I was supposed to. When my companion was going to bed with that girl, I just sat in the front room like a good soldier. I kept my nose clean, and I thought President Carlson was going to make me district leader. What good did it do me? Now I'm in disrepute, and I'll never be a DL. All I wanted was a chance to show everyone that I could be as good a DL as any one of you Americans. You guys come over here so smug and self-righteous, thinking you know everything. Well, we South Africans should be the district leaders and zone leaders, and now it's not going to happen. Tell me, how many people have you baptized, Elder?"

He didn't pause for Sam to answer, even had Sam been willing to answer such a brash question.

"Well I've baptized twelve," Elder Beesler continued. "Twelve people have come into the Church because of me. And what do I get for it? I'm accused of being lazy and that I'll never make mission leadership. Now I don't even want to finish this miserable mission. And here you are to dog me and make sure I don't do anything wrong." He paused for a moment, but Sam didn't interrupt the silence.

"I want you to know that I hate your guts, and nothing you do is going to change me. If President Carlson hadn't lied to me, I would have felt differently, but nothing is going to stop me from enjoying the rest of my mission. I am going to be a missionary and not do anything to be sent home, but you can bet that I'm not going to be kissing up to President Carlson, and certainly not to you. So keep your holier-than-thou baloney to yourself."

Sam's head was swimming. Elder Beesler sneered at him and jammed his foot onto the accelerator. They zipped past other cars and swerved dangerously into oncoming traffic. Elder Beesler made an obvious show of getting within inches of cars he was passing so that the other motorists would jerk away from them. Each time he did, Beesler gave Sam a glaring "I-dare-you-to-say-something" look. Not many minutes later, flashing lights appeared behind them, and a police officer pulled them over.

Elder Beesler swore in Afrikaans as he pulled over but spoke calmly and rapidly to the policeman in Afrikaans, mentioning his name and Sam's several times. Sam had difficulty following the conversation.

The following morning, they went to court and waited and waited. The courtroom was a large theater-like room, with the judge, prosecutors, and attorneys on a low stage in front of stair-stepped seats. The judge sat behind a raised pulpit where he could look down on everyone in his court. He wore an elaborate black robe. It reminded Sam of an old-time courtroom in England. The only thing that was missing was the white, powdered wig.

The prosecuting attorney wore a simple, black robe but seemed to have great authority in court. He directed everything, telling people what they could say or do. He often became belligerent or insulting and would occasionally turn to the judge and make sarcastic observations about the witness. The judge seemed to have almost no control over what occurred in the courtroom, except to render judgment after evidence had been laid out. At times, the prosecutor appeared to give legal advice to the person on trial, even making suggestions on what to do. It was entirely different from the Perry Mason movies Sam remembered. What was more amazing was how swiftly they did things. Usually the judge formed his opinion quickly, often banging down the gavel and pronouncing judgment in the middle of someone's testimony.

Sam watched as dozens of people were brought before the judge. The trials were conducted in Afrikaans. Late in the day, Elder Beesler was finally called to testify. He spoke in Afrikaans, periodically pointing back at Sam. Sam could barely tell what was happening.

After a long time, they called him to the stand and began to question him in Afrikaans. He asked them to switch to English, which they did.

The prosecutor spoke excellent English, though with a heavy accent. It made him sound British but with a guttural overtone. He dropped r's on the end of words, and rolled r's amid words. Words that ended in "uh" were pronounced "er."

"America" would have come out "Amerrricer," with the rrr being rolled like a child making an engine noise for his toy truck.

"You are accused of speeding, dangerous driving, and evading arrest. How do you plead?" the prosecutor in the long, black robe said with his heavy accent, obviously annoyed that Sam did not speak Afrikaans.

Sam was mystified. "I . . . I wasn't driving. I was the passenger. Elder Beesler was driving." The prosecutor laughed and exchanged a knowing look with the judge. "So you were the passenger?"

"Yes, sir."

He produced the ticket and pointed to the signature. "Is this your name?"

Sam studied the signature, and was surprised to see his name on the ticket. "That's my name, but it's not my signature."

The prosecutor smiled and took back the ticket. "Do you have another piece of identification with your signature on it?"

Sam thought for a moment. "No, sir. I don't. Not on me."

"That's what you told the officer, too. The citing officer asked for your license, and you said you were from America and didn't have any on you. Mister Beesler, who is a citizen of South Afrrrica (he pronounced it "Off-rrre-kuh") has told us that you were, in fact, driving the car. Why are you lying about it?"

"I'm not lying. I wasn't driving. I haven't driven a car in South Africa yet. You drive on the wrong side of the road, and I . . ."

"Why would he lie about driving the car?" the prosecutor demanded.

"He was angry with me, or just angry with the world, and was driving like an idiot to try to scare me."

The prosecutor spoke to the judge in Afrikaans, and the judge banged the gavel. "Guilty," he said in a heavy accent. "I sentence you to a fine of two hundrrred rrrand."

Sam sputtered. "I'm not guilty! I don't have two hundred rand!"

"Then twenty lashes and ten days in jail." The judge banged his gavel again, and an armed guard took Sam by the arm. Sam caught sight of Elder Beesler, who sneered at him, turned, and left the room. They took him to a hall, down a flight of stairs, and to a small room with concrete walls. There, they took everything from him, including his shoes, socks, belt, shirt, and tie. When they were done, he only had his pants left. They took him down a flight of stairs to a small room. They quickly clamped his hands to the wall and his ankles to the floor. He was facing the wall, with his feet behind him so he had to lean against the wall awkwardly on his elbows. Someone fumbled with his snap, and pulled his pants and underwear to the floor. He was too terrified to protest. He had no idea what was going on. For a moment, he thought they were going to rape him. A stiff canvas was unrolled from near the ceiling until it covered his entire backside. The canvas smelled of sweat and blood.

Nothing happened for several moments. He could hear people moving around in the room. A man's voice whispered and another laughed. Suddenly, he heard a whistling sound, and something exploded across his back. He had never felt such incredible pain. If felt as if someone had hit him with a sword and severed his body several inches deep. Someone said "twenty" in Afrikaans. Again, the whistling sound, and the pain exploded a little lower. His legs buckled as he lost all feeling except the horrendous pain in his buttocks. He became aware of his wrists nearly breaking off in the manacles, and struggled to stand just as another blow struck near his shoulders. "Eighteen," the voice said. Just as the feeling began to return from the first blow, another landed atop it. This time his scream drowned out the "seventeen." He felt his mind retreating further inside with each blow. Each blow seemed to land in a new spot between his knees and neck.

With a start, he heard the voice say "six," and he suddenly realized that he had passed out. He wished oblivion would return as the lash whistled again. It seemed as if the moment lasted forever, the screaming of the whip, the agony of knowing it was going to flail his flesh, and the terror of not knowing where it would hit. When it struck, it landed just above his waist and wrapped around his body, so that the greatest force of the blow landed on his side. The force of the blow caused his feet to slip, and he fell against the wall. He tried to stand, yet his feet slid again on something wet. He looked down and was surprised to see a puddle of water, and he realized he had lost control of himself. The humiliation was almost greater than the pain, and he cried out even before the lash landed again. By the time the voice said "one" his body collapsed in incomprehensible agony. His legs refused to support him, and he hung helplessly by his wrists.

What seemed like hours later, but was in fact just a few moments, they undid Sam's shackles. Two guards held him, or he would have crumpled to the floor in his own urine.

They helped him stand and pulled his pants back up. He heard someone scream and was startled to realize that he had done it. It sounded as if it came from someone else. Each step caused his wounds to rub against his clothing, and his mind refused to move his legs, even when he ordered them to take a step. They half drug him to a cell and laid him face down on the cot. They were surprisingly careful with him, considering they had just flogged him. A moment later, a man in a white smock came in and rubbed ointment on his back and legs. He explained something matter-of-factly in Afrikaans, which Sam could not understand. He wondered at the dichotomy—how they could be brutal and passionless in one minute and then sympathetic and almost gentle seconds later. He sensed that it was just their job, and knew that they would have just as emotionlessly executed him had they been instructed to do so.

There were no windows, and the cell smelled of disinfectant. The cot was hard, and the only blanket was thin but clean. He alternately felt feverish and freezing cold. He had felt this way before and knew he was slipping into shock. He focused his thoughts on prayer and felt a vague peace come over him for a while; but his mind could not ignore the pain for long. His back felt on fire, and he feared that his clothing would stick to the wounds and become infected.

Struggling to the toilet was further torture, and sitting was beyond agony. The toilet in Sam's cell had no seat on it, only the porcelain fixture, and the water from the sink was cold. In spite of a weakly offered prayer, he fell into despair and finally into a tormented sleep.

The following morning, no one spoke to Sam or brought him any food. It was nearly noon before someone appeared. It took him a second to recognize the prosecuting attorney without his robes. He spoke to him through the bars. Sam struggled and finally managed to stand up. His back no longer felt aflame but felt as if every muscle had been stripped from his skeleton and carelessly replaced in all the wrong places.

Sam tried to understand what was being said, but finally, in his best Afrikaans, said, "I am much sorry. I don't speak Afrikaans. Could you please speak English?"

"That's what I thought," the man said in English and motioned to an armed guard that Sam hadn't noticed. "You don't speak Afrikaans." The guard unlocked the bars.

"Well, I have been learning, but I'm afraid most people speak too fast for me to catch everything." Sam stumbled into the hallway, and the jailer slammed the door shut.

The attorney gave him a sympathetic look, almost an apology. "Last night," the attorney said, "as I was going to sleep, something was bothering me about your conviction. I woke up in the middle of the night and knew what it was. I know the officer who cited you, and he does not speak English—not even a little. This morning I called him, and he said you spoke excellent Afrikaans and described you. His description could have fit either you or the other man who was with you—except you don't speak Afrikaans, and he does."

"I wasn't driving the car," Sam said, hope rising in his heart.

"I believe you. Why didn't you say something when he was accusing you?"

Sam struggled to think that far back. It seemed a century ago. "He said it all in Afrikaans. I had no idea . . ."

"Yes, of course. I should have seen that. Well, I can get the charges dropped."

The prosecutor then averted his eyes, and almost looked chagrined. "I have to apologize for the lashes," he said at last. "It's unusual to sentence someone to lashes for a traffic violation, although perfectly legal. The judge was angry because you were—or at least at the time appeared to be—lying and refusing to speak in Afrikaans when the citing officer and the other missionary said you spoke the language perfectly. The judge also hates Mormons. His brother and sister-in-law have joined that church, and it has divided the family. I'm afraid you were the first Mormon missionary in court since then, and he was, shall we say, somewhat severe."

The attorney brightened a bit. "However, the good news is you will find that the scars are more psychological than physical. The canvas is to keep the whip from cutting. You will only see bruises for a few weeks. You will heal quickly. Perhaps you can look on this as Peter did? Not many people get to take stripes for their faith, now do they?" Somehow, the man's words almost made Sam feel better, but they did not take the sensation of being skinned alive from his backside. Each step was agony. He could not believe that a human body could be made to hurt so badly from such a short event. He was in greater pain than when he was beaten by the boys at the lake—far greater. "Do you have someone you can call to come get you?" the attorney asked as he lead Sam down the hallway. "And do you know where that other fellow is? He is guilty of perjury and the speeding citation. He will no doubt be sentenced to lashes for letting you unjustly take his place."

Sam stopped amid stride. "I don't know where he is. If my opinion means anything, I beg you not to whip him. If there was ever a circumstance that whipping was unjustified, it would be for traffic violators." This he said passionately, and the attorney nodded as if he agreed.

"One more thing," the prosecutor said, turning to face Sam. "This is not America, and you have no rights here. Our laws are very specific toward noncitizens. If you complain to anyone about your treatment, or start any legal action, you will simply be expelled from the country. My suggestion to you is that you tell no one, for your sake and for the sake of your church being able to continue to do missionary work in this country. I realize your treatment was unjust, but there are many who would like to lash all Mormons and send them back to America smarting. Do you understand?" He was dead serious, and Sam believed him.

They walked to the prosecutor's small office that was filled with books. It had no windows and looked as much like a cell as the room they had imprisoned Sam in the previous night. The prosecutor showed him the phone on his desk and turned to leave.

Sam interrupted his departure. "Thank you for liberating me. I applaud your sense of justice. I realize you could have left me in there just as easily." The prosecutor bowed slightly. But Sam was not finished. "However, you were wrong about my not having any rights in this country. No matter what your laws are, and no matter how insignificant my standing before your law is, there is a higher law. I am a servant of Jesus Christ, and before His law, I stand innocent. All men will one day be judged by that higher law. I would rather be flogged to death unjustly according to the laws of men than to stand before the bar of God having ordered that flogging."

The prosecutor's face slowly drained of color, and Sam felt his heart burning with the Holy Spirit. He suspected for a moment that he might be thrown back into the cell, but the prosecutor just nodded and said, "Let me know when you have finished your call, and I will bring you something to eat."

The prosecutor walked to the door, opened it, but then turned back to face Sam. "It's high irony to me that you can barely walk, and with a word I could confine you to prison for a very long time. Yet you speak boldly to me, and for reasons that escape me, I feel no anger toward you. You stand to lose a great deal by your boldness, yet I am the one who trembles." He stared at Sam in wonder.

President Carlson picked up Sam three hours later. Sam had spent the intervening hours talking to Prosecutor Van der Kerk, who had canceled his court duties for the day. During that time, Sam taught him the gospel and bore testimony in a way he had never experienced before. They talked a great deal about justice, mercy, and judgment. The attorney listened intently and occasionally made notes on a yellow pad. Sam was not surprised to find the prosecutor extremely knowledgeable about the scriptures, and highly intelligent. Mr. Van der Kerk would quote a scripture that seemed to contradict what Sam was saying, and immediately Sam would quote the verse before it, or another verse, which brought the meaning into true perspective. The wonderful part was that the scriptures quoted came to Sam's mind from only a cursory reading of the New Testament in seminary before his mission. Yet, he could visualize the verses and even quote them as if he were looking at the page. It was a marvelous experience, and by the time President Carlson arrived, they had become, if not friends, at least respected opponents. There was a feeling of spiritual discovery, and the glow of the Holy Spirit was upon them.

President Carlson had brought a member who was also an attorney. They arrived with flames shooting from their nostrils. Sam wouldn't have believed it possible for President Carlson to become this incensed. They would have launched into the prosecutor with a blue vengeance, except for the feeling of peace that existed in the room as they entered. It became obvious that there was no need for a defense, and the Holy Spirit overshadowed their indignation.

Sam introduced President Carlson and briefly explained Van der Kerk's role in setting him free, without mentioning his role in getting him lashed. They shook hands, and as they were about to depart, Van der Kerk pressed a business card into Sam's hand.

"You have impressed me, young man. I wish I had your simple faith and your black-and-white perspective of the world. I would to God that it was as simple as you say."

Sam transferred the card to his pocket and clasped the prosecutor's hand in both of his own. "With all my heart, I know that it is true," he said softly.

Looking deep into Sam's eyes, he replied, "That is what's most troubling about you, young man. I know you know it's true. Your simple faith is more powerful that any sophisticated argument I have ever heard. And believe me, I have heard many."

"God bless you," Sam said, and released his hand.

"I think he already has," was Van der Kerk's sincere reply.

* * *

Immobilized, Sam stood outside the car, looking down at the soft seat. He could not bring himself to lower his bruised flesh onto it.

"Get in Elder, and let's go," President Carlson urged him. Sam looked up at him, tears pooling in his eyes.

"President, would you give me a blessing so I can get into the car?" President Carlson came around to his side of the car and drew within whispering distance.

"What's troubling you Elder? How can I help?" So saying, he placed a hand in the middle of Sam's back, which made Sam groan and turn away.

President Carlson's eyes grew big with disbelief. "What did they do to you?" he demanded, anger rising in his face. He glanced back toward the courthouse and then at Sam. Sam could tell he was on the verge of marching back into the building.

"President, please give me a blessing so I can bear to sit in the car. Everything else is as it should be. Just my body needs help." Sam gave him a calm but pleading look.

President Carlson surprised Sam by suddenly raising his arm to the square, and in a voice of authority saying, "In the name of Jesus Christ, and by the authority of the holy Melchizedek Priesthood, I rebuke the power of evil over you, and command your body to be at rest and to heal according to the timetable of the Lord. In the name of Jesus Christ, amen."

No sooner had he said these words than the pain changed in his flesh. It didn't go away, but it became different—tolerable, or perhaps even acceptable. Sitting was still agony, but his heart soared with joy. He was overcome by a feeling of peace and the knowledge that God had accepted his sacrifice.

As they drove home, Sam related all that had happened, including the prosecutor's warning. President Carlson wanted to drive him immediately to a hospital, but Sam insisted he would be fine. They drove straight to the mission home, where he was given a proper meal and a soft bed.

Sister Carlson wept when she saw his back. He fell asleep as she gently rubbed ointment onto his wounds.

* * *

Sam awoke with a start when someone's alarm went off. He felt refreshed and considerably better. For the first time, he looked at his back in the mirror. He was surprised to see twenty distinct red welts surround by pools of black and blue. He expected to see open wounds and bleeding sores. Nowhere was his skin broken. The damage was deep and debilitating, but it would heal.

It was later that evening when the deep musical chimes of the front door announced the arrival of an unexpected visitor. All the Elders were out on teaching appointments, and only he and President Carlson were at home. President Carlson was startled to see Prosecutor Van der Kerk and a successful-looking woman at the door. In the circular drive was a limousine and two police cars. For a moment, he was stunned into inaction.

"Excuse us for just dropping in. We have come to speak to Sam Mahoy. Is he available?" Van der Kerk asked.

President Carlson smiled and invited them into the foyer. Sam was wearing the loosest clothing he could find and studying the scriptures when President Carlson popped into his room. It took him a few minutes to get himself looking like a missionary.

When Sam arrived in the big living room, President Carlson was explaining the history of the mission home. As soon as Sam walked in, Mr. Van der Kirk stood, as did the woman. They seemed awkward, almost intimidated. There was a moment of discomfort between them that seemed to stretch into eternity. Sam didn't know what to say and was grateful when the woman stepped forward to shake his hand.

"I'm pleased to meet you," she said. "You have made quite an impression on my husband. He spoke so highly of you that I insisted on meeting you. I couldn't believe you were not angry for the rough treatment you received. I can see from the expression on your face, however, that anger is not part of what you are feeling. What are you feeling, Sam?"

Mrs. Van der Kerk was a slender woman in her mid-forties. Her demeanor was regal, and her carriage proud. She had dark, almost black hair and vibrant blue eyes, which sparkled with keen intelligence. Her face was friendly and most pleasant to look at. Sam liked her. It was obvious they were wealthy and comfortable with status, position, and power. However, Sam did not get the feeling that she used her status to indulge pettiness. Instead, she seemed to use her position as a means to a greater end. He could not guess what that end might be, nor how he fit into it, but he was sure the Van der Kerks would not be there if he didn't figure into it some way.

Sam cleared his throat, and still holding her hand, he said, "I'm feeling like I should tell you why I'm in South Africa. Why don't you take a seat, and with your indulgence, I'll tell you."

The Van der Kerks took a seat on the large velvet couch, and Sam stood near the piano. He began telling of his youth and the faith his parents taught him. He told them about Jimmy and the lessons his passing had taught him. He told them why he'd come on a mission and what joy it had already brought into his soul. He told him how much the gospel meant to him, and how he knew it was true.

He concluded by saying, "You asked me what I am feeling. I'm feeling overwhelmed with His love and with the breathtaking beauty of His eternal plan. And I'm feeling very grateful for this opportunity to explain my feelings to you, Brother and Sister Van der Kerk."

During the nearly forty minutes of his recitation, Mrs. Van der Kerk remained intent, occasionally nodding, sometimes laughing, sometimes frowning with deep thought. When he finished, she stood and walked to where he stood. When she was directly in front of him, she studied him intently until he began to feel foolish.

Finally, she said, "We are members of the Dutch Reformed Church and hold responsible positions therein. We have fought the incursion of your church and several others into our country with all our energy. Our efforts are directly responsible for the limited number of representatives your church is allowed to have in our country at any one time. I have always seen your missionary efforts as an invasion of sorts. When my husband came home speaking highly of one of these—please forgive me, detestable Mormon missionaries—I decided I would meet you and discredit you before his eyes."

She cocked her head to one side. "My husband is the city prosecuting attorney and in line to be elected regional prosecutor of the whole nation. I am a lawyer of no small consequence myself in powerful circles. When he came home raving about you, I had planned to reopen his eyes to the threat that your religion poses to our way of life, and to belittle your gracious response to his rough treatment of you in jail as a ploy to win him over. After all, it would have been quite a conquest to win over one of your greatest opponents to your way of thinking, would it not?"

She turned and spoke to her husband as if he were the judge in a criminal trial. "However, I would bet considerable money that Sam was completely unaware until this moment of who we are, or the threat we represent. He has said nothing of his ordeal and has spoken quite plainly from his heart. He has rendered my cross-examination impotent and silenced the voice of opposition without even knowing I had come here to disembowel his arguments."

She turned back to Sam. "Either you are the most ingenious liar of all time, or you are speaking the truth. In either case, I beg your permission to hear you again on this matter to determine which of the two it might be."

Sam wasn't sure that what she said made sense, but he nodded. Her husband stood, and as they were turning away, Sam's mouth opened without his permission and said, "Until tomorrow evening then."

They paused as if considering, then nodded, and replied, "At seven." President Carlson ushered them into the night, and they were gone, but a sweet spirit rested upon those remaining in the mission home.

* * *

April 5, 1974

Yesterday, I had the dubious privilege of being falsely accused and whipped. They gave me twenty lashes. I have never felt such incredible pain in my life. They placed a canvas over my back to keep the whip from cutting my skin, and still my back is a mess, which will take weeks to heal. I can't imagine what Christ must have endured when they scourged him. He must have nearly died from that alone. Prior to that, He had suffered unknown horrors in the Garden and would later be crucified. It causes my mind to balk and my soul to anguish. It makes my soul cry out in His behalf just to think of His pain.

The man who prosecuted me later released me. I felt no anger toward him, and he found my behavior novel enough that he and his wife came to the mission home. I bore my testimony and taught them a little. They asked if they could come again. I think they still hope to convince themselves that my faith is insincere. They don't realize that they are investigating the Church and already have a testimony.

Missionary work is so amazing when it's done the Lord's way. I think this whole lashes thing was an elaborate door approach.

* * *

The Van der Kerks came the following evening prepared to debate, and brought several pages of notes that they carefully referred to. As soon they were seated, they began with the first item on their list and laid siege to Sam and President Carlson. Sam was aghast at the change in their demeanor, and had almost nothing to say.

Accordingly, they shifted their assault to President Carlson, who entertained their questions and tried to answer as plainly as he could. Even though the tone was friendly, it was still a debate, and they clearly intended to win. President Carlson had been a lawyer, even a federal judge, and knew how to debate very well; but it was evident from his posture that he was not enjoying the evening. The Van der Kerks were, however, and with each question President Carlson could not answer to their satisfaction, their attitudes were more triumphant.

After nearly an hour, Mrs. Van der Kerk suddenly turned to Sam, who had become a non-participant in the discussion. "Why have you stopped participating in the discussion, Elder Sam?" she asked. He had earlier asked them to call him Elder, and she had misinterpreted his words, so he became Elder Sam.

Without preamble, he said exactly what was on his mind. "I didn't come six thousand miles to debate doctrine. And you didn't come here this evening to learn. Given those incongruities, this evening was futile from the moment you walked through the door. Neither of us is being edified. If you wish to strengthen your own beliefs, then go talk to your minister. I'm not interested in wearing a bull's eye on my forehead so you can bolster your own opinions by lobbing arrows at me to see which ones stick."

Mr. Van der Kerk smiled. "That's pretty direct. You seem to have a way of cutting to the chase, Elder Sam. Since we have monopolized the evening with our debate, would you care to occupy the last remaining moments in whatever format of which you approve? It was, after all, you who initiated this event through your unfortunate experiences in my jail, and we are but guests in your home."

"Yes, Elder Sam. Please do," Mrs. Van der Kerk encouraged. "We are both lawyers and are most comfortable with debate and crossexamination. You choose the format that is most comfortable to you, and we will listen."

Sam was suddenly on stage without a script. He paused, waiting for the right thing to come to mind. The Van der Kerks waited patiently. When it came to him, it was so bold that it startled him, yet peace washed over him, and once again, he knew what the Lord desired. As before, he prayerfully sought the courage to speak the Lord's words.

"Brother Van der Kerk," Sam began, "when you released me from jail, you said I was like Peter who was whipped unjustly for preaching Christ and that I should see it as a blessing. I have endeavored to do that. After all, your words initiated the peace I now feel concerning those events. In that same spirit, I would like to propose that both of you are like Saul of Tarsus. You have gone about with great conviction attempting to destroy the work that God is bringing forth through The Church of Jesus Christ of Latter-day Saints."

The prosecutor looked stunned, and Sam continued, this time speaking to both of them. "Like Saul, you both have believed with all your hearts that you were doing good, and that the Church is a threat to your way of life. As a result, you have persecuted the Saints and unjustly cast some into prison and caused others to suffer unjust punishment. And, like Saul, because your hearts were good but your actions misguided, the Lord has seen fit to interrupt you on your road to Damascus. He has sent you a witness of sufficient power to turn your hearts away from your misguided course and to cause you to look upon His latter-day work with a new perspective and to feel within your hearts the need for change.

"I now say to you in words to echo in your souls as they did in Saul's: Brother Van der Kerk, Sister Van der Kerk—why persecute thou the Church of God? It is hard for thee to kick against the pricks." Sister Van der Kerk fell back into the couch as if struck in the face, and Brother Van der Kerk held his chin between thumb and forefinger, elbow upon his knee, as if deep in contemplation. A long silence fell upon them as they pondered his words.

Brother Van der Kerk finally broke the silence. "Saul's vision was accompanied by a sign. He was struck blind and dumb as I recall. Your invocation of his vision is well chosen, but impotent without an accompanying sign. What sign shall we expect to accompany our conversion on the road to Damascus?" he asked. His voice was soft, but it held an edge of disbelief, of challenge.

"This is the sign I give you," Sam heard himself say. He had no time to wonder what the sign was before he said, "You are an adulterous man."

Four people gasped simultaneously, including Sam and President Carlson. A stunned silence hung over them as the accusation seemed to bounce back and forth across the room. Sister Van der Kerk stared at Sam with contemptuous indignation, waiting for her husband to slam him into the ground with his denial; but when no denial came, her expression turned to disbelief and her gaze reluctantly swung toward her mate.

"Deny it," she hissed in Afrikaans, barely loud enough for Sam to hear.

After a long pause, he looked into his wife's face. His eyes were pleading, but his words were more startling than a denial.

He spoke in Afrikaans, and, unexpectedly, Sam understood every word as easily as if he had spoken in English.

"I asked for a sign, and this is indeed a true sign. Only God has known these many years, and it could only have come from Him. Would you have me add to my crimes, perjury before God? Would you rather be married to a lying adulterer or just an adulterer?"

Mrs. Van der Kerk bolted to her feet, grasping her handbag.

"I think it's time to leave" she stated tersely and turned toward her husband, who remained immobile on the couch. "I will get a ride home in one of the escort cars." She took two hasty steps toward the door before Sam's voice brought her to an abrupt stop.

Without knowing why, or even how, he spoke in Afrikaans. His pronunciation was awful, and his sentence structure sloppy, but his message was perfect. "There is one more lesson Saul learned from his sign, which you both will learn when you come tomorrow night."

Mrs. Van der Kerk turned toward him, her face red with anger. Her voice hissed with wrath as she stabbed the air with her finger, punctuating her words. "What lesson could possibly change the fact that my husband is an adulterer who has betrayed my trust and our marriage vows?"

Sam cocked his head to one side and whispered in Afrikaans, "Forgiveness."

* * *

They did not come the next night at seven, or even eight o'clock. It was nearly nine o'clock when a Mercedes pulled up in front without a police escort. It was almost ten minutes later when the doorbell rang. President and Sister Carlson met them at the door. This was the first time the Van de Kerks had met Sister Carlson, and she greeted them warmly.

Sister Van der Kerk seemed especially grateful to have Sister Carlson join the meeting. Brother Van der Kerk seemed oppressed and brooding. They were not in a pleasant mood, and whatever portion of the Spirit of the Lord that had been at the house seemed to evaporate with their arrival. When they were seated, Sister Carlson brought them rooibos tea.

The prosecutor and his wife sat on the couch several feet apart, an almost visible barrier of enmity separating them.

President Carlson suggested they begin with a prayer, something they had failed to do in their previous meetings with the Van der Kerks. Their guests immediately stood and bowed their heads. President Carlson offered a beautiful prayer. When everyone was seated, all eyes turned to Sam. He knew this would happen, yet he honestly didn't have a clue what to say. Still, knowing this would occur, he had resisted the urge to prepare something, preferring to wait upon the Lord to fill his lips with words of truth. He even suppressed the urge to ad lib as the seconds pushed toward a minute.

Still nothing came, and the second minute came and went in silence.

"Elder?" President Carlson asked quietly, but Sam just shook his head.

Silence stretched on for several minutes until everyone but Sam grew uncomfortable. Finally, Sister Van der Kerk asked impatiently, "Why haven't you said anything?"

Brother Van der Kerk answered her question. "Because, like before, we didn't come here to learn. We came here to be angry, and nothing he could have said would've made a difference. Silence is the only thing that could penetrate the wall I came here with. In reality, I am the one who should speak."

Turning to his wife, he said, "I need to beg your forgiveness and God's forgiveness. Believe me when I say that my crime was many years ago and was never repeated. I have anguished over it for years and wanted to tell you and to wash this taint from my soul, but I have never known how. I didn't understand how you could ever forgive me. I only knew that telling you would break your heart. And I couldn't bring myself to do that."

At this exact moment, Sam's heart flooded with understanding, and he opened his mouth and taught them the truths that could heal their souls. He began with the Garden of Eden and told of Adam's long separation from the Lord because of his transgression.

He told them of Adam's eventual understanding of the mission of Jesus Christ, and the unspeakable joy of becoming a participant in the Atonement. He told them of human nature, the natural man, and how all men are sinners. He taught them about the restoration of priesthood power in our dispensation and the cleansing power of baptism. He invited them to be washed clean and become whole through the power of that holy ordinance.

As Sam spoke, Sister Van der Kerk softened visibly. Her husband wept, and she held his head against her bosom and comforted him. When he could speak, he asked Sam to arrange for his baptism, and to help him prepare so that the cleansing would be absolute.

Of all the beautiful things Sam had ever seen, the look of love on Sister Van der Kerk's face was the sweetest. He thought of how the Savior might look as He gazes down upon a humble, repentant soul, and considered that the tender look on her face was a reflection of that perfect love and forgiveness.

The Van der Kerks came nearly every night for the next two weeks and were baptized sixteen days from the day Sam stood before Brother Van der Kerk in court. Their baptism was a solemn and joyful affair.

Since Brother Van der Kerk worked for the government, and the Dutch Reformed Church controlled the government, he fully expected to lose his job. Already, dozens of friends had abandoned them and heaped ridicule upon them. Family had disowned them, and their closest allies had rejected them. Yet, they considered it a small price to pay, and gladly walked away from it all with no apparent remorse. It was what they knew Jesus Christ wanted them to do, and their sacrifice was of little consequence to them. Over 150 people attended their baptism, not a single one of them from their former circle of friends and family.

Days later, Brother Van der Kerk was fired from his job. Sister Van der Kerk was demoted at her law firm until she finally quit. They lost their home after a few months, and eventually moved into a small apartment. They sold most of their possessions to pay for their needs, but inwardly rejoiced. Their faith was fantastic, and their joy in finding the true Church was utter and complete. They brought a sense of renewal and determination to the entire ward, and their courageous example revitalized and blessed everyone who became their new friends. The ward rallied around them and formed an impenetrable circle of safety. Their humility and gracious acceptance of the cost of righteousness won them friends of everyone they met. In time, their incredible story was told and retold among members and missionaries alike, until those who did not know them thought it was sheer fabrication. Yet, every word of it was true. The Van der Kerks had indeed sacrificed everything, other than life itself, for the truth.

In time, Brother Van der Kerk ran for election as the regional prosecuting attorney. His new friends in the ward donated all the money. His opponent ran his entire argument on the basis that Van der Kerk was a Mormon. Every advertisement published bashed him for his membership in the "Mormon cult," but Brother Van der Kerk ran on the campaign slogan that he had the courage to do what he felt was right, regardless of the cost. The campaign caught national attention, since his opponent became bitter and hateful. Brother Van der Kerk remained aloof, pressing his message of courageous honesty. In congregations throughout the nation, sermons were taught, with no other message than to urge people to "defeat the Mormon threat." The government itself donated money to the other man's campaign, and armed guards had to be stationed outside Van der

Kerk's apartment at night.

Because of the vigor of the opposition, Brother Van der Kerk's campaign cost very little. He had all the publicity he could have desired. In the end, he won a decisive victory. Everyone in the nation knew that a Mormon had been elected to high national office for the first time in their history, and missionary work surged ahead with unprecedented energy.

June 1, 1974

> *I have spent almost a month in the mission home. My back is healed enough so that I can get around without much pain. I still can't sleep on my back or right side. The skin is still black and blue and has shrunken, or at least it feels tight. I have been doing stretching exercises to try to regain full movement. Sister Carlson has been wonderful, and every evening she rubs ointment on my back. She also massages the muscles to keep them from balling up. Her ministrations have greatly lessened my suffering.*

> *About the only missionary work I have done is teaching the Van der Kerks. They were baptized on May 29. It was a glorious experience. I baptized them both, and President Carlson confirmed them. Brother Van der Kerk bore his testimony after the service and said that he had felt the burden of sin lifted from his shoulders. He turned toward me and asked me to forgive him for the abuse he had heaped upon me. No one except President and Sister Carlson and me knows about the lashes, and everyone wondered what he meant. Afterward, I gave him a hug and told him I loved him. He wept on my shoulder, and I on his.*

> *President Carlson told me today that I was being transferred back to Germiston. At least I will be in the same ward with Brother and Sister Van der Kerk. It just occurred to me that I didn't know their first names until I asked for their names in the waters of baptism. His first name is Joseph, and hers is Emma. Because of*

reasons that are obvious, their names became precious to me the moment I heard them. What a fantastic, almost poetic coincidence that they should possess the names of the greatest prophet of all time and his beloved wife. They didn't realize their names had significance in LDS history until I explained it to them. They both wept and proclaimed themselves unworthy.

My new companion is Elder Snider, also from the mission home. He is not happy about the transfer. He was President Carlson's personal secretary and wanted to become assistant to the president. He sees this as a demotion. This last month I hated to be around him. He is arrogant, demanding, and self-centered. I just hope he's a good missionary. I can put up with almost anything except not doing the work. I guess we'll see.

* * *

Sam and Elder Snider loaded the VW beetle and drove away from the mission home in silence. At almost the exact spot where Elder Beesler told him that he hated him, Elder Snider cleared his throat. Sam winced and waited. Elder Snider gave him a surprised look and smiled.

"Elder Mahoy, I know you have been in the mission home recovering from an illness. I also know that you think I'm an insufferable brat. I guess I am, at that. But we have something in common. We both love the Lord. If you will be patient with me, I will be the best senior companion you have ever had. What do you say?"

Sam could hardly believe his ears, and he relaxed.

"Elder," Sam answered, "I just want you to know that I recognize you as the senior companion, and I will do whatever I can to serve the Lord and be a good junior. Let's give it a try."

They drove to a different boarding house than the one he had spent that one night at with Elder Beesler. This one was a big old building apparently built as a boarding house. They were on the third floor, and there were no elevators. On their floor were perhaps twenty-five rooms, and all the tenants on the floor shared one big bathroom.

The first morning there, they went into the shower together. They were obligated by mission rules to remain within one another's sight, which included public restrooms. The shower was a large room with showerheads on three walls. Each showerhead had a stubby enclosure on two sides about armpit-high, but was open to the main room. At one time, there had been shower curtains, which had long since vanished.

Sam had just about finished showering when he heard a woman's voice mutter something about forgetting shampoo. He turned in time to see a completely naked woman stepping into the shower next to his. He was so stunned that he froze for a few seconds and only began to breathe again when she asked to borrow his shampoo. He handed it to her without looking her direction.

At that very moment, his eyes took on a will of their own, and even as his mind was shouting no, his eyes swept across her bare body as he turned. He hurriedly left without a second thought about his shampoo. As he and Elder Snider were leaving, two younger women walked past them. One had a towel wrapped around her waist, naked above that, and the other was completely naked except for a towel tossed across one shoulder. Sam bumped into Elder Snider three times before either one of them found the door. All three girls were giggling as Sam and Elder Snider bolted from the shower. They ran to their rooms soaking wet, each with only a towel around them.

They sat in their room, breathing heavily, shivering even in the heat of the African summer. Finally, Elder Snider stood and suggested that they both fast. Sam thought it was a wonderful idea. He could not get the image of the women from flashing in his mind. Even when he read the scriptures, he periodically had to force the images from his mind. To make matters worse, they were attractive women. He wondered if the images would be more or less haunting if they had been ugly. He derided himself for even having wondered that, but could not force the images to leave for any length of time.

The next morning they waited until the girls left. They took a quick shower in lukewarm water. It made them shower about an hour later than they would have otherwise, but at least they were alone.

The water was heated by a big wood-burning boiler that the landlord stoked up each morning except for Sunday. He kept the water warm until about eight o'clock. After eight, the Elders could have the shower to themselves, because the water quickly went cold. If they timed it right they could shower alone, but still catch the last few minutes of warm water.

Their actual room was not much larger than a walk-in closet. There were two beds with about two feet separating them. At one end of the room was a wooden wardrobe large enough to hang their shirts.

The next Saturday, a servant girl came by and collected laundry. They gave her their shirts. She returned them that evening all washed and pressed. She had done a good job, and they paid her several rand.

However, when they put them on, there were little black spots all over the shirts. They questioned her about it the next week, and she only shrugged. They were out tracting the next afternoon and came upon the same girl washing their shirts and garments. She was sitting on the curb in front of a house. The curb was running with water from the street. She had a lump of asphalt in her hand pounding a shirt on the curb. Their garments were spread out on the grass in a long row to dry, plainly visible to passing motorists. They were aghast, and scooped up their wet clothes, paid the girl, and left. The little black spots were from her lump of asphalt.

Sister Van der Kerk heard about this and insisted on doing their laundry thereafter. They were grateful beyond words.

Elder Snider turned out to be an incredibly hard worker. The Elders diligently tracted many hours each day. They worked and worked and worked, all without success. Without exception, every door was closed in their face. The more success they didn't have, the harder Elder Snider pushed. They began tracting several hours more each day than required by the rules, but still had zero investigators.

Sam suggested a special fast, which Elder Snider readily agreed to. They decided they needed extraordinary help, and planned a two-day fast. The weather was turning cooler but was still hot, about ninety degrees with eighty percent humidity. They physically strained themselves to complete the fast. Still, they had no teaching opportunities.

The next Sunday at church, Bishop Fanstein handed them a referral. These people were friends of his, and even though he had not discussed it with them, he felt they might be receptive. He asked the missionaries not to use his name. They were disappointed about that but agreed, grateful for the referral.

That evening, Sam and his companion drove to the subdivision indicated on the referral card, which stated the street name and house number. The subdivision was new and extremely large. The houses were nearly identical, with hundreds of them in tidy rows. However, there was not a single street sign. They could not tell which house was the correct one. Several dozen houses even had the same house number.

"Well Elder, the only way to work this is to knock on every house with that number and introduce ourselves," Sam's companion announced. "Let's do it."

Sam sat in the passenger side of the vehicle, frustrated that Elder Snider did everything the hard way. He had once suggested that they could rely on the Spirit to guide them in their tracting, and by doing so, they would not have to rely on their own wisdom to find investigators. Elder Snider had frankly told him that was foolishness. He insisted that they were to "find" the investigators and not expect the Spirit to dump them in their laps. He refused to entertain the thought of divine guidance in anything except at special times or in desperate circumstances.

"Elder Snider, if we willing to rely on the Spirit, it would guide us to these people," Sam pleaded. "The Lord knows where they live. Why don't we just try?"

Elder Snider gave him an indulgent look, as if Sam were a child who needed to be taught a lesson. He brought the VW to a complete stop near the entrance to the subdivision and turned to Sam.

"Okay, smart guy, here's what we'll do. As I pull up to each intersection, you listen to the Spirit and tell us which way to turn, okay?"

Almost immediately, Sam felt his heart burn and responded, "I have a better idea. You're the senior companion. As we pull up to each intersection, you tell me which way you would go. After that, we will go in the direction I pick. Good enough?"

"Yeah, whatever you want. And when we're done goofing around, we'll go tract them out like real missionaries." He drove to the first intersection, which was a "T."

"Turn right," Elder Snider said.

Sam did not know the way, but what he did know was that he had been prompted to chose the opposite of whatever Elder Snider said. "Left," he countered. They turned left.

Shortly they came to a four-way intersection. Snider chose right again, which would have taken them into the heart of the subdivision. "Left," Sam countered.

At each intersection, they went the opposite of every choice Elder Snider made. Finally, they ended up on a street still under construction. It was a dead-end street, and none of the houses had yard lights on, so they could not see the house numbers. There were no streetlights yet, and it was impossible to tell which house was which without pulling into each driveway and shining their headlights onto the house. "Wellyoulose. We'reonadeadend,"Elder Snidersaidtriumphantly.

Sam chose the opposite and said, "This is the right street. You choose a house."

Elder Snider gave him a "Don't you ever give up?" look and drove slowly down the dirt road until he picked a house on the left, which looked like someone was home.

Sam pointed to a dark house on the opposite side of the street. "That one," he said. They pulled into the driveway and saw that it actually had the correct house number.

"Well, that's pretty amazing, but we'll never know. No one's home. Let's leave," Elder Snider said.

Sam chose the opposite. "I say we knock."

Snider shrugged, willing to put this foolishness to rest.

They walked up to the door and knocked. It was dark inside, and they knocked again. Just as Elder Snider was turning to leave, footsteps sounded in the house. The porch light snapped on.

"Good evening," Elder Snider said to the woman who came to the door.

"Are you guys Mormons?" she asked suspiciously. Sam had heard that question a thousand times. It was usually followed by a door slamming in his face.

"We're from The Church of Jesus Christ of Latter-day Saints. People sometimes call us Mormons," Elder Snider answered with his best missionary smile.

"Really?" she replied. "For a minute I thought you were Jehovah's Witnesses. They have been around a lot lately. Let me get my husband. His best friend at work is a Mormon bishop. I think he's been wanting to learn more about the Mormon Church. Could you come in for a minute?"

Sam gave Elder Snider a smile and led the way into their investigator's home.

Brother and Sister Solomon were golden beyond golden. Teaching them was like giving the discussions in the LTM. Their answers were almost verbatim with the mythical "Brother Brown" in the discussions.

Elder Snider insisted on giving the first discussion wordperfect, and the Solomons enjoyed every word. The Spirit was strong and they rejoiced. Before the evening was over, the Solomons had happily committed to continuing on with the discussions, and they even discussed baptism.

On the way home, Elder Snider was quiet. He drove with both hands on the wheel, his eyes straight ahead. Sam knew what was on his mind. He was disturbed about how they had found the Solomons' home.

"Elder?" Snider said finally, stealing a glance at Sam. Sam didn't reply but waited for him to continue. "I have been thinking about what you did in directing us to the Solomons' house. I have to admit that you were right. I still can't believe that every decision I made was wrong. That hurts."

When Elder Snider didn't continue, Sam said, "It wasn't me who directed us to their home. It was the Lord through the whisperings of the Spirit. I had little to do with it. I think the Lord wanted you to have a graphic lesson in what the Spirit is able to do if you use it."

"Tell me the truth," Elder Snider responded almost instantly, a note of disbelief in his voice. "Did the bishop draw you a map to their home? You must have known how to get there, and you set me up. Huh? Come on, tell the truth."

"The truth is that it happened exactly as you saw it. I had no map. You can ask the bishop if he gave me a map. Remember that you were the one to say which way we should go at each intersection. All I knew was that I was to pick the opposite of whatever you said. I got that instruction from the Spirit, and I was willing to be obedient."

Snider gave him a sidelong glance. "Well," he said, "I find this all hard to swallow. I know that the Spirit doesn't work like that. I'm as spiritual as any missionary, and I tell you it just isn't like that. You have to work things out for yourself and then ask for confirmation. The only way the Spirit could have led us to that house is if we stopped and fasted and prayed at every street corner. Even then, I doubt the Lord would have shown us. He expects us to do the work, not the other way around. We're here to serve Him, not for Him to serve us." Sam felt his heart sinking. If Elder Snider couldn't see the truth of such a powerful example of guidance by the Spirit, nothing Sam could say would penetrate his heart. Sam bowed his head and said, "I know where you're coming from." That seemed to satisfy his senior companion, and they drove home in silence.

June 22, 1974

We have been teaching the Solomons for nearly a month. Each of our discussions has been wonderful. Their baptism is scheduled for this coming Friday. They are excited, especially Sister Solomon.

The Solomons are our only investigators. We have tracted the soles off our shoes, and there just doesn't seem to be anyone to teach. Elder Snider works harder than any missionary I have seen, but he still refuses to listen to the Spirit. He told me that when he returns home, he wants to be able to say that he served a good mission. He doesn't want to report that the Spirit served a good mission and that he was and wants to serve the there to provide backup. I feel sorry for him. He has a good heart and desperately wants to serve the Lord, but is inflicting unnecessary pain upon himself. Except for a few times when I suggest things that he agrees with, he has completely ignored me, and the Spirit as well.

I received another letter from home today. It was in the mail for over a month. The family has settled in the Matanuska Valley near Wasilla, Alaska. They just finished building a new chapel and have divided the ward. Dad was made the bishop of the new Wasilla ward. Because he was made bishop, he has quit his job on the Trans-Alaska pipeline and is looking for work in Wasilla or Anchorage. The pipeline job was two weeks on, two weeks off, and he knew he couldn't be the bishop with that kind of schedule. They have been living in a camp trailer and almost have enough saved to build a house, but they are waiting until Dad finds other work before they start building. They have to do something before winter comes. Dad says winter in Alaska is fierce, and everyone tells him he doesn't want to go through it living in a camp trailer.

* * *

As soon as they pulled up to the Solomon's drive, Sam knew something was wrong. A bad feeling surrounded the house.

"Do you feel that, Elder?" Sam asked. "What?"

"That negative feeling. I think the Solomons are in trouble."

"The Solomons are fine. I think you have an overactive imagination."

Sister Solomon let them in. Her eyes were puffy and red. She didn't offer them a seat.

"Elders, I'm sorry. My husband has decided that we're not being baptized. He doesn't want you to come around anymore." Sam was thunderstruck but not surprised. The feeling inside the house was like a cold shower.

"Are you sure this is what you want?" Elder Snider asked. He was terribly disappointed. "If it's what you really want, then we won't come back. It's your decision, but I would like you to be very sure."

Sister Solomon glanced toward the back of the house as if unsure and then nodded bleakly. "I don't think he'll ever change his mind. I've seen him like this before, and he is adamant. I'm sorry. I know the Church is true, but it wouldn't be right for me to be baptized against his will. It would probably cause a divorce. Please leave now, before he becomes more agitated."

Elder Snider nodded sadly and turned toward the door. He was half-way through it before he realized his companion had not followed. He placed a hand on Sam's arm, but Sam shrugged it off.

"Sister Solomon? May we speak to Brother Solomon? I feel like we need to talk to him directly."

Her eyes brightened a bit and then sank back into despair. "I don't think he'll come out, and if he does, it won't be pleasant. He'll probably scream at you, just like he . . ." She cut herself off. "Let me see." She disappeared into the back of the house.

She was gone for a long time before returning. After a few minutes, Brother Solomon stomped into the room, his hair standing on end and his clothing crumpled. His face was white with fury, and his eyes were wide and darting like a wild animal.

No sooner had he rounded the corner than he snarled at them, "My wife told you to leave this house. You and your evil religion are to never come back. Do you understand? Now go. Go before I get my shotgun!"

Elder Snider was pulling on Sam's arm, urging him to leave, but Sam's feet seemed riveted to the floor. A quiet urging brought his arm to the square, and he heard his voice begin to speak as if he were a spectator.

"In the name of Jesus Christ, I command you to come out of him." No sooner had these words escaped his lips than Brother Solomon took two steps backward as if slugged in the chest. He fell to one knee, and his head fell into his hands. Sister Solomon gasped and rushed to his side. After a minute, he stood and struggled to a chair. Sam backed up to open the way.

It took several minutes for him to recover. His eyes were tired but normal as they fastened on Sam. "Elder. I don't know what to say. For the last three days, ever since your last visit, I have fought a terrible battle. Every evil thought, every temptation, every hour of every day has been hell. I haven't been able to sleep or eat for three days. I feel as if I have literally wrestled with the devil. And at this point, I'm not sure if I lost or won."

"Brother Solomon," Sam began, but was cut off by a wave of Brother Solomon's hand.

"I don't want to hear it. I strongly suspect that the Church is true. My wife says it is, and for a while, I believed it was. But if I have to go through this to be a member of God's true church, then I'm not willing to do it. It's just not worth it. The first time I felt relief was when I told my wife to tell you to never come back. As soon as you stepped inside this house, the battle returned. It went away when you raised your arm, but I feel it returning. Please go now. Let's end this like gentlemen rather than with me threatening to shoot you. Believe me, ten minutes ago I would have done it, just to stop the battle in my head. Now, please go."

This time, Sam let Elder Snider tug him toward the door, but before he closed the door, Sam said, "Brother Solomon?" Brother Solomon looked up at him with an expressionless face. "You lost," Sam said, and closed the door behind him.

Elder Snider chastised him all the way home about opening his mouth without permission and not following his senior companion's instructions. Sam ignored his tirade.

August 3, 1974

I received a transfer notice today. I am going to be transferred to Rhodesia. It's another country north of here. Elder Snider has been a good companion as far as teaching me diligence and work. I feel bad that we never really got any missionary work done. I think he blames me for our lack of success. He has hinted at it but not said why. In Rhodesia, I'll be co-senior with Elder Palmer. He came out of the LTM in the group just behind mine. I am looking forward to finally being able to get some missionary work done the way I feel inspired to do it.

August 5, 1974

I am on the train to Rhodesia. This is day two of a five-day trip. The train is a coal-burning puffer belly and never goes over 20 mph. I am in the third car from the engine, and the cabin spends about half the time filled with coal smoke. I am constantly coughing.

The countryside is beautiful beyond description. It is rolling hills covered with low trees and brush. The colors are breathtaking. An unbelievable number of animals roam here. We have gone past many herds of deer-like animals, and I have seen lions, elephants, a bazillion monkeys, and other animals that I had no idea existed. I have taken many pictures.

The train stops at every black village it passes to let off packages and people. We usually spend about an hour at each village. We are not allowed off the train. While we are stopped, armed guards walk up and down the train to keep people from sneaking onto the train. The little kids of the village come up to the windows and sell things, such as oranges and bananas. They also sell lots of hand-carved animals and trinkets. I have bought a few because they are so cheap, but I don't have much money. The kids start out begging, and then as the train starts to warm up, they tell us we are selfish—rich and selfish. They demand that we buy something. As the train pulls away, they curse at us for not buying enough of their stuff. What an interesting sales tactic.

One cute little boy picked out a lady in the car ahead of mine and was saying, "Very beautiful rich lady, please buy an orange. I am so hungry." As the train began to move, he was saying, "Hey rich lady, why you so selfish? I think you very mean to me, rich lady. Please, my baby sister is so hungry." Then as we were pulling away, he said, "Hey mean rich lady. Why you hate me? You are too ugly to be nice. I hate you, ugly, mean, rich lady!"

It was funny. The kid was obviously not malnourished. He was as plump as the rich lady.

BULAWAYO

By the time Sam arrived in Bulawayo, Rhodesia, he was sick from coal fumes. His new district leader met him at the train station and drove him and his companion to their new area. He let them off on a street corner.

"Elders, this is a new area. Missionaries have never been here before, and there is no boarding. Your first tracting assignment will be to find boarding. I will come back to this street corner at six o'clock to deliver your bags. If you haven't found any, you will have no place to sleep." He hopped back into the car and drove away.

This was something unexpected, and neither Sam nor Elder Palmer had a clue what to do. Finally, Elder Palmer suggested that they have a prayer. Standing there on the street corner, they bowed their heads and Elder Palmer offered a prayer. When he was done, they walked down the street as if they both knew where they were going. Without a word or signal, they turned into the fourth house and knocked on the door. An older woman answered the door. She seemed surprised and openly pleased to see them.

"Good afternoon, Ma'am," Elder Palmer said. "We're missionaries for The Church of Jesus Christ of Latter-day Saints, and we're looking for accommodations in this area. Do you know of anywhere we might inquire?" She said she thought a Mrs. Whiting took in boarders, and gave them directions. They walked several blocks and found the house.

Mrs. Whiting was indeed looking for boarders and welcomed them. They offered the amount the district leader had suggested, and Mrs. Whiting's eyes grew big. She declined that amount, but insisted on a lesser amount. Their room was a large bedroom with two beds, a large wardrobe, an attached bathroom, and a beautiful view. It was almost more than Sam or Elder Palmer could believe. They paid her the first month's rent, and she gave them a key to the house.

Elder Palmer was over six feet tall, almost two inches taller than Sam. Where Sam's weight was compact and hard, Palmer's was loose and flabby. The skin on his face sagged and looked sallow. Sam wondered about Elder Palmer's health. In time, he learned that his companion was suffering from various health problems and had to get special permission from the First Presidency to go on his mission. Perhaps that was why he took missionary work so seriously, because it cost him dearly to do it. He was exhausted when they got home each day.

They tracted for the rest of the afternoon before realizing they were lost. They really had no idea which corner the district leader had left them at. It was approaching six o'clock when they rounded a corner, and quite miraculously, ended up at the right place. Minutes later, the district leader pulled up, and they climbed in. They drove to their new boarding and unloaded their bags.

* * *

Rhodesia is a small country of about 150,000 square miles. It sits on some of the most beautiful and mineral-abundant real estate in the world. The soil is a dark red in some places, a bluish-black in others, and in others still, a deep green. The soil colors change according to the type of minerals present. Red soils indicate iron deposits; blueblack soils indicate gold or silver, and green indicate copper deposits. The missionaries discovered that it was common to go into someone's home and see gold nuggets as large as tennis balls on the mantelpiece. Rhodesia was a country settled by whites from England, originally as an English commonwealth. Their neighboring country, Northern Rhodesia, was a commonwealth as well. In the late sixties, their English charter expired for both countries, and England began the process of turning the country over to the indigenous peoples, the blacks of the Xota, and other tribes.

Northern Rhodesia was renamed Zambia by the new government. It was a thriving colony because of their vast copper mines. At one time, they had the largest copper mine in the world and exported more copper than any nation in Africa. They also exported more chromium than any nation on earth.

Less than one year after their charter expired, a local black man made himself king of Zambia and ordered the whites to work without compensation. In response, the white people flowed across the border into Rhodesia, leaving him without technical workers in the mines. He ordered his troops to kill any white person fleeing the country, and a blood bath began that ended in civil war.

Before this king was overthrown, over thirty thousand whites had been slaughtered, and tens of thousands had been taken into slavery. In the meantime, the mines had flooded with water. When the white workers failed at the impossible task of evacuating the mines of the water, many of them and their families were slaughtered. Some escaped in daring rescues by friends and relatives from Rhodesia.

Rhodesia's charter expired in 1965, and England began the process of dismantling the local government. The settlers, led by then-president Ian Smith, rebelled. An election was held, and the people, black and white, overwhelmingly reelected Smith and commissioned him to issue a declaration of independence.

England condemned Rhodesia before the United Nations, and the United Nations voted to sanction Rhodesia. Member nations were no longer allowed to trade anything except certain humanitarian supplies with Rhodesia. Trade with South Africa continued unaffected.

The economic shock was catastrophic. The high-production gold, copper, and silver mines shut down overnight. Without a buyer, even gold became valueless. Since South Africa already produced huge quantities of these minerals, they had no need to buy Rhodesia's. Needed repair parts to keep vital utilities running became impossible to find, and utilities failed. Electricity only ran at certain times of the day, and water and fuels became scarce. Gasoline was rationed, jobs were nonexistent, and money, currently the British pound, became scarce.

President Smith coined the phrase, "Prosperity through independence", and asked people to report to their jobs without expectation of pay. He ordered the printing of the Rhodesian "dollar" and asked the citizens to accept it without question. They did. In time, textile mills were built from smuggled parts. Machine shops made parts for automobiles. Utilities became more reliable as they learned to manufacture their own repair parts. People created cottage industries to create things normally purchased overseas, and the economy of the nation stabilized. In less than ten years, they became an independent, though struggling, nation.

The year Sam arrived, President Smith announced the completion of the nation's only auto manufacturing plant. It cranked out a small vehicle oddly similar to a Toyota Corolla. The Church bought one of the first models to roll off the line. The district leader drove that vehicle. To Sam's eyes, it was a half-baked mess. It had holes drilled in the body for chrome trim, but none was installed. The front and rear bumpers were painted iron rather than chromed steel. The car had no heater, no radio, no horn, and air constantly blew through the heater vents. The clutch chattered, and the engine belched black smoke; but the car ran, and it soon became a symbol of national pride.

One thing Sam quickly learned was that everything was cheap in Rhodesia—cheap in cost and construction. When he arrived in the country, his first purchase was a new pair of shoes. They cost him less than four American dollars. They were handsome, lightweight shoes.

They lasted great until Sam stepped into the first puddle. In three steps, they fell apart. He walked back home in his socks. The shoes were literally made of paper. The soles, sides, and everything else on the shoes were made of paper. But since all the shoes in Rhodesia were made that way, he simply bought another pair and avoided puddles.

Sam's second pair of shoes lasted about a month, after which he had to buy another pair. No wonder they were so cheap. The new shoe industry thrived on a marketing necessity impossible under any other circumstances.

Unlike South Africa, black people were welcome to participate in the economy in any way they chose. As many black students as whites attended college. Black doctors, dentists, and lawyers, many of whom excelled at their trades, saw many white clients.

The race barrier was still there, but it was much thinner than in their large neighbor to the south. The people were divided into classes along economic lines, with almost no middle class. Those who understood business started one and invariably found success. Mansions dotted the hillside outside of town, and large cars were smuggled into the country. Those who understood only labor were paid paltry wages and lived in small, nearly-unfurnished homes. It amazed Sam that one could walk four blocks and go from mansions to shanties. What even amazed him further was that they found their greatest missionary success among the near-slums of Bulawayo.

The only difference between these rows of tiny houses and a true slum was pride. The people loved their country, understood sacrifice, and willingly gave of themselves. There was no filth, no litter, no chronic malcontent, and little, if any, crime. Everyone who wanted a job had one. The opportunity to progress was wide open, and people felt no limitation on their future. They had seen the country go from bankruptcy and despair to economic stability and hope. They believed in their future, and it showed.

* * *

Elder Palmer and Sam divided the days into even and odd. Sam would act as senior on odd days, and Elder Palmer on even days. It soon became obvious that Elder Palmer was a hard worker. He understood, at least on an instinctual level, the workings of the Spirit. Sam soon found out that his companion had a grasp of the scriptures that made Sam's head swim.

The mission published a list of four hundred scriptures for missionaries to memorize. They were encouraged to memorize one each day until they knew 365 of them. The remaining thirty-five were bonus scriptures. Elder Palmer knew nearly all of them, and Sam less than a third. On Elder Palmer's days, they played scripture chase while they tracted. The object was to quote a portion of a scripture, and then your companion had to finish the scripture and give the reference. If they failed, they lost a point. At lunchtime, whoever was behind bought the other a soft drink. Soft drinks in Rhodesia contained no artificial flavors since they had no technology to create them. They were pure, carbonated fruit juices. Sam found them delightful, and he decided to win as many of them as possible. Because neither of them could afford many soft drinks, whoever lost had to watch the other drink it, usually to appropriately exaggerated sighs of delight.

Elder Palmer also taught Sam how to "tip" rocks. This was done by placing the inside of his shoe beside a rock as he was walking. Just as he was about to lift his foot, he would flip his toe. The rock became a projectile inflicting non-lethal damage to Sam's shins. Elder Palmer was a pro, and for weeks, Sam had bruised ankles.

With a little practice, Sam also learned to tip rocks; however, Elder Palmer would give a little skip whenever Sam tipped one at him, and the rock would invariably miss.

At first, it seemed like a brutal, unmissionary-like sport, but there was a small satisfaction in it that allowed the release of pent-up frustrations that otherwise went unexpressed. They soon developed a set of de facto rules: No rocks bigger than a golf ball; never in the tracting area or other public places; only when walking to and from the tracting area, and so on. It kept it friendly and relatively private.

In a short time, they had teaching appointments, and their missionary hearts soared. The first Sunday meeting was a shock for Sam. They walked nearly two miles to the chapel. It was on a major thoroughfare and visible for miles. It was nearly the biggest building in that part of town, and certainly the biggest church.

As soon as they stepped inside, happy members mobbed them. They were escorted to seats on the stand and were treated like visiting General Authorities. They were each invited to bear their testimonies and tell where they were from. The branch president was Brother Braythwaite, formerly from England. He conducted the services with a humble heart, and the Spirit was present in abundance.

The talks were simple yet inspiring, and the music was sung without accompaniment. The congregation consisted of ten families, with about sixty people attending sacrament meeting. After the meeting, Sister

Braythwaite invited them to lunch at the Braythwaite's home. The Elders gratefully accepted.

While they were waiting for President Braythwaite to finish his branch president business, Sam investigated the organ in the chapel. It was locked, but he found a key in the bench. He was amazed to find it was a new Allan organ, made in America. It still had a manufacturer's sticker on the keys to keep them from vibrating during shipment. He removed the strip and turned the organ on. The sound was rich, full, and inspiring. He played "I Am a Child of God," and before he began the second verse, people had drifted back into the chapel and were singing. By the time the song finished, the entire congregation had returned.

Someone called out a page number. A request for "The Spirit of God like a Fire Is Burning" thundered through the small chapel. Sam had never heard it sung more enthusiastically or with such righteous feeling. He knew that angels were also singing with them. He played for nearly two hours before he finally could play no more. He had not played an organ since the ward in Idaho, yet it was a wonderful experience. The Braythwaites were ready to go, so he turned off the organ to loud but loving protests.

Sister Braythwaite bundled them off to her home, which was in a somewhat affluent section of town. The entire ward came too, all sixty or so of them. Sam could not believe his eyes. Everyone who came also brought food. They ate, laughed, and eventually held a testimony meeting. It was fantastically spiritual, and the fellowship was like nothing he had previously experienced. It felt to him as if he had entered a small portion of the celestial kingdom. The Braythwaites had no children, and Sister Braythwaite was not shy about telling everyone how desperately she wanted a baby.

Sister Braythwaite, Sharon as she preferred to be called, was thirty-five, blond, blue-eyed, and unusually beautiful. She had a model's body and a dazzling smile to melt any man's heart. Her laughter was second only to her keen sense of humor. She loved her husband with deep passion. A recent convert to the Church, she possessed a spiritual depth that bore testimony of premortal greatness. From her high-energy enthusiasm, to her fast speech and zest for life, she almost seemed to be living life in double time.

Yes, Sharon had everything—including leukemia. She was not expected to live much more than two to three years. The doctors insisted she did not have the health to carry a child full term. She had tried and had suffered three miscarriages. They feared that another attempt would be fatal to her. Reluctantly, she had given up her immediate hope of bearing a child, yet steadfastly maintained her faith that she would have her precious child before she left this earth. Her greatest hope was to go to America, where she just knew she could be cured of her disease and have her baby.

Sam and Elder Palmer looked at one another when she said this, but neither of them tried to disabuse her of her dream.

* * *

Missionary work in Bulawayo was a joy. They rarely had a door slammed in their faces, and at least among the poorer class of people, most everyone they met seemed pleased they were there. They were a curiosity, an anomaly in that land, and people hungered for news of the outside world. Their challenge became finding a way to determine who was interested in the gospel and who was just interested in them as visitors from another planet. They would often be walking down the street and have someone open their door and call them over to visit. It was so different from South African missionary work that Sam wondered if he were walking in a dream. Still, the bulk of their investigators came from the poorer section of town.

Elder Palmer was also a joy to work with. He was sensitive to the Spirit and as obedient as Sam. Together, they taught with power, and people began requesting baptism.

* * *

The day was over, and they were walking down a darkened street through an area they had previously tracted. It was nine o'clock and time for them to hurry home. They were both tired and footsore. As they came to the middle of the street, both of them came to a stop. It was Sam's day, so he said what they were both feeling.

"Elder, I think we need to knock on one more door."

Elder Palmer nodded and started up the walk directly in front of them. Sam grabbed his arm and pointed across the street.

"Just testing you, Elder," Palmer said, laughing. Together they crossed the dark street.

The house was unusually small and had no porch light on. Only a dim light in one of the rooms gave any hint of occupation. Sam knocked and waited as someone walked noisily through the small house. In a moment, a woman opened the door. Her hair was stringy and disarrayed.

She snapped on the porch light as she opened the door, but left the screen door closed between them.

They could see very little of her features, except that she was tall and dressed in a loose fitting cotton smock that was torn at the neck. A small child clung to her left leg and was making whimpering noises. Her expression was not unfriendly, but it definitely was not welcoming. A feeling of darkness and despair emanated from her that Sam found oppressive. He started to give a door approach when something unusual came from his lips.

"Good evening, Ma'am. We are missionaries for The Church of Jesus Christ of Latter-day Saints. We have come to tell you about the family home evening program, which strengthens families and draws them closer together. Would you have a few minutes for me to explain it?"

"Do I have to buy somethin'?" she asked suspiciously.

Sam chuckled. It was the first time he had been asked that. "No, nothing to buy," he answered.

She nodded meekly and pushed open the screen door.

The room they entered was smaller than Sam's bedroom at home. It had a rough wooden floor and a single couch against one side. She turned on a lamp without a shade, which made a harsh glow in the room. She brought a chair from the kitchen and put it against the opposite wall of the room. When the Elders sat down, their knees were less than three feet apart.

The woman lifted her daughter to her lap. The child was beautiful and wore a thin cotton dress. Both mother and daughter were barefoot. Sam noticed that the little one's front teeth were missing, and the mother had the remains of a black eye. She introduced herself as Elaine Knight and her daughter as Eleanor. Eleanor buried her face in her mother's chest and curled up into a ball. Sam guessed her age at about four years old.

"Mrs. Knight, the Church of Jesus Christ of Latter-day Saints is led by a living prophet, and one of the things he has given us is the family home evening program. It's where families meet together each Monday evening and share gospel stories and have fun together. It strengthens families and builds bonds between them."

Mrs. Knight stared at him as if she did not understand a word he was saying. He continued. "Would you be interested in having us come back and share a family home evening with you to show you how it may benefit your family?"

"Does it have to be a Monday?" she asked. Sam was surprised that she had understood that much.

"No. Any night. We would like to do it when your husband is home though."

Her face soured, but she shrugged it off. "How about this Friday? I think that's the day Thomas is coming home."

Sam consulted his pocket diary, and they made an appointment.

Within minutes, the Elders were back out in the street, and the porch light snapped off. They made their way back to their boarding in silence. Palmer didn't tip a rock at him once.

Friday came, and they found themselves standing a half-block away from the Knight's home. Elder Palmer was not sure he liked what Sam proposed.

"I've never done a family home evening with an investigator. What are we going to do?" Sam shifted his weight to one foot. He wasn't sure himself but was sure they needed to follow through. "We are going to have a family home evening with them, just like they were our own family. We'll say the prayers, sing the songs, and teach the lesson. I have some cookies Sister Braythwaite baked for us, and we'll share them. It may be a bust, but we have to try."

"Elder, I sing like a dying cow."

"Me too," Sam admitted, and they both laughed.

"We'll soon know if you were inspired or just at wits end, won't we?" Elder Palmer said quietly as he rang the buzzer.

A tall, balding man answered the door. He looked too young to be going bald. The man scrutinized them for a second and pushed open the screen. Sam introduced them just as Mrs. Knight came and stood beside her husband.

"You should know that we are Jehovah's Witnesses and aren't interested in Mormonism," he said in reply. His voice was gruff. Mrs. Knight punched him in the side, and he laughed.

"Just kidding. Come on in. You going to show us how to have a happier family? If anyone in the world needs that, we do. Sit over there," he said, indicating the only couch in the room.

They sat in exactly the same spot as before. Sam asked Elder Palmer to offer the opening prayer. Afterward, he slowly recited the words to the first verse of "I Am a Child of God." The idea was for the investigators to join in. It didn't happen, and he and Elder Palmer sang the verse alone. Neither of the Knights made an attempt to sing. Elder Palmer had told the truth. He did sing like a dying cow.

During their song, Mr. Knight struggled to keep a smirk off his face, and Mrs. Knight punched him in the side again.

Sam gave a short lesson on trust. He told a story about a little girl who had the job of taking her daddy's lunch to him each day while he was digging a well. Each day the well was a little deeper, and eventually she had to drop his lunch down to him. Each day she would hear her daddy catch the bag, and she would return home.

Finally, the well was so deep that she could not see her father, only hear his voice from far below. Even when she couldn't see him, he caught the lunch every time.

One day, as she came to the well, she found that the forest was on fire. She was too small to climb down the rope, and her father did not have time to climb up to her. She was afraid, and the heat of the fire was growing nearer. She called down to her father who called up to her with a single word. "Jump!"

Sam turned to Eleanor, who was cuddled on her mother's lap. Her mother called her "Ellie."

"Ellie," Sam said. "What do you think happened? Do you think her daddy caught her in his arms?"

Ellie looked at her father with large, frightened eyes. Then she looked at her mother and back at Sam. She stuck two fingers in her mouth, which her mother pulled back out with a loud sucking noise. Finally, Ellie nodded.

"You're right. Her daddy did catch her, and they were safe from the fire. Sister Knight, why do you think the little girl was able to jump into that dark well?"

"Because she trusted her daddy and knew he wouldn't drop her." Her voice was sure, and a little accusatory. She glanced at Thomas.

"Is it possible for us to help our children develop trust in our love for them so that when the need arises, they will trust us like the little girl in the story?"

"I would like to know how," Brother Knight said in all seriousness. "I would never trust someone with my life like that. Nobody ever inspired that kind of trust in me."

Sam smiled at him encouragingly. "How we do it is by earning that trust. A little at a time, the little girl in the story came to trust her daddy to catch the lunch sack. As the well grew deeper, her trust grew stronger. We can earn our children's trust. That's what this lesson is about. In the absence of learning to trust, children fear and mistrust. But it can be earned if we are willing to take the effort to do it."

Through all this, the Knights had sat with wooden faces, hardly involved in the meeting and obviously not enjoying it. An air of strained discomfort hung in the room.

Sam felt foolish and wondered why he had felt inspired to get into this mess. They passed out the cookies, skipped the closing song, and had a closing prayer. With no desire to remain in the uncomfortable situation a moment longer, they both stood as if on cue. As they were leaving, Elder Palmer handed Brother Knight a Joseph Smith pamphlet and told them about living prophets in the Church today. Brother Knight tossed it on the sofa without giving it a glance.

They both breathed a sigh of relief when they regained the street. It had been an uncomfortable experience, and they were both glad it was over.

As the days slipped by, the Knight family evaporated from their minds. It was nearly two weeks later when they were again walking past their home that the Elders both came to an abrupt stop.

"I think we . . ."

"Should visit the Knights," Elder Palmer finished for him.

They both wondered why as they crossed the street, but they were there to do the Lord's work, and both felt impressed to stop. Their previous FHE still rang a dull tone in their memories, and neither looked forward to another meeting.

Mrs. Knight opened the door. As soon as she saw who it was, her face brightened, and she called into the house. "The Mormons are back!" In moments, Thomas joined her, and pushed open the screen.

They went inside. Thomas brought two chairs from the kitchen, and Elaine got the pamphlet. As soon as they sat down, she held it open for them to see. Many paragraphs were underlined in red.

"We read the pamphlet together about the new prophet," Thomas said. "We had no idea there was another prophet on earth. I read it three times before I realized the dates. I assume Joseph Smith is dead now? Who's the current one? Is there a current one? What's his name? Why isn't this in all the newspapers? This is important, you know!" Thomas told them with some urgency in his voice.

A brief, yet lively discussion followed about living prophets. A missionary's greatest happiness is teaching someone ready for truth. It follows then, that a missionary's greatest joy would be teaching someone of simple and pure faith, literally starving for truth. Sam was tasting the sweet, sweet fruits of missionary joy, and it thrilled him to the center of his soul. The Knights questioned them with eagerness, and simply believed. There was no doubt, no cross-examination, and no dispute or debate. Their hungry souls simply received the truth with childlike faith.

After being told about a current living prophet, Elaine poked Thomas in the ribs. "Told ya," she said. "Tom said that Joseph Smith died and there wasn't another one. But I told him God wouldn't start something and then just let it die out again. Told ya!" Her husband chuckled at her.

Thomas leaned forward. "I have been trying to do the trust thing with little Ellie, and guess what?" He leaned forward as if he were going to tell a secret. "It's working a little. She hasn't trusted me since I busted her teeth out. Don't blame her none, but I was drunk, and I didn't even remember doing it. I gave Elaine a black eye too. Don't remember that either. I still feel terrible about it, but it was the drink, not me. The best thing is that Ellie is acting better toward me already." He leaned back. "I just need to figure out how to get trust with Elaine now. She still won't let me sleep at home. Don't blame her though."

Elaine punched him in the side and gave him a meaningful look.

He gave her a frown, but his eyes were smiling.

At that moment, Ellie came from the back of the house. She was in pajamas and clutching a threadbare teddy bear. She scanned the room and walked over to Sam. She held up her arms, and he lifted her onto his lap. She was as light as a feather. She curled up against him and started sucking her fingers. With her other hand, she twisted his tie.

Thomas cleared his throat. "Elder Palmer, would you give us an opening prayer so we can get started with learning about this new prophet?" Palmer's mouth dropped open, but he quickly recovered and offered a simple but lovely prayer.

As soon as they said "amen," the Knights peppered them with more questions. It was all the Elders could do to answer one before they came up with another. Every answer given was accepted. It was as if they had been starved for months and were now being allowed to savor a great feast. During the meeting, both of them smoked constantly. In a short time, the room was dense with smoke, making it unpleasant in the cramped and stuffy little home. Thomas noticed this and opened the front door.

Several hours passed before the Elders finally left. It was later than they should have stayed out. The Knights begged them to come again the next evening, which they did.

The following evening, the Knights looked restless and fidgeted with their hands. After the opening prayer, they announced simultaneously that they had quit smoking.

The missionaries were astonished, and asked them why. "Well," Sister Knight said matter-of-factly, "my parents are Jehovah's Witnesses, and they told us that you Mormons don't smoke or drink. They are furious that we are talking to you chaps, because they have been trying to convert us for years."

"So," Thomas interjected, "we figure if we're going to join the true Church, we had better start acting like it. So, we gave up smoking. Well, actually, Elaine gave up smoking, and I'm about half way there. She gave it up just like that." He snapped his fingers. "I'm struggling with it, but I'll make it."

"He will too," Elaine said. "He's bullheaded like an ox. When he sets his mind, it's set. He said he wants to join the Mormon Church, and that's that. So, I had to scramble to make up my mind. I know it's true, I just don't know much about it. Know what I mean? So you better teach me fast."

"And I want to know," Thomas added, "if it's true that we have to give up tea and coffee."

"Yes. Isn't it wonderful how much Heavenly Father cares about us?" Sam replied, a smile on his face.

"Damn!" Thomas said, and Elaine poked him in the ribs. "Oh, sorry. What I mean is, I'll get to that next. Smoking first, drinking next, and then tea and coffee. Damn! I mean, darn." She poked him again.

"Ask them about tithing," Elaine urged. "Ask them."

"Tithing too?" he asked.

"A tenth," Sam said.

"Only a tenth? That's not much. I spend more than that on cigarettes. I'll get healthier, we'll pay tithing, and we'll still have money left over. This will be great. When can we start? Do we have to be baptized first, or can we start paying tithing next Sunday? Do you Mormons pass a basket for donations? How do we pay it?"

"You put it in an envelope and privately hand it to the branch president."

"I like that way much better. There's so much pressure when they pass the basket. I never thought it was right for God's Church," Thomas said.

Elaine's voice was excited as she informed them, "We want to come to church next Sunday. Is that all right?"

"Absolutely. It will be wonderful to have you," Sam responded, his head spinning.

Elder Palmer gave him a bewildered look. Neither of them would have been surprised if the Knights had both jumped up and shouted, "April fools!" Except they knew the Knights were serious.

By this time, Ellie had twisted Sam's tie until he was choking. He took it from her sticky little hands and untwisted it. Then he put it back into her hands. "Here, twist it the other way for a while." Ellie smiled and whispered, "Okay."

Thomas bolted to his feet, and Elaine clapped a hand over her mouth. He turned to his wife and exclaimed, "Did you hear that?"

Elaine nodded, tears forming in her eyes. "What?" Sam asked, completely baffled.

"Ellie has never spoken to a stranger. Not one word. Not ever. This is the first word we've heard her say to anyone but us. She said, "Okay." It's a miracle. A miracle!" her mother cried.

"Okay," Ellie said again, and furiously twisted Sam's tie.

"Well, she's still pretty young. Some kids are shy for a long time. How old is she, about four?" Elder Palmer asked. "She's almost eight," Thomas said.

Sam felt tears pooling in his eyes. Somehow, the twisted tie felt sweet against his neck.

"Okay?" little Ellie asked, and Sam could only nod.

* * *

That first Sunday, Brother and Sister Knight acted nervous. Sister Knight wore excessive makeup, and Thomas had polished his shoes until he wore through to the paper. Ellie sat on Sam's lap and twisted his tie. Sam had tried to explain that they should wait until they were baptized to take the sacrament. When it was passed to them, they both partook. Elaine leaned over to him and whispered, "Sorry, but in our hearts, we are already members, you know." She poked him in the ribs.

Sam just nodded. In his heart, he knew her words were true.

As the days progressed into weeks, the change that came over the Knights was miraculous. Each time the Elders visited, they felt a sweeter spirit in the home. Thomas surprised Elaine by buying her a refrigerator with money he had saved from not smoking. It was an old, American-made model with the large coils on top. It was probably fifty years old, but it worked, and it made cold air. To them it was a miracle. Their kitchen was so small that they had to put it in the living room, where they proudly showed the Elders the carton of milk for Ellie.

Each day, Ellie spoke a little more until she practically became a jabber box. Sam had to bring trinkets for her to play with just to keep her quiet. Without exception, if Sam was in the room, she was in his lap. He loved little Ellie, and his heart ached for her. She was so small, and her heart so hungry, that he wished he could give something to feed her body and soul all the nourishment she had missed in her short life.

With the extra money they had from not smoking, they ate better, and Ellie began to grow. Elaine sewed her a new dress, and she began to laugh and play like a normal child. Every once in a while, she lapsed into the tie-twisting silence, but that became less frequent, and eventually vanished.

The branch nearly swallowed the Knights whole. They lavished unfailing love upon them. In a short time, the Knights were friends with everyone and would have continued to attend church even if they had been denied baptism. Sam watched all this with a sense of wonder and thought about how this little branch, a thousand miles from anywhere, was more like Zion than any place he had ever been.

The Knights were baptized exactly four weeks from the night of the botched family home evening. Sam baptized Thomas, and Elder Palmer baptized Elaine. The entire branch was there. Every priesthood holder present stood to confirm them. It was a token of the absolute unity they felt one toward another.

Afterward, they held a dinner party to celebrate. Ellie ate about half the food on the table. Her parents consumed as much love and fellowship as their souls could absorb.

The next Sunday, Thomas was ordained a deacon, and he helped pass the sacrament. Tears streamed down Sister Knight's face throughout the entire service. Her eyes were glued to him as he moved reverently from row to row. It was as if she were repeatedly shouting, "I love you! I love you!" Everyone in the chapel sensed it, and few eyes were dry, including Sam's.

The following Monday, they met with the Knights. They taught them how to study the scriptures and how to use the index and Bible dictionary. It was a fun meeting. When they were about to leave, a feeling of concern came over Sam.

"Brother and Sister Knight, I have a concern I want to share with you."

"Sure, Elder. What's on your mind?" Brother Knight replied. "World-wide, about half the people who are baptized later fall away."

"Oh, I'm surprised," Sister Knight said. "I can't imagine anyone falling away."

"I know what you mean," Sam agreed. "However, you can also imagine that your joining the Church is a great disappointment to Satan."

"I hadn't really thought of it that way. Well, let the old bugger be disappointed. I don't care," Brother Knight said, laughing.

"Still, I feel impressed to tell you that I have observed a particular pattern that Satan seems to use in trying to get people to leave the Church. It usually starts by someone giving them anti-Mormon literature. So, I want you to tell me when that happens, okay?"

"As a matter of fact, it has already happened," Sister Knight said as she stood and walked out of sight. In a few seconds, she returned with a handful of pamphlets. "My mom and dad brought these over. We weren't going to read them, but I did anyway, and they are disturbing. I just figured they were lies, but even still, it makes one wonder about things. Did I do wrong by reading them?"

"No, let's talk about your questions. It's like I said, apostasy usually starts this way. You can just accept it as a witness that you have done the right thing. The gospel is true, but Satan has a plan that works to deceive people from the truth—so he uses it over and over."

"We can talk about the anti-literature in a minute. I'm curious, what's the next thing that usually happens?" Sister Knight wanted to know. She picked up a pad and began making notes.

"Usually, the next thing is that the new member is offended by a member of the Church. This is a big one and usually works. The members of the Church are wonderful, but they are just people, and Satan can usually get one of them to give an offense. Many new members leave because they are offended or embarrassed. When it happens, you have to overlook it, forgive them, and go on."

"Okay, we'll let you know when that one happens. What's next?"

"Next, people come across doctrine they thought they understood, but they find out it's different than they thought, which challenges their testimonies. When that happens, you need to fast and pray and perhaps get some council from Church leaders. The Church is true, and the doctrine is beautifully complete. You just have to be humble enough to have the faith that our understanding of it is never complete."

"That's a good one. Okay, what's next?"

"Well, at some point, a person in a position of leadership will make an error or even commit a sin against the new member. At least, this may appear to be the case. The key to overcoming this is to forgive the leader and allow him to be human and make mistakes. Sometimes this one gets harder when they don't seem to be repenting. Even then, the principle is the same. We have to forgive, and we have to remember that the truthfulness of the Church does not crumble because a leader makes a mistake."

"Well of course not," she asserted. "Okay, what's next?"

"From here, I don't know of any particular pattern. By this time, you should be strong enough in the faith that you can handle most anything that comes along. Just remember that your faith and testimony are more important than anything else, and never sacrifice them to justify your pride or punish another for some offense."

It was barely two weeks later when both the Knights came up to the Elders outside the church. They seemed excited to get them where they could talk privately.

"Guess what, Elders," Sister Knight said excitedly, placing a hand on each of their arms. "It happened! Someone offended me and embarrassed me right in Relief Society. I gave the opening prayer, and the lesson was on prayer and about not doing almost everything I had done. I was so embarrassed! It was awful, and for a few minutes, I thought about stomping out of the room and never coming back. Then I remembered what you told me, and I walked right up to that sister and asked her to forgive me for saying the prayer wrong. She was surprised, because she didn't realize she had offended me. She got this look on her face of total embarrassment when she realized what she had done. She said she was thinking about her lesson during the prayer and hadn't really heard it. She was so ashamed and asked me to forgive her. We hugged and are friends now. It was wonderful, and I am so grateful for the warning. We are going to watch closely for those other things and not let them throw us off. Just thought you'd like to know!"

* * *

In the Southern Hemisphere, winter comes in May and lasts for several months. Winter consists of two months of rain, sheet lightning, terrifying thunderstorms, and wind. The temperature never drops below 50 degrees and the humidity not below 80 percent. The first rainstorm of the season caught Sam and Elder Palmer out walking.

The rain hit the pavement so hard that it bounced back up. They ran nearly a mile home, arriving thoroughly soaked.

When they were almost there, a clap of thunder sounded above them, and a flash of lightning exploded in the sky from east to west and rolled horizontally along the underside of the clouds until the entire sky was a huge, dazzling, blinding electrical discharge. In less than a heartbeat, it had roared across the sky from north to south with a crackling scream that was terrifying. Seconds later, Sam was lying on his face, covering his head with his arms, and Elder Palmer was kneeling beside him, his face a sheet of white, his hair standing on end.

"What was that?" Sam yelled.

"Satan!" Palmer yelled back, only half joking.

"Run!" they cried together, and they ran the remaining several blocks home, half crouching as they went. Each time the sheet lightning exploded over them, they fought the urge to hit the ground. They found out later that sheet lightning is one of the most spectacular and least dangerous of lightning phenomenon.

They dried off in their room and put on dry clothes, except that clothing is never dry in 90 percent humidity.

In a tropical country like Africa, homes are not heated. The inside of the house was the exact temperature as outside. They shivered in their damp clothing as they tried to study the scriptures. When they finally went to bed, the thin blankets did nothing to warm them. After a few hours, Sam got back up and pulled a rug off the floor onto his bed. He began to warm a bit after that, and he finally slept. He was still cold when he awoke. His first thoughts were of a hot bath, and he hurried to draw the water. In Africa, trees and lumber are scarce, and homes are constructed of brick and concrete. The bathtub sat on a concrete floor, and by the time he climbed in, the water was already lukewarm. Even filled with hot water, the tub was cold on the bottom. Before he climbed out, he felt colder than when he had gotten in. He hurriedly toweled off in the cold room, put on damp clothing, and shivered the entire day.

Sam had never been so cold in his life. The only time he got warm was when they walked briskly to their tracting area. As soon as they stopped, however, the breeze would whip through their damp clothing and the cold would return. Being inside a house made no difference. Most homes were not made tight against the wind. The main rooms were open at the eves of the roof to let air circulate. To seal a house tightly was to condemn it to destruction by mildew and mold. The doors had no thresholds to keep out the breeze. Even in snowstorms and subzero temperatures at home he had not felt this cold this long. The next time the district leader came around, he informed the Elders that he had challenged the city basketball team to a game. Sam couldn't believe his ears. Elder Tingley was tall and wiry and had played basketball in college. His companion was short and quick and almost as good as Tingley. Sam had never played basketball because of his poor vision. Elder Palmer said that Sam could hit the basket if he tried hard enough. Two other missionaries were coming from a neighboring town to join them. The only reason Sam consented to this humiliation was that he figured it was a good way to get warm.

The game was scheduled for the following Monday. They arrived at the field house, which contained a nice basketball court and bleachers.

The stands were packed with townspeople. Almost all the members of the Church came, along with several hundred others.

Someone handed him the local newspaper. The front page held a story about the "Americans" challenging the local team. The article only mentioned in passing that they were all missionaries for the Church.

Since there were six players, Sam took a welcome position on the bench. He was grateful, because his basketball skills were badly underdeveloped.

The referee blew the whistle, and Elder Tingley out-jumped the other center and grabbed the ball. In less than thirty seconds, he flew to the other end of the court and made a basket.

The other team put two players on him, and it was the last free basket he got. The other team was good, and in less time than Sam believed possible, they had scored three baskets. The score was 6–2.

Tingley was all over the court, running constantly, shooting every time he got the ball. But he was double-teamed, and few of his efforts were fruitful. The other four missionaries on the court did almost nothing. When the score hit 12–4, Elder Palmer called a time out.

Elder Palmer quietly scolded Elder Tingley for trying to win the game by himself. Elder Tingley nodded, sweat running down his face. Elder Palmer suggested that they pass the ball around and see what the other members of the team could do. He mentioned that if he was outside the key, Elder Tingley should toss him the ball. He wouldn't let them down.

The ball went to Tingley, who dribbled it to the key, quickly became surrounded, and bounced the ball to Palmer who was standing at the top of the key. Elder Palmer tossed the ball toward the hoop as if it were a wad of paper. The ball swished through the hoop.

The other team missed their shot, and the ball came back to their end. Palmer had stayed about half court. Tingley's companion rebounded, and tossed the ball to Palmer. He turned, took two steps, and swished the ball.

As the game progressed, the strategy became one of getting the ball to Palmer, who generally stayed between half-court and the key.

He hit the vast majority of the shots he attempted, some of them from nearly half court. When the other team ganged up on Palmer, he passed the ball to Tingley, who easily made the open shots in the key. The other Elders dribbled and passed and had opportunities to make a few baskets themselves. The crowd roared with approval. They cheered every time either team made a basket. They had come to watch basketball, and who won was secondary to the fact that this was real entertainment, real people, and real basketball.

By half time, Tingley insisted Sam go in for him. Sweat was pouring down his face, and he was approaching exhaustion. Sam huddled with the guys and only made one request. "Throw the ball to me slowly, or bounce it, or I won't even catch it." In the first few seconds of his entering the game, Palmer bounced the ball to Sam. He turned and made a basket. The ball rolled around the rim sloppily and went it, but it was worth as many points as Palmer's swishes. It was the first basket Sam had ever made in his life, and the only basketball game he'd ever participated in. It felt electric to hear the crowd roar their approval. Sam was also flattered when two of the other team members started guarding him. However, they soon figured out that he was no threat and went back to Palmer. As soon as he was not guarded, Sam's team members tossed him the ball, and he made another sloppy basket.

Sam stayed in nearly the entire quarter, during which time the other team got ahead. He really wasn't much help, and the other team easily stole from him. He learned by sad experience what double-dribbling, traveling, and a host of other violations were, but no one became impatient or ordered him off the floor. As he became familiar with the ball and his own ability to actually catch it, he played in earnest and ran until his legs were quivery. In the end, he made six baskets, which was a lifetime high for him.

When Elder Tingley replaced him, the score was 35–47 in the other team's favor. It was the fourth quarter, and everyone was exhausted.

Happy to be back on the bench, Sam wiped sweat from his face and cheered the guys on. Tingley passed the ball more than he shot it, and Palmer continued to swish nearly every shot he threw. The other team began surrounding Palmer, and the other missionaries took advantage of the open court. When the game ended, they lost by a decent margin of 62–65. The crowd roared and ran out onto the floor. The Elders were slapped on the backs until it hurt, but the crowd was delighted. Everyone who shook the Elders' hands got a Joseph Smith tract. It was unusual missionary work, but in that setting, the people thanked them like they had received a precious, American-made souvenir for free.

When the crowd started thinning out, the other team came over and enthusiastically shook their hands. They said repeatedly that they were amazed they had beaten a team from America. They were so impressed with themselves that no one had the heart to tell them that they were just a few missionaries and not the Harlem Globetrotters.

Sam and Elder Palmer baptized three more families before Sam was transferred. One of them was Sister Knight's Jehovah's Witnesses parents.

In all, they spent eight months together, and both of them wept when the letter came announcing Sam's transfer. The branch quickly organized a going-away picnic at the chapel. After the meal, they herded Sam to the organ and he played for nearly two hours while the Saints of God sang with great zeal.

Finally, Sam played "God Be with You Till We Meet Again." He could barely see the music for the tears in his eyes. He played the last verse almost without anyone singing, for their hearts were too tearful to make more than a whisper. He closed the organ lid and slid from the bench. He quickly shook every hand, hugged those closest to his soul, kissed sweet Ellie on the cheek, and slipped out into the night. His heart was soaring with both rejoicing and anguish. He loved these people and knew he had righteously served the Lord among them. He also knew that in his lifetime, he would never again visit this part of Zion.

10

A DISTANT MELODY

The train left Bulawayo on April 28, 1975, and headed south.

During his previous train ride to Rhodesia, Sam had gotten sick from coal smoke. It was approaching winter again, and Sam was dreading the ride and breathing coal smoke and fumes for five days. However, the weather was cool, and the windows were kept closed. His cabin had a heater in it, which actually blew warm air. He huddled by the register and let the warm air blow up his pant legs. It felt sweeter than any feeling he could remember. Every few seconds his body shivered with delight.

On the second day, late in the afternoon, the train suddenly lurched. Sam felt the wheels beneath his car lock up and scream in protest. He grabbed onto the seat for support. A series of sharp jolts was followed by his car pitching to the left. For a moment, it felt like the car might roll onto its side, but then it settled back. A series of minor jolts followed in rapid succession as the cars behind slammed into the couplings. A large escape of steam roared from the engine a few cars ahead, and the heater quit blowing hot air. That made Sam feel like crying. Simultaneously, the lights in the train went out.

Sam watched out the window as armed guards ran to positions beside the train and patrolled back and forth. Sam pushed open the sliding door to his cabin and took a single step into the hallway beyond.

Other people were emerging into the hall, some pressing bandages to their heads or other injured areas. He stooped to look out the windows and could clearly see the engine lying nearly on its side a short distance from his car. The train had derailed. The car immediately following the engine was nearly on its side. His car was the first one still upright. Nearly an hour later, the conductor came through his car. He explained what had happened. The rails had been sabotaged, and the engine was hopelessly derailed. They had radioed for assistance and expected another train by morning. The conductor said people from the forward cars had to be evacuated and asked if some could join Sam. Sam had a private berth, but his room included four seats and four beds. He agreed without hesitation. The Church had bought the three extra tickets to his cabin to give him privacy. The thinking was, rather than send another missionary along to be his companion, keeping him isolated on the train would serve the same purpose. Consequently, Sam had three empty seats in a nearly-full train.

In just a few minutes, the conductor introduced him to two young women, Marcia and Melody MacUlvaney. The girls were sisters, traveling to boarding school in Cape Town. Both were frightened and refused to share his cabin. Marcia was eighteen, and Melody, sixteen. They insisted that they would have nothing less than a private cabin.

"I understand your concerns," the conductor said with thinly veiled impatience. "However, there are only three sleeper cars on this train, and yours is lying on its side, as you recall. The third one is full, and this one has two rooms with space. The other one has two young men your age, also traveling away to school. This gentleman is an American mission-ary—a Mormon. They have the highest moral decency, and I trust you would be best served here than in with the other two gentlemen, who are in the process of getting drunk even as we speak. There simply are no other options." So saying, the conductor threw up his hands without waiting for a reply, and stomped away.

The girls stood outside Sam's cabin, still uncertain what to do. Sam cor-rectly interpreted the look on their faces as terror, and stood on impulse.

"Forgive me. I'm not thinking clearly," Sam said. "I'll go spend the night with the college students, and you two take my cabin. That will be better, I think. Then you won't be afraid to have me here with you." Mar-cia nodded, and Melody shook her head. They both wore long, brown riding coats that covered them from neck to ankle, and huge wool caps and gloves. They were dressed warm enough for Alaska, let alone Africa. The few soft curls of hair that hung from their hats were light brown. He could see very little of their faces because of their large caps.

It was Melody, the younger, who finally spoke. Her voice quivered as she spoke, but the words were calm. "No. I should be ashamed to put you out of your own cabin to accommodate us. No, I think not. You are kind to offer, and your kindness settles my fears somewhat. I think perhaps we can trust the American missionary. Ne?" she asked, turning to her sister. She spoke with a musical, lilting accent some British people acquire after living in Rhodesia. Her accent almost sounded Australian.

Her sister merely walked past Sam, sat down primly, and turned her face toward the window. Sam couldn't tell if she was disappointed, angry, or terrified. Melody sat beside her and pulled off her large wool cap. A tidal wave of hair spilled over her shoulders and flowed nearly to her waist. Sam was amazed so much hair could have been inside that cap. She pushed the flows of hair away to reveal an unusually beautiful face. Her eyes were dark brown, her nose small and turned upward. Her lips were full and seemed as if they might be comfortable with laughter and smiles.

Under different circumstances, he would have found himself smitten by her beauty. The thought didn't occur to him that her beauty was anything other than good looks, which, under the circumstances were meaningless to him since he was a missionary. Before sitting, he pulled the door to their cabin closed and latched it. He took the seat opposite the girls. The cabin was sufficiently small that their knees were nearly touching.

Sam felt the chill seeping into the cabin and pulled his jacket from his bag. Without heat in the train, it was going to be a cold night. It was only a few hours before dark, and without the engine running, there would be no electric lights in the train. The guards were building large fires on both sides of the train to keep the night from overtaking them entirely.

Before there was time for an awkward silence to develop, the lock on the door spun open, and the conductor shoved the girls' bags into the cabin, banging them against their legs. Sam helped Melody stack the bags in the luggage rack overhead. Amid the luggage were two violin cases. He picked up the first and held it for a few moments before carefully placing it on top of their other luggage.

Melody cocked her head inquisitively. "Do you play?" she asked. "Not really. A close friend showed me a few things, and I tinkered around. But I've never had any lessons or anything."

"I see," she replied, disappointment in her voice. There was a meaningful pause before she continued. "We are going away to continue our studies on the violin. Papa wants us to play professionally. Mama played beautifully before . . . anyway, we are going to school at Jan Smutt's Conservatory of Music. So, you might say, we love and hate the bloody things."

This earned a snort from Marcia. In this culture, bloody was a curse worthy of a hardened criminal, not a proper young woman on her way to boarding school. Melody seemed unrepentant, and Sam smiled in response.

"Good," she responded resolutely. "You're not a prude. I just wanted to see if you were going to lecture me on cursing."

"Did I pass the test or fail it?" Sam asked suspiciously.

"Fail," Marcia muttered simultaneously with Melody's "passed."

Sam chuckled. At that instant a rifle fired, and then another. With each report, Marcia slumped lower and lower in her seat, and Melody flinched as if she herself had been shot. Sam wasn't sure whether to be scared or curious. After a moment, another detonation sounded from the other side of the train. Sam could hear someone in the car behind him begin to cry. It sounded like a small child. Someone cursed in the distance, and something banged inside the train. It sounded more like someone threw some baggage around than anything more dangerous, but it had an electric effect on the passengers.

Panic seemed to become palpable, and people were running in the hall outside their door. Voices shouted, demanding explanations. Melody looked up at him anxiously. A tear slipped down her cheek. At that moment, the door to their cabin was wrenched open.

Two young men teetered in the opening. One had a bottle clutched tightly in his hand. They were drunk.

"Came to see if you ladies," he slurred the word sarcastically, "needed some comforting?"

"Go away, Kirt," Marcia said sternly. "We don't want anything to do with you."

"Why not?" he demanded. "Oh, I see, you got some other dandy to twattle with, then?" he said, motioning toward Sam.

"Don't be rude, Kirt," Melody demanded. "This gentleman is a Mormon missionary, and much more pleasant company than you and your liquor." The latter she said with a poisonous tone to her voice.

"Yes, well, I promised your father I'd take care of you two, so you're coming back to my cabin. We can keep each other safe and warm— and whatever else comes to mind." The man behind Kirt laughed drunkenly.

In a single motion, Kirt stepped into the room and grabbed Melody's arm. She struggled to free herself but could not. He pulled her to her feet. At exactly that same moment, Sam came to his feet, his heart pounding, his fists doubled. He was furious, and every muscle was tensed for battle. He took a step forward but was brought short by a blow to the chest, not from any visible source. It felt as if he had run into a wall of solid air. It brought no pain, but had the effect of completely stopping him. A feeling of calm swept over him, and he raised his arm to the square.

Kirt was shouting and Melody screaming protests so that neither of them heard him say, "In the name of Jesus Christ, and by virtue of the Melchizedek Priesthood, I command you to come out of him and trouble us no further."

Whether Kirt heard it or not, it had an immediate effect. He suddenly released his hold on Melody and staggered back, shaking his head as if dazed. He turned his eyes toward them, and Sam saw confusion and remorse in them.

"Melody . . . what?" Kirt stammered as Sam turned him toward the door and helped him out. In seconds, it was over, and the door was shut. Sam fiddled with the locks until he found the one that could not be opened from the outside. He slammed it home with finality. He was getting tired of the door bursting open. Besides, there was near pandemonium in the hall. People were running in both directions, knocking one another down in the narrow passageway.

When he sat again, Melody had a look of confusion on her face, but Marcia was staring at him with piercing brown eyes. He realized that she had heard every word. Without preamble, she said, "You cast an evil spirit out of him, didn't you." It was not a question.

Sam didn't know what to say. He wanted to explain, to tell them about the priesthood, but didn't know where to start. Just then, another rifle fired, and someone started fighting in the hall. The train jolted as bodies grappled not far from their door. Men cursed, and the sound of blows echoed in the train.

On impulse, Sam stood and quickly strode to the violins. "May I?" he asked. Melody nodded, and Sam retrieved one of the violin cases. He opened it to find an expensive instrument neatly packed in velvet. He picked it up and strummed the strings. The instrument was in perfect tune. It smelled of wax as he tucked it under his chin. He pulled the bow across the strings and made a long, solemn tone. Then he slowly began to play the only tune that came to mind, "Abide with Me; 'Tis Eventide." He played slowly, carefully, his fingers unsure what to do next. He was grateful to find that even though his fingers may be unsure, his soul was not, and the music swelled within him, flowing out of the little violin. He played with feeling, and peace settled over him.

Somewhere in the middle of the song, the brawl in the hallway stopped abruptly. Sam switched to another hymn and played with deep feeling. After two or three hymns, he stopped. The silence in the train was almost as if everything outside their door had ceased to exist. Even the crying in the adjacent cabin had stopped. From far away, a small, frightened voice called, "Sing Amazing Grace."

Sam loved that song. He played it with a sense of joy, and was vaguely aware of voices singing in the distance. Marcia stood and retrieved the other case as he played. She lovingly lifted the instrument and tuned it quietly. Afterward, she handed it to Melody, who tucked it under her chin.

Sam began the second verse as Melody played a quiet harmony. It was the most beautiful thing he had ever heard. He watched her eyes close and felt the power of her love for the instrument she held. She played with great skill, her touch sure and masterful. She allowed the harmony to flow unrestrained. The complexity and unabashed beauty of her music made Sam's contribution seem rather amateurish; yet her powerful music was like a full orchestration, the perfect accompaniment to Sam's simple melody.

Another request came from outside the train. The name of the song was French, and unfamiliar to Sam. Melody smiled and pulled the bow across the strings in quick, sure strokes. A joyful melody danced through the train, lifting hearts and causing toes to tap everywhere.

After the tune capered to its conclusion, someone requested "I Am a Child of God." Sam knew the person must be a Latter-day Saint, and it warmed his heart. He lifted the bow and played with a joyful heart. Melody listened carefully and joined him on the second verse, again quietly playing harmony. It was breathtakingly beautiful. The person who had made the request began to sing in a powerful tenor voice. The words of the precious hymn rolled through the train like a summer breeze. Peace settled upon them. Few even noticed the next few rifle shots. Sam and Melody certainly did not. All they heard was the music in their souls as it spilled from the strings.

They played for over an hour, mostly answering requests shouted from their unseen audience. They played until someone rapped on their door. It was the steward, who handed them a tray of bread, cheese, and mineral water. A single candle burned in the middle of the tray. Darkness had descended completely during their playing, and the candle brought a cheery glow to the room.

As they unfolded the table from the wall, the steward explained that the rifle shots were intended to keep lions and hyenas at bay. If they did not fire periodically, they would sneak up on the train. He told them to ignore the intermittent shots. Sam accepted the explanation, yet wondered what threat wild animals could be as long as they remained inside the train. He wondered if there wasn't another explanation.

They were hungry, and the food was unexpected and welcome. They ate in silence. By now, it was dark outside, and people were settling down. Sam could hear others pulling the bunks down in adjoining cabins. The steward came and showed them how to pull down their beds. There was a moment of awkwardness after he left. Sam excused himself and walked the length of the train. Candles had been left burning at intervals in the hallway. With darkness on every side being haltingly held back by the flickering candle glow, Sam felt as if he were inside a medieval castle.

Everywhere he went, people were humming to themselves and speaking in hushed voices, a sweet contrast to the previous sounds of terror. The effect of the music upon the people had been magical. They, of course, had no idea that Sam and Melody had played the music. It was somewhat mystical to walk the halls, nearly invisible in the darkness, and enjoy the peaceful effect of his music. What the people could not guess though, Sam thought, was that the peace they felt did not come from the music at all; it came from God. The music had only opened their hearts to the divine. Praising the music for calming their souls would have been like applauding the velvet curtain at a performance. The curtain only opened their view; it was the Master Musician who performed the miracle.

When Sam returned, Marcia and Melody were both in bed, their coats and dresses hung on hooks on the wall. He pulled off his shoes and tie, and climbed into bed fully clothed. There were extra blankets, and in a few minutes, he was warm and surprisingly comfortable. He could hear the girls' breathing slowing and deepening. He blew out the candle.

From the darkness, a soft voice asked him, "What did you do to Kirt?"

He could not be sure which of them asked the question, but he was fairly certain it was Marcia. "I relieved him of his motivation to hurt," Sam responded.

"You mean you cast an evil spirit out from him, ne?" she asked, using a colloquial expression of polite inquiry, which roughly meant, "Is this not true?"

"That's one way to put it, I guess," Sam replied. He knew evil spirits afflicted people but was completely aware of his imperfect knowledge concerning them. This was only the second time he had used the priesthood to cast one out, and he was not exactly sure about what he had done. He only knew that he did what he was prompted to do.

"Why? Why do that instead of fighting him? You are bigger and look capable."

Sam thought about this. It was actually a good question, and he didn't have an immediate answer. When the answer did come, it was just as informative to him as it was to Marcia.

"To be a disciple is to do the bidding of the master. I did as I was directed to do by the authority of Him who directed me. Nothing more."

There was a long pause before Melody asked, "I didn't know anyone could command evil spirits to depart in these times. I thought that all ended with Bible times."

So Melody was awake as well! Sam waited until the right answer formed in his heart. It was important to him to give them the right explanation.

"It did," he replied. "It was lost shortly after that and was not on the earth again until a new prophet was called in 1820. As a missionary and Elder of that restored Church, I hold the authority of the priesthood, which has been passed down from that new prophet to this day. It's a wonderful thing. If you like, I will tell you about it in the morning."

Silence reigned for a few minutes. Then he heard, "Sam?"

"Yes, Melody?"

"Can such an explanation wait until the morning? I think I should not be able to sleep for wondering what this all means. Would it be too much of an imposition to ask you to explain tonight, please?"

Sam was still quietly explaining the restoration of the gospel as the sky began to lighten outside. He realized with a start that he had been teaching and testifying the entire night. He started to apologize as he heard Marcia yawn, but they both urged him to continue. He concluded by bearing his testimony and promising the girls that he would continue after a few hours' sleep.

It was the most peaceful sleep he had ever had. The Holy Spirit blessed their little cabin with its sweet presence, and they slept the sleep of angels.

* * *

Sam awoke with a start to a sudden volley of gunfire. He rolled from his bunk and hopped to the floor. He was surprised to see his breath in the morning air. He raised a blind just as another volley of gunfire exploded from the small circle of men guarding the train. At that moment, he heard something thud against the train, and a split second later, the distant report of a gun. The guards answered with a volley. Silence followed for a few seconds before a spatter of bullets again thudded into the train. He heard people shouting in adjoining cars, and several people screamed.

Marcia and Melody tumbled from their bunks and pulled their dresses on over their heads. Sam kept his back turned, intent on watching the day dawn on the drama outside his window.

He noticed for the first time that they were in a large valley surrounded by low, rolling hills. The train track cut through the lush desert on a raised bed of red gravel about three feet high. A short distance beyond the gravel pad, the bush began abruptly. What everyone called bushes were actually small trees, each somewhat taller than a man. The larger bushes were a milky, olive green, with darker green plants growing in clumps closer to the ground. The ground was covered with a patchwork of grasses and wildflowers.

The guards were kneeling on the gravel pad to give them the advantage of height. They had brought some wooden crates from the train to act as a barrier to protect them. The closest guard was only about six feet from his window.

While he was observing this, he spotted a figure darting between the bushes in the distance. The guards responded by firing toward the figure. Seconds later, the sound of breaking glass was followed by a distant report.

Without warning, about ten men suddenly appeared in the bush, fired at the train, and quickly disappeared. Bullets ricocheted through the air, and glass shattered on the train. A guard near Sam's window lurched backwards, spun in the air, and landed on his face, a red stain quickly forming on his side. He thrashed on the ground for a moment before rolling over onto his back. A similar stain was forming on his shoulder, near his neck. Sam could clearly see his face pinched in pain. The man pulled a white cloth from his pocket and pressed it against his shoulder. It quickly turned red. Another volley from the bush smashed against the train, and the guards began backing from their wooden crates. They grabbed their wounded comrade, and retreated to beneath the train. At least they would have the big steel wheels to give them some safety.

"Sam?"

Sam had momentarily forgotten about the two girls and turned toward them. They were huddled on the floor, against the door, as far from the windows as possible. As he watched, Melody pulled Marcia's head onto her chest and held her, stroking her hair. With each gunshot, Marcia flinched as if she, herself, had been shot. Marcia was immobilized by fear, while her younger sister seemed grimly determined. Melody's face was a study in conflict between terror and icy, cold determination. It created an expression on her face something like a young mother might have while confronting a charging lion to protect her child.

"Sam, aren't you afraid?" Melody asked incredulously, her young voice quivering.

It suddenly occurred to him that it was unwise for him to stand in the window, and he knelt down. He wondered for a moment if he was just too stupid to be afraid or too American to comprehend that people actually attack passenger trains. Maybe he thought he was watching TV and the violence could not get past the glass of the window. Melody's question was a good one, and he pondered his feelings. When he knew the answer, he spoke it.

"No," he said honestly. "I'm not afraid."

At that moment, he heard a whistling sound that grew louder and higher in pitch until it ended in a deafening explosion near the train engine. The entire train shuddered and jolted from the impact. It was the loudest thing Sam had ever heard, and he wondered if he was now permanently deafened. They were only two cars from the engine, and the explosion sounded as if it actually hit the derailed engine. Seconds later, another whistling sound arched toward the rear of the train. It landed farther away, but still the train bounced on the tracks. It seemed their attackers had bigger weapons than rifles. The obvious occurred to Sam and to everyone who was not too terrified to think: their attackers had no particular interest in capturing them alive.

"Why? Why are you not afraid?" Melody asked, ignoring the explosions.

He wondered how to answer her question and waited for the right answer to form in his heart. When it came, it answered his own question as well as hers.

"When I made the decision to be a missionary for the Lord, my father gave me a blessing in the name of Jesus Christ. My dad is a high priest in the Church, a former bishop, and a man I know to be close to God. Among other things, he blessed me that if I was obedient to the commandments and to the promptings of the Holy Spirit, that I would serve a wonderful mission, bless many lives, and return home safely. As he spoke those words, I felt the Holy Spirit confirm their truth. I'm not afraid because I have implicit faith in the promises made to me in His name."

Melody pondered this as another bomb whistled directly overhead and exploded on the far side of the train, not far from their car. The glass on the opposite side of the train shattered with a roar, and the train rocked against the explosion.

Finally, she said, "I envy your faith, Elder Mahoy. I have always believed in Jesus, yet my faith is not sufficient to bring me your sense of safety. I guess my faith just isn't strong enough to know He will keep us safe."

"Many people believe in Christ," Sam replied. "Not many are able to believe Christ."

"I don't understand the difference," Marcia said, turning frightened eyes toward him. Sam was glad to see she was listening.

"Many people believe in Christ and that He is the Savior. What they don't believe is that He will keep His promises. He promises us great blessings if we obey Him and keep His commandments. Many people don't keep His commandments because they don't think He will bless them as promised. They doubt He will give them something as exciting and wonderful as what they think they are getting from their sins, so they keep sinning. If we really believed Christ, we would trust Him to keep His promises. I have the added comfort of having my father give me a blessing in Christ's name, in which I also have great faith. I believe Christ, I guess you might say."

"Okay, I guess I understand that. If we truly believe in Christ, then we should believe He keeps His promises. That feels true. I guess I wish I had a blessing from your father, too, and your faith to believe in it," Melody replied, her eyes lowered.

At that exact moment, a blaze of machine gun fire erupted like the roar of a demon. Bullets impacted the train from one end to the other, and glass exploded into their cabin. Fortunately, it was safety glass and did not cut them, but they were suddenly buried in a avalanche of broken glass. Sam could see a half-dozen bullet holes in the walls not far above their heads. Marcia buried her head in Melody's bosom and trembled there. She was too frightened to scream.

Melody cocked her head to one side and studied Sam through squinted eyes, as if trying to see through him. "You really aren't afraid, are you?" she observed.

Sam did not answer that question. He was thinking of her earlier statement. "Melody, I hold the same priesthood power that my father does. If you want, I could give you a blessing, too. I don't know what its content will be. That's up to the Lord. But I know it will be true, and I know it will help you."

Marcia raised her head and turned her tear-filled eyes toward him. "Oh, please. Please, could you give us your father's blessing?" she implored. Melody merely nodded and smiled weakly.

Sam crawled the short distance that separated them until their knees were touching. He reached out and placed a single hand on Marcia's head. She trembled beneath his hand as she lowered her head onto Melody's chest.

"Marcia, in the name of Jesus Christ, and by the power of the holy Melchizedek priesthood I hold, I give you a blessing of comfort and peace. Fear not the battle of men or the harm they can do. You will live many years beyond this day and will see your dreams fulfilled. You will become a noted musician and teacher of music. In time, you will reflect upon this day as a happy memory and tell it with wonder to your children, about the day God saved you from sure destruction by the power of His arm and simple faith in His love. In the name of Jesus Christ, amen."

Marcia looked up, an expression of wonder in her eyes.

Since Melody was closer, Sam placed both hands on her head. As he did so, he was suddenly filled with glowing warmth and a powerful sense of her magnificent spirit. The impressions that crowded into his mind were so sudden and powerful that he gasped involuntarily. It was as if he knew Melody, perhaps had always known her, and this sudden realization took his breath away. It took him a moment to speak.

"Melody, in the name of Jesus Christ, and by the power of the holy priesthood I hold, I also give you a blessing of peace and comfort. You are a noble daughter of Heavenly Father and a precious spirit in His sight. In order for you to fulfill the measure of your creation, you will be called upon to endure many trials, the present difficulties being a mere shadow of what will follow. You are the first and the last. You are the last to inherit the curse of your fathers, and the first to triumph over it. Your quest will take you to many nations and bring you full circle. When you finally find what you seek, you will have returned to this moment, and it will bring you joy. In the name of Jesus Christ, amen."

She looked deeply into Sam's wet eyes as he took his hands from her head. Her eyes were pooled with tears, and when she blinked, they coursed down her cheeks. A deep feeling unexpectedly stirred within Sam, which he suppressed almost without noticing it. He could not help but feel the familiar sweetness and purity of Melody's spirit, and it thrilled him in a way he had never before experienced.

"Sam, your blessing both comforts and frightens me. Do you understand the words?" Sam merely shook his head no. "I thought not," she continued, "but I felt the warmth and the peace. I believe that what you say will be, and it will bring me joy."

"I think you gave part of Melody's blessing to me," Marcia said. "She's the great musician, and I'm the one who's always getting into trouble." Her voice was brighter, almost peaceful.

Sam smiled but did not answer her. He had given them the blessings the Lord intended. He reached for his scriptures on the seat behind him, opened it to a blank page in the back, and wrote down the two blessings as nearly as he could remember them. When he finished, he signed it, wrote the mission home's address beneath his name, carefully tore it from his scriptures, and handed it to Melody.

She and Marcia read it together.

At that moment, an amplified voice boomed across the desert. The voice spoke in heavily-accented English. Oddly, Sam thought the accent sounded almost Spanish.

"You will be now throwing your guns away now! We have much bombs and will kill you all very much badly! Immediately surrender! Now!"

The guards beneath the train responded by firing. The detonation seemed to come from directly beneath their train car. They fired again and again, and a hail of machine gun bullets riddled the train. Some of them hit below the windows but did not penetrate the thick steel of the old train cars. At that moment, another bomb whistled toward them and exploded outside their window, showering them with dirt through the open windows. Sam's ears were ringing, and he found himself huddling with the girls. They pressed themselves against him and tried to make themselves small. Another bomb exploded a distance away, and then another. Sam did not hear the guards from beneath the train return fire.

Sam could hear men shouting in a foreign language outside the train, while sporadic gunfire came from beneath them. At that moment, a machine gun of much larger caliber belched with a deafening roar. It was so obviously a larger gun that it made the former machine gun sound like a toy. This gun spat bullets in a slower, more booming roar of heavy weaponry. The gun belched in short, authoritative bursts. Sam knew such a gun would easily penetrate the steel of the old train, yet no bullets hit the train. All he could hear were the shouted commands and curses of the men outside.

Suddenly, an engine roared a short distance away, and the big machine gun belched. This new vehicle sped past their car as the big gun bellowed its rage. No bullets hit the train for a full minute, and the shooting from under the train ceased. Sam heard men cheering outside. He crawled toward the window on shattered glass. What he saw outside was the most beautiful sight in the world.

An old vintage, armored World War II personnel carrier spun around on its huge rubber tires, spraying the bush with bullets from twin machine guns mounted on the top. The big gun blazed and threw a flame six feet from the end of the barrel. Off in the bush, Sam could see figures scurrying away from the train. Cheering began up and down the train as more and more people recognized their salvation.

Sam heard the telltale whistle of incoming artillery, and an explosion nearly flipped the old vehicle on its side. It slammed back to the ground, its wheels on one side falling into the bomb crater. It tipped into the crater and sat there immobile as if stunned. There was the whistle of another shell just as all six wheels on the faithful old machine churned the ground. It lurched up out of the hole in a roar of smoke, dust, and bravado. Seconds later, another shell landed in the exact spot where it had been. Sam could see that the left side of the armor was dented in nearly a foot, but the old machine roared ahead, blazing from the twin machine guns overhead. It zigzagged through the bush, firing almost steadily. It was gone nearly half an hour. When it returned, it was nearly destroyed. It limped back to the train, its wheels on the side of the explosion bent and wobbling severely. One of the big guns was drooping as if it had gotten too hot. Its side was pocked with bullet holes, some appearing to almost have penetrated its armor.

Then the big machine halted, spun slowly to face outward, and the motor clanged to a stop. A steel hatch slammed open on top, followed by a blue cloud of smoke. A head appeared in the smoke and looked around. A large man climbed out onto the top of the tank. He looked much too large to have been inside the tank. He was dressed in a khaki-colored uniform and had a huge handlebar mustache. He was broad of shoulder and slim of hip. His whole demeanor was confident and yet shaken. His smile displayed a wide gap between his front teeth. "Daddy!" Melody and Marcia screamed simultaneously, and bolted from the cabin. "Daddy! Daddy!" they cried as they pushed past people in the narrow hallway and leaped from the train to the ground. Sam was just jumping to the ground as their father caught them both. In an effortless move, he lifted them, one in each arm, and swung them around. "Daddy! Daddy!" they cried, holding onto him with all their passion and love.

"I made it!" he bellowed repeatedly in a voice much too loud. "I found my babies in time! I came for you! I did it!" His voice was huge, booming. He made no effort to suppress the tears running down his cheeks.

"Daddy! You came for us! Thank you!" Marcia nearly screamed at him.

"You lost your shoe?" he shouted at her, looking perplexed. "No Daddy, I'm happy you came!"

"What's the same?" he shouted back. The girls gave each other worried looks. "Daddy, what's wrong?"

"This is no time for a song," he shouted, and roared with laughter. Sam tapped Melody on the shoulder. She merely glanced at him. "He's deafened by the gunfire and explosions," he said to her back. She nodded. She had already figured that out.

Melody made hand signs to him, and he nodded. "Yes," he shouted. "The bloody explosion and bloody machine gun bloody deafened me. It will pass. Just give me a few minutes. It better bloody well pass."

Marcia said something about cursing, which he misinterpreted.

She ignored his nonsensical response.

Two other men climbed from the old war machine and were surrounded by cheering people. They were equally deaf but had no difficulty understanding the joy and adulation the people lavished upon them. When everyone on the train had come to thank their rescuers, there were about a hundred and fifty people.

In a few minutes, his hearing improved, and he demanded to speak to the engineer. A man in a conductor's uniform informed him that the engineer had been killed in the wreck. It took a few minutes to get the people back onto the train and to assemble the remaining railroad passengers. Marcia, Melody, and Sam were invited to stay.

Melody introduced Sam while they were waiting for the passengers to return to the train.

"Daddy, this is Elder Sam Mahoy. He took good care of us while you were coming. He is our friend, our very good friend," she added. "Donavon MacUlvaney," he said, taking Sam's hand in a powerful grip. "So, you're the Mormon missionary on the train. I thank you for taking care of my babies. You will find that my gratitude means something, young man. Thank you."

"Pleasure, sir," was all Sam could think to say. A part of him wondered how he knew he was "the" Mormon missionary on the train. He dismissed the thought once the railroad people had gathered. Donavon started speaking without preamble or introduction. "I have just driven over two hundred kilometers. Four vehicles started out, but the rest broke down part way here. Thank God they have weapons and food though, and are expecting reinforcements. My poor vehicle is out of petrol and out of ammunition," he said as he looked at the old armored vehicle. "I'm afraid the old girl has fought her last battle," he added wistfully. Then his demeanor quickly turned businesslike.

"We are in the bush lands of Botswana, as you know. Shortly after the train left Bulawayo, a rebel faction declared civil war and threatened to disrupt transportation. As soon as I heard that, I organized a private force and launched out after this train and my girls. I was afraid I wouldn't get here fast enough. Thank God . . ." his voice trailed off.

"The point is, we can't expect help from Rhodesia, as they are trying to negotiate a treaty with Botswana as we speak. We can't expect help from South Africa, since this is a Rhodesian Express train and they have no legal right to interfere. In short, we're on our own. We can't stay here. The rebels will go for reinforcements, and as soon as they realize I am by myself, they will attack with everything they have. As some of you may have correctly surmised earlier, they are not after hostages. They intend to kill us after they have . . ." Donavon didn't finish the sentence. It required little imagination to understand what he didn't say.

"We must get started immediately. My chums are about a day's march away. If we march all night, we can reach them by late tomorrow. If we stay here, we are surely doomed." A chorus of agreement rose from the passengers.

Sam was about to agree but felt a reluctance flow through him. He pondered this for a moment, trying to determine its origin. He bowed his head and supplicated with all his soul. The stakes were high, and he did not want to misunderstand. He closed his eyes and sought guidance, searching the inner reaches of his soul. A feeling of peace flowed over him, and he rejoiced.

"Sam? Sam?" He started when he realized Melody was speaking to him. He opened his eyes and was startled to realize everyone was looking at him, waiting.

"Sorry," he mumbled.

"Sam, what is it? You look troubled," she asked, placing a hand on his arm solicitously. "I . . ." He wondered what he should say. He didn't know what they should do; he only knew what they shouldn't do. They should not start walking back toward Rhodesia. "I don't think we should start walking toward Rhodesia," he said quietly.

"Why not, man?" Donavon demanded in a booming voice. "We're less than fifty kilometers from the Rhodesian border. We can't stay here, and it's over three-hundred kilometers to South Africa."

"I'm not sure. I only know that we shouldn't go toward Rhodesia."

"Look, lad," Donavon said, his voice lowered in a patronizing way.

"I know you're scared. I am too, but I have been fighting these bloody rebels for over twenty years. I know how they think. They'll be back about daylight tomorrow morning. There are food, ammunition, and friends less than fifty clicks from here. Logic dictates that we go that direction."

"I'm not speaking of logic. I'm saying I feel that we should not head north. If we must leave, it should be to the south."

"What you're saying doesn't make sense, lad."

"I'm not claiming it does. I'm just saying it's the right thing to do."

"Well, okay. Let's put it to a vote." He raised his voice. "All who want to head north, raise your hand." Everyone except Sam raised his or her hand.

"All who want to go south, raise your hand." Sam timidly raised his hand. He was the only one. However, just as Donavon was about to speak, Melody raised her hand.

"Melody, what are you doing, baby? You're coming with me, back home," Donavon thundered, his voice sure and demanding.

Melody cleared her throat, all the time looking steadfastly on Sam. Without lowering her hand, she said, "I'm going with Sam, Daddy. You take the others and go north."

"But why?" he thundered. "The Mormon doesn't know this country. I do. I came to take you home, and that's what I'm going to do," he concluded with finality.

Without looking away from Sam, she said. "Are you prepared to hogtie me and carry me screaming and kicking for fifty kilometers? No? Then I'll be going with Sam."

"Tell me why. At least give me the satisfaction of explaining your foolishness. Give me something to write on your grave marker, at least," he concluded with frustration.

"Daddy, forgive me. I trust you, and I'm so grateful you came for us. But, you see, before you saved us, there were bombs bursting, and machine guns firing, and people screaming, and I was terrified. But Sam wasn't. I asked him why, and he said because he knew we were going to be safe. Daddy, he knew something that seemed illogical at the time. He believed something that seemed foolish and impossible."

Donavon grunted, as if to say that what Sam was now going to do was foolish as well.

Melody ignored her father. "When Sam told us those things, he had a particular look on his face, a look of calmness and peace. He has that same look now. Look at him, and you'll see it."

"I don't see a bloody thing. I see a bleedin' Yank Mormon fool. That's what I see." Donavon leered at Sam, as if pretending to see beyond the obvious.

Sam was surprised at Melody's words, yet they were true. He didn't want to be their leader or to be contrary to Donavon. He just knew as surely as he knew anything that he should not be going north with them. If necessary, he would remain here alone. While these thoughts were going through his mind, Donavon's expression changed and softened somehow.

Unexpectedly, Marcia turned toward her dad. "I'm staying with Elder Sam too. I can see that expression, same as before. Daddy, please don't make us go north. I'm afraid we'll all be killed. Do what Sam says. Please," she pleaded.

"Bloody!" Donavon exploded. He scrubbed his face with both hands, as if dry-washing it. "You two stubborn women will be the death of me. You're just like your mother, God rest her sweet soul. And you, Sam the Mormon, are going to be the death of us all. If you are wrong, we are all dead. You know I won't leave my babies. But you'd better know this, if you're wrong, I'm going to save my last bullet and put it between your eyes. Do you understand me?"

Sam swallowed hard. This was a serious threat. He considered apologizing, or offering a compromise, or waffling somehow, but he knew he should not. Instead, he excused himself and walked out into the bush. When he had gone a short distance and was beyond hearing, he knelt upon the sandy red soil and prayed with all the energy of his soul. It seemed as if a long time elapsed before he felt comfortable with what he must do. He returned to the train, and found Donavon, who was still grumbling.

"Donavon? I wish to travel south. Since Melody and Marcia are planning to come with me, and I know nothing about the bush or survival in the bush, I would be very grateful for your company and leadership. I don't mean to cause you problems, and I am humbly asking for your help and protection."

Donavon stood and faced him. A multitude of expressions crossed his face before he merely nodded. He turned toward the train employees. "Tell the passengers I am leaving to travel south. I will conduct anyone who wishes to go with me. Tell them no guarantees. It will be hard and dangerous but less dangerous than staying here. Tell them if they wish to travel north, they should just follow my old tracks. Divide whatever food is left equally among the passengers. We leave in thirty minutes."

The group scattered to pass the word. Melody and Marcia returned to the train to get spare clothes and their violins. Sam tied some things into a small bundle around his scriptures. He picked up his coat, camera, and an extra roll of film. Everything else would have to catch up with him later, if ever.

It was nearly noon by the time they struck out. Approximately half the passengers on the train joined them. About fifty people remained aboard the train, and about twenty people started north, toward Rhodesia. Most of the railroad employees remained with the train.

Of the nearly seventy-five people in their group going south, well over half were black. They picked up their bundles of food, balanced their baggage on their heads, and strode off with an easy gate. They hummed or sang as they walked and seemed perfectly at ease. Sam picked up a box filled with loaves of bread and carried it under one arm. Under his other arm, he held his bundle of clothes. In just a few minutes, his arms were aching, and he was struggling to hold onto the box. A young African girl caught up with him and through hand signals made him understand that she wished to carry the box. Though awkward, it wasn't heavy, and Sam felt silly surrendering it to a young woman. She persisted, and he handed it to her. She wrapped a sweater around the top of her head and deftly balanced the box on her head. She smiled at him, took her own small bundle of clothes, and tossed it onto the top of the box. It landed neatly in the middle of the box. With one hand on a corner to steady it as she turned, she began walking briskly away. He smiled and caught up with Melody.

They walked along the train tracks, stepping from tie to tie. The black folks seemed to prefer walking among the bushes, weaving in and out to make their way. He could see parcels bouncing just above the tops of the bushes on both sides of the tracks. Donavon led the way, walking at a moderate pace. His eyes constantly scanned the countryside, but they heard and saw nothing but an endless reach of train track and desert. As it began to grow dark, they stopped and built small fires.

Donavon insisted that they build small, smokeless fires. He had to show them how. The blacks already knew how and deftly built small cook fires. They passed out their meager rations. Sam got two slices of bread and a tin of sardines. He hated sardines, but he was so hungry they actually tasted good. He sat by Melody as they ate.

During the entire hour that they ate and rested, neither of them spoke. But they communicated just the same. It was spiritual and deeply personal. When it was time to leave, Donavon carefully extinguished their campfires and strode off into the twilight. At first, Sam found it impossible to walk on the ties in the darkness, but he soon got the rhythm of it and found that he could do pretty well. Eventually, he ended up holding Marcia's right hand and Melody's left. Between them, they could keep lined up on the tracks and stop each other from falling and hurting themselves.

When daylight finally peeked above the horizon, they were bone weary, and their ankles, shins, and knees were scraped and raw from numerous falls. Donavon called a halt, and again they built small fires.

Sam nibbled on bread while Melody slept against his shoulder. Marcia found her father and curled up beside him. He let them sleep for several hours. Sam awoke to the feeling of warmth on his face. He opened his eyes to broad daylight and the welcoming African sun.

Melody had slumped to the ground, her head resting lightly in his lap. He resisted the urge to stroke her hair. Instead, he took off his jacket and laid it over her. She stirred and seemed to sleep more peacefully.

They were just beginning to stand and stretch their limbs when Sam heard the distant thrum of a helicopter. Donavon shouted for everyone to get into the bush. They ran into the trees and tried to hide. In a few minutes, a big helicopter passed over them, moving fast and low to the ground. It suddenly looped around and came back to their campsite. Sam could see men through the cockpit glass. A man stood at a machine gun in the open side door. There were no markings on the helicopter other than it being painted in a sand-colored camouflage pattern.

A speaker squawked, and a man's voice boomed across the desert. "Greetings from the South African Air Force. Glad to see you are all right." The voice bore a heavy, South African accent and sounded cheerful. "We will radio in your location and proceed on to the train wreck. Please remain at this location. A train is on its way and should arrive at your position in several hours. You are safe here. Good luck. Goodbye." The big chopper turned and powered away. It was obvious they were in a hurry.

Everyone cheered and hugged each other. Melody hugged Sam and ran to find her father. They built a roaring fire and consumed all the rest of their food and water.

Donavon sought out Sam. He arrived with a daughter on each arm. They sat down by him, and after a few minutes, Donavon handed him another tin of sardines with a smile. It was as much of an apology as the big man had ever made, and it was sufficient.

The train arrived as promised, and concerned men in uniforms helped them onboard. There were no sleeper cars, only military-style coaches. Sam sat by himself, and Donavon and his daughters squeezed onto a bench meant for two. The train was heavily armed, with soldiers in every car. One of the cars ahead of them was a train version of an army tank, with a heavy cannon and many machine guns protruding from slots in its sloping sides. Sam felt perfectly safe and was soon asleep.

He awoke later as the brakes squealed. They ground to a stop. Sam followed Donavon out onto the ground. They had arrived back at the train wreck. The train had been heavily bombed. Only a few people had survived. They told a tearful story of trying to fight against hopeless odds. The helicopter had finally delivered them from certain destruction.

The survivors were helped aboard the train. The big helicopter settled onto a flatcar on the train and refueled. A short time later, it headed north. It was gone just a little over an hour when it returned. It landed back on the flat car, and the train began its journey south. Except for meals, Sam slept the entire trip.

They arrived in Pretoria twenty-three hours later. President and Sister Carlson met Sam and hustled him away. As they were leaving the train station, they unexpectedly ran into Donavon, Marcia, and Melody climbing into a cab. Donavon waved vigorously and trotted up to Sam, the girls close on his heels. Sam introduced him to the Carlsons, and they shook hands. Without preamble, Donavon said, "Did you hear about the group who walked north toward Rhodesia?" Sam shook his head. He was not anxious for more bad news. "They were ambushed. No survivors."

Sam dropped his head, his heart heavy. It seemed such a short time ago.

"When I agreed to follow your illogical suggestion and head south," Donavon said, interrupting his thoughts, "I threatened you. I meant what I said. What I didn't say, however, was that if you were right, I would be profoundly grateful. I owe you a great deal, young man. If there is ever anything I can do for you—anything at all . . ."

"It just so happens there is something," Sam said, pulling his leather-bound Book of Mormon from his small bundle of possessions. He held it out. "I will consider the debt settled if you will read this book and sincerely pray about it." Donavon took the book, looked at the title, and smiled.

"You Mormons don't give up easily do you?" he said, chuckling. "I'll gladly do as you ask. God bless you, Elder Sam Mahoy," he added, as he squeezed Sam's hand without shaking it. The grip was so fierce that it brought tears to Sam's eyes, but they were tears of joy. Donovan shoved a hand into one of the many pockets in his vest and pulled out a tiny parcel tied in a white cloth. He nodded to Sam and handed him the little bundle. Then he spun on a heel and walked briskly away, hands clasped behind his back.

Marcia gave Sam a warm hug and turned away. Melody paused briefly, unsure of what to say. Then she impulsively held him for a while. It was much more than a hug. She kissed him on both cheeks, and blinking tears from her eyes, she turned and walked away. No words could have been adequate to express the feelings of deep sadness mingled with joy that coursed through her heart.

Sam and the Carlsons had driven many miles in heavy silence before Sam remembered the little bundle. He carefully unwrapped it, and to his astonishment, found a perfectly cut diamond the size of his thumbnail.

May 12, 1975

I only have one more thought to add to what I have already written about Rhodesia. I find myself thinking about Melody. Not in a romantic or worldly way, but in a way that makes me feel as if our lives will intersect again. I wish I had kept a copy of the blessing I gave her on the train. I remember something about her going full circle and coming back to that moment. I don't know what it means, but I feel myself involved in her life again, perhaps in the distant future.

I take that back, I do feel romantic. Strike that too. I love her. I suddenly realize that I have never loved a woman before. Not like this. It is exquisitely sweet and sharply painful. I don't like the feeling of discovering love and losing it at the same moment. And it is also not the kind of feeling any decent missionary should have, so I won't tell a soul.

President Carlson has kept me at the mission home for nearly a week. He doesn't let me go out tracting, teaching, or anything. I have been filing papers in the mission office. He says I need a rest. He spends a lot of time on the phone. I know he is trying to find out exactly what happened on the train.

I told him the entire event and showed him the diamond. He took it without promising to return it. He didn't seem angry but also didn't seem pleased. I think I get into too many unusual problems for his perception of a good missionary.

Well, I can now add one more item to my list of things I never want to be when I grow up. I don't want to be a clerk or a typist.

* * *

"Elder Mahoy, my boy, come, sit down," President Carlson said cheerfully, waving Sam to an overstuffed leather chair. Sam sat, a feeling of weariness settling over him. He wasn't looking forward to this interview.

President Carlson pulled his chair from behind the ornate desk around to where they were nearly touching knees. He smiled and sat with one elbow propped on the corner of his desk.

"Elder, I apologize for keeping you cooped up in the mission home this last week. I know you've been anxious to get on with your mission. In all candor, I have spent the last ten days on the phone with nearly every government agency in South Africa and Rhodesia. Almost without exception, they have been glowing in their reports of your conduct on the train. The glaring exception to this is the Rhodesian embassy, who feels that your involvement in urging the people to go southward was an affront to the rebels they were negotiating with, and doing so inadvertently led to the attack on the remainder on the train . . ."

"President, I . . ." Sam began but was cut off by an upraised hand and a friendly smile of dismissal.

"No need to defend yourself, son. I'm satisfied that your actions saved many lives. I'm also certain that if you had stayed, you would have been killed along with the rest. The difficult part of all this has been keeping you away from reporters and out of the newspapers. They have been clambering for your story. I hope you don't mind that I have shielded you from that." It was not a question, and Sam shook his head slightly and stared at his hands in his lap. All this was news to him, and he honestly did not want publicity. Notoriety would make the rest of his mission impossible.

With a thoughtful look, President Carlson leaned back in his chair and mused, "What I don't understand is how you manage to get yourself into so many difficult circumstances. Mind you, I know you don't plan them, but you do seem to attract them. You're the only missionary—the only one—for whom I have had to intercede with the government: once to bail you out of jail after being flogged, and again to keep you from becoming a national hero. You are a most unusual young man, Elder Sam Mahoy."

Sam didn't know what to say, so he kept quiet. This only seemed to make President Carlson more curious. Sam sensed what his question was, but waited until he asked it.

"Elder, why do you have these astonishing experiences?"

Sam evaded the question. "President, my grandfather used to say, if you aren't making waves, you don't have your oars in the water."

President Carlson chuckled but waited politely for Sam to continue. He wasn't going to be put off by a clever answer. In reality, Sam was aching to understand it himself.

"President, I'm not sure I understand myself why these things happen to me. I certainly don't want them. I would be grateful if you would explain it to me. I'm afraid I am not good for the mission. I seem to get into a lot of trouble without asking for it. If you want to send me home, I wouldn't blame you," he said meekly.

"Nothing could be further from my intent," President Carlson replied, his voice filled with surprise. "My only reason for asking is to see if you understood what is going on in your life."

"I sure don't," Sam responded dejectedly.

"Have you studied the life of Joseph Smith, Elder Mahoy?"

"A little, but not as much as I'd like to."

"You are, of course, aware that he lived a life that moved from one difficulty to another. His life was a continual course of tragedies and setbacks, along with unsurpassed spiritual peaks."

"He certainly paid a high price for his righteousness," Sam observed. "And that is the key," President Carlson added quickly. "Opposition is always meted out in direct proportion to righteousness. The greater our efforts and ability to serve God, the greater the opposition. It is my opinion that you experience what seems to be more than your share of trials because you try harder than most to be obedient and effective in your calling."

"It doesn't seem fair," Sam observed quietly.

"Oh, but it is! It's perfectly fair and just, and according to divine law. Through all the ages of time, those who have set the course of their lives in service of God have, by that same course, brought into their lives great trials. Consider this, my boy, that every one of these truth-seeking saints rejoiced in their trials, as well as in their spiritual blessings. I am convinced that if we were able to question them, they would bear powerful testimony that the reward is gloriously worth any price.

"I am concerned about you, it is true. But you must understand that my concern is not that you have trials. My concern is that they don't defeat you. You must never interpret that having opposition in your life indicates that God has abandoned you or that you are failing in your calling. Do you understand?"

"Yes and no," Sam admitted. "I do feel like a failure at times, and I sometimes feel I won't be able to bear up under my trials. I constantly feel I need to apologize to you and to the Lord. Yet, in my heart, I feel Heavenly Father's never-failing love, and I do rejoice in my blessings. It is kind of confusing to feel both ways, President."

"No doubt, Elder. Of course, I think it's important to observe that we can bring trials into our lives through unrighteousness and disobedience. It would be foolishness to assert that all trials are a result of opposition arising from righteousness."

"I understand that, President."

"I'm sure you do. However, I think it is equally important to point out that these trials on your mission are obviously a result of your righteous efforts to serve the Lord. That being the case, I want you to fast and pray until you no longer feel like a failure because of your trials. All such feelings do not come from the Holy Ghost."

"I hadn't considered that," Sam admitted, his mood lifting. "Think about it until you understand and believe it with all your heart. At the same time, pray for courage and strength equal to your faithfulness. It would be tragic if you were not able to endure the trials that your strivings for righteousness ordained. Along with the spiritual fortitude to press forward into righteousness, we must call upon God to give us the moral courage to endure the outcome, which includes fantastic blessings and great trials."

"I'm not sure I have the courage you speak of. I have felt utterly defeated so many times on my mission that I could write a book about it."

President Carlson chuckled and made a dismissive motion with his hand. "You say that, but here you are, ready to move forward. I think you have plenty of courage. Perhaps you need to rely less on your courage and more upon the Lord. You will have to work that out with Him, but never let your heart faint or become discouraged in these matters."

"I will try, President. I really will."

"Very good!" President Carlson said enthusiastically, ending the subject. "Now, I have one more item to discuss with you."

"Yes, sir?" Sam replied, unsure again.

"I am calling you to serve as the district leader in the Natal District. You will have a new missionary directly from the States and will be leaving this afternoon for your new assignment."

May 20, 1975

Transferred again. This time to Durban, in Natal, near the Cape. I will have a new companion straight from the LTM and will be the district leader in the Natal District. President Carlson is wonderful. He expressed the utmost confidence in me when he called me to this position. After talking to him, I feel a new hope and lifting of my spirits.

Who's counting, but I only have seven months left on my mission. I feel like I haven't gotten anything done yet.

11

THE ATHEIST

Elder Kim Hall was straight from the LTM and as green as grass. Sam picked him up at the bus station. He was dark-haired and black-eyed. He stood half a full head shorter than Sam and was half his size. Elder Hall was smiling when Sam picked him up and still smiling when they arrived at their digs. Sam liked Elder Hall. He was so eager to please and willing to serve that Sam rejoiced inwardly.

"Where you from, Elder Hall?" Sam asked as they entered their small room.

"It's hard to say," Elder Hall replied blandly.

"Why is that? Most people know where they're from," Sam replied with a chuckle.

"It's like this. My parents' current domicile is in San Jose, California—well, my dad is actually my stepfather, but he's like a real father to me. My biological father, who is less of a father figure than my stepfather, currently lives in San Francisco with his wife, who is more like the sister I never had than a stepmom. I've spent every other six months of the past twelve years in one or the other of those two places, so that I really don't know which one I owe the prestigious honor of calling my home. So you see, it's difficult to say."

"I see what you mean," Sam said. "How old are you?"

"Why do you ask such an inconsequential question?" Elder Hall asked.

"Just curious. You talk like a college professor," he replied as he unloaded pamphlets from his pockets.

"Would it cause a substantial shift in your opinion of me if I told you I was just nineteen?"

"Uh . . . no," Sam answered, not sure if Elder Hall and he were from the same planet.

"I'm nineteen."

Finally, a sentence with just two words in it, Sam thought. "Sorry, Elder Mahoy. I'm used to communicating on a substantially higher level than is usually considered conversant in nonacademic circles."

"Are you speaking English?" Sam asked teasingly.

"Actually, no. I'm speaking Stanford. It's quintessentially Californian and somewhat more expressive, though a little more verbose and snooty than village English. Some call it "high English" as a joke. It's required of anyone in graduate school—and a bad habit, now I see."

"You're a graduate student at Stanford?" Sam asked, amazed.

"I had hoped to avoid this subject," Elder Hall replied dejectedly.

"You brought it up. And why would you want to avoid it? It's cool."

"Because few people find me socially tolerant when they learn that I speak high English, am a graduate student at Stanford University, and am only nineteen years old. I guess I've grown defensive over the years."

"You've also grown vocabularily abusive."

"There's no such word, Elder."

"I know," Sam admitted. "But it was the only big word I could come up with on the fly."

Elder Hall laughed so heartily that Sam decided for sure that he liked him, and Elder Hall found Sam a welcome relief and a gentle introduction to missionary work. Kim made a promise to himself to drop the high English and speak like everyone else.

Sam was thinking along the same lines when he said, "Tell you what. I know a perfect way to slow your English down to mere village English. Let's go through the discussions in Afrikaans. I was in Rhodesia for seven months, and they only spoke English there. It would be a good refresher for me."

"I don't know them in Afrikaans. They cut our stay in the LTM short, because our visas came through early. I only learned through the second discussion in Afrikaans."

"In that case, why don't you study the third in Afrikaans while I fill out these district reports. Okay?"

"Sure," Elder Hall replied. He grabbed his book and curled up on his bed in what appeared to Sam to be a very uncomfortable position.

Sam filled out reports until his head spun. When he finally looked at the clock, he was startled to observe that three hours had passed, and it was time for bed. He also noticed that Elder Hall was reading his scriptures.

"I thought you were going to work on the discussions," he said with mild rebuke in his voice.

"Did it. Got it here," Elder Hall replied, tapping his temple.

"You memorized the third?" Sam asked in amazement. The third discussion was a long one on the Word of Wisdom, and had taken Sam days to memorize.

"Not actually."

"What do you mean, not actually?"

"I didn't just memorize the third. I memorized all of them."

"You what?" Sam exclaimed with disbelief in his voice. Elder Hall nodded curtly and went back to reading.

Sam flipped open the book and thumbed to a random place in the fourth discussion. "Give me the third concept of the fourth."

Elder Hall rattled it off in Afrikaans word-perfect. Sam corrected his pronunciation in several places. Sam turned to various places in the discussions and was startled to find that Elder Hall had spoken the truth. He knew them verbatim.

"How did you do that?" Sam demanded.

"I have a small gift. I memorize easily. Actually, I read it once, and I basically have it. I'll read it again tomorrow, and it will stick forever. It's nothing. I have always been able to do it."

"Do you understand what you've memorized?"

Elder Hall looked up with a quizzical expression on his face. "Ah now, there's the rub. I don't have a clue what it means. They are all just sounds to me. I would appreciate you going through them and giving me the translation. That would help immeasurably."

Sam was more flabbergasted. Elder Hall had memorized the entire set of discussions in three hours, in a foreign language, without having a clue what the words meant!

As the weeks progressed, Elder Hall became more and more of an astonishment. He was studying medicine at Stanford, was in his second year of graduate school, had a 4.0 GPA, and was president of a fraternity. The fraternity he created and was president of was called the "Anti-Protest Fraternity." They opposed anyone who opposed anything. He said it started as a joke but became popular because it gave kids a chance to have a voice against the radical groups so prevalent on campus. If someone held a sit-in to protest a rule not allowing men and women to live in the same dorm, Elder Hall's group staged a protest to support the rule.

In time, his group had more members than any radical group on campus, and their protests drowned out the real protesters. He grew long hair, a scruffy beard, and wore beads and torn Levis. Because they looked their part, the real protesters were not offended by their antiprotesting, and Stanford University was delighted by their effect. They even offered to fund Kim's "Anti-Protest Fraternity." He published the scathing letter about demonstrations in the school paper, and then held several anti-protest demonstrations himself.

Equally as astonishing was that Elder Hall had been a member of the Church just a little more than a year. One of the protests staged during the spring of '71 was against the building of a Mormon institute of religion on campus. His group had anti-protested in favor of the Mormons. Consequently, he met a few Mormons. One of them was a redheaded coed from San Diego. He described her as a "glow in the dark" kind of Mormon. Sam supposed he meant that she radiated the

Spirit. Kim said she radiated everything—happiness, virtue, beauty, and spirituality. His glowing description made Sam want to meet her, just to see if she were actually mortal.

Her name was Olivia, and Kim had wanted to know what made her "glow in the dark." She told him, and he believed her. He investigated the Church, read all (Sam wondered if he memorized) the standard works, was baptized, and proposed marriage to Olivia, all within three month's time. Olivia told him she had her heart set on marrying a returned missionary. In reality, she was already engaged to a returned missionary. However great as this disappointment was to him, the seed of being a missionary was planted, and Elder Hall patiently waited the year required between baptism and going on a mission.

* * *

Sam had no concept of what it meant to be a district leader.

Like every other missionary who wasn't one, he assumed it would be glorious, filled with exhilarating spiritual experiences and opportunities to do super-power missionary work. The district leaders he had known were spiritual giants in his estimation, and he desired to be just like them.

The reality of the situation was that being a district leader was a lot of work that had nothing to do with teaching. There were lots of meetings, interviews, traveling between cities, solving problems, finding boarding houses, transferring Elders, taking Elders to doctor's appointments, and the paperwork. He hated the paperwork.

It seemed futile, and demanded time he would have preferred to spend teaching people.

As the weeks turned into months, Sam slowly accepted the fact that he was no longer able to proselyte full-time. He did his job with as much energy as he could, but he continued to grow more disillusioned with his new position. He desperately missed teaching the people and yearned for the opportunity to bear testimony to humble souls. Without time to tract, they did not meet many people, and consequently, the only investigators Sam met were when they worked with the other Elders.

Sam saw the remaining precious months of his mission slipping through his fingers like fine sand. He mourned and wept inwardly. He didn't want to finish his mission this way. He felt locked into an administrative position, unable to meet the people or teach them. He felt useless and depressed. It seemed that the more depressed he grew, the hotter the fire burned inside him until it seemed as if he might burst from the unresolved conflict.

It was late at night, and Elder Hall had long since slipped into deep sleep. Sam knelt on the concrete floor beside his bed, and tears of frustration slid down his cheeks.

"Oh, Father. How could I have come to this dark hour? How could I have accepted this job where I have no power to bless the people? Father, my soul is on fire. I desire every minute of every day to be teaching the people, but I cannot. I know the job of district leader is important. The other Elders depend on me and look to me for encouragement. I know I did before I became the DL.

"I promised I would do anything thou asked me to do. I have done that, and will continue to do that with all my heart and soul. I most humbly apologize that I will not be baptizing any more . . ." He had to stop as tears flowed down his cheeks. Even his silent voice could not continue for the lump in his heart.

"Dearest Lord, I beg thee to forgive me. I cannot do the missionary work my heart yearns for. Forgive me. Forgive me. Still Father, with what little I have left to give, I give it all. Freely. Completely. I beg thee to use me for what little I am worth and allow me to complete my mission in righteousness."

A heightening of the Spirit flowed into him, and he felt his heart and mind quicken.

"Father, I know thou lovest me. I feel it in my soul. And even though I have little to offer, I covenant with thee that I will be obedient to every command. From now until the end of my life, and throughout all eternity, I will obey thee and do thy will, and walk in the paths of righteous, as thou will reveal them to me. I confess my profound love for thee, and do it in the name of Jesus Christ, amen."

A feeling of warmth flooded over Sam like a flow of warm water. He felt the tiredness of his heart lift, and he suddenly felt like singing. He lifted his head toward heaven and silently spoke the words that vibrated through his soul. They were more than language, more beautiful than poetry, and lovelier than angelic singing. They flowed from his soul in an unending symphony of love. So much honor, praise, and glory came from his heart that he wept as he worshipped. He felt the earthly world roll back to reveal a powerful outpouring of love from the eternal realm.

He lost track of time as his soul became immersed in praise such as he had never considered possible.

Hours later, he climbed into bed, his body cold and stiff, his soul burning with joy. He drifted off to sleep in the embrace of divine love, and dreamed dreams of great services performed in God's service.

*   *   *

When the alarm went off, Sam awoke with a warm burning in his bosom. Even though he had slept less than three hours, he felt completely rested. His heart was buoyant with joy—almost giddy. Everything was sweetly perfect, and he rejoiced.

Elder Hall took one look at him and covered his eyes with his forearm as if shielding them from the sun. "Glowing!" he said in mock surprise. "Glow-in-the-dark Elder!" he exclaimed.

Sam ignored his companion along with the pile of reports waiting for him. They hurried from their apartment and drove to their tracting area. They did have a tracting area, even though this was the first time they'd actually gone to it in weeks. They picked a block of small homes and knocked on the first door. His heart thrilled as he waited for the door to open. Though not interested, the man behind the door hesitated and looked at them quizzically.

"What you see is our testimony," Sam told him. The man gave them a puzzled look and slowly closed the door. Sam slid a Joseph Smith tract under the door.

Each door was an exciting experience. Even those who slammed them did so after feeling something. Before they broke off for lunch, the Elders had three appointments to teach. By the end of the day, they had taught a first discussion and had five appointments, two for that evening.

As they were walking back to the car, Elder Hall turned to Sam. "What happened last night? I saw that you stayed on your knees after I went to bed. I awoke hours later, and you were still there. What happened?"

"Elder, I'm not sure," Sam confessed. "I did pray long into the night. I've done that before, but this time was different. Something happened to me. I feel different. There's something different and wonderful inside me now. I have so much joy that I feel as if I'm going to burst. My bosom is burning so hotly that it would be painful if it didn't feel so wonderful. I don't understand it. It just is."

"Elder, when I first laid eyes on you this morning, I knew something had happened. You remember me calling you a 'glow-in-the-dark Elder?'

Well, you were—I mean, you are! You have to tell me what you said, what you did last night. I want to do it too."

"I'm sorry, Elder. I really don't understand it myself."

"I've never seen such a transformation in a person. You speak differently, you bear testimony more powerfully, and you make suggestions instead of commanding. You are friendlier, you laugh more, your prayers are sweet and loving, and you talk to everyone with patience and respect. Elder, if you don't tell me what you did or at least how you did it, I'll be very disappointed."

"Well, I don't want to disappoint you," Sam laughed. "I'll try, but it's not a simple story."

"I have two years," Elder Hall answered. They both laughed.

Sam began with Jimmy's death, with the lessons that had been impressed into his mind. He taught Elder Hall how to distinguish the voice of the Holy Spirit and how critical it is to obey it. He repeated several times, "Obedience is the key to righteousness." Sam told Elder

Hall about his experiences in Rhodesia, about the train wreck and saving people's lives by listening and having the courage to obey.

He described, as nearly as he could, his mighty prayer the night before. He spoke of his feelings of worthlessness and believing that he had nothing more to offer, and yet covenanting to obey and serve with all his soul, for the rest of his life. He explained that immediately after he told the Lord these things, he felt the powerful influence of the Holy Ghost flow over him.

Elder Hall listened intently, asking only questions that brought out rich, inspiring answers. By the time he concluded, it was late at night and they were in bed.

"Elder," Kim said quietly after a long silence. "There is a scripture that describes your experience exactly. It's in Mosiah, chapter 5." He sat up and pulled on a pair of pants. It was July, the middle of winter, and even though the days were often in the 80's, it still dropped to the 40's at night, far too cool to be without clothing.

"Let me read verse one. It describes the change you have experienced."

> And they all cried with one voice, saying: Yea, we believe all the words which Thou hast spoken unto us; and also, we know of their surety and truth, because of the Spirit of the Lord Omnipotent, which has wrought a mighty change in us, or in our hearts, that we have no more disposition to do evil, but to do good continually (Mosiah 5:2).

"Does that fit your feelings, I mean, having no more disposition to do evil, but to do good continually?" Elder Hall asked.

"It does," Sam replied. "I've read that verse many times, and it never occurred to me that I might be able to do the same thing as King Benjamin's people. I guess I have always considered it an experience unique to the ancients, not an indication of what might happen to me."

"There's more. This is verse five."

> And we are willing to enter into a covenant with our God to do his will, and to be obedient to his commandments in all things that he shall command us, all the remainder of our days . . . (Mosiah 5:5)

"See, they made a covenant of obedience similar to what you described."

Sam thought about this. "It seems they are making this covenant after they experienced a mighty change, while in my case, it preceded it."

"Not necessarily," Elder Hall replied after some thought. "The next verse says this is a covenant they had already made. The gospel only works one way, Elder. If it worked this way for you, it is going to be the same for all people."

"I believe that's true as long as we are all dealing with the fullness of the gospel."

"Sure. Let me read verses six and seven."

> And now, these are the words which King Benjamin desired of them; and therefore he said unto them: Ye have spoken the words that I desired; and the covenant which ye have made is a righteous covenant.
>
> And now, because of the covenant which ye have made ye shall be called the children of Christ, his sons, and his daughters; for behold, this day he hath spiritually begotten you; for ye say that your hearts are changed through faith on his name; therefore, ye are born of him and have become his sons and his daughters. (Mosiah 5:6–7)

"Oh my!" Sam exclaimed.

"Elder Sam Mahoy, I believe you have been born again—in the fullest sense."

"Oh my!" Sam repeated. There was a protracted silence while he tried to understand.

Finally Sam said, "I just find it hard to believe something like this could actually happen to me. I'm nobody special. I just try to do what's right. I make mistakes—lots of them. I'm not perfect. In fact, I'm far from it. I find it hard to accept. Perhaps this is something else."

Elder Hall persisted. "I know I'm your junior companion and you are my teacher in these things, but let me give you some spiritual counsel. Don't doubt the gifts of God. Don't let your humility interfere with your blessings. Accept it. Rejoice in it. It's true. You said you are nobody special? I tell you, you are a son of God in the purest respect, and that is very special."

Sam took his companion's counsel and rejoiced with all his soul. He recognized that doubt is not a gift of the Spirit, and when doubt in his rebirth came, he rejected it without exception. Each time he did, his soul rejoiced until he felt as if his blessings were too great for him to possess them all.

June 2, 1975

It is with great joy in my heart tonight that I record that I have recently experienced the rebirth. It was unexpected and far from my thoughts. I was completely depressed and felt as if I had failed the Lord. I thought I was going to go home having been a failure as a missionary. It pained my heart to the point of death, and I fell down and begged the Lord to forgive me.

While I was feeling so devastated, I still had this powerful desire to dedicate what was left of my soul to the Lord. I spent many hours in prayer and covenanted myself to absolute obedience. It was more than a promise. It was pure, profound, and absolute. Even though I was mostly worthless as a servant, I still wanted the Lord to have whatever I had left.

A marvelous feeling then swept over me, and my depression evaporated as quickly as fog before the bright sun. The Holy Spirit enveloped me, and I felt unbridled joy so intense that it confused me. I have never experienced joy so profound. It was joy in the Lord, and His joy in me as His child, all rolled together. I was completely changed in that moment. I came away from the experience a different man.

Since that time, I cannot think of sin without feeling repulsed. I look upon the world with different eyes. The things that previously excited me and I looked forward to with great hope no longer interest me. Money, a problem throughout my mission, has suddenly become meaningless. The only things that matter are people and my relationship with God.

My heart is continually filled with prayer. Every waking moment is prayer, and I find myself rejoicing continually. As soon as my heart turns to prayer, the Holy Ghost overflows me, and I am directed to speak like never before.

My words flow like a mighty river and come forth in more beauty than the loveliest music. It seems as if at times the words rhyme and have meter. When I am fully caught up in prayer, it becomes pure, absolute praise, and my soul rejoices in it. When I thus pray under the influence of the Spirit, I seem to get everything I ask for.

I feel absolute humility. Having had a small portion of the perfections of God opened to my understanding, I am struck with the fact that He—the God of all existence—loves me. He actually loves me!

Such unspeakably beautiful words: He loves me! Tears come to my eyes to think of it. I am His son. Think about it. He who is the most perfect, powerful, loving, kind, and holy being in the universe, is my Heavenly Father. And His Son is my loving Savior, who has snatched me from the dredges of hell. Hell is what I earned, but He has given me heaven.

For the first time in my life, I understand how the gospel can bring us to a measure of the stature of the fullness of Christ. In a way too beautiful for mortal man to understand, through obedience we qualify for His grace, which brings this mighty change, this rebirth, this remaking of the soul, and then changes us to become like unto Him—not perfect yet, but more like Him who is perfect.

I have long believed that we had to become perfect largely through our own labors. We had to develop faith, humility, love, kindness, hope, charity, and all other Christlike attributes. After we had done all of this, I believed that He would then apply His Atonement and wash away our sins so we would finally be like Him. It all seemed so distant, so incredibly hard and remote that even the most brave-hearted seeker would faint by the way.

What I now understand from this experience is that the primary thing Heavenly Father wants us to learn in this life is obedience. Through our agency we choose to forever obey, which triggers the Savior's grace and empowerment in our lives. The Spirit then purges our natural man, and we are born again—firm in our resolve to obey, and joyfully empowered by Christ to be submissive, meek, humble, patient, full of love, and flawlessly obedient. This grace-sustained obedience is the key that unlocks the doors of righteousness and eternal bliss.

Having at last the faith that leads to obedience, a key has been turned, and I now joyfully understand that the attributes of godliness are gifts of the Spirit. What a wonder it is to finally see clearly! It opens a thousand doors and brings the gospel into sharp focus. It makes it all things doable, *unscrambles the scriptures, casts bright light upon the straight and narrow way, and illuminates the darkness of the world.*

In a tiny way, I now perceive the perfection of the plan of salvation.

Every mortal born lives their lives surrounded by the voice of revelation, and all have an equal chance to hear and obey. To hear and obey is to be led along the path of righteousness until we experience a mighty change that makes us new creatures in Christ, as Paul expressed it. Suddenly, Paul's words make sense, whereas before they were nonsensical to me. Paul understood the rebirth profoundly, because his experience with it had been profound. With every letter he penned, he taught about the power of the change that had saved his soul from destruction.

Oh, how I rejoice in these things, and worship Him whose plan this is!

* * *

The Elders' first appointment that day was with Mr. and Mrs. De Bruyn. The De Bruyn's home was small, yet tidy and clean.

Mrs. De Bruyn opened the door and smiled. She was a refined dark-haired woman in her late thirties. Inside the door was a huge drafting table that took up most of the foyer and part of the living room. On the table were immaculately drawn electrical drawings. Sam studied the drawings. He had taken drafting in high school, and these were professionally done. He was bending over the drawings when Mr. De Bruyn came from the back of the house.

Sam extended his hand. "Good evening. I'm Elder Mahoy, and this is Elder Hall."

"Anchenama Kennis (pleasure to know you)," Mr. DeBruyn replied, switching to Afrikaans and shaking both their hands. Sam noticed Mrs. De Bruyn give her husband a quizzical look. He just smiled at her and turned his attention to the missionaries.

It was considered rude to change the language being spoken. If someone started speaking English, it was socially correct to continue in that language. They had just spoken with Mrs. De Bruyn in English. Sam knew they both probably spoke English as well as he did. He felt a momentary pang of panic. He hadn't had a conversation in Afrikaans in eight months, but he knew the language somewhat, and felt confident that the Holy Spirit would aid them.

After polite conversation, Sam told them briefly about the apostasy and restoration. He asked them if they would be interested in hearing more about the man who had been called to be a prophet in this dispensation.

They both expressed interest. Sam began the first discussion, and they went through the apostasy in detail. The De Bruyns understood and agreed. He then told them about Joseph Smith, and the first vision. As soon as he mentioned the appearance of God to the boy prophet, Mr. De Bruyn objected. He said no one had seen God, and stood to retrieve his Bible.

Sam could see that his Bible was well worn and marked in many places. Mr. De Bruyn turned to and read a verse that stated no man had seen God. Sam had not read the scriptures in Afrikaans, and it took him extra mental effort to translate the words into English. He recognized the verse and was about to reply when Mr. De Bruyn launched off into another verse. From there, the conversation deteriorated into an argument, except that no one was participating in it except Mr. De Bruyn.

Sam grew restless as Mr. De Bruyn pounded them with scriptures, not waiting for a reply or, in fact, not being interested in one.

"Wait!" Sam shouted just as Mr. De Bruyn was about to thumb to another verse. The sheer volume of Sam's voice brought the conversation up short. He filled the silence by saying, "I have sat here and listened to you attack my faith without allowing me to answer a single accusation. This is not the way Christ would have us do. You just read a scripture in First Corinthians."

Mr. De Bruyn nodded and glanced back at his book. He had not given the reference and was impressed that Sam knew it. In reality, Sam could not remember reading that particular verse in either English or Afrikaans, but, nevertheless, he knew the reference with great certainty. "Read the two verses prior to the one you read," Sam directed. Mr.

De Bruyn did so. Sam had difficulty following the words, yet knew through the Spirit what they said. "As you see, those two verses show us that it actually is possible to see God."

"You are misinterpreting the scripture," Mr. De Bruyn replied. "One must consider each verse separately. Each is inspired, and each bears its own message. To apply the meaning of prior verses to warp the meaning of the next is to twist the scriptures. Each verse stands alone," he stated haughtily and with indignation. "You say that God has called another prophet. I say that none is needed. We have the holy book of God, the Bible. It is all we need."

He thumbed quickly to a verse and read, "Search the scriptures; for in them ye think ye have eternal life: and they are they which testify of me."

This he read with great emphasis, punctuating the words by stabbing his finger in the air. He had switched into high Afrikaans, which was only used for preaching sermons and powerful prayers. It was never used when speaking to another person, and was considered a great insult.

"So you see, you poor, misguided Mormons, that salvation is in the scriptures. You don't need a prophet. Your whole argument is void. You have come to deliver a message that is false. Go back to America and quit wasting your time and ours."

Sam remained calm. "When Christ spoke these words, he was speaking to highly educated men who refused to accept him as the Christ. They used exactly the same argument you just did. They said they had the scriptures, the law and the prophets, and had no need of a living prophet."

"That is not true," Mr. De Bruyn insisted.

"Read the verse just prior to the one you quoted," Sam requested.

He had no idea what that verse said, but the fire was burning in his bosom, and he knew the words he spoke were true.

"And ye have not his word abiding in you: for whom he hath sent, him ye believe not."

Silence filled the small room after the reading. Sam let it linger for a few moments.

"Jesus was being sarcastic," Sam replied. "He was saying 'Search the scriptures all you want if you think they will save you, but they are they which testify of me. And if you don't accept me and those I send to you, then you cannot find eternal life in the scriptures alone.' How can you come unto Christ if you reject His prophets? Read the next verse, please."

Mr. De Bruyn slowly looked back at his scriptures, and after a pause, he read, "And ye will not come to me, that ye might have life."

Sam waited until the Spirit moved him. "Mr. and Mrs. De Bruyn, I want you to know that a prophet has been called anew in this era. His name was Joseph Smith. He was a prophet in the same respect that Moses, Peter, and Isaiah were prophets. I want to bear you my testimony that the true and living Church of God has been restored to the earth. All the blessings that were found in the ancient Church are found today. I know you feel the burning in your soul, testifying this is true. In the name of Jesus Christ, amen."

Mr. De Bruyn sat silent for almost a full minute. Finally, he closed his Bible and set it on a table beside his chair. His eyes studied each of the missionaries in turn before fixing upon Sam. For a moment, his face was aglow with wonder, but darkness began to seep across his face, and his brow furled into a frown.

"You two are dangerous," he finally said. "You almost deceived me. Very clever. I will inform the pastor about you two, and we will see that you have no success teaching in this town. I will also see to it that you two are miserable in every possible way. You take my words as true and consider my words prophetic, for they shall surely come to pass. You are evil!"

Sam stood suddenly. Elder Hall followed, gathering up their things. "Mr. De Bruyn," he began, "you have been given the true witness, and you felt the power of it. In all fairness, I want you to understand that you will be held accountable . . ."

"Hold on there!" Mr. De Bruyn bellowed. "Be careful what you say! Your words are being recorded in heaven and will echo in the halls of justice. Don't condemn me to hell unless you wish to go there yourself." This he nearly shouted.

Sam lowered his voice and held his gaze. "You, sir, will be called to account on the day of judgment for the testimony I have borne to you this day, and which you know to be true. Good night."

So saying, he walked solemnly to the door, opened it, and stepped out into the night. He was vaguely aware of Mr. De Bruyn storming into the back of the house. His wife quietly closed the door behind them without a word.

Sam stood on their porch for a long moment. Elder Hall stopped half way down the walk and turned just in time to see Sam lift each foot and brush the dust from each sole.

They climbed into their VW Beetle. "Elder," Kim said as soon as the engine chugged to life. "I thought you didn't speak Afrikaans that well."

Sam looked at him and shrugged. It hadn't occurred to him that he had spoken far beyond his abilities.

"Don't shrug this off. I just heard you speak for an hour, bearing testimony, quoting dozens of scriptures, answering difficult questions, and all of it in flawless Afrikaans. I know you don't speak it that well, and I know you haven't read the Bible in Afrikaans—yet you quoted those scriptures verbatim. You used words I doubt you had ever heard before, and quoted scriptures you probably never read before. Have you studied the Old Testament?"

"I've read at it, but I haven't gotten clear through it yet."

"Then how were you able to quote those scriptures from Isaiah?"

"I did that?" Sam asked, having difficulty remembering. Now that the power of that spiritual moment was subsiding, his memory of what he had said was fading as well. It felt to him as if someone else had conducted that interview, and he had merely watched the event. He had vague memories of quoting scriptures and of answering questions, but his memories included statements he had made in Afrikaans, which even now he had difficulty understanding.

"You did. And how about those scriptures in Jude, and in first John? Had you memorized those? They're not on the memorization list."

"No, I guess not."

"What about that scripture in John? Had you ever before considered what he meant when he said, 'Search the scriptures for in them ye think ye have eternal life'?"

"No, I had never really considered the meaning of that scripture."

"That's what I thought. I can hardly wait to get my hands on my journal tonight."

They drove in reverent silence all the way home. Sam turned off the car and put a hand on his companion's arm.

"Elder Hall, thanks."

"For what?" he asked with a puzzled expression.

"For helping me to more clearly see the blessings of the Lord. I think I have taken many things for granted without rejoicing over them. Tonight was special, and I probably would have overlooked the sweetness of it without your comments. Thanks."

Elder Hall closed his eyes in thought. When he opened them, they were moist.

"No. Don't thank me. I was just a witness of tonight's miracle. I'm astounded that I actually followed the conversation. I heard hundreds of new words I have never heard in my life and understood them perfectly. This is literally my first experience in actually hearing a complete conversation in Afrikaans. When he first started railing at us, I didn't understand a word he was saying. But as soon as you started speaking, I felt the Holy Ghost come over me, and I instantly understood every word. I tried several times to make comments, but even though I could understand perfectly, the words would not come to my tongue. I could say nothing. It seems obvious that you had the gift of tongues tonight. I guess I had the gift of ears." They both chuckled. Then Elder Hall put his arm around his companion's shoulder.

"Elder Mahoy, we have much to be grateful for."

"We certainly do, my friend."

* * *

At church that next Sunday, Bishop Van Halen stopped them in the foyer. "Elders, have you tracted out a family named Whitehall in the Sunny Side subdivision?"

"Yes, Bishop, we've already given them a first discussion," Elder Hall replied.

"Good. Very good. The wife is a friend and coworker of my wife. They have been friends for years. She has been anxious for the missionaries to meet them but didn't want to directly refer them. When you see my wife, she has something to tell you about them."

They had no trouble finding the bishop's wife. She was a happy, active woman who seemed to be the heart and soul of the ward. They found her setting up pictures in the Relief Society room.

"Her name is Judy," she told them as she motioned for them to sit down. She sat on the edge of the table before them. "I have known and worked with her for years. She has always resisted my attempts to share the gospel with her."

Elder Hall cleared his throat. "We taught her a first discussion, and both she and her husband seemed interested, or at least polite. They did invite us back."

Sister Van Halen clapped her hands together in joy. "Oh, wonderful!" she exclaimed. "Just wonderful. She told me at work that some missionaries had knocked on her door, and she thought they were from my church. She also told me something else. I'm not sure I should tell you."

"Why is that?" Sam asked, his curiosity piqued.

"Well, I don't want it to influence your teaching or make you go too quickly."

"We will teach them as quickly as the Holy Spirit directs, Sister Van Halen, regardless of what you tell us," Sam assured her.

"Yes, of course. I'm sorry! It's just that I've been working with her for so many years, you know."

Sam smiled at her. "We do understand. Don't worry, we'll teach her as carefully as we can. What she chooses to do with it will depend on whether she gets a testimony, as you know."

"Well, that's what I wanted to tell you. She already has a testimony."

"Oh?" both Elders said in unison.

"She told me at work and actually swore me to secrecy. She said that one evening about a week before you tracted them out, both she and her husband had the same dream. She said she saw a sea of faces, as if it were the entire world. They were wandering back and forth in her dream, without paying any attention to her. She felt lost and afraid. She could tell that some of the people were bad, because darkness surrounded them. Some people were good, because their faces were surrounded by light. She told me that one face in the crowd glowed brighter than all the others and was coming toward her. She watched, anxious to know who it was. Finally, it got close enough that she could distinguish the features, and it was a young man she had never seen before.

"At that moment an authoritative voice told her, 'This is my true messenger.' She knew it was the voice of God, and it frightened her. She was afraid she wouldn't find the person or recognize him. About a week later, you two knocked on the door, and she opened it with the determination to send you two packing. Imagine her surprise when one of your faces was the face in her dream!"

Sam glanced at Elder Hall, who looked back with raised eyebrows. They both wanted to ask which one of them she had seen, but neither did.

"She said she was so amazed that she didn't even say hello, but just ran to get her husband."

"I remember that now," Sam interjected. "I thought she was going after a gun or something. Instead, she brought her husband, who immediately invited us in. I thought it was strange at the time, but I was so glad to be able to teach them that I had forgotten about that." Sister Van Halen nodded. "My point in telling you this is so you will understand how precious they are. Heavenly Father must really want them to accept the gospel. Aren't you curious which of you she saw?"

"I'd rather not know," Elder Hall replied, and Sam agreed. He would feel more comfortable not knowing.

They had an appointment with the Whitehalls on Wednesday evening. They fasted and made spiritual preparations. As they walked up the path to the Whitehalls' front door, Sam had a bad feeling.

"Elder, do you feel that?" Sam asked in a hushed voice.

"I sure do. Something's blacked out inside." It was Elder Hall's way of saying there was a negative spiritual feeling from the house. Sam and he had felt it before, and it invariably ended up with them being asked not to return.

Sister Whitehall opened the door before they knocked and pushed open the screen door. She was solemn and barely greeted them. It did not look good to Sam. She left to get Brother Whitehall. He came into the room with a young man about Sam's age.

"This is our son, Neil. We invited him to come hear your message tonight. We hope that's all right."

"Certainly," Sam said cheerfully as he shook Neil's hand. It was like shaking the hand of a spiritual corpse. Darkness emanated from his eyes. This young man was one of the most completely evil people Sam had ever met. It caused his skin to crawl.

"Brother Whitehall, would you ask someone to pray?" Sam asked. Neil coughed, chuckled derisively, and half under his breath said,

"To what?"

Elder Hall gave a nice, though brief, prayer, during which Neil snorted at every mention of God.

"Thank you for having us by this evening," Sam began, not sure how to approach the situation. He wanted to teach the Whitehalls, but knew Neil would not allow it. He prayed silently for the Holy Spirit to inspire his words. "It's a pleasure to meet with you again."

"That's precious. Begin your teaching with a lie," Neil snorted. "What do you mean?" Sam asked.

"You lied. It's not a pleasure for you to have me here. You feel alienated from me because I represent the exact opposite of what you represent. You feel uncomfortable around me, and it's not a pleasure. Let's at least be honest. You claim to represent God. At least you can do it without lying." His voice was insulting and charged with hate.

Sam was taken back by his assault. He considered arguing that he was pleased to be with the Whitehalls tonight, and that was the truth, but he knew it would only derail their discussion.

"Truth," Sam began, "is what we are here to discuss. Truth in its purest form, as God has revealed it . . ."

"Another lie!" Neil bellowed. "God reveals nothing! There is no God." He turned to his father. "Do you really expect me to sit here and listen to this tripe? He can't say one sentence without lying. They're like all the rest. They have this mindless fixation on a being that does not exist, and the audacity to say they are His spokesmen. They aren't even entertaining. At least I got to laugh in the stupid faces of the others. These guys are just congenital liars," Neil proclaimed.

His father blanched and raised a hand as if to restrain his son, but Neil ignored him.

"Prove to me there's a God!" he demanded, turning back to Sam.

"Prove to me there's not a God," Elder Hall interjected hotly. Sam knew the discussion had just gotten out of hand. There was really nothing else to lose, so he let Elder Hall trade logic with Neil for a while. Elder Hall had apparently conducted this argument with some intellectual atheists before, and handled himself well. Still, the Spirit departed, and nothing of worth was being taught. Neil certainly wasn't going to change his mind, no matter how sound the logic Elder Hall might bombard him with.

Neil leaned forward and lowered his voice. "Just this morning in the paper, it told a story of a little girl who was abducted, raped, and murdered. An innocent little girl. Tell me where God was while she was crying and screaming, begging for her life. Where was God while she was being stabbed several times? Tell me. I'm really curious."

Elder Hall sputtered, and Neil jumped down his throat with both feet.

"You can't explain it, because there is no God," Neil said sarcastically. "If there was a God, that kind of insanity wouldn't happen. God would stop them. Or, if God chose not to stop it due to some all-mighty plan of his, then he would surely punish them on the spot. Make them hurt as much as that little girl."

"We all have agency," Elder Hall insisted, "and sometimes people use it unwisely. God doesn't stop people from exercising their free will."

"God doesn't stop them because He can't. God doesn't stop them because He doesn't exist." He sneered at them. "You call God 'Heavenly Father,' right?"

"Yes," Elder Hall replied.

"Father? What kind of a father, an all powerful, all mighty, all knowing, all loving father would allow his little girl to be brutalized before his eyes and not intervene? Would you? I know you think I'm a wolf, and I am, but I still wouldn't allow someone to do that to my daughter. I'm better than God, and I'm a scumbag."

"I . . ." Elder Hall started to speak.

"Excuse me," Sam said politely, interrupting Elder Hall's reply. "There is no excuse," Neil bellowed. "Either you produce God, or you shut up. If God exists, give me a sign. Prove to me that God exists, and I'll prove to you that he's a damn-hateful God. Make God come stand right here, and I'll scream in his face and tell him he's a failure as a god. A God who can't save his little girl, and thousands like her! Who would even want to believe in such a being, let alone worship him? It's pathetic."

"I will give you no such sign," Sam replied calmly.

"Why not? Because you can't, that's why. If there truly was a God, and you truly were his representative, you would be able to give me a sign. None of the others could—and you can't. There is no God."

"You're right. I can't. But if you insist on a sign, then let God give you one."

"Well, isn't that a convenient, coward's way out? God doesn't exist, so here we are back to the original lie." Neil threw his hands in the air in fake exasperation, a smile of triumph on his face.

Sam was unmoved. "I said that I personally can't give you a sign, but, as God's mouthpiece, I can give you His sign." Sam heard his own words with curiosity and wondered what the sign would be. It would be whatever the Lord directed, and he waited with anticipation to hear it.

"This ought to be precious," Neil said sarcastically, crossing his legs, and lounging back into the sofa. "What are you going to do, strike me blind?"

"Here is your sign. Your best friend raped and murdered that little girl."

"What!?" he screamed, bolting to his feet. His parents leaped to their feet at the same instant. For several minutes pandemonium reigned while his parents shouted—not at the Elders, but at their son. Demands, accusations, and denials punctuated the air. While they fought, Sam and Elder Hall sat in silence, barely hearing their words.

Sam pondered why he had said such a thing. It had just come out. His heart had been aflame with the Holy Spirit, and he had been speaking the words that came into his heart. The words had come out of his mouth without him changing them in any way. At the instant he said them, the thought occurred to Sam that Neil's best friend was actually Satan, and that the evil one had inspired the deed in someone unknown to Neil. However, the more Sam contemplated the words, the more he realized that they were literally true. Neil's hot denials proved their truth. If he had perceived it as a lie, he would have calmly called it such, as he had all evening. Without a word from Sam, the argument came to a sudden stop.

Neil took his seat. "Let me tell you all something," he began smoothly, his voice like a knife. "I'm sure you read the papers just like I did. My parents undoubtedly told you that the little girl's father is my best friend. What you said was an incredibly cheap shot. He is more devastated by his daughter's death than you can imagine, and your accusing him is just another indication of how hollow your claims to truth are."

What Neil did not know was that missionaries were not allowed to read newspapers, and until Neil mentioned it, Sam did not even know there had been a little girl murdered.

"Besides, that's not a sign," Neil continued vigorously. "A sign has to be irrefutable, undeniable. All you did was start an argument, not give me a sign. You'll have to do better than that." He pushed his long, black hair from his face and flipped his head to keep it there. His eyes were filled with hatred and defiance.

Once again, Sam felt the flow of words begin and steeled himself to speak them. It took courage to allow his voice to speak words he chose not to edit.

"If you want another sign, you choose it. By your own words, you will know the truth."

"Oh, this ought to be fun," Neil said mockingly. "Okay, let's see. Blindness? No, too obvious. Disease? No, too common. Shot by a jealous husband? No, too unlikely to happen. I think I'll go for a body part— something small, but important. Nothing crippling, but big enough to be obvious. What do you think, Mister Mormon Missionary? You call it."

"As you wish," Sam heard himself say. "The part of your person you value most will be denied to you until you repent of your sins. As a further witness, the curse will begin the next time you curse God."

"Well, damn it, let's get the show on the road! Consider your phony God cursed," he shouted and stood up. "I've had all of this foolishness I can stand. Besides, I have a doctor's appointment to get to." So saying, he nodded to his parents, strode to the door, and slammed it behind him.

Sam and Elder Hall spent the next short while speaking with Neil's parents, who were mortified by what had happened, and apologized profusely. They had hoped their son would be as touched as they had been. The Elders stayed until the Spirit returned to the home. They made another appointment and left them with a prayer.

Late that night, an insistent knocking at their door awakened Sam and Kim. It was about three in the morning.

"Who is it?" Sam called through the door.

"Bishop and Sister Van Halen," the voice came through the door.

They scrambled to get their clothes on and let them into their small room.

Sister Van Halen explained, "I just received a call from my friend, Virginia Whitehall. Something has happened to their son Neil, and they want you to come to the hospital. She didn't know how to get in contact with you, so she called me. Can you come with us? It's a long drive."

The Elders got ready quickly and climbed into the Bishop's Mercedes. They drove for more than an hour before coming to a large hospital on the outskirts of the city. It loomed before them like a lost city in the dim light of dawn.

Neil's room was on the twelfth floor and down a long hall. The hospital was surprisingly busy for so early in the morning. Of greater interest was that no one attempted to stop them or ask where they were going.

"Thank you for coming," Mrs. Whitehall said as she pressed Sam's hand. She led him to the side of the bed. Neil's black hair looked stark against the sea of white sheets and pillows. His face, however, was nearly the color of the sheets. He was looking away, toward the opposite wall as if ignoring them. After a few moments, however, he slowly turned his face toward them. He had been weeping. Most of the darkness was gone from his eyes. In its place was a total absence of light. It was still unnerving.

"How did you know?" he asked Sam, his voice barely audible.

Only Sam heard him clearly since he was closest to the bed. The others whispered his question behind Sam's back until all understood. "Know what, Neil?" Sam asked, his voice soft but not patronizing.

He felt the presence of the Holy Ghost and knew he had a further task to accomplish for the Lord. He also knew that Neil would not like what he had to say, even though Sam had no idea what it was.

"That my friend Charles was the murderer?" he said, his voice almost tiny.

"I personally didn't know. I told you what the Lord wanted you to hear. Until this minute, only my faith told me that it was true."

"I was certain you'd say something like that," he said, and turned his eyes toward the far wall. His voice was still filled with doubt, but it was no longer dripping with vitriol. Neil spoke without looking at Sam. "Charles and I have been . . ."

"Lovers," Sam interjected, surprised at the words himself.

A long pause followed, and Neil echoed the word, "Lovers." His parents gasped.

"We have been . . . lovers for many years. His daughter lives with her mama and is the cutest thing. She was ten years old. I loved her, and Charles loved her. I just don't understand . . ." There was another long pause.

"When she . . . when she died, Charles was devastated, and so was I. He wept, mourned, and howled. He thrashed on himself so badly that I was afraid for him. I did not believe that he could or would do such a thing. A few minutes after the doctors gave me their bad news, Charles called me and told me the entire story. He's in jail now, awaiting sentencing. He'll probably be executed before the week is out."

Bishop Van Halen explained softly when he saw Sam's puzzled look, "In our country, a confession coupled with evidence to support it cancels the need for a trial. There is a sentencing hearing, and the criminal is put away. In this case, he will almost certainly be executed." Sam understood and nodded. He had heard that justice—or injustice, as the case may be—was swift in this country. He had experienced some of it himself.

When Neil turned his head back toward Sam, his eyes were pooled with tears. At first, Sam believed Neil was weeping for the loss of his lover, but when Neil spoke, Sam learned that something else was torturing his soul.

"I have cancer," Neil said, and he and his parents wept. When he regained control of his emotions, he continued, "You'll recall that I had a doctor's appointment after our meeting yesterday. I came here for what I thought was a urinary tract infection. I have had several. It's one of the hazards of being—how can I say it delicately—attracted to men." The term "gay" had not yet been coined. At that time, in that country, there was no polite term for homosexuals.

"The doctor ran a lot of tests and finally informed me that I have an advanced stage of prostate cancer. He says it's probably the result of my deviant lifestyle." He laughed ruefully and paused to reflect. When he began again, his voice was filled with irony.

"If they don't operate, I will die within a few weeks. If they do, I may live, but I'll lose the use of my . . . my sexuality," he said, obviously struggling for words. "Do you want to know the hardest part of all this?" he asked, looking into Sam's eyes. Sam did not respond.

"It's knowing that you were right. You have given me a sign I cannot deny."

"God has given you a sign," Sam corrected him in a sad voice.

Neil pondered Sam's words and finally said, "God has given me a sign." Behind him, Sam heard Neil's mother begin weeping again. She mumbled something about it being too late. Sister Van Halen held her in her arms.

"You know?" Neil continued. "If it had just been Charles being guilty, I would have discounted it and rationalized that you must have guessed his guilt, but with that and this cancer taking away the part of my body I value most, it's beyond dispute. Checkmate," he said with finality.

"I'm sorry you had to go through this," Sam said, not sure what else to say. "In the long run, I know you can use it to your advantage by now believing that there is a God."

"Oh yes, I'm convinced of that. The problem is, I'm also convinced He hates me. A few hours ago, I would have argued that I don't want to believe in a hateful God. Now now I believe, and I still think He hates me. It's an awful feeling."

"Why do you consider His treatment of you hateful?" Sam asked. "Since there is a God, there is also salvation and, conversely, damnation."

Sam smiled faintly. "I think we would all agree that you were on the fast track to damnation a few hours ago. At least, now you have the choice. Your eyes have been opened by this experience. Now, when you choose, you can choose salvation. I know this experience is difficult for you, but this sounds like the work of a loving God to me, not a hateful one."

"I hope you're right, Elder Sam," Neil said quietly. "I do hope you're right. I know God loves you, because you keep the commandments and you're on a mission for Him. It's easy to see why God would love you. But me? I've done everything wrong a person can do. I've broken every commandment except murder, and I'm not so sure I didn't contribute to that one too. I've been in and out of jail a dozen times. If I were put in jail for every criminal act I've committed, I'd still be in jail. I have hated God and literally worshipped what you would call evil. I reveled in it, rejoiced in it, and bathed my entire soul in it. I don't see how I can be forgiven. I can't imagine a God willing to forgive such a long list of sins. I am not just bad, I'm vile," he said with deep conviction.

"Your words are the beginnings of repentance. Whether you understand it or not, you just confessed your sins. It is a beginning. It's up to God, but I believe you can be forgiven. What do you have to lose by trying?"

"That's certainly true. I have nothing at all to lose. Nothing." His voice trailed off into silence.

Sam patted him on the shoulder and turned to leave. "Elder?" Neil called to him softly.

"Yes, Neil."

"Before you go, can you remove the sign? I recognize the evilness of my life. Isn't that enough? Can you undo what you did? Can you release me from the sign?" His voice was childlike, desperate, and pleading.

"I cannot," Sam said sadly, but without hesitation. "It didn't originate with me. It's up to God to release you from it, not me. I simply can't do it."

Neil sobbed uncontrollably as Sam backed away. It was as if his last hope for life had been yanked away from him. His mother rushed to comfort him. Even in the hall, Neil's voice wafted through the heavy door, the long, forlorn, wail of an anguished soul. Sam heard it for what it was—the beginnings of a long, hard repentance. He didn't know if Neil would make it, but at least the process was begun.

As he climbed into the car, Sam suddenly realized that he was exhausted. He leaned back in the soft leather seat and slept deeply.

June 22, 1975

After leaving Neil's hospital room, I was so exhausted that I slept all the way home. I had a vivid dream about Alma the Younger. It was almost as if I were there, watching him fight against the Church, angry and vengeful. I watched in my dream as he was struck down and went through an accelerated repentance process. I couldn't help but wonder if the dream was meant to parallel Neil's experience.

I no longer view Neil as an evil, unredeemable soul. I can see that there is real power and the potential for goodness in him. He could be a great asset to the Church if he put as much effort into serving God as he did into hating Him.

Elder Hall is a great blessing to me. He is the first companion I have truly loved. All the others I have appreciated, valued, or been friends with. Kim is like a brother, and when the time comes, I will be most sad to leave him.

* * *

The Whitehalls delivered a message through the bishop's wife that they would appreciate not being visited by the missionaries until after Neil's operation and recovery. They promised to contact them when they were ready to resume their discussions. Sam took the note and carefully folded and dated it. He put it in an envelope with all the other notes like it and sighed.

12

DAWN BROUGHT THE SUN

A high concrete wall surrounded the subdivision, and armed guards stood outside the gate. Sam came to a stop by the guard's window. The man leaned out the window and waited for Sam to speak.

"Mr. Oliver Pauley requested that we pay him a visit," Sam told the guard, not sure what else to say. He passed the referral slip to him. It was a two-inch strip of paper, cut from the visitor's book at Temple Square in Utah. Mr. Pauley had signed it, indicating he would be glad to have a visit from a representative of the Church.

The guard disappeared inside for several minutes. When he leaned back out the window, the big iron gate started to swing open. Sam felt like he was in "Alice in Wonderland." The guard handed him back the slip and said, "Number 224, move forward."

They drove past buildings that were more like palaces than normal homes. It took them awhile to find 224, yet they did not mind slowly driving past all the beautiful houses. Every one of them was newer and more beautiful than the mission home.

Deep within the subdivision, they found another large fence and gate. On one of the massive gate towers was 224. The gate was open, so they drove in. They followed the narrow road, lined with flowering bushes and immaculately sculpted shrubs, until the road forked. A small sign directed all deliveries to the left. Sam took the right fork. Almost immediately, the road grew wider, with a low stone wall on either side. The wall was of gray stone, designed to look like a castle wall with regularly spaced turrets. Flowers grew from the turrets. When they spotted the house a second later, it was like driving into another world. It was, in fact, a true castle, complete with drawbridge and moat. They stared open-mouthed as they rounded a bubbling fountain before the huge front door. Everywhere they looked, the gardens and trees were immaculate. They could see an Olympic-size swimming pool far to the right, also decorated castle-like. A single figure, obviously female, lounged on a chaise beside the pool.

The only difference between this castle and a real one was that everything here was smaller, yet it was proportionately correct, giving the appearance of being much larger than it actually was. It was a carefully crafted optical illusion. The two-story walls appeared to be four stories tall, with small windows cut in the walls to complete the illusion.

They walked across the drawbridge, over a moat filled with goldfish and flowers, and knocked on the massive door. No one appeared. They were just about to give up and leave when they heard a bolt click back. The heavy door opened with an appropriate groan to reveal a young woman standing in the shadows. She had apparently been the girl by the pool, for she wore nothing but a bikini and had a large towel draped over one shoulder. She stared at them with a curious expression.

"Hello?" she said, more as a question than a welcome.

Elder Hall recovered first. "Good afternoon. I'm Elder Hall, and this is Elder Mahoy. We were asked to visit Mr. Oliver Pauley. He visited Temple Square in Salt Lake City, Utah, and requested that we visit him."

"Oh, yes!" the girl responded happily, pulling the door open wider and motioning for them to come in. "I was there with him. We had a wonderful time and loved the temple." She directed them to a large couch before a fireplace taller than Sam's head and twice as wide. "Would you excuse me? I need to put something on. I was just by the pool. I'll be right back." She smiled apologetically and disappeared up the circular stairs in the foyer.

Both Elders walked slowly around the room, looking at the unusual decor. The room, while very large, felt like it was almost too small. The illusion of the building gave the feeling of a huge castle. Now they were in a room that should have been vast to complete the illusion, yet it was not much more than a large living room. It was still impressive. The room was two stories high, with tall slotted windows. The wall to their left held a huge tapestry that covered the entire wall from side to side and nearly to the ceiling. All around the room near the ceiling were rows of animal trophies. There were lions, bears, water buffalo, rhinoceros, zebra, and a host of others. Medieval suits of armor with swords and spears stood in all four corners of the room. The opposite wall held a collection of massive portraits. The figures all wore the ornate clothing of medieval times, but the dates on the portraits were more recent.

They had barely begun discovering all the strange trappings in the room when the girl returned. She had pulled on a silken robe over her bathing suit. In reality, the robe did little to cover her and only added to her beauty. Sam had the fleeting unmissionary-like thought that she looked stunning as she came down the large staircase. But by the way she hopped down the stairs two at a time, he seriously doubted she was trying to impress them.

"My name is Dawn Pauley," she said breathlessly, offering Sam a slender hand.

"Don? D-O-N?" Sam asked, taking her hand. It felt warm and delicate, almost as if it might break if handled roughly.

"Dawn," she repeated, "as in the rising of the sun." She pronounced her name by prolonging the vowel sound. It came out "Daauwn" when she spoke it, and sounded exotic and magical.

"Oh, excuse me, Dawn. Pleasure to meet you."

She smiled at him and graciously shook Elder Hall's hand. She motioned for them to sit and took a large chair by the fireplace. She crossed her legs, and the robe slid open, leaving very little to the imagination.

"Look at the floor," Sam whispered to his companion, whose eyes were having a hard time staying in his head. Elder Hall nodded and obediently looked at the floor with an obvious effort.

Sam felt as if the huge couch was swallowing him. He had never sat in a chair with such massive cushions. Since it was Elder Hall's day, he resumed, still looking at the floor.

"Dawn, as we said earlier, we are from The Church of Jesus Christ of Latter-day Saints. We're glad you enjoyed your visit to Temple Square. Your father indicated that he would like a visit from us, so here we are."

"Do you chaps realize that we visited Temple Square over two years ago?"

"I'm sorry," Elder Hall replied, glancing at her face and then back to the floor. "They don't date our paperwork. This far from Utah, it sometimes takes a long time to follow through."

"That's fine. It's actually sweet that you remembered after all this time. Daddy will like that. But he isn't home. He usually gets home about six o'clock." She glanced at a huge grandfather clock to her left. It read a little before three. "I wouldn't want him to miss meeting you. He was very impressed and has been anxious to have someone call from the Church. If you like, you can join me in the pool. We have lots of bathing suits. That would be a fun way to spend the next few hours. Daddy usually comes home and takes a dip anyway. It would be perfect."

"Actually," Elder Hall explained, "as missionaries, swimming with attractive, young women is one of the things we aren't supposed to do. Appealing as your invitation is, I hope you will forgive us if we decline." He handled it so smoothly that Sam was proud of him.

She let her bottom lip slip forward in a pout and then smiled at them. "I should have guessed as much. Of course you can't. I meant no disrespect. Well, then the best I can do is to invite you back at seven. He will be pleased to receive you then." She stood gracefully, and adjusted the gossamer robe around her. Sam had to look away to keep his eyes off her body. He felt ashamed that he had no more self-control than that.

Once back in the car, they both wiped sweat from their brows, and not from the heat. "That was as close as I want to get to being tempted by a beautiful woman, Elder," Kim said with a sigh. "And she wasn't even trying to tempt us. Man, I need a three-day fast!"

Sam laughed and nodded agreement. He had liked the young lady, but sincerely hoped for their sakes that she had more in her wardrobe than the bikini and a silk robe.

Seven o'clock found them again knocking on the huge door. This time, a butler answered the door. He was dressed in a butler's uniform and invited them in with a sweeping bow. He led them past the big living room and into a study.

"The master will join you shortly," he said matter-of-factly, and closed the double sliding doors. The study walls were lined on three sides with bookshelves. It reminded him of the study in the mission home. Like in the mission home, many of these books were old and probably very valuable. This room was also tall, with the bookshelves extending far higher than any person could reach. Above the shelves, a silent zoo of smaller trophies stared at them with glassy eyes. One shelf held birds, some with their wings fully extended; Sam noted that they were all birds of prey. Another wall held a fine collection of small cats. He saw several that reminded him of the American bobcat. While the collection was impressive, the carnage made him feel slightly uncomfortable. A lot of animals had died to decorate these walls.

The Elders were so intent on the trophies that neither of them heard the study doors open. "It is an impressive collection, isn't it?" a voice said behind them. They both turned to see a middle-aged man dressed in a red smoking jacket and silk pants. He held a pipe in his teeth. He was slender and obviously athletic, with sandy hair and a slim mustache. His eyes were a pale blue. He smiled and shook their hands. When he spoke, his accent was heavily British. It completed the impression of the great white hunter.

"Damn decent of you to finally look me up after all this time," he said. "Please, take a seat." They pulled plush chairs toward the desk and sat. He took a seat behind the desk.

"Dawn told me you're from the Mormons?"

"Yes sir, The Church of Jesus Christ of Latter-day Saints," Elder Hall replied.

He nodded and puffed a cloud of blue smoke that rose slowly toward the ceiling. The pipe had a sweet, fruity smell that Sam did not find at all objectionable. It smelled more like fruit and roses than tobacco.

"As you know, Dawn and I visited there two years ago. Very impressive and most enjoyable. We went to every little performance and attended every tour. Had a splendid time. Had you come the day I returned to Africa, I probably would have joined your church without much of a to-do. As it is, I've kind of lost interest. Don't want to put you two lads off your feet, but I'm not interested in discussing religion. I hope that doesn't offend you. I know you've traveled a damn long way to visit me. Terribly sorry and all."

Elder Hall straightened in his chair. "Mr. Pauley, we live here in South Africa. We didn't travel from America for the sole purpose of visiting you, so you don't owe us an apology. We are on a mission for the Church and will be here in your country for two years."

"Quite right, of course. Much the better then. Splendid that I haven't put you out as much as I had originally thought. Still, I have to say that I anxiously awaited your coming for several months. Perhaps I'll go back some day, and that will rekindle the spark."

At that moment, Dawn entered the study carrying a tray of silver with four teacups. This time she was wearing a soft blue dress that extended from under her chin to her ankles and left everything to the imagination. In many ways, it made her even more beautiful. For the first time, Sam noted how finely chiseled her face was. She had her hair done up in soft ringlets. She could have walked from the room and attended any formal ball.

"Ah, there you are, Dawn. Thank you, my dear. Very thoughtful of you. Elders? Would you care for red bush tea?" he asked, using the English name for rooibos tea. "Dawn says you can drink it. Not real tea or coffee though, I understand, hey?"

They nodded and accepted the teacups she handed them. After offering them cream and sugar, she took a seat near Sam and sipped her own tea.

"Dawn," Mr. Pauley continued. "I was just telling these lads that I'm no longer keen to become a Mormon. What about you, dear? Do you still want to listen to these chaps?" He said it all so calmly, that it sounded as if they were discussing whether to have one lump of sugar or two.

"Daddy, you were the one who was so enthusiastic back then. I'm surprised you've lost it. You have often talked about it. To be honest, I have anticipated the missionaries coming only because of your interest. But now that you're no longer interested . . ." she said, pausing.

Sam could feel the rejection hovering in the air. He silently braced himself. He had been sent away so many times that another rejection would be just that—another rejection. He had long ago overcome the sense of personal failure at each refusal. Still, his heart ached as each of Father's children turned away from their opportunity to know Him better.

He looked into Dawn's eyes and saw more than a lovely woman. He saw a precious, spiritually significant daughter of Heavenly Father, and he prayed her heart would feel the need as keenly as his did. She reciprocated his gaze, then looked back at her father.

"I think I still want to know more. Would that be okay, Daddy?"

"Sure, my dear. You check it out. If it's really good, let me know, and maybe I'll come listen in," he said, blowing a blue cloud of smoke and leaning back in his chair. He suddenly stood up. "I'm going for a dip in the pool. You three carry on without me. Cheerio," he said, and left the room.

They taught Dawn the first discussion, which she enjoyed. It was a delight to teach her since she was sweet, unassuming, and believing. Her questions, while deep, were to explore the truth, not to challenge or dispute.

As they came to know her, they learned more about the Pauley family and their amazing house.

The castle had been built by her grandfather and passed on to his son, Dawn's father. The grandfather had made a great deal of money as a newspaper publisher. He loved castles and could afford to make his dream home look like one. The castle was, in fact, much larger than it appeared. There were over one hundred rooms, twenty-five of which were bedrooms. There was a six-car garage, two pools, two tennis courts, an indoor squash court, four formal living rooms, two libraries, two kitchens, four dining rooms, several game rooms, and a host of other rooms. Since her mother's death, they had closed off most of the huge building and occupied only a small portion of the whole.

One evening after the third discussion, on impulse Dawn stood and walked to the bookshelves. "Daddy doesn't like me showing these things to people. I only found this one a few weeks ago while cleaning." She pulled down on piece of trim near the third row of books. A latch clicked, and the bookshelf silently swung inward. She motioned for them to follow.

Dawn flipped on a light switch and they found themselves in a narrow, carpeted hallway. The walls were expensive wood, and the carpeting a plush green, though coated with dust. A few feet away, the hall came to a "T." She led them to the right, and they soon approached a stairway.

"This stairway rises in a cavity below the stairs in the foyer. It goes up and leads to secret openings in most of the bedrooms upstairs." She walked past the stairs to a blank wall. She placed the palm of her hand on the panel and slid it to the left. Beyond was a dark piece of glass. Sam stepped forward and moved closer to the glass. He could see a darkened room beyond, and immediately recognized it as the main living room. They were looking through the large mirror on the wall! Dawn slid the panel closed and led them past the hall they had just entered, which opened more panels to their view.

"Many of these panels open to allow you to see into other rooms. Some of them open into secret doors. I spent most of my childhood exploring these passageways. I know more about them than Daddy. He doesn't seem to be too interested. I can get from one end of the castle to the other without stepping out of these secret hallways."

By now she was walking so quickly that the Elders had to practically run to keep up. "I have found several rooms that have no other entrance than by these halls. One of them has a lot of guns and things. Several of the doors are thick and locked. I think Grandpa was afraid someone would discover these secret passages, so he locked even some of the secret doors. I don't know who has the key, or if anyone does."

She turned left, and then right, and stopped by a panel. She pushed left, and it slid open. A gust of frigid air rushed through the opening. She chuckled when the Elders seemed startled. She stepped through and flipped on a light. She was standing in a cooler. Stainless steel shelves filled with food surrounded her. They followed her through.

The secret door slid closed on its own. She pushed open the heavy door to the cooler, and they stepped out into a huge kitchen.

"I sometimes go this way to get a midnight snack," she confessed sheepishly as she led them to a counter that held a plate under a domed crystal cover. She lifted the cover to reveal three huge cinnamon rolls. "The prize at the end of the maze," she said happily, and carefully lifted one roll onto a china plate. She handed it to Sam and then another to Elder Hall. She then led them to a small dining area, where they talked and laughed as they ate the sticky sweet rolls.

Sam found Dawn's father intriguing. Oliver Pauley was forty-seven years old, and a diamond cutter by profession. One evening, instead of teaching Dawn immediately, they listened to him describe his line of work.

"I'm a cutter," he explained. "And without being presumptuous, I'm one of the best. I have a type of spiritual connection with the stones which you chaps might understand. I can feel their inner beauty and instinctively know how to cut them. However, I haven't cut a stone for years. I presently manage a cutting house for Goldstein, Goldstein, and Meyers. I direct the other cutters on how to find the magic in each stone."

"Wow," Elder Hall exclaimed, "it must pay really well."

"In fact," Oliver replied, drawing deeply on his pipe. "I work for nothing."

"How can that be?" Sam asked.

"Come on, Daddy. Tell them the whole thing," Dawn urged, her voice childlike.

He laughed. "When they offered me the position, they gave me two options. One was a handsome salary. The other was the pick of any stone that went through their shop, at their cost. The only limitation is that I cannot sell any stones in this country. I chose the latter. It has proven to be a wise decision."

"But if you can't sell any diamonds in this country, how can you make a living?" Elder Hall asked.

"Twice a year, I take two or three of my favorites, mount them in jewelry, and Dawn and I go on a vacation. First, we go to England, where we sell the stones for a handsome profit. Since they are mounted in jewelry, there is no import duty. We deposit the proceeds from the sale in a Swiss bank and head off to some new exotic destination for a couple of weeks."

"Wow, that's amazing," Sam said. "It makes me wonder why more people don't do it."

"Few people can buy stones at the cutter's cost. The only reason they let me is that I make them millions of rand each year. They know I could get a similar or better deal anywhere I go. Few people have my affinity for the stones, you see."

"Amazing," Sam said again.

"As a matter of fact," Oliver continued, leaning forward as if this were especially important. "I'm looking for people to do the traveling for me. Anyone with an American passport would be perfect. If I trusted them, we could do some lucrative business. I have a South African passport, and if I go more than twice a year, the customs laws allow them to tax my stones whether they are mounted in jewelry or not. They wouldn't pay any attention to a person with an American passport."

"What are you getting at?" Elder Hall asked, a suspicious tone to his voice.

"I'm a business man, and this is a business proposal. It has nothing to do with your teaching Dawn or with your mission. Here's the deal, lads. After your mission, you go home and raise $10,000 dollars. Come back to me, and I will sell you $50,000 dollars worth of diamonds, already mounted in jewelry. I'll introduce you to my buyers in England, where they will help you set up a Swiss account and transfer the money for you. You return home with $40,000 dollars in your hands. I make $5,000 on each transaction. I have enough buyers that you could make the trip once a month and never go to the same place twice."

He stopped to exhale another curl of blue smoke. "I have several people doing this already. They make their entire living doing it, and they live well. It works to everyone's advantage. You could make nearly half a million a year and travel all over the globe."

"I don't mean this to be an insulting question," Elder Hall said, "but, is it legal?"

"Certainly. It's a common practice. I've had several international lawyers check the various customs and import laws, and they all concluded that it is perfectly legal. You are welcome to read their letters so stating, if you wish."

* * *

Elder Hall could not sleep that night, thinking about diamonds. Mr. Pauley's proposal was indeed intriguing, and he considered it over and over. It was still on Kim's mind when they returned three days later to teach Dawn, and he had some more questions to ask. However, Dawn was home alone.

"I'm so sorry," she said as soon as she opened the door. "But I have an unexpected matter I need to attend to. A neighbor has lost their youngest son in a tragic accident. He was killed while playing soccer at school, of all things. Broke his neck." She sighed and stepped out onto the front porch. "They are having a gathering of friends at their home, and I really need to go. They have been friends for years. I hope you understand."

They did understand and assured her it was fine. They made another appointment for the following day and were just climbing into their car when she walked toward them, a smile on her face.

"I just thought of something. Why don't you come with me? They know I'm studying with the Mormon Elders, and they were supportive of the idea. It might be nice to have you come. What do you think? Afterward, if you still have time, we could do our discussion."

They exchanged glances and said in unison, "Sounds good." She smiled and turned away. She trotted several steps toward the garage and stopped suddenly.

"Do you chaps want to ride with me? Daddy said I could take the Jaguar. I'm a good driver, and I don't speed." She pronounced it "jagyour." They watched as the third garage door opened smoothly and the roar of an engine filled the yard. A sleek, red Jaguar convertible backed out into the lane. Sam noticed it was an XKE. It had a V12 engine and looked as if it were faster than a bat out of the hot place.

Sam climbed into the passenger seat, and Elder Hall squeezed into the tiny space behind that passed for a back seat. Sam gripped the door as she shoved it into gear. She touched the gas and the car jolted forward, belching smoke in a roar of burning rubber.

"Oops," she said and gave him an apologetic look. "I always forget how powerful this thing is." She started again, this time rolling smoothly down the lane. When she reached the road, she carefully powered onto the road. Even driven conservatively, the mighty roadster was a thrill. Sam felt his heart pounding as Dawn touched the gas and it leaped down the road. She took them on a short but dizzying journey deeper into the subdivision. Every home they passed was a palace.

Finally, they pulled up to a huge English Tudor-style home. She stopped on the curb and killed the engine. There were nearly a dozen other vehicles parked nearby. Sam counted four Rolls Royces and two Cadillacs. A butler met them at the door and ushered them into the living room. It was palatial in size, with two huge gold and crystal chandeliers at opposite ends of the high ceiling.

At the far end of the room, a couple stood side-by-side, their faces gripped with grief. They tried to entertain their guests, but every few minutes, one of them would have to turn away. Sam watched as the mother turned away from the crowd, and her shoulders shook with silent sobs.

He was transported back to the tragic days following Jimmy's accident, and it was as if he were watching his own parents grieve again. His heart felt as if it would break. Without waiting for an invitation, he walked directly toward them. He was only vaguely aware of Elder Hall following in his wake through the crowded room.

Dawn arrived at his side, and after embracing her friends, she turned and introduced Sam and Elder Hall. To their left, a picture of a handsome young boy was displayed on a grand piano. It was surrounded by cut flowers.

"Mr. and Mrs. Feinstein, this is a friend of mine, Elder Mahoy," Dawn said, and Sam and Elder Hall shook the couple's hands. The father was a short, balding man in his late forties with sandy blonde hair and a Roman-style beard. He shook Sam's hand without enthusiasm, and almost immediately looked back at the photo on the piano.

Mrs. Feinstein grasped Sam's hand and looked into his eyes. She was somewhat younger than her husband and possessed the most penetrating ice-blue eyes Sam had ever seen. A twin course of tears spilled down her cheeks, and he suppressed an urge to take her into his arms to comfort her. Somehow, she sensed his concern and smiled wanly.

A powerful urge to give them something swept over Sam, and he pondered what he possessed that might ease their pain. He had no flowers, no sympathy card, no poetry, and no inspiring thoughts. He glanced at the piano and realized that he did possess something. The music that endlessly played in his mind was there—sweet, flowing, and comforting. He stepped back, and Mrs. Feinstein released her grip.

He nodded toward the piano. "May I?" He asked.

Her eyes brightened, and she nodded, taking a step toward the big, black piano.

Sam sat and raised the lid. It was a Knabe piano, considered by many to be the finest piano in the world. Made in America, they routinely sold in Africa for sums exceeding $50,000 dollars. He played a brief chord and found it perfectly tuned. The music was there, waiting in his heart, but something was missing. He wanted to give them something permanent, more lasting than just music that evaporates into memory when the last note is played.

"Do you have a tape recorder?" he asked.

Mr. Feinstein nodded at a servant who was standing near the arched hallway. The servant disappeared, then came back a few minutes later rolling in a cart containing a large reel-to-reel recorder. He placed a microphone on top of the piano, and aimed another at Sam as if he expected him to sing.

Instead, Sam picked up the mike and handed it to Mrs. Feinstein. She took it hesitantly. The servant clicked on the big recorder, and the reels moved ahead slowly.

"Mrs. Feinstein, what was your son's name?"

"Lawson," she said hesitantly, "Lawson Levi Feinstein, Junior." Her voice was filled with pride, which wilted as soon as the words escaped her lips.

"Tell me about Lawson. Start with his age and tell me the special things about him, what he liked, the things he loved doing—all his favorite things and what made you love him most. When I start playing, I'd like you to keep talking. Speak up so I can hear you. Whatever comes to your mind, just say it, okay?"

She looked a bit self-conscious, but slowly began to speak. "Lawson was twelve. I guess his favorite thing in the world was camping. We all love to camp. We have this favorite place, where there's a small waterfall and a brook with clear, cold water."

Sam could almost see the waterfall, and the music it made as it happily tumbled over the rocks. He began to play, light and happy, spilling, rolling. His fingers caressed the keys, and the music became a giggling waterfall on a warm summer day.

Mrs. Feinstein stopped, momentarily mesmerized by the music, and Sam nodded at her to go on.

"I believe it was by that stream that his father first showed him how to kick a soccer ball. He was eight years old and took to it immediately. We played all afternoon. We ran, laughed, and kicked that ball until we were all so weary and happy that we could hardly walk."

Sam closed his eyes, and the ball flew through the music in long, intricate runs and bounced happily from person to person.

"It was almost dark, and my husband kicked the ball one last time. Lawson missed it, and the ball rolled into the stream. We tried to catch it, but it was quickly gone in the dark." She paused, remembering, as if she were there once again. "Lawson cried."

The music tumbled, turned minor, and rumbled like thunder, but then, just as suddenly, became happy again.

"Besides camping and soccer, I think he loved Mickey Mouse the most. I'll never forget the first Mickey Mouse cartoon we took him to. We had to stay and watch it three times!" She laughed as the music played M-I-C, K-E-Y, M-O-U-S-E. Everyone in the room chuckled and clapped their hands.

"His favorite movie was Doctor Zhivago, which surprised me at the time, because it is such an adult movie. But he loved it, especially the part where they meet again after so many years in that mansion filled with ice and snow. I remember watching him cry as he thought of their sadness and joy. He was an unusually mature child, I think."

The music became the dark days of the Russian revolution, and the bittersweet love story of Doctor Zhivago rolled majestically from the piano.

"I think the thing I will miss most," his father said, now standing close, facing his wife, both of their hands on the microphone that was now forgotten, "is his laughter. He was so alive and so happy," he said. "He was a bright star, a flash of sunlight in my life. Every time I saw him, he smiled at me, even when he was angry with me for punishing him or missing a soccer game. I can't remember one time when he didn't smile . . ."

"Yes," his wife agreed, "that was our son. I wish I knew where he is, if he's happy, if he still loves soccer . . ." her voice trailed off into silence. The music continued for almost a full minute, aching, wondering, weeping, and seeking answers.

"Let me share something with you," Sam said. The Feinstein started and looked at him as if seeing him for the first time. She nodded and, as an afterthought, set the microphone back on the piano.

"I want to tell you what my heart tells me, what my faith tells me." As he spoke, the music quietly turned to "I Am a Child of God."

The music flowed magically from Sam's soul, as if inseparably connected to his words.

"I believe we are children of a loving Father in Heaven—all of us. Since we are children of an eternal being, we also possess the seeds of eternity within us. As tragic as dying seems, it is not an end, but a beginning. We leave this life and enter the next still the same person, but freed from the limitations of mortality. It is my firm conviction that Lawson still lives as a spirit in the presence of God. It is my great joy to have complete faith in the truth that you will one day hold your son in your arms again. Until then, we endure this brief separation we call death with faith in God."

He turned back to the piano and finished the song with a reverent and beautiful flourish. He lifted his hands, and quite unexpectedly, a voice carried across the room. It was a man's voice, high and melodious. The voice carried across the room, as if from another world, rich and pure. It was as if an angel had come to add his testimony to Sam's. The crowd parted once again, and a man walked forward, singing "I Am a Child of God." He sang with reverent passion, pressing both fists to his chest, raising his chin, as if singing directly to God. His eyes glistened as he stopped beside the piano. Sam began once again, playing, not the melody, but an intricate harmony. His fingers did a ballet on the keys as the stranger's voice penetrated every soul.

The singer knew all three verses, and he sang them as if they were the final act of his life. Sam's heart soared, and tears ran down his cheeks. For him, nothing now existed but the music and the words he had known since childhood:

I am a child of God
And He has sent me here.
Has given me an earthly home
With parents kind and dear.

I am a child of God
And so my needs are great.
Help me to understand His will
Before it grows too late.

I am a child of God
Rich blessings are in store.
If I but learn to do His will
I'll live with Him once more.

Lead me, Guide me,
Walk beside me.
Help me find the way.
Teach me all that I must do
To live with Him someday.

The music ceased, the tape recorder clicked off, and Sam slowly closed the lid on the piano. He stood up, and Lawson's mother embraced him and held him as she laughed and wept on his shoulder. "Thank you," she said quietly in his ear. "I will long treasure this moment and the memories you have created for us. I did not realize until now that I know in my heart that Lawson is still alive— somewhere, somehow. We are Jewish by descent, although we are not religious; yet I believe what you have said to be true."

She wiped the tears from her cheeks, then glanced back at her husband, who nodded in agreement. "Would you come back and teach us what the words of that song mean? Come back and teach me why, against logic and hope, I still believe that Lawson lives."

Sam nodded at her, and smiled them both. She released Sam, new tears of joy and relief streamed from her eyes. She stepped back and was swept into an embrace by Dawn.

Mr. Feinstein took Sam's hand in both of his. "Thank you," he mouthed, no sound coming from his lips.

His purpose done, Sam walked quickly to the door and out into the hot afternoon. He was sitting in the passenger seat of the Jaguar waiting for Dawn when the stranger with the beautiful voice appeared outside the house. He caught sight of Sam and walked directly toward the car. Sam opened the car door to greet him.

"Elder," the man said, taking Sam's hand. "I am Sir Philip De Vries. I doubt you know me, but I sing opera with the South African Operatic Company. It may surprise you to know that I was once a member of your Mormon Church, although I confess I have not returned in twenty years. I have long known that simple song "I Am a Child of God,"—every word of it. When you started playing, I was so deeply touched that the words literally burst from me. I hope you will forgive me if I upstaged you. I didn't mean to."

Sam shook his head.

"I thought not," the man continued, a smile softening his face. "Even though I have stayed away from the Church, that song still speaks to me as a testimony of the eternal nature of the soul. Today as I sang it, my heart again received a sweet witness of the truthfulness of those words. I felt as if I could see into heaven and glimpse the endless joy God ordains for those who return to Him with unstained hands." He paused. Something was on his mind, and he was searching for words that seemed hidden to him. He continued in a voice soft with emotion.

"I am intimately familiar with the performing arts and persons of vast talent. Yet, I must say, my young friend, that your music is superior to all of them. Not because you possess a greater talent. Indeed, almost all my acquaintances could perform circles around you. No, it is because of the purity of your soul. You believe the message of your music with all your heart. For this reason, your music is truly divine." His voice faltered, and he grasped Sam's hand again. "Thank you, Elder Sam, for showing me the music the angels sing. Thank you for rekindling the bright flame of truth in my soul again. I will return to those truths I had forgotten for so long. Yes, I will return to God and His restored Church, beginning this very moment. My soul truly rejoices!"

So saying, he released Sam's hand and quickly departed. Sam stood on the pavement in stunned silence, then bowed his head in joy.

* * *

That evening, as they studied the scriptures before going to bed, they were surprised by a knock on their door. Sam straightened his tie, and answered the knock. Two uniformed officers stood before him. A moment of panic swept over him as the grim-faced officers handed him an envelope. His panic vanished as he read "Elder Sam" in flowing script. The envelope bore the return address of the Regional Prosecutor. The letter inside was in Sister Van der Kerk's flowing script.

My Dearest Elder Sam Mahoy,

It has come to our pleasant attention that you are now stationed in Durban, Natal. Since Brother Van der Kerk won the prosecutorship, we have purchased a new home in Pretoria to be near the seat of government; however, we spend three months each year in Durban. We are presently here and anxious to meet you once again.

Some good friends want missionary discussions, and we hoped you would teach them.

We know they are out of your teaching area, so all the above is just a ploy to see you again!

We formally invite you, your companion, and all your fellow missionaries in your area to join us for dinner this Friday evening. Be sure to bring everyone and a hearty appetite.

If you are able, please send word with the gentlemen who delivered this letter. They will pick you up at 6:00 p.m. that evening, if you agree.

Until then, we leave our love.
Brother and Sister Van der Kerk

Six o'clock Friday evening found Sam's small room crammed with eight Elders. When their car arrived, it was a stretch limousine, into which they all comfortably fit. The Van der Kerk's home was spread out over a hill near the coast. Sam's heart pounded in his chest as they drove up the cobblestone drive.

Sister Van der Kerk flung open the door and ran to the car as it pulled up. As soon as Sam emerged, she swept him into her arms and kissed both of his cheeks, releasing him only after the other missionaries cleared their throats.

"Well," Elder Hall said under his breath, his voice alive with humor, "I'll bet that greeting was against mission rules." She heard, and turned toward him.

"I have vast experience getting rules changed. If need be, young man, we'll change this one. It must be a stupid rule anyway."

She laughed at her own humor, and laced an arm through Sam's. She led him into the large foyer of her new home. She explained that it was owned by the government, set aside for the use of government officials. It seemed as if no expense had been spared. She led them from room to room, letting them "ooh and aah" at the lavish furnishings and grand design.

"Our home in Pretoria is much smaller. You would be proud, Elder Sam," she said happily. "Since joining the Church, our desire for opulence has diminished to zero. Our home is just adequate. It is kind of embarrassing to live in this great home, but we suffer along as best we can." That brought a laugh from everyone, including her. However, she was serious.

She led them to a huge dining room that held a table adequate for seating as many as forty guests. The ceiling was arched with open woodwork of great skill and beauty. Along one side, near the ceiling, were flags of the various cities. Along the opposite side were flags of the nations. The table was spread with a single white cloth and set with gold tableware. She showed them to their places and indicated a place for Sam near the end. She sat on the end, leaving a vacant seat beside her for her husband. A door closed, and Brother Van der Kerk scurried into the room. Sam stood and embraced him. He had been detained but was finally there. A servant took his briefcase and coat and they both sat down. Brother Van der Kerk asked Sam to pray.

The meal began with half an avocado stuffed with chilled shrimp. It was the size of an ostrich egg, sweet and smooth. The shrimp was in a light cocktail sauce and was the finest Sam had tasted. Sister Van der Kerk urged them to only sample each dish. The combination of avocado and shrimp was unique and difficult to just sample. Sam allowed himself to slowly savor the exotic flavors. Next came a soup made of water buffalo and black beans. The taste of the soup was so complete that it awakened taste buds never before used.

Next came a fruit salad in half a pineapple shell. It was made entirely of kiwi, grapes, pineapple bits, and narchi. The narchi was a large, grapelike fruit with its single pip removed. The meat immediately around the narchi seed was so bitter that no human could eat it. Once the bitter fruit was removed, there was no sweeter fruit than a narchi. The effect was so exotic and sweet that it should have been a dessert.

Following the salad came a plate with a single Lorenzo Marx prawn upon it. The large prawn was the size of a lobster. The missionaries had never seen a shrimp so large or ugly. Some of them just stared, their eyes growing large at the idea of eating such a grotesque monstrosity. Sister Carlson lifted hers and demonstrated how to open the shell and get the sweet meat within. After some encouragement, the missionaries gamely pried, twisted, and poked, until they succeeded. The meat was rich beyond belief. One taste was all it took to make them believers. Sam's mouth almost refused to believe that something this succulent existed. Each bite was a tiny bit of heaven. He found himself wishing there had been ten of them on his plate rather than one. Yet, by the time the shrimp had deteriorated to a pile of loose shells, he was full.

Next, the servants brought a frosty parfait glass filled with a bubbling liquid. Deep inside the liquid were three tiny scoops of ice cream. They sipped the almost-bitter liquid and ate the ice cream with long-handled spoons.

As they ate, Sister Van der Kerk explained, "In a traditional feast, what you have just eaten would be the appetizers. This drink is unsweetened mineral water, with a tiny bit of ice cream for sweetness and flavor. It settles the stomach and freshens the palate. In a moment, you will begin to feel hungry again, which is a good thing, because we have prepared what we hope is a very American treat."

At her words, servants placed large bowls of food before them. All around them swirled familiar smells. As each plate was set before them, Sister Van der Kerk described it. There were mashed potatoes from Idaho, candied yams from New York, corn on the cob from California, honeyed ham from Kentucky, corn fritters from Kansas, crayfish from Louisiana, and a host of other dishes, all from the States.

As each dish was introduced, the missionaries sighed with delight. The Van der Kerks had done their homework. A feast was prepared for each elder, carefully chosen to remind him of home.

The last dish to appear was a gigantic turkey. No one was disappointed. Sam later found out that they had telephoned the parents of each elder and asked what his favorite dish was.

Sister Van der Kerk's love for the Elders and her desire to please them was reflected in the great cost of international phone calls to the States, which was nearly a hundred dollars each.

By the time dessert was to be served, not a single soul could eat a bite more. Sister Van der Kerk stood and disappeared for a few minutes. She returned with a New York cheesecake, complete with blueberry topping. Sam loved blueberry cheesecake above all other foods. Atop the cake were twenty-one candles burning brightly. Behind her, a stream of servants brought in deserts for each Elder, each different, each burning cheerily with birthday candles. Elder Hall's dessert was a huge cantaloupe half, filled with orange sherbet ice cream, his favorite dessert. She set the cheesecake before Sam and sang "Happy Birthday." Though a little confused, everyone joined in. Birthdays are the hardest days for missionaries. They often go unnoticed, uncelebrated, and unsung.

"I know it isn't anyone's birthday today," she said as soon as the singing ceased. "I also know that you often don't celebrate them much because your families are so far away. This is my way of showing you my love and saying thank you. I am so grateful you came to our land. Please, make a wish and blow out your candles before you have to eat wax." They all laughed and blew.

A cloud of smoke wafted up from the table. Servants appeared with plates and deftly cut huge pieces of dessert for everyone, while another scooped ice cream of exotic flavors.

Not a single fork moved as they stared at the enormous plates of dessert, yet the sweetness was not on their table but in their hearts, and they treasured the joy of the moment. The only one who finished his dessert was Elder Hall, who also ate the other half of the cantaloupe.

An hour later, Elders were sprawled all over the huge living room, groaning in various states of blissful consciousness. With the exception of Elder Hall, they had all dismantled the word of wisdom with their forks.

Sister Van der Kerk found Sam lying on an oriental rug and indicated with a nod that she wished him to follow her. With some difficulty, he rolled to a kneeling position and pushed himself to his feet. She chuckled at him from the doorway. Elder Hall stood to follow him. She led them through several rooms and halls until they came to a game room. Brother Van der Kerk sat on the edge of a large billiards table, which was illuminated by an elaborate stained glass lamp hanging low over the table. He was holding a cue.

He handed them both a cue, and Sister Van der Kerk pulled one from the rack.

"Elders, have you ever played billiards?" he asked, motioning to the oversized table. It was larger than a pool table. Neither of them had. He explained the rules. They played one game, and then Brother Van der Kerk grew serious. "Elder Sam, I have looked forward to this opportunity for nearly a year now. We haven't spoken since our baptism, and I have longed for this day."

Sam turned to face him. Sister Van der Kerk walked to her husband's side and slipped her arm through his. It was clear that what he was about to say was important to them both.

"I have some unfinished business," he said, his voice breaking. He lowered his head. There was a long moment of silence. Elder Hall made a loud shot and mumbled something about the seven ball. It was his way of not being involved in the conversation, and it was appreciated. "Elder . . . ," he said and then paused. "Sam, my soul has been tormented almost without respite. I wake up in the middle of the night in a sweat and can't sleep. It is the one part of my life that my baptism did not wash away, and I need your help."

Sam was mystified and a little frightened by his words. "What is it? How can I help?" he asked, his voice echoing his deep concern. These were people he loved and cared about deeply.

"How you can help, is by hearing my confession," Brother Van der Kerk said.

Sam felt an electric bolt of fear stab through him, but before he could say a word, Brother and Sister Van der Kerk exchanged a quick glance, and Brother Van der Kerk continued.

"Well, that isn't what I mean, exactly. I guess what I need is to beg your forgiveness."

"Whatever for?" Sam demanded, his voice curious.

"For having you whipped that day in court," he said, his head lowered. His hands trembled, and tears dripped onto the deep green carpet.

Sam wanted to brush it aside but was stopped by a gentle urging from the Spirit. Instead, he said nothing.

"You see, I was so arrogant, so . . . official. I felt no remorse at the time. I thought you would learn a lesson, that we didn't want you in South Africa, that we were willing to cause you physical torment to deliver that message. I thought you deserved it for bringing a false religion into my beloved country." He fumbled with the cue, his wife still holding onto his arm.

"Yet, you know well the effect that event has had upon me—upon us. We have found the truth. Heavenly Father, through you, gave us truth and love and hopefully eternal life in response to my evil treatment of you."

Sam took a step forward and laid a hand on his arm. He didn't know what to say.

Brother Van der Kerk continued, "I was the one who made the observation that you were like Paul who had been whipped for teaching Christ." He paused and sobbed. "What I was blind to at the time, was that I was like the wicked men who ordered Paul scourged. Since this thought entered my heart, I have lain awake nights, terrified that I have jeopardized my exaltation. I allowed a representative of Jesus Christ to be scourged. It is the same as if I had stood by and allowed Christ himself to be whipped when it was within my power to stop it. My soul mourns more than words can express that I had so little valor that I willingly stooped to such evil. I can scarcely pray since my guilt is so heavy upon my soul. If God were to walk into this room, I would beg the house to fall on me, to hide me from His presence."

It seemed to Sam as if the only reason he did not fall to his knees was because Sister Van der Kerk still held his arm. It was as if the weight of damnation were upon his soul.

Sam stood quietly, with tears trickling down his cheeks, until his heart flowed with the right words. "There are two observations I want to make, if you'll allow me," he replied.

The Van der Kerks nodded solemnly.

"First, as you already know, I do forgive you. In fact, I look back on those events with rejoicing. I consider it a small price to pay to be able to find you and teach you. I love you, and you need never think otherwise."

"We know this is true," Sister Van der Kerk said softly. "Second, I believe your answer lies in a statement you made."

Brother Van der Kerk looked up, an expression of confusion and doubt on his face.

"You said, 'I can hardly pray, my guilt is so heavy.' Do you remember?" Brother Van der Kerk nodded.

"There's a scripture in Mosiah that says in part that it is the evil spirit that teaches a man not to pray. The effect of this long, painful, process of dwelling on the past and being harrowed up with awful feelings has taught you not to pray. Brother Van der Kerk, you are laboring under the effects of a false spirit. You have been listening to the wrong voice."

Brother Van der Kerk looked up, his eyes hopeful yet confused. "I don't understand," he said. "I thought this was the effect of the Holy Spirit working on me, bringing me to godly sorrow, to repentance, to the recognition of my woeful state."

Sam allowed a doubtful look to cross his features. "The process of repentance is often painful. It does bring a person to recognize their need for repentance and feel bad for their sins. But it never teaches a person they are worthless, lost, or beyond redemption. And it certainly never teaches them to stop praying. When the Holy Spirit works with a person, the end effect is peace and joy and brings a person closer to Christ—not further away. The Holy Spirit leaves one with an intense desire to pray, not to hide under the rubble of a tortured soul.

Sam stopped for a moment to let his words sink in, before he continued. "A scripture in Galatians that I memorized awhile ago goes like this: 'But the fruit of the Spirit is love, joy, peace, longsuffering, gentleness, goodness, faith, meekness, temperance' " (Galatians 5:23). "Nowhere in that scripture does it list shame, fear, hopelessness, alienation, shrinking from the presence of God, or any of the negative emotions you described as coming from this experience. I think you need to reevaluate this experience. You have needlessly allowed yourself to be tormented by events long past and long forgiven."

Brother Van der Kerk stared at him in wonder. "So, all this time that I have felt worthless and believed that God no longer loved me, I was actually being deceived by Satan." It was not a question. He straightened, laying his cue across the table. The pain that formerly twisted his features was gone. He took a deep breath and smiled. "I feel so much better. I was to the point of not wanting to go to church because I felt unworthy. Now that I understand, it seems so plain, so simple. I will remember from now on. If the effect of a thought process makes me feel worthless and like not praying, then those thoughts are not inspired."

"Or, they were inspired by an evil source," Elder Hall said. He had remained quiet, his presence in the room forgotten, and everyone turned to look at him. "I couldn't help but hear what was said," he explained, apologizing.

"Quite all right, Elder," Brother Van der Kerk said with an airy wave of his hand. "Your thoughts are most welcome."

"I'm grateful to have been here," Elder Hall replied earnestly. His face lit up with a smile. "I have been learning the same lessons from Elder Mahoy. One of the things he has taught me is that spirits can be discerned in the same way people are."

"Come again?" Sister Van der Kerk asked.

"I didn't say it well. We can judge if a person is inspired in what they do and how they live their lives. If their fruits are good and they bring people to Christ and teach them to pray and love and serve God, then we know they are inspired of God. Most people come to know Joseph Smith was a prophet by reading the Book of Mormon, one of his fruits of divine origin. The same is true of books, movies, talks in sacrament meeting, and many other things. If their fruits are good, they came from God. In the same context, if a spiritual experience leaves us feeling uplifted and teaches us to pray and worship, then it came from God."

Brother Van der Kerk was nodding vigorously. "I see. Yes, of course. Since all good comes from God, and all bad comes from Satan or one of his tempters, then we can discern them by their fruits as well. What a fascinating tool. If I had understood that, I would have rejected messages of self-loathing and the desire to hide from God and saved myself months of sorrow. Well," he concluded, rubbing his hands together briskly as if trying to warm them. "I'll be better armed next time."

"I wonder how all-encompassing this principle is," Sister Van der Kerk said aloud. "I will sometimes be thinking and suddenly have an angry thought or feel grumpy. Those kinds of feelings don't come from the Holy Spirit. Does that mean they came from an evil spirit? It makes me wonder how much the evil ones affect our lives. It's kind of spooky to think about." She shuddered and wrapped her arms around herself.

Sam thought about this for a moment. Her question was one he had pondered himself. In reality, he was unsure and was unaware of any prophet speaking on this subject.

"I really don't know the answer to that question," he replied. "I'm unsure what impact they have on our daily feelings, but I am sure that blatantly negative reactions are often evil in origin. I also know that if thoughts lead us away from righteousness or make us feel like not praying, they are definitely from Satan. I prefer to stay on the safe side and not attribute much to evil spirits. On the other hand, it really helps to understand what's going on when we have an experience that leaves us feeling alienated from the gospel or Christ. There's a scripture in Moroni, chapter 7, that says that the evil one entices and urges us to sin continually. I'm not sure we can interpret continually to mean every thought we have, but I'm sure they do everything in their power to drag us down."

Sister Van der Kerk nodded. "I've noticed that the big things start small. What I mean is, when Satan does succeed in getting me to feel disobedient or to feel alienated from the gospel, it usually starts as a small thing. It might have been something someone said that offended me that Satan worked on until it grew into something grotesque. I agree that Satan may not directly inspire every little negative feeling we have, but he apparently is able to pick up on them and try to use them against us. For my part, I prefer to avoid them all if I can," she added thoughtfully.

Sam sat on the corner of the billiard table. "You are wise," he agreed. "There are two great forces at work in our lives. On the one side, there is Christ and the Holy Spirit. They enlighten and entice us for good and strive to bring us unto righteousness.

"On the other side, and in direct opposition to Christ, are the forces of Satan and the unholy spirits. These continually entice us to depart from righteousness and choose anything that interferes with our eternal progression, whether it is blatant sin or just something mindless that saps our strength and keeps the Holy Spirit away.

"Somewhere in the middle is the mind of man. We are continually exposed to these two great sources of revelation. I know it sounds odd to call temptations revelation, but in a sense, they are.

"We are continually given the opportunity to choose between these two. The scriptures indicate that we will be exalted or damned— or stopped in our progression—according to which voice we choose to obey."

Brother Van der Kerk pulled up a chair and sat down. His thumb and forefinger were on his chin, and his elbow on one knee. He didn't realize it, but this was his trademark position. It made Sam smile.

"I'm always hearing complex conversations in my mind," Brother Van der Kerk said. "This is especially true since my baptism. They almost sound like arguments and can be confusing. I have been having a hard time determining which is the voice of the Holy Spirit and which is not. Like this last episode, I have sometimes listened to the wrong voices, even while trying very hard to do what is right."

Elder Hall responded, "I have had vast experience following the wrong voice. Before my baptism, I became quite familiar with sin and grew accustomed to that voice. Since my baptism, I have been able to avoid those enticements to sin simply because I recognize the flavor of the evil voice. Since deciding to be obedient to all revelation from the Holy Ghost, I am just as familiar with the voice of truth and can recognize the Holy Spirit much better now. It might be a matter of experience."

Sam nodded. "That, and testing the messages against the words of the prophets and scriptures. If I were to receive a prompting to steal something, I would immediately know it was of an evil origin because it conflicts with known truths. Conversely, a prompting to say my prayers is easily identified as a true prompting because it harmonizes with known truth.

"Something else that helps me identify the source of various promptings is to notice their order. As an example, when I receive an impression that I should bear my testimony, immediately following that prompting, I almost always hear a barrage of reasons of why I should not."

Sister Van der Kerk laughed. "That's what I hear all the time! I'm beginning to understand. It's like a cross examination in court. The defense makes a statement that supports their case, and immediately thereafter, the prosecution offers a series of rebuttals, often many more than necessary to prove the point. I do it myself in court. That's fascinating!" Her voice was animated, filled with excitement and discovery.

"In fact," Sam continued, "it is one of the evil one's weaknesses to continually tirade against what the Holy Spirit says."

"Of course," Brother Van der Kerk mumbled, "of course."

"The Lord expects us to search diligently in the Light of Christ, or our conscience, to determine the difference between the two," Sam added.

"As a matter of fact," Elder Hall said. "There's a scripture in Moroni, chapter 7, that speaks of what we've been discussing. He closed his eyes as if viewing something only he could see. "It goes like this," he said, and recited the verses word for word.

> But whatsoever thing persuadeth men to do evil, and believe not in Christ, and deny him, and serve not God, then ye may know with a perfect knowledge it is of the devil; for after this manner doth the devil work, for he persuadeth no man to do good, no, not one; neither do his angels; neither do they who subject themselves unto him.
>
> And now, my brethren, seeing that ye know the light by which ye may judge, which light is the light of Christ, see that ye do not judge wrongfully; for with that same judgment which ye judge ye shall also be judged.
>
> Wherefore, I beseech of you, brethren, that ye should search diligently in the light of Christ that ye may know good from evil; and if ye will lay hold upon every good thing, and condemn it not, ye certainly will be a child of Christ. (Moroni 7:17–19)

Brother Van der Kerk stood, picked up his cue, and said, "Elders, every time I talk to you I feel as if I'm a newborn babe spiritually, and I'm growing frightened about what I will do after you both leave Africa. I seem to easily be diverted from the straight course. When I talk to you, it seems straightforward again. You don't suppose I could offer you well-paying jobs and entice you to stay on, do you?" Brother Van der Kerk was very serious, and the missionaries smiled at one another.

"Probably not. But we do have time for a game before we have to get back," Sam said with a wink.

* * *

The following evening they met with Dawn. It was to be her fourth discussion. She met them on the porch, her face tear-streaked, and her eyes red and puffy.

"Daddy has forbidden me to continue with our discussions," she said without introduction. She sniffled and wiped her eyes with a silk handkerchief. "He says his boss is upset that I am studying to become a Mormon and has commented that he would not feel comfortable doing business with someone who let his daughter be abducted into a cult."

"Dawn," Sam said softly, suppressing an urge to place a hand on her arm. "I'm so sorry. Of course, we'll respect your wishes. I'm really sorry this has brought you so much sorrow."

Dawn's face turned from sorrow to anger in a flash. The transformation was so sudden that it startled the Elders. "How dare you assume what my wishes are, and how dare you assume that I am so spineless that his objections would deter me from finding and serving God!"

Sam opened his mouth to apologize, but she cut him off with a small shake of her head. "I'm sorry, Elders. I didn't mean to snap at you. It's just that I have been fighting this battle in my heart for two days, and I thought you, of all people, would understand how important this is. I'm sure you do. My emotions are just frazzled."

"What do you plan to do, and how can we help?" Sam asked.

"I plan to continue taking the missionary discussions. I plan to join the true Church," she replied simply.

"Then I have to ask you several questions. How you answer them will determine whether we will be able to continue teaching you, okay?" Sam said.

"Yes, I understand."

"Okay. Are you legally emancipated?"

In Africa, a teenager could become an adult any time after sixteen if they filled out the paperwork and filed it with the court. Until a person was legally an adult, the mission rules forbid them to teach them without parental consent.

"Daddy had me file for emancipation last year. That way I could have my own passport, and we could export more gems. So, I am."

"Good. Next question. Will your father react violently, throw you out of the house, or disown you?"

"I think he will. I know he loves me, but he is a worldly man, and I don't think he will sacrifice his business to let me become a Mormon."

"Last question. Are you willing to pay that high of a price to join Christ's true Church?"

"I am," she said without hesitation. "In fact, I want to accelerate the discussions and be baptized as soon as possible. Is that possible? I want to do it while the power of my decision is still strong and before I can be persuaded against it."

Sam considered this for a moment.

"It's possible," he said, "but I don't advise it. I suggest you allow enough time to elapse so that the fire of your decision does cool. When you go into the waters of baptism, I want your decision to be as hard and as cold as steel. I want it to be sufficient to carry you through the rest of your life. I don't want you to look back on that day and wonder if you acted hastily, or if you should have done it differently. I want you to rejoice every time you think of your baptism."

Dawn let her lip slip into a pout but quickly recovered and smiled. "I agree. I would still like to accelerate the lessons though, but out of a desire to learn. If we finish too soon, we can go through them again or pursue other teachings, but I want to learn as quickly as possible. I will stick with the baptismal date we originally set. I think it's wise, and I think Daddy will eventually see the light."

*   *   *

When Dawn told her father of her decision, he tried to persuade her otherwise, and failing at that, asked her to move out. Both she and her father wept as she walked down their long drive. He wouldn't even let her borrow the car to move away. He didn't close the door until she was out of sight down the long drive. She walked to the Feinstein's home, where she stayed for a few days. Eventually, she moved in with Bishop and Sister Van Halen. They wrapped their arms and their love around her.

Sam and Elder Hall were teaching Dawn the sixth discussion in the Van Halen's home when the phone rang. Having been isolated from the sound of telephones for almost two years, it startled them. It sounded like a fire alarm. Sister Van Halen answered the call and handed him a note. He waited until Elder Hall was giving the next concept before glancing at it. What he read more than surprised him.

> Elder Mahoy, Neil Whitehall called to request that you come to the hospital and talk to him, tele number 23-5225, room 1128.

They had been expecting a call from the Whitehalls, but their wayward son Neil was the last person they were anxious to meet again. Sam judged him to be one of the most evil men he had ever known. Nevertheless, they used the bishop's phone to call as soon as the discussion was over. Neil was abrupt and merely made an appointment for the following Thursday. Sam was not looking forward to it.

The hospital looked smaller in the daylight. Sam knew little about hospitals. This one seemed modern but had an air of backwardness that he found frightening. On the main floor was a large room filled with dentist chairs. He had never seen such a thing. The room was roughly the size of a basketball court yet had a dentist chair every ten feet in all directions. About a third of the chairs had someone in them. The chairs each had the old cable-operated drills. The sound and smell of drilling teeth drifted from the room. Sam was old enough to have had a couple teeth drilled using the old cable drills, and it made his teeth hurt to remember.

The Elders found the elevator and made their way to the eleventh floor.

Neil's room was windowless and felt cheerless. They found Neil lying in bed, his skin pallid and pasty-looking.

"Hello, Neil," Sam said, much more cheerfully than he felt. Neil rolled his head toward them, and without changing expression, motioned them to enter. The bed was high enough that sitting would have made them invisible to Neil, so they stood.

When Neil spoke, his voice was raspy. Without any attempt at pleasantries, he got directly to his point. "I have been lying here for almost three weeks now, with nothing else to do than think about how I got here. I have gone over and over it in my mind, trying to figure out how you two fit into it all.

"Logic tells me that I had this disease long before I met you in my parents home, and you telling me I would have a disease that would take away my most valued body part could have been wishful thinking on your part.

"Logic also tells me that you probably heard my parents mention that my best friend's daughter had been murdered, even though they say they did not. And logic tells me that you may have guessed or suspected that her father was the criminal." He paused as if struggling to find his next words.

"Logic . . . what a fickle thing," he mused aloud. "It is beyond logic, however, that you could have gotten all three of those things right. I have tried every avenue of logic, and none come close to explaining how you could've correctly guessed three incredibly obscure things about a total stranger.

"Logic—my faithful companion, my guide in hating God, my sword Excalibur in battling religious stupidity—has betrayed me and now suggests that the only way you could have known these things is that you are either clairvoyant or inspired of God. I personally prefer the former explanation; yet logic is as equally agnostic toward things paranormal as it is toward the entire idea of God."

He fixed his eyes on Sam with such intensity that Sam felt like turning away, but something in his gaze pulled at Sam's heart. His intensity was as much a cry for help as it was a tirade against all things spiritual.

"So, you see, I have asked you to come, and if you would be so kind to explain yourself. You know how I hate falseness, flattery, false religion, false spirituality, false emotions—anything false. I beg of you, tell me only the truth, and I will do my best to believe your words. I'm floundering here, and for the first time in my life, I am reaching out to a fellow mortal to help me. Help me, Elder Mahoy. Please."

Sam was surprised when he felt the familiar warmth of truth in his bosom. He had judged Neil as unrepentant, unsalvageable, and had personally written him off. The truth that touched him was a chastisement, a rebuke from the Lord, and it stung him to silence. Sam had wanted the truth to be a lesson for Neil, but it was a lesson for himself. No words could come to his lips. The rebuke lashed against his soul in firm yet loving admonition. Here was a son of God, a son that the Father loved as much as He did Sam, a precious soul needing help! God had prepared him, had conditioned his soul for teaching, and Sam had failed to see anything but the facade Neil had erected around himself.

Tears formed in Sam's eyes as he struggled to repent, to readjust his soul, and to see Neil in a purer light. Neil saw his inward struggle, and without understanding the source of it, was touched.

"The truth," Sam said, "is that I owe you an apology." Both Neil and Elder Hall were stunned. It was not what either had expected.

"I don't understand. If any apologies are due, they should be from me. What . . .?"

Sam cut him off with a small shake of his head. "When you asked me for the truth, I felt overwhelmed by the Spirit. It's a familiar feeling and often comes when it's time to teach. Yet, the truth that came to me was a rebuke. I stand rebuked by God for judging you and for not seeing your worth in God's eyes. I completely overlooked the thing I preach, which is His great and abiding love for you as His son."

"I don't understand . . ."

"At this point, it is only important that I understand, and that you please forgive me for prejudging you."

"Elder, I'm stunned. Your words shatter my thinking to splinters. I wanted to debate the existence of God with you, and you beg my forgiveness! What kind of a person are you?"

"I'm a person who has wronged you and is humbly asking for your forgiveness. That's all," Sam said, his voice small. He felt convicted of his sins, and of his failure as a disciple of the Lord. He only knew that he had been very wrong, and that he must beg for Neil's forgiveness, no matter the outcome.

"Elder Mahoy, I can see that you are in dead earnest here, and to whatever extent you have offended me, I do forgive you. However, I have to say that I can't think of a single way that you have. You have been civil with me in every way, so perhaps you could explain in what way you feel you have offended me. It wasn't at all what I wanted to hear from you but has certainly gotten my attention." He pushed himself up higher in his bed and rearranged his pillows behind his back.

"I am a disciple of Jesus Christ, one who loves Him with all my soul. Nothing is more important to me than to represent Him well and to lead others to understand and love Him as well. As near as I understand Him, His greatest attribute is love. He loved us so much that he was willing to die for us, all of us, whether we loved Him back or not, whether we knew about Him or believed in Him.

Sam hung his head. "When I first met you, I disliked you and decided that you were beyond redemption. I concluded that you were one of the most despicable men I had ever known, undeserving of God's love and forgiveness. In this way, I offended you. In reality, I offended God even more to believe that He would not love you in spite of your anger toward Him. It wasn't until I was overcome by the Spirit and felt His love for you that this became apparent, and it has been a great lesson to me."

Neil lay in his bed, his face stony. "So, God used me to teach you that He loves me," Neil replied. It was not a question but a summation of Sam's words.

"It has been a stunning revelation to me," Sam said, almost immediately realizing that Neil might take offense at his words, but before he could say anything further, Neil merely added, "Me too."

After saying this, Neil seemed amused and threw back his head in a hearty laugh that echoed around the room. It was the most amazingly rich laugh Sam had ever heard, and he felt his heart lifting. He was soon laughing too.

"Now, I want to get something straight," Neil said, still smiling. "This Spirit you mentioned that said God loved me, and that you said was a familiar feeling—what does it feel like?"

Sam was about to explain when Neil interrupted. "No, let me explain it, and you tell me if I'm right. It's a feeling in the center of the chest, almost a warmth or comfortable feeling. Am I right?" Sam and Elder Hall nodded.

"And the general effect it has upon the mind is one of peace and joy," he added.

"You've obviously felt this before," Elder Hall observed.

"Just now, a few seconds ago, just before I laughed. As a matter of fact, I believe that was why I laughed. I have lain here for three weeks in utmost turmoil, confusion, and bitterness, and when that feeling of peace hit me, it was absolute. What I mean is, not only did it bring me peace concerning what you were saying but also concerning my illness, my future, my eternal welfare, and everything else. For just a moment, I felt complete, total peace. I don't believe I have ever felt real joy before. It was unexplainable, unreasonable, illogical happiness. It felt so good, all I could do was laugh for joy."

"You have described it perfectly," Sam replied.

"Do you want to know what is odd? I felt it so strongly for a moment that I will never doubt for the rest of my life that it was real, although I can hardly feel it now. I seem to have returned to my former feelings of depression. Explain that to me."

"I don't understand why the Lord does a lot of the things He does," Sam answered, "but one possible explanation is that He wanted you to have a taste of His love for you. We are messengers for Christ and His Church, and if the people are ready when we speak, the Holy Spirit bears witness that our words are true. I suppose that since we were talking of His love for you, His way of bearing witness of that fact was to let you feel it for a moment."

"Fascinating! I would like to try that again. You don't suppose you could tell me about His love for me again, do you?"

"Let's try another subject. You already have that one down! Elder Hall will tell you about a young man who learned about the existence of God in a way that is similar to your own. This young man was confused about God and which church he should join. His name was Joseph Smith."

Elder Hall did most of the rest of the teaching that evening. Sam was grateful, because his soul was weary and burdened by the recent chastisement from the Spirit. He had never felt such a thing before, and even though he felt cleansed and much blessed by all that had happened, he still felt as if the experience had inexplicably drained his spiritual batteries. Elder Hall was filled with the Spirit, and his words were inspired and inspiring. Neil was a demanding student and asked pointed and detailed questions, but his questions were now to discover the truth, not to challenge it.

Neil continued with his chemotherapy during many more visits with the missionaries. Each time they came, he was weaker and seemed sicker. Yet, as his body weakened, his spirit strengthened until it seemed as if his body was an unfit habitation for his mighty spirit. Like Paul of Tarsus who had persecuted the Church and turned away from his sin in a single moment, Neil changed in a mighty leap toward righteousness. His face glowed with the Spirit, and his words rang with conviction. He read the Book of Mormon almost in a single sitting and rejoiced in it. He devoured every book they brought him and begged for more. He coerced them into coming every day for a while to complete his spiritual education.

Three weeks from the time they first visited Neil in the hospital, they came to find him too weak to sit up in bed. He greeted them weakly but with a big smile. His face was aglow with the Spirit, and he radiated hope and love. This marvelous change in him seemed as miraculous as the raising of Lazarus from the dead.

"Elders, come closer so I don't have to shout," he said, chuckling. His voice was small and seemed to wheeze from his emaciated body.

"The doctors tell me I am too weak to undergo the operation. It seems I have wasted much quicker than they suspected. Without the operation, I will die. If they operate, I will die. So you see, I am going to die. They told me to get things in order."

Tears formed in Sam's eyes, and he knew Neil's words were true. He fervently wished that the Lord had let them heal him, to lift the curse he had pronounced upon himself by his own words. In all their hours of teaching Neil, he had never once asked them to bless him to remove the curse. He had, however, expressed the thought many times that his curse was a blessing, because it brought him to the depths of humility where he was finally able to find the Lord.

"I have one thing that remains undone, which I know with absolute certainty I must do before I can face God without shrinking from His presence."

"What is that?" Sam asked, his voice breaking.

"I want to be baptized, by authority, for the remission of my sins. Without this, I fear death with all my being. When my sins are washed clean, I can die in peace."

"Neil, I rejoice in your desire to be baptized," Sam told him joyfully. Elder Hall expressed similar feelings. "We'll need to come up with a way to do it, though, since there is so little left of you that I'm not sure the doctors will let you travel to the chapel, let alone be baptized. Have you thought of a way to do it?"

"I have," Neil replied. "I wouldn't survive a trip from the hospital. However, one of the nurses said there is a small indoor pool they use for therapy right here in the hospital. The doctors have reluctantly given their permission to allow me to be baptized there. Will you do it?"

"Absolutely! When?" was all Sam could think of to say.

"Now. Tonight. As soon as my parents and Bishop and Sister Van Halen can get here. I feel a powerful urgency to do it tonight, almost as if I won't be able to tomorrow. Please, help me do this!"

Sam went to the pay phone in the hall near Neil's room. He dialed Neil's parents. They were already planning to visit Neil, and when Sam explained Neil's desires, they were excited and said they would be there in a little more than an hour.

Sam finally found the bishop in his office. He was in the middle of an interview but said he would immediately get Sister Van Halen and they would come. He would make the appropriate phone calls and bring the necessary paperwork. He would also be there in a little more than an hour.

Two interns rolled Neil's bed through the double doors that led to the pool. Dawn came with Bishop and Sister Van Halen. Neil's parents brought Neil's older sister, who the Elders had never met.

Word spread through the hospital, and one doctor and two nurses, who were LDS, joined them. Sam asked the doctor to offer the opening prayer. One of the nurses asked if she could sing a special musical number, and Sam asked Elder Hall to give a talk on baptism.

Bishop Van Halen handed Sam a bundle of white clothing. Sam had completely forgotten that he needed to wear white when performing the ordinance. He was grateful for the bishop's thoughtfulness. Neil was no problem, since everything he wore was hospital white. Sam quickly changed.

Bishop Van Halen conducted the meeting. The prayers were sweet and brought the Holy Spirit in rich abundance. The nurse sang like an angel, her voice clear and vibrant in the small room. Elder Hall's talk was brief yet inspired. Finally, it was time.

Sam stood and approached Neil's bed. All his tubes had been disconnected and needles removed. He stopped by the bed, unsure how to help Neil into the water. Before he could utter a word, Neil's father stepped between them. He was not much larger than Neil himself, yet without effort, reached into the bed and lovingly lifted his son. Their eyes locked, as if truly connecting for the first time in their lives.

Sam entered the pool. The water was comfortable. Neil's father slipped off his shoes and carried his son into the water until he was waist deep. He carefully transferred his son to Sam.

Neil's emaciated body had wasted to nothing, which startled Sam with its lightness. He carefully lowered Neil's legs into the water. Neil looped his arm around Sam's neck. Even with Sam's help, Neil had barely enough strength to support his own weight, even in the weightlessness of the water. Neil's body trembled with anticipation and joy. Sam whispered in his ear. "Neil, I'll support you all the way. Trust me and keep your arm around my neck." Neil smiled and nodded.

Sam raised his right hand to the square, and in a voice of quiet authority said, "Neil Eugene Whitehall, having been commissioned of Jesus Christ, I baptize you in the name of the Father, and of the Son, and of the Holy Ghost, amen."

Sam slowly knelt down. Neil closed his eyes with a look of ecstasy. Sam only closed his at the last moment. He continued to lower himself and Neil into the water until his entire body went under the water and Neil's arm around his neck was completely submerged. Just as carefully, he swiftly lifted him from the water. Neil came up, his face beaming with joy.

"It's done!" he cried in a hoarse voice. "I can finally meet God with a peaceful heart. I'm finally ready!" A single reverberating laugh of exquisite joy flowed from his throat, and he fell silent, his strength completely spent.

Neil's mother wept with joy, and his father carried him out of the water to his bed. The nurses efficiently removed his wet clothes and dried him. Within minutes, he was dry and back in his own room.

Neil insisted that he be confirmed immediately. So, despite his weakened condition, all the priesthood holders laid their hands gently on his head, and Elder Hall bestowed the sacred gift of the Holy Ghost. Among the words he spoke were these: "Neil, you have fulfilled the words that were spoken to you. The curse is lifted, and you are made whole through your faith."

The doctors, nurses, and others left quietly, and only Neil's parents, the bishop, and the Elders remained. It was time to go, but it was hard to say farewell. Everyone suspected this parting might be the last. Neil was listless upon his pillows, yet his face glowed with joy. It was as if death were only waiting for them to leave so it might bear him away.

Sam held Neil's hand for a few minutes and then tearfully and quietly said goodbye.

The Elders were a dozen steps down the hall when Elder Hall suddenly skidded to a stop. An idea had suddenly come to him. It was so sudden and incredibly pure that he instantly recognized its source. He spun around, leaving Sam walking a few more steps alone. He ran back into the room. Every eye turned toward him as he slid to a stop on the slick floor. Sam plowed into his back, his mind whirling with wonder.

"Neil," Elder Hall said, trying to control his voice. "I have some bad news."

"The first time I met you I told you not to lie to me, Elder," Neil said sternly and then laughed weakly.

"You're not going to die!" Elder Hall exclaimed as if the burden of his message was too big for his heart to keep inside.

"What?" everyone exclaimed simultaneously. Elder Hall was barraged by questions, none of which he answered until it again grew quiet.

"Neil, I don't think I ever mentioned it, but I dropped out of medical school to come on a mission. I was a junior in my masters program. But that isn't my point really."

"No, I didn't know that," Neil replied, his voice tired but tinted with hope.

"Well, you know how your cancer has not responded to any of the treatments?"

"Yes . . ." he slowly answered. "And has actually grown worse?"

"Yes."

"Well, I know why. It came to me just as I was leaving."

"Tell me," Neil urged, his eyes brightening with hope. "It's because you don't have cancer!"

"What? What do you mean? All the doctors said I have it. All the tests, everything indicates cancer. What would I have, if I don't have cancer?" he asked, his voice filled with wonder.

Sam was skeptical at first as he listened to their conversation, until the Spirit swept over him like a soft breeze. Peace entered his soul, and he knew Elder Hall was right. He stepped forward and laid a hand on Neil's knee.

"Listen to him, Neil. Listen to your heart. Listen to the Holy Ghost."

Elder Hall glanced at Sam and smiled. He continued, "I'm not saying this because I studied medicine. I'm saying this because the Spirit wrought on me a few minutes ago and gave me this message. I know it's true because of learning to listen and implicitly trust the promptings of the Holy Spirit. It hasn't responded to cancer treatment because it isn't cancer. It's an infection, or something similar. Have the doctors do another test. Have them look for something simple. Force them to give you antibiotics no matter what they find, and take you off the cancer drugs."

"But they said stopping the drugs would immediately let the cancer kill me," Neil replied, his voice worried.

"Stop thinking with your logic and use the gift you just received. Let the Holy Ghost guide you. Feel instead of think. Let the Holy Ghost take you beyond your mind's ability to understand. Think back on the original words of the sign you asked for. 'The part of your person you value most . . .'"

"Will be denied to you until you repent of your sins," Neil finished quietly, as if intimately familiar with that fateful sentence. "'Until' implies there will be something after, that the effect is not permanent," he realized as he spoke.

Neil pondered Elder Hall's words a minute longer, and then reached up and pulled the tape from his arm where the nurses had already reattached his tubes. He pulled a needle from each arm, and with his father's help, one from his ankle.

"Elders, my soul has finally triumphed over my brain. I have repented of my sins, and the words are fulfilled. Whether I live or die now is irrelevant. I have finally triumphed." He asked his father to find the doctor and bring him to his room. With these words, he fell back onto his bed and closed his eyes.

*　*　*

It was several days later, during the sixth discussion with Dawn, that the bishop's phone rang once more. Again, Sister Van Halen handed Sam a note. This time, he did not wait but interrupted himself to open it.

> Neil Whitehall called to tell you his tests still indicate cancer, but he has refused further cancer treatment. He says to tell you he has succeeded in convincing the doctors to give him antibiotics and feels stronger each day. He sends his love.

It took two weeks for the cancer results to disappear from Neil's tests. The doctors were mystified and to the end maintained that his cancer had spontaneously cured itself. Several were insistent that Neil's baptism had cleansed him, which was interesting since they were not LDS. However, they gave zero credence to the idea that the antibiotics had anything to do with his healing. It was interesting to Sam that they were far more protective of their medical beliefs than their spiritual ones.

Neil was released from the hospital, and after a brief convalescence at his parents home, began his life anew, completely cured of both cancers previously robbing him of life—cancer of the body and of the soul.

*　*　*

Dawn's eyes were bright with happiness when Sam told her Neil's good news. She had enjoyed his baptism, and it made her look forward to her own. Her own baptismal date was still a few weeks away.

"I just knew he would recover," she said, her accent even more British than usual. "I just knew he would. I felt it—here." She pressed a palm to her heart. "Elder Mahoy, how much longer until you return to America?"

Sam had to think for a moment. "Six weeks," he answered. "Just six weeks." It still seemed to him as if he had much more to accomplish, and the short time remaining pressed upon him.

"I want to ask you something. I hope you won't get mad, but I have thought about this a lot, and . . ." She paused as if unsure.

Sam was surprised at her timidity. Dawn was many things, all of them wonderful, but timid was not one of them.

"What is it, Dawn? What do you want to ask me?"

"I want to go to America," she said in a rush.

Sam nodded slowly. "Well, I'm sure some day you will . . ." he began, but she cut him off.

"No, you don't understand. I want to go to America with you, six weeks from now." Her eyes sparkled with hope and fear. She blinked rapidly, as if trying to keep the tears from gathering. He could tell she was serious and feared his rejection.

Sam took a deep breath. He could almost hear President Carlson's lecture. President Carlson's fear would be that he was taking Dawn to America because he had fallen in love with her. It was true that he loved her, but he was not in love with her. He hoped the distinction would be sufficient for President Carlson.

On the other hand, Dawn was without home, family, support, and work. She was too young to provide for herself entirely, yet old enough to make her own decisions. Sam knew his mother would wrap her arms around Dawn and love her as much as her own children. He could imagine his father's reaction and their inevitable conversation, probably late that first night, about Sam's questionable relationship with Dawn. But in the end, his father would be satisfied.

No, the obstacle was President Carlson, and it was no minor roadblock. Mission rules were explicit about taking people home from the mission. The obstacles were vast, and everywhere Sam's mind turned, he saw another and another. It seemed impossible, yet at this moment, it felt right to him. Somehow, it felt right. He glanced at Dawn, who was fighting an unsuccessful battle to keep tears out of her eyes. She had lowered her head, tears falling silently onto her fists bunched in her lap. She had interpreted his silence as rejection, and her hope was quickly evaporating.

Again, he drew a deep breath. "I think it's a marvelous idea," Sam told her.

"You do?" Dawn burst out, her head snapping up so quickly that he wondered how she didn't get whiplash. She jumped up as if to rush to him, but then thought better of it and sat back down. She clapped her hands silently, and bounced her feet in excitement like a small girl.

Elder Hall whistled, which sounded like a bomb falling. The metaphor was apropos.

"Dawn," Sam said as he closed his scriptures and set them aside. "I really do think it would be wonderful. I know my parents will welcome you with open arms."

"They will?" she said, marvel in her voice. "I was thinking of getting a room, finding a job, and maybe going to college. But your parents would take me in for a while—a total stranger?"

"They love everyone and would treat you like their own daughter," he answered with absolute confidence. He had seen them do it many times.

She clapped her hands together and held them to her lips as if in prayer. Again, her eyes misted with tears of happiness.

"You need to begin immediately to get your papers in order and say goodbye to your father. I need to talk to President Carlson. I'm not looking forward to that at all." He glanced at Elder Hall, who rolled his eyes. "Do you have money for plane fare?"

"Elder Mahoy, I have more money than you can imagine. My father has been salting away a fortune in Swiss bank accounts in my name since I was a baby. I'm not sure, but I could probably buy the airplane as easily as a seat on it."

"Won't your father transfer the money to another account now that you've moved out?" Elder Hall asked impulsively.

"In the first place, I don't think he would do that to me. Second, he can't. Since the day I became a legal adult, I have meticulously moved all the funds into accounts he has no knowledge of."

"Oh," Sam and Elder Hall said simultaneously. Dawn seemed so naive, trusting, and unassuming. Seeing this side of her was surprising. Part of her personality was very capable, and maybe even a little shrewd.

* * *

Sam had tried to imagine what it might be like to kneel at an altar across from a beautiful woman all dressed in white. He had replayed the scene many times in his mind, each time altering the face, the room, or the dress she wore; yet he had never imagined a woman more beautiful than Dawn, dressed in a simple white gown as she slowly walked down the steps and toward him in the baptismal font. Her face was radiant with happiness and aglow with the Holy Spirit. Sam's breath caught in his throat, and tears came to his eyes. Still a step away, she extended a hand toward him, a momentary look of wonder in her eyes. He reached out and felt her slender hand slide into his. She smiled, partly at him, but mostly at the joy of the moment.

The road from Dawn's front door to this sacred moment had been eventful. Her father had kicked her out of her home and refused to talk to her. She had repeatedly called, wrote letters, and even gone to visit him. The butler had tearfully refused to allow her to enter even the foyer. Sister Van Halen told Sam that Dawn often cried herself to sleep, or called out her father's name in her sleep.

The day after she asked to go to America with Sam, Dawn had gone to the bank to check on her accounts. She was told that none of them existed. Her father was shrewder than she. One moment she thought she could afford to buy an airplane, and the next, she was destitute. Yet here she was, standing before him, radiating joy, and anxiously awaiting the first of many ordinances on her road to exaltation.

Thoughts such as these flowed across Sam's mind, and warmed his soul. Here stood a beautiful, precious daughter of Heavenly Father, a woman of truth and light, and it was his privilege to baptize her. His heart thrilled.

He directed Dawn to stand to his left. He gazed into her eyes for a moment and then swept them across the Saints standing at the side of the font. He was ready. He raised his right arm to the square. A short moment of deep silence followed before he spoke the sacred words.

"Dawn Olivia Pauley, having been commissioned of Jesus Christ . . ." At that moment, a door opened and closed, and a man's voice boomed across the crowd.

"Wait!" the voice said urgently.

People parted, and the man came forward and knelt before the font.

"Daddy?" Dawn asked with wonder in her voice. Mr. Pauley reached out, and Dawn took a step toward him. Both of his hands closed over hers. What he said was so soft that only Sam and Dawn heard it in the hush that had fallen over the room.

"I love you," he said. So saying, he released her and nodded at her and then Sam. She returned to Sam's side. He raised his arm to the square, and in a voice of quiet authority spoke the words of salvation. "Dawn Olivia Pauley, having been commissioned of Jesus Christ, I baptize you in the name of the Father, and of the Son, and of the Holy Ghost, amen."

He opened his eyes to find hers fastened upon his. It was as if their souls touched and something electric passed between them.

He slowly lowered her into the water, her eyes still upon his. As the waters rose, she closed her eyes, and the water flowed over her. Beneath the water, her face was angelic.

Sam carefully lifted her from the font. When she opened her eyes, they were still on him. Immediately she flung her arms around him and held him close.

"Thank you," she said quietly in Sam's ear. Breaking free from him, she cried, "Daddy!" She rushed toward the stairs in a swirl of water. Her father ran to meet her, and they fell into one another's arms with a watery sound. Dawn laughed and wept loudly, and her father kept repeating, "I love you. I'm sorry."

* * *

It was Church policy for President Carlson to interview every missionary prior to him or her going home. Sam had dreaded it for several weeks.

He entered the now-familiar office and took a seat on a richly upholstered chair. It occurred to him that he had sat in the same chair every time he had entered the room. Not every experience here had been sweet, and he fully expected this one to trend toward bitter. Yet, the interview was rich with warmth and praise—both for him and the others who had entered the mission field with him. The requisite worthiness questions were asked and answered, and President Carlson was satisfied. "My dear boy, what an asset you have been to this mission, to me personally, and to the people of this continent. You can rest assured that you have made a lasting impact upon all who have known you. I have never known a missionary more willing to serve, more willing to do the Lord's work—or more prone to cause problems!" He laughed, and Sam knew that President Carlson's opinion of his problems did not include any blame for wrongdoing. His mission was difficult in many ways, yet he had fought a good fight, and his heart soared.

"Do you have any questions?" President Carlson asked unexpectedly. "Well, yes, there is something I'm curious about. Whatever happened to Elder Beesler?"

President Carlson frowned and turned his chair until he was profile to Sam. He seemed to be considering his answer.

"Generally," he finally said, "we do not make public mention of what happens to other missionaries. However, I feel that you deserve an explanation, especially considering the circumstances. Elder Beesler did not return to his mission duties after leaving you at the courthouse. He just disappeared with the mission's vehicle. He was found several weeks later in the Cape and arrested. He was accused and convicted of perjury, several traffic violations, and car theft. The latter was dropped because the Church declined to press charges. He received a one-year jail sentence and is presently serving that sentence. However, I received a phone call just yesterday asking if he had been here. At first, I thought it was a member calling, but the more I thought about it, I wondered if it could be the police. I fear he may have escaped and means mischief toward the Church."

President Carlson interlaced his hands over his chest and lowered his chin as if in deep thought. Then he straightened and resumed his narrative.

"As a result of leaving the mission field without permission, and the crimes he committed, he was excommunicated from the Church. It is all a sad affair. You may be interested to know, however, that he expressed considerable remorse for leaving you to be whipped. He said it didn't register to him what your sentence had been until after he had left the building. By then, he realized it was probably already in progress and he didn't have the courage to go back and put a stop to it. The reason he ran away was that he was ashamed of himself. When the Lord's will was made manifest to me that he was to lose his membership, I was shocked, because I considered his remorse genuine. However, when the verdict was announced, he was extremely angry. He cursed and raged and had to be taken from the room. I am certain the Lord's verdict included past acts much worse than those of the present.

"Since going to jail, he has called this office many times asking for your address so he could write you a letter and ask your forgiveness. I did not give it to him, because I felt you had enough to deal with without being exposed to his emotions. Besides, I had a hard time believing he was sincere after his outburst, and suspected he had darker motives for wanting your address. I hope I did the right thing."

"I'm grateful you told me these things," Sam said. "I'm especially grateful that Elder Beesler was not whipped."

"Before I officially give you my blessing to leave the mission field, I feel as if there is something you would like to bring up. What is it, Elder?"

Sam was taken aback by his perceptiveness, but he knew that President Carlson was a spiritual man upon whom the mantle of his office rested fully.

Sam cleared his throat and struggled to find the right words. There were no right words to find. Finally, he just blurted it out.

"The young woman we just baptized . . ."

"Sister Pauley," President Carlson interjected, a look of understanding crossing his features.

"Yes, well, she was disowned by her father."

"I'm familiar with her story. Her father came to the baptism at the last moment, and they were reconciled. It's a touching account."

"That's mostly accurate. He has forgiven her and asked her to come home, but she knows if she does, her father will lose his business. For some reason, his employers hate Mormons. So now they are at odds again, but from opposite positions. He wants her to come home and she refuses. She is determined to go to America with me. I honestly don't know what to do."

President Carlson was silent for a long moment. Sam waited, breathless. "There's nothing you can do," President Carlson finally said as he slipped a sheet of paper back into the file folder on his desk. "It's a free country, and she's a legal adult. Even if she wants to go to America on the same plane you're on, I don't see a big problem with that. Nor do I see why her doing so impacts you or your mission."

"But I know there are strict guidelines about missionaries doing this sort of thing."

"Elder, you taught me a valuable lesson, actually several of them. I know what the mission rules say, and in the strictest sense, this violates them. However, I feel at peace about the situation and choose to ignore the entire thing. You have served an honorable mission, that's all I need to know. My challenge to you is that you never allow yourself to forget what you have learned here. You have great potential for good and, consequently, great potential for failure.

He paused to consider his next words carefully. "Everything has its opposite—its opposite that is equal in power. You taught me this. Your spiritual greatness will bring you a lifetime of joy and a life filled with trials of great intensity. You have the power to realize the promise of exaltation in this life, but also the power to become a son of perdition. These are your possibilities. You will not end up with something in between. Beware, my boy. For God's sake . . . for your sake, beware all your life."

There were tears in President Carlson's eyes, and he spoke barely above a whisper. Sam received the warning with an open heart.

* * *

Sam and Elder Hall arrived at Jan Smuts airport three hours early. Bishop and Sister Van Halen met them at the door and relieved Sam of his only suitcase. As they walked toward the ticket counters, others joined them, until nearly fifty people pressed around him.

Most everyone he loved was there: The Van der Kerks with an armed escort; Tom and Linda Snodgrass with their new baby; and Neil, still looking frail, and his parents. The only people missing were Marcia and Melody, whom he presumed were still in Rhodesia, the Knights, still in Rhodesia, and President and Sister Carlson. Sam suddenly realized with a start that Dawn was nowhere to be seen. He knew she had tickets on this flight, and wondered if all was right with her.

The crowd of well-wishers migrated to an unused boarding area. Soon everyone was laughing and telling stories of Sam's deeds and misdeeds. He was embarrassed by the attention, yet his soul rejoiced in his dear friends, and simultaneously ached at their impending separation. This was going to be much harder than leaving his family back in Salt Lake City. At least there, he knew he would return.

There was still an hour to go when Dawn arrived. Her face was aglow with happiness as she directed the servants carrying her many bags. Her father attended her like another servant, anxious to do anything to help. She kept one arm laced tightly through his the entire time. When she spotted Sam, she hurried over and kissed him on the cheek. Elder Hall gave a meaningful cough.

Dawn shot Elder Hall a meaningful glance. "He's almost not a missionary anymore, so I can almost give him a kiss. When we get to America, I'm going to lay a proper one on him." Everyone laughed, and Elder Hall threw up his hands in mock resignation.

As the hour grew closer, the group grew more sober, until all eyes were misty and words no longer seemed adequate. Sam found himself in a daze, looking at faces he loved, suddenly aware that he would probably never see them again. Bishop Van Halen looked at his watch and pointed toward the gate.

"It's time," he said. A murmur of disappointment simultaneously escaped many lips. Sam stood and found himself facing Tom Snodgrass. "Sam, I want to give you something. I know it's small, and you said you no longer want one, but I felt impressed that this would be the most important thing I could give you." He held out a narrow box wrapped in colored paper. As soon as Sam touched it, he knew what it was. The feel, the weight, the very essence of the package was familiar to him. His eyes filled with tears. He didn't want it, yet his soul cried out in relief that he now owned one once again.

He tore open the paper and flipped the shiny latches. A beautiful silver flute lay nestled in blue velvet. He snapped the lid closed and hugged Tom and Linda.

Neil stepped up next and handed him a long envelope. Sam pulled a bound manuscript from the envelope. The title read, Atheists Never Die Atheists by Neil E. Whitehall.

"I already have a publisher," he said, as Sam studied the cover. "I was so heavily involved in the atheistic movement that my conversion to Christianity has created quite a stir. This is my way of being a missionary." His voice broke. "Thank you for all you've done for me." They shook hands and then embraced.

Brother and Sister Van der Kerk approached next and held out a small package. He took the small package with wonder in his eyes. He opened it to find a piece of knotted leather about six inches long, mounted inside a small viewing box that could not be opened. A small brass plaque held the following: Acts 5:41, "And they departed . . . rejoicing that they were counted worthy to suffer shame for his name."

"Is this . . ."

"It is," they replied simultaneously.

"In reality," Brother Van der Kerk told him, "it is your gift to us. I had two made and keep the other on my desk. By your stripes, I came to know Christ. I hope someday I can repay the great debt of your gift to me. God bless you . . ." His voice faltered. They embraced. He held Sister Van der Kerk's hand until she kissed him on both cheeks and turned away.

Everyone present came forward until his hands and pockets were full. Dawn preceded him through the gate, and just as he was turning to go, President and Sister Carlson ran toward them.

"Elder Mahoy!" they called from a short distance. They hurried toward him as the speaker announced the final boarding for his flight.

As he hugged Sister Carlson, he couldn't help noticing that she smelled of smoke.

"Elder," President Carlson said as he grasped his hand. "We almost missed you. You would not believe what has happened. We awoke this morning to a smoke-filled house. We barely got everyone out. The mission home has burned to the ground!"

"No!" Sam cried. His mind reeled at the thought of all the beautiful paintings, marble statues, and other treasures being destroyed in the fire.

"The terrible part is that the police say it was arson. Whoever set the fire also blocked the outside doors to trap us inside. We climbed through a window. It was a blatant attempt at murder, I'm afraid. Following my suggestion, they checked on Elder Beesler, and he has been released from prison. His parents had arranged for him to be deported to his hometown, and he was taken to the airport, but apparently, he didn't get on the plane. Everyone is looking for him now. I'm afraid if they find out he had anything to do with this fire, they won't let him be deported but will put him in prison for a long time."

"Do you really think it was Elder Beesler?" Sam asked, his hands trembling. It was standard procedure for missionaries about to go home to spend their last few days in the mission home. By special permission, Sam had not gone back to the mission home—but an arsonist would not have known that, Sam thought grimly.

"Perhaps it's unjust of me to suspect him without greater evidence . . ." President Carlson said, his voice trailing off into thoughtful silence.

"So much destruction," Sam replied, his mind walking through the plush interior of the old mansion. "So much destruction . . ."

"Yes, it's a tragedy, but no one was injured, and we were able to save most of the mission records. Only a few pieces of art were saved. I did have the presence of mind to grab something very important, though." He pressed a small package into Sam's hand.

Sam opened the box to find a gold tie clasp holding a perfect diamond the size of his thumbnail. He inhaled sharply when he recognized the stone Melody's father had given him in gratitude for his part in saving his daughters. Others leaned over the box and gasped. Even in South Africa, where large diamonds were commonplace, this was an exceptional stone.

"May I?" Mr. Pauley asked, and he took the box from Sam's hands.

He produced a loupe from his pocket and held the stone to the light.

He frowned and lowered the diamond. "I know this stone!" He said in an excited voice. "It was cut in my factory. It's a full twenty-two carats, D in color, ice blue, flawless under an X10 loupe. It's almost priceless. I tried to purchase it and couldn't. It was sold to a wealthy land baron in Rhodesia. How did you come by it?"

"I don't have time to explain," Sam said, taking the stone back. "It was a gift. President Carlson can explain." He shoved the box into his pants pocket. He gave both the Carlsons a hug and turned toward the gate.

"Elder," Mr. Pauley persisted. "I want to buy that stone. I will give you its wholesale value here and now."

Sam stopped walking. Dawn came back and slid her arm into his. She whispered, "Leave the stone with Daddy. Let him buy it or send it to you later. It really is too valuable to carry around."

"How much is its wholesale value?" Sam asked.

Mr. Pauley leaned forward to whisper in his ear, "Millions of dollars," he said. Sam's eyes grew wide, and he seriously considered it, but he felt only confusion, not peace, and he rejected the idea. He shook his head slightly.

"Elder, I strongly suggest you leave the stone with me. I'll ship it to you if you don't want to sell it."

"That's okay, I'll just take it with me." Mr. Pauley was about to say something else, but Sam turned away. He did not see the worried look that crossed Mr. Pauley's face.

Dawn kissed her father on the cheek. She whispered something quickly and then hurried away with Sam. Their plane was about to leave without them.

At the door to the concourse Sam turned once more to wave, and then proceeded onto the plane.

He, Dawn, and Elder Palmer had adjacent seats. She took her seat and slid her hand into his. He wondered if that was against mission rules, but concluded that it didn't matter. Elder Palmer was too excited to care what they did. Almost immediately, the engines began to turn, and the steward came to check their seat belts.

"That diamond," Dawn whispered in his ear, "is too valuable to transport this way. Too many people now know that you have it. There are those who will kill us both to get it. Believe me, I have done this many times, and I know. You should have sold it to Daddy, or given it to him to send to America for you. We have ways of safely transporting diamonds. This way is very risky."

Sam nodded. "I wasn't sure what to do, and there wasn't time to think."

"I know. There wasn't time to convince you that Father would deal honorably with you. You should have trusted me."

Sam thought about this. He was relatively certain it would have taken weeks to convince him to surrender the stone to Dawn's father, especially when he blamed Sam for her joining the Church. Even though Mr. Pauley had forgiven Dawn, he would barely talk to Sam. She was right, though; Sam should have trusted her. In fact, he did. At the time, leaving the diamond with Mr. Pauley hadn't seemed like an issue of trusting Dawn or not.

"What should I do?"

"For now, give it to me. I know exactly what to do. We'll be making a twelve-hour layover in England. When I kissed Daddy goodbye, I told him to have our contact in England meet us at the airport. He will come. Believe me when I say that you will not make it back to America with that stone in your possession. Diamond smuggling and diamond theft is a highly developed art in this country. They watch the airport twenty-four hours a day to spot this exact thing. I can guarantee that someone is on the phone this moment planning how to relieve you of it before you reach America. I don't expect them to try anything until we get to England. We'll be safe until then. Our problem will be to get it to our contact before the thieves get to us. We can do it . . . if we're lucky," she added.

Sam was worried. "I had no idea," he said as he slid the small box into her hand. She transferred it to her purse.

"I'm sure you didn't. We will be all right until we reach England," she said in a whisper. With a start, he realized she was right. Many people had seen the stone, including stewardesses and other people passing by. Naively, they hadn't even attempted to conceal the fact that he had it. Thinking back, he could remember several strangers being particularly impressed with the stone. He had a sinking feeling in the pit of his stomach and wished he were still just doing missionary work. He missed it already and was dreading the transition back to "normal" life.

"Why is my life always so complicated?" he mumbled under his breath. He lay his head back on his seat, and the big plane roared into the sky.

13

THE PRICE

Sam fell asleep holding Dawn's hand. Just as his mind slipped into un-consciousness, he had a small thrill of wonder. He had been released from his mission while still in Africa. Now, for the first time in two years, it was okay for him to sleep during the day. A part of him wondered in that same instant why he was more fascinated with a nap than with holding a beautiful woman's hand. This question remained unanswered as he drifted off to sleep. It took over twenty-four hours and two refueling stops to reach Heathrow International Airport in England. As the plane descended toward the runway, Dawn became increasingly more nervous. Finally, she leaned over to him and spoke softly in his ear.

"Sam, as you know, my father and I have transported many diamonds out of South Africa and into England. It is perfectly legal, but still a tricky and sometimes dangerous business. I need you to trust me and do as I ask."

Sam nodded for her to go on, a look of concern on his face.

"I need to tell you what I suspect will happen after we land. I'm positive someone from customs will try to steal the diamond here at Heathrow. I don't expect to be mugged or robbed, but they'll try to trick us into just handing them the diamond. The way they usually do that is by telling you that you must declare all gems and jewelry in your possession. If you're dumb enough to just hand them the gems, they impound them for customs, and you never see them again."

Sam stared at her with wide eyes. "We don't have to declare the gems?" he asked.

"No," Dawn assured him, "we don't. The truth is, this airport terminal is international soil, and as long as we don't leave the terminal, we are not legally in England. You don't have to declare anything unless we take it out of this terminal. So, don't let them trick you. Besides, when we step foot off this plane, we won't even have the stone in our possession, because I'm going to leave it on the airplane."

"But . . . how?" Sam stammered. Dawn ignored him, continuing with urgency. The plane was in a steep descent.

"It doesn't matter how. What matters is that the people we are dealing with are powerful and ruthless. They will use every means both legal and illegal to take the stone from us. They think we have a stone that is worth upwards of a million dollars, and they will be very nasty about getting it. They will probably search us, threaten us with jail, and everything else they can think of. They can do little more than attempt to intimidate us into handing them the stone. Our best defense is that we don't even know what they are talking about."

Sam shook his head as if trying to clear it. "That isn't entirely the truth. I can buy everything else, but I actually do know what they're talking about."

"I know, I know. But it is a very small white lie," she said, holding up her thumb and finger almost touching. "It is only to keep us out of the grasp of some horrible people. If we play dumb, and they can't find the stone, they won't have any reason to keep us from boarding our plane out of here." Dawn paused and lowered her head. "But, there will undoubtedly be several hours of unpleasantness before they will let us back on the plane."

Sam nodded. "I'll just have to repent later, I guess," he said with mock gravity.

Dawn smiled. "This is serious," she said. "Don't underestimate them."

Sam's smile faded to a reflection of the dismay he felt boiling within his soul. "I hate this," he said with quiet fervor. Dawn nodded sadly. "The only thing that really matters is that we get back on the plane. Do you understand? No matter what, get back on the plane, okay?"

"I understand," Sam said above the roar of the plane.

"I'm sure Daddy has been working to get our people in place to avoid problems. However, they really haven't had much time. I don't know what's going to happen. I'll do my best, but unless Daddy has succeeded, we have little hope of keeping the diamond."

Sam thought about this for a few seconds. They had just touched down on the runway, the big engines straining to bring the jet to a stop. The entire cabin was shaking as if it would come apart. Somehow, it felt appropriate for the circumstances they found themselves in.

"Dawn, listen. That diamond isn't important to me. It was a gift, and I don't really care if it's lost. What I do care about is that you don't get yourself into trouble or get arrested. I would feel terrible if you got in trouble trying to keep my diamond safe. I just don't care that much."

"I understand," she said, placing a hand on his arm. She smiled warmly. "Just promise me one thing. Go with the flow. Act perfectly innocent and naive. Play the dumb American. And, no matter what happens, just get back onto the plane. This is important. No matter what you see, get back onto the plane. Promise me you'll do that."

"Why? I mean, if you are in trouble, I couldn't just walk away . . ."

"Listen to me, we are almost at the terminal. No matter what you see, just get back onto the plane. This is more important than I can explain right now. Promise me," she said in a voice burdened with anxiety.

"All right, you promise me that you know what you're doing, and I'll promise to do as you say on faith alone. You have to know I don't like it, though."

"I know what I'm doing. So?"

"All right, I promise."

At his words, she relaxed visibly.

* * *

It didn't take long for it to happen. They deplaned through the rear door, and walked down a short hall. Dawn stopped in the ladies' room for a few minutes.

An arrow directed them to the left, and they came to a large room. Through the middle of the room was a row of glassed booths. An armed guard sat in each booth with another armed guard at the far side of the booth. Low metal railings formed paths up to the booths.

"This is where we split up," she whispered cryptically, and veered to the left. Sam had no time to do anything but walk toward a booth to his right. The line was long, and it took a while to reach the booth. He listened carefully to the conversation of the passenger before him. The guard in the booth was a woman. She looked the passenger in the face as she took his passport and thumbed to the picture on the first page. She turned to her left and tapped into a computer terminal. After a moment, she nodded.

"You are required to declare anything you intend to import or sell in England, items of value in excess of one thousand pounds, regardless of whether or not you intend to sell them, and items which you bought in a country other than your country of origin. Do you have anything to declare?"

"No," the man said.

"It is illegal to import drugs, any live plants or animals, or weapons of any type. Do you wish to declare any of these?"

"I have a prescription drug for my illness is all," he said. "Prescription drugs are exempt," she said. "Do you intend to stay in England, or are you just passing through?"

"I will be staying about two weeks."

"The purpose of your visit?"

"I'm visiting family outside London."

Again, she tapped into her terminal and then stamped a page in his passport.

"Thank you, sir. Have a nice stay in England." She gave him a cold smile and shoved the passport through the small window.

Sam slid his passport through the slot. She studied his face for a moment as she took the passport. She thumbed to the picture, and looked up at him again for a split second. She typed rapidly on her keyboard and waited for a moment. A frown crossed her face, and she typed again. After a moment, she picked up a phone and dialed. He could not hear her conversation, but she glanced at him several times. Finally she motioned for Sam to go through the gate. "Mr. Mahoy, would you come with me please?"

The gate buzzed as he pushed it open. She motioned for him to follow her. The other guard fell into step behind him. His heart began to pound. He wondered what they wanted, and strongly suspected it was the diamond.

Sam was perplexed and frightened as he followed her a short distance to a door which she opened with a key. The room was about ten feet square, dingy, and poorly lit by a small fixture high overhead. Its only furnishings were two grimy metal chairs and a small table.

Sam stopped apprehensively just outside the room. It was as if his feet had suddenly become heavy. The female guard impatiently motioned him inside and directed him to take a seat. She left him and locked the door.

He waited for over an hour, spending the entire time worrying about Dawn. He was startled from his worries when a key suddenly rattled in the door. It opened, and a man in coveralls carried Sam's only suitcase into the room and laid it on the table. He left without a word.

After a few minutes, a young woman in uniform entered.

She was short and slight of build. Her hair was short and dark brown. While not attractive, she was what some might consider cute. Sam felt his nervousness relax a little. She smiled engagingly at him, and walked forward to shake his hand.

"Sorry to keep you waiting, Mr. Mahoy. I'm Rita," she informed him. Her accent was heavily British, though somewhat musical. Sam wanted to pepper her with questions, but restrained himself by merely nodding in reply. "I've been asked to conduct a routine customs inspection. We do this randomly to ensure compliance with our customs laws. There is no particular reason you were selected, so please relax." Sam nodded, but could not bring himself to relax.

After asking him the same questions the lady in the glass booth had, she asked, "Do I have permission to search your baggage? You have the right to refuse, in which case I will be required to seek a court order, which may cause delays to your travel plans."

"I don't care," Sam said. "Thank you. Do I need a key?"

"No, it's not locked." She turned the case toward her and opened the latch. She took out each article of clothing and felt along each seam. She carefully refolded each item and laid it on the table. It went slowly, and finally Sam sat back down. She continued until she came to a gift-wrapped box. She carefully opened the paper with a penknife, then the box. It was a small beaded purse for Beth. She opened the purse, and felt inside and thenclosed it all up, opened a drawer in the table, and took out a roll of sticky tape.

When she had finished, it was difficult to tell it had been opened.

She did the same for each gift.

After a long while, every item was lying on the table. She carefully ran her hands around the inside of the case until she satisfied herself it was not concealing anything. Finally, she began putting Sam's belongings back into the suitcase. When she was finished, his case was packed more neatly than when he had done it.

"Thank you, Mr. Mahoy," she said and smiled. She opened the door with a key and quickly left. This time, he waited for almost another hour before a key again slipped into the door.

This time, a man accompanied Rita, the girl who had searched his bag. He also seemed friendly, but was somewhat agitated, or perhaps impatient.

"Mr. Mahoy, I understand you are returning from a mission in South Africa for the Mormon Church?"

"That's right," Sam said.

"Were you given anything of value in South Africa which you brought aboard the plane?"

Sam's mind snapped into high gear, searching for an honest answer that did not include mention of the diamond. "Well, I received several gifts in the airport. Someone gave me a flute . . ." He paused as his mind spun.

"Oh gosh, I think I left my flute on the plane," he said, his voice filled with despair.

"Don't worry, sir, we can get it for you. Your plane is not set to leave for a few hours. Please be patient," she said. They gave each other a congratulatory glance and left. They returned a while later with his flute case.

She set it down on the table and opened it. Again, she carefully inspected each piece and set it on the table. She took her knife, cut the lining around the edges and lifted the interior. This she carefully inspected until she was satisfied. She shook her head at the man, whose face fell. They both left without a word, leaving the flute case dismantled on the table. Sam stood, and put it back together as best he could. The case was ruined, but it would hold the flute until he got home. He placed it inside his suitcase.

His stomach was rumbling by the time they returned.

This time there were two men. He was sorry the girl was not there, and considered they had upped the stakes.

"Sorry to keep you waiting," the first man said perfunctorily. He was not in the least sorry. "We have reason to believe you are concealing a certain illegal item on your person. We need permission to search your body. You have the right to refuse, in which case we will seek a court order, which may cause substantial delays to your travel plans. If you consent, you will be out of here in a few minutes."

Sam thought about it for a moment. They were determined enough that he knew he would eventually have to submit. He frowned, and nodded.

"Please remove your outer clothing, sir."

He took off his suit jacket and tie. They searched these thoroughly, and placed them on the table. They continued to ask for certain items of clothing until he was standing before them in his underwear. When they asked for them, he hesitated.

They merely asked again. He reluctantly surrendered. "Just one more thing, Mr. Mahoy . . ."

When Sam was finally escorted from the room, he truly felt violated yet oddly vindicated. His greatest concern was for Dawn. Maybe they had not connected her to him. He hoped not. If they were willing to do this to him, there was every likelihood they would do the same to her—or worse. But he was finally free to leave.

It was late in the day, and he only had an hour before his plane left. He bought something to eat, and walked to the boarding area, hoping to find Dawn. She was not there. His heart sank as he took a seat next to Elder Palmer, who seemed in a trance of expectation.

As they waited, four other missionaries they had not seen before joined them and they chatted about their missions. Two were returning from England, one from France, and another from Denmark. They were traveling together at least as far as the States.

By the time the final call came to board his plane to New York, Dawn was still missing. Sam paced back and forth, waiting, hoping, and debating what to do. Everything in him told him to get on the plane. He prayed earnestly and peace settled over him. He knew he should march onto the plane.

However, the peace departed abruptly as he watched the big plane roar into the sky. He knew it was an error to remain behind, yet he could not bring himself to abandon Dawn. He just could not. He hoped Heavenly Father would forgive him and still protect him. He hoped with all his heart that this disobedience would not in some way make things worse for Dawn.

He wasn't worried about the Church objecting. President Carlson had released him from his mission in South Africa. His plane tickets would still be good, so he wasn't stranded.

He had some money for food, but not enough for a hotel. He would have to act quickly to find Dawn. His resources were limited.

Sam found a pay phone and placed a collect call to his parents. It was a difficult call to make. When he finally hung up, they were still objecting and insisting he get on the next flight out. He lied to them and told them he would, even though he had no intention of doing so. In that day alone, he'd told more lies than in the previous two years. He was ashamed, and a feeling of defiance settled over him. They just didn't understand. Besides, he could take care of himself. All he had to do was find Dawn.

He immediately made his way to the airport security office. The door opened to a small room containing a single desk. He approached the bored-looking woman behind the desk. She slowly looked up from a pile of papers and regarded him expressionlessly.

"I need your help," he began. "I arrived here with a traveling companion. I think she was detained by customs. I haven't heard anything about her, and I want to know what's going on."

He thought he had used the right mixture of pleading and demanding. He didn't want to seem helpless or overbearing.

The woman asked him several questions. She asked to see his passport, and after thumbing through it, handed it back. She turned to the computer terminal beside her and typed. Sam tried to count her keystrokes to see if it was Dawn's name or his. He couldn't tell. He could see by her eye movements that she was carefully reading the screen. She occasionally stole a glance at him, which served to further increase his apprehension. After what seemed like a long time, she turned back to him.

"I will arrange for you to speak to my supervisor."

Sam thought he detected a hint of accusation in her voice. He wondered if she knew something damning which he did not. He wanted to scream at her to tell him, but he corralled his raging fears with difficulty. She flipped off her terminal and left through a back door. He studied the yellowed ceiling tiles and dented furniture. It seemed as if he were back in the interrogation room, and he felt his innards knot up. After a short while, she returned and led him down a hall to a larger room and left him alone. He was relieved she hadn't locked him inside.

After a few minutes, Rita walked in. He was relieved to see her. He stood as she entered.

"Mr. Mahoy," she said with a note of surprise in her voice. "I thought you were on your way to America. I'm surprised to see you still here. What can I do for you?" Her tone seemed genuine, and he decided to speak candidly.

"I wish I was on my way to America. However, I arrived here with a young woman I was escorting to America. I promised her father to see her safely to the States. She missed her flight, and I could not leave without her. Can you help me find her?"

"What was her name?" she asked as she produced a pad from her hip pocket.

"Dawn Pauley," he said, and was dismayed to note that she didn't write it down. Instead, she shoved the pad back into her pocket.

"How well do you know Miss Pauley?" she asked guardedly.

"I met her in South Africa and was involved with her as a missionary. She joined my church and wanted to come to America. I was to accompany her there. After that, she had her own plans."

"I see. So you weren't lovers?"

"No," he answered. The question shocked him. "I was a missionary," he replied indignantly. "We don't have lovers."

"Yes, of course," she replied. "Were you business partners?"

"Once again, I was a missionary. I had no business dealings at all. I was her escort and her friend in the Church. I'm concerned about her."

"Did you know she was wanted on an outstanding warrant for smuggling?"

"Smuggling? You mean from some prior trip to England?"

"Yes. You had no knowledge of this?"

"No, certainly not. Why would I? I taught her the gospel, and she said nothing of having gone to England, and certainly nothing of smuggling."

This was the truth. Dawn's father had explained their business dealings and had made it all sound legal. Sam knew he was walking a fine line, but it was the truth. Besides that, he seriously doubted that the accusation was even legitimate.

"It is illegal to bring anything over a certain value into this country with the intent of selling it. This is especially true of gems or jewelry. Were you aware of her bringing anything of this type into this country to sell?"

Sam bridled. "Our travel plans didn't even include leaving the airport. Check our reservations if you doubt it."

She nodded as if this had already occurred to her. She smiled and indicated for him to sit. He took a folding chair.

She pulled a worn wooden chair to where their knees were nearly touching. She leaned forward and studied his face.

"I took the Mormon missionary lessons last year. I didn't believe what they were telling me and didn't join."

"I'm sorry," Sam replied honestly. It felt like a great loss, and he wanted to probe into her rejection of the gospel but did not.

"You're sorry? Why?" She seemed genuinely bothered by his answer.

Sam sat for a moment waiting for the familiar urgings of the Spirit to guide. He was surprised when nothing happened.

The thought that entered his mind was that he had removed himself from the Spirit, not the other way around. He was grieved at his disobedience, yet he knew what he wanted to say.

"You seem like a nice person. I can see goodness in your eyes. I can't believe you seriously investigated the Church without coming to a knowledge of its truth. I said I was sorry because you would have been very happy with the gospel in your life."

"I'm not unhappy now," she said defensively.

"I'm glad," was all he answered. Without the Spirit, he hardly knew how to have a conversation on spiritual things.

Sam wanted to bear his testimony, to teach her, to touch her heart with truth, but he could not.

Rita shook her head as if weary of the conversation and abruptly changed the subject. "Well, I guess that has little to do with your friend, Dawn. I'm afraid she's in deep trouble, and there is little you can do about it."

"Actually, it has everything to do with it," Sam replied abruptly. The Spirit had moved him so suddenly that he had nearly blurted out his answer before she had finished speaking. He was so relieved to have guidance again that he felt giddy with relief.

"What has my taking the missionary lessons to do with Dawn's legal problems?"

"It has to do with truth," Sam replied evenly. "Truth?"

"Truth, and the courage to obey it."

Rita cleared her throat as if annoyed. "I don't appreciate—"

"You know the Church is true," he interrupted.

"What?" she demanded hotly.

"When the missionaries taught you, you gained a testimony."

"What gives you the right to assume you know what I felt back then?"

"Truth," he replied again.

"I don't know what you are talking about. I'm not going to . . ."

"You can't escape the truth by walking away. The truth is, you still know what the missionaries told you is true. You chose not to be baptized because you didn't want to live by yourself." His answer puzzled him, yet he knew it was true by the urgings of the Spirit, and by the stunned expression on her face. There was a long moment of silence.

"Even if what you say is true, it has no bearing on Dawn," she replied defiantly but in a small voice.

"Actually, it has everything to do with it. Let me explain."

"Please do," she said loudly. She was both repelled by this conversation and inwardly stunned. It was as if her soul demanded to hear his words, and another part of her wanted to throw him in jail. The mixture of emotions was both puzzling and frightening.

"You chose not to join the Church, not because it isn't true, but for other considerations."

"Perhaps," she allowed.

"Those other considerations were important, but they have now evaporated, and you feel betrayed. My point is that you sacrificed truth and the lasting happiness it brings for what turned out to be a lie, and you are now miserable."

"I wouldn't call myself miserable, I'm just . . ."

"Now, you are faced with the same dilemma. The truth is, that neither Dawn nor I have broken any laws of this country. You have searched our baggage and our persons and have found nothing. The charges you are holding Dawn on are fictitious. You know this, yet there are other considerations."

"Assuming you are correct," Rita replied in a small, but defensive voice. "What other considerations might you be talking about?"

"You don't want to lose your job," he said. She fell back in her seat as if hit across the face.

He wasn't finished, or better stated, the Spirit wasn't finished. "Truth, once again, and a course to lasting happiness in doing what is right, is being confronted by your need for temporary gratification."

"You are making wild assumptions which . . ."

"Which we both know are true. If you wish, I will tell you how to bring happiness back into your life."

There was a long pause. Her voice was small, almost plaintive. "How?" she asked finally.

"First, release Dawn."

"I can't. It is not within my power. You don't know what would happen. Not only would I lose my job, but I'd probably be charged with a crime myself. No, it isn't possible."

"Second," he said.

She looked at him with amazement, a "Don't you ever give up?" look on her face.

Sam continued. "Second, go back and restudy the gospel. This time, when you feel the power of its truths, submit yourself to baptism. These two things will start you once again on the road to happiness."

"Even if I believed what you said was true, I . . ."

"You do believe," he interrupted softly.

Rita frowned. "Even if all that were true, this is also true: I have no power to release Dawn. She has been charged with a serious felony. I'm sorry."

Sam was deflated. Once again, the Spirit departed, and he was left to himself. He felt orphaned and sick at heart. His soul had been alive and energized while the Spirit was upon him.

Now, he felt helpless and sick to his stomach with fear. He was about to abandon himself to it when he remembered the calmness and courage he had briefly felt a few moments ago. He knew those sweet feelings to be real; these feelings of despair had to be a lie, even if they were very believable at this moment. He struggled to pump up his courage.

A look of compassion came on Rita's face, and she patted him on the knee. Her next question surprised him.

"Do you love her?"

"Yes," he replied without hesitation. It was true, but probably not in the context she meant. His love for her was real, large, and beautiful, but it was not romantic. He felt no urge to explain his answer.

"If you will tell me where the diamond is, I can get her released," she said candidly. "That's all they want. Tell me, and I can have you out of here in just a few minutes."

He was about to blurt out everything he knew about the stone, about handing it to Dawn, about her contact in England, everything. He opened his mouth to spill it all, but was suddenly constrained by the familiar feeling of the Spirit. When he spoke, something entirely unexpected came out.

"Is it against the law to transport jewelry through this country?"

"No, of course not," she replied.

"If Dawn had any jewelry on her, it was her intent to take it to America. The truth, if it matters to you at all, is that she has broken no law, and you know it." Sam lowered his head as tears came to his eyes. "Apparently, truth is no longer the issue."

Rita thought about this for a moment. "Actually, it still can be," she countered thoughtfully. "The truth is, someone wants that stone and is willing to do anything to get it. If you know where it is, you had best tell me. Otherwise, Dawn is going to languish a lot of years in prison."

"If I knew, if I even had a clue, if I knew anything that would release her, I would tell you. That is also the truth."

"I believe you," Rita replied almost reverently. She stood and left the room. She returned later with a sandwich and soft drink. She smiled sadly as she handed them to him and departed without a word. He wondered why it would make her sad to give him a sandwich. Just the same, his stomach grumbled its appreciation as he hastily ate. He felt as if he had an ally at least, even though a useless one. After eating, he rapidly grew sleepy. The world seemed to be slowly spinning counterclockwise. Sleep swept him away just as he realized something was very wrong.

* * *

Sam had no idea where they took him. He tried to force himself to remain awake, but fell asleep again watching telephone poles whiz by in the darkness. Several times, he awoke to loud voices. His body felt leaden and exhausted until sleep took him away again. He had a vague memory of stumbling to another vehicle, perhaps more than once. He slept soundly for what seemed a long time and was awakened as the car rolled to a stop on a gravel road. Someone opened the door from the outside. He stumbled out into the night. His mind felt fuzzy and refused to analyze his surroundings. All he could think about was going back to sleep.

Without a word, the driver closed the door, climbed back into the car, and drove into the night. The night was cool, and even though it was not cold enough to harm him, Sam felt a chill seep into his bones. The darkness was complete and impenetrable, and except for two red taillights rapidly diminishing in the distance, he could see in neither direction.

In a daze, Sam walked two steps, felt the ground disappear from under his feet, and rolled down a grassy embankment. He came to a harmless stop on flat ground and landed face down in long grass. He pushed himself to his feet and found the bank. It seemed pointless to climb back onto the road, so he lay down in frustration. In moments, a troubled sleep almost forcibly took him.

Sam awoke to sunshine on his face and gnawing hunger pains. He realized as he awoke that he had not eaten since the night before. He was lying on a sloping bank of grass. Not far from the bank, a dense stand of trees began. He stood and surveyed his surroundings before climbing the short hill to the road. Massive trees surrounded him in every direction, and majestic, mist-shrouded mountain peaks towered above him.

Sam turned in a complete circle. "This doesn't look like Kansas," he said aloud and chuckled darkly. "It doesn't even look like England." Deciding to take inventory of his assets, he fumbled in his pockets and was shocked to find his wallet and passport missing. He found a single piece of paper money. It was not American currency, and as near as he could tell, not English either. He shoved it back into his pocket.

He assumed that the driver had taken his things while he had been asleep in the car.

The road was narrow, scarcely more than twin dirt trails in dense grass growing thickly upon a wide lane cut through the forest. It was winding and hugged the mountainside above precipitous canyons below. It was obviously seldom traveled. It reminded him of a mountain maintenance road more than a highway.

Resigning himself to the idea of a long walk, Sam picked up a stout stick about four feet long that reminded him of a baseball bat. A childhood memory stirred. He selected a small rock and hit it solidly with the stick. It whined loudly as it flew into the woods, striking something with a loud thunk. Sam almost smiled. It was so satisfying to bop something soundly that he did it several times more.

Finally, he headed in the direction he surmised the car had departed into the night. He walked for most of the day, seeing nothing but dirt road and endless trees. He did not see a single car all day. Whenever he grew weary or bored, he clobbered a few more rocks. It gave him a childish sense of being in control, at least of the rock.

Night was beginning to settle when Sam came on a small stream. He climbed down a short grassy slope. The water looked clean and tasted sweet. He drank until he was full. He slept cold and miserable by the stream.

The second day of walking was even harder. His body rebelled against the hunger and he felt nauseous. He continued to walk until hunger, thirst, and fatigue overpowered him. He stopped by another stream, drank until he no longer felt hungry, and surrendered to bone-chilling sleep.

Day three found Sam too weak to do much more than stumble along the dirt road. Finally, he could move no more and sat on the grassy side of the road. It suddenly occurred to him that he was in desperate circumstances. Whoever had dumped him in the woods had picked a road few people traveled. He wondered if the road was even open to the public. In three days, he had seen no cars. For the first time in his life, he felt completely hopeless. Not only was there an incredible emptiness in his gut, but there was an absence in his soul which felt worse than any starvation. The emptiness was so profound that he had trouble identifying its cause.

When the truth finally caught up with his sluggish brain, Sam was shocked to realize that this emptiness was the absence of the Holy Spirit from his soul.

A word, a thought, a concept crystallized in his mind: "chastisement." At first the word meant nothing, yet the concept was crystal clear. Sam had offended the Lord through his disobedience. He had walked away from what he knew was right and relied upon his arm of flesh. A blackness settled over his heart that seemed to grip it with an iron fist. It was so compelling that he felt as if he had to struggle to draw each breath.

As this thought jelled in his mind, Sam felt coldness creeping up his spine. A touch of something unholy brushed through him, and he shuddered. Darkness settled on his soul, and he contemplated his disobedience, his undeniable failure, and his worthlessness.

Sam considered all these things with harsh self-loathing, and he laughed at the sudden plunge he had made to a telestial reward. But his laughter was bitter, and the sound of his voice called forth tears. Once the first drop was spilled, it was like a river overrunning its banks, and he wept, at first silently, then violently, until every tear within him was unleashed and his sobs rent his soul.

Suddenly an electric sensation slapped his consciousness, and Sam's head snapped up. A familiar warmth surged through him and just as quickly left. But it was enough, and his soul fed on the warmth, and sucked at the light like a drowning man sucks at air through clenched teeth, scarcely able to believe water no longer surrounds his face. In one blinding instant, he saw this long dark reverie for what it was, and President Carlson's words echoed in his mind as loudly as if he were there. "Beware, my boy. For God's sake . . . for your sake, beware all your life."

When tears came this time, they were tears of humility, repentance, and sweet surrender. He fell on his knees in the cold, damp darkness and poured out his soul to God. As desperate as his circumstances were, as empty and weak as his body was, these things were no part of his plea. His were the words of repentance, of humble acknowledgment of sin, and of sincere commitment to obedience. The wave of darkness assailed him many times and lashed him with its cold fury. Yet, so sweet was the peace of his surrender to the love he felt overflowing him that the darkness soon spent its last lie and departed.

All the night through Sam sought forgiveness. At times, his prayer was a terrible struggle, held back by his own fear of unworthiness. At others, it was as sweet as the purest love and as warm as an angel's embrace. When his mind finally returned from this grand communion, it was early morning and the sun was just finding its way toward the tops of the trees.

Sam woke up on his side, his knees drawn up as if he were kneeling, his hands clasped before him. He was surprised to find he was shivering, for he felt nothing but deep internal warmth and a glorious feeling of forgiveness. He closed his eyes again, and for a long while poured out his gratitude in worship more powerful than speech, more lyric than poetry, and more beautiful than choirs of angels. It seemed to him as if his voice for a time ascended unto God and joined the myriad beings who sing His praises both day and night.

Suddenly, without warning, and much to his regret, it was over, and he stood with sudden purpose. He was almost too weak to walk, yet he felt no fear, no hesitation, and no doubt. He turned toward the forest.

After a short struggle through dense undergrowth, the trees seemed to spread out and open into a pleasant, sunlit clearing. The same stream by which he had slept wandered through the glade. Had he not been so far from home, it would have been a glorious discovery, an almost magical find as if from a storybook of castles, kings, and queens.

For the first time in many days, it seemed obvious to Sam what he must do. Each thought came to him separately, without explanation. Without understanding why, he removed his suit coat and tie and hung it carefully over a branch. Next, he unlaced a shoelace from his shoe and tied it to a willow so that it bent into a small bow. Selecting several dried branches, he looped the bow over one, and carefully began drawing it back and forth. The dried stick twirled back and forth. One end of the stick he spun against a dry piece of bark, the other on a rock in his hand. In a surprisingly short time, a spiral of smoke arose from the branch. He laid a small bundle of grass next to it, and in a moment, a tiny yellow flame appeared. He nursed it carefully until he had a small fire burning warmly. He laid on a little more wood, and in not many minutes was warming himself by the fire. Sam shivered violently and realized how close he had been to succumbing to the effects of hypothermia. He fed the fire and waited for the warmth to penetrate to his limbs. With the return of warmth came a return of energy.

Sam was, of course, still hungry but not devastated by it. He actually considered intentionally continuing his fast as one of gratitude for his deliverance but felt an urging to the contrary. He simply obeyed. Memories of things he had done as a Boy Scout popped into his mind, and he returned to the small stream. He lay in the shadow of a tree and inched on his belly toward the stream. He had tried this many times as a scout and had always been unsuccessful. It did not surprise him to see a small fish against the bank swimming slowly in the current.

Moving as slow as it is possible for a human to move, Sam inched his hand into the water, moved it under the fish, and slowly closed his fingers. The fish fought for freedom, but his hand closed tightly around it.

In minutes, the fish was on a stick and turning slowly over his fire. The smell was divine and wafted gently through the trees. Sam intentionally cooked it slowly, lengthening the cooking time from a few minutes to half an hour. His body screamed for the food. His logic urged him to eat the fish—stick, guts, and all.

Yet, within him, a quiet, simple urging kept him from consuming the food now available to him.

Following an urging from the Spirit, he slowly turned the fish near the fire for nearly an hour, just keeping it warm. Sam heard a branch snap in the distance. He smiled to himself, an almost giddy sense of happiness sweeping through him. The happiness he felt had nothing to do with the distant sound of brush and twigs being disturbed, but the quiet joy of obedience. Whatever was making the sound grew nearer until it stopped a short distance from his clearing, waiting warily in the bushes.

"I believe this is done cooking," he said loudly. "Come have some breakfast."

A ragged figure pushed through the bushes with a strangled sob. He stood as Dawn limped toward him at a run. He caught her in his arms, and held her until she released him. Tears had made muddy tracks down both cheeks. Her hair was tangled with dirt and debris, her dress was smudged and torn. Her eyes were lackluster and sunken. He stepped back a little and raised the fish between them. It was deliciously cooked and still warm.

He pulled a piece of white meat from it with his fingers and held it to her lips. She took the small bite. Her eyes rolled back into her head in an ecstasy of taste. He continued to feed her and himself until the small fish was gone.

They sat near the fire, where Dawn curled up against him and fell asleep. He continued to feed the fire as he held her. Sam pondered the significance of the fact that she had said nothing from the moment she had found him until she had fallen asleep.

He knew it meant something, something both important and unique, yet his mind refused to understand it.

It was late in the afternoon when she awoke. He had also slept, and they both struggled to make their bodies move again.

Even though Sam's only meal had been tiny, it seemed to have rejuvenated him, and he felt strong once again. Dawn seemed less recovered, and swayed back and forth while standing.

A moment of awkward silence passed, and then they both tried to speak at once. Dawn held up a hand, and Sam fell silent.

"I'm so sorry, Sam—" she began, but tears cut her short.

Sam was stunned. It was he who had failed to obey! He reached out to her, but she pulled away. He simply could not understand her words or her rebuff.

"Dawn, what's wrong? You haven't done anything to me! Why are you crying?"

She looked up at him with such pathos that he wanted to hold her, stroke her hair, and tell her everything would be wonderful again. He could not.

"Oh, Sam, you have no idea what I've done to you. I thought I could beat them. I thought I knew what they would do and how to get the stone past them. They threatened me with all kinds of horrible things, but I thought I knew what to do. I held out, played innocent, and acted stupid. I did all that until they laid your passport on the table. It was then that I knew they had detained you. They said you were in custody to be tried for smuggling and would not be allowed to return home. I panicked and took them to the stone. I gave it to them."

Sam laughed. "Dawn, I don't care. It was never worth all you went through for it. I'm glad you gave it to them. I just don't care."

"You don't understand. I took them to the restroom on the airplane. What we do is flush the stone down the toilet in a special bag. One of our people retrieves it, and that's all there is to it. Well, they went through the sewage, and it was there. They took it out, and it was a fake."

"A fake?" Sam exclaimed.

"Well, it was a real diamond, the right size, but it was almost valueless, deeply flawed and discolored. All that effort was to protect a stone of very small value. They were furious and swore you would still be prosecuted. They drugged me and brought me here three days ago. I have no idea why they dumped me in the forest. I thought they were going to kill me."

Dawn paused as the memory of her terror marched through her like an invading army. "I have been wandering through these woods, praying you would be all right. For a while, I just wanted to give up and die. I felt so ashamed for causing you all this pain. I'm still so ashamed! I—"

"Dawn, they lied to you."

"What?"

"They lied. I wasn't detained. I intentionally missed the plane. I didn't keep my promise to get on the plane and went back to search for you. I asked about you and insisted on them releasing you. They were using us against each other. I was never in any real danger. I didn't fully realize they drugged me until you said it just now, but they dumped me out here three days ago too. Apparently after they found out that the stone was relatively worthless, they just wanted us to get lost."

"But why not just give us back our passports, and order us to leave?"

Sam shrugged. "There is the possibility that we might complain to the authorities, I guess, but out here, without identification, we can do nothing. By the time we either find our way out or perish, there will be no evidence of their actions against us or even of our having entered this country, I suspect. They probably assume that if we ever did find our way home we will not have the inclination or proof to accuse them of any wrongdoing. If we do, they will probably accuse us of being in the country without visas or something. Our best option is to just quietly leave the country. I'm sure they are counting on just such a course of action from us."

"I'm scared, Sam. I'm really scared. I'm afraid they will change their minds and come after us. Or they'll be setting us up so that when we finally get to a town, we will be accused of some gross crime and be arrested. I'm afraid—"

"I'm afraid," Sam interrupted her, hoping to lighten her mood, "that you've been watching too many cheap American movies."

"I hope so," she said fervently. She smiled and turned to walk slowly toward the stream, dusting dirt and leaves from her dress. It was another beautiful, sunny day.

"You know what I find amazing?" Sam asked as he began picking up twigs.

"No," she responded meekly, as if her mind was on many other things.

"That you found me. We've been wandering in the woods for three days and could have gone in a dozen different directions, but you found me. How did you manage that?"

"Very simply," she replied, her lips softening into a half smile. "I could hear you."

"Hear me? That's seems impossible," Sam insisted.

"Even though we have both been in the woods for three days, we have never been very far apart. On the very first day I heard a loud pop, and a sound somewhat like a bullet whizzing through the trees."

"That was me, bopping rocks!" Sam laughed, suddenly happy he had revived his childhood preoccupation with "rock bopping."

"Bopping?"

"That's what I used to call it on the farm," he explained sheepishly. Dawn smiled broadly. "A piece of your childhood that became my salvation," she assured him. "Several times a day I heard the same 'bopping' sound. At first I thought it was someone firing a gun. It scared me to death, but I thought it could be someone besides my kidnappers, and I decided to follow them at a distance. If it was a hunter, I didn't want to be shot by mistake. I only wanted to follow them to a road or a town."

She hesitated, and Sam waited for her to continue. "I didn't have any other means of finding another human," she said at length, her voice sounding lost again. "It seemed like my only hope. It wasn't until I smelled food cooking that I overcame my fear and tried to sneak close enough to see who it was. I was immensely relieved to see it was you, but I felt so ashamed that I almost ran away . . ."

Feeling a need to leave this subject, Sam said, "After I build the fire back up, I want to tell you about my struggle with the devil and of my repentance. I think there is a purpose in all this for both of us, and not just some random opposition." He began blowing on the smoldering coals. They quickly came back to life.

"Do you think we will find our way home?"

A warm confidence surged through him. He straightened from where he was kneeling by the fire and smiled. "Yes I do."

Dawn felt the same assurance and replied, "I believe you."

"It won't be easy," he added with some emphasis.

Dawn's voice was resigned when she replied a moment later. "I believe that too."

DELIVERANCE

It took hours of trying before Sam finally pulled another brook trout from the stream. This one was larger and gave them almost enough food for a satisfying breakfast. Sam cleaned his hands in the stream and carefully took his suit coat from the branch where he had hung it. It still looked clean.

"You know what's odd to me?" Dawn asked as she prepared herself to move on.

"I think I can guess, but go ahead and tell me."

"This forest doesn't seem like anything I've ever heard about in England."

Sam nodded. "No fog, no ocean breezes, and relatively high elevation. I'm not sure, but I don't think England has any tall mountains, yet we're definitely in some now."

"Yes . . ." Dawn agreed without enthusiasm.

"Well, let's find out where we are. I'm sure we're still in Europe," he said.

"Why?" she asked.

"Because the stars at night are wrong. I didn't recognize the sky at all. I know the South African sky and the American sky. This one is different."

"Where do you think we are?"

"What is a country near England they could drive to in a single night, which also has mountains?"

"I have a vague memory of being in a helicopter, I think," Dawn said with uncertainty. "We could be almost anywhere. Perhaps France?"

"If they took us in a helicopter we could be anywhere. France, or even further."

"I speak French," she commented as they started back toward the road.

"I doubt this is France."

"Why?"

Sam pushed his way through the tangle of undergrowth and held it open for Dawn. The road stood a few yards before them. There was still no sign of cars. They were standing on the road when he finally answered her question. "Because, it would be too obvious. There has to be some element of implausibility. If the suggestion is ever made, they need to be able to laugh at the idea that they hauled us that far in a single night just to get rid of us."

"Where then?"

Sam reached into his pocket and pulled out the paper money, studied it for a second, and handed it to her.

"It's a Swiss franc," she said with some amazement. "That's what I thought too."

Sam and Dawn wearily continued on, stopping to build fires and hunt for food. Time seemed to drag to a near-crawl, and the unending forests stretched to some parody of eternity.

They had been lost for five days when they unexpectedly heard distant rock and roll music on the wind. They quickened their pace, and a few ,minutes later, they hesitantly walked into a village.

At the edge of the town, the dirt road turned to cobblestone. The shops and homes were decidedly old, made of large timbers and stone. They had steep, red-tiled roofs, and looked like an illustration from a Hansel and Gretel storybook. The people in the village were all afoot. The few cars they saw were parked and dusty. The entire village was several blocks long and seemed to consist of a single row of buildings. They were primarily boutiques, clothing stores, gift shops, and ski equipment shops.

"It's a ski village," Dawn said with sudden understanding.

Sam nodded. "A tourist village. See that big lodge? Let's go there. Perhaps we can get help there." Dawn nodded silently.

As they walked, Sam put on his jacket and dusted off his pants. Because he had been careful with is jacket and tie, he looked fairly fresh. His six days growth of beard was long enough to look intentional. Dawn tried to tidy herself with somewhat less success. As long as no one got close enough to smell either of them, they would pass for tourists.

For a ski village in the middle of summer, there was an amazing number of people milling around. Behind the lodge were two double chairlifts reaching up the mountain. One of them was operating. Approximately every third chair had someone in it. It seemed as if the mountain attracted visitors all year around. Sam had to admit it was a charming village whose attractions were magical.

The sprawling lodge was built of massive logs and dominated the village. It looked like a woodland castle and gave an enchanted quality to the scene before them. Everything about the structure was larger than life. They walked up the steps onto the covered porch. A brass plaque beside the door informed them they had arrived at the world-famous Schöner Berg. An ornate set of doors stood invitingly open before them.

Inside, the room was a stunning mixture of rough logs, red velvet furnishings, and crystal. A huge crystal chandelier hung from the tall ceiling directly over an ornate grand piano. Golden lamps with silken shades stood beside French Renaissance furniture. Over the polished wooden floor lay rich Persian carpets.

To the right they saw a plush restaurant almost entirely decorated in red and gold. To their left sprawled a long hotel counter of highly polished wood. Their hunger commandeered their feet, and they turned right. A waitress showed them to a seat without as much as a glance at their crumpled clothing. She said something in another language, handed them menus, smiled, and left.

"What language was she speaking?" Sam asked, leaning toward Dawn.

"I'm sure it's German. A shame. I speak French, Italian, English, and Afrikaans, but I don't speak German."

Sam picked up the menu and tried to interpret it. Finally, he found a page written in English. After pointing it out to Dawn, he studied it carefully. A few minutes later, he pulled the note from his pocket. It was a ten franc note. The items on the menu started at six and went as high as fifty. They found a sandwich for eight francs and ordered it on two plates. It was ambrosia and nothing had ever tasted more divine to either of them. They ate slowly, sipping ice-cold water.

It surprised them that they could just barely finish their half sandwich. They sat and talked for a long time but finally admitted that they had no idea what to do next.

When the waitress came to take away their plates Sam asked, "Excuse me, do you speak English?"

"Yes, but a little," she replied in voice heavy with guttural tones. She was young, about their age. "I did study just some English in school," she continued. "How are your holidays happening?" She placed emphasis on her words in funny places.

"We are having quite an unusual holiday," Sam answered congenially. The South African people also called vacations holidays.

"So pleased. Did you have the long walk?" she asked, nodding toward their crumpled clothing.

"Oh, yes. Well, actually, we got lost and walked longer than we wanted to."

"So sorry to get you lost," she said sympathetically, as if she were responsible. "Next time, we take map at hotel counter. It will not get you lost, yes?"

"Thanks. We'll take a map next time."

"So good. Is anything else wanting you to eat it?"

"No. We're fine. Thank you. What's the nearest city?"

"Bern is the closest large city."

"Is there a bigger resort nearby?" Sam asked on impulse, having no real reason to want the information.

"Why yes. The most popular is the Alpen Stein. It's on the next mountain range. It's very much biggest as this one is not."

Sam handed her his only money. She nodded and slipped away. She returned moments later with change. Sam left some of it on the table, and they walked back out into the sunshine. It was pushing into afternoon.

Dawn tugged on his sleeve. "Sam, we need to find a phone and call my dad. He can wire us some money."

"That's a good idea," Sam agreed. He was glad for the suggestion since he otherwise had no idea how to get money. They returned to the hotel and, after going through three clerks, found one who spoke English. The clerk finally understood that they wanted to make a collect phone call and directed them to a phone on a small table between two plush red chairs.

Dawn had difficulty getting an operator to understand her. At length, she put her hand over the mouthpiece.

"It's ringing," she said happily.

When no answer was forthcoming, the operator interrupted the call. Dawn hung up the phone unhappily. "Father's apparently not home. What about your parents?"

"They just moved to Alaska. I had their new number in my wallet, but I don't have my wallet any more. Let me try information."

Sam took her place, and after half an hour hung up the phone in frustration. He had not been able to make anyone understand his request for information. Several had been willing to connect him to American information but wanted long distance fees. He longed for the simple "dial zero for an operator" convenience of American telephones.

Sam stood in frustration. Dawn's eyes followed him with concern. Sam looked down at her. "I think we struck out. We can try again in a few hours. Maybe your father will be back by then."

"Perhaps. However, I doubt my father knows anything's gone wrong. But, even so, it's odd that he didn't leave someone to answer the phone in case I called. There's almost always a maid or butler at home. In time we'll get through." Dawn's eyes filled with tears. "Oh, Sam, we just have to come up with a plan, or we're going to be sleeping outdoors and eating garbage. I'm not at all anxious to be arrested for vagrancy or panhandling in a foreign country."

Sam did his best to reassure her, even though his own assessment of the situation was bleak. They sat in dejected silence for nearly an hour before a thought suddenly came to him. Since emerging from the forest, they hadn't thought to pray about their dilemma. Sam looked around. Where they sat by the phones was private.

Sam bowed his head and leaned close to Dawn. He prayed aloud, speaking in a whisper. His prayer was so spiritually satisfying he had to remind himself nothing had changed yet to help them. Yet, the peace was as significant as if all was exactly as it should be. Afterward, they both felt the answer to their petition had already been granted, and all they needed to do was wait for the Lord to lay it before them.

Sam opened his eyes to rest upon the large grand piano standing majestically in the center of the large room. It was upon a small raised dais beneath the large chandelier, surrounded by a dozen plush chairs in a semicircle. Suddenly, quite unnervingly, he knew what to do. The solution was simple yet more brash and bold than any part of him could have conceived. However, it was the answer to their humble prayers, and Sam rejoiced even while his heart trembled.

He stood and found the English-speaking clerk. "Can I speak to a manager? One who speaks English?" The clerk frowned as if unsure one even existed, then hurried away.

"What are you going to do?" Dawn asked.

"I'm going to put into motion the answer to our prayers," he explained happily. Dawn smiled at him, a quizzical look on her face.

A short time later, an older gentleman walked briskly toward them. As he approached, his eyes took in their crumpled condition. His smile was forced and seemingly superficial. "How may I assist you?" he asked pleasantly.

Sam stuck out his hand, which the manager shook. "I'm Samuel Mahoy, a musician from America. My companion and I are traveling in your country. We are apparently obliged to spend a few days in your village. We seem to now have an opportunity to rest from our tour."

The manager seemed pleased and a bit puzzled. It was as if he were playing through his memories to find any mention of an American musician named Samuel Mahoy staying at his hotel. Sam decided to lay the rest of his plan in motion before questions or objections began flying.

"After arriving here, we realized we were brought here by mistake. Our luggage and instruments have been sent to another destination, perhaps back to America or to the Alpen Stein. We don't know. So, we have no reservations here."

"Ah, yes. I see your dilemma," the manager nodded thoughtfully.

The mention of his competitor's hotel made him flinch.

"Fortunately, it is summer, and we can accommodate you. Would you like me to book you a room?"

"Thank you. We will need your best room, of course."

"Certainly," the manager said smoothly.

"We will need room service to bring most of our meals to the room, and a telephone."

"It will be as you say," he soothed. The manager made a note in a pad. "Anything else, Herr Mahoy?"

"There is something else," Sam said smoothly. "I need to practice my instruments. I would prefer a private practice room if you have one. At the Alpen Stein I would probably be doing several evening performances, but this will be much better. I will just practice."

The cash register in the manager's mind clanked happily. "Our finest piano is the large one in the lobby, which you are most welcome to use. In exchange for the use of the piano, would you allow me to announce your, um, practices? Perhaps more people would come. Would you mind if we charge admission? It is the slow season, after all. A little more revenue would be appreciated."

"I said I want to practice. If this is to be a performance, I will find no rest in it," Sam answered haughtily. "Perhaps, I will just skip the practicing."

"No, no. Forgive me. Perhaps we could benefit one another here. As I said, it is the slow season, and our rooms stand empty. If I made your room, meals, and daytime tours complimentary, you could relax as you like during the day, and provide us with but several small, shall we say 'practices,' during the evenings? Would that be agreeable?" Playing her part to the hilt, Dawn placed a slender hand on Sam's arm solicitously. "Don't do it, Samuel. You need your rest," she said in a silken, pouty voice.

Sam patted her hand. "Yes, my love, I do. Perhaps if I call it a practice and it's brief. The rest would be grand. And the manager is being so generous. A few public practices would be much more relaxing than an actual performance. I've never done anything like it."

"It's up to you, as always." She smiled sweetly and gave him a long-distance kiss.

Sam hesitated a few moments before turning to the manager, who was anxiously awaiting his reply. "All right, then," Sam agreed in apparent reluctance. What he was really doing was frantically trying to pump up his courage to say what had just popped into his mind. Accompanied by the glow of the Spirit, he knew the idea was right, but it was more than he could normally force from his mouth.

Sam took a deep breath. "I can promise no more than three public practices. After that, we shall see. I will expect a week's accommodations, meals, and tours, all complimentary. I will also expect one half of gross ticket sales. We will reimburse you for other expenses at the end of the week from ticket sales."

"That will be acceptable," the manager said in a tightly controlled voice. "I will have the bellman show you to your room. It will take me a while to find instruments for you. Do you require any other than the piano?" he asked as he made notes.

"Just a flute and a violin," Sam replied as if bored.

"Do you have a preference concerning the instruments, such as manufacturer, or anything else I should ask for?"

"They must be the highest quality. And have the piano tuned. If it is the slightest out of tune, I will not perform, regardless of how many tickets you have sold."

"Certainly, certainly. I agree. Well, I have my afternoon cut out for me. You two enjoy your rest. Would seven o'clock be agreeable for your first performance?"

"Practice," Sam corrected him. "Yes, of course."

"I will be down at seven."

"Splendid." The manager shook his hand, bowed to Dawn, and hurried away.

* * *

Their room was the same stunning mixture of rough and regal. The walls were hewn logs, and the furnishings French. The bedspread was an intricately stitched silken comforter the color of cream, with huge pillows of the same color. Their room was large enough to be an apartment. Dawn walked through it feigning dissatisfaction and then accepted the keys from the bellman. The bellman held out his hand for a tip. Dawn gave him such a disapproving frown that he lowered his hand and backed out the door.

Dawn frowned as if ashamed of herself. "I'll make it up to him later," she said and turned in a full circle, inspecting the room with a childlike smile. "This is wonderful! Would you mind if I clean up first? I feel so filthy!"

"Please," Sam said, bowing and motioning toward the large bath. "Ladies first."

As soon as the door was closed, Sam returned to the elevator and to the lobby. There were several shops in the foyer, one of which had beautiful dresses. He found a long, lovely dress for Dawn, light blue with delicate white lace. He also bought her a pair of jeans, a sweatshirt, and tennis shoes, charging them all to the room. It took longer to find a pair of white dress shoes, but he was satisfied.

When he explained they had lost their luggage, the sales lady became nearly indignant at the few things he had purchased for his "wife."

After asking him several specific questions about Dawn's age, weight, and height, she rounded up a whole box of things, including make-up, underwear, and other items. He wasn't sure how they knew Dawn's sizes, but the saleslady seemed supremely confident in her selections. Unsure of what some of it was for, and afraid to see a single price tag, Sam quit watching halfway through. In the end, he had quite a bundle of things for Dawn.

For himself, Sam bought a white shirt, a new tie and socks, a pair of jeans, and a sweatshirt. He also bought a wristwatch.

He left his suit jacket to be laundered. He insisted that he have it back by six. For an extra fee, they guaranteed it. He charged it all to their room.

Dawn was still in the bath when he returned. He left the clothing he had purchased for her on a chair outside the bath. He slipped into his new jeans, and called for room service to pick up his crumpled suit slacks. He ordered a meal delivered at six, and lay down. He was asleep before he got the pillows adjusted.

Sam awoke to a gentle chiming on their door. He glanced at the clock on the wall, and was surprised to see that three hours had passed in an instant.

Dawn was asleep beside him, her hair splayed out in a rainbow of luxuriant gold. She looked childlike and innocent in her sleep. At that moment, she stirred and stretched slowly. He stood, walked into the next room, and opened the door. A cart filled with food was rolled in. Heavenly aromas emanated from the covered dishes. He added a generous tip to the ticket and signed it. The waiter smiled and backed out of the room.

Dawn came out of the bedroom wearing the jeans and sweatshirt.

They ate in silence, their bodies still unaccustomed to food.

Sam's suit arrived by the time he stepped from the shower. He looked clean and professional. Dawn looked stunning in her new dress. She turned smoothly to show it to him.

"Oh, Sam, thank you for buying me this dress! It's beautiful, and just what I would have picked out for myself. It was very thoughtful of you and unexpected." She thanked him with a kiss on the cheek.

He dismissed it with a mock aristocratic wave of his wrist. "Our public demands it."

Dawn grew serious, and sat on the edge of the bed with a somewhat defeated air. "Are you up to this?" she asked skeptically.

"Truthfully, no," he admitted. "I'm not a professional performer, and they will be able to tell that. During my mission, I baptized a wonderful couple that owned a music store. I must have spent a thousand hours playing in his store. I found, or maybe rediscovered, that I could play anything, in almost any way I liked. It was an amazing unveiling of this musical being within me."

"You never told me that! That makes me feel a lot better about tonight," Dawn said with relief.

Sam shrugged apologetically. "We baptized quite a few people who came to hear us. When I was younger I was ashamed of my musical ability, and I guess I just refused to let others see it. I'm confident I can entertain them tonight. I know lots of music, but I'm just as sure that I'm nowhere near a world-class musician." Sam scratched his head thoughtfully. "That's why I insisted on this being a practice. I haven't been able to put together a program in my head. If I'm not convincing, they will cancel the whole deal, and we will be out on the street again—or worse."

Dawn stood gracefully, raising a hand in a pose of someone about to perform. "Sam, I have some voice training. I'm not a professional either, but I've been told I could be."

Sam brightened. "That's right! I've heard you sing, and you really are good. What do you know that I can play?"

"Well, I know many of the Church hymns. I know some opera, and some Christmas music."

"Christmas won't help. What else?"

"Lots of things, but probably not much you would know. Wait. What about "The Lord's Prayer"? I can do that in Latin and English."

"Yes. That would be wonderful. Do you do Gounod's version?"

"Yes, I believe that's the arrangement I learned. Is that the most famous one?"

Sam didn't answer her question but stood in silence for a moment.

When he looked up, his eyes were confident. "Dawn, I just had an idea."

"What, Sam?"

"We have a wonderful opportunity to bless people's lives with this performance. It is obvious that Heavenly Father has intervened in our affairs. I feel strongly that if we do it His way and use this as an opportunity to bear testimony, we will be successful, because it truly is who we are. We won't be pretending, and people will recognize that.

"I feel impressed to give them music that is uplifting rather than just entertaining. What if we shift the whole emphasis to something we both love? Let's testify of the Lord's love for us with music this evening. Let's give people something to warm their hearts and uplift their souls."

Dawn clasped her hands and pressed them to her lips, her eyes sparkling with happiness. "I know this is what we should do! It feels so right. If we fail to impress the hotel, at least we will do some good. I love the idea!"

Sam nodded and knelt down before a plush sofa. Dawn joined him and placed her hand atop his.

"Heavenly Father, we are so grateful for this chance to be a blessing to the people here in this hotel. We confess our dependence upon Thee, and our weakness. I know my own disobedience has plunged me into this trial, and I humble myself and beg forgiveness of Thee. I am sorry for the guile that I used this day. No matter how great our needs, Father, we would like to bear testimony of Thy love and Thy gospel this evening. And we ask Thy Spirit to work upon those who hear that they will be touched, uplifted, and brought nearer to Thee. We thank Thee for hearing our plea and give Thee all our love, honor, and praise. In the name of Jesus Christ, Amen."

"Amen," Dawn echoed solemnly.

During the prayer, a feeling of peace fell over Sam. He knew no more of the outcome of their "practice" than before, but he knew somehow they would succeed. Even if they were pitched out of the hotel on their ears, someone among those who heard would be blessed and would eventually be led to salvation because of their performance. It seemed more than sufficient, and both their hearts relaxed. Everything else seemed trivial.

The hotel management had done a thorough job of getting an audience. Sam and Dawn arrived a little early, and Sam had a few moments to inspect the instruments. As people jockeyed for the few remaining seats, he quietly tuned and warmed the instruments. The violin was very old, and its tone was rich and vibrant.

The flute was newer and had a sweet, mellow tone that he liked. The big grand was perfectly tuned. He quietly played part of an intricate piece to limber his fingers. The instrument was superb. An appreciative hush fell across the audience as they listened to him warming up. By the time the manager stepped before the piano, there were a little more than a hundred people gathered.

"Good evening, ladies and gentlemen. My name is Herr Johann Muhlestein, general manager of the Schöner Berg. We are pleased to welcome Samuel Mahoy, a famous musician from America, to our hotel." This he said in English and then added, "Guten Abend Damen und Herren. Mein name ist Herr Johann Muhlestein, Generaldirektor des Schönen Berges. Wir freuen uns, Samuel Mahoy, ein berühmter Musiker aus Amerika zu unserem Hotel zu begrüßen."

He was answered with moderate applause. "Herr Mahoy is with us this evening unexpectedly and has agreed to share with us a short evening of music. This is not a scheduled performance, and he prefers to call it a practice. We thank him warmly for his indulging us in this. Without further ado, we present Samuel Mahoy."

Sam stepped forward and bowed slightly. He held out a hand toward Dawn, and she joined him. As he spoke, the manager translated.

"Thank you very much. May I introduce my companion, Dawn." Again, more light applause. "Dawn rarely performs with me, yet since this is, in fact, a practice, she has graciously agreed to join me this evening. I hope you will enjoy her." Dawn bowed graciously to polite clapping.

Sam smiled genially. "Usually when I perform, I am obliged to play whatever I consider my audience wishes to hear. However, since this evening is, for me, a practice, I have set my heart upon playing what I like. Will you indulge me in this?" He was answered with the same low-key applause.

Sam sat at the piano and adjusted his seat. The audience grew quiet. He threw his head back majestically and then forward to study the keys as if preparing himself for some great feat of musical extravagance. In reality, he had not yet decided what to play, and the longer he waited, the less sure he became. He placed his fingers upon the keys and still had no idea what to play. He felt a restless stir from the audience. He gave a silent prayer for help, and a long-forgotten song popped into his head. It was a preposterous choice, yet it was all that came to mind.

He had been expecting to play something devotional, worshipful, or inspirational. Instead, his fingers danced across the keys in a lighthearted rendition of "Dizzy Fingers." The music was lightning fast, running up and down the keyboard in a comedy of misplaced accidentals and playful harmonies. It was almost jazz, almost ragtime, and exactly perfect. People tapped their toes, and by the end of the number were clapping in time.

He prolonged the piece by repeating the showy part and ended with a sudden flourish.

The applause was spontaneous and hearty. Sam relaxed, and so did Dawn. He had won his audience, and hereafter, anything he played would be acceptable to them. He glanced at Herr Muhlestein, who was beaming from ear to ear. He nodded enthusiastically toward Sam, who sent him a smile full of confidence he had not felt just seconds before.

"Thank you very much," he said, still seated at the piano.

"You like American ragtime, I see." The applause came in loud agreement. "I do too. Ragtime is an American convention. It started in the early 1900s and continues to be a favorite in some parts of America today. Almost any song can be played in ragtime. Do you recognize this?" He played a line or two of "Happy Birthday." He was pleased when the applause came back affirmative.

He shifted the bass to a slow ragtime. The people laughed and clapped. He picked up the pace, and finished the song with a vigorous splash. While they were still clapping, he played a long, minor run, flowed into a minor key, and played a heavy, booming introduction of massive nature.

"This is how Bach would have played Happy Birthday." He continued to play a thunderous bass, majestically interspersing the melody into the song.

He switched to a rousing march rendition of the same song. "This is how John Philip Sousa would have played it."

"Happy Birthday" marched through the hall as precisely as a military brass brand.

Without waiting for a break in the applause, he transposed the song into a flowing waltz. Before he could say a word, someone shouted "Johann Strauss," from the audience. This rendition of Happy Birthday seemed to please everyone, and he played it through twice.

People were still clapping as Sam began to play the few passages he knew of the introduction to Beethoven's ninth symphony. He knew he couldn't finish what he had started, and wondered as he was playing why he had begun it. He came to an abrupt halt and turned toward the audience. A startled look was on their faces.

"Beethoven was a very sick man, I think. I'm told he suffered from constipation." A ripple of laughter flowed across the room. The manager quickly interpreted in German, and more laughter rolled toward him.

"As a matter of fact, some believe he wrote special music to celebrate his successes, and this is why we call them movements today." Sam began to play the same overture again and interrupted himself to say, "He wrote this to celebrate his ninth." He was still playing when the interpretation brought a peal of laughter from the crowd. When silence followed, he added, "My apologies to Victor Borga." This also brought laughter from his audience.

Sam's fingers floated across the keys, changing both mood and tempo. His heart felt full as the music changed, deepening in feeling. He changed keys, progressing through a rich succession of major sevenths and ninths. He had never played quite this way before, and as he changed keys again, a familiar feeling came over him. Quite unexpectedly, "As the Dews from Heaven Distilling" came forth in worshipful yet joyful harmony.

He glanced at the audience, and noticed some there with looks of recognition, a few with peace on their faces. Still playing, he said, "I see some of you know this beautiful music." A scattering of applause affirmed his suspicion. "This is the theme song of the Mormon Tabernacle Choir," he told them while still playing. Applause encouraged him to continue.

"I love another song the Choir sings. Do you want to hear it?" A chorus of ja, yes, and oui signaled their happy agreement. The music switched to "The Lord's Prayer."

There was power in the air, and as his heart sang, his fingers gave life to his joy. He nodded to Dawn who walked to the side of the piano. Her voice was steady, sweet, and rich. Even with knowing that she sang well, he was stunned by the beauty of the sound from her lips. She clasped her hands before her and sang in a voice more rich and vibrant than any he had heard. Tears rolled down her cheeks as she sang, "For Thine is the kingdom, and the power, and the glory! Forever, Amen."

Sam stood and embraced her as the applause thundered in the large room. Few eyes were dry. A song came to mind with sudden impact. Sam leaned forward and whispered a question. She smiled and nodded. Without comment, he began the introduction to "O, Divine Redeemer."

Dawn's voice was plaintive as she began, then powerful, sure, and worshipful. He had never heard a more glorious rendition of this precious and powerful music. Dawn sang it as if she, herself, had written every word. Sam's heart thrilled to the very marrow of his soul as she sang the glorious words.

> Ah, turn me not away, receive me though unworthy.
> Ah, turn me not away, receive me though unworthy.
> Hear Thou my cry, hear Thou my cry,
> Behold, Lord, my distress!
> Answer me from Thy throne,
> Haste Thee, Lord, to mine aid!

Thy pity show in my deep anguish,
Thy pity shew in my deep anguish.
Let not the sword of vengeance smite me,
Though righteous Thine anger, O Lord!

Shield me in danger, O regard me!
On Thee, Lord, alone will I call!

O Divine Redeemer, O Divine Redeemer!
I pray Thee grant me pardon, And remember not,
Remember not my sins!
Forgive me!

O Divine Redeemer, I pray Thee, grant me pardon,
And remember not, remember not,
O Lord, my sins!

Save in the day of retribution
On Thee, Lord alone, will I call.
O Divine Redeemer, have mercy!
Help me, my Savior!

For the briefest second after the music ceased, there was a silence of deep reverence and then an explosive applause that seemed to go on indefinitely.

Sam glanced at the clock and was surprised to see that over an hour had elapsed. He returned to Dawn's side, and waited for the applause to end. When it ended there was an electric silence in the air.

After thanking them for their kindness, Sam said, "It is time for us to depart. We have had a wonderful evening with you."

A rumble of polite protest came from the crowd, and the manager came forward, his hands raised, palms down, to quiet them.

"Please, my friends. Herr Mahoy, and the lovely Dawn have traveled far, and they must rest. They have consented to play again tomorrow. Please tell your friends. There will be a small admission to cover their expenses, but the performance will be longer." He glanced slyly at Sam, who nodded slightly.

This brought a happy murmur from the crowd.

"Aber Sie haben weder die Flöte noch die Violine gespielt! But you have not played the flute, nor the violin," a man protested from the first row. At least give us one small piece on one of them and we will be content. We insist!"

"Ah!" the manager cried following his translation into English. "A command performance then!" He turned to Sam. "What do you say? I think they will not leave quietly if you refuse."

Sam nodded, and the crowd burst into applause.

Dawn turned to follow the manager away, but Sam caught her elbow. He whispered something in her ear, and she nodded.

He asked something further, and again she nodded. He smiled and picked up the flute.

He turned back toward the crowd. "Since it is almost bedtime, I think it fitting to play a piece I learned as a child, and one which my mother used to sing me to sleep with. Perhaps it will put you to sleep, too." The crowd laughed as he put the flute to his lips.

He played an introduction of lilting, breathy runs, which evolved from intricate to worshipful. His heart remembered his mother's voice, then his little brother, Jimmy, who had once loved this song so well. The music went on until it became subdued with reverence.

At this moment, Dawn began to sing in Italian, "I am a Child of God." Sam had never heard the words in Italian and found them more beautiful, more melodious, and more wondrous than ever before. He himself became a spectator, an onlooker with wondering eyes as her beautiful voice bore witness to the most important relationship one may discover in this life.

When it was over, the crowd jumped to their feet in ovation. Sam felt overwhelmed and somewhat embarrassed. He had expected no such ovation and certainly claimed no credit for this evening. He just knew his prayer had been lavishly answered, and lives had been touched for good. They walked from the piano hand in hand, the applause still thundering behind them. It did not cease until the doors to the elevator closed behind them.

Back in their room, they knelt in prayer, and Dawn thanked Heavenly Father for this marvelously unexpected blessing. A short while ago, they had been fugitives, penniless, and friendless. Where all had been bleak and starvation seemed their future, now they were being applauded and treated like celebrities. It was a fascinating turn of events.

Sam quietly made himself a bed on the long sofa, and Dawn closed the door between them. It was a night of great peace for them both.

* * *

Sam awoke slowly to a gentle chiming. He pulled on his pants and stumbled to the door. A waiter rolled a food cart into their room. Sam signed the ticket. "Complimentary" was written in big letters across the bottom. The cart contained every breakfast food known to him and a few unknown. There was also a bottle of chilled wine, which made him smile. The waiter rolled the cart to the table and quickly laid out the food. In a few minutes, he was gone. Dawn emerged a few moments later with her head wrapped in a towel. She kissed him on the cheek, and sat opposite him. After prayer, they ate a hearty breakfast.

Shortly after breakfast, they reached Dawn's father by telephone. He was tremendously relieved to find her safe. He took their address and arranged to deliver money and a copy of her passport by courier.

Sam was still not able to reach his parents, but he did get his Uncle in Alaska, who promised to relay the message. Sam was also able to reach the American Embassy in Bern and arranged to get another passport. It seemed as if their troubles were nearly past. In the meantime, they had an entire day to do nothing but relax.

The next evening's "practice" was more successful than the first. Over two hundred people attended it. The third and final performance was attended by upwards of four hundred people, many of them standing, with every inch of the big hall filled. As with the prior two performances, the Holy Spirit was there, and their humble petition was granted. Lives were touched, and they were able to bear witness both in song and word.

In addition to the money Dawn's father sent, their little concert tour was a monetary success. Sam learned that some of the people had paid fifty dollars a seat for the final performance, and many were turned away. By the time they were ready to leave the hotel, they had purchased new luggage, a fair wardrobe, plane tickets home, and had nearly a thousand dollars in traveler's checks. Sam's heart rejoiced as they waited for the train to arrive to take them down the mountain. Since the small train station was but a short walk from the hotel, the manager accompanied them carrying Dawn's bag. He seemed subdued. "Herr Mahoy," he finally said. By his tone, Sam knew he had something serious on his mind. "Please to tell me something?"

"If I can."

"Are you really a famous musician from America?"

Sam shook his head and glanced at Dawn who was smiling coyly, awaiting his answer with obvious interest.

"I didn't say I was famous."

Johann, the manager, nodded. "Yes, I recall the conversation. The distinction did not occur to me at the time. How did you come to our village? I assume you are not on tour either?"

"I have been on tour, but only part of it was a musical tour. I was a missionary. We came here because we were kidnapped and dumped here."

"Is this so? Have you contacted the police? Are you still in danger?" Herr Muhlestein asked all in one breath.

"It was someone in English customs who did it. We aren't sure who. We had something valuable they wanted, and they eventually took it from us. We feel lucky to have gotten away with our lives."

"Acht," he said and spat on the ground symbolically. "The English are mad men. I trust them less than lions." Sam laughed and the manager smiled, but he was mostly serious. Sam was surprised Herr Muhlestein did not pump them for more details, but he seemed satisfied by that simple explanation. In fact, something more important was on the manager's mind.

"Herr Mahoy, when I first saw you sitting in my lobby, I decided before you spoke to me you were either lost or on the run. You both had that trapped and helpless look upon you. Would you like to know why I did not have you both thrown out into the street and arrested?"

Sam was startled by his candor. "Why, yes," he answered, more than a little curious.

"There were two reasons actually. The first was that despite your crumpled appearance, your suit jacket was neat and clean. For some reason that impressed me, since you had obviously been through . . . How do you Americans say it? Through Hades, I think?"

Dawn chuckled. "They do have a similar expression, I believe."

Johann smiled, pleased at having made Dawn laugh, but quickly grew serious again. "Second, it was because you asked me for nothing but waited for me to ask you. I have always found that when someone is trying to cheat you they will make their proposal first and very convincingly. This impressed me that you were confident enough to wait for me to propose a solution to your dilemma."

"I had no idea. I just knew what I had been impressed to do."

"It is very good that you were obedient to your feelings. I routinely expel undesirables from my hotel. You will never know how close you came to being in a Swiss jail."

"Actually," Sam said thoughtfully, "we were never in any danger. We were on God's errand and in His hands. There is no greater safety."

"I can see this is so," Herr Muhlestein agreed enthusiastically. "So, now you will continue your tour?" Sam took Dawn's hand in his before answering. His voice was wistful. "I wish I could, but that's finished. Now we will go back to America."

"I see," Johann replied, and after a pause, he added, "I must tell you that as soon as you began to play, I decided immediately you are not a professional musician. Don't misunderstand me, I think you play as well, but you have not the polish, you see." Sam nodded.

The manager continued. "However, I have scarcely ever heard more beautiful or more heart-touching music. How can this be? Tell me what is the difference about you. Why is it that I feel happiness inside when you make the music? Many make the music of the ears. You two make the music of the heart. This I must know why," he said emphatically.

Sam pondered this as the train slid next to the platform.

"I will tell you why, and you will have to decide what the truth is. It is because with every song, we are testifying that Jesus is the Christ. Every note professes our love for Him. When people with an honest heart hear such music, it makes them happy inside. It touches their heart."

Herr Muhlestein nodded thoughtfully. "I understand this answer you make. I also believe in Jesus. But, it is a quiet place in my heart where He lives, and I do not know Him as a joy to fill my whole soul as you do. How did you come to know Him so well?"

Sam took a step closer to him. "I will tell you because you are a good man, and because perhaps the whole purpose of our coming to this part of the world was to deliver this message to you. I came to know him because God has once again called a living prophet upon the earth, and because His true church is alive once again. Millions of people have come to know Christ in exactly the same way as I have."

"I wish this for myself and my family also, please!" he replied loudly. "Tell me where is this church, and where may I find this joy in my Christ."

"Its official name is 'The Church of Jesus Christ of Latter-day Saints.'"

"I have heard this name before. I am remembering that my wife had two young ladies that were nuns in this church come teach us one time."

"Nuns?" Dawn asked, surprised.

"Yes, they were sisters in this Latter-day Saints Church—nuns," he explained soberly.

Sam chuckled. "We don't have nuns. Sister is not a title but a means of recognizing their dedication and service as missionaries."

Their host seemed genuinely relieved.

"Acht!" he cried, "I thought at the time they were very young to be nuns. This seems much better, yes. So, I know a little of this Church of the latter days. My wife very much liked and believed about it, but I did not listen so carefully to their words. They spoke in heavy American accents, and I grew weary of listening. So, I came to think it was not so true at the time the nuns came," he replied, his voice serious but jovial. "Is it really as you say? Has God made once again the prophets to speak?"

"With all my heart, I testify that it is so today as it was when Peter walked the earth."

"What you say both thrills and confuses me. But, I have felt something from your words and songs that I have not felt before, and I promise I will once again investigate this latter-day prophet and this joy that lights your faces. I think this is a good thing," he concluded.

"I am convinced it is," Sam agreed as Dawn voiced similar feelings.

After exchanging addresses, the kindly manager helped them board the small, open cars.

"I now have your address, and I shall write you when I also know when I have found the prophets and this Jesus of whom you have taught me. God bless you, Samuel Mahoy, and Dawn with the angel's voice," he said as he bowed formally.

Sam's voice was subdued. He reached outside the small train and shook Johann Muhlestein's hand in a firm grip. "Thank you my friend," he said. "May the Lord bless and keep you."

"May the Lord lift up His countenance upon you and give you peace. Goodbye," Johann replied.

The train moved slowly away from the platform.

* * *

Neither Sam nor Dawn had ever so much as heard of a cogwheel train, let alone been on one. It looked as if it belonged in a carnival. The cars were only two persons wide, and open on all sides. One could reach out and catch leaves from slowly passing trees. On level ground, the seats reclined back almost forty-five degrees, making it like sitting back in a recliner chair. The small steam engine had a large geared wheel in the exact center. Between the two rails was a cogged rail. The big gear in the engine ran on this center rail, thus propelling the train. They soon found out why this was so.

The train left the station, turned a corner, and almost immediately began a steep descent. In minutes, the train was going down an incline so steep that Sam and Dawn found themselves sitting perfectly upright in the car. Had the seats been in a normal position, the passengers would have fallen forward out of the train.

At this steep angle, they could see over the top of the forward cars and were able to look right into the small engine. One man was busily shoveling coal, and another was studiously watching the track ahead with his hand on several levers. The little train puffed and hissed its way for many minutes to the bottom.

Upon arriving at the lower station, Sam and Dawn walked a hundred yards to another terminal.

Dawn inched up to the handrail and gasped. Before them a drop of many thousands of feet yawned like the edge of the world.

"Did I ever tell you I'm afraid of heights?" she whispered urgently. Sam looked at the panorama beyond the guardrail. "Are you?"

"Uh, I wasn't until just a second ago," she said seriously.

"Now I think I am." Sam took her arm. "At least we'll die together."

"Wrong answer," she replied and smacked his arm.

They boarded a gondola swinging on a cable that appeared far too frail for the job at hand. They began a dizzying descent from a fantastic height. They dropped quickly to a lower terminal and got out.

Dawn looked back up. "We have to go back up," she said nervously. "Why?"

"I think my stomach's still up there!" They found their bus to Bern and showed their tickets. The bus drove for several hours down steep, winding roads. They stopped twice at small villages that appeared to have been peeled from a picture postcard.

Each village had narrow, cobblestone streets, a dozen small shops, two dozen ancient, Swiss chalet-style homes, and a small picturesque Catholic church. Each village also had a large, ornate fountain in its main square. They were nestled against a long lake on one side and the steep mountains on the other.

Not even the fact that Sam and Dawn were anxious to pursue their journey home could detract from the magical charm of the ancient countryside.

They were walking past a watchmaker's shop when Sam suddenly stopped walking.

"What's wrong?"

"My camera! I no longer have my camera. We're in the middle of the most photographed country on earth, and I don't have a camera!"

"You're right!" Dawn cried, glancing at her watch. "We have time to get one before the bus leaves."

They quickly located a shop and bought a modest camera. Sam nearly wore it out before nightfall.

They finally arrived in Bern and took a hair-raising taxi ride to the American Embassy where Sam picked up his duplicate passport.

Standing outside the embassy, Dawn gripped Sam's arm to stop him from hailing a taxi. "There's no way I'm getting back into another one of those again!" she groaned. "I'm still shaking from the last ride." Sam agreed. They finally found a bus to the airport.

It seemed like a long time since they had left South Africa. It seemed like two months instead of just over two weeks ago. At last, they were on their way home.

Dawn finally felt like talking about her ordeal with the English customs police. It had been much worse for her than for Sam. He listened in horror as she described her experience in detail. They had been determined, thorough, and brutal. They had terrorized her, deprived her of food, privacy, and even sleep. They had repeatedly forced her to disrobe, submit to protracted personal indignities, and then left her without clothing for hours, shivering on a cold metal chair.

Though they left no physical scars, Dawn walked away with wounds aplenty that would take many years to heal.

Sam held her hand as she concluded her tale of terror.

"I'm so sorry this happened to you," he told her through clenched teeth. "It makes me furious."

Dawn shrugged. "I've been thinking about it—a lot, actually. In the end, they won. I broke down and told them what they wanted to know. I caused us both a lot of unnecessary pain."

Sam disagreed. "You know what I think? I think it was probably the fact that you did break that saved our lives. When they retrieved the stone from the sewage tank, they knew you had told them everything you knew. You said the stone they found was nearly worthless? Why would your father's people switch stones?"

"I've thought about that too. If they had found nothing, they would have continued to brutalize me. When the stone turned out to be nearly valueless, they knew two things: first, that I had told the truth; and second, that someone with a lot of power and money knew they were holding me. They let us go because they were afraid to do anything else," she concluded with certainty.

*　*　*

Including layovers, it took three days to fly to Alaska. During those days, Sam and Dawn talked, ate, and slept—all in the same seats. By the time they were able to get off the plane for good, their legs could barely support them. Halfway between Seattle and Anchorage, Sam shaved and combed his hair in the tiny restroom on the plane. Dawn also freshened up and somehow emerged looking tired but beautiful.

The Anchorage airport was surprisingly large for such a remote location. Sam watched the buildings glide by, his heart pounding in his ears. Even though he had called his parents to let them know his plans, he had no idea if he would be welcomed with a loving embrace, a hero's welcome, so to speak, or meet in embarrassed disgrace. It seemed as if he had been gone four years—two wonderful years serving the Lord, and two nightmare years trying to get home.

Finally, the plane jerked to a stop, and the rattle of seatbelt buckles signaled the end of their long journey. Sam could not bring himself to stand. Tears strained to escape his eyes, and his heart seemed to skid to a stop. He felt a hand on his, and looked up into Dawn's eyes. She was standing, smiling down at him. It seemed almost as if she were a foot taller than normal, and he had the impression he was looking sharply upward to see her.

"Your family loves you," she said, as if she had read his mind. "They will always love you. You are their eldest, beloved son and hero. Nothing could change that, and you know I speak the truth, for the Spirit is upon me."

Sam closed his eyes and realized the warmth of the Holy Spirit was upon him as well. It vanquished all his fears, and he stood with confidence. When he looked back at Dawn, she had shrunk back to her normal size. He blinked twice, knowing he had just seen a miracle of sorts. He paused long enough to fervently thank Heavenly Father for His gentle mercies and love—most of all His love.

All of Sam's family were there crowded as close around the door as the velvet ropes permitted. They spotted him as he rounded the first corner, and they laughed, pointed, and shouted. His parents looked the same as when he left. Mom was crying, as it should be. Dad was beaming, also as it should be.

Angela and Beth, the twins, were grown up. They were eighteen, beautiful, and dressed exactly alike. They both cried tears of joy as they waved at him.

Benjamin was thirteen and bigger—much bigger. He had lost the softness of youth and taken on the angles of manhood. Sam had to look twice to realize it was his little brother standing there grinning at him.

Little Rachel was eleven and no longer so little. Of all those who were there to meet him, she had changed the most. She had grown from a child to practically a young woman, and the change was startling. Had they not sent him photos, he could not have picked her out of a crowd. She radiated joy as she pranced from foot to foot.

Sam and his family rushed toward one another with a united shout of joy. With the rope still between them, they fell into his arms. He felt his back being patted, his arms, hands, and fingers being patted and held, and his face covered with kisses and tears. It was all he had imagined, and much more. It was perfect. Suddenly, they were asking questions—so many questions. He tried to answer them, to tell them of his joy. No one mentioned his two-week delay. There would be a lot of fence mending, but until then, it was enough to be home.

With a sudden realization, he remembered Dawn. As politely as he could, Sam untangled himself and turned to Dawn. She was waiting almost directly behind him. He motioned for her to join him. He was surprised to see there were tears in her eyes as well. There was a wistful, almost lost expression on her face.

"Mom, Dad, everybody, this is Dawn."

There was the briefest moment of awkwardness, and then his Mother gathered her into her arms. A moment later, he was standing alone, watching his family make her one of their own. He had to smile, for he knew what she was experiencing. He had watched them love and welcome strangers into their home many times. It was a powerful thing, an almost palpable sense of belonging. He felt his heart sing as the expression on Dawn's face turned from lost, to loved. Suddenly, quite unexpectedly, she was home as well.

"She does look like a princess," Ben said almost to himself. As if he had said something startlingly vulgar, everyone turned toward him. He blushed and blustered, "Well, you said she lived in a castle. Doesn't that make her a princess?"

"I suppose it does," Sam laughed. He turned to Dawn. "How does it feel to suddenly be royalty?"

Dawn blushed. "Your family is far more wonderful than you could have ever told me, Sam! It makes me feel like royalty to feel so loved and accepted." She lowered her eyes. "But I became royalty when you baptized me, and I became a daughter of God."

It was such a perfect answer, such a noble response, that she quietly changed identity in everyone's mind. She evolved, emerged, and was born again. She became not just a princess, but Princess. From that moment on, it would be the only name they called her, and it thrilled her to the very center of her being.

Home—suddenly the word meant worlds more than ever before.

She was home, and her soul rejoiced.

307

THE LAST FRONTIER

Sam's parents, Jim and Laura Mahoy, had brought a motorhome made from an older Greyhound bus to get him and Princess.

By the time everyone was inside with all their baggage, the passenger section with its three rows of big chairs was fully loaded. They put Sam in the front passenger seat that had been swiveled to face backward. His mom took the opposite seat, and his Dad drove. Dawn sat in a chair behind the table, and everyone else found seats nearby. The twins took posts on either side of Dawn and held her hands in theirs. A happy chatter drowned out all else as they pulled away from the airport. Above the rumbling of the big diesel engine and happy talk, Sam could hear Princess's clarion laughter. It was like the tinkling of a silver bell to his soul.

Anchorage was a surprisingly bustling city. Sam marveled at all the new construction, new homes, and new roads. It seemed almost as if the city had recently awakened and was rushing to recover from a long sleep. They drove through road construction almost the entire way until the city suddenly ended and a lush birch forest crowded the road on both sides.

It was a beautiful, sunny day, and Sam watched the breathtaking beauty of rugged mountains so close that in winter some parts of the city were in perpetual shade. The mountains were pristine, as if newly made. They were grand, majestic mountains of granite, balustraded with outcroppings of stone as unscathed by time as if cut only yesterday from virgin stone. Though deep into summer, they still sported white patches of snow snuggled into deep ravines. Everywhere he looked was green. Having so recently come from Switzerland, the comparison between these two mountain worlds was inescapable.

The Glenn Highway wound its way through lush forests, until the Cook Inlet squeezed them tight up against the towering Chugach Range. For the briefest distance, it seemed as if there would be insufficient room for a road between these two unyielding forces of nature. At the last moment, the road turned left, crossed the Knik and Matanuska Rivers in a series of low bridges, traversing the tidal flats at the mouth of the inlet.

Sam was amazed to see several moose grazing knee-deep in the lush grasses of the tidal flats. They turned left onto the Parks Highway, which almost seemed to be a black-velvet ribbon positioned across the gentle rolling hills of lush birch and spruce forest. There were few businesses, few homes, and few signs of man until they approached the small city of Wasilla.

Wasilla had little to recommend itself except stark beauty. The city was unincorporated with no commerce, no industry, and no reason for its existence except its relative closeness to Anchorage.

"Dad," Sam asked above the din of the bus. "What fuels Alaska's economy, and where do the people in Wasilla work?"

Sam listened as his dad explained the odd economics that made the little town work.

"The Trans-Alaska Pipeline is just being completed. The eight-hundred-mile engineering marvel is bringing a forty-eight-inch steel pipe from the furthest north shores of the state to the tiny village of Valdez on the south. It crosses two major mountain ranges, including the Brooks Range, one of the most rugged in North America. It crosses four major rivers, including the Yukon, and hundreds of lesser ones. Its entire length is primarily above ground, on refrigerated pillars, and insulated its entire length. It has eleven major pump stations that use Rolls-Royce jet engines to pump the hot crude across the incredible distance. Operating to full capacity, it is capable of pumping nearly two million barrels of prime Alaska crude a day."

Sam was amazed. "That's a lot of crude. What's a barrel of crude go for?"

Jim, obviously interested and conversant on the subject, answered, "At a spot price of fifteen dollars per barrel, the pipeline pumps out thirty million dollars in gross revenues a day, nearly a billion dollars a month. Of that incredible sum, some 10 percent goes directly to the State of Alaska as royalties."

Dawn was listening closely. "It's no wonder all of Alaska seems to be in a frenzy of construction everywhere you look!"

"It's really amazing," Jim replied. "Anchorage is nestled on a narrow strip of land between the Chugach Mountains and the Cook Inlet. After nearly ten years of booming pipeline prosperity, there's very little room left for development. People had to look toward Wasilla.

"Nearly every parcel of land that could be developed was, and land prices were soaring. With costs so high and the economy so vigorous, people soon looked for cheaper ground. They found it in the nearly unlimited lands of the valley. With so much land available, prices dropped, and the people came in droves—one hand on a shovel, and the other with a mortgage. That's why I started building homes," Jim explained.

"Even though there's not much more than a grocery store and a post office," Jim went on, "Wasilla has more than forty thousand residents. Hundred dollar bills seem more common than ones, and there are too many new homes to count."

Laura, Sam's mother, spoke up. "Even so, part of the charm of Wasilla is that the dense birch forests hide most signs of development, and the valley has maintained its beauty."

At the main intersection in town, the motorhome turned left, once again toward the Inlet. They drove through lush forest for five more miles before turning left onto a dirt road, right again for several miles on a very winding road, and right a short distance up a lane. They stopped before a large wood frame home. It was unfinished inside and out, but Sam could see the promise of a beautiful home in its graceful lines. The Mahoys had purchased a five-acre piece of land for not much more than a signature, a hundred dollars down, and a hundred dollars a month. Once the loan for the land was paid off, every dime they made went into building materials. Though the home was not much to look at, in time it would be, and it was theirs. In keeping with the Alaskan spirit of stark individualism and rugged self-sufficiency, they had no mortgage on their home.

It was the most breathtakingly beautiful setting for a home Sam had ever seen. They had cleared away a part of the dense birch forest to reveal that their property sat on a bluff overlooking the Cook Inlet. The Chugach Mountains rose majestically across the glistening waters. Anchorage sat nestled far to the right, barely visible in the afternoon sun.

Before going into the home, Jim took them to his garden just south of the house. Sam could not believe his eyes. Jim pointed out a row of cabbage plants with heads approaching three feet in diameter. He then directed their attention to a row of pea vines as tall as a man's armpits, each laden with peas nearly four inches long.

They pulled thick orange carrots from the rich soil as sweet as candy, and ate raspberries as big as his thumb. They walked slowly through the greenhouse and ate cucumbers as succulent as if they had been marinated in some divine nectar, and tomatoes as large as his fist.

Dawn, now Princess, had never seen a vegetable garden, let alone a garden in Alaska. By her definition, a garden had roses, sculpted shrubs, and fountains. It seemed entirely novel to her that a garden could yield edibles. She walked up and down the rows, asking questions, laughing, wondering, sampling, and sifting the rich loam through her hands.

Jim and Princess remained in the garden several hours after Sam and all the rest had gone inside. Several times Sam glanced at them out the dining room window and caught them laughing, or saw Jim peeling a large kohlrabi with his pocketknife. He wondered how many people in this world could turn a garden into a loving introduction to a phenomenon called home.

The inside of the home lacked everything. All the floors were plywood with the exception of the kitchen and one bathroom. Though they were obviously living in an unfinished home, there was no wanting for signs of industry. All the plywood floors had been sanded and painted. Only half of the walls had sheet rock on them, the other half were pink insulation covered with plastic. Even these had pictures, small shelves with family treasures, and signs of loving habitation. The one completely finished room in the house was the upstairs bath.

It was massive, with both an oversized bathtub and a separate shower stall, accessible through different doors to be used simultaneously. It included a laundry chute that dropped the dirty clothes into a cupboard directly above the washing machine. Two sinks had been installed, one of which was outside the bathroom in an area always available even when the doors were locked. There was a large closet inside the bath and a large window overlooking the inlet. Even Princess proclaimed it "magnificent," high praise from one who grew up in a castle.

Princess made a collect call to her father and assured him all was well.

Everyone finally ended up sitting together in the large living room, looking out the big windows across the Inlet. It grew quiet, and everyone drew a breath of peace and togetherness. It was one of those rare moments when for just a moment, despite their unfinished surroundings, everything was perfect.

"Well, it's late," Jim said as he slid to his knees. Sam watched in wonder as the life-long tradition continued. He could not remember a night in his youth when this scene had not been replayed. Sam knelt and felt Beth's hand slip into his left and Princess's into his right. Even though he was exhausted, it seemed too early for bed. He glanced at the old grandfather clock and was amazed to see it was nearly midnight. Outside it was still daylight, just moving beyond twilight.

"Sam, will you pray for us?" his father asked quietly. A gentle peace settled over Sam, and he nodded. It was indeed good to be home.

16

BABYLON THE GREAT

Born in Devonshire, England, to wealthy parents, Melody was the youngest of three. Winston was six years older than Marcia, and Melody three years younger than Marcia. At nine years Winston's junior, she was truly the baby in the family.

Melody's father, Donavon Winston MacUlvaney III, was the proud inheritor of the family tradition and a considerable fortune. Serving in the army in his youth had taken him all across Europe and Africa. His campaign had taken him into the tiny African country of Rhodesia, where he fell in love with the vast open spaces and arid-tropic beauty. When on the first day out in the veldt (bush lands), he had kicked up a gold nugget the size of his thumb, and he knew he had discovered heaven.

He returned home, sold much of what he owned, bundled his family onto a steamer, and journeyed to their new home in South-Central Africa. Melody still remembered the two-month trek across two oceans, two continents, and three nations to arrive there.

He had served in the military when the little country had been a British commonwealth that was thriving economically, mineralogically wealthy, and politically stable— a veritable grab bag of opportunities. Donavon had moved his family to Rhodesia with the plan of mining gold. He had purchased a tract of land near Salisbury, staked a claim, purchased mining equipment, hired workers, and refined his first bar of gold by the time Rhodesia split politically with England by declaring independence in 1965.

At England's insistence, the United Nations immediately slapped an embargo on the fledgling country. Without the ability to sell it outside of Rhodesia, Donavon's gold became virtually worthless.

Even though independence had literally bankrupted Donavon overnight, he supported his new country's independence, more from a sense of injustice done to Rhodesia than as an act of treason against his beloved homeland. In the end, his thinking in the matter made little difference to those who labeled him an outlaw and stripped him of his family titles, ancestral lands, and remaining wealth. Now, besides being broke, he was also stranded in Africa.

Not one easily defeated, Donavon had loaded his gold bars into an old truck, and taking with him all his food, fuel, and a small, well-armed army to defend it all, he had driven nearly eighteen hundred miles into neighboring South Africa. Much of the way there were no roads, no bridges, or signs to point the way. He followed his compass and his luck. The journey took weeks.

When he finally arrived in South Africa, he sold the gold for enough money to more than justify all his labors. He tarried in Africa, purchasing trucks, equipment, medical supplies, books, musical instruments, furniture, and diamonds. He carefully cultivated new friends, bought loyalties, and secured patronage. He returned home after nearly a year's absence.

While his wild gamble had been completely successful at salvaging his fortune in their new land, tragedy struck with mindless fury during his absence. Rebels from neighboring Botswana had swept into the poorly defended country, killing, raping, and looting in the long tradition of African tribal warfare. Donavon tragically lost his wife and only son in the raid.

Marcia had been raped and then allowed to escape without clothing into her father's fields. Melody, just seven at the time, had been hidden in a wine cupboard by her mother and had watched her family's horrible fate. Had she even whimpered or flinched, she would have certainly shared Marcia's fate.

Donavon was inconsolable, and could not forgive himself. After doing all in his power to make sure his family was safe and healing, he had borrowed military equipment from the small Rhodesian army, collected a group of angry settlers, and retaliated by tracking the rebels to their homeland and lynching all involved. It wasn't hard to find the guilty ones, for they had smeared themselves with the blood of their victims as a token of bravery. He simply hung every man who smelled of death. He returned a hardened, bitter man and a national hero.

At great personal cost to his own soul, Donavon had revenged his family's losses, but healing was still decades away and forgiveness an eternity away. His little country was immensely grateful and deeded him ten thousand acres of rich, tropical desert in token of its gratitude. The former Brit's new kingdom included some of the greatest mineral wealth on the face of the planet—all of little value. He took the money he had recovered and drilled wells, a thing almost unheard of in that land. His wells brought forth an almost unlimited supply of life-giving water, and he put his vast holdings to the plow. He spent months clearing the land with his own hands. He laughed bitterly many times as he watched softball-sized gold nuggets roll beneath the rich, red soil.

His new homeland was literally starving. Food was in scarce supply, and without a local economy, it was impossible to buy or sell. Donavon planted vast tracts of wheat, barley, and corn. The indefatigable Englishman traveled to Salisbury and convinced the Rhodesian president, Ian Smith, to print currency. Donovan promised to accept the new currency in exchange for his grains, personal possessions, lands, and home.

Encouraged by Donavon's confidence in Rhodesia, President Smith borrowed a printing press from South Africa and printed their new money on newsprint. They picked the name of the most stable currency in the world, the US dollar, and named their currency accordingly, hoping a tiny portion of faith in the US dollar would rub off on Rhodesian dollars.

Donavon sold his entire crop for what amounted to basket loads of paper. This he used to pay his workers and promised to redeem the currency for any crop he grew or item he possessed. He treated the money with respect, bargained with suppliers for better prices, and gave nothing away. His workers took the new money to market and exchanged the paper for scarce goods based on the rich farmer's promises. In time, faith in the currency grew, and it became accepted without comment.

In the meantime, Donavon had considerable amounts of the paper money. He planted more crops including tobacco, cotton, soy, tea, and every variety of fruit tree. It seemed as if anything would grow in the red soil. In a matter of a little more than ten years, he had parleyed his investment into great wealth.

By this time, South Africa was accepting the Rhodesian dollar, and Donavon traded every slip of paper he possessed for anything of value. He acquired the great stone he eventually gave to Sam as a reward for saving his daughters.

Throughout all of this, Melody and Marcia struggled to recover from the horrible experiences of their youth. Their healing began the day they first picked up a violin. They immediately exhibited unusual talent, and daddy Donavon lavished the finest teachers on them. Soon, however, their talent exceeded the best available in the small backward country, and it was decided they should travel south to seek better education. It was with great anticipation that the two young women made plans to go away to the great metropolis to the South.

It was during this happy exodus that Sam had met them on the train as he was leaving Rhodesia following his missionary duties there. He could not have known how terrifying it was for them to once again be surrounded by African raiders. It was also little wonder that Marcia had been paralyzed with fear. She still remembered in far too graphic detail what it was like to be brutalized for sport, not knowing if she would ultimately live or die, but actually preferring the latter.

When Sam laid his hands upon Marcia, her fear had evaporated as the power of the Holy Ghost bore witness of the truth of his words. She had instantly recognized the eternal significance of what had occurred. From that moment on, she searched until she found the true church and had joined with palpable joy. Her journey to healing reached a perfect climax when she stepped out of the waters of baptism on her twenty-third birthday in Devonshire, England, her ancestral home.

When Sam gave Melody her blessing, it was powerful yet hard to interpret. It became evident that for Melody, the journey would be much longer and fraught with peril.

The Lord, speaking through Sam, told her of a long quest that would take her to many nations and bring her full circle. The blessing had promised, "When you finally find what you seek, you will have returned to this moment, and it will bring you joy."

Those words were a monument in the halls of his cherished memories. They were sweet confusion that Sam would often remember with wonder—words without meaning, yet rich with power.

For Melody, those words remained troubling—food for forced forgetfulness and a stony ground that refused her fervent attempts to plow. Many years would pass before she realized what precious promises awaited their fulfillment in her.

* * *

The morning following his arrival in Alaska, Sam arose early with his father and Ben. They traveled to the site of their construction project. Jim was good at two things. The first—his greatest love—was farming. However, in Alaska, there was little call for commercial farming. The cost of equipment, labor, fertilizer, and everything else was too high, and food could be trucked and air freighted in much cheaper than it could be raised locally.

At one time, the Matanuska–Susitna Valley, which held Wasilla in its rich embrace, was the breadbasket of Alaska and raised almost all of its staples. Numerous farms that had once been prosperously appointed with large barns, grain silos, and lush fields were all abandoned now, unused, neglected, and tumbling down in some cases.

The other thing Jim was good at was speculative real estate development. He had a sixth sense for a good deal and an artist's eye for a well-designed home. On that morning, Jim, Sam, and Ben pulled up to a partly framed home that was one of Jim's current construction projects. While not as dramatic as the Mahoy's estate, the setting was beautiful, wooded, quiet, and secluded. They unloaded tools, and after studying the blueprints briefly, began laying out walls. Ben went right to work, having his father's easy familiarity with tools and building.

Sam, on the other hand, had to be shown everything to do. He had never built a home and watched and learned with interest. By the time they stopped for lunch, the outside walls on the upper floor were standing, complete with windows installed. When it was time to go home, they had all the roof trusses standing.

Sam was amazed at how many muscles he had not used on his mission. Now, after a single day's work, every one of the several hundred of them was sore.

Several months later, the home was completed, and new owners were moving in. Jim stopped at the bank, deposited a sizable check, and they drove home, exhausted but happy. For the next several days, they worked on their own home, adding sheet rock, installing carpet, and painting the exterior of the house. It was a happy interlude—one performed with loving care.

During all this time, Princess wrote letters, made phone calls, and said little of her plans. She was a delight to have around. She always seemed cheerful, willing to help, never too busy to assist, and genuinely pleased to learn new things.

She fell in love with fishing and gamely baited hooks, hauled in salmon too large for her to lift, and amid squeals of disgust, cut and cleaned her fish. Sam watched her with growing admiration and wonder. In his eyes, her new name was a label of love and a title of distinction, both well-suited to her noble soul.

When the package arrived, it was marked with customs stamps and colorful postage. Princess laughed happily as she carried the box to the kitchen table. Sensing something important in the offing, the whole family gathered around as she carefully cut the tape and opened the box. Princess grew quiet, almost reverent as she lifted the carefully packed items from the box.

Because Sam had been around her father, he immediately recognized each item as she unwrapped and laid them on a velvet cloth she had also withdrawn from the package.

First, came a jeweler's loop with two lenses. Next, she lifted a small but elaborate scale from the parcel. Following this, she set out tweezers of various sizes and a handful of other tools. When she finally reached the bottom, she lifted a small leather package no larger than a box of wooden kitchen matches. She carefully unzipped the pouch and folded back the lid. Inside was a row of small white envelopes. Princess took the first in the row, placed it flat on the table, and without lifting it from the surface, deftly unfolded the edges. Inside was a thin layer of bluish tissue, and lying in the fold of the envelope, three small diamonds.

A collective gasp went up from round the table, but Princess did not hear it. She was in a world where only she existed. She clamped the first stone into tweezers and lifted it to the light.

Satisfied she could see no flaws, she studied it with the 10x loupe and then the 20x. She studied a color chart for a moment before declaring, "This is a good stone. Eye pure, with slight flaws at ten, nice color, about 'I.' Good cut, good edges—a nice stone."

"What's it worth?" Benjamin asked impulsively. Without looking up, she unfolded the scales, laid the stone in one dish, and placed small weights on the opposite side. The scales were soon balanced.

"It's a little larger than a third carat," she said. "Stones in America are higher priced. I would judge this to be worth about four hundred dollars wholesale, nearly double that retail."

"Wow!" Benjamin said enthusiastically. "Can I look at it?"

"Sure," Princess said happily. She made sure it was clamped securely in the tweezers and showed Ben and everyone else how to look through the loupe.

"You hold the loupe to your eye without moving it. Next, you turn to the light and move the diamond back and forth until it comes into focus. By moving it slightly, you can focus on the surface of the stone, or actually inside the gem. Some internal flaws are only visible once you learn how to focus the loupe inside the stone."

While they were learning to use the loupe, she continued to inventory her gems. In all, she had exactly fifty stones. They were all relatively small and in sizes of greatest demand. She confided to Sam later that their retail value was over fifty thousand dollars.

The next afternoon, she and Sam drove to Anchorage. They were between construction jobs, and Sam happily accepted her request to drive her to a meeting. She was still not comfortable driving on what seemed to her to be the wrong side of the road.

All Sam knew of their trip was that she was going to sell some of her diamonds. Princess talked happily about diamonds on the drive to Anchorage. She directed him to an address that was more of a warehouse than an office. How she had discovered this place was beyond Sam. On the outside of the building, a small brass plaque held the cryptic name "Blumstein and Noble." There was no indication of what Blumstein and Noble actually did.

Princess introduced herself to a secretary, and stated she had some "quality goods" to display. The secretary left for a moment and returned to usher them into a back room. The room was well lit, with plain, white tile floors. In a few minutes, an older gentleman entered the room and introduced himself as Mr. Blumstein.

Mr. Blumstein was a short, balding man in his sixties, with silver-streaked hair and a pencil-thin mustache. He wore a black, pinstriped suit that looked as if it had been pressed moments before.

Princess made no introductions but simply laid out her wares. Mr. Blumstein sat at the small table, pulled a loupe and tweezers from his breast pocket, and examined several of the stones.

"Hmmm," he said aloud. "South African, I see. Good cut, good color, nice clarity, good size. How many do you have?"

"I have about thirty carats total, all similar," she told him.

Without examining the rest of the stones, he looked her squarely in the eye. "Your source?" he asked pointedly.

"My father is a diamond cutter in Johannesburg. These stones come through Danbers to my father, and then to me after cutting."

"How good is your supply?"

"I can bring over as many as you need. At this point, I am establishing my delivery schedules and will need several months to come to full potential, but beyond that, it is basically unlimited."

"I see, very good. I presume you have a sales receipt."

"I do," she said, and pulled a small certificate from her purse detailing the stones and her right to sell them. The man was satisfied.

"Price?"

"To begin with, 75 percent of appraised wholesale by lots, 85 percent of wholesale by the piece." The man's eyebrows went up as dollar signs appeared in his eyes. It took him barely a moment to recover his composure.

"Will you place them on consignment?" he asked.

"Not at that price. For full wholesale, I will place them for thirty days to begin with. In the future, I will be able to extend to the customary sixty days. My apologies," she replied smoothly.

Sam was amazed at her professional presentation and confident demeanor.

"Very good. I will give you 75 percent of wholesale for this lot," the man said. "I will have the stones appraised independently and forward you a check."

"That would be acceptable," she said as she stuck out her hand.

The man shook it once, looked her in the eye, and smiled. "Pleasure doing business with you, Miss . . .?"

"Pauley. Princess Pauley," she replied. The man's eyebrows went up slightly, and he bowed formally from the waist.

"Princess," he said simply. "May our association be long and mutually profitable."

"Thank you," she replied. He left the stones sitting where they were and escorted them to the front door.

"That's it?" Sam asked. "No contracts, no receipts, a handshake and you give him fifty thousand dollars' worth of stones?"

"He won't cheat me," she said simply.

"You don't know him from Adam," Sam objected.

"Yes I do. He deals in diamonds. There are no dishonest diamond wholesalers."

"How can that be?"

"Because it is not allowed. You don't understand, but you will. The diamond industry is tightly regulated. It is more closely watched than you can imagine. This sale I have made is already known and approved by Danbers. If not, my father would never have acquired the stones in the first place, and I would have never received them. Selling diamonds is like an exclusive religion. You can only get in if you have family already inside, and to cheat another diamond merchant would be like cheating family, which is unthinkable. Should it happen, they would be kicked out and never touch another diamond as long as they lived. My diamonds are more secure in his hands than if they were in a bank."

Princess walked through the door that Sam held open for her. She smiled at him for his thoughtfulness, and Sam smiled back. Her gratitude was one of the small things he admired about her. She appreciated small kindnesses and smiled easily. He would have opened a hundred-ton door for her to see that brief smile.

Sam helped her into the car and got behind the wheel.

"It seems odd that the first place you stopped at you sold all the stones almost without effort."

Princess laughed and turned to face him. For a moment, he was lost in her beauty, and somewhere inside of him, a warning bell went off. He mentally shrugged and concentrated on her words. "My father 'suggested'

I contact this man. I told you, the sub-wholesale diamond trade business is a big family. He knew I was coming before I ever set foot in his store. He knew what stones I had and approximately the price he would pay. He was pleased to get them, because I am now his primary supplier of stones."

* * *

Exactly three days later, an envelope came in the mail addressed to "Princess Gems." Sam read the name and smiled. He knew the name was the creation of Mr. Blumstein. It said all that needed to be said. Princess laughed when she read the name and asked if Sam would drive her to the bank. He gladly agreed.

One might expect a small city bank to have little exposure to international banking, yet when Princess declared her intent to make a deposit into a Swiss account, the bank manager smiled and handed her a deposit form. It was a full sheet of paper. She handed Sam the check after endorsing it and filled out the rather lengthy deposit form. He gasped when he read the amount, which was for $22,000. It was the largest amount of money he had ever seen. He felt as if he should be glancing over his shoulders for robbers.

Sam was deep in thought when she slid the paper over to him and handed him the pen.

"What's this?" he asked.

She pointed to a section of the form labeled "Account holder."

"You sign by the 'X,'" she said simply.

"Why? This is your money, not mine," he objected, noticing the bank manager suppressing a smile. It apparently seemed unlikely that anyone would refuse so much money.

"Do you trust me?"

"Absolutely."

"Then sign. I'll explain when it's time. Until then, I just need you to trust me."

Sam twirled the pen in his fingers while he studied her face, which, he decided, was just as pretty with a frown on it as it was with a smile. He quickly signed the document and the banker whisked it away. In minutes, they were back in the car.

Every few weeks another package arrived for Princess. After a while, the family lost interest, and just the two of them sorted through the stones. The first few months the stones were carefully graded and sorted so that every stone in the batch was similar in size and value. As the quantities became larger, the stones were more varied, until no two were exactly alike.

"Isn't it dangerous to have that many diamonds here at home in a cardboard box?" Sam asked, suddenly wary.

"That brings up the next subject. We need an office in a secure building. We also need several safety deposit boxes in different banks. Sooner or later, someone is going to find out we have the stones here and make an attempt to steal them. They will easily succeed the way we keep them now."

"Well, I don't see a problem with getting an office. I'll help you find an office tomorrow afternoon after work if you like. You may enjoy having your own office anyway," he said. It sounded like fun.

"You don't quite understand. The office isn't for me. It's for us. I can't handle everything that's going to be taking place. We will need to hire a bookkeeper, arrange for armored-car delivery of stones, all kinds of things. We need to make trips overseas to secure new delivery routes and better prices. I am tempted to go to Asia and purchase colored stones. This is much bigger than I can handle alone. I really need your help, if you'll have me as your partner."

Sam was stunned. Since the first small parcel of diamonds had arrived, he had considered this her business. It even bore her name. The idea of working for Princess had never occurred to him, let alone working with her as a partner. It made his head buzz.

She took his silence as a rejection and turned away from him, busying herself with a stone under a loop. A quick glance at her revealed a glistening tear hovering in her eye.

"Why are you doing this?" Sam asked.

"What do you mean?" she replied without looking away from her stone.

"Why are you setting up this business and involving me in it? We both know you don't need the money. Your father restored all your assets he took away before your baptism. You have more money than I could ever hope to make in a lifetime. You have your father's inheritance on top of this business. Besides, you know I'm planning to go away to college next spring, and you mentioned going to college too. You put my name on the Swiss bank account without explanation, and now you are involving me in your business. Why are you doing all this? You said several months ago you'd explain it when the time was right. Maybe now would be a good time."

Princess turned toward him. A blink sent a single tear streaking down her cheek. He reached out and brushed it away. As he did so, she leaned her face into his fingers, and for a moment, he found it difficult to breathe.

"The time isn't right," she said cryptically.

"Let me ask you something else, then. Are you doing this for yourself, or for me?"

"For myself," she replied, smiling and added, "Well, mostly for me. I have another motive, but it's of no consequence right now."

"And you really need my help? You're not just making that up to be generous or something?"

Princess turned to look him full in the face. "I honestly need your help, and I am trying to be generous. I owe you a lot, but this is not repayment for that. I don't know. It's just that I want you to be with me in something I feel is very important."

"You're not going to tell me why." It was not a question. "No," she replied simply.

"I didn't think so." He realized he was bumping into that part of Princess's personality that was very stubborn. Well, so was he, just on different matters, and not nearly to her level. She was a curious combination of generous to a fault and as stubborn as a rusted—make that welded—hinge. When something was important to her, nothing— that is, no earthly thing—could make her budge. It made Sam chuckle that she could be more headstrong than he was.

"What are you laughing about?" Princess asked suspiciously. "That you are more stubborn than I am."

"Get used to it," she replied cheerfully but without any attempt at apology.

"I'll do it," he said without further delay.

"Thank you," she replied as if he had given her a great gift. Her smile was so wide that he wondered again what deep plot she was brewing. It was something of great significance to her. He thought it might be some time, if ever, before he knew what it was.

The following afternoon they found an office above the National Bank of Anchorage, which occupied a new building in the middle of Wasilla. It was exactly what she needed. They would have easy access to their safety deposit boxes, and the building was unusually secure. They arranged to have a quality security system installed. Princess paid the lease a year in advance.

Their new office consisted of a lobby and three large offices. It was bare except for carpeting. They spent several days in Anchorage arranging for office furniture. Princess insisted that they rent the furniture rather than purchase it. Since he knew she had access to considerable sums of money, it surprised him. However, he considered it pointless to debate the issue. Since he had no idea what her agenda was, he could not guess at her motives for the decisions she made. He decided to simply trust her. Accordingly, Sam took the first office, Princess the second, and a book-keeper the third.

Princess had been involved in the diamond trade since her youth. Af-ter her mother's death at age eight, it was her main tie with her father. His life was diamonds, and she had made it hers in an instinctual need to con-nect with him. She showed a genuine aptitude for the business, which her father had recognized, fondly kindled, and encouraged. All of her current wealth stemmed from prior involvement in the trade. Only twenty-two years old, she already possessed her father's prodigious knowledge of the diamond trade.

It was precisely six months from their return to America that they purchased tickets and returned to South Africa. The whirlwind trip be-gan at Princess's childhood castle and continued on to diamond mines in Germiston, diamond-cutting houses in Johannesburg, and finally the diamond works in West Africa. By the time they returned home, Sam could describe every aspect of a diamond's journey from a mine half a mile beneath the earth's surface to a woman's finger. It was a fascinating, exhausting journey.

Of all he learned, of all he saw, of all things made plain to him in this long journey, the greatest of these was the preciousness of Princess's soul. Over the course of the past year he had seen her in every condition possible—happy, sad, excited, terrified, disappointed, fresh, exhausted, healthy, sick, laughing, and weeping. No matter the circumstances, she radiated a noble quality that seemed unassailable. There was no thin ve-neer, no cheap facade to Princess. She was simply a princess, both in name and quality.

The plane was four hours out of England, and Princess had fallen asleep beside him. They had flown first class for the express purpose of "giving him more leg room." (It was just one of a thousand thoughtful things she did for him.) He was tired, and his mind and body demanded sleep, but he was too troubled to rest. He tried reading the scriptures, but his eyes passed over the words. His mind did not register their meaning, for his thoughts were upon another puzzle so pressing it refused to give him peace.

It was barely ten days ago that they had walked up to that imposing front door of her father's castle together. As the heavy door groaned open, it was almost as if those first moments played out again when he had first stood there as a missionary.

He looked across that vast room, and could almost see Dawn walking through it in her swimsuit and gossamer robe. As the evening progressed from laughter, through dinner, and to small talk, certain words seemed to trigger flashes of memory for Sam, and he would be transported away with a memory of her.

He saw her serving tea in her father's study, leading them through the secret passages of the castle, serving them cinnamon rolls and cold milk in the vast kitchen after a missionary discussion. In his mind, he listened again with wonder to her golden answers to their missionary questions and saw the tears stream down her face as she acknowledged for the first time that she knew it was true.

By far, Sam's most powerful memory was of that eternal moment when he had pronounced the words of divine cleansing and lowered her into the waters of baptism. She had looked at him, her intense blue eyes lovingly fastened to his, only closing as the waters washed over her. As she emerged, her eyes reopened to his as if nothing in eternity could separate them. How he thrilled then to her purity, to the spiritual feast it was to teach and baptize her, to the sheer joy of that unity that forever binds a spiritual child with her first teacher.

Now, nearly a year later, they were once again on a plane, headed toward his home, which was now her home. They had spent nearly every intervening day together, either living in his parent's home or working in the same office. Each day had revealed a new side of her inner beauty until he was awed into silence.

It was true she was flawed in some ways, but the flaws were like the tiny specs of flint he had learned to find in an almost perfect diamond. The flaws did much more than signify imperfection. Truly, one great flaw lowered the value of an otherwise precious stone, but many small flaws attested to the fact that this was indeed a diamond. A flawless stone did not exist in nature, and any stone without some imperfection was labeled valueless as a cheap laboratory creation.

It was not her flaws he constantly saw but the brilliance of the diamond surrounding them. Any mortal can put on a perfect facade for a period of time, and like the laboratory mockery, its sparkle is artificial. There was no facade in Princess though. Her flaws were naked, visible, and honest. Sam saw her flaws as evidence of the fact that this was her soul, utterly unadorned, in bright light, under a 20x loupe. It was this, and a thousand other brilliantly special things that made him love her. However, this was not the puzzle now twisting his soul into knots.

What puzzled Sam was that he had come to love her with great intensity but had not "fallen in love" with her.

He knew it was a distinction worthy of some great philosopher's treatise or a poet's inspired lyrics. It was a distinction smaller than dust, yet greater than the vastness of space. It bound him to her forever, and in the same mighty stroke, it separated them for eternity.

Still greater than his dilemma was hers, for there was little doubt she was not encumbered by this subtle, yet steely distinction. Her every gesture spoke of her love for him in a way he recognized in the deepest, most precious part of his soul. She made every effort to hide it, to treat him as a friend or perhaps a sibling. Manhood had placed the usual brown paper bag over his head in regard to female subtlety, but the message slowly seeped into his heart after countless hours, days, and weeks of exposure to it. Princess loved him.

It brought tears to his eyes and anguish to his soul to know that one day he must tell her that he did not love her in a romantic way. He knew it would tear a great hole in her noble heart and simultaneously a hole in his own.

"Oh, Father," he heard himself cry out in the silent anguish of his soul. "Thou knowest how I love Thee, and how I love to feel Thy arms around me. Thou knowest how in the simpleness of my heart I have longed to be a blessing to Thy daughter. Oh, Father, how it pains me to know that I must tell Thy precious daughter that I can't love her the way she needs and deserves. I have no idea why this is, and I would give all, Father, to spare her that hurt. Father, I—"

A stirring next to him interrupted his prayer, and he turned to watch Princess lean over until her head rested on his shoulder. Long blond hair spilled over his shoulder, and a smile played briefly across her lips. It was almost more than he could stand. His heart cried out in love for her; yet, the brick wall in his heart refused her entrance any further. A flash of pure truth suddenly penetrated Sam's thoughts as cleanly as a beam of light through total blackness. He saw the wall her love had hit and recognized for the first time that he had constructed it.

It was not a fixture of his nature but a construct alien to the landscape of his soul. Every way Sam looked at it, he saw his handiwork, his thinking, and his peculiar craftsmanship. Almost with a palpable feel of stone on his fingers, he picked up a brick and looked at it from every side. It was made of cold resolve. It was the color of his mission and the texture of the mission rules. It was every female on his mission whose feminine call had gone unanswered. Suddenly, with great relief, he mentally tossed the brick away. It had outlived its purpose.

He examined another and saw it was made of the same stone as Princess's castle home, from the first time he had seen her. It was the color of her swimsuit and the softness of her skin. On impulse, he brought it to his nose and smelled the sweetness of her perfume as the movement of the big door wafted it to his nose. He knew why he had placed this brick on the wall and tossed it aside as well.

Brick after brick he examined in his mind. He found dozens of them had the texture of the missionary lesson guide. Each was the color of a different piece of clothing she had worn. He pulled down another one for every missionary lesson he had taught her and one for every time he had forced himself to see inside her soul and not dwell on her physical beauty.

He was surprised to find many bricks the color of pine trees and the texture of rough-hewn logs. They had crystal for ends and gold for corners. He lifted one to his ear and heard her voice singing those angelic evening performances in Switzerland. He found one for every time he had looked at her, loved her, and remembered who she was and who he was.

He found one with velvet sides, textured like silken bed sheets, the color of her hair as it spilled across the pillow beside him. It smelled of expensive soap and freshly scrubbed skin. He turned it over in his hands and savored its softness and beauty. He rejoiced that he had made it a part of his brick wall. And then with joy, he mentally tossed it aside and watched it vanish to non-existence. Dozens of bricks were made of Alaskan birch wood, the color of her bathrobe, and the texture of her skin. One smelled of shampoo and swirling steam from a hot bath.

Dozens of them had been placed into the wall in his father's home, each a little different but each adding to the thickness of the wall keeping her out. One was slick like porcelain, the smell of chlorine, moist to the touch, the color of her swimsuit atop the pinkness of her skin.

Each of these he examined with care, savored the memory, remembered their function, valued their purpose, and then discarded them. At length, no wall stood, no barrier prohibited her. He looked around, searching, hoping, and waiting for her love to try the wall again.

He rejoiced that now it could pass, now it was free—no, in reality, now he was free. The contemplation of the happy moment when she came and found the wall gone thrilled him, and he laughed. The sound of his own voice delighted him, and he laughed again.

Something moved against his shoulder, and that peculiar sensation of sudden awakening surrounded him. He hadn't realized he had fallen asleep. He blinked opened his eyes to see her sleepy face pulled into a puzzled smile.

"You were laughing in your sleep," she said and chuckled softly at the memory.

"I was dreaming, I guess," he explained and found his eyes drinking in her beauty in a way he had never allowed before.

She pushed herself away from him as if she had been trying to focus on something too close. Her smile turned to happy puzzlement. She blushed. "Why are you looking at me that way?" she demanded, happy yet confused.

"Don't you recognize this look on someone's face?"

"No," she responded playfully. "Should I?"

"You'd better get used to it."

"Why?"

"It's the look of love, Princess. It means that I have loved you from the first moment I saw you, and that my life will never be complete unless you are a part of it."

"Sam!" Princess stammered. She fumbled nervously with her hands, her eyes falling from his face to her hands. "I think you're still asleep," she finally managed to say.

"Then I wish to never awaken. If this is a dream, let me dream it through eternity." He reached out, took her hand, and brought it to his lips. Twin tears streaked down her cheeks.

"Don't tease me. I couldn't stand it if . . ."

"Dawn." His voice softened, and he touched her cheek lovingly. "Princess, I love you. I think I have always loved you. Before this world began I loved you, and as long as the smallest speck of dust exists anywhere in all eternity, my love for you will be what it's made of."

His eyes clouded with tears, and his hands trembled. Tears fell on her hand as he pressed each finger to his lips and kissed it tenderly.

"I know this is unexpected," he continued, "and I know we have talked of little other than the gospel and diamonds, but I will burst if I wait another second! Princess . . ." He paused to regain control of his voice. "Princess, will you stay with me for the rest of eternity? Will you make my journey through this dismal world meaningful and marry me?"

The sound that came from her lips was at once a cry of joy, a laugh of sweetness, and the sound of bitterness escaping. She looked at him, her face wet with tears, her lips moving, trying to say the right words, but they would not come. She laid her face against his chest and wept. At first they were tears of happiness and then tears of long-held fear that had suddenly, unexpectedly been released. He held her gently against his chest, his cheek on her head as she cried until only sweetness remained.

Finally, she raised her head and rubbed away tears with both hands. She smiled and tried to speak, but her mouth was again overcome with emotion. When she did speak, it was so small he nearly had to read her lips.

"Yes," she whispered, and with great happiness she added, "Yes, a thousand times! Yes, an eternity filled with them! My answer has always been yes. I just feel like I have been waiting a million years for you to ask me the right question." Her voice was soft and breathless.

Princess's face was close. Sam placed his hand on her cheek. She turned her face and kissed his palm. "Perhaps," he said, gazing into her eyes with an intensity that was both new and intoxicating. "Perhaps if one counts the premortal world, it has been that long. Since you have had to wait so long, do you mind if I ask you again?"

She shook her head wordlessly, a beautiful smile glowing on her face. How like an angel she seemed to him at that moment. Sam swallowed hard, his heart pounding nearly beyond control. He slipped out of his seat, kneeling in the aisle, holding both her hands in his.

"Princess, will you make me the happiest man among all of God's creations and marry me?"

"Oh, yes!" she cried. "I will," and fell into his arms.

Without explanation, without warning, without regard for the sanctity of what had just occurred, a passenger nearby began to clap, and then another and another. As seconds turned into minutes and whispers into shouts, the entire plane erupted into applause. People cheered, some of them whistled, many laughed, and a few cried. Princess and her beloved prince nestled down into their seats oblivious to anything but one another and the miracle of perfect love.

17

PERFECT LOVE

In the morning of June 14, 1975, Sam waited nervously in the long hall below the Salt Lake Temple, his clothing entirely white. His heart raced like a chariot of fire, and his eyes continually pooled with tears. He had tried all his life to imagine this moment—this frightening, celestial moment. He had rehearsed and replayed this image in his mind a thousand times, and each had been less in every respect than what he felt now. He had imagined less fear, less nervousness, less love, less sheer joy.

A rustle of skirts to him was like the parting of the veil, and he turned to see the heavenliest of all God's creations coming toward him in a wedding dress. Oh, how he strained to imprint that image in his mind, to remember every detail, every nuance of her beauty, the glow of her righteousness, the halo of love that surrounded her face! He wanted to be able to replay this moment every day of his life and remember the intensity of the love that was now filling his soul to overflowing.

Surrounded by his mother, family, and friends, Princess walked toward him like a glorious preview of the Second Coming. Her dress was rich and full, entirely made of lace with thousands of lace rosebuds in an intricate pattern. He marveled, wondered, and felt his heart race. She was lovelier than any dream mortal man could devise—awake or asleep—and she came to him, of all people.

He reached out to her and felt her silken hands slide into both of his. He pulled her to him and was immediately hindered by billowing lace. He laughed to himself for joy, happiness, and love and leaned forward to kiss her lightly. Her face was radiant. Her lips moved without making a sound.

"I love you," she whispered. It was the most perfect thing she could have said.

Princess had received her endowments that morning. Sam had been there, heard her say the words, repeated them with her at the dividing of worlds, and seen her step through the eternities to meet him. "Glorious" was too small a word to describe that moment, and the promises were richer and more profound than he had ever realized. The symbolism was deep and eternally significant. He wondered what it all meant and longed for the day when the promises were all granted. Almost as if the world skipped a step, Sam found himself holding Princess's hands across the altar, her face a halo of love and serenity. He listened to the words of the ceremony with rapt attention, trapping them in his mind and heart. He had never heard such beautiful words or such profound promises and pronouncements. It was as if the Savior Himself was pronouncing the vast promises, and Sam knew, as he had never known anything else before, that they were true.

Was it a minute, an hour, or an eternity later that he heard God's authorized spokesman say those words that made Princess his for time and eternity? Sam leaned across the altar, cradled her face in his hands, and kissed her as if all his love had to be expressed in that single act. He heard, saw, felt, and knew nothing else but that she was his forever. A hand suddenly rested on his shoulder and demanded his attention. His father laughed and suggested saving some for later. Sam chuckled and reluctantly surrendered her face. She opened her eyes to his as if awakening from a dream, her eyes childlike with utter joy. So much happened in the next few hours that the newlyweds almost had no time to see each other. They zoomed from place to place; from breakfast to lunch, to friends' houses and home again, and then to receptions, photos, gifts, and thank you's. Night fell suddenly, and then it was goodbye.

When at last they climbed into their car and drove away, they were exhausted. They drove the short distance to the Hotel Utah, which was east of the Salt Lake Temple, and checked in. They knelt in prayer beside their bed, fell atop it fully clothed, and were soon sound asleep. Sam awoke with a start to the warmth of sunlight in the room.

He sat up in a daze. It took several moments to remember where he was and how he had gotten there. A memory seized him and left him spellbound for a split second before he turned to the bed behind him. Only a white wedding dress lay there carefully arranged. It was then that he realized the door to the bathroom was closed. He could hear soft movements beyond it and felt his heart quicken with . . . anticipation? Fear? Passion? So complex were his emotions that the only feeling he was entirely sure of was love. On his side of the door and on hers, love was the power of life.

The door stayed closed a long time until he wondered if it might actually be vacant and his princess had fled.

He lifted the phone and ordered breakfast for two. He had lived in the same house with his new bride for the last year and knew exactly what she liked. He ordered it with every side and trimming he could think of. It was more food than ten people could eat.

The bathroom door clicked softly just as he hung up the phone. It opened slowly, and an angel stepped into the room. For a moment his heart stopped, his eyes glued themselves open, and he felt his face heating up. He had never seen so lovely a creature as his princess as she walked slowly toward him.

He stood to meet her and she came to him, her arms open wide.

They held one another for nearly an eternity, their hearts melting into a single inseparable whole. He kissed her, softly, slowly, tenderly, until the world ceased to exist except her love, which she gave to him completely, utterly, passionately, and perfectly.

* * *

Sam and Princess had no recollection of receiving or eating breakfast and lunch, yet the carts of half-eaten food testified to the reality of their having done so.

It was hard to do—very hard. Anyone who has tried it will testify that it is nearly impossible to pack a suitcase when you can't look at the luggage because your eyes are glued in near worship to your new spouse's face. But somehow, perhaps as a result of a miracle, they both left the room with most of their possessions.

His last comment to his bride as they closed the door to their honeymoon suite was, "I wonder what housekeeping is going to think when they see the mess we left behind."

"They're going to be jealous," she replied shyly.

He sighed, and she laughed softly like a wind chime in the distance. She looped her arm through his.

"They should be, my Princess. If they knew, they surely would be."

"I'm going to hear you say that when you are eighty years old," she whispered in his ear. He felt a thrill of delight travel up his back. He couldn't help sighing again, for in the fabric of his soul, he believed her, and it thrilled him through and through.

* * *

As far as their family knew, they were flying to Hawaii for two weeks. In reality, Hawaii was a jump on their way to Paris, Switzerland, Greece, and South Africa. Having been raised a struggling farmer's son, it was hard for him to adjust to the idea that the least of their concerns was financial. In the eight months since Princess had started importing diamonds, they—actually she—had done far better than well.

His demure bride, however, had grown up in affluence and seemed perfectly at ease with the astronomical prices demanded to dip one's tongue in the syrupy sweetness of luxury.

They flew, ate, slept, and honeymooned first class. They spent more money during those two weeks than he could have earned in a year of building houses. It didn't really matter, for life had been good beyond reason, beyond their wildest dreams, beyond any hope of permanency. It was a walk in the full sunshine of utter happiness and wild joy. It was paradise, and they rejoiced in its perfection.

*　*　*

The Atlantic's cold waters churned thirty thousand feet below them as Sam hovered somewhere between sleep and wakefulness. He had been watching Princess sleep for almost an hour, and it seemed as if she grew more precious with each breath she drew. She was lying on her side facing him, and he found that he could not sleep with her this close.

Their honeymoon had been more glorious than anything he could have imagined. He had been invited with passion into a new and glorious world previously unknown to him, and he found himself in a constant state of giddy happiness. Being married was everything he had hoped it would be, and a thousand times better. Without reservation, he considered himself the luckiest man alive.

At that moment Princess's eyes flickered open, and a smile transformed her face when she realized he had been watching her. Her hand gently touched his cheek and flopped sleepily back into her lap.

"Why do you watch me so? You could give a girl a complex," she said, her voice indistinct from sleep. She was like a sleepy child, and he chuckled.

"I find I can't sleep with you near when there is light in the room."

"Oh? Why not?" she asked, straightening and stretching in her seat.

"Because, I feel like we're the luckiest people on earth," he replied after a moment's silence.

"I don't want to even think like that." Her voice was suddenly somber.

"How come?"

"Well, because luck is fickle and temporary and eventually turns bad. I don't want to be lucky. I just want to enjoy the good things while they are mine. That would be sufficient for me."

"Me, too," he agreed. "But is that really what you believe? That happiness is temporary?"

"On some level I do, I guess. I've been here before. Well, not nearly this happy, and not nearly this in love, but I've seen happiness turn to tragedy more than once," she concluded quietly.

"Like when your mother died?" Sam asked. "Yes."

"And, when your father kicked you out of the house?"

"Why are you bringing up these unhappy memories at such a happy moment? I don't want to think about those things." Her voice sounded pouty, not angry.

"Sorry. I only wanted to understand your personal philosophy about happiness."

"I understand. I'm not angry. I don't think I could be angry with you. Let's change the subject." This she said with a hand on his knee. It felt good there, and he placed his hand on hers to soak up as much of her as he could.

"Are you afraid of happiness?" he asked.

She gave him a stern look and then smiled. "I thought we were going to change the subject."

"Are you?" he asked, ignoring her protest.

"My love, I could give you a thousand-word essay on my attitude about happiness."

"Distill it to one word."

"Just one?"

"Please," he said.

She took that moment to readjust her skirt and push a loose strand of hair out of her face.

Princess opened her mouth, her face suggesting a long explanation. "Just one word," he reminded her.

"In a word. Yes," she said forcefully, throwing her hands into the air in frustration. Then more subdued she added, "I sometimes get the feeling that God does not want me to be happy very long. Every time something gets wonderful, it goes away, usually violently. I guess whenever I feel strong happiness I begin to resent God, because I fear He is going to take it away from me. It's almost as if He does not want me to be happy about anything except Him. It makes it hard for me to have great faith in Him sometimes. Does that make you think less of me?"

"Nothing you can say could make me think less of you."

"See? See why I love you? You always know the perfect thing to say to make my heart sing."

Princess sat quietly for a while. Sam wanted to ask her more and to assure her that he would never let tragedy strike her again, but he knew it was not within his power to promise such a thing. Still, he was pained for her unhappy outlook on things.

Finally, she looked him squarely in the eyes. "Tell me something? Are you afraid of happiness?"

Even though he had broached the subject, Sam was still taken back when it was his turn. He had to think hard to come up with the correct answer. Most of all, he had to push aside some pride to give her an honest answer.

"Afraid isn't the right word. I'm . . ." he began, but she wagged a finger in his face.

"In a single word," she insisted. "Then I would have to say no."

"Really? I'm surprised. From the stories you tell, you have had some awful things happen to you too."

"Not really," he disagreed.

"Oh? What about Jimmy's death? What about those guys beating you up at the lake and trying to hurt your sister? What about being whipped on your mission and thrown in jail? What about those things? Don't they make you doubt that happiness can be permanent?"

Something occurred to him, and he asked a new question rather than answering hers.

"Is that why you are so intense and passionate about enjoying life, love, money, and beauty because you think they will all end abruptly?"

"Not fair!" she said.

"The court directs the witness to answer the question," he said sternly.

Princess smiled and sat up rigidly in her seat. "Yes, Your Rudeness. I am guilty. I intend to squeeze every milliliter of happiness from my life while it is available to me. I'm passionate about things because they don't last."

"That's kind of sad," he said.

"Tripe," she said sternly, and it made him laugh. Tripe is a filthy-tasting dish made from the lining of a sheep's stomach. It tastes so bad that it had become a common curse to define something as such. Sam had eaten—or more correctly—had tried to eat tripe in Africa, so the curse was graphic to him.

"You owe me an answer," she insisted. "What was the question?"

"Haven't the awful things in your life given you the sense that happiness is temporary?"

"Oh, kind of."

"Then how can you say you are not afraid of happiness? You know it won't last, and the happier you become, the more devastating the inevitable disaster is."

Sam turned as far as he could in his seat until their knees were touching. He took her hand and gently massaged it as he tried to answer her question.

"There was a time in my life when I agreed with you. I sometimes went to the extent of avoiding happiness because I didn't want to experience the misery and unhappiness I thought would inevitably follow."

"Yes, that's how I am sometimes. But you said that's how you used to be. What's different now?"

"I discovered what true happiness is," he replied.

"Really? Tell me what it is," she said playfully.

Sam laid his head back in his seat. "True happiness is finally understanding who you are in God's eyes. It is thereafter knowing you are worthy and acceptable before the Lord and feeling His love to the marrow of your bones."

Princess looked disappointed. "I thought you were going to say something incredibly romantic. You know, like loving me was true happiness."

"Loving you is the most wonderful emotion I have ever experienced and by far the sweetest thing that has happened to me."

"That's what I thought you were going to say the first time," she said happily. Then her mood turned serious. "I don't understand why having my love isn't the ultimate happiness."

"I know you don't, and I'm not sure I can explain it in a way you can. I'm not sure anyone can understand it without experiencing it. But your fear that God will take away any happiness you achieve is a part of what I am trying to say."

"Keep trying until I get it," she said. It made him laugh.

"Okay. Suppose you were a parent and had a beautiful little girl about four years old."

"Hmmm. I like this scenario. I plan to make it come true."

"Me too. Well, suppose our beautiful daughter discovered chocolate. The first time she tasted it, she fell in love with it and thought it was the ultimate happiness in life. As her mother, would you forbid her to eat chocolate?"

"No, of course not."

"Let's add to the picture. In time your daughter became so addicted to chocolate that she thought it was the most wonderful thing on earth."

Princess laughed. "Who's been telling you about my childhood? I was like that once."

"Aha, a true confession!"

Princess laughed. "Get on with your story! This imaginary daughter sounds adorable."

"It gets better! Your daughter refuses to eat anything but chocolate. You can see that her health will be affected by her addiction. Would you become concerned? Would you begin to restrict the amount of chocolate she could have?"

"Yes, of course."

"Do you think your daughter would understand or appreciate your restricting her chocolate diet?"

"I'm sure she would fight it."

"Might she not think you were mean or cruel?"

"I know I would if I were that child."

"But since you have greater wisdom and you love your daughter enough to risk making her hate you, you take away the very thing she thinks is necessary for her happiness."

Princess sat quietly for a moment before replying. "I hadn't thought about it that way. I can see why Heavenly Father would do that, even if we don't understand that too much happiness can hurt us. What I don't understand is how having a loving home, or a baby brother still alive, or other things that appear to be good would be harmful to us."

Sam clasped his hands and shoved them into his lap. He arched his shoulders and then relaxed.

"Princess, I don't know the answers to all these things. I'm not claiming to know why everything happens or if those things we lose were actually bad for us. What I do know is that in order for us to achieve the ultimate happiness, the eternal type of happiness that we are capable of, we must be absolutely focused on Jesus Christ. I think what happens isn't so much that everything we lose was bad for us but that we still are not aligned with the gospel."

He studied her intently and then continued. "Perhaps it's just that our temporary joys make us complacent and we think we have all we need, and we don't realize our total dependence upon God. It seems to me that our trials keep us from being lulled into foolishly trusting in ourselves and becoming spiritually immobile. I know that when I am comfortable and happy in my life, I don't want anything to change, even if it means progressing to greater happiness."

Princess nodded her head, albeit somewhat tentatively. "I can understand that. I'll have to think some more about it. But it still doesn't seem fair."

"At times it certainly doesn't—perhaps even most of the time. I think that's the purpose faith serves in our trials, to give us the assurance that our trials have a greater purpose and will ultimately be a blessing to us if we trust in God and bear them well. Speaking from my own life's experience, I have gained tremendous blessings from every trial I endured. I wouldn't change any aspect of my life. As near as I can tell, my life in its present form is as perfect as it can be. It would terrify me to think of taking some other path that might lead to another outcome in my life. Though it's been hard, it's brought me great blessings, not the least of which is loving you."

Princess smiled, leaned forward, and kissed him on the forehead. "You keep reminding me why I love you," she said. "However, you do admit that happiness is temporary and sometimes ends abruptly— even tragically. But you're not afraid of happiness because you believe the outcome of your trials will be wonderful in the end."

"I can honestly say that I have enjoyed every year of my life more than the one before it. I can also say that each year has been harder than the one before."

"So, just because we're deliriously happy together, you don't fear that it will come to a tragic end?"

"It may."

"Oh! That wasn't the right answer," she cried as she punched him on the shoulder.

"No, but it's the truth, and the truth of this entire discussion is that no matter what happens, as long as we are faithful and obedient, all things will work together for our eternal happiness. I expect to say that I have enjoyed every year of my life more than the one before even when I'm a hundred years old!"

"I hope I'm there to hear you say it," she said pointedly.

"If you aren't, I won't be able to say it, because it won't be the truth anymore."

"Now," she asserted, a beaming smile on her face, "that's the right answer!"

SUMMER OF JOY

It did look too big. "It sure looks bigger in reality than on paper," Princess admitted as she stood outside the massive log structure that was soon to be their home. Sam had to agree.

They had pored over the plans for months, moving walls, adjusting window sizes, moving bathrooms, shrinking, enlarging. It had been a happy yet frustrating experience for them both. Their backgrounds were so varied that their vision of the perfect home was quite different.

Princess had been raised in a castle—literally. She had been waited on by servants, pampered beyond reason, spoiled rotten, and indulged in every whim. Sam had been raised in a small home on a farm. He had worked hard, been taught discipline, temperance, sharing, and had received but few of his greatest desires.

One would have thought that Princess would have wanted another castle home and Sam a smaller, more functional home. However, it was an odd twist that this was not so. Sam wanted what he had never had—a large home with many rooms, secret passageways, a formal dining hall, and several garages.

Princess wanted what Sam took for granted—closeness, love, family, and a strong sense of home. Since she had not found these things in her castle, she feared to move into another one.

Their compromise had produced a home not entirely unlike the Swiss hotel with rough-hewn logs and crystal chandeliers.

It looked comfortable, homey, and peaceful to her and big and successful to Sam. Its rooms were small enough to be livable, and large enough to be spacious. One side of the house was a four-bedroom home not unlike any other. The other side was a collection of rooms not clearly defined in their purpose. They existed for the purpose of being, having, and living with excess. The rooms were appropriately connected by a hidden hall and cleverly crafted secret doors. One room could only be entered through the secret hall. To add a splash of functionality to soften the sense of foolishness he felt, Sam also made the secret hall the quickest and safest way to leave the big home in the case of a fire. This was the unused east wing in his castle, and he valued every empty square inch.

Princess decorated the livable part of her home in warmth, lace, and love. His side of their castle was rich, luxuriant, velvet, and crystal. It suited them, and they could afford it.

Their log mansion sat beside beautiful Lake Helen on one end of a twenty-acre paradise of dense birch forest. Sam had the area around the home cleared and planted in grass and formal gardens.

Princess had the grounds near the lake cleared of underbrush, planted in grass, and left to its natural beauty. She also had sand hauled in for a small beach and had a boat dock built.

Walking from one end of the house to the other, one passed from exquisite formal gardens to lush grasses and virgin forest. All of it pleased them both and symbolized their jigsaw-puzzle love.

Sam had an airstrip cleared near the house, bought a single-engine plane, and immediately began studying for his pilot's license. In 1976, Alaska had more private aircraft per capita than any other place on earth. With its low altitude, cool dense air, and vast expanses of unpopulated land, it made a perfect location for small aircraft.

They moved into their new home on October 31, 1976— Halloween day. Sam's entire family showed up to help them move.

Even though they had been married just over a year, they had acquired a considerable array of possessions, especially when they decided to build the log castle. They had purchased anything they felt might go well in their new home. They were both amazed at how much of it was junk that had no real place in their new abode.

A light snow fell most of the day as they unloaded the big truck. They backed the truck into the large garage and had a warm place to unload the boxes. They carried them down the ramp of the truck, up two steps into the laundry room, through the family room, past the kitchen and dining room, and into the spacious living room.

Sam was regretting the size of his home long before he carried the last box inside. While the men finished the last of it, Princess and Sam's mother slipped away to make a treat.

Mom had previously made an apple pie, and Princess prepared some red bush tea (also known as rooibos tea in Africa) to go with it. Sam's family had all come to appreciate the tea's rich, herbal flavor.

Apple pie was unknown in South Africa, and to Sam's knowledge had never been served with red bush tea. They found that the two made a delightful combination.

It was nearly midnight before everyone left, and Sam and Princess flopped down exhausted on the big sofa in the main living room. They silently surveyed their accomplishments and were pleased. In all, they had come a long way, and it seemed wonderful to finally have a home of their own. In front of them, a natural rock fireplace stood two stories high. On either side of the fireplace were recessed bookshelves. On the opposite side of the room, a large grand piano sat majestically on an oval oriental rug. Another set of sofas surrounded the opposite side of the piano. Various groupings of Victorian chairs were scattered around the room. The ceiling was high with large open beams. Beautiful woodwork had been laid diagonally across the beams. The effect was stunning.

"I am so tired," Princess mumbled. "I think I'll go to bed." She smiled at him and levered herself to the edge of the sofa.

"I'll help you make the bed," he offered. He knew their bedding was still in boxes.

"That's nice, but your mom and I already did that. All I have to do is go pass out between the sheets."

Sam laughed and then sighed. "When are you going to tell me?"

"Tell you what?" she asked innocently.

"Your big secret."

"You mean about the diamond business?"

"No, about our family," he said.

"I don't know any secrets about your family."

"You don't understand, my love. Yours and my family—us."

"Oh? Do you think I'm keeping a secret from you?" She asked mischievously.

"Either you are keeping a secret from me or you don't know yourself."

"Know what, you silly? What are you talking about?"

"Are you sure you want me to say it? I thought it was something women wanted to announce themselves," he said in all seriousness.

"What are you talking about?" she demanded, her curiosity piqued.

"Why, I'm talking about your being pregnant," he said happily.

"I'm not!"

"Yes you are."

"If I was I would know it before you. Why do you say that?"

"I say it because it's so."

"You can be such a tease sometimes. I'm going to bed."

"Wait," he said and caught up with her partway up the stairs. She received him happily, and wrapped her arms around his neck. Princess by nature was a snuggly person and never seemed to tire of physical affection. It was another of her many virtues that made her priceless in Sam's heart.

"I may be wrong, but I don't think so. I watched my Mom have four babies. Every time I knew she was expecting before she told the family. I could tell."

"How?" she asked, her head cocked to one side, her brow furrowed. "Well, there's a different look about a mother-to-be. A new softness. A gentleness not there before. Kind of a glow. It's the way they walk and move. A new peace. Almost a kind of reverence, I guess. For about a week I have been seeing that in you, and I have been wondering when you were going to tell me."

"You amaze me," she said, and since she was standing on a step above him, she kissed him on the forehead. "I have been feeling different, and kind of sickish in the mornings. I actually have a doctor's appointment next Monday. You speak with great conviction about something that is an unknown to me. Maybe you're right. Maybe not."

"I'm right," he replied with emphasis.

"Are you ready to be a daddy?" she asked, her face lowered, a hint of a pout on her lips.

"I can think of nothing finer. What about you?"

"I'm not ready to become a daddy," she said and laughed at her own joke.

"You've got to learn to keep a straight face," he said.

"I know. I'm working on it. To be honest, I'm scared."

"Of being pregnant?"

"Well, that too, but mostly I'm scared of being a mother."

"Why?"

"Because my mother died when I was young, somehow I have always assumed that the same thing would happen to me."

"I can see how you might come to that conclusion as a child, but surely, as an adult, you can see that your mother's death didn't set a precedent. Her circumstances were unique to her. There's no reason to believe the same thing would happen to you."

"I know all that, of course, but ever since I was a child, every time I thought of the day when I would have children, I've had a feeling that my life would end shortly thereafter. I suppose it may be a childhood delusion, but it's always been there. I guess I have ceased to question it anymore."

Resignation and sadness was in her voice. She deeply believed what she was saying, and it disturbed Sam.

"You said children. Does this mean you think you will have more than one before you die?"

"Well, yes, I guess. I have always thought I would have several before I was called home."

"Okay then," Sam said, acting much more cheerful than he felt. "This is baby number one, so nothing is going to happen. Before baby number two comes, we will work on your bad attitude about living. At any rate, I don't think there's anything to it at all."

Princess brightened somewhat. "I know it sounds silly, but I've told myself everything you just said, and it doesn't help. It's probably nothing, but it bothers me. Sometime appropriate, will you give me a blessing? I'd like that."

"I will, I promise," he said, wishing there was something he could say to take away her fear.

"I just hope I'm a good mother," she added seriously. "I haven't had a role model. An English nanny raised me. She was wonderful to me, but not the same as a mother. I really want to be a good mother."

"I can't imagine you being anything other than a perfect mother. I'll give you a pointer though."

Princess nodded. Sam paused for effect and then continued with exaggerated seriousness, "The most important thing to being a great mommy is to pamper the new baby's daddy."

Princess laughed. It was a silken, joyful sound. She stepped down to his level. "Let's start your pampering right now."

* * *

Melody had gone on to study music in South Africa. It was a tearful and frightening transition for her. This time she flew from Rhodesia with Marcia by her side. Their studies lasted approximately a year. After a brief visit to Rhodesia, they packed again and headed to England. Marcia's talent was technically superior to Melody's. Marcia's technique and prowess showed great promise, but for Marcia the violin was merely an instrument.

Melody's music was charged with emotion. Her violin was far more than music; it was a love affair. She played with what some described as genius. Her instructors considered the missing technical skills something that could be learned, and her love of the violin divinely inspired. Hence, Melody showed greater promise and was courted by prestigious orchestras.

Marcia studied until she met and married a warm and loving Englishman.

Melody returned to Rhodesia after two years in England's finest music schools. Her timing was unfortunate for she had returned on the exact day the rebels once again attacked their home.

This time, however, her father, Donavon was prepared. He had quietly purchased a small army, complete with cannons, armored personnel carriers, one WWI vintage tank, and a considerable supply of small arms and ammunition. Melody had loaded guns for what seemed like days on end as her father, and a few faithful friends, defended their fortress-like home.

On the sixth day of the attack, Melody fell asleep on the couch in utter exhaustion. All had traded turns taking short naps, but the strain was most telling on her, and her father had ordered her to sleep. She awoke with a start to the feeling of someone nearby. Her eyes fluttered open to see her father kneeling beside her. Tears were streaming down his face; yet, when he saw her awake, he quickly fumbled with something in his hands. She knew very well what it was.

"Daddy, I know you can't bear the thought of me being captured by the rebels, but I don't want you to kill me, even out of love, even if you know in your very heart of hearts that it's the best thing to do. Do you understand?"

"Oh, Baby, I'm sorry you saw that," he whispered, and stroked a grizzled hand through her soft hair. "During the night they brought up an army tank. Until now I thought we could hold out. It's only a matter of hours before the sun comes up, and they attack. There's no way we can defend ourselves. Forgive me, precious one, but I couldn't bear to have them take you and . . . and . . ."

"And do things to me like they did my mother, and Marcia," she finished for him. He merely nodded without looking at her.

She sat up and wrapped her arms around his neck, laying her head on his broad shoulder. He held her tightly, and wept for not much more than ten seconds. With a sudden resolve so typical of him, he straightened, kissed her on the cheek, and smiled as if nothing at all was amiss.

Melody was frightened by the sudden change. "Daddy, I want you to listen to me. I know you have already decided to do what you think is unavoidable, but I want you to consider my words, then reconsider your decision. Will you do that?"

"It's the least I could do," he admitted, still kneeling a short distance from her. She placed a soft hand on either cheek, and kissed him on the forehead.

"When I was on the train and you came to rescue me, do you remember that?"

344

"I remember it bloody well," he said grimly.

"There came a time when bullets were smashing into our cabin, glass was flying everywhere, and we could hear the rebels just outside our window. We knew it was but a few minutes before we would be captured, and they would begin . . . well, you understand."

"I was certain I would be too late," he said with a grimace.

"At that moment when we could not possibly survive, that Mormon missionary who was with us . . ."

"Elder Mahoy," Donavon supplied.

". . . Elder Mahoy gave me a blessing."

"You told me about it, but not many details, honey."

"He wrote it down. It's actually fairly short. What it said in essence was that we would not be harmed by the attackers, but that it was a type of other trials that I would have in my life.

"The important part is that he promised me that I would survive them—all of them, including this one. Do you see what I mean?"

"Do you honestly believe what the blessing said?" her father asked intensely.

"I do, with all my heart. When he gave it to me I felt a great warmth rush through me, and a sense of peace I had never felt before. I feel that same peace now, Daddy, and I want you to honor my faith, and not try to save me by . . ." She couldn't bring herself to say it.

"I have never felt such a peace. I've heard others describe it though. Your mother spoke of it . . ." He seemed lost in memories for a moment, his eyes focused on distant scenes. He quickly returned his attention to Melody.

"I will make you a promise."

"Okay," she replied.

"I will wait until the rebels are actually in the house, and coming for you. But, I promise you, I will not let them take you alive. It's the best I can do, my precious child."

"I understand, Daddy, and I thank you for that. But, there's one other thing you need to understand."

"Which is?"

"If the rebels kill me, I will be dead."

"That seems apparent," he said, and chuckled with dark humor. "If you kill me, you'll be dead."

"What do you mean?"

"As awful as it seems to both of us for me to be tortured and killed, it would be much, much worse if you killed me, even to save me. My blood would be on your hands, and you would not be guiltless. I'm afraid you could not come where Mama and I would be, and that would be the greatest tragedy of all," she said emotionally.

"I'm afraid my hands are already stained with many people's blood, child. One more, as an act of mercy, couldn't make a difference."

Melody persisted, "Tell me, tell me what my heart already knows. Have you ever killed someone except in the line of duty, or in defense of what was rightfully yours?"

"No, of course not," he attested.

"Then killing me would be an act of horrible, unforgivable shedding of innocent blood. Oh, Daddy, don't you see, the Bible says a person who sheds innocent blood can't ever go to heaven. Please, Daddy, for your sake, for Mama's sake, for my sake, please rethink this, I beg you." Donavon's shoulders hung low, his face became a forsaken mask, and he hung his head. She had never seen him so defeated.

Even while he could not accept allowing his youngest daughter to be brutalized, he loved her too much to deny her this request. Unknown to her, he silently vowed to stay by her side until they either both escaped, or both perished. It wouldn't be his bullet that spared her, but he would not draw his last breath until she had been spared in one way or another. It was a solution far too risky to give him any peace. And, it cost him more courage than he actually possessed to agree to risk her so needlessly. But, it was how it would be.

He stood and looked down at her still sitting before him.

"I will do as you say. No matter how awful it seems, I will not interfere by taking your life." Then he added, "I never break my word."

"Thank you, Daddy," Melody cried with tears of gratitude. She jumped to her feet and embraced him fiercely. He held her for a moment, nodded, spun on one heel, and marched away, barking orders as he stomped into the other room.

During all this time, months of negotiations had been underway in Salisbury for the unconditional surrender of Prime Minister Ian Smith's government to the new communist-backed government seeking to take its place. Ian Smith finally capitulated to stop the killing, and a truce was set in place.

The so-called truce was nothing more than an unconditional surrender of the former British citizens to their indigenous neighbors, many of whom had chafed under the apparent unequal distribution of wealth. Now in power, their former employees began a systematic punishment of those upon whom they had relied for so many years for their welfare.

Thousands of British farmers, business owners, owners of industry and merchants were forced from their homes and businesses at gunpoint. Their daughters and wives were ravaged before their eyes, their sons murdered, and they were either jailed as enemies of the state, or executed on the spot.

A week of relative calm came and went as the new government enacted laws outlawing persons of British descent from ownership of land larger than one acre, or buildings larger than one thousand square feet. All other properties were immediately forfeit and subject to resettlement. All mortgages and financial obligations on the land were to remain the burden of the former owners, who would be jailed if they did not immediately pay in full, in cash.

Food became scarce as those taking over the vast farms and factories neglected to plant crops, or simply lacked the expertise to run the equipment. Famine loomed, the economy plummeted, and anger raged. Those in power loudly blamed the prior government of Ian Smith, and by association, all of British descent; and mobs, with the sanction and assistance of government troops, began systematically killing their former employers.

Thousands of former British citizens escaped across the border into neighboring Botswana, hoping to make their way into South Africa.

Less than half of them made it. Surrounded on every side by hostile troops, Donavon and all with him were not able to sneak away. Though a proud man, and as stubborn as hardened concrete, he would have gladly abandoned all to spirit Melody away to safety.

The day following the enactment of these new laws saw the fiercest fighting yet. The tank was brought forward and fired three shells. One overshot the MacUlvaney house, the second blew away the whole south corner, killing two defenders, and the third blasted completely through the front of the house and out the back without exploding. It left a three-foot hole in the front, and a ten-foot hole in the back. Miraculously, no one else was killed.

Inexplicably, they never fired the big gun again. Melody would never know that the fourth shell had only partially fired, killing the tank crew, and jamming the shell in the barrel beyond repair.

The shooting stopped suddenly about seven p.m., and Melody found herself deafened from the shelling. A man approached cautiously with a white flag and informed them everyone but Donavon could leave in safety if they would leave their home and possessions and never return.

For the safety of his daughter, Donavon agreed and surrendered his weapons, his fortune, his home, and his life before Melody could object.

Melody and the others were allowed to escape in a battered old truck with two flat tires. They drove away not knowing what would become of Donavon.

The last Donavon saw of Melody, she was crying hysterically, clawing at the back window of the truck.

The last Melody saw of her father, he was surrounded by armed guards in military uniforms, his eyes fixed upon her. As soon as he was certain she was truly being set free, his chin rose defiantly. He smiled broadly and turned to face his captors.

Donavon was immediately arrested as an enemy to the new state of Zimbabwe. When asked how he would plead, he said "bloody guilty," with great feeling. Minutes later he was hanged on his own front porch. He was noble to the end, and as a last request asked to wax his mustache. The amazed soldiers watched as he carefully waxed and curled his great mustache, fitted the rope carefully around his own neck to avoid disturbing it, and nodded. He was buried in an unmarked grave in his own front yard with an odd smile on his face.

Melody learned of her father's fate a few days later at the same time she learned she had also been declared an enemy of the state. She was smuggled out of Zimbabwe on an airplane inside a mailbag, taking with her great faith, bitter memories, and her violin.

* * *

The day after Princess and Sam moved into their log castle, Sam's parents' home was burglarized, or rather, vandalized. The only evidence was a big diamond shape scratched onto the mirror hanging above the living room sofa. The diamond shape was carefully faceted and faced to look like a real diamond. The number 22 had been deeply etched beneath it.

They all felt violated, and careful precautions were taken to preclude another break in. The police were truly stumped by the weird vandalism, and the fact that the door had been professionally picked. There was nothing to suggest a motive.

Robbery was ruled out as nothing had been taken.

Sam and Princess returned home in deep silence. Neither needed to ask the other if they knew what the 22 represented.

It was the exact weight of the diamond they had attempted to transport through England many months ago. The fact that only a diamond could cut the carefully drawn image in glass, and the number below it, incontrovertibly connected it to the lost gem.

Suddenly, what was forgotten history was terrifyingly present. They had no one to whom they could turn for advice or protection. They were on their own, and what minutes before had been the number before 23, was now a looming, invisible threat in their lives. They both knew the reason his family's home had been vandalized. It was a warning, and it meant someone still wanted the stone.

* * *

Princess found she loved being pregnant. From the beginning she felt a deep sense of love and unity for the precious life she carried. As her tummy grew in size, her love grew to match.

Each day she became more anxious to finally meet the sweet spirit inside her. She would find herself talking to her unborn baby, and then blush and stop in embarrassment.

Sam came home unexpectedly one Friday afternoon and found her sitting in the rocking chair, singing Primary songs to her baby. Between each hymn she stopped and told her baby the meaning of the words, and how important it was to understand. Sam listened a long time as tears trickled down his cheeks. He felt as if he had quietly stepped into the celestial room in the temple, and interrupted an angel singing to her child. How he valued that moment in years to come, and how sweet its memory was in his soul.

"How long have you been standing there?" Princess asked when she finally realized he had been listening to her.

"Minutes," he answered, then amended it to "A lifetime."

Princess blushed, and turned away from him quickly. "I didn't know you were there. You caught me being silly."

"I caught you being the perfect mother you were concerned about. Our baby is so lucky, how could you call yourself silly?"

"I just love this baby so much," she said, rubbing her tummy tenderly. "Sometimes my heart has to express it. I find that singing fulfills my need to express my love. But, I . . . I hadn't planned on you seeing me."

"I shall always treasure the memory of watching you sitting there singing softly. It is a moment of joy I would not want to have missed."

Princess smiled softly at him, and looked down with a tender twinkle in her eye. "Baby, I want you to meet the person I love most in this whole world. His name is Samuel, and he's your father. He loves you just as much as I do, and one day, he is going to teach you how to grow up strong in faith and goodness. Listen my child, listen as Mommy and Daddy sing to you." Tenderly, quietly, she began to sing, "I am a child of God, and He has sent me here . . ."

Sam started to sing with her, but memories toppled in upon him, and his voice broke. He had vivid memories of singing this precious song to his little brother the morning he had died. He had loved Jimmy with all his being. Somehow, singing it again to a child tugged at his heartstrings beyond endurance.

He stood and walked to the big piano. Softly, ever so softly, and with every fiber of love he possessed, he played the precious hymn as she sang the words to the child of their love.

In some way unknown, unrecognized, and unexplainable, something healed deep within his soul. When the music came to a reverent end, he was enriched beyond his understanding.

For Princess, this was a moment of sweet awakening. For the first time in her life it became sweet and acceptable to be a mommy. She suddenly felt free to be a tenderhearted mother who could talk to her children in loving baby talk, quietly sing songs, read nursery rhymes, and express unabashed love.

As the weeks progressed, Princess became unchained from the restraints of stuffy societal mores of the wealthy who had been her role models. In ways too important for her to understand, she evolved from a woman to a mother, and the change was liberating beyond expectation. Even though she did not understand the glorious change which had come over her, she did rejoice in its purity.

* * *

Since their marriage, Sam had been too busy to give little thought to anything other than Princess and their growing business. It came as a shock, then, when his father asked if he would come to the church. Jim, his father, had been serving as bishop of the new Wasilla ward since its creation two years ago.

The Wasilla ward boundaries extended from the city limits of Palmer to the outskirts of Fairbanks, over three hundred miles to the north. The ward extended thirty miles south, and four hundred miles east to Valdez, the new terminus of the Trans-Alaska Pipeline. With nearly twelve thousand square miles of area, their task was daunting.

Sam wasn't sure if he should be suspicious or afraid as his father closed the door behind them, and offered him a chair.

"Thanks for coming, Sam. I know you are wondering why I couldn't talk to you at home, but I wanted this to be official. I hope you don't mind."

"Sure, Dad. What do you need?"

"It's not what I need, but what the Lord needs." The Spirit began to burn in Sam's soul. He sat up straighter.

"As you know, my first counselor is moving away from Alaska. I have spent many days fasting and praying to know who the Lord has prepared to fill this position. Each time the answer came to me, I didn't have sufficient faith to accept it, I guess. Time after time I have gone back to the Lord to seek a reaffirmation of His will. At last, the Lord has confirmed His will in such a way that I am left a bit chagrined for being so slow to respond."

Sam didn't know what to say but was beginning to feel considerable suspense over his father's words. "What is it, Dad? You're making me nervous."

"I am calling Brother Linus to be my counselor. As you know, he is presently my elder's quorum president. So, I'm in need of a faithful priesthood holder to fill that position. I have submitted your name to the stake and received authority to ask you to be my new elder's quorum president. There will be an official call by a member of the stake presidency, of course. But since you're my son, I asked if I could tell you myself and was given permission to do so."

Sam's shoulders relaxed. "Wow. For a moment I had thought you were going to ask me to be your counselor. I was wondering how the people would react to that. They would probably think you did it because I was your son, not because I was who the Lord wanted."

"I think that is the very reason I have been so slow to hearken to His words. I wanted to be sure this call was correct. Now that I know it is, I am anxious to work with you. Whether or not the people accept you in this position is up to them, and largely up to how you labor in your calling."

"It is an odd situation. I don't think I've ever heard of a son being an elder's quorum president to his father."

"Me either. Well, will you do it?"

"Yes. Certainly. However, I want to talk to Princess first. I already know how she'll feel. But let me talk to her, and I'll let you know."

"I understand. I'm proud of you, son, and I know you will make a faithful elder's quorum president. If you accept, I'd like to put you to work immediately. You could be set apart by a member of the stake presidency this coming Sunday. Thank you for being a faithful member, and a wonderful son."

Sam had forgotten what it felt like to have the mantle of authority settle upon his shoulders. On his mission, his authority had been limited, and the burden was light to be borne. The mantle of responsibility of being the elder's quorum president was a burden of considerable consequence.

His first task was to find two brethren to serve as his counselors. He studied the list of elders and was dismayed to find that out of nearly ninety names, all but six of them inactive. Of those six, all but one already held responsible positions in the ward. The sixth came to church but refused to accept any positions. Most of the ninety had no addresses or phone numbers. They were merely names on a list. He prayerfully selected two brethren he had never met, drove to their homes, and succeeded in calling them to be his counselors. From the day of their calling, both brethren remained stalwart in the church and faithfully labored with him in the daunting task of creating a brotherhood from a list of unwilling names.

* * *

The rebel soldiers had been ordered to let all leave except Donavon and his family. In their haste to capture the man responsible for leading the retaliatory raid into their own villages, the generals had not identified Melody as Donavon's daughter. She had moved out nearly two years prior, and her presence was unexpected. Several of those attacking their home were former employees, who recognized her but said nothing, fearing implied guilt by prior association. Her release and subsequent escape from the country cost at least three of these former so-called friends, and one officer, their lives.

Their orders were to search all those leaving the farm to ensure they were taking nothing valuable with them. When it came Melody's turn to be searched, their attention turned from finding valuables, to having their hands on her body. As repugnant as their rough groping was, it was totally ineffective, and she left with a small collection of gems embedded in a plastic clip in her hair. It was not a lot, but it would just be sufficient to see her to England.

Donavon had had many friends in South Africa—mostly people who had profited substantially from his frenzied purchases during the years of his wealth. She quietly contacted these until she found one willing to help her—for a price of course.

Melody booked passage on a steamer. She did not have a passport and could not pass through customs at any airport. Discrete inquiries found a captain of a small freighter who would take anyone anywhere for a price. Once he learned she was a refugee from Rhodesia, his sympathies were aroused, and he accommodated her comfortably on the long voyage. He, however, did not lower his price.

The passage to England was uneventful except that she had nothing but her violin and the clothing she wore. She was forced to wash her dress in the sink in her cabin and let it dry before she could once again emerge. During the two-week voyage she spent many sweaty days cooped up inside her cabin waiting for her long black dress to dry in the humid heat.

Her arrival in England was unceremonious. She simply walked off the gangway and down a narrow street. There was no one there to meet her, no one she could contact, and nowhere to go. It was true that Marcia was in England, but Melody was not even sure what city she was in. Since Marcia had joined the Church, she had moved to a new apartment closer to the chapel, which had been some thirty miles away in a different city. Which city, Melody could not even guess.

Melody's only money was a few South African rand. Even in a large bank, it was difficult to exchange rand for pounds. No bank anywhere would exchange less than one hundred rand, and she had far less than that. They were, for all intents and purposes, worthless pieces of paper. When she had asked the captain of the ship to exchange them for any amount of local currency, he had laughed at her, and told her there were better ways for a beautiful young woman to make money, "If ye know wha' I mean, missie," he said as he winked at her. More than merely leaving, she had fled from his ship in disgust.

Melody's only real advantage was in the simple fact that they had landed in England in the morning hours. She had eaten her last meal aboard ship a few hours ago, and would not be in desperate need of either food or lodging for most of the day. It was not much, but it would have to be enough.

The ship had landed her in the port of Swansea, Wales, a sizable city, yet not a usual destination for ships bearing passengers. As a result, the waterfront was a narrow strip of piers and warehouses jammed against the ocean. It was an ideal location for anyone without a passport because there were no customs agents within three hundred miles.

A few blocks inland all trace of the waterfront vanished into a dirty slum. Melody kept to the busiest streets she could find, and felt very grateful she was not making this foot journey at night. Many people stared, a few asked questions, several even offered directions. Not a soul threatened her. She walked swiftly toward the busier part of the city, not sure what she planned to do, but compelled to escape the squalor of this section of the city.

In a short time she began passing small shops, clothing stores, and other signs of culture. By the time she found the main business district she was very tired, thirsty, hungry, and disheartened. She had been able to keep her courage up while she had a goal, but now she was without a clue as to what she should do.

The young, frightened refugee sat on a bench near a small park and kicked off her shoes. Her feet ached from the long, hot walk. She watched the bustle of the big city, and studied the faces of people walking by. Though fearful, she was very glad to be safely among people who had no intention of either exploiting her desperation, capitalizing on her beauty, or arresting her for her political leanings.

While she rested, Melody took stock of her assets. They were pitifully few. She had nothing, knew no one, and had no passport, no work papers, no money, and no way of getting any.

She was unwilling to prostitute her body for money, and could not think of anything else she had except her violin.

Thinking of the precious instrument brought her a concern, and she opened it for the first time since boarding the ship. She had packed it with several bags of table salt to keep it dry. These she pulled from the case and set aside. She lifted the instrument and turned it over to inspect it. Thoughts of having to sell or pawn it filled her with sadness. The afternoon sun reflected off the highly polished surface in rich reds and browns. When she was satisfied it was in perfect condition, she plucked at the strings to satisfy herself that they had not grown limp from moisture.

"Do you know any Mozart?" she heard a man's voice ask her. She looked up to see an old, kindly-faced gentleman leaning on a cane. He was not much taller than she, and spoke with what seemed to be a German or Swiss accent. She quickly concluded his question was completely innocent, and meant nothing more than the actual words he spoke.

"I do," she replied. Then as if struck by her instructor's baton, she suddenly realized what he was asking. He wanted to hear some Mozart, not just learn whether she knew any.

She stood slowly, looked around self-consciously, and quietly tightened the strings until they were in pitch. She suspended her bow over the strings without any sure idea what she would play.

At that moment a lively gavotte by Mozart, well loved, and oft played, came to mind. It was too showy, she thought, and tried to force it from her mind, but it persisted. Without any other thought than to quickly get this over with, she drew the bow quickly downward. The music danced out into the park, its clarion tones and obvious quality apparent to everyone who heard. As she played, other passersby walked up slowly. Initially she played simply to fulfill his request, but shortly she was playing for the simple joy of the music, and for the great peace it filtered into her soul.

The gavotte ended happily, and people clapped. Melody opened her eyes to see about ten people applauding. She curtsied politely, which looked very old fashioned in England and brought a chuckle of delight from those watching.

The old man who had requested the piece stepped forward and dropped a five-pound note into her open case. She looked at it in surprise and almost handed it back. She didn't want him to pay her for her music. She had accommodated his request as a favor.

As if he had just purchased a ticket to a concert, he requested another piece by Strauss, the beautiful Emperor Waltz. It was a piece she had played many times, though never as a solo. However, it was well within her range of talent to improvise as she played. She played with fervor, and a man and woman began waltzing on the grass.

Others dropped in paper money and coins, and made their requests. She had so much fun playing for such a happy and appreciative audience, that she had not noticed her case filling with bills and coins. The older gentleman who had first asked her to play stepped forward and stacked most of the bills, leaving a few in the case. He folded them carefully, and handed them to her.

"Never leave too many in the case, and always leave just a few. Come here during lunch time and afternoon to early evening only. Never stay after seven in the evening. There's a clean little hotel called The Royal Roost several blocks north on Queens Avenue, with a little cafe in the lobby. I'll come check on you tomorrow." So saying, he bowed slightly, took one step backward, turned, and walked quickly away. Though the walking stick clicked on the pavement, it seemed as if he hardly needed it. His instructions surprised her, yet she was grateful for the advice, and did exactly as he suggested.

The lunch hour ended shortly thereafter, and people simply stopped walking in the park. She counted her little pile of bills and was amazed to find over one hundred pounds in various notes. With a racing heart she walked north and found the hotel and café. She ate a simple meal, hired a small room, and fell onto her bed in exhaustion. That evening Melody played from five to seven, exactly as the old gentleman had suggested. During that time she made another 126 pounds. That evening the park was alive with jugglers, mimes, musicians, pundits of politics, and hucksters of religion. She was in good company, and enjoyed the fact that she was one of many doing the same thing.

The following day the old gentleman reappeared as promised. He paid her another five pounds after she had played several of his requests. He nodded, smiled and limped away without a word.

That evening she started early, eager to find the best spot. She played with extra fervor, and found her take growing larger. When seven o'clock came, people were still listening, and she played on until nearly eight.

After finishing the final number, Melody noticed that at least half of those listening were ragged young men who were looking at her in the wrong way. She quickly packed her instrument and started away. For a moment she was lost in the evening rush of people, but when she turned onto Queens Avenue, they were there before her. She turned around and found herself facing more of them.

* * *

As the mantle of his office fell upon Sam, something unexpected occurred—it was the beginnings of the sure understanding of the Lord's will concerning His quorum.

Sam began to exercise himself in obedience to the Spirit's direction, and small miracles began to occur. After all, it was the Lord's priesthood, and however essential his calling as elder's quorum president might be, it was subservient to He whose priesthood it was. As he obeyed, Sam's faith grew in the Lord's willingness to use him as His servant and the miracles followed.Friday evening found Sam driving home from work. It was late, and he was tired. It was his habit to visit a different member of the ward each day on his drive home from work.

Even though their ward area was immense, those for whom Sam actually had addresses lived within an hour's drive from his home. His ambition was to visit a new member of his quorum every day on the way home from work. However, because he was especially tired this evening, he had convinced himself to go straight home. The long shadows of summer were warming the verdant green landscape as Sam made his way home. He drove slowly, enjoying the idea of coming home an hour earlier and surprising Princess. As he approached the turn-off to a small subdivision he felt a sudden urging to turn in. He signaled, slowed, and drove into the subdivision. Under the urging of the Spirit he turned left, then right, and then left into a driveway. He was pleased to see the name of a family he recognized. He had not previously known where they lived. This would be a pleasant visit, since they were active in the church, and stalwarts in the ward.

As he approached the house it felt cold and dark, as if someone had left a window open to a winter breeze. He rang the bell and waited. When she finally answered, it was with an ironic tone in her voice.

"Oh, Brother Mahoy," Sister Williams said. "I'm surprised to see you here. What can I do for you?"

"Sister Williams, I'm here because the Lord sent me. May I come in?"

She hesitated. "Well, sure. Brother Williams is in the living room," she said, gesturing in that direction. Sam walked the three steps into the living room to find Brother Williams sitting on the sofa hunched over. He stood slowly as Sam entered and came around the coffee table to shake his hand. There was an atmosphere of tension and sadness in the air, which chilled Sam.

"President Mahoy, to what do we owe this visit? Here, take a seat," he said, pointing toward a large chair.

"You owe it to the Lord, Brother Williams. I was on my way home and was directed to swing in. You will have to tell me why I'm here."

Brother Williams glanced at his wife, and then sat back on the couch, resuming the cowered posture Sam had seen upon first entering. "Well," Sister Williams began. "Perhaps it's just as well. We sent the kids away for the evening so we could have time to ourselves. We have been sitting here all afternoon discussing our divorce."

An electric moment came and went. "I see," Sam replied in surprise, then suddenly was filled with the Spirit, energized with truth, and the mantle of his office. "As you are aware, I am your quorum president, and have priesthood stewardship over your family. I know that sometimes couples split up, and sometimes it's not only justifiable, but also necessary. I don't know what has brought you to this dilemma, and don't mean to be judgmental in any way. However, since the Lord interrupted my journey home to come visit you at this critical moment, how do you suppose He views your plans to divorce?"

It was a startling question, and Sister Williams lowered her head, her eyes pooling with tears. Sam thought her reaction was one of sadness, but quickly changed that estimate to defiance and frustration.

Brother Williams straightened as if a new hope had suddenly entered him. "I would say He doesn't want us to split up," he said with conviction.

"Why do you say that?" Sam asked.

"Well, he wouldn't send you over here to urge us to divorce, or to help us break up. It could only be that he disapproves."

"What do you think, Sister Williams?" Sam asked quietly.

She seemed stunned into silence. Her mouth moved, but no words came out. The Spirit moved within him, and he knew it had been her idea, and upon her insistence they were considering divorce. She wanted out and was reluctant to have that plan aborted.

"Sister Williams, do you mind if I ask you a question or two?" Sam asked. Without looking up she shook her head from side to side.

"Do you love the Lord?"

Her head snapped up, then lowered slowly. With fervor she said, "I do."

"Do you think He loves you?"

"Oh yes, I know He does," she replied with equal emphasis.

"If He asked you to give up your life for Him, would you do it?"

"In a heartbeat," she said, and she meant it.

"Would your eternal reward be better or worse for having given your all to obey His will?"

"Better by far," she replied.

"Let me ask you again. In the light of His having sent me here to your home, what is His attitude toward your divorce?"

"I think he is repelled and sickened by the idea," she said.

The intensity of her answer surprised both Sam and Brother Williams.

"Regardless of whether you understand why, are you willing to have faith in His love for you, and obey Him in this matter of your divorce?"

"Do you really think we can be happy?" she asked pointedly.

"That isn't the question. The question is one of obedience. Even so, do you trust Him? Do you really think He would send you down a path designed to make you unhappy?" Sam asked with tenderness. She did not answer his question.

Sam stood and walked to the kitchen, picked up a wooden chair, and set it near the sofa.

"Sister Williams, I have a blessing for you, if you'll receive it." She looked startled, then stood and walked slowly to the chair. She glanced up at him before she sat. Tears streaked down her cheeks. Her face was sober, resigned, and fearful.

Sam placed his hands on her head and waited for the glow of the Spirit to fill him. After a long moment it came upon him so powerfully it gave him a sense of great courage. It took him a moment to recognize that it was courage he was feeling. This was the second time he had felt this empowering emotion in response to the Holy Spirit. The first time had been on a train in the bush lands of Botswana, expecting to die at any moment.

"Sister Anna Williams, in the name of Jesus Christ, and by His holy priesthood, I give you a blessing this day according to the will of God, and under the direction of His Holy Spirit. For your sake, and as a witness unto you of the source of your anger and adverse will, I rebuke the power of evil within you and command it to depart.

"Sister Williams, you are a precious daughter of Heavenly Father, beloved of Him, and glorious in His sight. All God's children, with the exception of Christ himself, have at times succumbed to the influences of darkness. This is not an indictment against your goodness, or an indication of your worth, but is a result of poor choices on your part. You have long listened to the anger within you until you have accepted this anger as your own. Yet, you are not an angry spirit, and have been tricked into thinking of your anger as justified, or worthy, at times, even righteous.

"Feel the liberty of being free, and rejoice in the purity of your native sweetness. It has been many years since you last felt it this pure and strong. I admonish you that from this day, and on throughout your life, that you rebuke this dark influence whenever it presents itself. Never again yield to its fury, for the choice is yours.

"Without doubt, and according to divine law, it will return. Satan and his angels have a divinely decreed right to infest our minds and hearts. Your anger will return after a brief absence caused by this blessing. But know that it is within your power to keep it from taking residence in your soul again. The choice was, is, and forever will be, yours.

"Your lack of happiness has nothing to do with your marriage but is a function of your yielding to the influences of darkness. Awaken your spirit, put on your beautiful garments, adorn your spirit with flowers and sweet perfume, and go forth henceforth in the glow of your premortal beauty. For great you were, and great you are, and glorious shall be your reward hereafter if you heed the counsel of this day. "I seal upon you this blessing according to divine guidance, and according to the stewardship of my office, in the name of Jesus Christ, amen."

Sam hadn't realized until he said the word amen that she was sobbing. She stood to find her husband standing before her with open arms. She fell into them with a sob. Sam heard her whispered apologies as Brother Williams soothed his wife with words of love.

"Brother Williams," Sam said at the appropriate moment. "It's your turn." For just a moment Brother Williams looked surprised, as if there was no need. Yet, there was much power in the room, and he nodded in submission and took the chair.

"Brother Williams, in the name of Jesus Christ, and according to His will, I also give you a blessing, a promise, and a warning. You are not blameless in the darkness that has overcome your home. This is your stewardship, and you have walked away in fear and resignation when you should have been fearless in doing that which is right. You have let your fear of your wife's anger drive you from your position to preside in love over this home. In the name of Jesus Christ I command you to reclaim it. It is your right to preside, and you must act in that responsibility in order to be exalted. Even though this anger originated from your wife, your response to it has been far less valiant than it should have been.

"You are a noble son of God, and a spirit of intelligence and unusual faith. Your love for your wife extends beyond this world, and has literally existed for millennia. Had you allowed your timidity and fear to end this love relationship that has existed so long, and has been a delight to your Heavenly Father, you would not have found true happiness in this world, nor in the world to come. My visit here today has been as much to save you from this eternal blunder, as to save your love from destruction.

"Arise, awake, and stand in the office where you have been called. Love your wife without reservation or qualification. Expect nothing, give everything. Teach your children by precept and example. Perform your church duties faithfully, and you shall open your eyes one day in the celestial kingdom of our God surrounded by your glorified wife and children and loved ones who shall for an eternity rise up and call you blessed.

"I seal upon you these blessings in the name of Jesus Christ, amen." Sam raised his hands from Brother Williams's head and walked directly to the door. They did not notice him leave as they held one another and wept. Sam basked in the glow of the Spirit for days thereafter. It was the first time he had experienced the pure joy of perfect service. The distinction had never occurred to him before. Always before he had done the best he could. This time, for the first time, he had done precisely as Jesus Christ would have done had He been there Himself. He had acted with absolute honor, and rendered that service which is perfect and eternal. Had Christ Himself visited this troubled family, He would have done precisely the same. For the first time Sam's service had truly been in the name of Jesus Christ, and it thrilled him beyond comprehension.

* * *

"Princess, can we talk a minute?" Sam asked as he wrapped his arms around her waist from behind. They were just finishing cleaning up the kitchen. Sam enjoyed working in the kitchen with her. This kind of surprised him, because he had hated it as a child. But there were two great paybacks for helping Princess. First, he got to be around her that much longer. Second, no matter how many times he helped, she never seemed to expect it, and was always truly grateful.

"Love to," she said as she dried her hands.

They walked to the sofa facing the piano and sat so that their knees were touching. Sam was thoughtful for a moment before speaking. "I learned something today, and I wanted to share it with you while it was fresh on my mind."

"Tell me about it," she replied with interest.

"Well, I made a stop at a member's home under the direction of the Holy Spirit. It was wonderful."

"You've done that before," she observed. "I know how hard you try to be completely obedient to the promptings you receive."

"Well, I do most of the time," he said. "But tonight something was different. It was almost as if I was a spectator there. I went in, and the Spirit was so strong that I knew exactly what to do, and what to say. I gave them both blessings, and the words were profound and I know will be honored by the Lord. The startling thing is that as I was leaving I had this overwhelming sense of power from the Lord. I have never felt such power."

"What kind of power do you mean?"

"It was the kind of power that comes from absolute faith. If God would have commanded me to move a mountain I would have simply turned and ordered it to move. And, it would have. That's the thing that's so startling. I know for an absolute fact that it would have moved. If He would have told me to raise the dead, or stop the world from turning, or to call down a pillar of fire, it would have happened. I have never felt faith like that. It was absolute."

"Wow," she said as she placed a hand on his knee. "I've never felt anything like that."

"Until tonight, I hadn't either. But actually, that isn't the part I wanted to talk about."

"There's something better?" she asked, a little astonished.

"I don't think better, just important. You see, I know why it happened. I know why this absolute faith came to me."

"I'd like to hear what that was. I want to try it."

"It was because for the briefest moment in time I was absolutely obedient. I had placed my life, my will, my whole being into His hands. I have flawlessly obeyed every prompting I have received for weeks. And as a result of walking in the Spirit so closely day and night for weeks, I finally arrived at the point where I could do precisely as Christ would have done had he been there himself."

Princess laid her hand atop his and looked into his eyes. "I think I understand what you are saying. It's kind of like becoming so obedient that your acts actually become identical with what the Savior would do if he were there himself."

Sam nodded, leaned back in the sofa and crossed his legs loosely. After a moment he said. "That's exactly the way I see it. It was fantastic, Princess! It was the most spiritually fulfilling experience of my life. I have finally tasted the sweet fruits of service, and it is sweet beyond my ability to comprehend it. It has filled me with an overwhelming desire to have this blessing again, and again."

"I have no doubt that you will," she replied with surety.

"I hope so. The interesting thing is how difficult it seemed to achieve, and how many small obediences it took to qualify for this great blessing. However, now that I have experienced it, it seems so natural and beautiful, and simple. It makes me wonder why I took so long getting to this point." He studied his hands for a moment before continuing. "It occurs to me that this is the fullest meaning of the phrase, 'In the name of Jesus Christ.'"

"That's an interesting thought. I'll bet it is," Princess agreed. She loved having these conversations with Sam not only for the spiritual blessing they were to her, but because she got to experience the most profoundly significant part of her spouse.

She did everything she could think of to make these discussions last longer. "We seem to say 'In the name of Jesus Christ,' for about every act we perform in the Church."

"That's true," Sam responded thoughtfully. He interlaced his fingers behind his head and stared at the ceiling. "I'm sure the way it's used in the Church is completely acceptable to Heavenly Father. But, it makes me wonder if that phrase doesn't actually carry a much heavier burden of meaning. And, if it does, it makes me wonder if we shouldn't be seeking to fulfill its higher implications."

Sam's voice took on a tone of wonderment. "The way we use it it's almost like saying 'Okay, that's all I wanted to say,' rather than, 'I have just spoken by revelation, and the words I used were from Jesus Christ Himself.' There's a big difference between the two."

Princess glanced at her husband, and then returned her gaze to the highly polished side of the grand piano. She could see their combined reflections in the curve of its glossy blackness. Their reflections almost seemed to merge into a single image. It felt symbolic to her at that moment. "I remember wondering about this very thing when I was taking the missionary lessons. Can't remember the missionary's name who taught me, but he made a comment that may be valid."

"You never can tell what a missionary might say in the heat of a teaching frenzy," Sam said with a tone of feigned cynicism.

"True, so true," she agreed in mock seriousness. "Anyway, that nameless missionary said that many things were true on various levels. He said that even in the Church things were understood on different levels, and each level could be true.

"Even the child who stands up and closes a talk he read in the name of Jesus Christ, even when he didn't understand a word he just read, is still speaking in Christ's name."

"I believe that," Sam allowed. "I'm just concerned that it has taken me so many years to gain a higher understanding of the meaning of those words. In reality, to hear someone truly, correctly say 'In the name of Jesus Christ' at the end of a talk, should literally send chills of spiritual ecstasy up our spines. We should correctly interpret that benediction to mean 'I have spoken as Christ would have had He been here Himself.' To correctly make such a statement would have a profound effect upon every listener."

Princess scooted toward him and laid her head on his chest. He wrapped an arm around her and kissed the crown of her head. "I get those sometimes," she said softly.

"What?"

"Thrills of spiritual ecstasy up my spine," she replied just as softly.

"Really? When?" He laid his cheek on the top of her head. "Whenever I think of spending eternity with you."

THE THRESHING FLOOR

"What do you want?" Melody demanded as bravely as possible, her voice tremulous with fear.

"We wan' yer money, sweetie," one of them said.

"An, maybe we wan' somethin' moah too," a bigger one announced with a grin. "You are about the prettiest bloody organ grindah ah've evah seen. It's obvious yer not from around heah, an, ya didn' know ya had te pay us, in order te play in our pahk. But, ya do, see?"

"I didn't know that. I honestly didn't," Melody said quickly, terrified. "I can pay. How much do you want? I'll pay you, just please don't hurt me."

"Oh, ye'll bloody pay, missie. But, ya messed up, an' ya gotta pay it all, or we gonna bust up yeh little fittle, and have some othah fun with ya. So give it all ovah. Now!" he shouted.

Melody jumped and dug handfuls of bills from the pockets of her dress. She was about to hand them over when upon sudden impulse, she tossed them into the air. The bills scattered in the light evening breeze. Her attackers cursed, and dove after the substantial quantity of fluttering money. Melody turned instantly and ran the opposite direction.

"Hey!" someone shouted. "She's gettin' away! Scooter! Devin! Catch the wench. We ain't done wi' 'er!" he ordered. Instantly, two of them sprang after her. One glance over her shoulder told her they were significantly faster than she, and her heart fell. She raced toward the nearest intersection where she could see cars passing in the approaching dusk. She knew she could not possibly beat them there.

A mere two paces separated them when a side door in one of the buildings opened and an old gentleman stepped backwards into the street.

"Good night, Melvin," he called into the building, and pulled the door closed with a bang. He turned just in time to catch her in his arms. She nearly knocked him over, but he spun around nimbly and kept them both standing. As he spun around his cane flew into the air and came down hard on the right shoulder of one of her pursuers. The action was so sudden it appeared an accident. The young thug fell to the ground groaning, clutching his shoulder.

"Oh! So sorry!" he exclaimed, bending over the young man on the ground. "I was in such a dither to have this handsome young lady crash into me, that I'm afraid I've dashed you with my cane. Are you all right?" he asked earnestly.

The ruffian still standing took a dancing step toward him, his hands punctuating the air in jabs of anger. "Hey, old man! You beta' walk away from this, oah' . . . what the bloo—!" His curse was cut off when the old man's cane flashed out and cracked loudly against his left knee. The street thug crumpled to the cobblestones with a yelp.

"I'm so sorry! I'm just mortified. It seems my cane doesn't like you. Perhaps you'd best leave, so my cane doesn't express its unhappiness with you any further, hmm?" he said in a voice of perfect calmness.

With the sudden appearance of this unexpected help, Melody's fear had turned from fear for herself, to fear for the old gentleman. However, upon seeing his composure, and the speed and precision with which his able cane expressed its dislike for her assailants, she grew calmer.

"Let's leave these gentlemen to nurse their wounds, shall we?" he said casually to her. He took her elbow and they walked slowly away as if taking a stroll to enjoy the cool of the evening.

He did not look back, but merely chatted amiably about the weather until they reached the intersection and turned toward her hotel.

"I thought I suggested you not stay in the park after seven," he said as pleasantly as he had discussed the weather. It wasn't until that moment that she recognized him as the same gentleman who had first asked her to play Mozart in the park.

He was dressed differently tonight, and was wearing a hat.

"It's you!" Melody said in amazement, looping her arm a little tighter around his.

"You didn't recognize me? I'm abashed," he winked, then chuckled happily. "You do remember my instructions?" he asked.

"I'm sorry. I guess I got greedy, and stayed longer. I am sorry," she replied contritely, almost the same as she might have if he had been her father.

"Well, no harm done, except you lost all your money. I see you did retain your instrument," he noted happily, indicating the violin case still securely tucked under her arm.

"Yes, I'm very lucky to not have lost it. I really have no other . . . ," she stopped, embarrassed to admit it was her only hope for survival.

"You do play so very well," the mysterious gentleman said cheerfully as they stopped at the bottom of the steps to her hotel.

"There you are my dear. Now, if you like, there's another park exactly four blocks east of here. I suggest you perform there tomorrow, and then come back here the following day. Follow that pattern, and don't get greedy, and all will be well. Are you quite able to make it to your room?"

"I am. I'm truly indebted to you, sir." She paused, cocking her head to one side, partly in apology, yet also in interest.

"I don't even know your name. I'm Melody, Melody MacUlvaney." She offered her hand, which he took in a warm, sure grip. She was surprised to find his hands strong and steady. It seemed inappropriate to his age and heightened her curiosity regarding him.

His smile was warm, his voice cheery. "Melody. What a beautiful and fitting name for one who plays so beautifully, and who is so beautiful as well. I am thoroughly charmed to meet you. Well, Melody, I bid you a very good evening," he said. Lifting his bowler from his head, he nodded formally and turned back the direction they had come.

"Good evening, and thanks again," she called to him. Without turning around, he raised his cane in the air, and twirled it slightly in response. It was almost as if he were saying "no big deal." It made her chuckle.

It wasn't until she was safely inside her room that Melody realized he had not told her his name.

The old gentleman met her each morning regardless of which park she played in. After four days she had sufficient money to move on. Her most pressing need was to find her sister. She still had no idea how to accomplish that.

* * *

Princess went into labor late the afternoon of July 3, 1977. They rushed to the hospital in Palmer, a short thirty-minute drive away. They were admitted to the maternity ward, checked in, and assigned a room in a matter of minutes. Princess changed into a gown and settled in for a long, frustrating wait.

Sam's mother arrived minutes later, and walked past Sam with little more than a concerned smile. She placed her hand on her daughter-in-law's forehead, smiled at her in a knowing way, and was thereafter in charge. Even the nurses bowed to her authority. Sam held onto his wife's other hand and spooned chunks of ice into her mouth. It was the extent of his duties. In a way, he was glad for the calm confidence his mother brought into the room. He certainly knew Princess appreciated it. Beneath his wife's calm exterior, she was terrified.

In another way, in a way too instinctual to even understand, he resented it. This was his baby being born, his night of joy and fear, wonder of wonders, and he was reduced to spooning ice as if he had suddenly become a moron barely able to do anything more complicated. It was almost as if he was the criminal who had caused his beloved wife this pain in her life, and he was not to be trusted with anything more important, lest he mess that up too.

To his astonishment, the more intense the labor became, and the more his beloved cried out in pain through clenched teeth, the more he felt isolated from the only woman he had ever loved. It was as if the very process of birth climaxed in an irony of rejection of the poor fool who had contributed to the pregnancy.

But Sam wanted with all his heart to be there and knew his feelings were childish, no matter how many millennia men had been feeling them. Every time she became paralyzed in pain and then fell back on her bed in sweaty exhaustion, he felt as if another thread had been torn from his heart. The only thing that kept tears from coursing down his own cheeks was the odd need he felt to present a courageous face.

Time became a blur of Princess's pain, his tangled emotions, and ice cubes. When he finally realized something was wrong, he was the last one in the room to comprehend it. The clock on the wall said 8:02 a.m. Princess had been in hard labor for sixteen hours. Yet the baby was not ready to be born. The heart monitor on the baby showed it was in distress. Doctors began coming through the door with increasing frequency, then huddling outside to consult one another.

Finally, a woman in a white coat walked through the door and approached Princess's bed. Sam stood as she entered. Somehow, everyone knew this was a pivotal moment, and this new woman was here for something important.

"Princess. Mr. Mahoy. My name is Dr. Sally Green," she said in a conversational tone. "Before the next contraction begins, I need to talk to you."

Princess pushed a pillow behind her head so she sat a little more upright. Her face was ashen, her hair soaked with sweat.

Her hands trembled as she shook the doctor's hand. "What's going to happen?" was her only question to the doctor.

"You are not progressing as expected. The baby should have been born by now. Both you and the baby have reached a critical stage. You both may be in shock. I have consulted with your attending physician, and we feel it is time to deliver your baby by cesarean. Do you know what this means?"

"Yes," Princess replied calmly, though Sam thought there was an increase of fear in her eyes. "I know what a cesarean operation is. Do you know how to do them?"

"I am an obstetric surgeon. I have performed many cesareans. There is nothing for you to worry about. The hospital is equipped for the operation, and I am ready to perform it. All I need is your consent and we will begin. You will be given anesthesia. You will wake up in what will seem to you like minutes later, and it will be all over."

"That sounds wonderful," Princess said weakly.

"Good. Let's begin then," Dr. Green said as she turned to give instructions to the two nurses standing behind her.

"No," Princess said emphatically. The room immediately fell into heavy silence.

"Excuse me? What did you say?" Dr. Green asked in a shocked tone.

"I said—no."

"But, Mrs. Mahoy, if we don't do this procedure, I cannot guarantee your baby's safety. I think it is essential for your own welfare as well."

"I'm sure it is," Princess replied wearily.

"Then, why do you object to the procedure?"

"I don't object to the procedure," Princess began, but her reply was cut off by the onslaught of a tremendous labor pain. She doubled over, then relaxed and puffed through her teeth. The contraction lasted nearly two minutes, which seemed to all present like two eternities.

"Please continue to explain your objection," Dr. Green urged as soon as Princess fell back onto the sweaty sheets.

"I don't object to the procedure. I object to you doing it," Princess replied, her voice small but determined.

"I am the only qualified surgeon in this hospital. It's a small hospital, and there is no one else here. I don't understand."

"I object on the grounds that you perform elective abortions. I don't want the same hands who take life from babies, to give life to my baby. I don't mean to be rude, but I am not willing to have you operate on me, or my baby."

Dr. Green walked up to the side of the bed and leaned over until she and Princess were eye to eye. "If I don't operate, I believe you and your baby will die. I'm sorry you object to my abortion practice. In my opinion it is immaterial. We don't have time to debate the moral issues surrounding abortions. You and your baby don't have any time left. I suggest you set aside your prejudice and let me help you. Do you understand?"

Princess did not blink an eye as she replied. "It's you who does not understand, Dr. Green. This baby inside me is no more precious than any of the hundreds you have killed in the pursuit of making money. If I let you deliver this baby, you will walk away feeling justified in your heart because you saved one. Because of that, you will go on to kill more, perhaps hundreds or thousands more. Don't you see? I can't let my baby's life grant you justification for killing others. If my baby's death will save a thousand other little babies, then it's a small price."

Sam was nearly beside himself with panic, and pushed himself between the doctor and his wife. His first impulse was to beg her to reconsider, to let the doctor help, not to sacrifice herself in a battle she could not win. His objections were stilled when he saw the calm determination in her eyes. Anything he might have said was swept away as another contraction gripped her.

"I regret your decision. If I had time, I would seek a judge's order to force you to let me operate. But there is no time. I will remain in the hospital for a time if you change your mind," Dr. Green said, and turned to leave.

Princess spoke through teeth clamped tight in pain. Her voice was nearly impossible to understand, yet the message was heard very clearly by the doctor. "Perhaps in a short time I will meet our Eternal Judge personally. The idea brings me peace. One of these days you will meet Him, too, and it terrifies me for you."

Her words brought the doctor to an abrupt halt. She stood there for the briefest time as if frozen in midstride. Just as suddenly, she lifted her chin and left the room.

As soon as she was gone everyone began speaking at once. Sam, his mom, and nurses all began pleading with Princess. She simply ignored them, a look of ashen calm on her face. One of the nurses began weeping and rushed from the room. Another wiped Princess's forehead gently, then walked slowly from the room.

"I'll be right back," Sam whispered to Princess, who seemed not to hear, and hurried from the room. He found a pay phone and made a dozen calls. His request was the same every time.

They began arriving only a few minutes later. About the third person to enter was his father, Jim Mahoy. Others came, many others. Less than thirty minutes after his first call almost a dozen priesthood holders surrounded Princess's bed. Sam was moved upon to ask his father to be the voice in the blessing.

Princess smiled as they placed their hands upon her and upon one another until they were all joined in the power of the priesthood.

Jim began in a whisper. "Princess, beloved daughter of God. We the elders of Israel combine our faith, and in the name of the Holy Messiah, and by the power of the Melchizedek Priesthood, we bless you with this one great blessing. You and your babies will survive this ordeal, and all will be as it should be. I seal this blessing upon you in the name of Jesus Christ, amen."

A chorus of amens was interrupted by the abrupt opening of the door to the small room. Dr. Green scuttled into the room with another doctor in tow by the sleeve. She plowed through the press of priesthood holders until she stood beside the bed.

"This is Dr. Green, my husband. He is a pediatric physician and has performed many delicate operations. He has never done an abortion and is philosophically opposed to them. He has assisted me in many cesareans and has agreed to do it while I direct his every move. I will stand back and assist only. Will that satisfy your objection?" She sounded breathless, angry, and frustrated all at once. Her husband looked as if he had just been abducted by aliens.

A collective sigh of relief went up from the overfilled room. "No," Princess replied breathlessly.

"Why not?" the woman demanded angrily. "I won't be doing the operation, just assisting."

"Because your soul is still in jeopardy. You learn nothing. You still feel vindicated, and you still perform abortions. Nothing has changed."

"I can't stand here and let you and your baby die!"

"Babies," Sam's father corrected.

"What?" at least four voices asked simultaneously.

"I said, there is more than one baby at risk. Babies. She is carrying twins."

"How could you know that?"

"I learned it in the blessing. Twins," he said with absolute surety.

Dr. Green had a look of panic on her face. "If that's true, it's even worse. I couldn't live with myself if I let you and your babies die. It isn't right!"

"Why are my babies any different? Women who opt for an abortion chose their baby's death. I choose the same for my own reasons. It's the same thing."

"It isn't the same!" Dr. Green objected loudly. "What you are doing just isn't right."

Princess's voice was breathy, barely a whisper. "Explain it to me. Why isn't it right?"

"Because your babies have a right to—" She stopped short.

"They have the right to live." Princess said. "I know they do, and I want that for them. But so do the thousands of others you will kill in your practice. Don't you see they all have the right to live?"

"This is not the right time for philosophy!" Dr. Green shouted. "You have very little time left."

"I have an eternity left. It's you who are out of time."

Tears began to spill down the doctor's cheek. "I don't want to be responsible for your death. I couldn't live with myself."

"I don't want to be responsible for the death of countless more. I couldn't live with myself," Princess replied, her strength gone. Another contraction gripped her, but she was too weak to deal with it and simply laid back, her eyes rolling up into her head. She had now been in labor nearly twenty hours.

"I will make you a deal," the doctor said loudly, hoping to get through to Princess.

Princess replied without opening her eyes. "You must make it with God. I will know when it is enough."

The doctor pushed herself away from the bed in frustration, spun around, and walked toward the door plowing into people with every step. She turned and returned to the bed in the same manner.

"Okay," she said.

"Whatever your deal is, it's not enough," Princess replied after a moment.

The doctor threw up her hands and repeated her assault on those in the room with greater energy. She stopped at the far side of the room, and placed her head in her hands.

Everyone waited with pounding hearts. All knew, including Dr. Green, that it was the final time she could make her arrangements with God. There was no more time for Princess and her babies. Finally she walked slowly back to Princess's bed. Time seemed to stand still, as if hours had passed in terrible waiting.

"Princess," she asked quietly. "Is it enough?" Princess remained quiet, almost as if she had not heard.

After a long moment she slowly moved her lips. "It is enough," they formed, almost without sound.

Dr. Green came to life, and began ordering people like a war general. In less than two minutes Princess was under anesthesia and being prepped for the operation. The last thing Dr. Green said to Sam as she bolted past him was, "I'm afraid we have waited too long."

Before the double doors slammed behind her she heard him say, "God will guide you. She will live."

The doctor stopped and turned back toward him. She nodded before disappearing beyond. When he had said it he knew it with absolute surety.

As soon as the doctor disappeared, doubt began to assail him.

* * *

Saturday morning Melody's kindly old friend stood and listened to her entire morning concert. Afterwards he gave her ten pounds, roughly thirty US dollars. As people began to drift away he remained. It pleased her, for over the last few days she had begun to realize how much she owed him. She wanted to thank him, and also to pepper him with questions. She had it in her mind to loop her arm through his, and not release him until he had satisfied her curiosity. She was just brain enough to do it.

"Beautiful concert, Melody," he said with his light, continental accent. "I'm pleased you enjoyed it. Would you have time to walk me to my hotel?"

"Delighted, my dear," he replied. "There's something I'd like to ask you."

"I have a question or two for you, too," she admitted, feeling smug that her plans were coming to pass so easily.

The old gentleman's face was kind as he asked. "Why are you still here in Swansea? Don't you have sufficient funds to complete your journey?"

She found it an odd but insightful question. "Actually, thanks to you, I have more than enough. I'm still here because I don't know where my sister lives. She's in England somewhere, but she moved recently, and I don't know her address. I don't even know what city she's in."

"Why did she move without informing you?" he asked congenially. Melody debated whether to give him a simple answer, or the long version. There was a lot of prejudice against Marcia's new religion, and she didn't want to offend or alienate her new friend by mentioning it. "She just joined a new church, and she moved to be nearer to the chapel. I had her new address at one time, but I left home rather suddenly and didn't think to pick up the paper. I can't remember what city it was. England has so many oddly named cities."

"It does indeed. What church did you say she joined?"

"I didn't," she said, then added almost apologetically, "It was the Mormon church."

"Truly? I may know someone who can help. As a matter of fact, they're right there," he said, pointing across the park toward a small gathering of people.

It was so common for people to cluster around a performer or actor, that Melody rarely paid much attention to little gatherings. She turned her attention to the group he indicated and saw a young man in a business suit and small black derby standing on a box, speaking. It seemed that someone in the audience was giving him a hard time.

"Who are they?" she asked.

"Why, they're Mormon missionaries," he said, his tone implying everyone on earth knew who they were. She gave him a remonstrative glance, and he hunched his shoulders as if she really should have known.

She gathered up her meager possessions and walked toward the gathering. She turned to ask her friend another question, but he was no longer near. She could see his gray head bobbing slowly away in the distance. She thought it odd that he had not even said goodbye.

"I don't know how many wives Brigham Young had," one of the missionaries was saying in an exasperated tone.

"How can you be a missionary for the Mormon church and not know?" the heckler wanted to know.

"Tell you what," the young man said in a heavy American accent. "When I get to heaven, I'll ask him."

"He's not in heaven!" the heckler called back. This brought a roar of laughter from the crowd.

"Then you ask him," the missionary shot back. This brought an even greater roar of laughter. The heckler lost interest and left the group. After that, the missionaries delivered a message to the crowd that Melody found uplifting. It was, in fact, her first exposure to LDS doctrine. In the years since meeting Sam on the train, she had either not had the opportunity, or had not taken advantage of the ones she had had to learn more.

The crowd was dispersing and the two missionaries were just turning to leave when Melody interrupted them. "Excuse me," she said shyly.

They both turned toward her. They were slightly older than she, about nineteen or twenty, she guessed. One of them was tall and quite good-looking. The shorter one was freckle-faced and red-haired. He seemed to be their spokesman, and smiled at her. "Can we help you?"

"I don't know," she replied honestly. "I'm looking for my sister who just joined your church."

"What's her name?" he asked. "Marcia MacUlvaney."

"Is she in this area?"

"I don't know what city she lives in."

"That makes it harder," he said soberly. "It's a big mission."

"I guess it was a long shot," she said sadly. "She's recently from Rhodesia, Africa," she added, hoping it would make a difference, "and she plays the violin."

"Elder," the taller one said, "Do you suppose that's the young woman President Farnsworthy spoke of at the last zone conference? Wasn't there a lady from Africa who played the violin?"

"Hey, I think he did say she was from Africa. It's worth checking into. Miss, if we can find a pay phone, I can call President and see if that girl is your sister. What do you think?"

"I would be ever so grateful. Please."

"Great!" the freckle-faced elder said, sticking his hand toward her enthusiastically. "I'm Elder Johnston, and my companion here is Elder Fleur. We're both from America." Melody shook both their hands with a sense of amusement mingled with gratitude. They were unusually helpful, as sincere as the Pope, and certainly seemed harmless.

"I'm pleased to meet you both."

"There's a post office a short distance from here," Elder Johnston suggested. "We could find a phone there. If we hurry we will probably catch our mission president still in his office."

"Thank you," she said walking in stride beside Elder Johnston as they hurried toward the middle of town.

The post office turned out to be nearly a quarter mile away. Her legs were aching from trying to keep up with them by the time they arrived.

Melody talked to President Farnsworthy, and they decided the woman in question probably was her sister; however, President Farnsworthy had no idea where she actually lived. He promised to find out. He would call the missionaries, and they would deliver the message to her. President Farnsworthy assured her she would have her sister's address sometime soon, possibly even tomorrow.

The missionaries were kind enough to escort her the considerable distance back to her hotel. During the whole journey they talked excitedly about someone named Smith, who had seen an angel, and had been given a golden book. They talked with so much animation in their thick accents that Melody had difficulty understanding their speech, and soon found herself lost. She was quite unsure what they were talking about, except that they believed it with all their hearts.

She made a shallow connection between the book Sam had given her father, and the gold book from the angel. Melody had never read the book, since Marcia had taken it with her when she left for England. If she had not, it would now be in the possession of the Rhodesian rebel army.

It took most of a week for the missionaries to deliver her sister's address. Each evening they met her in the park and escorted her to her hotel. During their walks they talked enthusiastically about various gospel topics. At first Melody only tolerated it because they were helping her find her sister. After a time she began to enjoy these brief talks, and looked forward to them.

The odd thing was that since the missionaries had begun escorting her home, she had not seen her friend, the older gentleman without a name.

Saturday she played in the park from noon to four. By now she had a small following of people who regularly came to the park to hear her play. It was rare for one of such extraordinary talent to be a street musician, and her impromptu concerts drew fairly large crowds. She found that she collected so much money in a four-hour concert that she could not safely carry it home for fear of being robbed. After several hours she closed her violin case, and refused further gifts.

The missionaries showed up around three, and politely worked their way through the crowd until they were nearly in front. They watched her closely, and closed their eyes in appreciation when she played especially beautiful passages.

Melody decided to give the two elders a treat, and searched through her memory for some music they might enjoy. She remembered a hymn her sister had played over and over after joining the Mormon church. It seemed perfect.

Waiting for the applause to die down, Melody lowered her violin. Thinking she was through, a collective sigh of disappointment drifted across the gathering. "I have one more piece to play today. It's a church hymn, a song especially for my two friends. I hope you enjoy it."

Melody raised her bow, paused, and brought it down in a long minor strain that seemed to weep with anguish. Slowly, with tender care she played the music. She glanced up and saw tears in the eyes of both missionaries. She did not know the words, but they did, and they began to sing, quietly at first, and then with gusto. Elder Fleur had a rich baritone voice. It rose up in impassioned strains, and she felt the hair rising on her arms as a thrill of spiritual yearning passed through her such as she had never felt before. It was as if her soul had suddenly discovered it was emaciated from life-long starvation, and had just tasted its first sip of the very nectar of the gods.

Come, come, ye Saints, no toil or labor fear; But with joy wend your way.

Though hard to you this journey may appear, Grace shall be, as your day.

Gird up your loins; fresh courage take. Our God will never us forsake;

And soon we'll have this tale to tell— All is well! All is well!

The music died in the autumn breeze, and Melody lowered her bow to appreciative applause. She had sat in grand halls and heard the world's finest voices. She had played in orchestras as virtuoso tenors thrilled thousands. But she had never heard anything like this.

This young missionary's voice wasn't trained. She knew he hadn't sat at the feet of a master teacher and practiced scales endlessly until his voice was flawless. She doubted he had sung for more than a hundred people in any one room. Yet, she had never heard someone sing with more joy and passion. His voice had reached far beyond the furthest ears in a large concert hall. It had reached deep within the soul of all who heard.

It was the second time simple music had touched her soul at its greatest depth. The first time was on a train in Africa. The parallel between then and now was inescapable; both times the music had unexpectedly come from a young Mormon missionary.

People wandered away reluctantly. Melody laid her violin atop the pile of bills and succeeded in closing it only after stuffing several handfuls into her pockets.

Elder Fleur waited until she looked up before speaking. His voice was husky with emotion. "Thanks, Sister MacUlvaney," he said, mispronouncing her name slightly.

"You're welcome, Elder." It tickled her that they insisted on calling her sister. It made her feel like a nun from a convent. Yet nothing she could say would dissuade them; she had finally given up.

"You were right," he continued. "It is one of my favorite songs. I hope you don't mind that I sang it. I didn't mean to butt in, but it just welled up in my throat, and I either had to sing, or burst," he explained.

Melody placed a slender hand on his arm. "I loved that you sang," she assured him. "I have to say that you have a beautiful voice."

Elder Fleur seemed quite abashed by the idea. "Oh, gosh. I don't know. I just love to sing. I know I can make a lot of noise, but that's about it."

"Don't be so modest," she admonished happily. "You do have a beautiful voice. Even without training you caused the hair to rise on my arms."

"I always thought that was a bad thing," he replied with wide eyes.

"No!" she laughed. "No, what I mean is you touched my heart. I think what touched me was how much you love that song, more than how fine your voice is."

"Sister MacUlvaney," he replied earnestly, "It isn't that I love that song."

"What then?" she asked, genuinely perplexed.

"It's that I love the Lord. This song causes all my hope and faith to come in great bursts of happiness. That's what you're hearing; not my appreciation for a tune, but my love of all it stands for."

His words entered her heart with power. "I stand corrected," Melody said and bowed toward him from the waist. When she arose she could see he was genuinely perplexed by her response. She laughed, her voice not unlike sleigh bells on a windless winter's eve. She turned to walk and beckoned them to join her.

She stepped between them, handed her violin to Elder Johnston, and took each by an elbow. "As much as I know about music," she told them, "You have added a dimension I never realized before."

"What's that," they asked almost in unison.

"Great music expresses great passion. I have always known this. What you taught me is that the nearer the passion of the performer mirrors the passion of the composer, the greater, and more life-altering a performance becomes. I think we heard you sing just as the composer might have sung had he been here."

"That's a wonderful thought," Elder Fleūr replied after another few steps, then turned to look at her. "I was just puzzled about why you bowed to me."

Melody stopped walking. Both young missionaries stopped, turning to face her.

"To me, music is everything," she explained. "It is the food I drink, and the air I breathe. Music comforts me, feeds me, and gives my soul wings. Yet, I have never understood what you just revealed to me. What you taught me would be somewhat analogous to when one of your investigators accepts what you teach them. I bowed because it is the way I was taught as a child to acknowledge when someone has given me a great gift."

Both missionaries stared at her with wide eyes, then as if they had rehearsed it many times, they both bowed to her.

"What's this!?" she laughed.

Elder Johnston's eyes sparkled as he replied, "Paybacks."

"Yeah," Elder Fleūr added. "Every single time we see you playing in the park we leave blessed and spiritually fed. Whenever we feel discouraged, we come to the park because your music sustains us and feeds our souls. You see, you have given us a great gift as well; not once, but many times."

Having received plaudits all her life for her beauty, charm, and considerable talent, Melody was still not prepared for their reply. Her eyes misted. She smiled happily and brushed a tear away with the back of her fingers. "Thank you," she said very softly.

Elder Johnston was about to say something else, when he suddenly remembered. "Oh! I almost forgot. We've got your sister's address," he said happily, and held out a copy of the Book of Mormon.

"What's this?" she asked with mock suspicion. She had twice refused to take a Book of Mormon.

Elder Johnston smiled slyly. "Well, we wrote the address in the fly leaf. See?" he said, holding open the book. There was an address, and a telephone number. Her heart leaped and she reached for the book, but he pulled it back.

"I know this is blackmail," he said in all seriousness. "But, I want you to have this book because it's true, not because it's got your sister's address inside. I don't care if you believe in it or not, I just want you to know why I want to give it to you. This book will eventually help you complete your life's journey. It will take you full circle. It is the most precious thing I possess, and I want you to have it." So saying, he held out the book.

Melody took the book in both hands, then shook her head in wonder. "What did you say?"

"Er—I'm not sure what . . ."

"I mean, about this book taking me full circle?" she inquired, her eyes narrowing.

"Yes, I think I said that. Did it offend you?"

Melody shook her head vigorously. "Not at all! Is this a common expression with Mormon missionaries?"

Both Elders looked at each other, then shook their heads.

It was Elder Fleur who said, "I've never heard anyone say it before just now."

Melody looked at the book, thumbed to her sister's address, then looked back at Elder Johnston. "Why did you say that? What does 'it will take you full circle' mean, do you think?"

The young missionary shrugged. "Honestly, Sister MacUlvaney, I have no idea. I was speaking from my heart, and the Spirit was upon me, and I just said it. I'm sorry, but I can't give you an explanation other than that it was the right thing to say."

Melody stared at him in deep thought before replying, "Elder Johnston, it was probably the only thing you could have said to make me accept this book other than just to get my sister's address."

She closed the Book of Mormon and held it before her with both hands. "Thank you, Elders. I will not forget what you have said. I believe you when you say this book is precious. I couldn't have said that one minute ago. Perhaps in time I will understand why you said what you did. Until then, I will accept your words on faith."

Her eyes focused on a far distant memory. "I knew another young missionary in Africa named Elder Mahoy, who used those very words in a blessing he gave me. I believe that blessing saved my life. Someday I hope to understand both his words, and yours."

Elder Fleur's voice was husky. "That's really great, Sister MacUlvaney. Without knowing anything specific about your life, I can promise you in the name of Jesus Christ that this book is essential to your finding what you seek. I just know it with all my heart." His accent was a heavy American drawl, and it strummed pleasant memories in her heart.

"Thank you, Elder. I believe it is too. Now, I just need to find out how." They escorted her directly to the pay phone near the post office and she called the number they had written in the book.

Her heart nearly stopped when she heard her sister's voice on the phone.

"Marcia!" she cried. But, before she could speak even one joyous word, she remembered that Marcia did not know. She had to swallow three times before she could make a sound come from her lips.

"Oh, Marcia!" she wailed. "Daddy is dead!"

* * *

The operation lasted three agonizing hours. When Dr. Green once again emerged through the double doors her face was drawn and weary. Except for his faith, Sam would have collapsed in an agony of sorrow. As it was, the look on her face was enough to tear at his fragile hope. Tears sprang to his eyes, and a terrible foreboding gripped his soul. He felt his knees folding beneath him. The doctor grabbed both his shoulders and lowered him back to his chair.

"Your faith has seen you this far. Don't give up yet," she said cryptically. "Princess has survived the operation. She shouldn't have. Three times she nearly bled to death, and three times we revived her. The second time we had no more blood. One of the nurses was her blood type and gave blood right there in the operating room. Each time I was on the verge of giving up, but something more powerful than logic urged me on.

"In the end, I would have to say that regardless of the seriousness of the procedure we performed, there was never any chance of her not making it. Her god has quite obviously delivered her from the jaws of death. She will have a long recovery, but she will be fine.

She continued wearily, "We don't know what effect the severe blood loss will have on her. She may suffer some memory loss, perhaps slight personality shifts, though I doubt anything severe. You can relax, Mr. Mahoy. You are the proud recipient of three miracles."

Sam slumped in his chair, his heart soaring in relief and silent prayers of thanksgiving. He didn't hear what else the doctor said until his father nudged him.

"What?"

Dr. Green was leaning forward, smiling. "I said, two of your miracles are identical twin daughters. They are perfectly healthy."

Sam was so amazed that his legs refused to support him further, and he dropped into his chair, stunned.

"When can I see them?" he queried.

Dr. Green frowned thoughtfully. "Princess is still under anesthesia. The babies will be in isolation for at least twenty-four hours. I suggest you go home and get some rest. Your wife won't be seeing anyone for at least twelve hours. Go get some rest."

Sam struggled to stand, and shook the doctor's hand. "Thank you very much for giving me back my wife, and new babies."

Dr. Green looked at him with some irony in her face. She merely nodded, and turned away as if in a hurry to be elsewhere.

Sam's family herded him to his car. His mind was in a fog of colliding thoughts and emotions. He would have happily gone home and slept for a small eternity, but was shocked to full awareness the instant he saw the driver's side window. Scratched deeply in the glass was a large 22.

Someone took him home and put him to bed. He slept for several hours in deathlike exhaustion. But, the implication of the hated numerals on his car at the hospital, so near his family, terrified him. He hurried back to the hospital as soon as his mind and body could function.

They named the girls Lisa Laura Mahoy, with her middle name after Sam's mother, and Bonnie Marie Mahoy, her middle name after Princess's mother. Princess came home ten days later. She was still too weak to care for the baby girls by herself. Sam's mother moved in with them to help. The babies thrived.

Princess seemed barely to have the will to survive. She had to be urged to eat, urged to sit up—urged to breathe it seemed.

She seemed to have little energy for her babies, though a look of love came on her face when she saw them. The first turning point toward recovery came when Grandmother Mahoy carried the twin girls to her, one in each arm. Princess was lying in bed, staring up at the ceiling.

"Princess, I have in my arms two little angels who have loved you since before time began. They depend on you for life itself. You have to eat, if for no other reason than so that you can nurse them. You chose life for them; now follow through on that commitment. You nursed them in the hospital, and they have thrived on your gift. But I refuse to feed these precious little ones cow's milk, not when you have the milk of life to give them."

Princess's face changed. She smiled weakly, and without a word she struggled to sit up. Sam hurried to help her, but a warning look held him back. She pushed herself to a sitting position, a look of pain on her face. She held out her arms and took one of the babies. The little one fumbled anxiously, and with a little help, began nursing noisily. Mother Mahoy propped a pillow under Princess's elbow to support her arm, which trembled from the weight of the baby. The other little one soon found her meal on the other side, and began drinking as daintily as her sister was noisy. A smile formed on Princess's lips as she looked from one tiny face to another, an expression of love on her face.

Sam took a seat on the edge of the bed to watch this precious moment. In response, Princess shot him a withering glance.

He stood as if shot by an arrow and left the room quietly. He went to his study and wept. He wept for happiness, sadness, joy, and tragedy. It was all more than he could endure. It was the first time Princess had ever looked at him with anything other than enduring love.

Princess slowly recovered, each day a little stronger. It was almost as if the babies fed her even as she fed them. In time she regained her health, and Mother Mahoy went home. But even after Dr. Green pronounced her physically well, Princess's former feelings of endearment for Sam seemed partly forgotten, or lost, or perhaps discarded.

* * *

That November the ward was divided and the Wasilla Second Ward was formed. Sam and Princess lived within the boundaries of the new ward, while his parents stayed in the former.

His father remained bishop of the old ward. Sam was immediately called to be elder's quorum president in the new ward. He rejoiced in the opportunity to serve, and pressed forward with determination. He and Bishop Dowling spent many evenings going from home to home, using somewhat the same methods his own father had used for so many years to build the wards in Downey and in Wasilla.

January of that year brought the worst winter storm ever recorded in the Matanuska Valley. On January 15, the temperature dropped to twenty-three below zero and a deep snow fell.

The odd thing was that it was too cold to snow; usually it will not snow when the temperature is below freezing. The snow was light and crystalline, almost glass-like, and it fell until several feet of fine powder lay on the ground like so much glitter.

Almost midnight on the next day the wind began to blow. It whipped up until the winds exceeded 120 miles per hour with gusts to 150. The big log house trembled as the winds hammered against it. The winds continued to pound the valley for nearly two weeks.

Sam's new home was thick and sturdy, but it was also large and hard to heat without electricity. The power went out within the first hour of the windstorm. Sam bundled up and brought in wood to stoke the big stove in the living room. The heat seemed to rise to the ceiling, leaving the floor cold and drafty.

He brought Princess and the babies into the room with the stove and hung blankets in the doorway and across the stairs.

The room slowly became tolerable, but hardly comfortable.

With no electricity they were left in darkness, and Sam quickly found he was unprepared for such things. Having only lived there for a few months he had yet to complete their food storage. They suddenly found themselves rationing things like matches, toilet paper, diapers, toothpaste, and drinking water. They had only a few candles and one kerosene lantern with one small bottle of fuel. The only thing that worked to their advantage was that their kitchen stove was propane and they had a full tank of fuel. Sam lit the oven and left the door open. He carefully monitored the level in the tank, which went down much quicker than he liked.

Princess seemed to accept the situation with a stoic sense of fate. She kept the babies wrapped against her body for warmth and cared for them as best she could. Sam melted snow for water and chopped wood. They ate everything in the house until all they had was wheat, beans, and canned goods of various unappetizing varieties. Sam ground the wheat to flour in a hand mill, and cooked it as many different ways as he could. The toilets in the house were frozen solid, and he set up a privy in the corner of the big room separated by curtains. Many times a day he took the bucket outside and emptied it.

The wind blew the powdery snow into great drifts as hard as concrete. One side of their house had a drift to the roofline. The drift grew around the house until the front door was blocked, then the windows. The only way to exit the house was through the garage doors. Every time he raised a garage door it felt as if the wind would take away the whole garage. The structure whined, and the roof rattled from the strain. He decided it was no longer safe to open those big doors.

Sam pried open the front door and shoveled a tunnel through the drift. After about ten feet he turned left and dug another six feet before breaking through. The opening faced away from the wind, and he could come and go without sending a gust of wind and snow into the house. Had he not had a sick wife and two six-month-old daughters, it might almost have been an adventure. Princess was getting sick of wheat and beans, and her milk was slowly dropping off for want of adequate drinking water. After two weeks they were on the last fifteen percent of their propane tank. Sam reluctantly shut it off as a source of heat. The winds died down to forty miles per hour on February first.

Sam knew they desperately needed supplies, and dressed up in everything he could put on. It was still nearly thirty below zero; with the wind chill it was well over one hundred below zero.

"Princess, I'm going to try to get into town today," he said, walking up behind her. He placed his hands on her shoulders and kneaded them gently.

"Sam, please be careful. But come back in when you decide what you're going to do, so I don't worry, okay?"

"Of course. I'll go see if the jeep will start."

"Be careful," she urged.

He made his way to the four-wheel drive jeep. He had unwisely parked it outside the night of the big blow. It was buried in three feet of rock hard snow. He chipped open an area sufficient to open the driver's door. When he hit the starter the engine would not turn over, but gave off a screaming sound. He raised the hood and found the engine compartment completely white. Only the air cleaner was above the snow.

After warming himself by chopping some more wood, he returned with a screwdriver and chipped the snow out of the engine compartment. As soon as the fan was clear the faithful old engine roared to life. The cabin immediately filled with exhaust. He shut it off and dug away the snow from the tailpipe.

By this time it was dark again, and he gave up.

The next day the wind was still blowing. He found the truck drifted back in, but this time the snow that had blown in was powdery. Sam started the vehicle, observed there was only a quarter tank of fuel, and shut it back off. With his snow shovel he chipped a narrow path through the solid drift until he came to an area nearly free of snow. In the fickle nature of snowdrifts, his transportation was buried nearly three feet deep, and a hundred feet away, the ground was bare. He chipped icelike snow for a whole day.

It was just twilight when he started the jeep and drove it without trouble onto bare road. In an Alaskan winter, twilight is around three in the afternoon. He went back inside to warm up.

"I've got the jeep on the road. I'm going to make a quick trip into town," he informed her as he piled more wood by the stove.

"Is the road open? Can you make it into town?"

"It has drifts, but seems to be passable. If I encounter anything too big, I'll turn around and come back."

Holding Lisa in her arms, Princess walked to the door with him. She was wearing Levis over pajamas, with a warm bathrobe over all that. She had one of his baseball caps on her head, and looked like a refugee. "Remember diapers, and please be careful."

"I will. Don't worry."

He brought with him a shovel, a candle, and a blanket. He drove a short distance down their lane before encountering another drift several feet deep blocking the road. He got out and walked across the drift. It was as hard as stone. Carefully, he drove up onto it. It easily supported the weight of the jeep. The other side was an abrupt drop off of three feet. It had turned dark by the time he was able to dig a ramp off of it and drive onto solid ground.

Turning left was the shortest way into town. In the headlights of the vehicle he could see many small drifts, while the other direction seemed to have larger ones. Favoring the most direct route, he turned left. The first drift he came to was powdery. It dissipated in the wind as he drove through it. Each drift he came to was powdery and easy to get through, though the larger ones required some speed to blast through them.

He was about a hundred yards from the intersection with the main highway when he came to a massive wall of snow. He got out and inspected what looked like the side of a mountain.

The drift was taller than the telephone poles, and stretched as far as he could see in either direction. It was simply impassable.

Had he not been shivering in one-hundred-below temperatures, and desperate to get food for his family, he would have been amazed.

As it was, he was disappointed to the point of explosive anger.

He struggled to regain his emotional stability, and climbed back into the truck. He was nearly on an eighth of a tank. Under normal circumstances, it would be plenty to get him into town.

Sam turned around and retraced his tracks, now blown nearly to nonexistence in the wind. He passed their drive, and felt an urging to return home. He wondered if it was the Spirit or his own thinking, but shrugged it off. All he could think about was food for his family. The thought of Princess smiling at him as he carried in bags of groceries warmed him, and once again, he drove past their drive. She hadn't smiled at him much at all since the babies were born, and he was willing to brave winds and storms, or dragons if necessary, to have the joy of it again.

The road beyond their driveway was nearly bare. He could see the brown gravel underneath the layer of snow slithering across the road like a thousand white snakes driven by the winds.

He came to the first big drift and eased the front of the jeep into it.

It was soft but too deep to drive through, and he got stuck.

He easily backed out and got a short run at it. The snowdrift exploded into white fury, and vanished in the brisk wind. He drove through onto hard ground. The next drift was smaller and likewise vanished when he hit it. Drift after drift gave way to him, until he thought little of finding another crossing the road.

The biting cold was frosting his windshield even with the defroster blowing full blast. He periodically scraped the inside.

The fuel gauge continued its plunge toward "E."

"Heavenly Father, I really need some help," he prayed out loud. "Please let me bring home food for my family."

Five miles passed with no major problems, his sense of success grew, and he thanked the Lord. The road turned right, and he only had another mile to go until he came to the highway. He was certain he would have no problems on the highway.

He had been listening to the radio. Power had been restored to the city of Wasilla. The main roads were being maintained, and stores were open. Secondary roads would be opened as soon as the winds died down.

As these thoughts were going through his mind he came to another drift. It was somewhat larger than the others and sloped on the side facing him. He stopped and pushed open the door.

The wind slammed it back shut before he could get out. The wind had picked up considerably. The world of cold on the other side of the glass caused him to shiver. The jeep rocked as it was buffeted by the wind. He suddenly felt very weary and decided not to brave the slamming cold to inspect the drift on foot.

An urging inside warned him against it, which he ignored.

He backed up the jeep and mentally judged what speed he would need to break through the drift. He decided on about twenty-five mph. He backed up a little farther and began forward. He carefully adjusted his speed until it was just under twenty-five. The drift approached, and he steered toward the lowest part. He came onto the drift and waited for it to explode.

Without warning the jeep launched into the air. His head snapped forward, hitting the steering wheel as the jeep took flight. He flew through the air for a dozen feet before landing with a jarring impact on the other side. Sam's head snapped back, and his neck screamed in pain. He slammed on the brakes and came to a stop. The engine was still running, but the jeep sat at an odd angle. He took inventory of himself, and decided he was all right, though his face was bleeding slightly above his brow, and his back and neck hurt.

Refusing to give up, he shut off the jeep and climbed back out. Hours passed in a frantic scramble between bone-numbing digging and partly warming himself in the jeep. He lost track of time. Outside, the wind pierced through him like nails shot from a gun. He did not dare run the truck long enough to warm himself completely. The wind was stronger now, and the path filled in as fast as he could dig. Despair slowly settled over him.

Sam returned to the jeep. He had been working in the headlights without the motor running, and for a frightening moment it seemed as if the faithful jeep would not start. At the last possible moment the engine barked to life and he slapped himself to keep warm until heat came from the jeep. He knew he could push himself no further, and steely fear swept over him.

He turned on the headlights and saw that the digging he had just done had blown back in. He laughed aloud with dark humor, then laid his head back. Something sharp snapped in his neck, and he shouted in pain. For the first time he realized he was seriously injured. Cold sweat beaded on his forehead as he slowly went into shock.

Faced with his own mortality for the first time in his life, Sam was startled to find that his greatest regret was regarding Princess. He did not want to die without having restored her love to his life. He pondered what the twins might become without him, but knew they would be cared for and loved. He pondered every aspect of his life, and found himself surprisingly in good repair. The only loose end he truly regretted was the inexplicable loss of Princess's love. This loss, he decided, was greater than the apparently imminent loss of his own life. As only the howling of the storm disturbed the quiet of the cold vehicle, his heart soared in prayer. No sooner had he begun to pray than the Holy Spirit swept over him, and he felt peace. Tears filled his eyes as he poured out his soul in prayer, not begging for physical salvation, but in words of love and worship. Without asking, without begging, with no more than a feeling of peace, he knew all would be well. He turned off the headlights and let darkness surround him.

The engine coughed and died. He did not try to restart it. Instead, he turned off the key. The blower quickly became cold, and he turned it off as well. Cold invaded the cabin immediately. He listened to the wind and estimated that it was almost up to one hundred again. He tucked his hands under his arms and prayed as feeling first left his toes, then his feet, then legs. He knew he was dying, and yet fear was not the emotion he felt—it was joy; joy that soon he would have the privilege of worshipping at the Savior's feet.

At first his benumbed mind thought it was the rumble of an earthquake. He felt it in his pants before he heard it. He decided it was an avalanche, yet he was nowhere near a mountain or hillside. He opened his eyes to what appeared to be a hurricane coming directly toward him. The hurricane had two blinding lights above and on either side of it. His mind struggled to comprehend, to understand what it might be. It roared even louder than the wind, and screamed as it sent snow and ice furiously in every direction. He decided his mind was playing tricks on him, and nearly closed his eyes when he felt a surge of warmth and a clear command.

"Turn on the lights," it said. He reached out and fumbled without feeling for the light button. It stuck to his fingers as he pulled on it. The headlights of the jeep flared into the night, and the hurricane stopped with a lurch just in front of his jeep.

Sam watched with stupid interest as the hurricane paused, then grew silent. As he watched, it died away, and magically became the gaping mouth of a giant beast with huge yellow teeth slowly turning in his headlights. He simply stared at it in dumb fascination.

A hand rubbed away the frost from the side window. A face appeared and quickly vanished. He heard voices and heard a shovel banging against his door. In a few moments his door was yanked open and Sam was swallowed by the wind. He felt irritated that whoever it was had opened the door and let in the wind.

Someone grabbed his arm and yanked him out into the storm.

He would have resisted, but he was too cold. Hands fumbled all over him, and he was lifted. It seemed like his feet were directly over his head, and snow blew into his pant legs. It was an odd sensation.

The next Sam knew, he was upright again and being pushed up a ladder. He tried to help and managed to climb. In a short while he was sitting in a large cabin with hot air blowing in his face. Someone shoved a cup against his lips and he swallowed a gulp of burning liquid. It tasted awful, and he wondered if they were trying to kill him. But the heat hit his stomach and flared outward. It felt so good that he took another swallow of the foul liquid. It burned his mouth and throat, but the warmth was magical.

Someone was talking on a radio, reporting something about a buried jeep. Someone else asked his name, and he tried to remember it. He took another swallow and almost as if a light switch had been snapped on, he remembered. With sudden panic he became fully aware, and couldn't help himself from yelling.

"Hey, you're okay. Here, take another swallow of coffee." Sam looked into the concerned face of a young man. He was wearing a military uniform. Sam looked around himself and decided he was in the cab of a big machine. From the fact that everything was drab green, it was a military machine. He took another swallow of the hot liquid before it registered that it was coffee. He handed back the cup and nodded his thanks.

"Judas Priest, we almost ground you to pieces!" the older man said as soon as he hung the radio microphone back up.

"You okay?"

"I think so. Where am I. What is this?"

"It's one of the National Guard's biggest snow blowers. We've been working for weeks to open up the back roads. We didn't see your truck until you turned on the lights. Another two feet and we would have ground you to shrapnel," he said with deep concern in his voice. Sam leaned forward and couldn't even see the top of the jeep over the big blower. The huge blower was a mere two feet from the front of the truck. Its vicious mouth was ten feet wide, and capable of chewing up an automobile without much more than a cough. Sam shivered inwardly, and sent a prayer of thanks for the urging to turn on the lights.

Sam noticed that both men were sweating. They had turned the heaters in the cabin up full blast to thaw him out.

"Mr. Mahoy, we need to take you to a hospital," the senior of the two insisted.

Sam shook his head. "I'm feeling much better, thanks to you. My family is out of food, and I need to get back."

"I can't force you to go," the man said, "but I think it unwise to not treat your injuries immediately. I can see that your neck hurts."

"I will be fine. I promise, I'll get medical attention as soon as possible."

"It's your call, Mr. Mahoy. I'm just so darn glad we didn't . . ." He shook his head.

In about an hour, Sam recovered enough to climb back out of the big machine. He was amazed to see how his jeep was dwarfed by the big machine a mere twenty-four inches from his bumper. They backed up and tied a chain to his truck. The little jeep hopped effortlessly onto smooth ground. They gave him a spare can of gas.

"You'd be surprised how many stranded motorists we have dragged out of snow drifts. We were ordered to carry extra gas, courtesy of the US government." The needle read half a tank when he climbed back in. He started the engine and waited until heat once again came from the blower. He could feel everything but his feet, which he was able to move stiffly, so they weren't frozen, just very cold.

The soldiers backed the big machine out of his way. The road was flat and smooth before him. Nearly four hours after his engine had died, he was once again able to continue his journey. He happened to glance in his rear-view mirror just as the big snow blower roared back to life, belching a column of snow and ice into the air. The drift that had thrown him into the sky vaporized into the night.

A few minutes later Sam pulled up to the brightly lit grocery store. He purchased many bags of food and milk, paper diapers, candles, kerosene, another lamp, matches, and toilet paper. He resisted the urge to buy the whole store.

The poor little jeep was sitting so low to the ground that the wheels almost rubbed the wheel wells. In the bright lights of the parking lot he inspected the damage. Three of the springs were broken, the fourth hopelessly bent. He got out the bumper jack and jacked it up. He had several pieces of two-by-four, which he laid between the frame and axle. He found some bailing wire and tied them in place.

He had to stop twice to put the blocks back in place. He finally arrived home about ten o'clock at night. He had left around three. His labors to dig out the driveway were wasted.

It had all blown back in, and he had to park by the road. He walked the long lane to his home carrying his treasures.

Princess was waiting for him and threw open the door. Her face was a picture of relief. She took the packages from him and he returned to the jeep for the remainder. When Sam finally arrived with the final load he was nearly as cold as when the National Guard had rescued him. His speech was slurred, and he was having difficulty concentrating. The wind had resumed its former ferocity.

Princess sat him by the stove and pulled off his gloves and boots. She massaged his feet and wrapped them in towels warmed on the stove. She worked on him for nearly an hour before he began to feel warm again and his shivering stopped.

"Thank you, Princess. I'm okay now, I think," he said, his speech nearly normal.

"Oh, Sam, I was so worried! I was afraid you had gotten into trouble. The babies and I said many prayers for you," she said earnestly.

"I did, actually. I got stuck and ran out of gas and nearly froze."

"Oh no! Sam, I was afraid something had happened. How did you get out?"

"The National Guard came along."

"Truly?" she asked in disbelief.

"They did. They were clearing the roads and pulled the jeep out of the drift. I broke all four springs hitting a snowdrift. I thought I was a goner." He left out the part about almost being ground to hamburger by their snow blower.

"I'm so grateful you're okay!"

"Thanks for worrying about me, and for warming me back up. It felt wonderful to have you care about me again."

Princess looked at him with a blank expression before turning away. "What did you bring us?" she asked in an obvious effort to change the subject.

* * *

Princess made regular visits to Dr. Green with the babies, and they seemed to be thriving. Sam decided to contact the doctor herself. Princess said very little about her appointments, and Sam was concerned. Even though she was much better physically, there was a vast change in her personality. Dr. Green invited him to come and talk about his fears.

Dr. Green's office was near the hospital. Sam arrived after hours and had to wait nearly an hour for the last patient to leave. The waiting room was decorated like a nursery, obviously for the comfort of expectant mothers. He could hardly believe this was the office of an abortionist. But that wasn't what he was here to discuss.

The doctor shook his hand and ushered him into a large office. Her office was all business and had none of the feminine trappings of the outer rooms. He felt as if he had entered a lawyer's office. Dr. Green took a seat behind a big walnut desk and came directly to the point.

"Mr. Mahoy, I understand you have concerns about your wife's health. How may I help?"

Sam cleared his throat and nodded. "It's not her physical health I'm concerned about. She seems to have had a personality change. She no longer seems to care about things she formerly loved." He wanted to say people but felt more comfortable saying it this way.

"I see. Has this all happened since the babies were born?"

"Yes. It has been sudden and dramatic."

"Hmm. Does she treat you differently?"

"Very much so."

The doctor frowned and leaned forward, steepling her hands on her desk. "I see. Let me make a couple of observations. First, pregnancy and birth require tremendous physiological changes in a female's body. Hormones change, body chemistry changes, her diet and routine all change. In addition to this, there are tremendous emotional burdens associated with giving birth. Sometimes there is a deep depression that lingers for several months following delivery. In the vast majority of cases these things wear off in a few months and the mother returns to normal."

"I know about those things," Sam interjected. "She was wonderful during the pregnancy, and seemed anxious for the baby to come. The changes have all been since the birth. It's been seven months now. She just isn't the same person." Sam felt as if he were whining, and had to struggle to keep tears from his eyes.

"Yes, I see," she said. "During the operation your wife lost a lot of blood. Several times her heart stopped and she had to be revived. These times were brief, but it is entirely possible that she suffered some minor brain impairment. In almost all cases related to blood loss, the impairment shows up first in small personality changes. In severe cases, there is loss of motor skills, or memory. She doesn't exhibit memory loss does she?"

"Not that I can tell. But she hardly talks to me anymore."

"I'm going to recommend that you take Princess to a specialist, Dr Spenard. He is not a psychologist but a doctor who deals specifically with long-term illnesses of this type. His methods are unusual and even controversial but are highly effective. I don't know if anything can be done to help Princess regain her former personality, but he may be able to help." With this she jotted a name and number on a prescription pad.

Sam took the slip and stood. He was about to leave when a thought occurred to him. "Doctor, I want to thank you for saving Princess and my babies. I know it was a traumatic affair for you. Anyway, thank you very much."

The doctor seemed to struggle with indecision before she motioned him back into his chair. Sam sat down uncomfortably.

"In all candor, Mr. Mahoy, your wife's behavior has troubled me deeply. What she did was either very brave, or incredibly stupid. I haven't decided which. She was willing to die rather than let me save her." She shook her head and appeared to be viewing the scene again in her mind.

After a moment she continued. "When I went to medical school they taught us repeatedly that a fetus was only tissue, that there was no more life in it than in your finger or foot. Because of my training I have had no qualms about performing abortions and have done so many times. I don't especially enjoy doing it and usually send new patients requesting an abortion to another doctor. But when an established patient requests it, I have obliged them.

"As you know there has been a great uproar in recent years about abortions. There are many who want to make it illegal. It made me angry that some group of people wants to shove their moral system down my throat and tell me what I can, or can't do. As a result, I have performed more abortions in the last two years than I would have otherwise; perhaps as many as three times more.

"However, I have never been so unhappy in my life. It seemed to me as if every time I returned from a procedure of this type, I felt more and more unable to care about the mothers and their babies who wanted a live birth. I began to view them as carrying unliving tissue inside them, and I felt indifferent toward their babies, who they loved deeply. I have lost some patients because of my attitude."

She sighed, then went on as if telling this story for the first time. "It had come to the point that I had almost decided to go into abortion practice exclusively. There is certainly more money in it and less risk of lawsuits. There is much demand, and many reasons to do such a thing. As a matter of fact, I had decided in favor of dropping my obstetric practice the very day I was called in to work with Princess. The reason I'm telling you all this is so you will understand my circumstances prior to meeting your wife."

"Sure," was all Sam could think to say.

"I felt both relieved and deeply troubled by my decision. I reasoned that in ten years I could retire wealthy from my abortion practice. It would take twice that long to achieve the same end with my regular practice. Yet when I realized Princess was willing to die rather than let me operate on her, I was stung. I was struck with such deep selfloathing that I could barely function. I know I displayed it as anger toward Princess, but it was really anger toward myself. I wanted her to recant, to let me help her."

There was a long pause. Dr. Green looked at her hands, which she laid flat on the desk. "She was right, you know. If I would have performed that operation on her I would have felt vindicated. My skills saved precious lives and eliminated unwanted tissue in the same noble stroke. What she actually did was force me to reevaluate my own morality. She forced me to look deep enough into my soul to see that I did not like what was there."

Sam cleared his throat nervously. He wasn't sure why she was telling him all this. "So," he asked. "Can you share what your decision was?"

"It wasn't a decision," she declared. "Princess said I had to make a deal with God. The first time I came back I had decided to reevaluate my position. Princess would not accept that. Even not knowing what my decision was, she would not accept it. When I went away the second time I realized if I was not sincere in my negotiations with God, and if it was not one hundred percent right, Princess and her babies were going to die. The thought of my trading their lives for my financial gain was so bitter in my mind that I literally felt ill."

The doctor stood and walked to the window so that her back was to Sam. She stared out the window at the towering mountains just beyond.

When she finally spoke, her voice was subdued. "When I returned the second time, I had made a deal with God. I told Him that if He would let me save Princess's life and her babies, I would keep my obstetric practice and not switch to abortion work. Just in case that wasn't enough, I also promised to only perform an abortion in limited cases where the mother's life was at stake. Any others I would send to another doctor.

"When I returned to Princess's bedside I knew it would be enough. I was not even surprised when she nodded. I wasn't sure we had not waited too long, though."

"It was a frightening and confusing event," Sam confided. "I'm extremely grateful you were able to come to a decision that allowed you to save her. It makes my gratitude doubly significant."

The doctor walked around the desk. Sam stood and accepted her hand. "So am I," she said softly. There was a brief hesitation before she added, "I am very grateful to Princess, Sam. Please tell her that. Tell her that, once again, I like what I see in the mirror."

* * *

Sam had dubious feelings as he escorted Princess to the door to Dr. Spenard's office. It was small and somewhat shabby compared to Dr. Green's. It was obvious he cared much less for fine trappings and acquiring wealth. Princess blushed when she shook his hand. He was in his thirties, medium height, and dark-haired. He had a thin mustache and bright blue eyes. His speech was animated and upbeat. He seemed larger than life. Even Sam thought he was good-looking and was impressed with his optimistic appraisal of his wife's condition.

After a thorough exam, which Sam attended, the doctor proposed a form of oxygen therapy which involved removing quantities of her blood, infusing it with oxygen, and injecting it back into her. He recommended the treatment three times a week.

Dr. Spenard sat on a small stool and faced Sam directly.

"I've never tried this therapy in a case such as this, but I'm optimistic Princess will benefit from it."

Sam nodded and took Princess's hand.

"It stands to reason that if oxygen deprivation has caused minor brain damage, then oxygen enrichment may reverse it," he told them confidently. "I suggest we try it. It is somewhat expensive."

Sam nodded. "That's not a problem." In addition, the doctor prescribed an extensive diet change and megavitamin therapy along with long exposure to sunlight and moderate exercise. They left his office feeling hopeful.

On the way home Princess unexpectedly began to cry. "Sam," she said after she regained her composure. "I know I've changed since the babies were born. I don't know why. I just don't feel the same. I'm so sorry. I really miss the wonderful feelings we had before. I desperately want them back. Will you forgive me and be patient with me?"

Sam fought back strong emotions. It was the first time she had acknowledged anything amiss. "Princess, I will always love you, no matter what. I will wait as long as it takes," he said with a lump in his throat. She smiled at him almost the way she used to. It warmed his soul.

Princess returned from her first treatment animated and happy. She laughed and seemed enthusiastic for the first time in months. She described her session with the doctor in glowing terms.

Princess continued her treatments every other day and Sam returned to work. The business had been running without him for months. He returned to find things badly needing his attention. He had left affairs pretty much in the hands of his salesman and the bookkeeper. He threw himself into his work with passion, feeling optimistic about everything for the first time in months. In a short time sales surged as word spread about the great deals he was offering. In reality, it was the first time a sub-wholesaler had done business in Alaska, and the market responded with near greed to the lower prices.

In a short time the opportunity came to expand into Washington and Oregon. Sam flew down for a couple weeks to investigate. He returned having signed a contract with several diamond wholesalers potentially worth millions.

Princess continued with her treatments faithfully. After each treatment she felt stronger and upbeat, but the effect wore off before the next treatment. She was afraid to stop taking them. On the day Sam returned home she came home from a treatment depressed.

"Dr. Spenard says I'm not responding to the treatments. The effect appears to be temporary. He wants to try something else."

Sam swore loudly. He had truly hoped it would help. Princess's eyes opened wide in shock. "I'm sorry," he added contritely. "I just really wanted this to work! What does he suggest?"

Princess dropped her purse onto the couch and took Bonnie from Sam's arms. "Well, he thinks I may have a chronic blood infection called Epstein-Barr virus. I have heard about it before. It drains a person's energy and causes depression."

"I've never heard of it," Sam admitted. "Why would you get a virus during an operation? Is there a cure?"

"Well, there really is no cure. There is a treatment. It involves a low-stress lifestyle, absolutely no sugar, and very little red meat. There is also some medicine you take with it."

"No sugar?" Sam asked a bit alarmed. He was particularly fond of sweets, as was Princess.

"None whatsoever, he says."

"Gosh. What do you want to do?"

"There's one other thing I haven't mentioned."

"What's that?" Sam wondered. From her voice he could tell she was reluctant to tell him.

"The no-stress part."

"Yeah?"

"Well, he runs a retreat. It's somewhere near Fairbanks. Every couple of months he takes a few patients up there for a month to six weeks. He describes it like a health spa of sorts. He said you relax, have lots of massages, eat raw, fresh food, have laugh therapy, play games, and take lots of natural medicine."

"It actually sounds fun," Sam admitted, although the thought of her leaving for a month sent panic through him.

"I'm reluctant to leave the twins," Princess said with sadness. It pained him that she wasn't reluctant to leave him. "And to leave you that long," she added as if she had read his mind.

He smiled at her and patted her cheek. They sat at their favorite spot on the big sofa near the grand piano. The babies were still asleep upstairs.

"Dr. Spenard says I would have to wean them. He says they have nursed long enough. He suggests doing it several weeks before the retreat so I'll be comfortable again. He really wants me to go and thinks he can cure me completely in that length of time." She sounded very hopeful.

Sam struggled with all this. It sounded both good and potentially bad. He didn't know Dr. Spenard any more than from one brief visit. He liked him but wasn't ready to trust his Princess on a nearly two-month trip to some isolated location.

"How many other people will be there?" Sam asked, forcing concern from his voice.

"Rob says about a dozen will be there, all female. No men at the retreat, except him of course. He'll only be there at the beginning to get it started, and the last two weeks to finish up. He may come up once in between."

"Rob?" he asked suspiciously.

"You knew his name is Dr. Robert Spenard, didn't you? He prefers being called Rob to Doctor. Most of his patients call him Dr. Rob."

"Dr. Rob," Sam said as if trying it on for size. He didn't like it. "What do you want to do?" he asked, hoping she would express doubt, or reservations.

"I want to go," she said simply. "Grandma Mahoy can handle the twins and would love it. The girls will be fine. You can manage, and when I return maybe things will be as they were before."

It was apparent to Sam that Princess had thought this all through. Even that concerned him. "Will you call, or does he keep you incommunicado?"

"That's another thing. No calls except for emergencies. He wants us to forget about the real world and just relax. He is optimistic that it will have a dramatic effect upon me. I really want to try. I need a break, and this could be the answer to my prayers. Please say it's okay. Please?"

"Princess, you don't need my permission to go. You're not my daughter. If you feel it's that important, I'll support you in it. I just want you to understand that I don't like it."

"Oh? Why?"

"I don't have a good feeling about it, that's all."

"Do you know why?"

"It has something to do with spending six weeks with a strange man in a paradise of back massages and laugh therapy. Maybe I'm just skeptical."

"Or jealous?"

"Should I be jealous?" Sam asked, unable to keep suspicion from his voice.

"Certainly not!" she replied heatedly. "Rob is my doctor, nothing more. If you think so lowly of me, maybe you're the one who needs some help. Have I ever given you reason to doubt my loyalty?"

"No," Sam replied truthfully, and humbly.

"Have I ever disappointed you?"

"No," he answered after a millisecond's delay. Even that tiny hesitation was enough to infuriate her.

"Oh!" she cried, stood, and stormed from the room. It was the first time she had blown up at him, ever. She had been angry at him before, but never over something so small. He sat on the couch in stunned silence.

Princess came home with a stack of baby bottles and formula the following day. From that moment on she was determined to go. Nothing he could have said would have deterred her.

* * *

Sam took Princess to the airport May 12. Dr. Spenard was there with three other patients and two nurses, all female. They were meeting others in Fairbanks, he said. Sam waited with a sinking heart until the plane was airborne. He did not like it, not at all. Princess had said goodbye happily, and kissed him on the cheek. She was far too cheerful at leaving for a six-week separation, far too cheerful for his comfort. Time dragged by painfully. Sam spent his days busy with business, which was thriving. Every week he sent enormous amounts of money to their accounts overseas. Grandma tended the girls and was in a heaven of her own. Soon the big house became too empty for him, and he slept at his parents.

Benjamin was gone on a mission by now, and there was an extra room. Sam settled in and restlessly awaited Princess's return. He could find no joy in the waiting, and every day ground by in anguish. He became so grumpy that his mother told him to lighten up or go back home. Sam apologized and tried to cheer up. Whatever good humor he displayed was purely superficial. The only time he felt peace was in doing elder's quorum work. He spent many evenings out until late doing the only thing that brought him comfort.

After a whole month of waiting he received a letter in the mail. It was addressed in Princess's flowery script. He tore it open with haste. The note was written on a single sheet of paper.

> *Dear Sam,*
>
> *How are you and the girls? I am doing much better and have decided to continue for the full six weeks. That way I can have the benefit of working with Dr. Rob the last two weeks. The rest and treatment have been very good for me. Thank you for supporting me in this. Kiss Lisa and Bonnie for me.*
>
> *I'll be home soon. Love, Princess*

Even though the message was upbeat, Sam read it like a funeral program. He threw it on the sofa and stormed from the house. Like a drum beating an unending cadence in his mind he kept hearing "Dr. Rob, Dr. Rob, Dr. Rob . . ."

* * *

Princess walked off the plane side by side with Dr. Rob, chatting happily. She smiled and waved at Sam as soon as she spotted him. She said something to Rob, smiled affectionately at her doctor, then turned her attention to Sam. She was cheery-faced and bright. As happy as she seemed, there was something unusual about her. Her face was deeply tanned, but that wasn't it. As he hugged her, Sam came to the startling conclusion that there was no light in her face. He hoped that this was just from not attending church for six weeks and nothing more.

Princess talked enthusiastically all the way home about the retreat and her progress. She spoke in glowing, almost reverent, terms about Dr. Rob and how he had worked with her endlessly to get her going again. She kept repeating how he had pulled her through in an almost miraculous way.

She pulled open her blouse to show him her tan. "Light therapy," she said happily and laughed. They gathered up the girls, and Princess cooed and snuggled them. She seemed so happy to hold them again. Grandma Mahoy handed them back soberly. Sam already knew she was dreading giving them back, and he suspected there would be some tears as soon as they left.

Once home Princess played with her babies for hours until they were exhausted. She fed them slowly, and bathed them with great care. Sam offered repeatedly to help, but Princess kindly refused. She was starved for their love, and she wanted to soak them up as much as she could. When they were finally put to bed, Princess disappeared into their room. Sam fought the urge to follow her and instead sat down at the piano.

The keys felt like old friends, warm and willing. He ran his fingers across the keys until the familiar unity came, and the music poured from his soul. For a time he was lost in the joy of music, and the sadness of the burden upon his soul. The music flowed from the piano in surging waves, at times thunderous and complex, at others, longing and sad. He played with his eyes closed, thinking of nothing else. At long last the music came to its own conclusion and he lowered his hands into his lap.

"I have scarcely ever heard you play with more feeling," Princess said from nearby. He had been unaware of her presence, and opened his eyes to see her sitting on the big sofa. She had on her soft blue robe. She came and sat beside him on the piano bench and laid her head on his chest. It was something she had not done in a long time, and though it pleased him, it also caused him to wonder.

They were still in one another's arms when the babies awoke crying at six in the morning. Princess winked at him, kissed him softly, and slid from bed.

She had never winked at him before. The only person he could remember who winked at people was Dr. Rob. It made his heart sink.

* * *

Sam stayed home all that day to be with his little family.

It was evening, and the babies were already sleeping when Princess came down the stairs. She joined him at their favorite spot beside the piano. Instead of snuggling up next to him as he expected, she sat with some space separating them.

"Is anything wrong?" he asked, not really believing anything could be wrong after last night.

"Yes, and no," she answered somewhat vaguely.

Sam put down the scriptures he was reading and turned to face her. "What's going on, Princess? Before you left you didn't want anything to do with me, and after you return, you climb all over me like it might be our last . . ." His voice trailed off. As soon as he said it, thunder struck inside his head.

"There's something I want to talk to you about," she replied. "Something has changed inside me. I don't know why, but it has. I don't know if it is brain damage from the operation, or just the way it is. At any rate, I'm different."

Sam felt his pulse quicken, his heart pounding in his throat. "Different in what way? You seemed so happy to be home."

"I am. I'm happy because I have made some decisions that were really hard, but that I had to make. Now that I've made them, I finally feel at peace."

"That's good," he said with a smile, though he didn't feel good.

"Yes, it is. But you may not think so."

"Why? What's wrong? You're killing me with suspense here. Whatever it is, we can work through it. I love you, remember? Love can conquer any obstacle."

"Two-way love can," she replied, placing a hand on his knee. "One-way love is not healing; it's entrapping."

"Princess, you're scaring me. Get to the point."

She smiled sadly. "Sam, this is hard for me too. What I'm trying to say is that I'm not in love with you—anymore."

"What!?" Sam stammered. He felt strangled, as if an iron hand had gripped his heart.

"I do love you, you see, but I'm not in love with you. I thought I was, but I've found that I'm not, and it would be unfair of me to keep you trapped in a relationship with someone who doesn't love you. Sam, I don't think I ever really loved you. I think I idealized you as a missionary, and wanted to be like you, and to have your faith and determination. I just don't think it was ever really love. I'm sorry it's just taken me this long to realize it."

"Princess, I can't believe this. I have seen such love in your eyes. I know you love me, or at least you did. How can you say this? It's not right. It's not true. It's not . . ." He couldn't think of anything else to say.

Princess averted her eyes and continued. "I know this is hard to accept. It was for me too, but the truth is that we will be happier apart. You will still be around the girls, and they will love you just the same. It's just that I can't live with you now that I . . ." She didn't finish.

"Now that you love Dr. Rob," Sam finished for her with sarcasm in his voice.

"Even if that were true, it would be beside the point," she said. "The important thing isn't whether I love someone else but that I no longer love you."

"You said you never loved me, and now you said you used to. Which is it?"

"Well, I suppose I used to, but not now."

"You said you do love me but don't love me. Which is it?" he demanded hotly.

"You're missing the point . . ."

"Why did we have such a wonderful night last night if you don't love me?"

"I felt I owed you that. I wanted you to feel the passion I felt . . ."

"With him?"

"Well, yes," she admitted. "If you want to be frank about it, yes."

"And did this passion express itself the same . . . ?"

"That's none of your business!"

"Of course it's my business! I'm your husband, for heaven's sake!"

"Not for much longer," she said hotly, but when she saw the slain look on his face, she instantly regretted it. She lowered her head and began to cry.

Sam began to cry too, and for a long time the only sound in the house was that of sobbing.

Finally, Princess lifted her head and dried her tears. "I'm sorry," she said. "I didn't want this to get ugly."

"It got ugly when you betrayed our vows," Sam said without looking up.

"I don't see it that way. I would never do that with someone I didn't love. But anyway, whether I did or not isn't the issue. The important thing is love, or the absence of it," she declared.

Princess stood and left the room. When she returned she had on her jacket. "I'll be back tomorrow to get the girls. They will be living with me. If you need to talk to me, and you can be rational, I'll be at Dr. Rob's home. His number is in the Anchorage directory." She turned toward the door.

"I love you, Princess," Sam said as she pulled it open.

She stopped and turned toward him. "I know you do," she said and left into the night.

Less than fifteen minutes later the phone rang. Sam let it ring a long time while he tried to compose his emotions. When it didn't stop, he picked it up.

"Sam, this is Mom. What's wrong? I have this sick feeling in my soul and it has something to do with you. Do you need me to come over?"

"Oh, Mom," Sam blurted in a sob. "She left me. She's gone to live with her doctor . . ."

"Oh, Sam! I'm sorry, Son. I was afraid when I saw her. I was afraid for her. Do you want me to come over?"

"Not now, please. I want to be alone."

"I'll come over first thing in the morning," she said, and after a long silence filled with love and support, bid him good night. He gave only passing thought to the fact that she had sensed his grief so far away. A mother's love is a powerful thing.

* * *

Melody arrived in Birmingham, England, late in the afternoon after a slow, two-hundred-mile train ride through densely populated countryside. It had rained the entire way, yet her heart sang with anticipation. Marcia and two other ladies met her at the train station. They ran into one another's arms in a tumultuous collision of joy and sorrow.

Marcia looked radiant, and notwithstanding the recent bad news of their father, happier than Melody had ever seen her. She still wore her hair long, her figure somewhat softer than before. But it all suited her very well. She spoke in glowing terms about her family, her husband, her new life, and her faith. Melody was almost motivated to accuse a new Marcia of living in the old Marcia's body.

Marcia was far too compassionate to say so, but to her eyes, Melody looked haunted and weary. It made Marcia's soul ache to receive her little sister in such battered condition.

They sat up until late that night as Melody divulged the details of the loss of their father and fortune, and her miraculous escape into Wales. Marcia wanted to know every detail, and wrung every scrap of information from her sister until Melody felt dry. Marcia's husband and children had long ago gone to bed.

Melody's eyes were closing without her permission when her sister stood, took one step to the center of the room, and knelt down. She beckoned Melody to join her. Melody had never seen such behavior in her life and joined her there with a befuddled mind. Marcia took her hand, bowed her head, and prayed.

"Heavenly Father, I just want to thank you that my sister, Melody, has come to be with me safely. Oh, Heavenly Father you know how much I love her and how many times I have prayed for her safety. I was beginning to think I might be bothering you, I asked so many times. I guess I don't really believe that, but I did ask a lot. I'm so grateful you answered my prayers. Thank you, Heavenly Father.

"We are so sad about our father. He was a good man, as you already know. By now you've already had some conversations with him, and I wouldn't be surprised if he was just as abrupt with you as he was with everyone else. But he was that way because he had to be. And we hope you'll forgive him, and send him missionaries to teach him the gospel. Please tell him how much I love Thy gospel, and tell him I'll be so happy if he will listen to the missionaries you send.

"Heavenly Father, I want to end this prayer by sending my voice to your throne in gratitude once again for bringing Melody safely to me, for sending the nice old man to help her, and letting the missionaries teach her a little and give her your book. It is all truly amazing to me, but you know how I'm always a little overwhelmed by how good you are to me. I love you. In the name of Jesus Christ, amen."

When Melody opened her eyes, Marcia's were still tightly shut. She had the distinct impression she was appending a silent PS to her prayer. She had never heard her sister pray. Actually, except for Sam, she had never heard anyone pray who was not a minister. She had been told that her mother prayed, but she was too young to remember. Her father certainly didn't pray, and all the prayers she had heard from ministers seemed formal and impersonal.

Her sister's prayer seemed as personal as if she were talking to someone right in the room. It was so filled with love and hope that Melody inwardly wanted Marcia to show her how she could pray that way herself. Wanting to be able to pray suddenly caused Melody to feel peace and warmth in a way she had never known before. The feeling was very small, but so beautiful it brought tears to her eyes. Quite unexpectedly her father evolved from being dead, to simply being absent. It lightened her grief, and unburdened her soul as nothing else could.

Her sister's simple prayer had brought her father back to life as surely as Jesus had raised Lazarus from the tomb. What had been an intolerable, inalterable dissolution of a man she dearly loved was now simply a separation of predictable duration. To her joy, with her father's sudden awakening in her heart, she found her mother similarly alive, and the joy was more than her heart could hold.

When Marcia opened her eyes, Melody's were closed, tears coursing softly down her cheeks.

It took months to get Melody legally admitted into the country. It was very difficult because England had no sympathy for Rhodesian refugees. It was England, after all, that had forced Ian Smith's government into economic poverty through the sanctions and orchestrated their overthrow.

Melody ultimately acquired citizenship through "alternative" means, at considerable expense. Melody paid for it all from the funds she had saved playing music in the park. She could easily earn several hundred pounds a day, approximately triple a working man's salary. She didn't like having to deal with the type of people who for a price could provide anything you desired; yet at the time it seemed she had no other choice. She was a fugitive, an illegal immigrant, political dissident, and undesirable foreigner subject to arrest and immediate deportation back to Rhodesia. It didn't take much imagination to realize what her fate would be in the hands of those who had killed her father.

After gaining citizenship, Melody simply became a young woman of modest means and considerable talent, moving through the English economic system in an unremarkable way.

During all this time Melody had been unemployed. As soon as she was legally able to do so, she scoured the area for any suitable employment. Without any formal training other than music, she could only find mind-numbing employment serving food, washing dishes, changing beds, or other menial labor. She considered going back to school to learn bookkeeping or some other trade, but her love was music and that alone. The thought of doing anything else filled her with frustration.

Accordingly, she soon gravitated back to the very thing she had first discovered, playing in the park.

Melody applied for and received a business license and permit to perform on the streets, a thing she had been lacking previously, and proceeded to play at the park twice a week. She made more than sufficient for her needs with minimal effort.

Besides, she loved it, was developing a devoted audience, and had plenty of time left for practicing the violin.

Her eyes first fell upon Theodore after having played a stirring collection of old English church hymns. She nearly always concluded each concert with those hymns, and it always pleased her audience, and consequently, topped off each day's tips. Theodore appeared older, though he was not quite thirty. Melody was just barely twenty-one at the time.

He had dark eyes that sparkled like sapphires, a straight jawline, and impressive dimples. His hair was parted on the top of his head, and combed down and back. Perhaps his most noticeable characteristic was his fine clothing and long, white scarf, which lay loosely over his shoulders in a fashion quite uncommon.

After nearly a year of making her living as a street minstrel, Melody had encountered nearly every form of human being possible. Of necessity she had developed ready answers, quick responses, and pat comebacks for every possible situation.

She had even taken the liberty of hiring the local street gang to watch out for her. Without exception, two or three longhaired boys showed up at each concert and watched after her solicitously. They hardly realized they were mostly protecting her from themselves.

When she looked up from packing away her violin, Melody saw three people remaining of the rather large afternoon crowd: one neatly dressed gentleman and two scruffy teens. The gentleman was watching her intently, while the street toughs were watching him maliciously. He was totally unaware of the dangerous position he had gotten himself into.

Melody looked at the boys and shook her head with a smile. They nodded and backed away, but did not leave.

"Evenin', Miss," the gentleman said, doffing an invisible hat. His accent was British, almost aristocratic. Doffing his nonexistent hat was a quaint gesture and intended to amuse her. It had the desired effect.

She curtsied, put a hand to her cheek and said, "Why, good evening, govnah." Her words were right out of a Charles Dickens novel she had just read, and at least a century more antiquated than his. Without intending to, she struck his funny bone a glancing blow, and he laughed so heartily for several seconds that she smiled in spite of herself.

"Oh! Oh, excuse me. If it weren't for your accent, I'd have accused you of being an American," he said, forcing himself to calmness.

"Not at all," Melody admitted cheerfully. "It's from a book by an Englishman actually."

"I thought as much. I haven't actually heard someone speak like that my whole life. Where are you from?"

"From around here," she replied as she tucked her violin under her arm. She rarely carried it by the handle. She had seen handles break, and the clasps sometimes popped open letting the precious instruments fall to the pavement.

"Your accent isn't English," he replied innocently.

She decided to take it innocently.

"My mother was from Australia," she explained. It was a partial truth, her mother had been born there, but had moved to England at age three. Her accent was decidedly not Australian, but only a linguist could have correctly labeled it Rhodesian.

"That would explain it," he replied cheerfully. "I have to admit that I have become a fan of yours. This is the fourth time I've come to the park to hear you play."

"I haven't seen you before," Melody said thoughtfully.

"The other times I wore my work clothes. You probably didn't notice me dressed that way. People often look the other way when I'm in my work clothes."

"That could be, I guess. I don't really pay much attention to faces," Melody responded. She started walking back toward Marcia's apartment, her two guardians tailing her at a distance. They would remain with her until she was out of their area. It felt kind of good having them back there. They had come in handy a couple of times on her walk home.

"My name is Theodore." He offered her a hand. "Theodore Lyman Tennison the Second," he said quite properly, bowing slightly at the waist. She took his hand and found it smooth, warm, and gentle, much different from her father's iron-like hands.

"Melody MacUlvaney," she replied.

"Ah, a good Scottish name."

"Irish, actually. My father's family were land barons in Ireland until sometime after the turn of the century." In reality, it had been a mere twenty-five years ago.

"Yes, I believe I've read some of your family's history. Come to think of it, there are some MacUlvaneys buried in the old church cemetery where I work," he said thoughtfully.

"You work at the church?" She found it an odd employer for one dressed so well.

"Yes," Theodore replied, his mind obviously focusing on something else.

"Uhm, what do you do there? What kind of work are you in?"

"Hmm? Oh, excuse me. I was trying to remember the dates on the tombstones. I'm what one might call a caretaker."

"You take care of the building?"

"That and other things. Why don't you play with some big orchestra? You certainly have the talent," he returned in an obvious change of subject.

Melody decided not to press him. He was apparently uncomfortable telling her his job. She didn't have a particular problem with the idea that he was a janitor, or gardener, but apparently he did. Her father had been a farmer, and dirty hands seemed normal on a man. Whatever he did, he could afford at least one change of nice clothes, for he was wearing them.

"I do play with the city orchestra, and I've been invited to play with the Liverpool Philharmonic when it comes here on tour next week," Melody explained happily. It was something she was looking forward to, and for which she was dedicating many hours of preparation.

"Truly? I simply must get tickets. Will you tell me when the concert is? I should be most disappointed to miss it. I love orchestra, and I love your playing immensely. I'd love to go see you. If I don't guard myself, I'm going to fall in love with—" This all came out in a rush. He blushed, cleared his throat, and concluded ". . . your music."

Melody found it quite admirable that Theodore was innocent enough to blush. It belied the sleek, confident facade that his clothing and demeanor implied.

He shuffled his feet. "Please forgive me. I didn't intend to . . ."

Melody mischievously decided to reward him for his impudence in the worst possible way. She leaned toward him, kissed him softly on the cheek, straightened, flashed him her most dazzling smile, and said, "Whatever for?" She walked past him without another word. She dared a glance back many minutes later, and he was still standing in that exact spot, a hand pressed to his cheek where she had anointed him with her lips.

"That'll fix him for about a week," she thought to herself playfully, fully intent on completely ignoring him the next time they crossed paths. It was a little mean, but he deserved it.

In reality, it fixed him for about the rest of his life.

* * *

Grandma Mahoy was with Sam when Princess came to get the twins. She arrived with a police car behind her. The officer stood with one hand on the butt of his pistol as Princess gathered the baby's things. The only thing she said to Sam was, "I'll be in touch." She and the officer left in a swirl of dust. Sam felt as if his whole purpose for living had just walked out the door.

The papers arrived a week later. Sam read them with deep regret. They outlined the details of their divorce. The important parts were that Princess wanted the home and all its furnishings except the piano. Sam could have the business and one car.

Princess acquired sole custody of the girls, and he had visitation rights every other week on Saturday and Sunday. He would pay her a sizable sum each month until the girls reached eighteen.

To him it was like reading an execution order. He tried to sign it and could not. The papers sat on the living room coffee table for weeks. Finally he wrote Princess a note explaining that he could not sign them and sent them back.

The next day he received a phone call from her attorney suggesting he contact an attorney because they were suing for divorce. With or without his signature it was going to occur.

That following evening Sam was alone in the big house. It felt like a tomb. He wanted to pack up and move out, to escape the memories. He sat at the piano and was filled with the vision of her sitting beside him, her head resting gently on his chest. He almost stood to escape it, but instead he lifted the lid, and laid his hands on the keys. He was about to play when the Holy Spirit flooded over him. There was a single message, one he had never heard before. "Record it," the sweet feeling said.

He stood and found a small cassette recorder. He placed it on the piano and set it to record.

For a long moment he waited until sadness overwhelmed him, then love, then peace. Somewhere in his mind he felt the joy loving Princess had been, and how it had felt so eternal, so very forever. He said aloud "I have always loved you," and the music came.

He had often felt the flow of music in his soul, but never like this. If there was a pure source of music, as there is a pure source of truth, he found it that night. Every note, every harmony, every delicate, breathlessly beautiful phrase was known to him. It was opened to his mind as clearly as if he had been taught this haunting melody in some premortal childhood, and had known it all his life. He played, and as he played he spoke the words that carried the burden of his love.

The music came to him in sweet flows of perfection, and he played with deepest feeling. When it was over, it was simply over, and the feeling passed. He reached up and clicked off the recorder. He popped the tape from the machine and dropped it into his pocket. He sat for a long time in silence.

On impulse Sam stood and went into his study. He addressed an envelope to a former missionary companion whom he knew to be successfully involved in the music industry. He dropped the tape inside, and mailed it the next day.

Two weeks later to the day he received a large brown envelope. He opened it and was surprised to find a piece of sheet music inside. It wasn't until he read the title that he began to understand. "I Have Always Loved You," was in bold type across the front page. He sat at the piano and opened the music.

The score was well done, and though somewhat simplified from the way he had played it on the tape, it was exactly as he remembered it. The words between the lines were his as well.

He was stunned to tears. There was a handwritten phone number on the first page.

* * *

"Mike? This is Sam Mahoy. I like what you did with my song."

"Elder Mahoy!" the voice on the other end exclaimed. "I haven't heard from you since our mission, and then I get this tape with this hauntingly beautiful song on it. Hey, Sam, I knew you played, but had no idea you wrote music as well. It is a fantastic piece, and I want to produce it."

"Well, I'm flattered," Sam said. "But it's deeply personal, and I'm not quite sure I want to throw it to the world."

"All love songs are deeply personal. All great love songs come from deep within the soul, from a place of beauty now scarred by pain," his friend observed quietly. "Anyway, this song is a masterpiece. Don't you realize that, Sam?"

"I don't know."

Michael persisted. "If you didn't want it published why did you send it to me?"

"I felt prompted by the Holy Spirit to send it to you," Sam replied candidly.

His friend cleared his throat meaningfully. "Well, let me rephrase the question then. If Heavenly Father didn't want it published, why did He prompt you to send it to me?"

"Good point," Sam replied at length, still unsure.

"Sam, if you want we can take your name off the title. You would still get the same money from it, but maybe that would help."

"I'm not concerned about money."

"Yeah, I heard you are doing really well. Listen, my friend, I'm going to publish this song one way or the other. You'll have to sue me to stop me. So what do you say?"

"I say, go ahead. I doubt it will go anywhere. It's just feelings I put to music."

"It's much more than that," Michael disagreed. "Sam, I've written and produced enough music to be able to spot inspiration. This music is timeless. If we go ahead you will become a music writing celebrity."

"I don't want to be a celebrity," Sam replied dejectedly. "What do you want?"

"I want my wife back," Sam said with more honesty than he intended.

There was a long silence from the phone. "I'll get to work on this immediately. If I have anything to say about this, you will be hearing this tune on the radio in less than a month."

A second package arrived two weeks later with a cassette tape and a bundle of papers. Sam listened to the tape. Michael had written his song into a duet for a man and woman. As Sam listened to the beautiful song he could scarcely believe it was his own. In fact, it was not. It was something that had come to him, not from him. The papers were a standard publication contract. Sam didn't even read them, but signed several places and sent them back.

Michael performed the piece at his next concert, included it on his next CD, and good to his word, Sam heard it on the radio a little more than a month from their phone conversation.

The best part of it all was that no one suspected that he was that Samuel Mahoy. The several times someone asked if he was related, he replied, "Not at all." How can one be related to oneself? Unthinkable. Had they asked if it were him, he would have replied that it was. He was happier with anonymity.

During the intervening weeks, it seemed to Sam as if he progressed through definite stages with his emotions. At first he just couldn't accept that she had really left him. He kept expecting Princess to walk through the door happily returning from shopping, or something.

After that he felt angry and wanted to kill the loathsome man who had taken her away from him. He fantasized about throwing a firebomb through the front window of Dr. Rob's medical practice, or even better, through the window of his home right while he and Princess were there. Let them see if they can be in love while their house burns down around them, he screamed in his mind. That lasted for a couple weeks.

After that, Sam begged Heavenly Father to work a miracle and let her come home and love him again. He made promises, bargains, deals with God to get her back. Even knowing that she was with a slime ball couldn't stop him from wanting her back. The thought of her being with someone else nauseated and disgusted him, but it didn't make him stop loving her.

The most difficult stage, though, was acceptance. In time it finally dawned on him that Princess was gone for good. When acceptance finally came to him he wept for three days, grew a beard, and pouted. In time though, he began to think his heart may heal.

Sam was not surprised when his attorney delivered the final papers to his office. Sam had attended none of the divorce proceedings, preferring to never see her again. His fear was that he would start loving her again, and he was not willing to go through all that anguish. He took the papers home and flopped them on the coffee table, intending to just sign them later. As soon as he did, he would have to move out of the house, and another phase of his life would come to an end. In many ways he dreaded moving from his dream home. In others, he was anxious to get on with his life.

It was not unusual for people to come visit, especially since word spread of Princess's absence. The ward had rallied around him, and someone came almost every evening to make sure he was all right and not suffering unduly.

When the doorbell rang its rich melody he was in the kitchen fussing with a Cajun dish he had just fixed. He lifted it from the oven and set it on top, then hurried to the door as it rang a third time. He switched on the porch light and pulled open the heavy oak door.

"Hello," she said quietly into the awkward silence. "Princess?" Sam gasped. He was both pleased and appalled.

He was torn between sweeping her into his arms, and strangling her there on the spot. He nearly settled the issue by slamming the door in her face, but remained paralyzed with indecision.

"May I come in, Sam?" she asked timidly, and glanced toward the big room uncertainly.

Sam realized he was blocking her way, and releasing the door, stepped aside. She smiled briefly and walked past. He caught a whiff of her perfume as she walked by, and it pierced him. Suddenly he was angry; angry that she and her perfume had left him, angry that she had betrayed him, and angry that she had returned to torture him.

"Why are you here? I'll be out in a few days, and it'll all be yours. You didn't need to come and torment me," he said bitterly with the door still open.

"Sam, I didn't come to torment you. I almost didn't come at all," she replied soberly and unbuttoned her coat. It was October, and the air was frosty with the promise of winter.

Sam closed the door a little too hard. Princess winced at the sound. "I wish you hadn't come," he said honestly, not intending to be cruel. Princess looked from the floor to his eyes, then back down again.

"I had to," she replied meekly.

"Why? To gloat? To see if I have suffered enough? To survey your castle while the former occupants can still see your triumph? To let me smell your perfume one more time?" he choked out. "Why did you come here?" he demanded.

"None of that, Sam. Nothing like that."

Hearing her say his name pierced through him like an arrow. His heart tried to beat harder, and stop dead all at the same moment. It was not a pleasant sensation. He realized with a start that he still loved her, and that made him even more angry. A battle started between love and hate, which tore at his soul. Tears formed in his eyes and he had to blink hard to keep them inside.

Princess walked to the piano and ran a hand softly across its rim. The lid was up, and Sam could see her face in the polished wood. He looked away.

"Is this where you wrote it?" she asked innocently. It was an odd question. "Wrote what?"

"My song."

"Your song?"

"The one that plays on the radio every fifteen minutes all day long," she said and rolled her eyes into her head in mock displeasure.

"Oh, it's not your song."

"Whose then? Who did you write it for? Who have you always loved? Is there someone I don't know about?" Princess asked, looking around the room as if expecting to find someone.

"You know there isn't," he replied quietly.

"Then you did write it for me?" It was not meant to be a question, but came out unsure.

"I wrote it about you, perhaps—not for you."

"What's the difference?"

"The difference is . . . that was before."

"Before what, Sam?"

"Before you betrayed me! Before you betrayed us!" he replied with more anger than he had intended. But the anger was there, hot and insistent. It caused his skin to crawl, and his fingers ached to throttle something, to destroy something that could never be fixed again.

Princess took a tentative step toward him. "Sam, the words say 'I will spend forever loving you.' Are you telling me that you no longer love me? Has forever ended so soon?"

Sam stood in silence, rocking back and forth as if standing on a ship. He had to hold onto the piano to steady himself. He couldn't believe he was having this conversation. If she hadn't come back to torture him as she claimed, she was doing a thorough job of it just the same.

"Forever came to an end when you walked out the door and went to his bed instead of mine," he said with a steely coldness.

To his surprise a tear sprang to her eye, and rolled down her cheek.

She made no attempt to wipe it away. "Then you don't love me anymore?"

Sam almost screamed at her, if for no other reason than to hurt her, but the words would not come, and his anger was hot, not cold. Hot anger flares to hurt back as a defense; cold anger craves revenge. A long silence passed.

"Princess," her name stuck in his throat. He swallowed hard. "I do still love you, I'm afraid."

A smile brightened her face. He wasn't finished. "But, I'm afraid that I can't forgive you," he said in a small voice. "I am trying as hard as I can to not love you. I have already started to succeed. At least I thought so thirty minutes ago," he said very quietly.

"Sam, I have listened to you tell me that you love me every fifteen minutes for the past two weeks. Every time I hear that music I want to cry. I can't escape your telling me you love me. You tell me in my car, in the grocery store, in the vehicles next to me at the stop sign—everywhere! I have heard it so many times, that I realized something I didn't understand a month ago."

"What's that?" he asked blandly, trying hard to convince himself he didn't want to hear her answer and altogether failing.

"I realized that I . . ." She paused to collect herself. When she continued her voice was very small. "I realized that not only do I still love you, but I'm hopelessly in love with you. Very, very much. I'm sooo sorry . . ." She paused a long time. "I want to come home," she said. Her voice sounded very childlike, afraid and lost. It made his heart ache even more, if that was actually possible.

Sam fell into the couch as if he had been slugged. He buried his face in his hands and silently wept. For a long time he wept, until the grief was past. When he was finished he looked at her. She had been crying too, silently, painfully. She looked at him and smiled hopefully, but he could not return it.

"I wish you had not come here tonight," Sam said. "It would have been easier if you would have stayed where you belong, with him," he added, not intending to emphasize the last word as much as he had.

"But, Sam. I just told you that I love you. Doesn't that mean anything?"

Sam stared at her with a wounded expression. "Yes! It means you are going to be much, much harder to forget. It means that now I am going to have to hate you and despise you in order to forget you. Before, I only had to be angry and unforgiving. Now I have to be disgusted by you. I didn't want that, Princess. Don't you see? You shouldn't have come!"

Princess choked back a strangled sob. "I know you love me, Sam. Do you really want me to just walk out that door and never come back? Even though you know I do really, honestly, love you? Is that what you want?"

"No! Yes! I mean, there is no choice."

"Why, Sam? Why?" she nearly shouted between sobs.

His face contorted with pain, Sam said, "Because every time I see you, I think of you with him. Every time I think of your face, I think of him touching it. Every time I see your lips, I see him kissing them. It isn't because I don't love you, or because you don't love me! It's because I can't look at you anymore! It's because I don't respect you. We have lost the glue that holds a relationship together—trust. It's not that I don't love you. It's that I don't want you!" He was shouting at her now. Princess flinched at each of his words as if they were bullets striking her. Her shoulders trembled as she wept. She buried her hands in her face, and her soul wailed as if dying. Suddenly, she stood. She moved with determination toward the door, clutching her coat about her. Sam looked away. He heard the door open and close and she was gone from his life—gone forever.

Sam's eyes fell on the divorce documents still lying where he had dropped them. He pulled a pen from his pocket, flipped to the last page, and signed with a flourish. He was angry again, and this time it was cold. He marched to the door and yanked it open. Princess had just started her car when she saw him coming in the headlights. She opened the door and stood again, a look of strangled hope on her face.

Sam stomped up to her and, jamming the papers in her face, opened his mouth to speak the last hateful words that would erase her from his life forever. Just as his voice began he felt a wash of power penetrate him, and a voice more powerful than a billion decibels blasted through his soul. Its message was unmistakable. These words thundered in his mind: "At the peril of thine own soul!"

He took a step back as if struck by lightning. He gasped, clutched his chest, and fell to the ground on his knees, divorce papers scattering on the frozen ground.

Princess was terrified by all this, and, slamming the car door shut, ran to kneel beside him. She put a hand on his forehead, then on his neck to see if he was having a heart attack.

She decided nothing obviously was amiss, yet something was terribly wrong.

She began to cry tears of true panic. "What's wrong, Sam? What's wrong? Please be all right. I'm leaving now, so just relax. I'm sorry I hurt you. You're right, I shouldn't have come. Can you get up? Just get up so I know you're okay, and I'll leave. I won't come back to hurt you again, I promise. Sam . . ."

She tugged on his arm. He looked up at her. Her hair had fallen onto his shoulder. It smelled that special smell that he had loved so long, so well, so perfectly.

Suddenly, unexpectedly, the anger left, the pride melted, the hurt burrowed out of sight, and he could stand it no longer.

Sam looped an arm around her neck and pulled her to him so hard she literally fell into his arms. He lifted her to him, slowly, gently, and kissed her with all the love he had thought gone and forgotten.

Startled, Princess stared at him wide-eyed, then feeling his tenderness, she closed her eyes and surrendered. Sam held and kissed her for a long while, bathing her face in his tears. Finally, chilled and feeling repentant, he stood and in a single powerful move, lifted her with him. She looped an arm around his neck, her lips still pressed against his. He carried her into the house, and stood her near the piano. Wonder, fear, doubt, and hope simultaneously played on her face.

Sam studied her face, then pulled her into his arms and held her, then pushed her at arm's length to study her again, then pulled her to him again. This he did many times, until they were both confused.

"Sam, please talk to me," Princess finally said as he held her fiercely against him.

"I love you," he said in simple explanation. It was exactly what she wanted to hear.

"I love you too," she sobbed back, her voice muffled against his chest. "But, can you forgive me? Can you accept me back, even knowing what I've done?"

"Princess . . . It feels so good to say your name again," he interjected. "Princess, inside me it still hurts. It hurts more fiercely than anything I have ever felt. But, I love you, and I want you, and I want to forgive you. In time, with Heavenly Father's help, I will. Until then, I'll just concentrate on what is, not what isn't."

"I'm so sorry," she sobbed, and wrapped her arms around him again very tightly. He held her for a long time. "I don't know what has come over me. I just know that I want to come home. More than anything in this whole world, I know that I love you, and I want to be with you. I want to be passionate like we used to be," she said shyly, but with certainty.

"One thing at a time," Sam responded sadly. "One thing at a time." He knew some healing had to occur first.

"I understand. Oh!" she suddenly said, pushing away from him. "I need to get the babies. They're in the car."

"They are?" Sam demanded. "Are they all right?"

"They were fine just a minute ago. Come on, let's get them. That is, if they are spending the night here?" she asked, not entirely sure.

"Where else?" he demanded happily. "This is where they belong." Then more softly, "This is where you belong."

At that moment they were startled to hear the high-pitched whine of a jet engine and the whup-whup-whup of a helicopter in the yard. They exchanged puzzled looks, and Sam walked to the door while looking at this watch. It was late. He pulled open the door to a hurricane of blowing snow. The helicopter was just settling a short distance from the house, its blades blasting a hurricane of snow at them. Sam pushed the door closed against the gale. Sam knew whoever was in the chopper would wait for the swirl of snow to die down before coming to the door.

"You don't suppose that could be your father, do you?" Sam asked in amazement.

Princess's eyes grew wider. "I don't know, but I wouldn't really put it past him."

"Me either," Sam agreed with mixed feelings. "It sure is odd timing though."

"Very odd," Princess agreed.

Suspicion quickly grew stronger than curiosity. "Sam, open the door! Open it back up!" Princess cried. Sam pulled the door back open. "Look!" she screamed. Sam's eyes followed her shaking finger. He stepped back with a gasp. The hated "22" screamed at them in large red figures from the door. Paint dripped from them like blood. At that moment they heard glass break.

Sam bolted through the door just a step ahead of Princess.

A "22" had also been painted on the windshield of the car. A figure was darting toward the chopper even as it lifted into the air. Sam and Princess ignored the whipping snow and ran to the car. The passenger door window had been smashed, but the door was still locked.

Princess had snapped the electric door locks even as she ran to help Sam. The childproof rear door locks meant the door could not be opened from either side while locked. It was the only reason their babies were still in the car. A baby blanket lay outside in the snow. The tightly strapped car seats had kept the thugs from removing car seat and babies together. It was obvious they had tried. One of the harness straps holding Bonnie into her seat had been cut with a knife.

Terrified, they carried their crying babies inside. Though frightened by the noise and blowing snow, the twins quieted quickly and went back to sleep. Princess and Sam put them in their cribs in utter silence. It was too terrible to contemplate, and both he and Princess were numb. But at least they were numb together, and that mercifully softened the blow.

* * *

Theodore was at Melody's Saturday afternoon performance in the park. He seemed impatient for the two hours to pass. He walked up to Melody straight away after the concert and held out four tickets with a huge grin as if they were winning lottery tickets.

"I've purchased tickets to all four performances!" His voice was almost squeaky with excitement.

She decided to carry through on the brush-off portion of his punishment but couldn't make herself be so rude as to completely ignore him. So she decided on a low-key response instead.

"You'll surely tire of it, then. It's the same program each night."

His face fell for just an instant and then brightened. "I'll enjoy the concert the first night, and I'll just enjoy watching you the other nights," he said, in what seemed to her to be an answer he had carefully crafted and rehearsed. It was, in fact, utterly spontaneous.

"That's nice. I'll see you there, then." Melody turned and walked away. She didn't need to look back to know he was standing there perplexed. Had she looked back, she would have seen a man with a wounded heart. It's a good thing she didn't, for as tender as her heart was, she probably would have run back, begged his forgiveness, and hugged him until he was thoroughly confused.

Theodore attended all four concerts. Melody caught sight of him out of the corner of her eye. His face was plainly enthralled. She played first chair and was guest soloist for one of the Beethoven pieces. She had played beyond herself each night, and the crowd was very appreciative. It was a glorious thing to be a part of such beautiful music.

Melody fully expected Theodore to come charging onto the stage after each concert to congratulate her, but he did not.

After the fourth night she fully expected it, but again he evaporated with the crowd. As she rode home in the cab, Melody could not help feeling a little disappointed.

Melody's enigmatic church employee did not show up for a performance in the park for almost three weeks. For the first week she felt angry that he would take her teasing so to heart.

The second week she felt angry at herself for skewering him so badly. The third week she just felt deeply disappointed.

When he did return, it was Melody's last outdoor performance of the year. The afternoons were beginning to be blustery with the first curtain call of fall. Soon the rains would begin and not relent until they turned to snow.

It was a brilliantly sunny afternoon, with a tease of crispness in the air. A light breeze brought the fresh smell of the ocean to the park. As if sensing this would be her last public performance until spring, and perhaps forever, loyal listeners turned out in large numbers. She no longer stood on the sidewalk, but had moved to the place of honor inside the small gazebo at the center of the park. The little building amplified sound, provided an impromptu stage with a pleasant backdrop.

She often wore a formal-length, deep blue velvet dress with a white collar, white fingerless gloves, and white high heels. To see one so attractive making such startlingly beautiful music was so unexpectedly grand that few passersby could actually pass by.

Theodore didn't arrive until late in the performance and stood far back in the crowd. When it was over he waited for the press of people to thin before coming toward her. He seemed unsure. She didn't blame him after her prank at his expense.

"Hello, Melody," he said quietly. "I'm sorry I've missed so many of your performances."

"I really don't blame you," she answered.

Theodore sounded baffled. "Oh? Why don't you blame me?" He was dressed almost as she remembered, except his white scarf was now soft wool rather than silk.

Melody blushed, which not only intrigued Theodore but also charmed him. "I owe you an apology for teasing you so shamelessly. I wouldn't have come to my concerts either."

His smile brightened. "Whatever are you talking about?" he asked, shaking his head from side to side.

"Well, when I . . . I mean because . . . Why didn't you come to my concerts?" she finally asked.

"I had final examinations this whole last month, plus I finished my thesis, so I just didn't have the time. I did miss your music terribly, though. I hope you don't think badly of me for not coming."

Melody looked at him incredulously, her eyebrows raised in surprise. "You're not mad at me? You just had to study?" she asked with wonder in her voice, at the same time laughing at herself. It occurred to her she had been pretty self-centered to think his whole world was in orbit around her as if she were the sun.

"Why would I be angry at you? I have thought nothing but fond thoughts about you this last month as I sat in dreary classrooms making hen scratchings on scraps of paper."

Melody gathered up her things as she tried to think of a graceful way to rescue herself from her own foolishness. "How did it go? Did you pass?" she asked in a blatant attempt to change the subject. He looked at her through narrowed eyes, then quickly smiled again.

"I did!" he finally said happily. "I'm now a full-fledged doctor of philosophy."

"Fantastic!" she cried, hardly able to comprehend the jump from janitor to student to doctor. She blinked her eyes rapidly as if the sun were too bright.

"You never mentioned you were studying to get your PhD," she finally said, a note of accusation in her voice.

"You never asked," he answered cheerfully. "I have an idea. Would you help me celebrate?"

She wasn't surprised really. She had been asked out to dinner quite a few times by handsome young men, and some not so young, and many not at all handsome. She would have been disappointed had he not asked her.

"Perhaps," she replied coyly.

He smiled and took a slip of paper from his pocket and wrote on it for a moment. When she took it she was surprised to see it held the name of a church, and a date about a month away.

"What's this?" she asked suspiciously, expecting some grandiose arrangement for a date with her.

"Part of my graduation requirement is to deliver a doctoral dissertation before the faculty and the public. I have the option of having some guest speaker or performer join me. I think it would be jolly wonderful to have you play something appropriate just before my speech. What do you say? Will you do it?"

"But, I thought . . ."

"Please don't say no. It would help me relax. I'm so tense about this, you see. Every time you play you exude confidence and peace. I just know having you play for me just before will make all the difference in the world. Won't you say yes?"

"Well, with that much fanfare I don't see how I could refuse," she replied a little too soberly. She had certainly not expected this.

"Jolly good," he exclaimed. "Well, I'll see you then," he concluded, and turned to walk away.

"Jolly good," she echoed, half in jest, half in sarcasm.

He walked away briskly. He didn't need to turn back to know she was standing there trying to figure all that out. It's a good thing he didn't, for had he, he would have seen an astonishingly beautiful young woman in a blue velvet dress standing there with tears in her eyes. As tender as his heart was in regard to her, he could not have restrained himself from running back, gathering her into his arms, and confessing the depth of his true feelings for her. Then they would have both been thoroughly confused.

Except for the name of the church, Melody had no idea how to reach him. A dozen times she stopped herself from marching over there, half to inquire what type of music he desired, the other half to find out what he really did at the church, and another half to plumb the depths of her own feelings concerning him. Of course that made more than two halves, but she did feel about twice confused concerning him.

* * *

Sam spent all the next day talking with the police, trying to neutralize the threat of the kidnapping attempt. After a full day of probing questions and toothless promises, the police finally left. Their filial suggestion was for Sam to hire a bodyguard. Their day had been so taxing that they had not had time to discuss Princess's miraculous return the night before, nor Sam's powerful change of heart just moments before the kidnapping attempt. They were just returning from putting two very sleepy little girls to bed.

"I'm exhausted," Princess said as they passed their room.

"I think I'll turn in. It's been an emotionally draining day," she said with a sigh.

"I'll grab a blanket," Sam said and hurried into their room. He returned with his pillow and a blanket. He smiled as he passed her near the stairs. Even sleeping apart, it seemed wonderful to have her home.

"Oh, there's something else I need to tell you," Princess said as he started down the stairs. He stopped on the third tread and turned back. He was tired of surprises and being devastated by sudden revelations. His face betrayed his angst.

"What's that," he asked a little petulantly.

"You remember Dr. Rob?"

Sam's face hardened. "Oh, definitely!"

"Well, last night you asked me why I was here. The reason I came here was because he threw me out of his house," she said a little sheepishly.

"So you came here because you had nowhere else to go?" he asked, feeling sick inside again. He thought she had returned because she realized she truly loved him, not because she was homeless.

"Sam, he threw me out the very first evening. I never did stay at his house. We spent the whole time with my friend Heather in Anchorage."

"You never did stay at his house?" Sam asked, his voice laced with disbelief.

"That's the wrong question," she replied brightly. "You're supposed to ask me why he threw me out."

Sam was on the verge of nausea, but he complied in a small voice. "Okay, why did he throw you out?"

"Because I refused to be intimate with him," she replied, her head lowered, her eyes fixed upon him.

"He kicked you out because you stopped sleeping with him? Is this supposed to make me feel better?"

"That isn't what I said. I said, he kicked me out because I refused to be intimate with him. You have to start something before you can stop it."

"Wait a minute. Are you saying you never did . . . ?" Princess's face lit up. She merely nodded.

"But, when you came home, you were so ... changed," he said, struggling for the right words. "How come ...?"

Princess drew a deep breath and blew it back out as if steeling herself for a difficult explanation. "That last two weeks at the retreat, Dr. Rob was very forward. He made so many advances at me. I denied him what he wanted every time. But, by the time I got home I was .... I, uhm, well, you were there!" she concluded, embarrassed.

"So you never ...?" was all Sam could stammer.

"No, never," she said, an odd look of quasi-justification mixed with shame on her face.

"You didn't ...?"

"No." Princess shook her head emphatically. "I didn't."

"And after you went to his house? You didn't ...?"

"Sam, I know you have lost faith in me, but think about it. I'm not promiscuous—it's not in my nature. I was confused, not sleeping around. I thought I had fallen out of love with you, but I was also uncertain about my feelings for him. I had been so sick, and he healed me. I was in love with love and hero worship, and perhaps with the idea of wild romance."

Sam shook his head unbelievingly. "But I accused you, and you didn't deny it! You just said you didn't see it that way, that the only thing that mattered was that you loved him, and not me. You led me to believe you had—uhm—been with him," he accused loudly.

Princess shook her head. "Sam, I'm sorry. But I think it would be more accurate to say I *let* you believe that, more than I *led* you to believe it. I was surprised you came to that conclusion, and it honestly just made me angrier. So, I let you continue believing it, partly out of spite. I was angry, and confused, and upset, and wanted you to hate me so I could feel justified in leaving you. But I never slept with him."

Sam wasn't convinced. "Didn't he try to seduce you that first evening?"

"Oh, yes!" she replied, her face reddening. "Constantly. He wooed me, dined me, and promised me the sky and stars. He told me, 'Where have you been all my life?' It was every girl's dream of being swept off her feet by a handsome hero."

She cleared her throat in an embarrassed way before continuing. "I do have a confession to make, although not as severe a one as you previously had expected."

Sam sat down heavily on the top step, and Princess knelt beside him.

"That first night after I left, he was so romantic, so persuasive and gallant," she admitted. "I felt so ... so ... female, I guess. I let him kiss me—a lot—and hold me. But, when he tried to do more, I just couldn't do it. I kept thinking about you, and I couldn't. Everything inside me cried out against it. At that point I knew I still loved you. I made him stop. It was very difficult, and he turned ugly. He was not a gracious loser. I almost had to fight my way out of his house. But, I did, and I left. I have slept at Heather's every night since then. I haven't spoken to Dr. Rob for over a month."

"Oh," was all Sam could say. The vision of her kissing him was playing before his eyes, and he didn't like it.

"Sam, listen to me," Princess said, interrupting his dark reverie. He looked into her eyes and saw love, and deep regret. "I know I sinned. And I know I offended and hurt you horribly. I was weak, but in a way, I was also strong. Do you have any idea how hard it is to let something go that far, and then tell them you won't go on? It was the hardest, most humiliating, devastating, embarrassing, *and stupid* thing I have ever done!" she said, tears gathering in her eyes. She composed herself and continued.

"At that point I knew I was in deep trouble, badly mistaken, and totally in error, standing in an evil man's home in jeopardy of my soul!" Princess shuddered involuntarily before she went on.

"As soon as I can arrange it I'm going to go talk to the Bishop, and I'll do whatever it takes to become pure again," she said soberly. "Sam, I'm so, so sorry. I know I offended you, and Heavenly Father, and the girls. I want to repent with all my heart. I want to *change*."

She began to sob, her entire body shaking. She looked up at him, her eyes swollen but determined. "I want to find my real self again--the woman that I know I am, the woman I can be. So, there is a favor that I must ask of you." She drew a ragged breath before continuing.

"Sam, I have let you and everybody else in Alaska call me 'Princess.' It was a sweet nickname, and I have been flattered by your kindness. But really, I am not a 'Princess.' I need to find the real me. I want to be true to myself once again." She looked beseechingly into his eyes. "Sam, I would like you to call me by my real name. I want you to call me 'Dawn.' Please, would you do that—for me?"

Sam was stunned to silence. It was all more than he could assimilate and understand. His heart felt like someone had been playing crack-the-whip with his emotions, and he had lost grip and been flung off into a thicket of thorns. But he could tell she was serious in her introspection and resolve.

He answered slowly. "I guess I can try," he said, looking at his hands. "After all, you were 'Dawn' when I first fell in love with you." His eyes fell on their family picture in the hallway. "But it will take me a while. All of this will take me a while--a long, long while."

"I know. Thank you," Princess whispered. Then she slowly took him by the arm and escorted him to their room. They spent the whole night in one another's arms. They were together, apart, in love, hurting, so close, so far away. Neither of them slept.

Dawn, as she now asked everyone to call her, was lovingly dealt with by the Lord's appointed judges the following Sunday evening. She cried bitterly in front of them. Sam had only been invited to attend a small portion of the proceedings, and it made him weep for her to have to go through it. Yet, afterward, she had a glimmer of hope and was filled with new determination. Paying a price was cathartic and even therapeutic to her as she sought to feel her way home. It was hard for her to pass the sacrament tray without partaking; it was hard for Sam to watch her do so. He felt a cautious love for his wife, but not trust, and he sought earnestly that he could learn to forgive, and perhaps one day to forget. He knew this could only come as a gift of the Spirit, and he prayed that it would be bestowed upon him.

Monday morning Sam contacted Crichton and Dangerfield, a nation-wide detective agency. Sam took photos, police reports, and everything he had collected regarding his tormentors. He laid $20,000 in cash on their desk and told them to use every resource to find who they were and what they wanted.

Crichton and Dangerfield declined to take the case. No amount of money would change their mind—nor would they explain why.

Sam walked from their office stunned. For the first time in his life he felt truly afraid. The police were willing but ineffective. The FBI was interested but not motivated since no real crimes other than petty van-dalism had been committed. Beyond all that, there were no telling clues, not even one.

As he was driving home, he prayed earnestly. For some reason, to Sam, driving was an invitation to pray. Almost every time he slid behind the wheel the Spirit would gently slide in with him. He often found solace, relief, and peace while driving. As he drove he felt the familiar stirrings of truth, and felt his soul relax and begin to soar. In a flash that warmed his soul, a memory surfaced of an account he had read in the newspaper about a year ago.

The article involved a man whose ex-wife had kidnapped his two young daughters and taken them to South Africa. The article gave a sketchy account of a daring rescue that involved international mercenaries, rekidnapping the girls, and lots of cash. The father only acted after waiting three years for word of his children. One evening he received a brief call from his oldest daughter, then fourteen, crying and begging him to come take them home. The call lasted less than twenty seconds. The planning and eventually successful rescue took over three years. Of course the man's name was not given in the article.

Sam immediately returned to Crichton and Dangerfield, who accepted $1,000 to find the man's identity.

Scarcely a week had passed. Sam was grading a small shipment of diamonds at his desk. A soft knock on his open door brought him eye-to-eye with a man standing stiffly in the doorway. Sam carefully folded the gems into their packet and slipped them into his desk. He stood as the man walked across the hardwood floor, his eyes darting quickly about.

His visitor wore old denim jeans, a dark brown leather jacket, and hiking boots. He wore a ponytail of dark brown hair, heavily streaked with gray. He was somewhat shorter than Sam, and walked with the ease of someone familiar with the outdoors. The man's eyes were a very light gray, and gave the impression of hidden intelligence. His face was heavily tanned beneath a leather Aussie hat whose left brim was fastened up with a gold medallion. All this gave the impression he had just returned from digging for treasure in Egypt. An air of confidence gave the added impression he had succeeded.

Sam offered his hand, which the man took in a strong grip. Sam judged his age a little shy of sixty. "I understand you've been looking for me, Mr. Mahoy," the man said with a gravelly voice, his eyes locked upon Sam's.

"I have no idea who you are," Sam replied as he motioned to a seat on the opposite side of the desk. Instead of sitting the man turned and swung the door closed, then took the offered seat.

"I was contacted by Crichton and Dangerfield. They said you wanted to talk to me."

"I understand now," Sam said, suddenly off guard. He struggled for a moment to know where to begin.

"What do you want?" the man asked in a steady voice.

"I need your help," Sam replied slowly.

"With . . ."

"There was a kidnapping attempt on my daughters a few days ago."

"Why contact me?"

"The police are at a standstill. There are no clues."

"Why contact me?" the stranger asked again.

"I am at a loss. I've got to do something. I read about your rescue of your daughters . . ."

"That was almost twenty years ago," the man interrupted. His voice was a little perturbed.

"The article gave no indication when it occurred. It seemed recent."

"Newspapers almost always get it wrong," he said without emotion.

"I've noticed," Sam replied, attempting to ease the tension in the room with a smile.

The man wasn't amused. "Before I walk out of here, I ask again. Why did you contact me?"

Sam leaned forward in his chair and steepled his fingers under his nose, his elbows on the desk. He did not know how to answer this question until he felt the Spirit move him. The answer was incredibly simple, because it was the truth. "I was praying urgently, seeking direction, and your name and story came into my heart. I contacted you because it was the right thing to do," Sam answered.

The man leaned back in his chair as if suddenly deflated. His slight edge of aggression seemed to evaporate. Almost a full minute elapsed in silence before he replied, "That is probably the only answer that could have stopped me from storming out of your office."

"Please explain."

"Mr. Mahoy—"

"Please call me Sam."

The man's demeanor, if anything, grew annoyed. "Sam, you have to understand. Rescuing my daughters sucked the life out of me. It took more courage than I actually had. It left me psychologically, emotionally, and financially bankrupt. The only good thing that came from it was that I got my daughters back, and I consider it all worth it. But, I have no desire to become entangled in some new international intrigue. I don't think I could survive it."

"That isn't exactly what I was hoping you would say," Sam replied quietly.

"I know. But it is the truth. Don't get me wrong. I owe God a great deal. Our little rescue was much more a miracle than a precision rescue. We did our best, but there is no doubt in my mind that we succeeded by divine intervention. I am willing to do what I can, but I'm afraid it's precious little."

"Apparently that will be enough," Sam said, opening both palms heavenward.

"I hope so."

"Me too."

Sam's enigmatic visitor hesitated before he spoke. "There is one tidbit of information that may help you. It's something the man from Crichton and Dangerfield told me. He mentioned that they had a client conflict with you."

"What do you suppose that means?" Sam asked.

"It means a bunch of things. First of all, it means that their firm apparently did some work for whoever is harassing you. They most probably didn't know they were assisting in a criminal act at the time. My guess is they were asked to gather and supply information about you."

"Telling you they have a client conflict couldn't have been an accident," Sam observed.

"I'm sure it wasn't."

"I'm sorry," Sam said. "I don't believe you ever said your name."

"No, I didn't. My guess is they are trying to help without getting themselves in trouble with their former client. They must realize now that their client is capable of nasty retaliation if they find out."

"They're afraid," Sam observed, forcing himself to not press further for the man's name. Sam was willing to play whatever games were necessary to save his family.

"They should be. There's something else I know that could help."

"Which is?"

"They don't necessarily want the twenty-two carat diamond."

Sam was amazed. "What do they want, then?"

"Most probably revenge."

"Why do you say that?"

The man's eyes became steely. "Because they tried to take your kids. That is an act of terrorism. They aren't after a refund. They want revenge—or they simply want your kids."

"But I haven't done anything to them!" Sam cried. "But you did."

Sam's shoulders slumped. "What? What did I do that would drive them to such dark depths?"

"Apparently only they know that. But you or your wife certainly did something, or they wouldn't be after you like this. There is one other possibility."

"Which is?"

"This has little to do with you. Perhaps there's someone they wish to manipulate, someone who would be devastated by the loss of your daughters."

Sam was momentarily stunned that this man knew his children were daughters but chose not to act upon it. "My parents, of course, are alarmed for the girls. But they don't have any enemies I know of. Besides, they haven't been contacted in any way."

"Your wife could be the target. Does she have any enemies?"

"It is inconceivable to me."

"Can you think of anyone who could use your children to manipulate your wife into something she might not otherwise be willing to do—like leave you, perhaps?"

"Who would want such a thing?" Sam asked, stunned.

"What about your wife's parents?"

"Her father lives in South Africa. He was very upset that my wife came to America with me. If it makes any difference, he's a wealthy diamond—"

"Let me guess," the man interrupted loudly, "He's a diamond merchant and/or smuggler. I understand in South Africa it's often about the same thing. I'll also wager he had something to do with this twenty-two-carat stone. My guess is he's been smuggling diamonds long before, and undoubtedly long after this incident. I'd guess the stone belongs to you, but he has it."

"Yes, yes!" Sam cried, astonished. This was, in fact, the first time Sam had realized that someone working for his father-in-law had retrieved the real diamond from the airplane, and yet Dawn's father had never even mentioned the diamond, let alone returned it.

"I think you just solved the puzzle—at least in part." The man sat contemplatively for a moment. "The possibilities I can see are that whoever is doing this is either after revenge against your father-in-law . . ."

When he didn't continue, Sam said, "Or?"

"Or it's your father-in-law who's behind it all."

"What?!" Sam cried.

His mysterious visitor gave him a steely look and stood.

"Either way, he's the key to this mystery, and either way, the only one who can stop it."

So saying, he pulled the hat from his head for the first time to reveal a shiny bald dome. It unexpectedly added ten years to his age, and made him look tired and vulnerable. He smiled and offered Sam his hand.

Before returning the handshake Sam reached into his desk and palmed a four-carat stone he had just been studying. He pressed the stone into the man's hand as they shook.

The old gentleman looked truly surprised. "I don't want anything for helping," he said, holding the stone toward Sam in the palm of his hand. It glittered like a tiny sun.

"You said you were financially bankrupt. That stone will easily reverse that."

"This stone is probably worth more than any home I've ever owned," he said in amazement.

"Then get a bigger one," Sam suggested. "Buy something nice for the girls." The man's hand slowly closed around the stone. His eyes clouded with tears, and he nodded once, turned, and disappeared through the door. Sam never saw him again.

Sam immediately opened his organizer and found Grandpa Pauley's phone number. The phone rang six times before Dawn's father answered, his British accent in full bloom. Sam quickly got to the point and related everything he had just learned. His father-in-law listened quietly. "I'll take care of it," he said in a terse voice and hung up without saying goodbye.

HARVEST

Six months elapsed before Dawn was restored to her former blessings. During all that time they heard nothing from the gang of 22. Sam hired a full-time bodyguard to stay near his family twenty-four hours a day. It made them all feel better, but was probably insufficient to thwart any real attempt on their safety.

That same September, Sam was called as first counselor in the bishopric. The calling both thrilled and frightened him. He knew he was willing to do anything for the Lord, and yet he was not sure he could summon enough inspiration to do it right. Old feelings from childhood, feelings of fear and inferiority, plagued him. For over a week he fought random impulses to decline the offered blessing. Yet, each time he prayed, he felt increasingly that, once again, the Lord would work a miracle that would make him adequate to the calling. After all, if God was able of these stones to raise up seed unto Abraham, as John the Baptist said, then God was able of Samuel Mahoy to raise up a humble servant of the Lord.

Sam knew it would have to occur in spite of him, not because of him. His weaknesses were too great, and his capacity too small to just change into a worthy man. He desperately needed the Lord to lay His hand upon his shoulder and give him strength he did not possess of his own.

Perhaps the thing that worried him most was that he might just blunder ahead and do things that might prove harmful to those he was meaning to bless.

With his calling came a startling glimpse into the tumultuous affairs of the ward. He was suddenly made aware of problems he had no previous idea were occurring. It almost seemed as if half the ward was having marital problems, and the other half was dying of some disease. Of the few who had nothing especially wrong, most were unemployed. He had to struggle to pull his heart out of a sense of despair. For the first time in his life he saw the church as a hospital, rather than a divinely appointed country club.

Of the many people with special needs was the Fowler family. Brother Fowler was a faithful brother who was nearly always away from his family driving truck. When he was at home, he seemed to have little energy for much more than long hours of watching television. Yet he responded willingly to any church assignment and attended to his home teaching faithfully. Sister Fowler was overweight by nearly a hundred pounds. It was a strain for her to walk from one room to the other. She seemed afflicted by the ailment of the month.

Her most pressing illness was multiple sclerosis which occasionally flared up and sapped her of energy and control of her limbs. She had brought three children into the world, all with severe handicaps. Their oldest girl was almost blind, deformed in the face and arms, and socially inept. Their next oldest boy was physically normal, but mentally little more than half his age.

Their youngest was physically perfect and unusually bright. He was also unusually active, literally bouncing off the walls and furniture. No one could control him, certainly not his mother who at times could barely move. Yet this little one was their sweetheart, and their family's only claim to any vestige of normalcy.

To make matters worse, the Fowlers were outcasts in a quiet way. The adults of the ward were friendly toward them, but none were friends. Perhaps inwardly most felt superior to the Fowlers and silently believed this family's misfortunes were their own doings, or the results of poor diet, poor work ethic, or poor genetics. Whatever the reason, they were what might be termed accepted but not truly embraced in the ward.

The children were treated with contempt by their peers. When no adult was present they were persecuted, physically tormented, and mentally harassed. If their personal problems were not sufficient to cripple them, the emotional abuse they received was more than sufficient to complete the debilitation.

Sam's first special assignment as a member of the bishopric was to fellowship the Fowlers. His assignment included special emphasis on helping the ward accept them as well as assisting them to fit in.

Sam and Dawn visited the Fowlers' home together several times. Dawn became nauseated the first time they walked into their home. The halls were stacked from floor to ceiling with newspapers, books, boxes, car parts, and dirty laundry. The smell of cat urine was so caustic that even Sam felt pressure rising in his throat. He could not help but wonder how anyone could be healthy in such an atmosphere.

The kitchen was piled high with dirty dishes and empty pizza boxes while the kitchen floor was not even visible underneath the grime and litter. The living room was piled deep in trash and dirty clothing. Obvious piles of cat and dog droppings lay in the corners of the room. The only clear spot of drab green carpet (probably not its original color), was between a new-looking leather recliner and the TV, which were also the nicest and newest pieces of furniture. Four dogs barked and danced around Sam and Dawn, jumping up to put stinking paws on their chests.

The Fowlers seemed to think this cute and made no attempt to restrain them. Numerous cats climbed and clawed everywhere one looked. Brother Fowler occupied the recliner directly in front of the TV. He alternately yelled at the kids, the cats, and his wife and spoke lovingly to the dogs as the TV blasted a dozen decibels above the threshold of pain.

Dawn flatly refused to go with Sam a third time. It did seem futile, as he could not carry on a conversation with anyone while there. The only discussions were held during commercials and usually centered on the plot of the show, movies playing at the theater, or would he like a cat to take home?

In the beginning Sam truly wanted to help them. As time went on he found them resistant to his urgings, suggestions of ways they could fit in, and easily offended by any suggestion regarding cleanliness, hygiene, or health. Slowly Sam felt his attitude being battered by what seemed impossible odds. Sadly, Sam was on the verge of concluding it was impossible to make any positive progress with the Fowlers when his heart was changed in an unexpected way.

Four days before Christmas the Fowlers' home caught fire and burned to the ground. The fire could have been started by a thousand things—their home was a firetrap. Oddly, the fire started from the electric cord going to the TV where it crossed a cat's latrine. The constant saturation of caustic urine had finally eaten through the insulation on the cord.

Sam rushed to their home in time to watch the firemen put out the last of the flames. Even the burning rubble put off a nauseating stench. Sam noticed that several of the firemen had wrapped cloths around their faces to fend off the odor of burning filth.

When Sam arrived, the Fowler family was huddled in their only remaining possession, a 1964 Dodge van that no longer had an engine. They had run from their burning home in their nightclothes and had sought shelter from the blaze, and the unrelenting cold, in their van. They had been kept warm by the heat from their burning home. Sam found them in an agony of grief. Their middle son, Anthony, had not escaped the fire and was lost. Sam had never seen such grief, such complete, unrelenting anguish. No words came to him. No comfort seemed possible in the face of such loss.

The Fowlers' plight was real and immediate. They had nothing left. In every sense they were helpless, homeless, naked in the cold night, and nearly friendless. Sam pondered the possibilities in his mind. They were few, pitiably few. There were no relatives to call on, no friends to lean on, no insurance to claim, no place to go, and little hope of finding one.

Bishop Dowling arrived while Sam was still trying to comfort them. Others came from the ward to see what had happened and to offer assistance. A team was formed to find housing for the displaced family. One brother offered a small camp trailer sitting behind his home. It was small, and it would need to have electricity and heat hooked up, but it was available. Another offered a garage with a bathroom that he and his wife had occupied while they were building their home beside it. Someone suggested renting a hotel room, another thought they should contact the Salvation Army. A thoughtful brother brought a large army tent and began pitching it on the front lawn of the burned home. Others saw his efforts and helped. Soon the tent was erected. A van arrived stuffed with clothing gathered from who knows where, and sisters began scuttling around searching for specific-sized clothes. In a short time the displaced family was clothed.

Sam watched all this with a sense of wonder and discomfort. While there were many people pitching in to help, they were working to "fix" the problem and return home. Everything he saw happening seemed somewhat less than what Sam felt this destitute family truly needed.

After a while the crowd of people began to dissipate. Vague offers of further help were often expressed just as the people walked away. Sam remained, unsatisfied, yet unable to think of anything more to do. While he was in the midst of making efforts to find them a running car, his mom and dad pulled up in their motor home. There was barely room for the big old bus amidst all the cars, but Jim found a place. Sam watched in quiet appreciation as the two people he most admired emerged from the bus, walked directly to the Fowlers, and hustled them into the bus. Before anyone fully comprehended what had occurred, Jim was backing away. With a roar of diesel fumes their problem family had disappeared into the night.

The remaining volunteers began taking down the tent with a defeated air. There seemed to be disappointment that their stopgap assistance had been upstaged in a way. Sam thought it most odd that few seemed to understand what had just happened. To Sam's thinking, the Lord had sent angels to assist His children in their desperate need.

* * *

Grandpa and Grandma Mahoy rearranged their home, their lives, and their finances to make a place for the Fowlers.

They wrapped their love around this lost family so completely that their only grief was for the loss of their son.

Sam visited his parents the next day and found their big home churning with orderly chaos. Grandma Mahoy immediately changed their diet to one of wholesome food. Their guests were too modest to comment about the nearly total absence of sugar from their diet and too astounded to complain when their health and energy radically improved. Young Bobby made a radical change in a mere few days. After a week of crying himself to sleep, begging for candy, and severe temper tantrums, he accepted his new diet and quietly changed into a pleasant little boy.

Their salvation came partly in the fact that the Fowlers were economically destitute and could not buy a single item of candy for him, for they surely would have done so just to shut him up. Grandma quietly restrained him, taught him, disciplined him with love, and doused him with a glass of cold water whenever he threw a tantrum. When young Bobby felt the need to explode, he did it as far away from Grandma Mahoy as possible.

The fits of rage invariably ended suddenly when he heard the water running in the kitchen. When the change came, it was quiet, sweet, unexpected (at least to the Fowlers), and permanent. Permanent, that is, as long as Bobby stayed completely away from sugar of any kind.

Grandma utterly, completely refused to let anyone in her kitchen, and the result was that the Fowlers had no choice but to eat wholesome food. They found themselves unavoidably, unexpectedly, and perhaps unhappily what they considered to be almost vegetarians.

Their former diet had been largely meat fried in hot grease. Their new diet, by comparison, was very little meat, usually in a thick stew or gravy. Grandma owned a big old skillet, but its only function in life was to fry eggs and zucchini. Yet when Sister Fowler unexpectedly lost fifteen pounds, and Brother Fowler found himself brimming with energy, they were very vocal in their acceptance of their new lifestyle.

Three days after their arrival, Sam's parent's TV mysteriously broke. Brother Fowler soon found himself outside the house pacing with unaccustomed energy. Before many days he was back driving trucks, but even that was too sedentary. He started looking for more energetic work and amazed himself when he found a job in a cabinet shop for a considerably higher wage. It turned out that he loved working with wood and was good at it too. He began a steady climb toward success in his new career.

Grandma ruled her home with the same gentle no nonsense she had used when Sam was a child. No pets came to stay. No litter touched the floor and stayed. No one ate without also helping clean up. Bathtubs were clean before and after a bath. Spills were wiped up by the spiller, and quarrels were quickly put away with good feelings on both sides. In short, the whole family restarted their lives, and for a time, they all called her Grandma Laura.

When the example had been set to a solid gel, she let Sister Fowler into her kitchen. Flattered that Grandma Mahoy trusted her in the inner sanctum of her sparkling kitchen, Sister Fowler produced a meal largely meeting the criteria of the mistress of the castle.

To shorten a rather lengthy tale, the lost family was found, clothed, cleaned, loved, and reborn. When they emerged from their temporary home nearly a year later, they were different people. The change was startling, nearly unbelievable.

Most startling of all was that the Fowlers recognized the miracle of their metamorphosis more keenly than anyone else. As they grew they looked back on their former existence with growing revulsion and loathing. In time they knelt in prayer together and thanked God for taking away their home so they could come to know the love of Grandpa and Grandma Mahoy and the joy of their new life.

Though this miracle was significant and life-changing, it was in reality very slow. Lessons were learned at a snail's pace, forgotten far faster, and repeated many times.

Although the change was miraculous, it was discounted by some in the ward. They attributed the squeaky cleanness, wrinkle-free clothes, and bright faces to Grandma Mahoy's tireless efforts, not to any true worth on the part of those souls wearing the new smiles.

In a way that surprised Sam, the Fowlers recognized this reaction in others as inevitable and refused to be resentful or to blame them. They simply changed and waited patiently for those around them to recognize it—or not, as the case may be.

In some ways they exhibited a higher level of nobility than those to whom these changes were invisible.

The Fowlers built a new, larger home on the foundation of their old one. With Brother Fowler's new job and new energy, the family could afford something a little better. Grandpa Jim worked tirelessly for weeks to build the new home alongside his friend.

Since it was being built out of pocket, Grandpa energetically campaigned for building materials to be donated from local businesses, members, neighbors, and charities. His efforts were rewarded, the materials arrived when needed, and the home rose from the ashes of their former plight. They moved into their new home in early December, just a little short of two years after the fire.

Sam spent many hours driving nails beside his father. It was good to have a hammer back in his hand again. He donated a few things as seemed appropriate, like a bathtub, plumbing, and other small things. Even though he could have financed the entire project without any difficulty, Sam chose to give his time, and to let others benefit from giving as well. The bulk of the donations came from nonmembers. When it was ready to occupy, it was a sweet feeling to stand back and look at their new home—painted, carpeted, clean, and very likely to stay that way when the Fowlers moved in. It still needed lots of work, but it was warm, sound, and all theirs.

* * *

Sam was in charge of the Christmas program for sacrament meeting that year. He worked energetically to arrange everything just right. He wanted this Christmas to be most special and worshipful. Yet, as perfect as every preparation seemed, there was still something missing. He troubled over what it might be right up to the Saturday before the Christmas program.

It was rather late when the phone rang and he was surprised to hear Sister Fowler's voice on the line. She was cheerful yet somewhat subdued, almost as if she were frightened. He had to coax out of her what was on her mind.

"Well, you see, Brother Mahoy, it's my oldest daughter, Catherine. She has wanted to sing a song at Christmas time for a long time. And you know, she's almost blind and all and not real pretty," she said in a whispered voice. "She can just barely read her music by holding it very close to her face. We never felt like people would appreciate her singing. But you see, she's turning seventeen, and next year she's going away to college."

This was a revelation to Sam. He had no idea that Catherine was even in school, let alone looking toward college. "Would you like me to put her on the program?" he heard himself ask. Even before she answered, he knew that this was the part that had been missing from the program.

He felt his heart rejoice as she replied. "Oh, would you? That would be so wonderful! Thank you. You're just like your parents. They are so special to us, you know. We just love them with all our heart. Why, they loved us like their own and taught us how to be real people. We were like little children playing house and not even knowing how. They saved us, did you know that? Well, of course you did. We just love them, that's all."

Sam thought to himself that everyone should experience being loved so purely by a friend. But rather than commenting on that, he asked, "Who will accompany her on the piano?" He considered they might ask him to do it.

"Why, I will, of course," she asserted brightly.

"I had no idea you played."

"Well, you couldn't see the piano in our first house. It was always buried under something, but it was there. I taught Catherine this song myself. She can do it pretty good. It will be good for her to finally get to sing this song. We've worked and worked on it. She's so shy, you know. She wants to go to college to study music. Did you know that?"

"No I didn't. I'm going to put her as the closing number. Is that all right?"

"Oh, gosh. I suppose so. We'll practice some more tonight." There was a moment's silence, and then she said with deep sincerity, "You're just like your dad," and hung up.

It was the greatest compliment she could have given him.

* * *

The Christmas program was beautiful. The choir sang like a chorus of angels, and each talk was inspiring. All through the program Sam felt his suspense growing until he was nearly ready to burst. He had listed the final musical number merely as "Special musical number . . . Mary's Lullaby." He had intentionally not listed who would perform. He did this for two reasons. One was to avoid embarrassment should Catherine decide she couldn't do it at the last minute. The second was to forestall the inevitable prejudice that would surround the inclusion of those names on the program.

Sam wanted the audience to have as little warning as possible, so that they might set aside their preconceptions and see Catherine in a new, positive light.

"Mary's Lullaby" is one of the most beautiful and touching Christmas pieces ever written. It is intended to be sung by a young, motherly woman. It describes Mary's love for her newborn son, and talks of her sure knowledge that He is the promised king who would die for His people. She sings a lovely, almost sad lullaby to the Christ child, proclaiming, "One day you will be King. But tonight you are mine."

Everyone was looking down at their programs to see who would sing the final number as Sister Fowler led her daughter toward the stand. Catherine tripped on the lowest step, and a deacon snickered. Sister Fowler whispered directions, and they climbed the steps to the stand and walked slowly toward the pulpit. Sister Fowler turned her daughter toward the microphone. It groaned loudly as she pulled it down.

As she made her way toward the piano, Catherine raised a piece of music very close to her face and studied it with what tiny bit of vision she possessed. Sam could see her screwing up her face into a deformed scowl. Even he had to cringe a little, and felt himself somewhat repulsed. The poor girl was a long ways from pretty and very nearly painful to look at. Someone coughed rudely, and others whispered too loudly. Sam began to feel annoyed by their un-Christian behavior. He and the bishopric were sitting in the audience or he would have bolted to his feet to stand by her until she could sing. As it was, she was on her own.

Sister Fowler began to play. Her light, sure touch on the piano pleasantly surprised Sam. He instantly recognized in her one who loved music and for whom the touch of the keys was a magic elixir that washed away hurt and brought peace and joy.

The music built to a crescendo, then fell to a hush. Sam waited and prayed.

Catherine lifted her chin, twisted her face into a mask of unpleasantness and sang. With the first crystalline note Sam felt his heart leap. The voice that came from that face certainly could not belong to one so deformed. The music flowed as peacefully and serenely as love itself. Each note was pure, vibrant, and sure. Her voice was far too mature, far too trained, far too beautiful to belong to one so young. Yet it did—with wonder and joy, it did.

The words told a story of Mary's love for her divine son, of a longing too pure to comprehend. For nearly four minutes, Catherine, the deformed, was Mary, the mother of God, and it stunned and electrified everyone in the chapel. Poor little Catherine, unsure, shy, disliked, repelled, and repelling, was for that brief moment in eternity the most beautiful creature on God's earth. Sam listened with joy as each note filled him with love, peace, and sorrow. How sorry he was that he had ever thought of anyone with such inner beauty as ugly. How sorry he was that the song must ultimately end. How sorry he was that he had not known her beauty long before.

He opened his eyes, and Catherine was different. Her face was aglow with love. Her hands were clenched to her breast as she filled every heart with the perfect love of she who had been chosen first among women. He saw tears of sweet sorrow running down Catherine's cheeks, and his own eyes filled. He watched those short, stubby arms form a cradle as blind eyes were turned toward the baby who would be the king of all; and he knew, he felt it, he lived it, he loved as she had loved, and it filled him with tragic joy of exquisite beauty.

The music flowed to an end too soon, far too soon. Sam could not help but hear the sniffles and quiet sighs that once had been whispers of derision. Total, reverent silence waited as Sister Fowler joined her daughter, who had remained motionless where she stood, her sightless eyes still gazing at the empty cradle of her arms. Her mother took her elbow, and she smiled.

It was a crooked, unbeautiful smile, but it was angelic, and it warmed every soul who beheld it. Breathless silence lay over the audience as the mother and her daughter walked slowly down the steps. Catherine stumbled on the bottom step and four people jumped up to assist. The same deacon who had snickered earlier was the first there. He gently took Catherine by the other arm, and stayed with her until they found their seats a long moment later. The whole time he stared in wonder at the little deformed face that housed an angel of uncommon beauty.

* * *

The twins turned two the same year Connie and Fred Chapman moved next to Sam and Dawn. The property already had a home on it when Sam had bought it. Sam and Dawn had built their log castle a distance away. In time Sam had repaired the old home, painted it, and put it up for rent.

They didn't need the money but felt it a waste to leave the home sitting vacant.

Fred was not a member of the Church and worked for the Alaska State Troopers. Connie was a baptized member but hadn't been inside the church since her baptism at age nine. She was a long-legged, blonde-haired, blue-eyed beauty from California. Fred was largeboned with a prominent brow, square chin, blond hair, blue eyes, and a ready smile. His face was the type one expects to see snarling inside a linebacker's mask. He was energetic, happy, obviously in love with his wife, and violently disinterested in the Church. They had a three-year-old boy, Freddie.

From the start, the Chapmans were good renters and good neighbors. Sam rarely began an outdoor project without Fred coming over with an appropriate tool to help. In time they became friends. In many ways Fred was the ideal neighbor, even better than was Sam himself. Yet whenever the conversation turned to religion, Fred either quietly left for home or simply changed the subject. The connection Fred and Sam shared was mostly the result of being close neighbors, and Fred's gregarious nature.

They had little else in common. Fred obviously took being neighbors as an obligation he faithfully honored.

Connie and Dawn shared no such bond. Whatever sparks of friendship might have flared were extinguished in their first meeting which was cool and brief. Both men were surprised by their wives' reaction. Both felt powerless to change it.

With two busy two-year-olds to care for, Dawn spent most of her time at home. By now Sam could handle any situation at work, and Dawn simply stopped going to the office.

She loved her days at home and pampered her girls until they thought the whole world revolved around their needs. In fact, it did.

Sam would have called the girls spoiled, but there was a definite line Dawn drew in the invisible sand of their lives that they did not cross without repercussion. They were obedient, polite, and well behaved. It was true that Dawn had drawn the line in a much more lenient spot than Sam might have. Yet this was Dawn's world, and he trusted her motherly instinct implicitly.

Dawn loved her twin daughters absolutely, and Sam doubted that anything in this world could go wrong with their childhood.

Even as two-year-olds, Lisa and Bonnie were strikingly beautiful and charming. Their long blonde hair sparkled from repeated brushings, and their baby pink skin shone and smelled of expensive soaps. They often wore identical outfits purchased at JC Penney. Though their clothes were new and cute, they were not expensive. Dawn was determined to raise two normal children, not two brats from the royal family.

As the weeks and months went by, Dawn saw very little of Connie, and there seemed to be no urge to change that situation. What ultimately forced a change was a love affair between Bonnie and three year-old Freddie. For reasons unfathomable, these two tykes fell hopelessly in love and would not be satisfied apart. Every other day either Freddie played at their house, or Bonnie and Lisa spent time at Freddie's house. As infant love affairs go, theirs was exceptional. They walked around holding hands, and often talked of when they would have their own house, and their own children. Dawn was charmed by it all, as was Freddie's mom.

One sunny afternoon Connie's eyes were puffy as she picked up Freddie. Dawn noticed immediately that she had been crying and invited her in. Dawn offered her a cup of Red Bush tea. Connie sipped silently until she finally burst open like an overfilled dam.

"Fred came home yesterday and said the Troopers were going to fire him for taking a bribe!" Connie told her in a rush. "He pulled over an out-of-state driver for speeding almost a week ago. The man explained that he was about to miss his plane at the airport, and Fred let him pay the fine to him. I didn't know that this was against department policy, but Fred did! He shouldn't have done it. But he was just being nice and was going to mail the fine that evening. No one would have known that the man hadn't mailed it himself. He was just doing him a favor. Fred's like that. He likes to help people," she said, her voice softening a bit.

Dawn nodded. Fred was exceptionally accommodating. "What went wrong?"

Connie's face grew disgusted. "Oh, Fred's so disorganized," Connie said with a sad smile, "he's always misplacing things. He said he just put the envelope on his desk at work and forgot about it! It got buried and forgotten."

"Oh dear!"

"Yes, well, the man who paid the fine contacted Fred's captain to see if the fine had been paid. It hadn't. Without saying anything to Fred, they searched his desk and found the envelope with the money and the ticket. They took it as evidence, suspended him on the spot, and sent him home without pay." Tears began to flow again. Dawn brought her a box of tissues.

"I just don't know what we're going to do. Fred's been with the Troopers twelve years. I know he doesn't look old enough, but he has. He has a big retirement built up, and if he gets fired for cause he'll lose it all. It's the only thing he knows how to do, and he won't be able to find a job with another police department for as long as he lives," she wailed, then broke down again and sobbed.

Dawn's heart went out to Connie. She put her arms around her and held her while she cried. When the tears finally stopped, something had changed between them. Though not strong, a bond had been formed.

"What would you do if you were me?" Connie asked after she had regained her composure.

"I'd pray," Dawn replied without hesitation. She realized after the fact that she had crossed the "no religion" line with her answer. Connie had wanted advice on how to solve a dilemma, not how to satiate her troubled soul.

Happily, Connie was not offended. She recognized Dawn's response as sincere not pushy.

"Pray? I hadn't thought of that. I don't see how it could help, though," she replied heavily. "We need a job, not a prayer."

Dawn waited until the correct answer came to her. When it came it felt right and comfortable. Even so, it took all her courage to obey. She slipped to her knees while Connie watched, a look of incomprehension on her face. "Come on. I'll show you how," she said.

Connie smiled weakly and slipped to the floor beside her.

As was her custom, Dawn slipped her hand into Connie's hand. Then, unseen by either of them, angels knelt with them, and for the first time in her life Connie heard someone talk to God. It unexpectedly warmed her through and through.

When Dawn had finished praying, she looked at Connie and nodded, indicating that it was her turn. Connie flinched, yet nodded back and lowered her head.

"Dear God," she began as if addressing a letter. "Until a minute ago I didn't even know how to talk to you. So, you'll have to forgive me that I never tried. Now that we're having this talk, I kind of remember things my mother said about you. I remember that she said we are your children, and you love us." Connie paused here as if the idea had struck her with some force.

"God, I know what it's like to love my children, and if your love is anything like that, I know that you care about Fred and me. So, without telling you what I think the answer is, 'cause I really don't know, would you help us out? Please?" There was a long pause. "Just one more thing. Thank you for Dawn and God bless her and the twins. Thank you. Uhm, Jesus Christ, amen."

When Connie looked up at Dawn she was surprised to see tears in her eyes.

Dawn squeezed her hand. "That was beautiful, Connie. I know He heard you."

They both stood. "I think so too," Connie admitted. "It felt good, and I feel peaceful now. Thanks for showing me that." They walked toward the stairs to collect Freddie.

"Dawn?"

"Yes, Connie?"

"How did you know I wouldn't hate you for trying to show me how to pray? I've certainly told you not to involve me in your religion often enough. Why did you do it?"

Dawn concentrated on climbing the stairs. When she reached the top she stopped. "Have you ever had your conscience urge you to do something you knew was good?"

"Yeah, I guess so . . . sure, lots of times, now that I think about it."

"It was like that," Dawn explained. "I just knew it was right, and I always try to obey my conscience."

"Why? Most of the time my conscience just nags me. It's almost like having my mother around telling me what to do. Most of the time it just annoys me, and I ignore it."

"Well, the conscience we hear is the voice of the Holy Spirit. It comes from God."

Connie gasped. "No!" she exclaimed. "Are you sure?"

"That's what the scriptures say. And, that's what my experience has been. I am always the happiest when I follow the whisperings of the Holy Spirit."

"Oh, my God!" Connie exclaimed, then slapped her hand to her mouth when she realized she had profaned. "Sorry," she added contritely. "It's just that, well, I had no idea. Oh my word! I'm going to have to do a lot of thinking. If what you say is true, I've been very, very naughty. If I was my mother, I'd spank me!"

They both laughed at that, and the bond between them deepened.

Dawn asked, "What would your mother have done if you were naughty?"

Connie chuckled. "She'd probably have done something to try to teach me to behave and to listen to what she told me. She was an inactive church member, you know. But she really believed it, even if she didn't go to church." It was obvious her memories of her mother were fond ones.

By this time they had arrived at the girls' room, and found them happily playing together with Freddie. They watched for a moment before collecting Freddie. Dawn felt the sweet stirrings again, and asked: "Why wouldn't a loving Heavenly Father do just the same so that we could be happy?"

"I suppose He would. Do you think that's what this is with Fred's work, a teaching thing from Heavenly Father?"

"I'm sure of it," Dawn replied.

"Then will it go away after we learn the lesson?"

"I don't know, Connie. It may, or it may not. What I do know is that whatever it costs you to learn this lesson, your lives will be much happier afterward. I believe we came to this life to be happy. I believe the only way to be truly happy is to learn the lessons Heavenly Father teaches us, and then our earthly happiness will eventually become eternal happiness."

"That's a beautiful perspective on life, I think," Connie replied softly. "I'll think about all this. Thanks, Dawn. You're a good friend. And a good Christian," she added hastily.

Nearly a week passed with little more conversation passing between them than what was needed to shuffle the kids back and forth. Dawn felt content to wait for Connie to broach the subject again. When she did, it was with a sense of wonder. They were once again sitting by the big piano, sipping Red Bush tea.

"Dawn, this past week I've thought and thought about what you told me. And, each time I ponder what you said, I feel a glowing feeling right here," she said laying her hand upon her breast. "I've been anxious to talk some more to you about it but wasn't sure how to bring it up."

"I think you just did," Dawn said happily.

"Right," Connie said with a smile. "Well, what I did in the meantime was to try out what you said. I've been listening very carefully to my conscience. And, guess what! It works! I couldn't believe it. Even Fred noticed the difference."

She paused here to sip her tea. Her face fell a little. "It's demanding isn't it," Connie observed.

"What do you mean?"

"Well, my house has never been cleaner. All my laundry is done. I've been reading the Bible every evening. I've been extra loving with Fred . . . and I'm exhausted!" she said emphatically.

"But you're happy," Dawn appended.

"Absolutely. I've never been so filled with peace in my life. I can't remember a time when my life was so fulfilling, so together. Fred's convinced that I'm pregnant. I got like this when I was first pregnant with Freddie." They laughed again.

Connie grew sober and set her cup aside. "Something else happened, something I don't understand."

"What was that, Connie?" Dawn asked with concern.

"Well, I have a cousin who lives in Talkeetna. She's the family rebel. She's single and has two kids by two different men she never married. She lives on welfare and is a drug addict. She pays for her addiction by selling herself to men. She lives in a filthy little apartment."

"Wow, I feel sorry for her," Dawn said unhappily.

Connie shrugged. "I never have. She chose her life, and did it against her own common sense and a lot of free advice. I barely know her, and I certainly don't like her. Anyway, she stopped at the house yesterday."

Dawn's eyes widened. "I saw a little beat-up white car pull up yesterday."

"That was her. She knocked on the door and asked me point blank if she could borrow a typewriter. She didn't even say hello, just 'Do you have a typewriter I can borrow?'"

"Did you loan her one?"

"I was going to tell her no. I knew she was going to go directly from my home to the pawnshop. She's done it before. My mouth was already open to say no when my conscience kicked me in the back of the head."

"I've had that happen," Dawn said sympathetically.

"I had made myself a promise that I was going to give this conscience thing an honest try. I really meant it, and knew it had brought me happiness so far, so I yielded to it."

"So, what did you do?" Dawn asked eagerly.

"What I said was that I did have one. I invited her in, and went to get it. I have two typewriters, and I got the better of the two. I actually carried it out to the car for her. I was about to ask when she would bring it back when out of my mouth comes, 'It's an extra machine. You can just have it.' Both she and I were amazed. She thanked me and actually smiled before she left. I just stood there in shock watching my typewriter drive away."

"You did the right thing," Dawn replied with certainty.

"I know. I was so shocked. And Fred? Fred was furious. He blazed around the house. Here we are, out of work, and I'm giving away valuable things. He was right, and I knew it. It was hard to explain to him why I had done it."

"Oh, Connie, I'm so proud of you! You are truly amazing. It must have been very hard—and very hard to explain to Fred."

Connie snorted. "You have no idea!"

"Perhaps I do," Dawn chuckled.

"But you know what the odd thing is, Dawn? I was about to make up a good excuse to Fred when my conscience butted in again and wanted me to tell him the truth, all of it."

"Really!" Dawn replied. "What happened?"

"Fred believed me. He listened to my explanation, and he accepted it. I was stunned . . . I think he was stunned."

"You can include me in that list," Dawn assured her, then more seriously. "Would you mind if I shared something very precious with you?"

Connie nodded happily. "I'd be honored," she said.

Dawn stood, crossed the room and returned with a leatherbound copy of the Book of Mormon. She didn't immediately hand it to Connie.

"I feel like we are good enough friends that I can give you this. I'm not doing this to try to force you to read it. That's not the point really. The point is, this book has brought me lasting joy. This is where the things I've been sharing with you largely come from. I don't feel like I would be a real friend if I didn't give you your own copy. Will you accept it in the same spirit I'm offering it?"

Connie slowly took the book and turned it so she could read the title. Her face was expressionless. She lifted the front cover and read the hand-written inscription inside. In Dawn's flowery script it said:

> To my dear friend, Connie.
> May joy always be the measure of your days.
> Dawn Mahoy.

Connie was slow to look up. When she did her eyes were bright with happiness. "I will treasure this book as long as I live, if for no other reason than for what you have written inside the cover. Thank you."

Dawn beamed. "You are most welcome."

"And," Connie continued a trifle uncertainly, "if my conscience tells me to read it, I will. I vowed at one time I would never touch this book again, but I'm learning so many wonderful things from you, I don't want to place any stupid limitations upon any of it."

"I can't imagine you doing anything stupid."

"You haven't known me that long," Connie asserted, then laughed heartily.

* * *

No sooner had Connie left the house than the phone rang. It was Sam. "I have bad news," he said without preamble. "Oh dear, what is it?"

"We were broken into last night."

"Oh no! By whom? What did they take? Have they been caught?" Dawn asked in one breath.

"I don't know, almost everything. They got away," he replied soberly, answering every question.

"How did they get past the alarms? Did the alarms even work?"

"They knew how to bypass them, I guess. It looks like a professional job, the police say."

"Did they get into the safe?" Dawn asked breathlessly.

"Yes, but I had taken everything down to the bank vault that evening. They didn't know that of course. They ruined the safe trying to open it. They used a cutting torch. Can you believe that? They almost burned down the building. The carpet was on fire at one point, and they used our fire extinguisher to put it out. The place is covered in a yellow powder. It's awful."

"Scum-sucking bottom feeders!" Dawn hissed. It made Sam chuckle with dark humor.

"They also took the sampler from my desk."

"Lowlifes!" she exclaimed.

"I agree. The sampler alone had about $10,000 our cost, but that's only a fraction of what could have been in the safe had I not taken it to the bank."

"Sam, we've got to do something. They'll be back. The next time, we may lose even more."

"Dawn, there's something else. They cut a big '22' in the door of the safe."

"Oh!" Dawn gasped. Then in a subdued voice she added, "I wish they had gotten the contents of the safe now. Maybe they'd leave us alone if they did."

"I know. I had the same thought. Somehow I still don't think it would be over. Just the same, we have to take strong precautions. How do they handle security in South Africa?"

"They have twenty-four-hour guards. Not just alarms, but live, armed guards."

"I do think we need an armed guard at least at night," Sam agreed.

"I think I know where we can find one," she said with sudden cheerfulness.

"I do too," Sam agreed. He had had the same idea before he dialed the phone. It pleased him that they were in sync again.

*　*　*

Fred resigned from the Alaska State Troopers just as the snow began to fall that year. He resigned before they had completed their investigation. By doing so they were forced to accept his resignation and leave his retirement intact, since no formal charges had been filed. They chose to simply drop the matter. It was an unexpectedly happy conclusion to a nasty affair.

Fred accepted Sam's offer of a job that same day. The pay was much better, the benefits not quite as generous, and the hours abysmal, but Fred was overjoyed. He strode through their offices making numerous suggestions. They did everything he suggested.

He was on guard that next night.

*　*　*

When the bank heard that Sam had hired a night guard, they offered to extend Fred's pay, improve his benefits, and add an elaborate lock box system if he would also patrol the bank below them. He readily agreed. In a short time he started his own security firm and launched himself into a career that provided handsomely for his family from that day on. It wasn't too long before Sam and Dawn subdivided the second house from their property and sold it to Fred and Connie. In addition to being great neighbors and business associates, they became dear friends.

* * *

Shortly after Fred went to work, Connie knocked on their door. Dawn was taking cupcakes from the oven and was slow getting to the door. When she opened it Connie stood there with a slip of paper in her hand, her face aglow with a childlike look of expectation. Without saying a word she handed Dawn the paper.

"You're pregnant!" Dawn cried.

"I am," she replied happily. "I think listening to the Spirit is to blame for this," she added. They laughed then hugged.

"Congratulations!"

"Thanks. There's something else I want to tell you. Something almost as wonderful."

"Come in. Sit. I'll get some Red Bush tea."

"Hear me out first."

"Okay. Is it that important?"

"It's that wonderful is all."

"I'm anxious to hear it," Dawn said as she settled in beside her. "You remember Angelica, my cousin?"

"The drug addict with your typewriter."

"Right. Well, this is all your fault, you know." Dawn laughed.

"Tell me what I did."

"You taught me how to listen to the Holy Spirit, and nothing's been the same since. Well, we have two cars, as you know. Fred's Suburban and my Subaru. I kept having this feeling that I should give my Subaru to Angelica."

"Give it to her? That's your only transportation while Fred's at work. And she's got that little white car. I saw it."

"Those were my thoughts too. Anyway, I kept getting this weird impression that I needed to give her my car. This was before you guys hired Fred, and money was a big problem. So for a time I ignored it, but it kept getting more insistent. Finally, I recognized that I was disobeying, and I reminded myself that every time I obey I receive wonderful blessings. So I loaded up Freddie and we drove the Subaru to Talkeetna."

"That's a long drive."

"Yeah, it took almost two hours. When we arrived at her apartment there was no white car outside. She had totaled it weeks earlier. I found her sitting in her filthy little apartment crying."

"That's so sad." Dawn shook her head.

"It gets worse," Connie assured her. "I just walked up to her and held out the keys to the Subaru. 'What's this?' she asked me. There were tears dried on her face where she hadn't even bothered to wipe them away. Her two kids were crying in the bedroom.

"I told her, 'I've brought you my Subaru. I don't need it any longer.' She just stared at me with big wide eyes. She looked at me like that for the longest time, then just broke down and cried uncontrollably. I held her and held her. It was so pathetic. My heart melted, and I cried with her." Connie stopped here to brush tears from her cheeks.

"Anyway, after she was done crying I asked her what was wrong. It was a stupid question, because everything in that child's life is wrong. She smiled sadly and told me the most incredible story, Dawn. Is it all right if I try to tell what she said in her own words?"

Dawn nodded for her to go on.

Connie nodded. "Angelica said, 'You know my life is messed up, Connie. You know I'm a bad person. I do drugs, I neglect my kids, I steal things to pay for my habit, and I sleep around for money. What you couldn't have known is that I hate myself, and hate what I've become, and hate where I'm going with my life. Two weeks ago I crashed my car. It was my fault. I was high, and I just plowed into someone. I didn't hurt his truck much. I slept with him, and he didn't file a police report, but it ruined my car. My car was my only security in life. It gave me freedom and mobility. I have been cooped up here now for two weeks. My kids are hungry, I'm broke and too beat up to even sell my body for money. In short, I'm at the end of my rope. I have nothing left physically, emotionally, monetarily, or morally. I have been sitting here wishing I could die, and lacking the courage to kill myself.'"

Dawn gasped. "Oh, no!"

Connie nodded grimly. "It was awful to hear. Then she told me, 'I didn't get out of bed this morning until almost noon. The only reason I did get up was because the kids were crying 'cause they was hungry. I fed them half a bowl of sugar puffs in water. It's all I had. I went back to bed and cried and cried. I cried until I was so depressed that I actually knelt down beside my bed and talked to God. You know me. I'm hard, and I'm defiant, and I'm bad. I ain't prayed to God since my mother last made me when I was six years-old. But I prayed. I says, God, I know you're up there, and I ain't never doubted that. But I can't imagine you even know I'm alive. God, everyone in my life has walked away from me except you. And, I suppose in that case I was the one who did the walkin'. God, I don't want nothin' from you, and I'm not worthy to ask for nothing. But I would like to know something. I would like to know if you are aware I even exist.'"

"Oh, Connie, this is depressing," Dawn said sadly.

"Yes, but listen to the rest. Angelica said, 'That was this morning. I have sat here all afternoon contemplating ways to end my life. If I had a phone I would have already called the Child Welfare people to come take my kids from me. I do love them, I really do, but I'm not good for them. Everyone knows that, even them. So when you walked up to me holding out those car keys, even before you said a word, this flood of warmth and love came over me.'"

Connie paused to wipe away a tear. "Then, Dawn, she stopped, crossed her arms over her chest, and hugged herself, a sad smile on her grimy little face. Angelica's voice was strangled as she said, 'I've never felt anything like it, and I knew . . . I just knew in some way deep inside me that this was my answer. God really does know me, and He really does care. What I felt at that moment was pure love. I've never felt that before from anyone, not even from God.'"

Connie's eyes refocused on Dawn. "I stayed there long enough to pack her and the kids up. I brought them home with me. I may be nuts, but I couldn't leave them there. I bought them food, and they ate like little piglets. You should see those poor babies. They're skin and bones. Mikey is six and looks three. Thomas is four and looks two. As soon as I got them home I gave them more food and put Angelica in the bathtub. She just sat there in a daze until the water turned cold. I warmed it up again and bathed her just like a baby." Connie paused as if reliving the experience. "I've never bathed a grown woman, Dawn."

Connie choked on her words and had to pause. When she continued, her voice was heavy with emotion. "Her body was covered with scabs, bruises, and sores. She's been beat up so many times, Dawn. Her body is absolutely devastated from disease and abuse. Her breasts are bruised, her arms are black and blue, she's almost skin and bones, and there are needle tracks on her arms and legs."

A look of horror, then compassion crossed Dawn's face.

Connie's eyes focused far away. "She just stood there like a child and let me care for her. She has absolutely no pride left, Dawn. Something happened there in that bathroom. I felt love inside me as if I were her mother and she my desperately ill daughter. I suppose I felt the way that father did in the scriptures when he placed the robe and gold ring upon his returning prodigal son. I know Connie felt it, too. She just stood there and smiled sadly as I attended to her. I was as gentle as I could possibly be, and yet everything I did was painful to her. I believe she is in constant pain and just says nothing because no one cares."

"Oh, that poor child!" Dawn exclaimed.

"I cried the whole time. As I washed her body, I think something was cleansed on the inside too. I dressed her in my best gown and tucked her in my bed. I even kissed her on the forehead and told her I loved her. When I left she was still sleeping. It was all more tragic and more beautiful than anything I have ever experienced before."

Connie was quiet for a long time, then added. "I've made arrangements to enroll her in a drug addiction clinic. She's agreed to go and really give it a try. Oh, Dawn, it's just the most pathetic thing I've ever seen in my life. Believe it or not, she's actually a member of the Church, and I've made arrangements for her to meet with Bishop Dowling."

She laughed an ironic-sounding laugh. "I haven't told you this, but I've been reading the Book of Mormon you gave me. I have a zillion questions, and now I'm going to be teaching Angelica. She needs the gospel desperately. I know the Church is true, Dawn. I think I've known it all along, but was too proud to live it, or too lazy, or something. I don't know, but I do know Angelica needs me to be solid, which I'm not. I need a crash course on religion, Dawn, and I need to know what times we meet on Sunday. I really need your help. I'm in way over my head!"

"And you feel happy inside," Dawn appended.

"Oh . . . oh yes," Connie replied softly.

* * *

Sam and Dawn invited the missionaries to their home to teach Angelica. Fred and Connie came and listened intently.

Because of their deep concern for Angelica's spiritual welfare, they turned their whole attention to acquiring truth, not filtering it through their own prejudices. They were so cooperative with the missionaries that Angelica probably never realized Fred was not a member and Connie hadn't been inside a church in over twenty years.

During the fifth discussion, the missionaries asked Angelica if she would like to be baptized after she was able to get her life in order. Angelica answered that she was already a member.

An awkward moment of silence followed while the missionary who had asked the question turned red. His companion poked him in the ribs with an elbow, and the room erupted into laughter. When solemnity returned Sam realized that Fred had not laughed.

"Fred," Sam asked. "Is something troubling you?"

"Yes," he answered frankly. "I'm grateful that Angelica is taking the missionary lessons and is finding the truth for herself. But I'm the non-member here, and nobody has bothered to ask me a single question."

There was a moment of silence while everyone, including Fred, pondered the meaning of his complaint. One of the missionaries started to apologize, and to promise to ask Fred more questions. But Sam politely interrupted him.

"Fred, would you like to be baptized?"

"Well, yes!" he almost shouted. Connie turned to him with an expression of total amazement.

"Fred!" she exclaimed. "I had no idea you knew it was true too!" Fred fumbled with his hands, then looked directly at his wife.

"I watched a miracle take place in your life and now with Angelica because of the gospel. I'm stubborn, Connie, but I'm not stupid. I know something good when I see it, and I want to be a part of it. I want to have these miracles a part of my life from now on. Yes, I know it's true." He smiled happily. "Don't look so amazed!"

"I'm sorry, Honey. It's just that I, well, you, I mean, we never—"

"When would you like to be baptized?" Sam asked, interrupting Connie's stammering.

"As soon as it can be arranged," Fred replied forcefully.

"That would be tomorrow night," the senior of the two missionaries replied. Fred merely nodded and smiled broadly.

* * *

Melody's life took on a pattern of quietude and security she had never known in her whole life. She filled her days practicing, playing in the park, and thinking of Theodore, whom she found a charming enigma. She decided to do a little quiet research and found that his last name, Tennison, descended from the wealthy Tennison family very prominent in English and American history. His family proudly wore the status, the title, and the old money that their name endowed upon them.

Melody was sitting in her sister's apartment rehearsing a complex passage in a Rimsky Korsakov work of sweeping minors and intricate rhythms when a firm knock at the door interrupted her concentration. She laid her violin aside and opened the door with some curiosity.

Two men in business suits stood officiously before her.

"Miss Melody MacUlvaney?" the shorter of the two asked without introduction.

"Yes?"

He nodded and pulled an official-looking envelope from his jacket. "You are hereby served to appear before the Magistrate to answer charges regarding illegal immigration and living in this country with forged papers. We suggest you hire a solicitor, Miss MacUlvaney. He can advise you of your rights."

Melody was thunderstruck. "What? I'm just—"

"Do you intend to appear?" the man asked, sparing her the need to reply.

Her mind spun in a thousand directions. Only one idea emerged with any clarity: deny everything! She opened her mouth with those words on her lips when a quiet urging literally lifted the words from her tongue even as she forced air through her lips to speak them.

"Of course," she said quietly.

Both men nodded as if satisfied. They had turned to leave when the taller of them turned back as if on impulse. His face was impassive, his voice apologetic. "Miss, it's good you said what you did. We'd have had to arrest you otherwise. Sorry to frighten you, but the department has received a tip from someone very respectable with some very damning evidence. There's an accusation that you may be a spy for the outlawed Rhodesian colony. These are very serious charges, Miss. I again suggest you get a very good solicitor," he said. His voice lost all hint of apology. "And don't attempt to flee the country. You are under close surveillance." So saying, he touched the rim of his small hat, nodded once, and walked briskly away.

* * *

Melody consulted the best solicitor she could find in their little town. The old barrister listened to her plight with interest as she explained through tears what had brought her to Wales, and then England, and of her struggle to obtain papers, then of her decision to "purchase" legality.

"I understand your decision, and the plight that motivated it," he concluded after listening carefully. "However, I am sorry to inform you that under English law, the truth of what has occurred is the controlling factor. That a law was broken, not why it was broken, is the rule of law. The magistrate will attempt to determine whether the charges are true, and if they are—since they are—there can be no defense. You will be found guilty of those charges and punished accordingly."

He leaned back in his chair and pondered for a moment.

"Even though your motivation for doing what you did has no bearing upon your guilt, it may soften the ultimate punishment. I suspect in the least you will be fined and deported."

Melody fell back in her chair, crushed and terrified. Her voice was frightened. "How much fine?"

"More than you possess, I'm sure. The purpose of the fine is to strip you of all your assets plus enough to prohibit your return to England."

"That's the best case? What's the worst case?"

"In the extreme the court could find you guilty of all charges, including espionage, and sentence you to a very large fine, and as much as twenty-five years in prison."

"Twenty-five years! But I haven't committed espionage!"

"Then all you have to do is prove you are innocent."

"How can I prove I am innocent? Is there no presumption of innocence?"

He raised his chin as if the idea were repugnant to his thinking. "The assumption is that you are guilty or you would not be accused. You yourself told me you are guilty of the lesser crimes."

"God help me," Melody whispered to nobody present.

"Indeed. God may be your best hope," the old gentleman replied pensively.

* * *

Sweet peace hovered over Sam and Dawn as they prepared for bed. The missionary meeting with Fred and Connie had been precious and spiritual. Both he and Dawn rejoiced deeply in Fred's desire to be baptized and in the blossoming of Angelica's soul.

"I'm going to go look in on the twins," Dawn said as she slipped a light robe over her nightgown.

Sam had just opened his mouth to say he was sure they were fine when they distinctly heard a door bang downstairs.

Sam looked at Dawn and bolted from their room out onto the landing. The door to their room was directly at the top of the large staircase. Below them the big front door was wide open, still moving ominously.

Dawn stifled a scream. Sam ran down the hallway barely ahead of Dawn. The twins' door was open. Sam flipped on the light, his heart paralyzed by fear.

Both beds were empty! On Bonnie's bed a dozen stuffed animals had been arranged into a large "22." Dawn screamed and ran from the room.

Sam spun to follow and was slammed by a sound that seemed to shake the organs within his body. It took his mind a few seconds to realize it was the report of a gun from inside his home.

EXCERPTS FROM *ANGELS OF FIRE*

Book Two of the Journey to Zion series

The hardest thing Sam ever did in his life, before or after, was to get out of bed the next morning and go to church. He had to force himself to take every footstep toward church. He turned back a thousand times, and waged a running battle inside his soul. By the time he was walking out to the car holding Lisa's hand he was sick to his stomach from conflict. Yet he was determined to do what was right, no matter the cost. This cost him more than he had inside and tore things apart that should be immune to such damage.

* * *

Theodore's uncle was dressed in a silk smoking jacket with a wide black collar and gold embroidered body. He was in his late seventies, and still hale, though somewhat stooped. He commanded a sprawling empire that stretched across most of Europe.

His name was universally honored and feared. His hair was full and perfectly white, which he wore full, to his shoulders.

Uncle's voice was booming with welcome. "Come into my study! What brings you out into the country? It must be urgent."

"Uncle, you know I love you," Theodore began in a warning voice. His uncle smiled, and holding up both hands, sat in a plush red chair.

"I better sit down for this one."

Theodore sat opposite him. "I just pieced together several statements I remembered your making last weekend."

His uncle smiled. "About the spy from Rhodesia?" 226

Excerpts from "Uncle, I met the person in question, and she's no spy."

"Of course not! But she is a person of unsavory background and hardly fit for association with one of noble birth," he said forcefully, though still amiably.

Theodore wagged his finger at his uncle. "Are you playing matchmaker again? I thought you were going to stay out of my love life."

"I do stay out of it!" he cried. Then his voice grew conspiratorial. "That is, unless you start gravitating toward gutter tripe and street musicians."

Theodore bridled. "Melody is a marvelous woman of great talent and depth."

"Melody. What an appropriate name for a street musician."

"Uncle, you're being haughty. She plays in the park for the love of music—"

"And to make money."

"She makes money because she is a world-class musician, and because our government denied her a visa and passport, and, with that, any possibility of making a living. A lesser woman would have turned to something menial or prostitution. I tell you she is a noble woman."

"Posh! She's a street musician."

"Uncle, if you met her you'd be charmed too, and probably ask her to marry you yourself."

His uncle laughed heartily. "You know I can never deny you. You charm me even when you defy me. What do you want me to do?"

"I want you to stop her prosecution. It was you who started it. Don't deny it."

"I do what I must to protect my kingdom," he said airily. "What's in it for me?"

"There's nothing you don't have, including my undying fealty," Theodore avowed with a regal wave of his hand from chin to knee.

Uncle grew serious. "I want you to marry in your class. I want you to possess all this," he said with an expansive wave of both arms, "after I am gone, or even before. I don't want you to sully my name by marrying beneath yourself."

"Then I will give you a challenge," Theodore said upon a sudden inspiration.

"You? Challenging me? You grow bold in your cleric's collar," he said jovially, but with an obvious nip of warning.

"A challenge even you can't resist."

"Intriguing, go on."

"Elevate whomever I choose to accompany me on life's journey, to whatever status you feel appropriate. Or perhaps you haven't the power to raise, only to tear down," Theodore said, his words tonal with jest, his eyes flashing with gravity.

"I can turn a potato into a princess of desire!"

"Then I challenge you to do whatever you must to satisfy your lusts, and still leave my happiness to my discretion. I'm afraid if you destroy this fragile flower, I shall be forever moody and sullen when I'm around you," he pouted only partly in jest.

"Happiness has nothing to do with women, love, or discretion. It has to do with power."

Theodore stood slowly. "Then I offer you the happiness of using your power to restore my street musician to her station. She needn't know anything of it, and I prefer she does not. I only ask that you cease to persecute her."

"It is an intriguing challenge," his uncle said as he took his chin in both fingers.

"You will do it then?"

"You know I can't say no to you," Uncle affirmed, once again amiable.

Still, there was a steely look in his eyes that conveyed strict warning.

Theodore smiled slyly. "A fact I was counting on. Still, Uncle, I thank you with all my heart."

"Posh. You just want my money."

"That too," Theodore laughed. "Get out of my house!"

"Yes, Uncle," Theodore smiled broadly and hurried to the door. Uncle Tennison watched him until the butler began to open the door.

"Theodore," he called across the large room. "Yes, Uncle?"

"Well played," he said softly.

*　*　*

"Excuse me, Sister Wadsworth," a man's voice said. Sister Wadsworth was standing in the row directly behind Sam and Dawn. She turned to see who had spoken to her. Sam was pleased to see the older gentleman from his quorum meeting the previous week. The old gentleman extended his hand with a warm smile.

"Sister Wadsworth, I just wanted to tell you how sweet your testimony was to my soul today. You made me remember my own mother, and I can tell you, at my age, that is no small affair." He chuckled to himself. "It was long, long ago." He smiled meaningfully. "You bore a sweet testimony. I shall remember your words a long time."

Sister Wadsworth smiled. "Well, thank you. I don't believe I've met you before. You already know who I am. May I ask your name?"

"Oh," he said as he leaned forward slightly. "I don't have a name. I'm just one of the three Nephites going around visiting the Saints." With this he released her hand, glanced pointedly at Sam, and turned away.

"What do you suppose he meant by that?" Sister Wadsworth asked Sam with a puzzled expression.

As she spoke Sam was watching his old gray head move slowly down the crowded row, greeting people as he went.

Reluctantly, he turned his attention to Sister Wadsworth. "I think he's telling the truth," Sam replied emphatically.

"I want to talk to him some more." Having so said they both turned to where the old gentleman had been but seconds before.

He was gone.

* * *

Six years had passed: six long, soul-stripping, desolate, debilitating years. For the first time in many years Sam knew he would survive, and his survival would be rich and rewarding, not as a refugee shivering in the cold blizzards of reality. With equal intensity he realized that his torment these last six years had also flowed from another untimely farewell. His soul had languished dreadfully from the absence of the Holy Spirit. Now that healing had begun, he felt as if an unjust sentence of death had been commuted.

* * *

She had sought out Sam at his sister's home to apologize, and to say goodbye, or so she told herself. In reality, she had gone to feed her aching heart, to hear his voice one last time, and to finally close a chapter of her life that had been too long open to the ravages of the cold winds of un-answerable love.

Somewhere inside, unseen, and unrecognized, she was also desperately hoping to unplug the storm drain in her soul that she might not utterly drown in the torrential downpour of a shattered dream.

Had his sister's home been another half-block away, she would have never made it. A dozen times she had turned back, and a dozen and one times, she had turned again and pressed forward. Walking with him in the cool evening, feeling his warmth beside her had not healed, had not saved her from drowning, but had in fact increased her pain. In a way only those who have faced imminent death can understand, the only reason she had not run from him was that to do so was to close the coffin lid on an already dead dream. She remained, without hope, without reason, in fact beyond all reason, simply because there was no other option.

She had asked foolish, intimate questions of Sam about love, and had run from him at last in embarrassment. He had kissed her then; beyond wonder, beyond hope, beyond dreams, he had kissed her. She had been too stunned to do anything but stand there. She couldn't even form her lips into a kiss, or close her eyes, but he kissed her, and love flowed into her until a huge steel door slammed shut in her soul, and the cold winds of despair ceased to ravage the landscape of her heart.

Then she had kissed him back, at first carefully, with breathless disbelief, then with wonder, and finally with passion fired by a desperation whose thunder voice had but a magic moment ago been rendered mute.

* * *

The opening through the veil grew smaller until it closed entirely, and Sam was left alone. . . . He slowly reached out and ran his fingers across the deep pile of the carpet that still held the precious imprint of two bare feet.

ABOUT JOHN PONTIUS

It was never John's intent to write LDS books or a doctrinal blog or website, but he decided early on to obey the voice of the Lord and discern His will in his life. Hearkening to the Lord's voice was not always easy, but John's difficult journey ended in a far better place than he ever dreamed possible.

After living thirty-three years in Alaska, raising a family there, and building several careers, the Lord sent John and his family to Utah. John and his wife, Terri, who is the love of his life, both grew up in Utah but spent the majority of their lives in "the mission field." Returning to Utah was like coming home and brought them nearer to additional family, children, and grandchildren. Together they have eight children and twenty-one grandchildren.

John had many opportunities to speak at firesides, write books, and begin and maintain his blog, UnBlogmySoul. He accomplished many unexpected and amazing things that only the hand of the Lord could have brought to pass. The Lord's hand took John places he did not want to go, but when he actually got there, he recognized them as his "far better land of promise."

John passed away peacefully in his home in 2012, after a lifetime of service to the Lord Jesus Christ.